D1137581

Mario Puzo

THE
GODFATHER

THE LAST DON

ARROW

This edition published by Arrow in 2002
an imprint of The Random House Group
20 Vauxhall Bridge Road, London SW1V 2SA

Copyright © Mario Puzo 2002

The right of Mario Puzo to be
identified as the author of this work has been
asserted by him in accordance with the
Copyright Designs and Patents Act 1988

The Godfather copyright © Mario Puzo 1969
The Last Don copyright © Mario Puzo 1996

Papers used by Random House UK Ltd are natural recyclable products made from wood grown
in sustainable forests. The manufacturing process
conform to the environment regulations of the
country of origin.

A catalogue record for this book is available from
the British Library

Printed and bound in Germany by Elsnerdruck,
Berlin

ISBN 0 09 188543 4

For Anthony Cleri

MARIO PUZO

The Godfather

Book 1

*Behind every great fortune
there is a crime.*
—Balzac

Chapter

×××××××××××××××××××××××××

1

AMERIGO BONASERA sat in New York Criminal Court Number 3 and waited for justice; vengeance on the men who had so cruelly hurt his daughter, who had tried to dishonor her.

The judge, a formidably heavy-featured man, rolled up the sleeves of his black robe as if to physically chastise the two young men standing before the bench. His face was cold with majestic contempt. But there was something false in all this that Amerigo Bonasera sensed but did not yet understand.

"You acted like the worst kind of degenerates," the judge said harshly. Yes, yes, thought Amerigo Bonasera. Animals. Animals. The two young men, glossy hair crew cut, scrubbed clean-cut faces composed into humble contrition, bowed their heads in submission.

The judge went on. "You acted like wild beasts in a jungle and you are fortunate you did not sexually molest that poor girl or I'd put you behind bars for twenty years." The judge paused, his eyes beneath impressively thick brows flickered slyly toward the sallow-faced Amerigo Bonasera, then lowered to a stack of probation reports before him. He frowned and shrugged as if convinced against his own natural desire. He spoke again.

"But because of your youth, your clean records, because of your fine families, and because the law in its majesty does not seek vengeance, I hereby sentence you to three years' confinement to the penitentiary. Sentence to be suspended."

Only forty years of professional mourning kept the overwhelming frustration and hatred from showing on Amerigo Bonasera's face. His beautiful young daughter was still in the hospital with her broken jaw wired together; and now these two *animales* went free? It had all been a farce. He watched the happy parents cluster around their darling sons. Oh, they were all happy now, they were smiling now.

The black bile, sourly bitter, rose in Bonasera's throat, overflowed through tightly clenched teeth. He used his white linen pocket handkerchief and held it against his lips. He was standing so when the two young men strode freely up the aisle, confident and cool-eyed, smiling, not giving him so much as a glance. He let them pass without saying a word, pressing the fresh linen against his mouth.

The parents of the *animales* were coming by now, two men and two women his age but more American in their dress. They glanced at him, shamefaced, yet in their eyes was an odd, triumphant defiance.

Out of control, Bonasera leaned forward toward the aisle and shouted hoarsely, "You will weep as I have wept—I will make you weep as your children make me weep"—the linen at his eyes now. The defense attorneys bringing up the rear swept their clients forward in a tight little band, enveloping the two young men, who had started back down the aisle as if to protect their parents. A huge bailiff moved quickly to block the row in which Bonasera stood. But it was not necessary.

All his years in America, Amerigo Bonasera had trusted in law and order. And he had prospered thereby. Now, though his brain smoked with hatred, though wild visions of buying a gun and killing the two young men jangled the very bones of his skull, Bonasera turned to his still uncomprehending wife and explained to her, "They have made fools of us." He paused and then made his decision, no longer fearing the cost. "For justice we must go on our knees to Don Corleone."

In a garishly decorated Los Angeles hotel suite, Johnny Fontane was as jealously drunk as any ordinary husband. Sprawled on a red couch, he drank straight from the bottle of scotch in his hand, then washed the taste away by dunking his mouth in a crystal bucket of ice cubes and water. It was four in the morning and he was spinning drunken fantasies of murdering his trampy wife when she got home. If she ever did come home. It was too late to call his first wife and ask about the kids and he felt funny about calling any of his friends now that his career was plunging downhill. There had been a time when they would have been delighted, flattered by his calling them at four in the morning but now he bored them. He could even smile a little to himself as he thought that on the way up Johnny Fontane's troubles had fascinated some of the greatest female stars in America.

Gulping at his bottle of scotch, he heard finally his wife's key in the door, but he kept drinking until she walked into the room and stood before him. She was to him so very beautiful, the angelic face, soulful violet eyes, the delicately fragile but perfectly formed body. On the screen her beauty was magnified, spiritualized. A hundred million men all over the world were in love with the face of Margot Ashton. And paid to see it on the screen.

"Where the hell were you?" Johnny Fontane asked.

"Out fucking," she said.

She had misjudged his drunkenness. He sprang over the cocktail table and grabbed her by the throat. But close up to that magical face, the lovely violet eyes, he lost his anger and became helpless again. She made the mistake of smiling mockingly, saw his fist draw back. She screamed, "Johnny, not in the face, I'm making a picture."

She was laughing. He punched her in the stomach and she fell to the floor. He fell on top of her. He could smell her fragrant breath as she gasped for air. He punched her on the arms and on the thigh muscles of her silky tanned legs. He beat her as he had beaten snotty smaller kids long ago when he had been a tough teenager in New York's Hell's Kitchen. A painful punishment that would leave no lasting disfigurement of loosened teeth or broken nose.

But he was not hitting her hard enough. He couldn't. And she was giggling at him. Spread-eagled on the floor, her brocaded gown hitched up above her thighs, she taunted him between giggles. "Come on, stick it in. Stick it in, Johnny, that's what you really want."

Johnny Fontane got up. He hated the woman on the floor but her beauty was a magic shield. Margot rolled away, and in a dancer's spring was on her feet facing him. She went into a childish mocking dance and chanted, "Johnny never hurt me, Johnny never hurt me." Then almost sadly with grave beauty she said, "You poor silly bastard, giving me cramps like a kid. Ah, Johnny, you always will be a dumb romantic guinea, you even make love like a kid. You still think screwing is really like those dopey songs you used to sing." She shook her head and said, "Poor Johnny. Good-bye, Johnny." She walked into the bedroom and he heard her turn the key in the lock.

Johnny sat on the floor with his face in his hands. The sick, humiliating despair overwhelmed him. And then the gutter toughness that had helped him survive the jungle of Hollywood made him pick up the phone and call for a car to take him to the airport. There was one person who could save him. He would go back to New York. He would go back to the one man with the power, the wisdom, he needed and a love he still trusted. His Godfather Corleone.

The baker, Nazorine, pudgy and crusty as his great Italian loaves, still dusty with flour, scowled at his wife, his nubile daughter, Katherine, and his baker's helper, Enzo. Enzo had changed into his prisoner-of-war uniform with its green-lettered armband and was terrified that this scene would make him late reporting back to Governor's Island. One of the many thousands of Italian Army prisoners paroled daily to work in the American economy, he lived in constant fear of that parole being revoked. And so the little comedy being played now was, for him, a serious business.

Nazorine asked fiercely, "Have you dishonored my family? Have you given my daughter a little package to remember you by now that the war is over and you know America will kick your ass back to your village full of shit in Sicily?"

Enzo, a very short, strongly built boy, put his hand over his heart and said almost in tears, yet cleverly, "*Padrone*, I swear by the Holy Virgin I have never taken advantage of your kindness. I love your daughter with all respect. I ask for her hand with all respect. I know I have no right, but if they send me back to Italy I can never come back to America. I will never be able to marry Katherine."

Nazorine's wife, Filomena, spoke to the point. "Stop all this foolishness," she said to her pudgy husband. "You know what you must do. Keep Enzo here, send him to hide with our cousins in Long Island."

Katherine was weeping. She was already plump, homely and sprouting a faint moustache. She would never get a husband as handsome as Enzo, never find another man who touched her body in secret places with such respectful love. "I'll go and live in Italy," she screamed at her father. "I'll run away if you don't keep Enzo here."

Nazorine glanced at her shrewdly. She was a "hot number" this daughter of his. He had seen her brush her swelling buttocks against Enzo's front when the baker's helper squeezed behind her to fill the counter baskets with hot loaves from the oven. The young rascal's hot loaf would be in *her* oven, Nazorine thought lewdly, if proper steps were not taken. Enzo must be kept in America and be made an American citizen. And there was only one man who could arrange such an affair. The Godfather. Don Corleone.

All of these people and many others received engraved invitations to the wedding of Miss Constanzia Corleone, to be celebrated on the last Saturday in August 1945. The father of the bride, Don Vito Corleone, never forgot his old friends and neighbors though he himself now lived in a huge house on Long Island. The reception would be held in that house and the festivities would go on all day. There was no doubt it would be a momentous occasion. The war with the Japanese had just ended so there would not be any nagging fear for their sons fighting in the Army to cloud these festivities. A wedding was just what people needed to show their joy.

And so on that Saturday morning the friends of Don Corleone streamed out of New York City to do him honor. They bore cream-colored envelopes stuffed with cash as bridal gifts, no checks. Inside each envelope a card established the identity of the giver and the measure of his respect for the Godfather. A respect truly earned.

Don Vito Corleone was a man to whom everybody came for help, and never were they disappointed. He made no empty promises, nor the craven excuse that his hands were tied by more powerful forces in the world than himself. It was not necessary that he be your friend, it was not even important that you had no means with which to repay him. Only one thing was required. That you, *you yourself*, proclaim your friendship. And then, no matter how poor or power-less the supplicant, Don Corleone would take that man's troubles to his heart. And he would let nothing stand in the way to a solution of that man's woe. His reward? Friendship, the respectful title of "Don," and sometimes the more affectionate salutation of "Godfather." And perhaps, to show respect only, never for profit, some humble gift—a gallon of homemade wine or a basket of peppered *taralles* specially baked to grace his Christmas table. It was understood, it was mere good manners, to proclaim that you were in his debt and that he had the right to call upon you at any time to redeem your debt by some small service.

Now on this great day, his daughter's wedding day, Don Vito Corleone stood in the doorway of his Long Beach home to greet his guests, all of them known, all of them trusted. Many of them owed their good fortune in life to the Don and on this intimate occasion felt free to call him "Godfather" to his face. Even the people performing festal services were his friends. The bartender was an old comrade whose gift was all the wedding liquors and his own expert skills. The waiters were the friends of Don Corleone's sons. The food on the garden picnic tables had been cooked by the Don's wife and her friends and the gaily festooned one-acre garden itself had been decorated by the young girl-chums of the bride.

Don Corleone received everyone—rich and poor, powerful and humble—with an equal show of love. He slighted no one. That was his character. And the guests so exclaimed at how well he looked in his tux that an inexperienced observer might easily have thought the Don himself was the lucky groom.

Standing at the door with him were two of his three sons. The eldest, baptized Santino but called Sonny by everyone except his father, was looked at askance by the older Italian men; with admiration by the younger. Sonny Corleone was tall for a first-generation American of Italian parentage, almost six feet, and his crop of bushy, curly hair made him look even taller. His face was that of a gross Cupid, the features even but the bow-shaped lips thickly sensual, the dimpled cleft chin in some curious way obscene. He was built as powerfully as a bull and it was common knowledge that he was so generously endowed by nature that his martyred wife feared the marriage bed as unbelievers once feared the rack. It was whispered that when as a youth he had visited houses of ill fame, even the most hardened and fearless *putain*, after an awed inspection of his massive organ, demanded double price.

Here at the wedding feast, some young matrons, wide-hipped, wide-mouthed, measured Sonny Corleone with coolly confident eyes. But on this particular day they were wasting their time. Sonny Corleone, despite the presence of his wife and three small children, had plans for his sister's maid of honor, Lucy Mancini. This young girl, fully aware, sat at a garden table in her pink formal gown, a tiara of flowers in her glossy black hair. She had flirted with Sonny in the past week of rehearsals and squeezed his hand that morning at the altar. A maiden could do no more.

She did not care that he would never be the great man his father had proved to be. Sonny Corleone had strength, he had courage. He was generous and his heart was admitted to be as big as his organ. Yet he did not have his father's humility but instead a quick, hot temper that led him into errors of judgment. Though he was a great help in his father's business, there were many who doubted that he would become the heir to it.

The second son, Frederico, called Fred or Fredo, was a child every Italian prayed to the saints for. Dutiful, loyal, always at the service of his father, living with his parents at age thirty. He was short and burly, not handsome but with the same Cupid head of the family, the curly helmet of hair over the round face and sensual bow-shaped lips. Only, in Fred, these lips were not sensual but granitelike. Inclined to dourness, he was still a crutch to his father, never disputed him, never embarrassed him by scandalous behavior with women. Despite all these virtues he did not have that personal magnetism, that animal force, so necessary for a leader of men, and he too was not expected to inherit the family business.

The third son, Michael Corleone, did not stand with his father and his two brothers but sat at a table in the most secluded corner of the garden. But even there he could not escape the attentions of the family friends.

Michael Corleone was the youngest son of the Don and the only child who had refused the great man's direction. He did not have the heavy, Cupid-shaped face of the other children, and his jet black hair was straight rather than curly. His skin was a clear olive-brown that would have been called beautiful in a girl. He was handsome in a delicate way. Indeed there had been a time when the Don had worried about his youngest son's masculinity. A worry that was put to rest when Michael Corleone became seventeen years old.

Now this youngest son sat at a table in the extreme corner of the garden to proclaim his chosen alienation from father and family. Beside him sat the American girl everyone had heard about but whom no one had seen until this day. He had, of course, shown the proper respect and introduced her to everyone at the wedding, including his family. They were not impressed with her. She was too thin, she was too fair, her face was too sharply intelligent for a

woman, her manner too free for a maiden. Her name, too, was outlandish to their ears; she called herself Kay Adams. If she had told
them that her family had settled in America two hundred years ago
and her name was a common one, they would have shrugged.

Every guest noticed that the Don paid no particular attention to
this third son. Michael had been his favorite before the war and
obviously the chosen heir to run the family business when the proper
moment came. He had all the quiet force and intelligence of his great
father, the born instinct to act in such a way that men had no re-
course but to respect him. But when World War II broke out,
Michael Corleone volunteered for the Marine Corps. He defied his
father's express command when he did so.

Don Corleone had no desire, no intention, of letting his youngest
son be killed in the service of a power foreign to himself. Doctors had
been bribed, secret arrangements had been made. A great deal of
money had been spent to take the proper precautions. But Michael
was twenty-one years of age and nothing could be done against his
own willfulness. He enlisted and fought over the Pacific Ocean. He
became a Captain and won medals. In 1944 his picture was printed in
Life magazine with a photo layout of his deeds. A friend had shown
Don Corleone the magazine (his family did not dare), and the Don
had grunted disdainfully and said, "He performs those miracles for
strangers."

When Michael Corleone was discharged early in 1945 to recover
from a disabling wound, he had no idea that his father had arranged
his release. He stayed home for a few weeks, then, without consulting
anyone, entered Dartmouth College in Hanover, New Hampshire,
and so he left his father's house. To return for the wedding of his
sister and to show his own future wife to them, the washed-out rag of
an American girl.

Michael Corleone was amusing Kay Adams by telling her little
stories about some of the more colorful wedding guests. He was, in
turn, amused by her finding these people exotic, and, as always,
charmed by her intense interest in anything new and foreign to her
experience. Finally her attention was caught by a small group of men
gathered around a wooden barrel of homemade wine. The men were
Amerigo Bonasera, Nazorine the Baker, Anthony Coppola and Luca
Brasi. With her usual alert intelligence she remarked on the fact that
these four men did not seem particularly happy. Michael smiled.

"No, they're not," he said. "They're waiting to see my father in private. They have favors to ask." And indeed it was easy to see that all four men constantly followed the Don with their eyes.

As Don Corleone stood greeting guests, a black Chevrolet sedan came to a stop on the far side of the paved mall. Two men in the front seat pulled notebooks from their jackets and, with no attempt at concealment, jotted down license numbers of the other cars parked around the mall. Sonny turned to his father and said, "Those guys over there must be cops."

Don Corleone shrugged. "I don't own the street. They can do what they please."

Sonny's heavy Cupid face grew red with anger. "Those lousy bastards, they don't respect anything." He left the steps of the house and walked across the mall to where the black sedan was parked. He thrust his face angrily close to the face of the driver, who did not flinch but flapped open his wallet to show a green identification card. Sonny stepped back without saying a word. He spat so that the spittle hit the back door of the sedan and walked away. He was hoping the driver would get out of the sedan and come after him, on the mall, but nothing happened. When he reached the steps he said to his father, "Those guys are FBI men. They're taking down all the license numbers. Snotty bastards."

Don Corleone knew who they were. His closest and most intimate friends had been advised to attend the wedding in automobiles not their own. And though he disapproved of his son's foolish display of anger, the tantrum served a purpose. It would convince the interlopers that their presence was unexpected and unprepared for. So Don Corleone himself was not angry. He had long ago learned that society imposes insults that must be borne, comforted by the knowledge that in this world there comes a time when the most humble of men, if he keeps his eyes open, can take his revenge on the most powerful. It was this knowledge that prevented the Don from losing the humility all his friends admired in him.

But now in the garden behind the house, a four-piece band began to play. All the guests had arrived. Don Corleone put the intruders out of his mind and led his two sons to the wedding feast.

There were, now, hundreds of guests in the huge garden, some dancing on the wooden platform bedecked with flowers, others sitting at long tables piled high with spicy food and gallon jugs of black, homemade wine. The bride, Connie Corleone, sat in splendor at a special raised table with her groom, the maid of honor, bridesmaids and ushers. It was a rustic setting in the old Italian style. Not to the bride's taste, but Connie had consented to a "guinea" wedding to please her father because she had so displeasured him in her choice of a husband.

The groom, Carlo Rizzi, was a half-breed, born of a Sicilian father and the North Italian mother from whom he had inherited his blond hair and blue eyes. His parents lived in Nevada and Carlo had left that state because of a little trouble with the law. In New York he met Sonny Corleone and so met the sister. Don Corleone, of course, sent trusted friends to Nevada and they reported that Carlo's police trouble was a youthful indiscretion with a gun, not serious, that could easily be wiped off the books to leave the youth with a clean record. They also came back with detailed information on legal gambling in Nevada which greatly interested the Don and which he had been pondering over since. It was part of the Don's greatness that he profited from everything.

Connie Corleone was a not quite pretty girl, thin and nervous and certain to become shrewish later in life. But today, transformed by her white bridal gown and eager virginity, she was so radiant as to be almost beautiful. Beneath the wooden table her hand rested on the muscular thigh of her groom. Her Cupid-bow mouth pouted to give him an airy kiss.

She thought him incredibly handsome. Carlo Rizzi had worked in the open desert air while very young—heavy laborer's work. Now he had tremendous forearms and his shoulders bulged the jacket of his tux. He basked in the adoring eyes of his bride and filled her glass with wine. He was elaborately courteous to her as if they were both actors in a play. But his eyes kept flickering toward the huge silk purse the bride wore on her right shoulder and which was now stuffed full of money envelopes. How much did it hold? Ten thousand? Twenty thousand? Carlo Rizzi smiled. It was only the beginning. He had, after all, married into a royal family. They would have to take care of him.

In the crowd of guests a dapper young man with the sleek head of a ferret was also studying the silk purse. From sheer habit Paulie Gatto wondered just how he could go about hijacking that fat pocketbook. The idea amused him. But he knew it was idle, innocent dreaming, as small children dream of knocking out tanks with pop-guns. He watched his boss, fat, middle-aged Peter Clemenza whirling young girls around the wooden dance floor in a rustic and lusty *Tarantella*. Clemenza, immensely tall, immensely huge, danced with such skill and abandon, his hard belly lecherously bumping the breasts of younger, tinier women, that all the guests were applauding him. Older women grabbed his arm to become his next partner. The younger men respectfully cleared off the floor and clapped their hands in time to the mandolin's wild strumming. When Clemenza finally collapsed in a chair, Paulie Gatto brought him a glass of icy black wine and wiped the perspiring Jovelike brow with his silk handkerchief. Clemenza was blowing like a whale as he gulped down the wine. But instead of thanking Paulie he said curtly, "Never mind being a dance judge, do your job. Take a walk around the neighborhood and see everything is OK." Paulie slid away into the crowd.

The band took a refreshment break. A young man named Nino Valenti picked up a discarded mandolin, put his left foot up on a chair and began to sing a coarse Sicilian love song. Nino Valenti's face was handsome though bloated by continual drinking and he was already a little drunk. He rolled his eyes as his tongue caressed the obscene lyrics. The women shrieked with glee and the men shouted the last word of each stanza with the singer.

Don Corleone, notoriously straitlaced in such matters, though his stout wife was screaming joyfully with the others, disappeared tactfully into the house. Seeing this, Sonny Corleone made his way to the bride's table and sat down beside young Lucy Mancini, the maid of honor. They were safe. His wife was in the kitchen putting the last touches on the serving of the wedding cake. Sonny whispered a few words in the young girl's ear and she rose. Sonny waited a few minutes and then casually followed her, stopping to talk with a guest here and there as he worked his way through the crowd.

All eyes followed them. The maid of honor, thoroughly Americanized by three years of college, was a ripe girl who already had a "reputation." All through the marriage rehearsals she had flirted with Sonny Corleone in a teasing, joking way she thought was permitted because he was the best man and her wedding partner. Now holding her pink gown up off the ground, Lucy Mancini went into the house, smiling with false innocence, ran lightly up the stairs to the bathroom. She stayed there for a few moments. When she came out Sonny Corleone was on the landing above, beckoning her upward.

From behind the closed window of Don Corleone's "office," a slightly raised corner room, Thomas Hagen watched the wedding party in the festooned garden. The walls behind him were stacked with law books. Hagen was the Don's lawyer and acting *consigliori*, or counselor, and as such held the most vital subordinate position in the family business. He and the Don had solved many a knotty problem in this room, and so when he saw the Godfather leave the festivities and enter the house, he knew, wedding or no, there would be a little work this day. The Don would be coming to see him. Then Hagen saw Sonny Corleone whisper in Lucy Mancini's ear and their little comedy as he followed her into the house. Hagen grimaced, debated whether to inform the Don, and decided against it. He went to the desk and picked up a handwritten list of the people who had been granted permission to see Don Corleone privately. When the Don entered the room, Hagen handed him the list. Don Corleone nodded and said, "Leave Bonasera to the end."

Hagen used the French doors and went directly out into the garden to where the supplicants clustered around the barrel of wine. He pointed to the baker, the pudgy Nazorine.

Don Corleone greeted the baker with an embrace. They had played together as children in Italy and had grown up in friendship. Every Easter freshly baked clotted-cheese and wheat-germ pies, their crusts yolk-gold, big around as truck wheels, arrived at Don Corleone's home. On Christmas, on family birthdays, rich creamy pastries proclaimed the Nazorines' respect. And all through the years, lean and fat, Nazorine cheerfully paid his dues to the bakery union organized by the Don in his salad days. Never asking for a favor in return except for the chance to buy black-market OPA sugar coupons during the war. Now the time had come for the baker to claim his rights as a loyal friend, and Don Corleone looked forward with great pleasure to granting his request.

He gave the baker a Di Nobili cigar and a glass of yellow Strega and put his hand on the man's shoulder to urge him on. That was the mark of the Don's humanity. He knew from bitter experience what courage it took to ask a favor from a fellow man.

The baker told the story of his daughter and Enzo. A fine Italian lad from Sicily; captured by the American Army; sent to the United States as a prisoner of war; given parole to help our war effort! A pure and honorable love had sprung up between honest Enzo and his sheltered Katherine but now that the war was ended the poor lad would be repatriated to Italy and Nazorine's daughter would surely die of a broken heart. Only Godfather Corleone could help this afflicted couple. He was their last hope.

The Don walked Nazorine up and down the room, his hand on the baker's shoulder, his head nodding with understanding to keep up the man's courage. When the baker had finished, Don Corleone smiled at him and said, "My dear friend, put all your worries aside." He went on to explain very carefully what must be done. The Congressman of the district must be petitioned. The Congressman would propose a special bill that would allow Enzo to become a citizen. The bill would surely pass Congress. A privilege all those rascals extended to each other. Don Corleone explained that this would cost money, the going price was now two thousand dollars. He, Don Corleone, would guarantee performance and accept payment. Did his friend agree?

The baker nodded his head vigorously. He did not expect such a great favor for nothing. That was understood. A special Act of Congress does not come cheap. Nazorine was almost tearful in his thanks. Don Corleone walked him to the door, assuring him that competent people would be sent to the bakery to arrange all details, complete all necessary documents. The baker embraced him before disappearing into the garden.

Hagen smiled at the Don. "That's a good investment for Nazorine. A son-in-law and a cheap lifetime helper in his bakery all for two thousand dollars." He paused. "Who do I give this job to?"

Don Corleone frowned in thought. "Not to our *paisan*. Give it to the Jew in the next district. Have the home addresses changed. I think there might be many such cases now the war is over; we should have extra people in Washington that can handle the overflow and not raise the price." Hagen made a note on his pad. "Not Congressman Luteco. Try Fischer."

The next man Hagen brought in was a very simple case. His name was Anthony Coppola and he was the son of a man Don Corleone had worked with in the railroad yards in his youth. Coppola needed five hundred dollars to open a pizzeria; for a deposit on fixtures and the special oven. For reasons not gone into, credit was not available. The Don reached into his pocket and took out a roll of bills. It was not quite enough. He grimaced and said to Tom Hagen, "Loan me a hundred dollars, I'll pay you back Monday when I go to the bank." The supplicant protested that four hundred dollars would be ample, but Don Corleone patted his shoulder, saying, apologetically, "This fancy wedding left me a little short of cash." He took the money Hagen extended to him and gave it to Anthony Coppola with his own roll of bills.

Hagen watched with quiet admiration. The Don always taught that when a man was generous, he must show the generosity as personal. How flattering to Anthony Coppola that a man like the Don would borrow to loan *him* money. Not that Coppola did not know that the Don was a millionaire but how many millionaires let themselves be put to even a small inconvenience by a poor friend?

The Don raised his head inquiringly. Hagen said, "He's not on the list but Luca Brasi wants to see you. He understands it can't be public but he wants to congratulate you in person."

For the first time the Don seemed displeased. The answer was devious. "Is it necessary?" he asked.

Hagen shrugged. "You understand him better than I do. But he was very grateful that you invited him to the wedding. He never expected that. I think he wants to show his gratitude."

Don Corleone nodded and gestured that Luca Brasi should be brought to him.

In the garden Kay Adams was struck by the violet fury imprinted on the face of Luca Brasi. She asked about him. Michael had brought Kay to the wedding so that she would slowly and perhaps without too much of a shock, absorb the truth about his father. But so far she seemed to regard the Don as a slightly unethical businessman. Michael decided to tell her part of the truth indirectly. He explained that Luca Brasi was one of the most feared men in the Eastern underworld. His great talent, it was said, was that he could do a job of murder all by himself, without confederates, which automatically made discovery and conviction by the law almost impossible. Michael grimaced and said, "I don't know whether all that stuff is true. I do know he is sort of a friend to my father."

For the first time Kay began to understand. She asked a little incredulously, "You're not hinting that a man like that works for your father?"

The hell with it, he thought. He said, straight out, "Nearly fifteen years ago some people wanted to take over my father's oil importing business. They tried to kill him and nearly did. Luca Brasi went after them. The story is that he killed six men in two weeks and that ended the famous olive oil war." He smiled as if it were a joke.

Kay shuddered. "You mean your father was shot by gangsters?"

"Fifteen years ago," Michael said. "Everything's been peaceful since then." He was afraid he had gone too far.

"You're trying to scare me," Kay said. "You just don't want me to marry you." She smiled at him and poked his ribs with her elbow. "Very clever."

Michael smiled back at her. "I want you to think about it," he said.

"Did he really kill six men?" Kay asked.

"That's what the newspapers claimed," Mike said. "Nobody ever proved it. But there's another story about him that nobody ever tells. It's supposed to be so terrible that even my father won't talk about it. Tom Hagen knows the story and he won't tell me. Once I kidded him, I said, 'When will I be old enough to hear that story about Luca?' and Tom said, 'When you're a hundred.'" Michael sipped his glass of wine. "That must be some story. That must be some Luca."

Luca Brasi was indeed a man to frighten the devil in hell himself. Short, squat, massive-skulled, his presence sent out alarm bells of danger. His face was stamped into a mask of fury. The eyes were brown but with none of the warmth of that color, more a deadly tan. The mouth was not so much cruel as lifeless; thin, rubbery and the color of veal.

Brasi's reputation for violence was awesome and his devotion to Don Corleone legendary. He was, in himself, one of the great blocks that supported the Don's power structure. His kind was a rarity.

Luca Brasi did not fear the police, he did not fear society, he did not fear God, he did not fear hell, he did not fear or love his fellow man. But he had elected, he had *chosen*, to fear and love Don Corleone. Ushered into the presence of the Don, the terrible Brasi held himself stiff with respect. He stuttered over the flowery congratulations he offered and his formal hope that the first grandchild would be masculine. He then handed the Don an envelope stuffed with cash as a gift for the bridal couple.

So that was what he wanted to do. Hagen noticed the change in Don Corleone. The Don received Brasi as a king greets a subject who has done him an enormous service, never familiar but with regal respect. With every gesture, with every word, Don Corleone made it clear to Luca Brasi that he was *valued*. Not for one moment did he show surprise at the wedding gift being presented to him personally. He understood.

The money in the envelope was sure to be more than anyone else had given. Brasi had spent many hours deciding on the sum, comparing it to what the other guests might offer. He wanted to be the most generous to show that he had the most respect, and that was why he had given his envelope to the Don personally, a gaucherie the Don overlooked in his own flowery sentence of thanks. Hagen saw Luca Brasi's face lose its mask of fury, swell with pride and pleasure. Brasi kissed the Don's hand before he went out the door that Hagen held open. Hagen prudently gave Brasi a friendly smile which the squat man acknowledged with a polite stretching of rubbery, veal-colored lips.

When the door closed Don Corleone gave a small sigh of relief. Brasi was the only man in the world who could make him nervous. The man was like a natural force, not truly subject to control. He had to be handled as gingerly as dynamite. The Don shrugged. Even dynamite could be exploded harmlessly if the need arose. He looked questioningly at Hagen. "Is Bonasera the only one left?"

Hagen nodded. Don Corleone frowned in thought, then said, "Before you bring him in, tell Santino to come here. He should learn some things."

Out in the garden, Hagen searched anxiously for Sonny Corleone. He told the waiting Bonasera to be patient and went over to Michael Corleone and his girl friend. "Did you see Sonny around?" he asked. Michael shook his head. Damn, Hagen thought, if Sonny was screwing the maid of honor all this time there was going to be a mess of trouble. His wife, the young girl's family; it could be a disaster. Anxiously he hurried to the entrance through which he had seen Sonny disappear almost a half hour ago.

Seeing Hagen go into the house, Kay Adams asked Michael Corleone, "Who is he? You introduced him as your brother but his name is different and he certainly doesn't look Italian."

"Tom lived with us since he was twelve years old," Michael said. "His parents died and he was roaming around the streets with this bad eye infection. Sonny brought him home one night and he just stayed. He didn't have any place to go. He lived with us until he got married."

Kay Adams was thrilled. "That's really romantic," she said. "Your father must be a warmhearted person. To adopt somebody just like that when he had so many children of his own."

Michael didn't bother to point out that immigrant Italians considered four children a small family. He merely said, "Tom wasn't adopted. He just lived with us."

"Oh," Kay said, then asked curiously, "why didn't you adopt him?"

Michael laughed. "Because my father said it would be disrespectful for Tom to change his name. Disrespectful to his own parents."

They saw Hagen shoo Sonny through the French door into the Don's office and then crook a finger at Amerigo Bonasera. "Why do they bother your father with business on a day like this?" Kay asked.

Michael laughed again. "Because they know that by tradition no Sicilian can refuse a request on his daughter's wedding day. And no Sicilian ever lets a chance like that go by."

Lucy Mancini lifted her pink gown off the floor and ran up the steps. Sonny Corleone's heavy Cupid face, redly obscene with winey lust, frightened her, but she had teased him for the past week to just this end. In her two college love affairs she had felt nothing and neither of them lasted more than a week. Quarreling, her second lover had mumbled something about her being "too big down there." Lucy had understood and for the rest of the school term had refused to go out on any dates.

During the summer, preparing for the wedding of her best friend, Connie Corleone, Lucy heard the whispered stories about Sonny. One Sunday afternoon in the Corleone kitchen, Sonny's wife Sandra gossiped freely. Sandra was a coarse, good-natured woman who had been born in Italy but brought to America as a small child. She was strongly built with great breasts and had already borne three children in five years of marriage. Sandra and the other women teased Connie about the terrors of the nuptial bed. "My God," Sandra had giggled, "when I saw that pole of Sonny's for the first time and realized he was going to stick it into *me*, I yelled bloody murder. After the first year my insides felt as mushy as macaroni boiled for an hour. When I heard he was doing the job on other girls I went to church and lit a candle."

They had all laughed but Lucy had felt her flesh twitching between her legs.

Now as she ran up the steps toward Sonny a tremendous flash of desire went through her body. On the landing Sonny grabbed her hand and pulled her down the hall into an empty bedroom. Her legs went weak as the door closed behind them. She felt Sonny's mouth on hers, his lips tasting of burnt tobacco, bitter. She opened her mouth. At that moment she felt his hand come up beneath her bridesmaid's gown, heard the rustle of material giving way, felt his large warm hand between her legs, ripping aside the satin panties to caress her vulva. She put her arms around his neck and hung there as he opened his trousers. Then he placed both hands beneath her bare buttocks and lifted her. She gave a little hop in the air so that both her legs were wrapped around his upper thighs. His tongue was in her mouth and she sucked on it. He gave a savage thrust that banged her head against the door. She felt something burning pass between her thighs. She let her right hand drop from his neck and reached down to guide him. Her hand closed around an enormous, blood-gorged pole of muscle. It pulsated in her hand like an animal and almost weeping with grateful ecstasy she pointed it into her own wet, turgid flesh. The thrust of its entering, the unbelievable pleasure made her gasp, brought her legs up almost around his neck, and then like a quiver, her body received the savage arrows of his lightning-like thrusts; innumerable, torturing; arching her pelvis higher and higher until for the first time in her life she reached a shattering climax, felt his hardness break and then the crawly flood of semen over her thighs. Slowly her legs relaxed from around his body, slid down until they reached the floor. They leaned against each other, out of breath.

It might have been going on for some time but now they could hear the soft knocking on the door. Sonny quickly buttoned his trousers, meanwhile blocking the door so that it could not be opened. Lucy frantically smoothed down her pink gown, her eyes flickering, but the thing that had given her so much pleasure was hidden inside sober black cloth. Then they heard Tom Hagen's voice, very low, "Sonny, you in there?"

Sonny sighed with relief. He winked at Lucy. "Yeah, Tom, what is it?"

Hagen's voice, still low, said, "The Don wants you in his office. Now." They could hear his footsteps as he walked away. Sonny waited for a few moments, gave Lucy a hard kiss on the lips, and then slipped out the door after Hagen.

Lucy combed her hair. She checked her dress and pulled around her garter straps. Her body felt bruised, her lips pulpy and tender. She went out the door and though she felt the sticky wetness between her thighs she did not go to the bathroom to wash but ran straight on down the steps and into the garden. She took her seat at the bridal table next to Connie, who exclaimed petulantly, "Lucy, where were you? You look drunk. Stay beside me now."

The blond groom poured Lucy a glass of wine and smiled knowingly. Lucy didn't care. She lifted the grapey, dark red juice to her parched mouth and drank. She felt the sticky wetness between her thighs and pressed her legs together. Her body was trembling. Over the glass rim, as she drank, her eyes searched hungrily to find Sonny Corleone. There was no one else she cared to see. Slyly she whispered in Connie's ear, "Only a few hours more and you'll know what it's all about." Connie giggled. Lucy demurely folded her hands on the table, treacherously triumphant, as if she had stolen a treasure from the bride.

Amerigo Bonasera followed Hagen into the corner room of the house and found Don Corleone sitting behind a huge desk. Sonny Corleone was standing by the window, looking out into the garden. For the first time that afternoon the Don behaved coolly. He did not embrace the visitor or shake hands. The sallow-faced undertaker owed his invitation to the fact that his wife and the wife of the Don were the closest of friends. Amerigo Bonasera himself was in severe disfavor with Don Corleone.

Bonasera began his request obliquely and cleverly. "You must excuse my daughter, your wife's goddaughter, for not doing your family the respect of coming today. She is in the hospital still." He glanced at Sonny Corleone and Tom Hagen to indicate that he did not wish to speak before them. But the Don was merciless.

"We all know of your daughter's misfortune," Don Corleone said. "If I can help her in any way, you have only to speak. My wife is her godmother after all. I have never forgotten that honor." This was a rebuke. The undertaker never called Don Corleone "Godfather" as custom dictated.

Bonasera, ashen-faced, asked, directly now, "May I speak to you alone?"

Don Corleone shook his head. "I trust these two men with my life. They are my two right arms. I cannot insult them by sending them away."

The undertaker closed his eyes for a moment and then began to speak. His voice was quiet, the voice he used to console the bereaved.

"I raised my daughter in the American fashion. I believe in America. America has made my fortune. I gave my daughter her freedom and yet taught her never to dishonor her family. She found a 'boy friend,' not an Italian. She went to the movies with him. She stayed out late. But he never came to meet her parents. I accepted all this without a protest, the fault is mine. Two months ago he took her for a drive. He had a masculine friend with him. They made her drink whiskey and then they tried to take advantage of her. She resisted. She kept her honor. They beat her. Like an animal. When I went to the hospital she had two black eyes. Her nose was broken. Her jaw was shattered. They had to wire it together. She wept through her pain. 'Father, Father, why did they do it? Why did they do this to me?' And I wept." Bonasera could not speak further, he was weeping now though his voice had not betrayed his emotion.

Don Corleone, as if against his will, made a gesture of sympathy and Bonasera went on, his voice human with suffering. "Why did I weep? She was the light of my life, an affectionate daughter. A beautiful girl. She trusted people and now she will never trust them again. She will never be beautiful again." He was trembling, his sallow face flushed an ugly dark red.

"I went to the police like a good American. The two boys were arrested. They were brought to trial. The evidence was overwhelming and they pleaded guilty. The judge sentenced them to three years in prison and suspended the sentence. They went free that very day. I stood in the courtroom like a fool and those bastards smiled at me. And then I said to my wife: 'We must go to Don Corleone for justice.' "

The Don had bowed his head to show respect for the man's grief. But when he spoke, the words were cold with offended dignity. "Why did you go to the police? Why didn't you come to me at the beginning of this affair?"

Bonasera muttered almost inaudibly, "What do you want of me? Tell me what you wish. But do what I beg you to do." There was something almost insolent in his words.

Don Corleone said gravely, "And what is that?"

Bonasera glanced at Hagen and Sonny Corleone and shook his head. The Don, still sitting at Hagen's desk, inclined his body toward the undertaker. Bonasera hesitated, then bent down and put his lips so close to the Don's hairy ear that they touched. Don Corleone listened like a priest in the confessional, gazing away into the distance, impassive, remote. They stood so for a long moment until Bonasera finished whispering and straightened to his full height. The Don looked up gravely at Bonasera. Bonasera, his face flushed, returned the stare unflinchingly.

Finally the Don spoke. "That I cannot do. You are being carried away."

Bonasera said loudly, clearly, "I will pay you anything you ask." On hearing this, Hagen flinched, a nervous flick of his head. Sonny Corleone folded his arms, smiled sardonically as he turned from the window to watch the scene in the room for the first time.

Don Corleone rose from behind the desk. His face was still impassive but his voice rang like cold death. "We have known each other many years, you and I," he said to the undertaker, "but until this day you never came to me for counsel or help. I can't remember the last time you invited me to your house for coffee though my wife is godmother to your only child. Let us be frank. You spurned my friendship. You feared to be in my debt."

Bonasera murmured, "I didn't want to get into trouble."

The Don held up his hand. "No. Don't speak. You found America a paradise. You had a good trade, you made a good living, you thought the world a harmless place where you could take your pleasure as you willed. You never armed yourself with true friends. After all, the police guarded you, there were courts of law, you and yours could come to no harm. You did not need Don Corleone. Very well. My feelings were wounded but I am not that sort of person who thrusts his friendship on those who do not value it—on those who think me of little account." The Don paused and gave the undertaker a polite, ironic smile. "Now you come to me and say, 'Don Corleone give me justice.' And you do not ask with respect. You do not offer me your friendship. You come into my home on the bridal day of my daughter and you ask me to do murder and you say"—here the Don's voice became a scornful mimicry—" 'I will pay you anything.' No, no, I am not offended, but what have I ever done to make you treat me so disrespectfully?"

Bonasera cried out in his anguish and his fear, "America has been good to me. I wanted to be a good citizen. I wanted my child to be American."

The Don clapped his hands together with decisive approval. "Well spoken. Very fine. Then you have nothing to complain about. The judge has ruled. America has ruled. Bring your daughter flowers and a box of candy when you go visit her in the hospital. That will comfort her. Be content. After all, this is not a serious affair, the boys were young, high-spirited, and one of them is the son of a powerful politician. No, my dear Amerigo, you have always been honest. I must admit, though you spurned my friendship, that I would trust the given word of Amerigo Bonasera more than I would any other man's. So give me your word that you will put aside this madness. It is not American. Forgive. Forget. Life is full of misfortunes."

The cruel and contemptuous irony with which all this was said, the controlled anger of the Don, reduced the poor undertaker to a quivering jelly but he spoke up bravely again. "I ask you for justice."

Don Corleone said curtly, "The court gave you justice."

Bonasera shook his head stubbornly. "No. They gave the youths justice. They did not give me justice."

The Don acknowledged this fine distinction with an approving nod, then asked, "What is your justice?"

"An eye for an eye," Bonasera said.

"You asked for more," the Don said. "Your daughter is alive."

Bonasera said reluctantly, "Let them suffer as she suffers." The Don waited for him to speak further. Bonasera screwed up the last of his courage and said, "How much shall I pay you?" It was a despairing wail.

Don Corleone turned his back. It was a dismissal. Bonasera did not budge.

Finally, sighing, a good-hearted man who cannot remain angry with an erring friend, Don Corleone turned back to the undertaker, who was now as pale as one of his corpses. Don Corleone was gentle, patient. "Why do you fear to give your first allegiance to me?" he said. "You go to the law courts and wait for months. You spend money on lawyers who know full well you are to be made a fool of. You accept judgment from a judge who sells himself like the worst whore in the streets. Years gone by, when you needed money, you went to the banks and paid ruinous interest, waited hat in hand like a beggar while they sniffed around, poked their noses up your very asshole to make sure you could pay them back." The Don paused, his voice became sterner.

"But if you had come to me, my purse would have been yours. If you had come to me for justice those scum who ruined your daughter would be weeping bitter tears this day. If by some misfortune an honest man like yourself made enemies they would become my enemies"—the Don raised his arm, finger pointing at Bonasera—"and then, believe me, they would fear you."

Bonasera bowed his head and murmured in a strangled voice, "Be my friend. I accept."

Don Corleone put his hand on the man's shoulder. "Good," he said, "you shall have your justice. Some day, and that day may never come, I will call upon you to do me a service in return. Until that day, consider this justice a gift from my wife, your daughter's godmother."

When the door closed behind the grateful undertaker, Don Corleone turned to Hagen and said, "Give this affair to Clemenza and tell him to be sure to use reliable people, people who will not be carried away by the smell of blood. After all, we're not murderers, no matter what that corpse valet dreams up in his foolish head." He noted that his first-born, masculine son was gazing through the window at the garden party. It was hopeless, Don Corleone thought. If he refused to be instructed, Santino could never run the family business, could never become a Don. He would have to find somebody else. And soon. After all, he was not immortal.

From the garden, startling all three men, there came a happy roaring shout. Sonny Corleone pressed close to the window. What he saw made him move quickly toward the door, a delighted smile on his face. "It's Johnny, he came to the wedding, what did I tell you?" Hagen moved to the window. "It's really your godson," he said to Don Corleone. "Shall I bring him here?"

"No," the Don said. "Let the people enjoy him. Let him come to me when he is ready." He smiled at Hagen. "You see? He is a good godson."

Hagen felt a twinge of jealousy. He said dryly, "It's been two years. He's probably in trouble again and wants you to help."

"And who should he come to if not his godfather?" asked Don Corleone.

The first one to see Johnny Fontane enter the garden was Connie Corleone. She forgot her bridal dignity and screamed, "Johneee." Then she ran into his arms. He hugged her tight and kissed her on the mouth, kept his arm around her as others came up to greet him. They were all his old friends, people he had grown up with on the West Side. Then Connie was dragging him to her new husband. Johnny

saw with amusement that the blond young man looked a little sour at
no longer being the star of the day. He turned on all his charm,
shaking the groom's hand, toasting him with a glass of wine.

A familiar voice called from the bandstand, "How about giving us
a song, Johnny?" He looked up and saw Nino Valenti smiling down
at him. Johnny Fontane jumped up on the bandstand and threw his
arms around Nino. They had been inseparable, singing together,
going out with girls together, until Johnny had started to become
famous and sing on the radio. When he had gone to Hollywood to
make movies Johnny had phoned Nino a couple of times just to talk
and had promised to get him a club singing date. But he had never
done so. Seeing Nino now, his cheerful, mocking, drunken grin, all
the affection returned.

Nino began strumming on the mandolin. Johnny Fontane put his
hand on Nino's shoulder. "This is for the bride," he said, and stamping his foot, chanted the words to an obscene Sicilian love song. As he
sang, Nino made suggestive motions with his body. The bride
blushed proudly, the throng of guests roared its approval. Before the
song ended they were all stamping with their feet and roaring out the
sly, double-meaning tag line that finished each stanza. At the end they
would not stop applauding until Johnny cleared his throat to sing
another song.

They were all proud of him. He was of them and he had become a
famous singer, a movie star who slept with the most desired women
in the world. And yet he had shown proper respect for his Godfather
by traveling three thousand miles to attend this wedding. He still
loved old friends like Nino Valenti. Many of the people there had
seen Johnny and Nino singing together when they were just boys,
when no one dreamed that Johnny Fontane would grow up to hold
the hearts of fifty million women in his hands.

Johnny Fontane reached down and lifted the bride up on to the
bandstand so that Connie stood between him and Nino. Both men
crouched down, facing each other, Nino plucking the mandolin for a
few harsh chords. It was an old routine of theirs, a mock battle and
wooing, using their voices like swords, each shouting a chorus in
turn. With the most delicate courtesy, Johnny let Nino's voice
overwhelm his own, let Nino take the bride from his arm, let Nino
swing into the last victorious stanza while his own voice died away.
The whole wedding party broke into shouts of applause, the three of

them embraced each other at the end. The guests begged for another song.

Only Don Corleone, standing in the corner entrance of the house, sensed something amiss. Cheerily, with bluff good humor, careful not to give offense to his guests, he called out, "My godson has come three thousand miles to do us honor and no one thinks to wet his throat?" At once a dozen full wine glasses were thrust at Johnny Fontane. He took a sip from all and rushed to embrace his Godfather. As he did so he whispered something into the older man's ear. Don Corleone led him into the house.

Tom Hagen held out his hand when Johnny came into the room. Johnny shook it and said, "How are you, Tom?" But without his usual charm that consisted of a genuine warmth for people. Hagen was a little hurt by this coolness but shrugged it off. It was one of the penalties for being the Don's hatchet man.

Johnny Fontane said to the Don, "When I got the wedding invitation I said to myself, 'My Godfather isn't mad at me anymore.' I called you five times after my divorce and Tom always told me you were out or busy so I knew you were sore."

Don Corleone was filling glasses from the yellow bottle of Strega. "That's all forgotten. Now. Can I do something for you still? You're not too famous, too rich, that I can't help you?"

Johnny gulped down the yellow fiery liquid and held out his glass to be refilled. He tried to sound jaunty. "I'm not rich, Godfather. I'm going down. You were right. I should never have left my wife and kids for that tramp I married. I don't blame you for getting sore at me."

The Don shrugged. "I worried about you, you're my godson, that's all."

Johnny paced up and down the room. "I was crazy about that bitch. The biggest star in Hollywood. She looks like an angel. And you know what she does after a picture? If the makeup man does a good job on her face, she lets him bang her. If the cameraman made her look extra good, she brings him into her dressing room and gives him a screw. Anybody. She uses her body like I use the loose change in my pocket for a tip. A whore made for the devil."

Don Corleone curtly broke in. "How is your family?"

Johnny sighed. "I took care of them. After the divorce I gave Ginny and the kids more than the courts said I should. I go see them once a week. I miss them. Sometimes I think I'm going crazy." He took another drink. "Now my second wife laughs at me. She can't understand my being jealous. She calls me an old-fashioned guinea, she makes fun of my singing. Before I left I gave her a nice beating but not in the face because she was making a picture. I gave her cramps, I punched her on the arms and legs like a kid and she kept laughing at me." He lit a cigarette. "So, Godfather, right now, life doesn't seem worth living."

Don Corleone said simply, "These are troubles I can't help you with." He paused, then asked, "What's the matter with your voice?"

All the assured charm, the self-mockery, disappeared from Johnny Fontane's face. He said almost brokenly, "Godfather, I can't sing anymore, something happened to my throat, the doctors don't know what." Hagen and the Don looked at him with surprise, Johnny had always been so tough. Fontane went on. "My two pictures made a lot of money. I was a big star. Now they throw me out. The head of the studio always hated my guts and now he's paying me off."

Don Corleone stood before his godson and asked grimly, "Why doesn't this man like you?"

"I used to sing those songs for the liberal organizations, you know, all that stuff you never liked me to do. Well, Jack Woltz didn't like it either. He called me a Communist, but he couldn't make it stick. Then I snatched a girl he had saved for himself. It was strictly a one-night stand and she came after me. What the hell could I do? Then my whore second wife throws me out. And Ginny and the kids won't take me back unless I come crawling on my hands and knees, and I can't sing anymore. Godfather, what the hell can I do?"

Don Corleone's face had become cold without a hint of sympathy. He said contemptuously, "You can start by acting like a man." Suddenly anger contorted his face. He shouted. "LIKE A MAN!" He reached over the desk and grabbed Johnny Fontane by the hair of his head in a gesture that was savagely affectionate. "By Christ in heaven, is it possible that you spent so much time in *my* presence and turned out no better than this? A Hollywood *finocchio* who weeps and begs for pity? Who cries out like a woman—'What shall I do? Oh, what shall I do?'"

The mimicry of the Don was so extraordinary, so unexpected, that Hagen and Johnny were startled into laughter. Don Corleone was pleased. For a moment he reflected on how much he loved this godson. How would his own three sons have reacted to such a tongue-lashing? Santino would have sulked and behaved badly for weeks afterward. Fredo would have been cowed. Michael would have given him a cold smile and gone out of the house, not to be seen for months. But Johnny, ah, what a fine chap he was, smiling now, gathering strength, knowing already the true purpose of his Godfather.

Don Corleone went on. "You took the woman of your boss, a man more powerful than yourself, then you complain he won't help you. What nonsense. You left your family, your children without a father, to marry a whore and you weep because they don't welcome you back with open arms. The whore, you don't hit her in the face because she is making a picture, then you are amazed because she laughs at you. You lived like a fool and you have come to a fool's end."

Don Corleone paused to ask in a patient voice, "Are you willing to take my advice this time?"

Johnny Fontane shrugged. "I can't marry Ginny again, not the way she wants. I have to gamble, I have to drink, I have to go out with the boys. Beautiful broads run after me and I never could resist them. Then I used to feel like a heel when I went back to Ginny. Christ, I can't go through all that crap aga

It was rare that Don Corleone showed exasperation. "I didn't tell you to get married again. Do what you want. It's good you wish to be a father to your children. A man who is not a father to his children can never be a real man. But then, you must make their mother accept you. Who says you can't see them every day? Who says you can't live in the same house? Who says you can't live your life exactly as you want to live it?"

Johnny Fontane laughed. "Godfather, not all women are like the old Italian wives. Ginny won't stand for it."

Now the Don was mocking. "Because you acted like a *finocchio*. You gave her *more* than the court said. You didn't hit the other in the face because she was making a picture. You let women dictate your actions and they are not competent in this world, though certainly they will be saints in heaven while we men burn in hell. And then I've watched you all these years." The Don's voice became earnest. "You've been a fine godson, you've given me all the respect. But what of your other old friends? One year you run around with this person, the next year with another person. That Italian boy who was so funny in the movies, he had some bad luck and you never saw him again because you were more famous. And how about your old, old comrade that you went to school with, who was your partner singing? Nino. He drinks too much out of disappointment but he never complains. He works hard driving the gravel truck and sings weekends for a few dollars. He never says anything against you. You couldn't help him a bit? Why not? He sings well."

Johnny Fontane said with patient weariness, "Godfather, he just hasn't got enough talent. He's OK, but he's not big time."

Don Corleone lidded his eyes almost closed and then said, "And you, godson, you now, you just don't have talent enough. Shall I get you a job on the gravel truck with Nino?" When Johnny didn't answer, the Don went on. "Friendship is everything. Friendship is more than talent. It is more than government. It is almost the equal of family. Never forget that. If you had built up a wall of friendships you wouldn't have to ask me to help. Now tell me, why can't you sing? You sang well in the garden. As well as Nino."

Hagen and Johnny smiled at this delicate thrust. It was Johnny's turn to be patronizingly patient. "My voice is weak. I sing one or two songs and then I can't sing again for hours or days. I can't make it through the rehearsals or the retakes. My voice is weak, it's got some sort of sickness."

"So you have woman trouble. Your voice is sick. Now tell me the trouble you're having with this Hollywood *pezzonovante* who won't let you work." The Don was getting down to business.

"He's bigger than one of your *pezzonovantes*," Johnny said. "He owns the studio. He advises the President on movie propaganda for the war. Just a month ago he bought the movie rights to the biggest novel of the year. A best seller. And the main character is a guy just like me. I wouldn't even have to act, just be myself. I wouldn't even have to sing. I might even win the Academy Award. Everybody knows it's perfect for me and I'd be big again. As an actor. But that bastard Jack Woltz is paying me off, he won't give it to me. I offered to do it for nothing, for a minimum price and he still says no. He sent the word that if I come and kiss his ass in the studio commissary, maybe he'll think about it."

Don Corleone dismissed this emotional nonsense with a wave of his hand. Among reasonable men problems of business could always be solved. He patted his godson on the shoulder. "You're discouraged. Nobody cares about you, so you think. And you've lost a lot of weight. You drink a lot, eh? You don't sleep and you take pills?" He shook his head disapprovingly.

"Now I want you to follow my orders," the Don said. "I want you to stay in my house for one month. I want you to eat well, to rest and sleep. I want you to be my companion, I enjoy your company, and maybe you can learn something about the world from your Godfather that might even help you in the great Hollywood. But no singing, no drinking and no women. At the end of the month you can go back to Hollywood and this *pezzonovante*, this .90 caliber will give you that job you want. Done?"

Johnny Fontane could not altogether believe that the Don had such power. But his Godfather had never said such and such a thing could be done without having it done. "This guy is a personal friend of J. Edgar Hoover," Johnny said. "You can't even raise your voice to him."

"He's a businessman," the Don said blandly. "I'll make him an offer he can't refuse."

"It's too late," Johnny said. "All the contracts have been signed and they start shooting in a week. It's absolutely impossible."

Don Corleone said, "Go, go back to the party. Your friends are waiting for you. Leave everything to me." He pushed Johnny Fontane out of the room.

Hagen sat behind the desk and made notes. The Don heaved a sigh and asked, "Is there anything else?"

"Sollozzo can't be put off any more. You'll have to see him this week." Hagen held his pen over the calendar.

The Don shrugged. "Now that the wedding is over, whenever you like."

This answer told Hagen two things. Most important, that the answer to Virgil Sollozzo would be no. The second, that Don Corleone, since he would not give the answer before his daughter's wedding, expected his no to cause trouble.

Hagen said cautiously, "Shall I tell Clemenza to have some men come live in the house?"

The Don said impatiently, "For what? I didn't answer before the wedding because on an important day like that there should be no cloud, not even in the distance. Also I wanted to know beforehand what he wanted to talk about. We know now. What he will propose is an *infamita*."

Hagen asked, "Then you will refuse?" When the Don nodded, Hagen said, "I think we should all discuss it—the whole Family— before you give your answer."

The Don smiled. "You think so? Good, we will discuss it. When you come back from California. I want you to fly there tomorrow and settle this business for Johnny. See that movie *pezzonovante*. Tell Sollozzo I will see him when you get back from California. Is there anything else?"

Hagen said formally, "The hospital called. *Consigliori* Abbandando is dying, he won't last out the night. His family was told to come and wait."

Hagen had filled the *Consigliori*'s post for the past year, ever since the cancer had imprisoned Genco Abbandando in his hospital bed. Now he waited to hear Don Corleone say the post was his permanently. The odds were against it. So high a position was traditionally given only to a man descended from two Italian parents. There had already been trouble about his temporary performance of the duties. Also, he was only thirty-five, not old enough, supposedly, to have acquired the necessary experience and cunning for a successful *Consigliori*.

But the Don gave him no encouragement. He asked, "When does my daughter leave with her bridegroom?"

Hagen looked at his wristwatch. "In a few minutes they'll cut the cake and then a half hour after that." That reminded him of something else. "Your new son-in-law. Do we give him something important, inside the Family?"

He was surprised at the vehemence of the Don's answer. "Never." The Don hit the desk with the flat of his hand. "Never. Give him something to earn his living, a good living. But never let him know the Family's business. Tell the others, Sonny, Fredo, Clemenza."

The Don paused. "Instruct my sons, all three of them, that they will accompany me to the hospital to see poor Genco. I want them to pay their last respects. Tell Freddie to drive the big car and ask Johnny if he will come with us, as a special favor to me." He saw Hagen look at him questioningly. "I want you to go to California tonight. You won't have time to go see Genco. But don't leave until I come back from the hospital and speak with you. Understood?"

"Understood," Hagen said. "What time should Fred have the car waiting?"

"When the guests have left," Don Corleone said. "Genco will wait for me."

"The Senator called," Hagen said. "Apologizing for not coming personally but that you would understand. He probably means those two FBI men across the street taking down license numbers. But he sent his gift over by special messenger."

The Don nodded. He did not think it necessary to mention that he himself had warned the Senator not to come. "Did he send a nice present?"

Hagen made a face of impressed approval that was very strangely Italian on his German-Irish features. "Antique silver, very valuable. The kids can sell it for a grand at least. The Senator spent a lot of time getting exactly the right thing. For those kind of people that's more important than how much it costs."

Don Corleone did not hide his pleasure that so great a man as the Senator had shown him such respect. The Senator, like Luca Brasi, was one of the great stones in the Don's power structure, and he too, with this gift, had resworn his loyalty.

When Johnny Fontane appeared in the garden, Kay Adams recognized him immediately. She was truly surprised. "You never told me your family knew Johnny Fontane," she said. "Now I'm sure I'll marry you."

"Do you want to meet him?" Michael asked.

"Not now," Kay said. She sighed. "I was in love with him for three years. I used to come down to New York whenever he sang at the Capitol and scream my head off. He was so wonderful."

"We'll meet him later," Michael said.

When Johnny finished singing and vanished into the house with Don Corleone, Kay said archly to Michael, "Don't tell me a big movie star like Johnny Fontane has to ask your father for a favor?"

"He's my father's godson," Michael said. "And if it wasn't for my father he might not be a big movie star today."

Kay Adams laughed with delight. "That sounds like another great story."

Michael shook his head. "I can't tell that one," he said.

"Trust me," she said.

He told her. He told her without being funny. He told it without pride. He told it without any sort of explanation except that eight years before his father had been more impetuous, and because the matter concerned his godson, the Don considered it an affair of personal honor.

The story was quickly told. Eight years ago Johnny Fontane had made an extraordinary success singing with a popular dance band. He had become a top radio attraction. Unfortunately the band leader, a well-known show business personality named Les Halley, had signed Johnny to a five-year personal services contract. It was a common show business practice. Les Halley could now loan Johnny out and pocket most of the money.

Don Corleone entered the negotiations personally. He offered Les Halley twenty thousand dollars to release Johnny Fontane from the personal services contract. Halley offered to take only fifty percent of Johnny's earnings. Don Corleone was amused. He dropped his offer from twenty thousand dollars to ten thousand dollars. The band leader, obviously not a man of the world outside his beloved show business, completely missed the significance of this lower offer. He refused.

The next day Don Corleone went to see the band leader personally. He brought with him his two best friends, Genco Abbandando, who was his *Consigliori*, and Luca Brasi. With no other witnesses Don Corleone persuaded Les Halley to sign a document giving up all rights to all services from Johnny Fontane upon payment of a certified check to the amount of ten thousand dollars. Don Corleone did this by putting a pistol to the forehead of the band leader and assuring him with the utmost seriousness that either his signature or his brains would rest on that document in exactly one minute. Les Halley signed. Don Corleone pocketed his pistol and handed over the certified check.

The rest was history. Johnny Fontane went on to become the greatest singing sensation in the country. He made Hollywood musicals that earned a fortune for his studio. His records made millions of dollars. Then he divorced his childhood-sweetheart wife and left his two children, to marry the most glamorous blond star in motion pictures. He soon learned that she was a "whore." He drank, he gambled, he chased other women. He lost his singing voice. His records stopped selling. The studio did not renew his contract. And so now he had come back to his Godfather.

Kay said thoughtfully, "Are you sure you're not jealous of your father? Everything you've told me about him shows him doing something for other people. He must be good-hearted." She smiled wryly. "Of course his methods are not exactly constitutional."

Michael sighed. "I guess that's the way it sounds, but let me tell you this. You know those Arctic explorers who leave caches of food scattered on the route to the North Pole? Just in case they may need them someday? That's my father's favors. Someday he'll be at each one of those people's houses and they had better come across."

It was nearly twilight before the wedding cake was shown, exclaimed over and eaten. Specially baked by Nazorine, it was cleverly decorated with shells of cream so dizzyingly delicious that the bride greedily plucked them from the corpse of the cake before she whizzed away on her honeymoon with her blond groom. The Don politely sped his guests' departure, noting meanwhile that the black sedan with its FBI men was no longer visible.

Finally the only car left in the driveway was the long black Cadillac with Freddie at the wheel. The Don got into the front seat, moving with quick coordination for his age and bulk. Sonny, Michael and Johnny Fontane got into the back seat. Don Corleone said to his son Michael, "Your girl friend, she'll get back to the city by herself all right?"

Michael nodded. "Tom said he'd take care of it." Don Corleone nodded with satisfaction at Hagen's efficiency.

Because of the gas rationing still in effect, there was little traffic on the Belt Parkway to Manhattan. In less than an hour the Cadillac rolled into the street of French Hospital. During the ride Don Corleone asked his youngest son if he was doing well in school. Michael nodded. Then Sonny in the back seat asked his father, "Johnny says you're getting him squared away with that Hollywood business. Do you want me to go out there and help?"

Don Corleone was curt. "Tom is going tonight. He won't need any help, it's a simple affair."

Sonny Corleone laughed. "Johnny thinks you can't fix it, that's why I thought you might want me to go out there."

Don Corleone turned his head. "Why do you doubt me?" he asked Johnny Fontane. "Hasn't your Godfather always done what he said he would do? Have I ever been taken for a fool?"

Johnny apologized nervously. "Godfather, the man who runs it is a real .90 caliber *pezzonovante*. You can't budge him, not even with money. He has big connections. And he hates me. I just don't know how you can swing it."

The Don spoke with affectionate amusement. "I say to you: you shall have it." He nudged Michael with his elbow. "We won't disappoint my godson, eh, Michael?"

Michael, who never doubted his father for a moment, shook his head.

As they walked toward the hospital entrance, Don Corleone put his hand on Michael's arm so that the others forged ahead. "When you get through with college, come and talk to me," the Don said. "I have some plans you will like."

Michael didn't say anything. Don Corleone grunted in exasperation. "I know how you are. I won't ask you to do anything you don't approve of. This is something special. Go your own way now, you're a man after all. But come to me as a son should when you have finished with your schooling."

The family of Genco Abbandando, wife and three daughters dressed in black, clustered like a flock of plump crows on the white tile floor of the hospital corridor. When they saw Don Corleone come out of the elevator, they seemed to flutter up off the white tiles in an instinctive surge toward him for protection. The mother was regally stout in black, the daughters fat and plain. Mrs. Abbandando pecked at Don Corleone's cheek, sobbing, wailing, "Oh, what a saint you are, to come here on your daughter's wedding day."

Don Corleone brushed these thanks aside. "Don't I owe respect to such a friend, a friend who has been my right arm for twenty years?" He had understood immediately that the soon-to-be widow did not comprehend that her husband would die this night. Genco Abbandando had been in this hospital for nearly a year dying of his cancer and the wife had come to consider his fatal illness almost an ordinary part of life. Tonight was just another crisis. She babbled on. "Go in and see my poor husband," she said, "he asks for you. Poor man, he wanted to come to the wedding to show his respect but the doctor would not permit it. Then he said you would come to see him on this great day but I did not believe it possible. Ah, men understand friendship more than we women. Go inside, you will make him happy."

A nurse and a doctor came out of Genco Abbandando's private room. The doctor was a young man, serious-faced and with the air of one born to command, that is to say, the air of one who has been immensely rich all his life. One of the daughters asked timidly, "Dr. Kennedy, can we go to see him now?"

Dr. Kennedy looked over the large group with exasperation. Didn't these people realize that the man inside was dying and dying in torturous pain? It would be much better if everyone let him die in peace. "I think just the immediate family," he said in his exquisitely polite voice. He was surprised when the wife and daughters turned to the short, heavy man dressed in an awkwardly fitted tuxedo, as if to hear his decision.

The heavy man spoke. There was just the slightest trace of an Italian accent in his voice. "My dear doctor," said Don Corleone, "is it true he is dying?"

"Yes," said Dr. Kennedy.

"Then there is nothing more for you to do," said Don Corleone. "We will take up the burden. We will comfort him. We will close his eyes. We will bury him and weep at his funeral and afterwards we will watch over his wife and daughters." At hearing things put so bluntly, forcing her to understand, Mrs. Abbandando began to weep.

Dr. Kennedy shrugged. It was impossible to explain to these peasants. At the same time he recognized the crude justice in the man's remarks. His role was over. Still exquisitely polite, he said, "Please wait for the nurse to let you in, she has a few necessary things to do with the patient." He walked away from them down the corridor, his white coat flapping.

The nurse went back into the room and they waited. Finally she came out again, holding the door for them to enter. She whispered, "He's delirious with the pain and fever, try not to excite him. And you can stay only a few minutes, except for the wife." She recognized Johnny Fontane as he went by her and her eyes opened wide. He gave her a faint smile of acknowledgment and she stared at him with frank invitation. He filed her away for future reference, then followed the others into the sick man's room.

Genco Abbandando had run a long race with death, and now, vanquished, he lay exhausted on the raised bed. He was wasted away to no more than a skeleton, and what had once been vigorous black hair had turned into obscene stringy wisps. Don Corleone said cheerily, "Genco, dear friend, I have brought my sons to pay their respects, and look, even Johnny, all the way from Hollywood."

The dying man raised his fevered eyes gratefully to the Don. He let the young men clasp his bony hand in their fleshy ones. His wife and daughters ranged themselves along his bed, kissing his cheek, taking his other hand in turn.

The Don pressed his old friend's hand. He said comfortingly, "Hurry up and get better and we'll take a trip back to Italy together to our old village. We'll play *boccie* in front of the wineshop like our fathers before us."

The dying man shook his head. He motioned the young men and his family away from his bedside; with the other bony claw he hung fast to the Don. He tried to speak. The Don put his head down and then sat on the bedside chair. Genco Abbandando was babbling about their childhood. Then his coal-black eyes became sly. He whispered. The Don bent closer. The others in the room were astonished to see tears running down Don Corleone's face as he shook his head. The quavering voice grew louder, filling the room. With a tortured, superhuman effort, Abbandando lifted his head off his pillow, eyes unseeing, and pointed a skeletal forefinger at the Don. "Godfather, Godfather," he called out blindly, "save me from death, I beg of you. My flesh is burning off my bones and I can feel the worms eating away my brain. Godfather, cure me, you have the power, dry the tears of my poor wife. In Corleone we played together as children and now will you let me die when I fear hell for my sins?"

The Don was silent. Abbandando said, "It is your daughter's wedding day, you cannot refuse me."

The Don spoke quietly, gravely, to pierce through the blasphemous delirium. "Old friend," he said, "I have no such powers. If I did I would be more merciful than God, believe me. But don't fear death and don't fear hell. I will have a mass said for your soul every night and every morning. Your wife and your children will pray for you. How can God punish you with so many pleas for mercy?"

The skeleton face took on a cunning expression that was obscene. Abbandando said slyly, "It's been arranged then?"

When the Don answered, his voice was cold, without comfort. "You blaspheme. Resign yourself."

Abbandando fell back on the pillow. His eyes lost their wild gleam of hope. The nurse came back into the room and started shooing them out in a very matter-of-fact way. The Don got up but Abbandando put out his hand. "Godfather," he said, "stay here with me and help me meet death. Perhaps if He sees you near me He will be frightened and leave me in peace. Or perhaps you can say a word, pull a few strings, eh?" The dying man winked as if he were mocking the Don, now not really serious. "You're brothers in blood, after all." Then, as if fearing the Don would be offended, he clutched at his hand. "Stay with me, let me hold your hand. We'll outwit that bastard as we've outwitted others. Godfather, don't betray me."

The Don motioned the other people out of the room. They left. He took the withered claw of Genco Abbandando in his own two broad hands. Softly, reassuringly, he comforted his friend, as they waited for death together. As if the Don could truly snatch the life of Genco Abbandando back from that most foul and criminal traitor to man.

The wedding day of Connie Corleone ended well for her. Carlo Rizzi performed his duties as a bridegroom with skill and vigor, spurred on by the contents of the bride's gift purse which totaled up to over twenty thousand dollars. The bride, however, gave up her virginity with a great deal more willingness than she gave up her purse. For the latter, he had to blacken one of her eyes.

Lucy Mancini waited in her house for a call from Sonny Corleone, sure that he would ask her for a date. Finally she called his house and when she heard a woman's voice answer the phone she hung up. She had no way of knowing that nearly everyone at the wedding had remarked the absence of her and Sonny for that fatal half hour and the gossip was already spreading that Santino Corleone had found another victim. That he had "done the job" on his own sister's maid of honor.

Amerigo Bonasera had a terrible nightmare. In his dreams he saw Don Corleone, in peaked cap, overalls and heavy gloves, unloading bullet-riddled corpses in front of his funeral parlor and shouting, "Remember, Amerigo, not a word to anyone, and bury them quickly." He groaned so loud and long in his sleep that his wife shook him awake. "Eh, what a man you are," she grumbled. "To have a nightmare only after a wedding."

Kay Adams was escorted to her New York City hotel by Paulie Gatto and Clemenza. The car was large, luxurious and driven by Gatto. Clemenza sat in the back seat and Kay was given the front seat next to the driver. She found both men wildly exotic. Their speech was movie Brooklynese and they treated her with exaggerated court-liness. During the ride she chatted casually with both men and was surprised when they spoke of Michael with unmistakable affection and respect. He had led her to believe that he was an alien in his father's world. Now Clemenza was assuring her in his wheezing gutteral voice that the "old man" thought Mike was the best of his sons, the one who would surely inherit the family business.

"What business is that?" Kay asked in the most natural way.

Paulie Gatto gave her a quick glance as he turned the wheel. Behind her Clemenza said in a surprised voice, "Didn't Mike tell you? Mr. Corleone is the biggest importer of Italian olive oil in the States. Now that the war is over the business could get real rich. He'll need a smart boy like Mike."

At the hotel Clemenza insisted on coming to the desk with her. When she protested, he said simply, "The boss said to make sure you got home OK. I gotta do it."

After she received her room key he walked her to the elevator and waited until she got in. She waved to him, smiling, and was surprised at his genuine smile of pleasure in return. It was just as well she did not see him go back to the hotel clerk and ask, "What name she registered under?"

The hotel clerk looked at Clemenza coldly. Clemenza rolled the little green spitball he was holding in his hand across to the clerk, who picked it up and immediately said, "Mr. and Mrs. Michael Corleone."

Back in the car, Paulie Gatto said, "Nice dame."

Clemenza grunted. "Mike is doing the job on her." Unless, he thought, they were really married. "Pick me up early in the morning," he told Paulie Gatto. "Hagen got some deal for us that gotta be done right away."

It was late Sunday night before Tom Hagen could kiss his wife good-bye and drive out to the airport. With his special number one priority (a grateful gift from a Pentagon staff general officer) he had no trouble getting on a plane to Los Angeles.

It had been a busy but satisfying day for Tom Hagen. Genco Abbandando had died at three in the morning and when Don Corleone returned from the hospital, he had informed Hagen that he was now officially the new *Consigliori* to the family. This meant that Hagen was sure to become a very rich man, to say nothing of power.

The Don had broken a long-standing tradition. The *Consigliori* was always a full-blooded Sicilian, and the fact that Hagen had been brought up as a member of the Don's family made no difference to that tradition. It was a question of blood. Only a Sicilian born to the ways of *omerta*, the law of silence, could be trusted in the key post of *Consigliori*.

Between the head of the family, Don Corleone, who dictated policy, and the operating level of men who actually carried out the orders of the Don, there were three layers, or buffers. In that way nothing could be traced to the top. Unless the *Consigliori* turned traitor. That Sunday morning Don Corleone gave explicit instructions on what should be done to the two young men who had beaten the daughter of Amerigo Bonasera. But he had given those orders in private to Tom Hagen. Later in the day Hagen had, also in private without witnesses, instructed Clemenza. In turn Clemenza had told Paulie Gatto to execute the commission. Paulie Gatto would now muster the necessary manpower and execute the orders. Paulie Gatto and his men would not know why this particular task was being carried out or who had ordered it originally. Each link of the chain would have to turn traitor for the Don to be involved and though it had never yet happened, there was always the possibility. The cure for that possibility also was known. Only one link in the chain had to disappear.

The *Consigliori* was also what his name implied. He was the counselor to the Don, his right-hand man, his auxiliary brain. He was also his closest companion and his closest friend. On important trips he would drive the Don's car, at conferences he would go out and get the Don refreshments, coffee and sandwiches, fresh cigars. He would know everything the Don knew or nearly everything, all the cells of power. He was the one man in the world who could bring the Don crashing down to destruction. But no *Consigliori* had ever betrayed a Don, not in the memory of any of the powerful Sicilian families who had established themselves in America. There was no future in it. And every *Consigliori* knew that if he kept the faith, he would become rich, wield power and win respect. If misfortune came, his wife and children would be sheltered and cared for as if he were alive or free. *If he kept the faith.*

In some matters the *Consigliori* had to act for his Don in a more open way and yet not involve his principal. Hagen was flying to California on just such a matter. He realized that his career as *Consigliori* would be seriously affected by the success or failure of this mission. By family business standards whether Johnny Fontane got his coveted part in the war movie, or did not, was a minor matter. Far

more important was the meeting Hagen had set up with Virgil Sollozzo the following Friday. But Hagen knew that to the Don, both
were of equal importance, which settled the matter for any good
Consigliori.

The piston plane shook Tom Hagen's already nervous insides and
he ordered a martini from the hostess to quiet them. Both the Don
and Johnny had briefed him on the character of the movie producer,
Jack Woltz. From everything that Johnny said, Hagen knew he
would never be able to persuade Woltz. But he also had no doubt
whatsoever that the Don would keep his promise to Johnny. His own
role was that of negotiator and contact.

Lying back in his seat, Hagen went over all the information given
to him that day. Jack Woltz was one of the three most important
movie producers in Hollywood, owner of his own studio with dozens
of stars under contract. He was on the President of the United States'
Advisory Council for War Information, Cinematic Division, which
meant simply that he helped make propaganda movies. He had had
dinner at the White House. He had entertained J. Edgar Hoover in
his Hollywood home. But none of this was as impressive as it
sounded. They were all official relationships. Woltz didn't have any
personal political power, mainly because he was an extreme reaction-
ary, partly because he was a megalomaniac who loved to wield
power wildly without regard to the fact that by so doing legions of
enemies sprang up out of the ground.

Hagen sighed. There would be no way to "handle" Jack Woltz.
He opened his briefcase and tried to get some paper work done, but
he was too tired. He ordered another martini and reflected on his life.
He had no regrets, indeed he felt that he had been extremely lucky.
Whatever the reason, the course he had chosen ten years ago had
proved to be right for him. He was successful, he was as happy as any
grown man could reasonably expect, and he found life interesting.

Tom Hagen was thirty-five years old, a tall crew-cut man, very
slender, very ordinary-looking. He was a lawyer but did not do the
actual detailed legal work for the Corleone family business though he
had practiced law for three years after passing the bar exam.

At the age of eleven he had been a playmate of eleven-year-old
Sonny Corleone. Hagen's mother had gone blind and then died
during his eleventh year. Hagen's father, a heavy drinker, had become a hopeless drunkard. A hard-working carpenter, he had never
done a dishonest thing in his life. But his drinking destroyed his

family and finally killed him. Tom Hagen was left an orphan who wandered the streets and slept in hallways. His younger sister had been put in a foster home, but in the 1920's the social agencies did not follow up cases of twelve-year-old boys who were so ungrateful as to run from their charity. Hagen, too, had an eye infection. Neighbors whispered that he had caught or inherited it from his mother and so therefore it could be caught from him. He was shunned. Sonny Corleone, a warmhearted and imperious eleven-year-old, had brought his friend home and demanded that he be taken in. Tom Hagen was given a hot dish of spaghetti with oily rich tomato sauce, the taste of which he had never forgotten, and then given a metal folding bed to sleep on.

In the most natural way, without a word being spoken or the matter discussed in any fashion, Don Corleone had permitted the boy to stay in his household. Don Corleone himself took the boy to a special doctor and had his eye infection cured. He sent him to college and law school. In all this the Don acted not as a father but rather as a guardian. There was no show of affection but oddly enough the Don treated Hagen more courteously than his own sons, did not impose a parental will upon him. It was the boy's decision to go to law school after college. He had heard Don Corleone say once, "A lawyer with his briefcase can steal more than a hundred men with guns." Meanwhile, much to the annoyance of their father, Sonny and Freddie insisted on going into the family business after graduation from high school. Only Michael had gone on to college, and he had enlisted in the Marines the day after Pearl Harbor.

After he passed the bar exam, Hagen married to start his own family. The bride was a young Italian girl from New Jersey, rare at that time for being a college graduate. After the wedding, which was of course held in the home of Don Corleone, the Don offered to support Hagen in any undertaking he desired, to send him law clients, furnish his office, start him in real estate.

Tom Hagen had bowed his head and said to the Don, "I would like to work for you."

The Don was surprised, yet pleased. "You know who I am?" he asked.

Hagen nodded. He hadn't really known the extent of the Don's power, not then. He did not really know in the ten years that followed until he was made the acting *Consigliori* after Genco Abbandando became ill. But he nodded and met the Don's eyes with his own. "I would work for you like your sons," Hagen said, meaning with complete loyalty, with complete acceptance of the Don's parental divinity. The Don, with that understanding which was even then building the legend of his greatness, showed the young man the first mark of fatherly affection since he had come into his household. He took Hagen into his arms for a quick embrace and afterward treated him more like a true son, though he would sometimes say, "Tom, never forget your parents," as if he were reminding himself as well as Hagen.

There was no chance that Hagen would forget. His mother had been near moronic and slovenly, so ridden by anemia she could not feel affection for her children or make a pretense of it. His father Hagen had hated. His mother's blindness before she died had terrified him and his own eye infection had been a stroke of doom. He had been sure he would go blind. When his father died, Tom Hagen's eleven-year-old mind had snapped in a curious way. He had roamed the streets like an animal waiting for death until the fateful day Sonny found him sleeping in the back of a hallway and brought him to his home. What had happened afterward was a miracle. But for years Hagen had had nightmares, dreaming he had grown to manhood blind, tapping a white cane, his blind children behind him tap-tapping with their little white canes as they begged in the streets. Some mornings when he woke the face of Don Corleone was imprinted on his brain in that first conscious moment and he would feel safe.

But the Don had insisted that he put in three years of general law practice in addition to his duties for the family business. This experience had proved invaluable later on, and also removed any doubts in Hagen's mind about working for Don Corleone. He had then spent two years of training in the offices of a top firm of criminal lawyers in which the Don had some influence. It was apparent to everyone that he had a flair for this branch of the law. He did well and when he went into the full-time service of the family business, Don Corleone had not been able to reproach him once in the six years that followed.

When he had been made the acting *Consigliori*, the other powerful Sicilian families referred contemptuously to the Corleone family as the "Irish gang." This had amused Hagen. It had also taught him that he could never hope to succeed the Don as the head of the family business. But he was content. That had never been his goal, such an ambition would have been a "disrespect" to his benefactor and his benefactor's blood family.

It was still dark when the plane landed in Los Angeles. Hagen checked into his hotel, showered and shaved, and watched dawn come over the city. He ordered breakfast and newspapers to be sent up to his room and relaxed until it was time for his ten A.M. appointment with Jack Woltz. The appointment had been surprisingly easy to make.

The day before, Hagen had called the most powerful man in the movie labor unions, a man named Billy Goff. Acting on instructions from Don Corleone, Hagen had told Goff to arrange an appointment on the next day for Hagen to call on Jack Woltz, that he should hint to Woltz that if Hagen was not made happy by the results of the interview, there could be a labor strike at the movie studio. An hour later Hagen received a call from Goff. The appointment would be at ten A.M. Woltz had gotten the message about the possible labor strike but hadn't seemed too impressed, Goff said. He added, "If it really comes down to that, I gotta talk to the Don myself."

"If it comes to that he'll talk to you," Hagen said. By saying this he avoided making any promises. He was not surprised that Goff was so agreeable to the Don's wishes. The family empire, technically, did not extend beyond the New York area but Don Corleone had first become strong by helping labor leaders. Many of them still owed him debts of friendship.

But the ten A.M. appointment was a bad sign. It meant that he would be first on the appointment list, that he would not be invited to lunch. It meant that Woltz held him in small worth. Goff had not been threatening enough, probably because Woltz had him on his graft payroll. And sometimes the Don's success in keeping himself out of the limelight worked to the disadvantage of the family business, in that his name did not mean anything to outside circles.

His analysis proved correct. Woltz kept him waiting for a half hour past the appointed time. Hagen didn't mind. The reception room was very plush, very comfortable, and on a plum-colored couch opposite him sat the most beautiful child Hagen had ever seen. She was no more than eleven or twelve, dressed in a very expensive but simple way as a grown woman. She had incredibly golden hair, huge deep sea–blue eyes and a fresh raspberry-red mouth. She was guarded by a woman obviously her mother, who tried to stare Hagen down with a cold arrogance that made him want to punch her in the face. The angel child and the dragon mother, Hagen thought, returning the mother's cold stare.

Finally an exquisitely dressed but stout middle-aged woman came to lead him through a string of offices to the office-apartment of the movie producer. Hagen was impressed by the beauty of the offices and the people working in them. He smiled. They were all shrewdies, trying to get their foot in the movie door by taking office jobs, and most of them would work in these offices for the rest of their lives or until they accepted defeat and returned to their home towns.

Jack Woltz was a tall, powerfully built man with a heavy paunch almost concealed by his perfectly tailored suit. Hagen knew his history. At ten years of age Woltz had hustled empty beer kegs and pushcarts on the East Side. At twenty he helped his father sweat garment workers. At thirty he had left New York and moved West, invested in the nickelodeon and pioneered motion pictures. At forty-eight he had been the most powerful movie magnate in Hollywood, still rough-spoken, rapaciously amorous, a raging wolf ravaging helpless flocks of young starlets. At fifty he transformed himself. He took speech lessons, learned how to dress from an English valet and how to behave socially from an English butler. When his first wife died he married a world-famous and beautiful actress who didn't like acting. Now at the age of sixty he collected old master paintings, was a member of the President's Advisory Committee, and had set up a multimillion-dollar foundation in his name to promote art in motion pictures. His daughter had married an English lord, his son an Italian princess.

His latest passion, as reported dutifully by every movie columnist in America, was his own racing stables on which he had spent ten million dollars in the past year. He had made headlines by purchasing the famed English racing horse Khartoum for the incredible price of six hundred thousand dollars and then announcing that the undefeated racer would be retired and put to stud exclusively for the Woltz stables.

He received Hagen courteously, his beautifully, evenly tanned, meticulously barbered face contorted with a grimace meant to be a smile. Despite all the money spent, despite the ministrations of the most knowledgeable technicians, his age showed; the flesh of his face looked as if it had been seamed together. But there was an enormous vitality in his movements and he had what Don Corleone had, the air of a man who commanded absolutely the world in which he lived.

Hagen came directly to the point. That he was an emissary from a friend of Johnny Fontane. That this friend was a very powerful man who would pledge his gratitude and undying friendship to Mr. Woltz if Mr. Woltz would grant a small favor. The small favor would be the casting of Johnny Fontane in the new war movie the studio planned to start next week.

The seamed face was impassive, polite. "What favors can your friend do me?" Woltz asked. There was just a trace of condescension in his voice.

Hagen ignored the condescension. He explained. "You've got some labor trouble coming up. My friend can absolutely guarantee to make that trouble disappear. You have a top male star who makes a lot of money for your studio but he just graduated from marijuana to heroin. My friend will guarantee that your male star won't be able to get any more heroin. And if some other little things come up over the years a phone call to me can solve your problems."

Jack Woltz listened to this as if he were hearing the boasting of a child. Then he said harshly, his voice deliberately all East Side, "You trying to put muscle on me?"

Hagen said coolly, "Absolutely not. I've come to ask a service for a friend. I've tried to explain that you won't lose anything by it."

Almost as if he willed it, Woltz made his face a mask of anger. The mouth curled, his heavy brows, dyed black, contracted to form a thick line over his glinting eyes. He leaned over the desk toward Hagen. "All right, you smooth son of a bitch, let me lay it on the line for you and your boss, whoever he is. Johnny Fontane never gets that movie. I don't care how many guinea Mafia goombahs come out of the woodwork." He leaned back. "A word of advice to you, my friend. J. Edgar Hoover, I assume you've heard of him"—Woltz smiled sardonically—"is a personal friend of mine. If I let him know I'm being pressured, you guys will never know what hit you."

Hagen listened patiently. He had expected better from a man of Woltz's stature. Was it possible that a man who acted this stupidly could rise to the head of a company worth hundreds of millions? That was something to think about since the Don was looking for new things to put money into, and if the top brains of this industry were so dumb, movies might be the thing. The abuse itself bothered him not at all. Hagen had learned the art of negotiation from the Don

THE GODFATHER · 56

himself. "Never get angry," the Don had instructed. "Never make a threat. Reason with people." The word "reason" sounded so much better in Italian, *rajunah*, to rejoin. The art of this was to ignore all insults, all threats; to turn the other cheek. Hagen had seen the Don sit at a negotiating table for eight hours, swallowing insults, trying to persuade a notorious and megalomaniac strong-arm man to mend his ways. At the end of the eight hours Don Corleone had thrown up his hands in a helpless gesture and said to the other men at the table, "But no one can reason with this fellow," and had stalked out of the meeting room. The strong-arm man had turned white with fear. Emissaries were sent to bring the Don back into the room. An agreement was reached but two months later the strong-arm man was shot to death in his favorite barbershop.

So Hagen started again, speaking in the most ordinary voice. "Look at my card," he said. "I'm a lawyer. Would I stick my neck out? Have I uttered one threatening word? Let me just say that I am prepared to meet any condition you name to get Johnny Fontane that movie. I think I've already offered a great deal for such a small favor. A favor that I understand it would be in your interest to grant. Johnny tells me that you admit he would be perfect for that part. And let me say that this favor would never be asked if that were not so. In fact, if you're worried about your investment, my client would finance the picture. But please let me make myself absolutely clear. We understand your no is no. Nobody can force you or is trying to. We know about your friendship with Mr. Hoover, I may add, and my boss respects you for it. He respects that relationship very much."

Woltz had been doodling with a huge, red-feathered pen. At the mention of money his interest was aroused and he stopped doodling. He said patronizingly, "This picture is budgeted at five million."

Hagen whistled softly to show that he was impressed. Then he said very casually, "My boss has a lot of friends who back his judgment."

For the first time Woltz seemed to take the whole thing seriously. He studied Hagen's card. "I never heard of you," he said. "I know most of the big lawyers in New York, but just who the hell are you?"

"I have one of those dignified corporate practices," Hagen said dryly. "I just handle this one account." He rose. "I won't take up any more of your time." He held out his hand, Woltz shook it. Hagen took a few steps toward the door and turned to face Woltz again. "I

BOOK I · 57

understand you have to deal with a lot of people who try to seem more important than they are. In my case the reverse is true. Why don't you check me out with our mutual friend? If you reconsider, call me at my hotel." He paused. "This may be sacrilege to you, but my client can do things for you that even Mr. Hoover might find out of his range." He saw the movie producer's eyes narrowing. Woltz was finally getting the message. "By the way, I admire your pictures very much," Hagen said in the most fawning voice he could manage. "I hope you can keep up the good work. Our country needs it."

Late that afternoon Hagen received a call from the producer's secretary that a car would pick him up within the hour to take him out to Mr. Woltz's country home for dinner. She told him it would be about a three-hour drive but that the car was equipped with a bar and some hors d'oeuvres. Hagen knew that Woltz made the trip in his private plane and wondered why he hadn't been invited to make the trip by air. The secretary's voice was adding politely, "Mr. Woltz suggested you bring an overnight bag and he'll get you to the airport in the morning."

"I'll do that," Hagen said. That was another thing to wonder about. How did Woltz know he was taking the morning plane back to New York? He thought about it for a moment. The most likely explanation was that Woltz had set private detectives on his trail to get all possible information. Then Woltz certainly knew he represented the Don, which meant that he knew something about the Don, which in turn meant that he was now ready to take the whole matter seriously. Something might be done after all, Hagen thought. And maybe Woltz was smarter than he had appeared this morning.

The home of Jack Woltz looked like an implausible movie set. There was a plantation-type mansion, huge grounds girdled by a rich black-dirt bridle path, stables and pasture for a herd of horses. The hedges, flower beds and grasses were as carefully manicured as a movie star's nails.

Woltz greeted Hagen on a glass-panel air-conditioned porch. The producer was informally dressed in blue silk shirt open at the neck, mustard-colored slacks, soft leather sandals. Framed in all this color and rich fabric his seamed, tough face was startling. He handed Hagen an outsized martini glass and took one for himself from the prepared tray. He seemed more friendly than he had been earlier in the day. He put his arm over Hagen's shoulder and said, "We have a little time before dinner, let's go look at my horses." As they walked toward the stables he said, "I checked you out, Tom; you should have told me your boss is Corleone. I thought you were just some third-rate hustler Johnny was running in to bluff me. And I don't bluff. Not that I want to make enemies, I never believed in that. But let's just enjoy ourselves now. We can talk business after dinner."

Surprisingly Woltz proved to be a truly considerate host. He explained his new methods, innovations that he hoped would make his stable the most successful in America. The stables were all fire-proofed, sanitized to the highest degree, and guarded by a special security detail of private detectives. Finally Woltz led him to a stall which had a huge bronze plaque attached to its outside wall. On the plaque was the name "Khartoum."

The horse inside the stall was, even to Hagen's inexperienced eyes, a beautiful animal. Khartoum's skin was jet black except for a diamond-shaped white patch on his huge forehead. The great brown eyes glinted like golden apples, the black skin over the taut body was silk. Woltz said with childish pride, "The greatest racehorse in the world. I bought him in England last year for six hundred grand. I bet even the Russian Czars never paid that much for a single horse. But I'm not going to race him, I'm going to put him to stud. I'm going to build the greatest racing stable this country has ever known." He stroked the horse's mane and called out softly, "Khartoum, Khartoum." There was real love in his voice and the animal responded. Woltz said to Hagen, "I'm a good horseman, you know, and the first time I ever rode I was fifty years old." He laughed. "Maybe one of my grandmothers in Russia got raped by a Cossack and I got his blood." He tickled Khartoum's belly and said with sincere admiration, "Look at that cock on him. I should have such a cock."

They went back to the mansion to have dinner. It was served by three waiters under the command of a butler, the table linen and ware were all gold thread and silver, but Hagen found the food mediocre. Woltz obviously lived alone, and just as obviously was not a man who cared about food. Hagen waited until they had both lit up huge Havana cigars before he asked Woltz, "Does Johnny get it or not?"

"I can't," Woltz said. "I can't put Johnny into that picture even if I wanted to. The contracts are all signed for all the performers and the cameras roll next week. There's no way I can swing it."

Hagen said impatiently, "Mr. Woltz, the big advantage of dealing with a man at the top is that such an excuse is not valid. You can do anything you want to do." He puffed on his cigar. "Don't you believe my client can keep his promises?"

Woltz said dryly, "I believe that I'm going to have labor trouble. Goff called me up on that, the son of a bitch, and the way he talked to me you'd never guess I pay him a hundred grand a year under the table. And I believe you can get that fag he-man star of mine off heroin. But I don't care about that and I can finance my own pictures. Because I hate that bastard Fontane. Tell your boss this is one favor I can't give but that he should try me again on anything else. Anything at all."

Hagen thought, you sneaky bastard, then why the hell did you bring me all the way out here? The producer had something on his mind. Hagen said coldly, "I don't think you understand the situation. Mr. Corleone is Johnny Fontane's godfather. That is a very close, a very sacred religious relationship." Woltz bowed his head in respect at this reference to religion. Hagen went on. "Italians have a little joke, that the world is so hard a man must have two fathers to look after him, and that's why they have godfathers. Since Johnny's father died, Mr. Corleone feels his responsibility even more deeply. As for trying you again, Mr. Corleone is much too sensitive. He never asks a second favor where he has been refused the first."

Woltz shrugged. "I'm sorry. The answer is still no. But since you're here, what will it cost me to have that labor trouble cleared up? In cash. Right now."

That solved one puzzle for Hagen. Why Woltz was putting in so much time on him when he had already decided not to give Johnny the part. And that could not be changed at this meeting. Woltz felt secure; he was not afraid of the power of Don Corleone. And certainly Woltz with his national political connections, his acquaintanceship with the FBI chief, his huge personal fortune and his absolute power in the film industry, could not feel threatened by Don Corleone. To any intelligent man, even to Hagen, it seemed that Woltz had correctly assessed his position. He was impregnable to the Don if he was willing to take the losses the labor struggle would cost. There was only one thing wrong with the whole equation. Don Corleone had promised his godson he would get the part and Don Corleone had never, to Hagen's knowledge, broken his word in such matters.

Hagen said quietly, "You are deliberately misunderstanding me. You are trying to make me an accomplice to extortion. Mr. Corleone promises only to speak in your favor on this labor trouble as a matter of friendship in return for your speaking in behalf of his client. A friendly exchange of influence, nothing more. But I can see you don't take me seriously. Personally, I think that is a mistake."

Woltz, as if he had been waiting for such a moment, let himself get angry. "I understood perfectly," he said. "That's the Mafia style, isn't it? All olive oil and sweet talk when what you're really doing is making threats. So let me lay it on the line. Johnny Fontane will never get that part and he's perfect for it. It would make him a great star. But he never will be because I hate that pinko punk and I'm going to run him out of the movies. And I'll tell you why. He ruined one of my most valuable protégés. For five years I had this girl under training, singing, dancing, acting lessons, I spent hundreds of thousands of dollars. I was going to make her a star. I'll be even more frank, just to show you that I'm not a hard-hearted man, that it wasn't all dollars and cents. That girl was beautiful and she was the greatest piece of ass I've ever had and I've had them all over the world. She could suck you out like a water pump. Then Johnny comes along with that olive-oil voice and guinea charm and she runs off. She threw it all away just to make me ridiculous. A man in my position, Mr. Hagen, can't afford to look ridiculous. I have to pay Johnny off."

For the first time, Woltz succeeded in astounding Hagen. He found it inconceivable that a grown man of substance would let such trivialities affect his judgment in an affair of business, and one of such importance. In Hagen's world, the Corleones' world, the physical beauty, the sexual power of women, carried not the slightest weight in worldly matters. It was a private affair, except, of course, in matters of marriage and family disgrace. Hagen decided to make one last try.

"You are absolutely right, Mr. Woltz," Hagen said. "But are your grievances that major? I don't think you've understood how important this very small favor is to my client. Mr. Corleone held the infant Johnny in his arms when he was baptized. When Johnny's father died, Mr. Corleone assumed the duties of parenthood, indeed he is called 'Godfather' by many, many people who wish to show their respect and gratitude for the help he has given them. Mr. Corleone never lets his friends down."

Woltz stood up abruptly. "I've listened to about enough. Thugs don't give me orders, I give them orders. If I pick up this phone, you'll spend the night in jail. And if that Mafia goombah tries any rough stuff, he'll find out I'm not a band leader. Yeah, I heard that story too. Listen, your Mr. Corleone will never know what hit him. Even if I have to use my influence at the White House."

The stupid, stupid son of a bitch. How the hell did he get to be a *pezzonovante*, Hagen wondered. Advisor to the President, head of the biggest movie studio in the world. Definitely the Don should get into the movie business. And the guy was taking his words at their sentimental face value. He was not getting the message.

"Thank you for the dinner and a pleasant evening," Hagen said. "Could you give me transportation to the airport? I don't think I'll spend the night." He smiled coldly at Woltz. "Mr. Corleone is a man who insists on hearing bad news at once."

While waiting in the floodlit colonnade of the mansion for his car, Hagen saw two women about to enter a long limousine already parked in the driveway. They were the beautiful twelve-year-old blond girl and her mother he had seen in Woltz's office that morning. But now the girl's exquisitely cut mouth seemed to have smeared into a thick, pink mass. Her sea-blue eyes were filmed over and when she walked down the steps toward the open car her long legs tottered like a crippled foal's. Her mother supported the child, helping her into the car, hissing commands into her ear. The mother's head turned for a quick furtive look at Hagen and he saw in her eyes a burning, hawklike triumph. Then she too disappeared into the limousine.

So that was why he hadn't got the plane ride from Los Angeles, Hagen thought. The girl and her mother had made the trip with the movie producer. That had given Woltz enough time to relax before dinner and do the job on the little kid. And Johnny wanted to live in this world? Good luck to him, and good luck to Woltz.

Paulie Gatto hated quickie jobs, especially when they involved violence. He liked to plan things ahead. And something like tonight, even though it was punk stuff, could turn into serious business if somebody made a mistake. Now, sipping his beer, he glanced around, checking how the two young punks were making out with the two little tramps at the bar.

Paulie Gatto knew everything there was to know about those two punks. Their names were Jerry Wagner and Kevin Moonan. They were both about twenty years old, good-looking, brown-haired, tall, well-built. Both were due to go back to college out of town in two weeks, both had fathers with political influence and this, with their college student classification, had so far kept them out of the draft. They were both also under suspended sentences for assaulting the daughter of Amerigo Bonasera. The lousy bastards, Paulie Gatto thought. Draft dodging, violating their probation by drinking in a bar after midnight, chasing floozies. Young punks. Paulie Gatto had been deferred from the draft himself because his doctor had furnished the draft board with documents showing that this patient, male, white, aged twenty-six, unmarried, had received electrical shock treatments for a mental condition. All false of course, but Paulie Gatto felt that he had earned his draft exemption. It had been arranged by Clemenza after Gatto had "made his bones" in the family business.

It was Clemenza who had told him that this job must be rushed through, before the boys went to college. Why the hell did it have to be done in New York, Gatto wondered. Clemenza was always giving extra orders instead of just giving out the job. Now if those two little tramps walked out with the punks it would be another night wasted.

He could hear one of the girls laughing and saying, "Are you crazy, Jerry? I'm not going in any car with you. I don't want to wind up in the hospital like that other poor girl." Her voice was spitefully rich with satisfaction. That was enough for Gatto. He finished up his beer and walked out into the dark street. Perfect. It was after midnight. There was only one other bar that showed light. The rest of the stores were closed. The precinct patrol car had been taken care of by Clemenza. They wouldn't be around that way until they got a radio call and then they'd come slow.

He leaned against the four-door Chevy sedan. In the back seat two men were sitting, almost invisible, although they were very big men. Paulie said, "Take them when they come out."

He still thought it had all been set up too fast. Clemenza had given him copies of the police mug shots of the two punks, the dope on where the punks went drinking every night to pick up bar girls. Paulie had recruited two of the strong-arms in the family and fingered the punks for them. He had also given them their instructions. No blows on the top or the back of the head, there was to be no accidental fatality. Other than that they could go as far as they liked. He had given them only one warning: "If those punks get out of the hospital in less than a month, you guys go back to driving trucks."

The two big men were getting out of the car. They were both ex-boxers who had never made it past the small clubs and had been fixed up by Sonny Corleone with a little loan-shark action so that they could make a decent living. They were, naturally, anxious to show their gratitude.

When Jerry Wagner and Kevin Moonan came out of the bar they were perfect setups. The bar girl's taunts had left their adolescent vanity prickly. Paulie Gatto, leaning against the fender of his car, called out to them with a teasing laugh, "Hey, Casanova, those broads really brushed you off."

The two young men turned on him with delight. Paulie Gatto looked like a perfect outlet for their humiliation. Ferret-faced, short, slightly built and a wise guy in the bargain. They pounced on him eagerly and immediately found their arms pinned by two men grabbing them from behind. At the same moment Paulie Gatto had slipped onto his right hand a specially made set of brass knuckles studded with one-sixteenth-inch iron spikes. His timing was good, he worked out in the gym three times a week. He smashed the punk named Wagner right on the nose. The man holding Wagner lifted him up off the ground and Paulie swung his arm, uppercutting into the perfectly positioned groin. Wagner went limp and the big man dropped him. This had taken no more than six seconds.

Now both of them turned their atttention to Kevin Moonan, who was trying to shout. The man holding him from behind did so easily with one huge muscled arm. The other hand he put around Moonan's throat to cut off any sound.

Paulie Gatto jumped into the car and started the motor. The two big men were beating Moonan to jelly. They did so with frightening deliberation, as if they had all the time in the world. They did not throw punches in flurries but in timed, slow-motion sequences that carried the full weight of their massive bodies. Each blow landed with a *splat* of flesh splitting open. Gatto got a glimpse of Moonan's face. It was unrecognizable. The two men left Moonan lying on the sidewalk and turned their attention to Wagner. Wagner was trying to get to his feet and he started to scream for help. Someone came out of the bar and the two men had to work faster now. They clubbed Wagner to his knees. One of the men took his arm and twisted it, then kicked him in the spine. There was a cracking sound and Wagner's scream of agony brought windows open all along the street. The two men worked very quickly. One of them held Wagner up by using his two hands around Wagner's head like a vise. The other man smashed his huge fist into the fixed target. There were more people coming out of the bar but none tried to interfere. Paulie Gatto yelled, "Come on, enough." The two big men jumped into the car and Paulie gunned it away. Somebody would describe the car and read the license plates but it didn't matter. It was a stolen California plate and there were one hundred thousand black Chevy sedans in New York City.

Chapter

❊❊❊❊❊❊❊❊❊❊❊❊❊❊❊❊❊❊❊❊❊❊❊❊❊

2

TOM HAGEN went to his law office in the city on Thursday morning. He planned to catch up on his paper work so as to have everything cleared away for the meeting with Virgil Sollozzo on Friday. A meeting of such importance that he had asked the Don for a full evening of talk to prepare for the proposition they knew Sollozzo would offer the family business. Hagen wanted to have all little details cleared away so that he could go to that preparatory meeting with an unencumbered mind.

The Don had not seemed surprised when Hagen returned from California late Tuesday evening and told him the results of the negotiations with Woltz. He had made Hagen go over every detail and grimaced with distaste when Hagen told about the beautiful little girl and her mother. He had murmured *"infamita,"* his strongest disapproval. He had asked Hagen one final question. "Does this man have real balls?"

Hagen considered exactly what the Don meant by this question. Over the years he had learned that the Don's values were so different from those of most people that his words also could have a different meaning. Did Woltz have character? Did he have a strong will? He most certainly did, but that was not what the Don was asking. Did the movie producer have the courage not to be bluffed? Did he have the willingness to suffer heavy financial loss delay on his movies would mean, the scandal of his big star exposed as a user of heroin? Again the answer was yes. But again this was not what the Don meant. Finally Hagen translated the question properly in his mind. Did Jack Woltz have the balls to risk everything, to run the chance of losing *all* on a matter of principle, on a matter of honor; for revenge?

Hagen smiled. He did it rarely but now he could not resist jesting with the Don. "You're asking if he is a Sicilian." The Don nodded his head pleasantly, acknowledging the flattering witticism and its truth. "No," Hagen said.

That had been all. The Don had pondered the question until the next day. On Wednesday afternoon he had called Hagen to his home and given him his instructions. The instructions had consumed the rest of Hagen's working day and left him dazed with admiration. There was no question in his mind that the Don had solved the problem, that Woltz would call him this morning with the news that Johnny Fontane had the starring part in his new war movie.

At that moment the phone did ring but it was Amerigo Bonasera. The undertaker's voice was trembling with gratitude. He wanted Hagen to convey to the Don his undying friendship. The Don had only to call on him. He, Amerigo Bonasera, would lay down his life for the blessed Godfather. Hagen assured him that the Don would be told.

The *Daily News* had carried a middle-page spread of Jerry Wagner and Kevin Moonan lying in the street. The photos were expertly gruesome, they seemed to be pulps of human beings. Miraculously, said the *News*, they were both still alive though they would both be in the hospital for months and would require plastic surgery. Hagen made a note to tell Clemenza that something should be done for Paulie Gatto. He seemed to know his job.

Hagen worked quickly and efficiently for the next three hours consolidating earning reports from the Don's real estate company, his olive oil importing business and his construction firm. None of them were doing well but with the war over they should all become rich producers. He had almost forgotten the Johnny Fontane problem when his secretary told him California was calling. He felt a little thrill of anticipation as he picked up the phone and said, "Hagen here."

The voice that came over the phone was unrecognizable with hate and passion. "You fucking bastard," Woltz screamed. "I'll have you all in jail for a hundred years. I'll spend every penny I have to get you. I'll get that Johnny Fontane's balls cut off, do you hear me, you guinea fuck?"

Hagen said kindly, "I'm German-Irish." There was a long pause and then a click of the phone being hung up. Hagen smiled. Not once had Woltz uttered a threat against Don Corleone himself. Genius had its rewards.

Jack Woltz always slept alone. He had a bed big enough for ten people and a bedroom large enough for a movie ballroom scene, but he had slept alone since the death of his first wife ten years before. This did not mean he no longer used women. He was physically a vigorous man despite his age, but he could be aroused now only by very young girls and had learned that a few hours in the evening were all the youth of his body and his patience could tolerate.

On this Thursday morning, for some reason, he awoke early. The light of dawn made his huge bedroom as misty as a foggy meadow-land. Far down at the foot of his bed was a familiar shape and Woltz struggled up on his elbows to get a clearer look. It had the shape of a horse's head. Still groggy, Woltz reached and flicked on the night table lamp.

The shock of what he saw made him physically ill. It seemed as if a great sledgehammer had struck him on the chest, his heartbeat jumped erratically and he became nauseous. His vomit spluttered on the thick flair rug.

Severed from its body, the black silky head of the great horse Khartoum was stuck fast in a thick cake of blood. White, reedy tendons showed. Froth covered the muzzle and those apple-sized eyes that had glinted like gold were mottled the color of rotting fruit with dead, hemorrhaged blood. Woltz was struck by a purely animal terror and out of that terror he screamed for his servants and out of that terror he called Hagen to make his uncontrolled threats. His maniacal raving alarmed the butler, who called Woltz's personal physician and his second in command at the studio. But Woltz regained his senses before they arrived.

He had been profoundly shocked. What kind of man could destroy an animal worth six hundred thousand dollars? Without a word of warning. Without any negotiation to have the act, its order, counter-manded. The ruthlessness, the sheer disregard for any values, implied a man who considered himself completely his own law, even his own God. And a man who backed up this kind of will with the power and cunning that held his own stable security force of no account. For by this time Woltz had learned that the horse's body had obviously been heavily drugged before someone leisurely hacked the huge triangular head off with an ax. The men on night duty claimed that they had heard nothing. To Woltz this seemed impossible. They could be made to talk. They had been bought off and they could be made to tell who had done the buying.

Woltz was not a stupid man, he was merely a supremely egotistical one. He had mistaken the power he wielded in his world to be more potent than the power of Don Corleone. He had merely needed some proof that this was not true. He understood this message. That despite all his wealth, despite all his contacts with the President of the United States, despite all his claims of friendship with the director of the FBI, an obscure importer of Italian olive oil would have him killed. Would actually have him killed! Because he wouldn't give Johnny Fontane a movie part he wanted. It was incredible. People didn't have any right to act that way. There couldn't be any kind of world if people acted that way. It was insane. It meant you couldn't do what you wanted with your own money, with the companies you owned, the power you had to give orders. It was ten times worse than communism. It had to be smashed. It must never be allowed.

Woltz let the doctor give him a very mild sedation. It helped him calm down again and to think sensibly. What really shocked him was the casualness with which this man Corleone had ordered the destruction of a world-famous horse worth six hundred thousand dollars. Six hundred thousand dollars! And that was just for openers. Woltz shuddered. He thought of this life he had built up. He was rich. He could have the most beautiful women in the world by crooking his finger and promising a contract. He was received by kings and queens. He lived a life as perfect as money and power could make it. It was crazy to risk all this because of a whim. Maybe he could get to Corleone. What was the legal penalty for killing a racehorse? He laughed wildly and his doctor and servants watched him with nervous anxiety. Another thought occurred to him. He would be the laughingstock of California merely because someone had contemptuously defied his power in such arrogant fashion. That decided him. That and the thought that maybe, maybe they wouldn't kill him. That they had something much more clever and painful in reserve.

Woltz gave the necessary orders. His personal confidential staff swung into action. The servants and the doctor were sworn to secrecy on pain of incurring the studio and Woltz's undying enmity. Word was given to the press that the racehorse Khartoum had died of an illness contracted during his shipment from England. Orders were given to bury the remains in a secret place on the estate.

Six hours later Johnny Fontane received a phone call from the executive producer of the film telling him to report for work the following Monday.

That evening, Hagen went to the Don's house to prepare him for the important meeting the next day with Virgil Sollozzo. The Don had summoned his eldest son to attend, and Sonny Corleone, his heavy Cupid-shaped face drawn with fatigue, was sipping at a glass of water. He must still be humping that maid of honor, Hagen thought. Another worry.

Don Corleone settled into an armchair puffing his Di Nobili cigar. Hagen kept a box of them in his room. He had tried to get the Don to switch to Havanas but the Don claimed they hurt his throat.

"Do we know everything necessary for us to know?" the Don asked.

Hagen opened the folder that held his notes. The notes were in no way incriminating, merely cryptic reminders to make sure he touched on every important detail. "Sollozzo is coming to us for help," Hagen said. "He will ask the family to put up at least a million dollars and to promise some sort of immunity from the law. For that we get a piece of the action, nobody knows how much. Sollozzo is vouched for by the Tattaglia family and they may have a piece of the action. The action is narcotics. Sollozzo has the contacts in Turkey, where they grow the poppy. From there he ships to Sicily. No trouble. In Sicily he has the plant to process into heroin. He has safety-valve operations to bring it down to morphine and bring it up to heroin if necessary. But it would seem that the processing plant in Sicily is protected in every way. The only hitch is bringing it into this country, and then distribution. Also initial capital. A million dollars cash doesn't grow on trees." Hagen saw Don Corleone grimace. The old man hated unnecessary flourishes in business matters. He went on hastily.

"They call Sollozzo the Turk. Two reasons. He's spent a lot of time in Turkey and is supposed to have a Turkish wife and kids.

Second. He's supposed to be very quick with the knife, or was, when he was young. Only in matters of business, though, and with some sort of reasonable complaint. A very competent man and his own boss. He has a record, he's done two terms in prison, one in Italy, one in the United States, and he's known to the authorities as a narcotics man. This could be a plus for us. It means that he'll never get immunity to testify, since he's considered the top and, of course, because of his record. Also he has an American wife and three children and he is a good family man. He'll stand still for any rap as long as he knows that they will be well taken care of for living money."

The Don puffed on his cigar and said, "Santino, what do you think?"

Hagen knew what Sonny would say. Sonny was chafing at being under the Don's thumb. He wanted a big operation of his own. Something like this would be perfect.

Sonny took a long slug of scotch. "There's a lot of money in that white powder," he said. "But it could be dangerous. Some people could wind up in jail for twenty years. I'd say that if we kept out of the operations end, just stuck to protection and financing, it might be a good idea."

Hagen looked at Sonny approvingly. He had played his cards well. He had stuck to the obvious, much the best course for him.

The Don puffed on his cigar. "And you, Tom, what do you think?"

Hagen composed himself to be absolutely honest. He had already come to the conclusion that the Don would refuse Sollozzo's proposition. But what was worse, Hagen was convinced that for one of the few times in his expereience, the Don had not thought things through. He was not looking far enough ahead.

"Go ahead, Tom," the Don said encouragingly. "Not even a Sicilian *Consigliori* always agrees with the boss." They all laughed.

"I think you should say yes," Hagen said. "You know all the obvious reasons. But the most important one is this. There is more money potential in narcotics than in any other business. If we don't get into it, somebody else will, maybe the Tattaglia family. With the revenue they earn they can amass more and more police and political power. Their family will become stronger than ours. Eventually they will come after us to take away what we have. It's just like countries. If they arm, we have to arm. If they become stronger economically, they become a threat to us. Now we have the gambling and we have the unions and right now they are the best things to have. But I think narcotics is the coming thing. I think we have to have a piece of that action or we risk everything we have. Not now, but maybe ten years from now."

The Don seemed enormously impressed. He puffed on his cigar and murmured, "That's the most important thing of course." He sighed and got to his feet. "What time do I have to meet this infidel tomorrow?"

Hagen said hopefully, "He'll be here at ten in the morning." Maybe the Don would go for it.

"I'll want you both here with me," the Don said. He rose, stretching, and took his son by the arm. "Santino, get some sleep tonight, you look like the devil himself. Take care of yourself, you won't be young forever."

Sonny, encouraged by this sign of fatherly concern, asked the question Hagen did not dare to ask. "Pop, what's your answer going to be?"

Don Corleone smiled. "How do I know until I hear the percentages and other details? Besides I have to have time to think over the advice given here tonight. After all, I'm not a man who does things rashly." As he went out the door he said casually to Hagen, "Do you have in your notes that the Turk made his living from prostitution before the war? As the Tattaglia family does now. Write that down before you forget." There was just a touch of derision in the Don's voice and Hagen flushed. He had deliberately not mentioned it, legitimately so since it really had no bearing, but he had feared it might prejudice the Don's decision. He was notoriously straitlaced in matters of sex.

Virgil "the Turk" Sollozzo was a powerfully built, medium-sized man of dark complexion who could have been taken for a true Turk. He had a scimitar of a nose and cruel black eyes. He also had an impressive dignity.

Sonny Corleone met him at the door and brought him into the office where Hagen and the Don waited. Hagen thought he had never seen a more dangerous-looking man except for Luca Brasi.

There were polite handshakings all around. If the Don ever asks me if this man has balls, I would have to answer yes, Hagen thought. He had never seen such force in one man, not even the Don. In fact the Don appeared at his worst. He was being a little too simple, a little too peasantlike in his greeting.

Sollozzo came to the point immediately. The business was narcotics. Everything was set up. Certain poppy fields in Turkey had pledged him certain amounts every year. He had a protected plant in France to convert into morphine. He had an absolutely secure plant in Sicily to process into heroin. Smuggling into both countries was as positively safe as such matters could be. Entry into the United States would entail about five percent losses since the FBI itself was incorruptible, as they both knew. But the profits would be enormous, the risk nonexistent.

"Then why do you come to me?" the Don asked politely. "How have I deserved your generosity?"

Sollozzo's dark face remained impassive. "I need two million dollars cash," he said. "Equally important, I need a man who has powerful friends in the important places. Some of my couriers will be caught over the years. That is inevitable. They will all have clean records, that I promise. So it will be logical for judges to give light sentences. I need a friend who can guarantee that when my people get in trouble they won't spend more than a year or two in jail. Then they won't talk. But if they get ten and twenty years, who knows? In this world there are many weak individuals. They may talk, they may jeopardize more important people. Legal protection is a must. I hear, Don Corleone, that you have as many judges in your pocket as a bootblack has pieces of silver."

Don Corleone didn't bother to acknowledge the compliment. "What percentage for my family?" he asked.

Sollozzo's eyes gleamed. "Fifty percent." He paused and then said in a voice that was almost a caress, "In the first year your share would be three or four million dollars. Then it would go up."

Don Corleone said, "And what is the percentage of the Tattaglia family?"

For the first time Sollozzo seemed to be nervous. "They will receive something from my share. I need some help in the operations."

"So," Don Corleone said, "I receive fifty percent merely for finance and legal protection. I have no worries about operations, is that what you tell me?"

Sollozzo nodded. "If you think two million dollars in cash is 'merely finance,' I congratulate you, Don Corleone."

The Don said quietly, "I consented to see you out of my respect for the Tattaglias and because I've heard you are a serious man to be treated also with respect. I must say no to you but I must give you my reasons. The profits in your business are huge but so are the risks. Your operation, if I were part of it, could damage my other interests. It's true I have many, many friends in politics, but they would not be so friendly if my business were narcotics instead of gambling. They think gambling is something like liquor, a harmless vice, and they think narcotics a dirty business. No, don't protest. I'm telling you their thoughts, not mine. How a man makes his living is not my concern. And what I am telling you is that this business of yours is too risky. All the members of my family have lived well the last ten years, without danger, without harm. I can't endanger them or their livelihoods out of greed."

The only sign of Sollozzo's disappointment was a quick flickering of his eyes around the room, as if he hoped Hagen or Sonny would speak in his support. Then he said, "Are you worried about security for your two million?"

The Don smiled coldly. "No," he said.

Sollozzo tried again. "The Tattaglia family will guarantee your investment also."

It was then that Sonny Corleone made an unforgivable error in judgment and procedure. He said eagerly, "The Tattaglia family guarantees the return of our investment without any percentage from us?"

Hagen was horrified at this break. He saw the Don turn cold, malevolent eyes on his eldest son, who froze in uncomprehending dismay. Sollozzo's eyes flickered again but this time with satisfaction. He had discovered a chink in the Don's fortress. When the Don spoke his voice held a dismissal. "Young people are greedy," he said. "And today they have no manners. They interrupt their elders. They meddle. But I have a sentimental weakness for my children and I have spoiled them. As you see. Signor Sollozzo, my no is final. Let me say that I myself wish you good fortune in your business. It has no conflict with my own. I'm sorry that I had to disappoint you."

Sollozzo bowed, shook the Don's hand and let Hagen take him to his car outside. There was no expression on his face when he said good-bye to Hagen.

Back in the room, Don Corleone asked Hagen, "What did you think of that man?"

"He's a Sicilian," Hagen said dryly.

The Don nodded his head thoughtfully. Then he turned to his son and said gently, "Santino, never let anyone outside the family know what you are thinking. Never let them know what you have under your fingernails. I think your brain is going soft from all that comedy you play with that young girl. Stop it and pay attention to business. Now get out of my sight."

Hagen saw the surprise on Sonny's face, then anger at his father's reproach. Did he really think the Don would be ignorant of his conquest, Hagen wondered. And did he really not know what a dangerous mistake he had made this morning? If that were true, Hagen would never wish to be the *Consigliori* to the Don of Santino Corleone.

Don Corleone waited until Sonny had left the room. Then he sank back into his leather armchair and motioned brusquely for a drink. Hagen poured him a glass of anisette. The Don looked up at him. "Send Luca Brasi to see me," he said.

Three months later, Hagen hurried through the paper work in his city office hoping to leave early enough for some Christmas shopping for his wife and children. He was interrupted by a phone call from a Johnny Fontane bubbling with high spirits. The picture had been shot, the rushes, whatever the hell they were, Hagen thought, were fabulous. He was sending the Don a present for Christmas that would knock his eyes out, he'd bring it himself but there were some little things to be done in the movie. He would have to stay out on the Coast. Hagen tried to conceal his impatience. Johnny Fontane's charm had always been lost on him. But his interest was aroused. "What is it?" he asked. Johnny Fontane chuckled and said, "I can't tell, that's the best part of a Christmas present." Hagen immediately lost all interest and finally managed, politely, to hang up.

Ten minutes later his secretary told him that Connie Corleone was on the phone and wanted to speak to him. Hagen sighed. As a young girl Connie had been nice, as a married woman she was a nuisance. She made complaints about her husband. She kept going home to visit her mother for two or three days. And Carlo Rizzi was turning out to be a real loser. He had been fixed up with a nice little business and was running it into the ground. He was also drinking, whoring around, gambling and beating his wife up occasionally. Connie hadn't told her family about that but she had told Hagen. He wondered what new tale of woe she had for him now.

But the Christmas spirit seemed to have cheered her up. She just wanted to ask Hagen what her father would really like for Christmas.

And Sonny and Fred and Mike. She already knew what she would get her mother. Hagen made some suggestions, all of which she rejected as silly. Finally she let him go.

When the phone rang again, Hagen threw his papers back into the basket. The hell with it. He'd leave. It never occurred to him to refuse to take the call, however. When his secretary told him it was Michael Corleone he picked up the phone with pleasure. He had always liked Mike.

"Tom," Michael Corleone said, "I'm driving down to the city with Kay tomorrow. There's something important I want to tell the old man before Christmas. Will he be home tomorrow night?"

"Sure," Hagen said. "He's not going out of town until after Christmas. Anything I can do for you?"

Michael was as closemouthed as his father. "No," he said. "I guess I'll see you Christmas, everybody is going to be out at Long Beach, right?"

"Right," Hagen said. He was amused when Mike hung up on him without any small talk.

He told his secretary to call his wife and tell her he would be home a little late but to have some supper for him. Outside the building he walked briskly downtown toward Macy's. Someone stepped in his way. To his surprise he saw it was Sollozzo.

Sollozzo took him by the arm and said quietly, "Don't be frightened, I just want to talk to you." A car parked at the curb suddenly had its door open. Sollozzo said urgently, "Get in, I want to talk to you."

Hagen pulled his arm loose. He was still not alarmed, just irritated. "I haven't got time," he said. At that moment two men came up behind him. Hagen felt a sudden weakness in his legs. Sollozzo said softly, "Get in the car. If I wanted to kill you you'd be dead now. Trust me."

Without a shred of trust Hagen got into the car.

Michael Corleone had lied to Hagen. He was already in New York, and he had called from a room in the Hotel Pennsylvania less than ten blocks away. When he hung up the phone, Kay Adams put out her cigarette and said, "Mike, what a good fibber you are."

Michael sat down beside her on the bed. "All for you, honey; if I told my family we were in town we'd have to go there right away. Then we couldn't go out to dinner, we couldn't go to the theater, and we couldn't sleep together tonight. Not in my father's house, not when we're not married." He put his arms around her and kissed her gently on the lips. Her mouth was sweet and he gently pulled her down on the bed. She closed her eyes, waiting for him to make love to her and Michael felt an enormous happiness. He had spent the war years fighting in the Pacific, and on those bloody islands he had dreamed of a girl like Kay Adams. Of a beauty like hers. A fair and fragile body, milky-skinned and electrified by passion. She opened her eyes and then pulled his head down to kiss him. They made love until it was time for dinner and the theater.

After dinner they walked past the brightly lit department stores full of holiday shoppers and Michael said to her, "What shall I get you for Christmas?"

She pressed against him. "Just you," she said. "Do you think your father will approve of me?"

Michael said gently, "That's not really the question. Will your parents approve of me?"

Kay shrugged. "I don't care," she said.

Michael said, "I even thought of changing my name, legally, but if something happened, that wouldn't really help. You sure you want to be a Corleone?" He said it only half-jokingly.

"Yes," she said without smiling. They pressed against each other. They had decided to get married during Christmas week, a quiet civil ceremony at City Hall with just two friends as witnesses. But Michael had insisted he must tell his father. He had explained that his father would not object in any way as long as it was not done in secrecy. Kay was doubtful. She said she could not tell her parents until after the marriage. "Of course they'll think I'm pregnant," she said. Michael grinned. "So will my parents," he said.

What neither of them mentioned was the fact that Michael would have to cut his close ties with his family. They both understood that Michael had already done so to some extent and yet they both felt guilty about this fact. They planned to finish college, seeing each other weekends and living together during summer vacations. It seemed like a happy life.

The play was a musical called *Carousel* and its sentimental story of a braggart thief made them smile at each other with amusement. When they came out of the theater it had turned cold. Kay snuggled up to him and said, "After we're married, will you beat me and then steal a star for a present?"

Michael laughed. "I'm going to be a mathematics professor," he said. Then he asked, "Do you want something to eat before we go to the hotel?"

Kay shook her head. She looked up at him meaningfully. As always he was touched by her eagerness to make love. He smiled down at her, and they kissed in the cold street. Michael felt hungry, and he decided to order sandwiches sent up to the room.

In the hotel lobby Michael pushed Kay toward the newsstand and said, "Get the papers while I get the key." He had to wait in a small line; the hotel was still short of help despite the end of the war. Michael got his room key and looked around impatiently for Kay. She was standing by the newsstand, staring down at a newspaper she held in her hand. He walked toward her. She looked up at him. Her eyes were filled with tears. "Oh, Mike," she said, "oh, Mike." He took the paper from her hands. The first thing he saw was a photo of his father lying in the street, his head in a pool of blood. A man was sitting on the curb weeping like a child. It was his brother Freddie. Michael Corleone felt his body turning to ice. There was no grief, no fear, just cold rage. He said to Kay, "Go up to the room." But he had to take her by the arm and lead her into the elevator. They rode up together in silence. In their room, Michael sat down on the bed and opened the paper. The headlines said, VITO CORLEONE SHOT. ALLEGED RACKET CHIEF CRITICALLY WOUNDED. OPERATED ON UNDER HEAVY POLICE GUARD. BLOODY MOB WAR FEARED.

Michael felt the weakness in his legs. He said to Kay, "He's not dead, the bastards didn't kill him." He read the story again. His father had been shot at five in the afternoon. That meant that while he had been making love to Kay, having dinner, enjoying the theater, his father was near death. Michael felt sick with guilt.

Kay said, "Shall we go down to the hospital now?"

Michael shook his head. "Let me call the house first. The people who did this are crazy and now that the old man's still alive they'll be desperate. Who the hell knows what they'll pull next."

Both phones in the Long Beach house were busy and it was almost twenty minutes before Michael could get through. He heard Sonny's voice saying, "Yeah."

"Sonny, it's me," Michael said.

He could hear the relief in Sonny's voice. "Jesus, kid, you had us worried. Where the hell are you? I've sent people to that hick town of yours to see what happened."

"How's the old man?" Michael said. "How bad is he hurt?"

"Pretty bad," Sonny said. "They shot him five times. But he's tough." Sonny's voice was proud. "The doctors said he'll pull through. Listen, kid, I'm busy, I can't talk, where are you?"

"In New York," Michael said. "Didn't Tom tell you I was coming down?"

Sonny's voice dropped a little. "They've snatched Tom. That's why I was worried about you. His wife is here. She don't know and neither do the cops. I don't want them to know. The bastards who pulled this must be crazy. I want you to get out here right away and keep your mouth shut. OK?"

"OK," Mike said, "do you know who did it?"

"Sure," Sonny said. "And as soon as Luca Brasi checks in they're gonna be dead meat. We still have all the horses."

"I'll be out in an hour," Mike said. "In a cab." He hung up. The papers had been on the streets for over three hours. There must have been radio news reports. It was almost impossible that Luca hadn't heard the news. Thoughtfully Michael pondered the question. Where was Luca Brasi? It was the same question that Hagen was asking himself at that moment. It was the same question that was worrying Sonny Corleone out in Long Beach.

At a quarter to five that afternoon, Don Corleone had finished checking the papers the office manager of his olive oil company had prepared for him. He put on his jacket and rapped his knuckles on his son Freddie's head to make him take his nose out of the afternoon newspaper. "Tell Gatto to get the car from the lot," he said. "I'll be ready to go home in a few minutes."

Freddie grunted. "I'll have to get it myself. Paulie called in sick this morning. Got a cold again."

Don Corleone looked thoughtful for a moment. "That's the third time this month. I think maybe you'd better get a healthier fellow for this job. Tell Tom."

Fred protested. "Paulie's a good kid. If he says he's sick, he's sick. I don't mind getting the car." He left the office. Don Corleone watched out the window as his son crossed Ninth Avenue to the parking lot. He stopped to call Hagen's office but there was no answer. He called the house at Long Beach but again there was no answer. Irritated, he looked out the window. His car was parked at the curb in front of his building. Freddie was leaning against the fender, arms folded, watching the throng of Christmas shoppers. Don Corleone put on his jacket. The office manager helped him with his overcoat. Don Corleone grunted his thanks and went out the door and started down the two flights of steps.

Out in the street the early winter light was failing. Freddie leaned casually against the fender of the heavy Buick. When he saw his father come out of the building Freddie went out into the street to the driver's side of the car and got in. Don Corleone was about to get in on the sidewalk side of the car when he hesitated and then turned back to the long open fruit stand near the corner. This had been his habit lately, he loved the big out-of-season fruits, yellow peaches and oranges, that glowed in their green boxes. The proprietor sprang to serve him. Don Corleone did not handle the fruit. He pointed. The fruit man disputed his decisions only once, to show him that one of his choices had a rotten underside. Don Corleone took the paper bag in his left hand and paid the man with a five-dollar bill. He took his change and, as he turned to go back to the waiting car, two men stepped from around the corner. Don Corleone knew immediately what was to happen.

The two men wore black overcoats and black hats pulled low to prevent identification by witnesses. They had not expected Don Corleone's alert reaction. He dropped the bag of fruit and darted toward the parked car with startling quickness for a man of his bulk. At the same time he shouted, "Fredo, Fredo." It was only then that the two men drew their guns and fired.

The first bullet caught Don Corleone in the back. He felt the hammer shock of its impact but made his body move toward the car. The next two bullets hit him in the buttocks and sent him sprawling in the middle of the street. Meanwhile the two gunmen, careful not to slip on the rolling fruit, started to follow in order to finish him off. At that moment, perhaps no more than five seconds after the Don's call to his son, Frederico Corleone appeared out of his car, looming over it. The gunmen fired two more hasty shots at the Don lying in the gutter. One hit him in the fleshy part of his arm and the second hit him in the calf of his right leg. Though these wounds were the least serious they bled profusely, forming small pools of blood beside his body. But by this time Don Corleone had lost consciousness.

Freddie had heard his father shout, calling him by his childhood name, and then he had heard the first two loud reports. By the time he got out of the car he was in shock, he had not even drawn his gun.

The two assassins could easily have shot him down. But they too panicked. They must have known the son was armed, and besides too much time had passed. They disappeared around the corner, leaving Freddie alone in the street with his father's bleeding body. Many of the people thronging the avenue had flung themselves into doorways or on the ground, others had huddled together in small groups.

Freddie still had not drawn his weapon. He seemed stunned. He stared down at his father's body lying face down on the tarred street, lying now in what seemed to him a blackish lake of blood. Freddie went into physical shock. People eddied out again and someone, seeing him start to sag, led him to the curbstone and made him sit down on it. A crowd gathered around Don Corleone's body, a circle that shattered when the first police car sirened a path through them. Directly behind the police was the *Daily News* radio car and even before it stopped a photographer jumped out to snap pictures of the bleeding Don Corleone. A few moments later an ambulance arrived. The photographer turned his attention to Freddie Corleone, who was now weeping openly, and this was a curiously comical sight, because of his tough, Cupid-featured face, heavy nose and thick mouth smeared with snot. Detectives were spreading through the crowd and more police cars were coming up. One detective knelt beside Freddie, questioning him, but Freddie was too deep in shock to answer. The detective reached inside Freddie's coat and lifted his wallet. He looked at the identification inside and whistled to his partner. In just a few seconds Freddie had been cut off from the crowd by a flock of plainclothesmen. The first detective found Freddie's gun in its shoulder holster and took it. Then they lifted Freddie off his feet and shoved him into an unmarked car. As that car pulled away it was followed by the *Daily News* radio car. The photographer was still snapping pictures of everybody and everything.

In the half hour after the shooting of his father, Sonny Corleone received five phone calls in rapid succession. The first was from Detective John Phillips, who was on the family payroll and had been in the lead car of plainclothesmen at the scene of the shooting. The first thing he said to Sonny over the phone was, "Do you recognize my voice?"

"Yeah," Sonny said. He was fresh from a nap, called to the phone by his wife.

Phillips said quickly without preamble, "Somebody shot your

father outside his place. Fifteen minutes ago. He's alive but hurt bad. They've taken him to French Hospital. They got your brother Freddie down at the Chelsea precinct. You better get him a doctor when they turn him loose. I'm going down to the hospital now to help question your old man, if he can talk. I'll keep you posted."

Across the table, Sonny's wife Sandra noticed that her husband's face had gone red with flushing blood. His eyes were glazed over. She whispered, "What's the matter?" He waved at her impatiently to shut up, swung his body away so that his back was toward her and said into the phone, "You sure he's alive?"

"Yeah, I'm sure," the detective said. "A lot of blood but I think maybe he's not as bad as he looks."

"Thanks," Sonny said. "Be home tomorrow morning eight sharp. You got a grand coming."

Sonny cradled the phone. He forced himself to sit still. He knew that his greatest weakness was his anger and this was one time when anger could be fatal. The first thing to do was get Tom Hagen. But before he could pick up the phone, it rang. The call was from the bookmaker licensed by the Family to operate in the district of the Don's office. The bookmaker had called to tell him that the Don had been killed, shot dead in the street. After a few questions to make sure that the bookmaker's informant had not been close to the body, Sonny dismissed the information as incorrect. Phillips' dope would be more accurate. The phone rang almost immediately a third time. It was a reporter from the *Daily News*. As soon as he identified himself, Sonny Corleone hung up.

He dialed Hagen's house and asked Hagen's wife, "Did Tom come home yet?" She said, "No," that he was not due for another twenty minutes but she expected him home for supper. "Have him call me," Sonny said.

He tried to think things out. He tried to imagine how his father would react in a like situation. He had known immediately that this was an attack by Sollozzo, but Sollozzo would never have dared to eliminate so high-ranking a leader as the Don unless he was backed by other powerful people. The phone, ringing for the fourth time, interrupted his thoughts. The voice on the other end was very soft, very gentle. "Santino Corleone?" it asked.

"Yeah," Sonny said.

"We have Tom Hagen," the voice said. "In about three hours he'll be released with our proposition. Don't do anything rash until you've heard what he has to say. You can only cause a lot of trouble. What's done is done. Everybody has to be sensible now. Don't lose that famous temper of yours." The voice was slightly mocking. Sonny couldn't be sure, but it sounded like Sollozzo. He made his voice sound muted, depressed. "I'll wait," he said. He heard the receiver on the other end click. He looked at his heavy gold-banded wristwatch and noted the exact time of the call and jotted it down on the tablecloth.

He sat at the kitchen table, frowning. His wife asked, "Sonny, what is it?" He told her calmly, "They shot the old man." When he saw the shock on her face he said roughly, "Don't worry, he's not dead. And nothing else is going to happen." He did not tell her about Hagen. And then the phone rang for the fifth time.

It was Clemenza. The fat man's voice came wheezing over the phone in gruntlike gasps. "You hear about your father?" he asked.

"Yeah," Sonny said. "But he's not dead." There was a long pause over the phone and then Clemenza's voice came packed with emotion, "Thank God, thank God." Then anxiously, "You sure? I got word he was dead in the street."

"He's alive," Sonny said. He was listening intently to every intonation in Clemenza's voice. The emotion had seemed genuine but it was part of the fat man's profession to be a good actor.

"You'll have to carry the ball, Sonny," Clemenza said. "What do you want me to do?"

"Get over to my father's house," Sonny said. "Bring Paulie Gatto."

"That's all?" Clemenza asked. "Don't you want me to send some people to the hospital and your place?"

"No, I just want you and Paulie Gatto," Sonny said. There was a long pause. Clemenza was getting the message. To make it a little more natural, Sonny asked, "Where the hell was Paulie anyway? What the hell was he doing?"

There was no longer any wheezing on the other end of the line. Clemenza's voice was guarded. "Paulie was sick, he had a cold, so he stayed home. He's been a little sick all winter."

Sonny was instantly alert. "How many times did he stay home the last couple of months?"

"Maybe three or four times," Clemenza said. "I always asked Freddie if he wanted another guy but he said no. There's been no cause, the last ten years things been smooth, you know."

"Yeah," Sonny said. "I'll see you at my father's house. Be sure you bring Paulie. Pick him up on your way over. I don't care how sick he is. You got that?" He slammed down the phone without waiting for an answer.

His wife was weeping silently. He stared at her for a moment, then said in a harsh voice, "Any of our people call, tell them to get me in my father's house on his special phone. Anybody else call, you don't know nothing. If Tom's wife calls, tell her that Tom won't be home for a while, he's on business."

He pondered for a moment. "A couple of our people will come to stay here." He saw her look of fright and said impatiently, "You don't have to be scared, I just want them here. Do whatever they tell you to do. If you wanta talk to me, get me on Pop's special phone but don't call me unless it's really important. And don't worry." He went out of the house.

Darkness had fallen and the December wind whipped through the mall. Sonny had no fear about stepping out into the night. All eight houses were owned by Don Corleone. At the mouth of the mall the two houses on either side were rented by family retainers with their own families and star boarders, single men who lived in the basement apartments. Of the remaining six houses that formed the rest of the half circle, one was inhabited by Tom Hagen and his family, his own, and the smallest and least ostentatious by the Don himself. The other three houses were given rent-free to retired friends of the Don with the understanding that they would be vacated whenever he requested. The harmless-looking mall was an impregnable fortress.

All eight houses were equipped with floodlights which bathed the grounds around them and made the mall impossible to lurk in. Sonny went across the street to his father's house and let himself inside with his own key. He yelled out, "Ma, where are you?" and his mother came out of the kitchen. Behind her rose the smell of frying peppers. Before she could say anything, Sonny took her by the arm and made her sit down. "I just got a call," he said. "Now don't get worried. Pop's in the hospital, he's hurt. Get dressed and get ready to get down there. I'll have a car and a driver for you in a little while. OK?"

His mother looked at him steadily for a moment and then asked in Italian, "Have they shot him?"

Sonny nodded. His mother bowed her head for a moment. Then she went back into the kitchen. Sonny followed her. He watched her turn off the gas under the panful of peppers and then go out and up to the bedroom. He took peppers from the pan and bread from the basket on the table and made a sloppy sandwich with hot olive oil dripping from his fingers. He went into the huge corner room that was his father's office and took the special phone from a locked cabinet box. The phone had been especially installed and was listed under a phony name and a phony address. The first person he called was Luca Brasi. There was no answer. Then he called the safety-valve *caporegime* in Brooklyn, a man of unquestioned loyalty to the Don. This man's name was Tessio. Sonny told him what had happened and what he wanted. Tessio was to recruit fifty absolutely reliable men. He was to send guards to the hospital, he was to send men out to Long Beach to work there. Tessio asked, "Did they get Clemenza too?" Sonny said, "I don't want to use Clemenza's people right now." Tessio understood immediately, there was a pause, and then he said, "Excuse me, Sonny, I say this as your father would say it. Don't move too fast. I can't believe Clemenza would betray us."

"Thanks," Sonny said. "I don't think so but I have to be careful. Right?"

"Right," Tessio said.

"Another thing," Sonny said. "My kid brother Mike goes to college in Hanover, New Hampshire. Get some people we know in Boston to go up and get him and bring him down here to the house until this blows over. I'll call him up so he'll expect them. Again I'm just playing the percentages, just to make sure."

"OK," Tessio said, "I'll be over your father's house as soon as I get things rolling. OK? You know my boys, right?"

"Yeah," Sonny said. He hung up. He went over to a small wall safe and unlocked it. From it he took an indexed book bound in blue leather. He opened it to the T's until he found the entry he was looking for. It read, "Ray Farrell $5,000 Christmas Eve." This was followed by a telephone number. Sonny dialed the number and said, "Farrell?" The man on the other end answered, "Yes." Sonny said, "This is Santino Corleone. I want you to do me a favor and I want you to do it right away. I want you to check two phone numbers and give me all the calls they got and all the calls they made for the last three months." He gave Farrell the number of Paulie Gatto's home and Clemenza's home. Then he said, "This is important. Get it to me before midnight and you'll have an extra very Merry Christmas."

Before he settled back to think things out he gave Luca Brasi's number one more call. Again there was no answer. This worried him but he put it out of his mind. Luca would come to the house as soon as he heard the news. Sonny leaned back in the swivel chair. In an hour the house would be swarming with Family people and he would have to tell them all what to do, and now that he finally had time to think he realized how serious the situation was. It was the first challenge to the Corleone Family and their power in ten years. There was no doubt that Sollozzo was behind it, but he would never have dared attempt such a stroke unless he had support from at least one of the five great New York families. And that support must have come from the Tattaglias. Which meant a full-scale war or an immediate settlement on Sollozzo's terms. Sonny smiled grimly. The wily Turk had planned well but he had been unlucky. The old man was alive and so it was war. With Luca Brasi and the resources of the Corleone Family there could be but one outcome. But again the nagging worry. Where was Luca Brasi?

Chapter

◆◆◆◆◆◆◆◆◆◆◆◆◆◆◆◆◆◆◆◆◆◆◆◆

3

COUNTING the driver, there were four men in the car with Hagen. They put him in the back seat, in the middle of the two men who had come up behind him in the street. Sollozzo sat up front. The man on Hagen's right reached over across his body and tilted Hagen's hat over his eyes so that he could not see. "Don't even move your pinkie," he said.

It was a short ride, not more than twenty minutes and when they got out of the car Hagen could not recognize the neighborhood because darkness had fallen. They led him into a basement apartment and made him sit on a straight-backed kitchen chair. Sollozzo sat across the kitchen table from him. His dark face had a peculiarly vulterine look.

"I don't want you to be afraid," he said. "I know you're not in the muscle end of the Family. I want you to help the Corleones and I want you to help me."

Hagen's hands were shaking as he put a cigarette in his mouth. One of the men brought a bottle of rye to the table and gave him a slug of it in a china coffee cup. Hagen drank the fiery liquid gratefully. It steadied his hands and took the weakness out of his legs.

"Your boss is dead," Sollozzo said. He paused, surprised at the tears

that sprang to Hagen's eyes. Then he went on. "We got him outside
his office, in the street. As soon as I got the word, I picked you up.
You have to make the peace between me and Sonny."

Hagen didn't answer. He was surprised at his own grief. And the
feeling of desolation mixed with his fear of death. Sollozzo was speaking again. "Sonny was hot for my deal. Right? You know it's the
smart thing to do too. Narcotics is the coming thing. There's so much
money in it that everybody can get rich just in a couple of years. The
Don was an old 'Moustache Pete,' his day was over but he didn't
know it. Now he's dead, nothing can bring him back. I'm ready to
make a new deal, I want you to talk Sonny into taking it."

Hagen said, "You haven't got a chance. Sonny will come after you
with everything he's got."

Sollozzo said impatiently, "That's gonna be his first reaction. You
have to talk some sense to him. The Tattaglia Family stands behind
me with all their people. The other New York families will go along
with anything that will stop a full-scale war between us. Our war has
to hurt them and their businesses. If Sonny goes along with the deal,
the other Families in the country will consider it none of their affair,
even the Don's oldest friends."

Hagen stared down at his hands, not answering. Sollozzo went on
persuasively. "The Don was slipping. In the old days I could never
have gotten to him. The other Families distrust him because he made
you his *Consigliori* and you're not even Italian, much less Sicilian. If
it goes to all-out war the Corleone Family will be smashed and everybody loses, me included. I need the Family political contacts more
than I need the money even. So talk to Sonny, talk to the *caporegimes;* you'll save a lot of bloodshed."

Hagen held out his china cup for more whiskey. "I'll try," he said.
"But Sonny is strong-headed. And even Sonny won't be able to call
off Luca. You have to worry about Luca. *I'll* have to worry about
Luca if I go for your deal."

Sollozzo said quietly, "I'll take care of Luca. You take care of
Sonny and the other two kids. Listen, you can tell them that Freddie
would have gotten it today with his old man but my people had strict
orders not to gun him. I didn't want any more hard feelings than
necessary. You can tell them that, Freddie is alive because of me."

Finally Hagen's mind was working. For the first time he really
believed that Sollozzo did not mean to kill him or hold him as a
hostage. The sudden relief from fear that flooded his body made him

flush with shame. Sollozzo watched him with a quiet understanding smile. Hagen began to think things out. If he did not agree to argue Sollozzo's case, he might be killed. But then he realized that Sollozzo expected him only to present it and present it properly, as he was bound to do as a responsible *Consigliori*. And now, thinking about it, he also realized that Sollozzo was right. An unlimited war between the Tattaglias and the Corleones must be avoided at all costs. The Corleones must bury their dead and forget, make a deal. And then when the time was right they could move against Sollozzo.

But glancing up, he realized that Sollozzo knew exactly what he was thinking. The Turk was smiling. And then it struck Hagen. What had happened to Luca Brasi that Sollozzo was so unconcerned? Had Luca made a deal? He remembered that on the night Don Corleone had refused Sollozzo, Luca had been summoned into the office for a private conference with the Don. But now was not the time to worry about such details. He had to get back to the safety of the Corleone Family fortress in Long Beach. "I'll do my best," he said to Sollozzo. "I believe you're right, it's even what the Don would want us to do."

Sollozzo nodded gravely. "Fine," he said. "I don't like bloodshed, I'm a businessman and blood costs too much money." At that moment the phone rang and one of the men sitting behind Hagen went to answer it. He listened and then said curtly, "OK, I'll tell him." He hung up the phone, went to Sollozzo's side and whispered in the Turk's ear. Hagen saw Sollozzo's face go pale, his eyes glitter with rage. He himself felt a thrill of fear. Sollozzo was looking at him speculatively and suddenly Hagen knew that he was no longer going to be set free. That something had happened that might mean his death. Sollozzo said, "The old man is still alive. Five bullets in his Sicilian hide and he's still alive." He gave a fatalistic shrug. "Bad luck," he said to Hagen. "Bad luck for me. Bad luck for you."

Chapter

4

WHEN Michael Corleone arrived at his father's house in Long Beach he found the narrow entrance mouth of the mall blocked off with a link chain. The mall itself was bright with the floodlights of all eight houses, outlining at least ten cars parked along the curving cement walk.

Two men he didn't know were leaning against the chain. One of them asked in a Brooklyn accent, "Who're you?"

He told them. Another man came out of the nearest house and peered at his face. "That's the Don's kid," he said. "I'll bring him inside." Mike followed this man to his father's house, where two men at the door let him and his escort pass inside.

The house seemed to be full of men he didn't know, until he went into the living room. There Michael saw Tom Hagen's wife, Theresa, sitting stiffly on the sofa, smoking a cigarette. On the coffee table in front of her was a glass of whiskey. On the other side of the sofa sat the bulky Clemenza. The *caporegime*'s face was impassive, but he was sweating and the cigar in his hand glistened slickly black with his saliva.

Clemenza came to wring his hand in a consoling way, muttering, "Your mother is at the hospital with your father, he's going to be all

right." Paulie Gatto stood up to shake hands. Michael looked at him
curiously. He knew Paulie was his father's bodyguard but did not
know that Paulie had stayed home sick that day. But he sensed tension in the thin dark face. He knew Gatto's reputation as an up-and-
coming man, a very quick man who knew how to get delicate jobs
done without complications, and today he had failed in his duty. He
noticed several other men in the corners of the room but he did not
recognize them. They were not of Clemenza's people. Michael put
these facts together and understood. Clemenza and Gatto were suspect. Thinking that Paulie had been at the scene, he asked the ferret-
faced young man, "How is Freddie? He OK?"

"The doctor gave him a shot," Clemenza said. "He's sleeping."

Michael went to Hagen's wife and bent down to kiss her cheek.
They had always liked each other. He whispered, "Don't worry,
Tom will be OK. Have you talked to Sonny yet?"

Theresa clung to him for a moment and shook her head. She was a
delicate, very pretty woman, more American than Italian, and very
scared. He took her hand and lifted her off the sofa. Then he led her
into his father's corner room office.

Sonny was sprawled out in his chair behind the desk holding a
yellow pad in one hand and a pencil in the other. The only other man
in the room with him was the *caporegime* Tessio, whom Michael
recognized and immediately realized that it must be his men who
were in the house and forming the new palace guard. He too had a
pencil and pad in his hands.

When Sonny saw them he came from behind his desk and took
Hagen's wife in his arms. "Don't worry, Theresa," he said. "Tom's
OK. They just wanta give him the proposition, they said they'd turn
him loose. He's not on the operating end, he's just our lawyer.
There's no reason for anybody to do him harm."

He released Theresa and then to Michael's surprise he, too, got a
hug and a kiss on the cheek. He pushed Sonny away and said grinning, "After I get used to you beating me up I gotta put up with
this?" They had often fought when they were younger.

Sonny shrugged. "Listen, kid, I was worried when I couldn't get
ahold of you in that hick town. Not that I gave a crap if they
knocked you off, but I didn't like the idea of bringing the news to the
old lady. I had to tell her about Pop."

"How'd she take it?" Michael asked.

"Good," Sonny said. "She's been through it before. Me too. You were too young to know about it and then things got pretty smooth while you were growing up." He paused and then said, "She's down at the hospital with the old man. He's gonna pull through."

"How about us going down?" Michael asked.

Sonny shook his head and said dryly, "I can't leave this house until it's all over." The phone rang. Sonny picked it up and listened intently. While he was listening Michael sauntered over to the desk and glanced down at the yellow pad Sonny had been writing on. There was a list of seven names. The first three were Sollozzo, Phillip Tattaglia, and John Tattaglia. It struck Michael with full force that he had interrupted Sonny and Tessio as they were making up a list of men to be killed.

When Sonny hung up the phone he said to Theresa Hagen and Michael, "Can you two wait outside? I got some business with Tessio we have to finish."

Hagen's wife said, "Was that call about Tom?" She said it almost truculently but she was weeping with fright. Sonny put his arm around her and led her to the door. "I swear he's going to be OK," he said. "Wait in the living room. I'll come out as soon as I hear something." He shut the door behind her. Michael had sat down in one of the big leather armchairs. Sonny gave him a quick sharp look and then went to sit down behind the desk.

"You hang around me, Mike," he said, "you're gonna hear things you don't wanta hear."

Michael lit a cigarette. "I can help out," he said.

"No, you can't," Sonny said. "The old man would be sore as hell if I let you get mixed up in this."

Michael stood up and yelled. "You lousy bastard, he's my father. I'm not supposed to help him? I can help. I don't have to go out and kill people but I can help. Stop treating me like a kid brother. I was in the war. I got shot, remember? I killed some Japs. What the hell do you think I'll do when you knock somebody off? Faint?"

Sonny grinned at him. "Pretty soon you'll want me to put up my dukes. OK, stick around, you can handle the phone." He turned to Tessio. "That call I just got gave me dope we needed." He turned to Michael. "Somebody had to finger the old man. It could have been Clemenza, it could have been Paulie Gatto, who was very conveniently sick today. I know the answer now, let's see how smart you are, Mike, you're the college boy. Who sold out to Sollozzo?"

Michael sat down again and relaxed back into the leather armchair.

He thought everything over very carefully. Clemenza was a *caporegime* in the Corleone Family structure. Don Corleone had made him a millionaire and they had been intimate friends for over twenty years. He held one of the most powerful posts in the organization. What could Clemenza gain for betraying his Don? More money? He was rich enough but then men are always greedy. More power? Revenge for some fancied insult or slight? That Hagen had been made the *Consigliori?* Or perhaps a businessman's conviction that Sollozzo would win out? No, it was impossible for Clemenza to be a traitor, and then Michael thought sadly it was only impossible because he didn't want Clemenza to die. The fat man had always brought him gifts when he was growing up, had sometimes taken him on outings when the Don had been too busy. He could not believe that Clemenza was guilty of treachery.

But, on the other hand, Sollozzo would want Clemenza in his pocket more than any other man in the Corleone Family.

Michael thought about Paulie Gatto. Paulie as yet had not become rich. He was well thought of, his rise in the organization was certain but he would have to put in his time like everybody else. Also he would have wilder dreams of power, as the young always do. It had to be Paulie. And then Michael remembered that in the sixth grade he and Paulie had been in the same class in school and he didn't want it to be Paulie either.

He shook his head. "Neither one of them," he said. But he said it only because Sonny had said he had the answer. If it had been a vote, he would have voted Paulie guilty.

Sonny was smiling at him. "Don't worry," he said. "Clemenza is OK. It's Paulie."

Michael could see that Tessio was relieved. As a fellow *caporegime* his sympathy would be with Clemenza. Also the present situation was not so serious if treachery did not reach so high. Tessio said cautiously, "Then I can send my people home tomorrow?"

Sonny said, "The day after tomorrow. I don't want anybody to know about this until then. Listen, I want to talk some family business with my brother, personal. Wait out in the living room, eh? We can finish our list later. You and Clemenza will work together on it."

"Sure," Tessio said. He went out.

"How do you know for sure it's Paulie?" Michael asked.

Sonny said, "We have people in the telephone company and they tracked down all of Paulie's phone calls in and out. Clemenza's too. On the three days Paulie was sick this month he got a call from a street booth across from the old man's building. Today too. They were checking to see if Paulie was coming down or somebody was being sent down to take his place. Or for some other reason. It doesn't matter." Sonny shrugged. "Thank God it was Paulie. We'll need Clemenza bad."

Michael asked hesitantly, "Is it going to be an all-out war?"

Sonny's eyes were hard. "That's how I'm going to play it as soon as Tom checks in. Until the old man tells me different."

Michael asked, "So why don't you wait until the old man can tell you?"

Sonny looked at him curiously. "How the hell did you win those combat medals? We are under the gun, man, we gotta fight. I'm just afraid they won't let Tom go."

Michael was surprised at this. "Why not?"

Again Sonny's voice was patient. "They snatched Tom because they figured the old man was finished and they could make a deal with me and Tom would be the sit-down guy in the preliminary stages, carry the proposition. Now with the old man alive they know I can't make a deal so Tom's no good to them. They can turn him loose or dump him, depending how Sollozzo feels. If they dump him, it would be just to show us they really mean business, trying to bulldoze us."

Michael said quietly, "What made Sollozzo think he could get a deal with you?"

Sonny flushed and he didn't answer for a moment. Then he said, "We had a meeting a few months ago, Sollozzo came to us with a proposition on drugs. The old man turned him down. But during the meeting I shot off my mouth a little, I showed I wanted the deal. Which is absolutely the wrong thing to do; if there's one thing the old man hammered into me it's never to do a thing like that, to let other people know there's a split of opinion in the Family. So Sollozzo figures he gets rid of the old man, I have to go in with him on the drugs. With the old man gone, the Family power is cut at least in half. I would be fighting for my life anyway to keep all the businesses the old man got together. Drugs are the coming thing, we should get into it. And his knocking off the old man is purely business, nothing personal. As a matter of business I would go in with him. Of course he would never let me get too close, he'd make sure I'd never get a clean shot at him, just in case. But he also knows that once I accepted the deal the other Families would never let me start a war a couple of years later just for revenge. Also, the Tattaglia Family is behind him."

"If they had gotten the old man, what would you have done?" Michael asked.

Sonny said very simply, "Sollozzo is dead meat. I don't care what it costs. I don't care if we have to fight all the five Families in New York. The Tattaglia Family is going to be wiped out. I don't care if we all go down together."

Michael said softly, "That's not how Pop would have played it."

Sonny made a violent gesture. "I know I'm not the man he was. But I'll tell you this and he'll tell you too. When it comes to real action I can operate as good as anybody, short-range. Sollozzo knows that and so do Clemenza and Tessio. I 'made my bones' when I was nineteen, the last time the Family had a war, and I was a big help to the old man. So I'm not worried now. And our Family has all the horses in a deal like this. I just wish we could get contact with Luca."

Michael asked curiously, "Is Luca that tough, like they say? Is he that good?"

Sonny nodded. "He's in a class by himself. I'm going to send him after the three Tattaglias. I'll get Sollozzo myself."

Michael shifted uneasily in his chair. He looked at his older brother. He remembered Sonny as being sometimes casually brutal but essentially warmhearted. A nice guy. It seemed unnatural to hear him talking this way, it was chilling to see the list of names he had scribbled down, men to be executed, as if he were some newly crowned Roman Emperor. He was glad that he was not truly part of all this, that now his father lived he did not have to involve himself in vengeance. He'd help out, answering the phone, running errands and messages. Sonny and the old man could take care of themselves, especially with Luca behind them.

At that moment they heard a woman scream in the living room. Oh, Christ, Michael thought, it sounded like Tom's wife. He rushed to the door and opened it. Everybody in the living room was standing. And by the sofa Tom Hagen was holding Theresa close to him, his face embarrassed. Theresa was weeping and sobbing, and Michael realized that the scream he had heard had been her calling out her husband's name with joy. As he watched, Tom Hagen disentangled himself from his wife's arms and lowered her back onto the sofa. He smiled at Michael grimly. "Glad to see you, Mike, really glad." He strode into the office without another look at his still-sobbing wife. He hadn't lived with the Corleone Family ten years for nothing, Michael thought with a queer flush of pride. Some of the old man had rubbed off on him, as it had on Sonny, and he thought, with surprise, even on himself.

Chapter

■■■■■■■■■■■■■■■■■■■■■■■■■

5

IT was nearly four o'clock in the morning as they all sat in the corner room office—Sonny, Michael, Tom Hagen, Clemenza and Tessio. Theresa Hagen had been persuaded to go to her own home next door. Paulie Gatto was still waiting in the living room, not knowing that Tessio's men had been instructed not to let him leave or let him out of their sight.

Tom Hagen relayed the deal Sollozzo offered. He told how after Sollozzo had learned the Don still lived, it was obvious that he meant to kill Hagen. Hagen grinned. "If I ever plead before the Supreme Court, I'll never plead better than I did with that goddamn Turk tonight. I told him I'd talk the Family into the deal even though the Don was alive. I told him I could wrap you around my finger, Sonny. How we were buddies as kids; and don't get sore, but I let him get the idea that maybe you weren't too sorry about getting the old man's job, God forgive me." He smiled apologetically at Sonny, who made a gesture signifying that he understood, that it was of no consequence.

Michael, leaning back in his armchair with the phone at his right hand, studied both men. When Hagen had entered the room Sonny had come rushing to embrace him. Michael realized with a faint twinge of jealousy that in many ways Sonny and Tom Hagen were closer than he himself could ever be to his own brother.

"Let's get down to business," Sonny said. "We have to make plans. Take a look at this list me and Tessio made up. Tessio, give Clemenza your copy."

"If we make plans," Michael said, "Freddie should be here."

Sonny said grimly, "Freddie is no use to us. The doctor says he's in shock so bad he has to have complete rest. I don't understand that. Freddie was always a pretty tough guy. I guess seeing the old man gunned down was hard on him, he always thought the Don was God. He wasn't like you and me, Mike."

Hagen said quickly, "OK, leave Freddie out. Leave him out of everything, absolutely everything. Now, Sonny, until this is all over I think you should stay in the house. I mean never leave it. You're safe here. Don't underrate Sollozzo, he's got to be a *pezzonovante*, a real .90 caliber. Is the hospital covered?"

Sonny nodded. "The cops have it locked in and I got my people there visiting Pop all the time. What do you think of that list, Tom?"

Hagen frowned down at the list of names. "Jesus Christ, Sonny, you're really taking this personal. The Don would consider it a purely business dispute. Sollozzo is the key. Get rid of Sollozzo and everything falls in line. You don't have to go after the Tattaglias."

Sonny looked at his two *caporegimes*. Tessio shrugged. "It's tricky," he said. Clemenza didn't answer at all.

Sonny said to Clemenza, "One thing we can take care of without discussion. I don't want Paulie around here anymore. Make that first on your list." The fat *caporegime* nodded.

Hagen said, "What about Luca? Sollozzo didn't seem worried about Luca. That *worries me*. If Luca sold us out, we're in real trouble. That's the first thing we have to know. Has anybody been able to get in touch with him?"

"No," Sonny said. "I've been calling him all night. Maybe he's shacked up."

"No," Hagen said. "He never sleeps over with a broad. He always goes home when he's through. Mike, keep ringing his number until you get an answer." Michael dutifully picked up the phone and dialed. He could hear the phone ringing on the other end but no one answered. Finally he hung up. "Keep trying every fifteen minutes," Hagen said.

Sonny said impatiently, "OK, Tom you're the *Consigliori*, how about some advice? What the hell do you think we should do?"

Hagen helped himself to the whiskey bottle on the desk. "We negotiate with Sollozzo until your father is in shape to take charge. We might even make a deal if we have to. When your father gets out of bed he can settle the whole business without a fuss and all the Families will go along with him."

Sonny said angrily, "You think I can't handle this guy Sollozzo?"

Tom Hagen looked him directly in the eye. "Sonny, sure you can outfight him. The Corleone Family has the power. You have Clemenza and Tessio here and they can muster a thousand men if it comes to an all-out war. But at the end there will be a shambles over the whole East Coast and all the other Families will blame the Corleones. We'll make a lot of enemies. And that's something your father never believed in."

Michael, watching Sonny, thought he took this well. But then Sonny said to Hagen, "What if the old man dies, what do you advise then, *Consigliori?*"

Hagen said quietly, "I know you won't do it, but I would advise you to make a real deal with Sollozzo on the drugs. Without your father's political contacts and personal influence the Corleone Family loses half its strength. Without your father, the other New York Families might wind up supporting the Tattaglias and Sollozzo just to make sure there isn't a long destructive war. If your father dies, make the deal. Then wait and see."

Sonny was white-faced with anger. "That's easy for you to say, it's not your father they killed."

Hagen said quickly and proudly, "I was as good a son to him as you or Mike, maybe better. I'm giving you a professional opinion. Personally I want to kill all those bastards." The emotion in his voice shamed Sonny, who said, "Oh, Christ, Tom, I didn't mean it that way." But he had, really. Blood was blood and nothing else was its equal.

Sonny brooded for a moment as the others waited in embarrassed silence. Then he sighed and spoke quietly. "OK, we'll sit tight until the old man can give us the lead. But, Tom, I want you to stay inside the mall, too. Don't take any chances. Mike, you be careful, though I don't think even Sollozzo would bring personal family into the war. Everybody would be against him then. But be careful. Tessio, you hold your people in reserve but have them nosing around the city.

Clemenza, after you settle the Paulie Gatto thing, you move your men into the house and the mall to replace Tessio's people. Tessio, you keep your men at the hospital, though. Tom, start negotiation over the phone or by messenger with Sollozzo and the Tattaglias the first thing in the morning. Mike, tomorrow you take a couple of Clemenza's people and go to Luca's house and wait for him to show up or find out where the hell he is. That crazy bastard might be going after Sollozzo right now if he's heard the news. I can't believe he'd ever go against his Don, no matter what the Turk offered him."

Hagen said reluctantly, "Maybe Mike shouldn't get mixed up in this so directly."

"Right," Sonny said. "Forget that, Mike. Anyway I need you on the phone here in the house, that's more important."

Michael didn't say anything. He felt awkward, almost ashamed, and he noticed Clemenza and Tessio with faces so carefully impassive that he was sure that they were hiding their contempt. He picked up the phone and dialed Luca Brasi's number and kept the receiver to his ear as it rang and rang.

Chapter

✕✕✕✕✕✕✕✕✕✕✕✕✕

6

PETER CLEMENZA slept badly that night. In the morning he got up early and made his own breakfast of a glass of *grappa*, a thick slice of Genoa salami with a chunk of fresh Italian bread that was still delivered to his door as in the old days. Then he drank a great, plain china mug filled with hot coffee that had been lashed with anisette. But as he padded about the house in his old bathrobe and red felt slippers he pondered on the day's work that lay ahead of him. Last night Sonny Corleone had made it very clear that Paulie Gatto was to be taken care of immediately. It had to be today.

Clemenza was troubled. Not because Gatto had been his protégé and had turned traitor. This did not reflect on the *caporegime*'s judgment. After all, Paulie's background had been perfect. He came from a Sicilian family, he had grown up in the same neighborhood as the Corleone children, had indeed even gone to school with one of the sons. He had been brought up through each level in the proper manner. He had been tested and not found wanting. And then after he had "made his bones" he had received a good living from the Family, a percentage of an East Side "book" and a union payroll slot. Clemenza had not been unaware that Paulie Gatto supplemented his income with free-lance stickups, strictly against the Family rules, but even this was a sign of the man's worth. The breaking of such regulations was considered a sign of high-spiritedness, like that shown by a fine racing horse fighting the reins.

And Paulie had never caused trouble with his stickups. They had always been meticulously planned and carried out with the minimum of fuss and trouble, with no one ever getting hurt: a three-thousand-dollar Manhattan garment center payroll, a small chinaware factory payroll in the slums of Brooklyn. After all, a young man could always use some extra pocket money. It was all in the pattern. Who could ever foretell that Paulie Gatto would turn traitor?

What was troubling Peter Clemenza this morning was an administrative problem. The actual execution of Gatto was a cut-and-dried chore. The problem was, who should the *caporegime* bring up from the ranks to replace Gatto in the Family? It was an important promotion, that to "button" man, one not to be handed out lightly. The man had to be tough and he had to be smart. He had to be safe, not a person that would talk to the police if he got in trouble, one well saturated in the Sicilians' law of *omerta*, the law of silence. And then, what kind of a living would he receive for his new duties? Clemenza had several times spoken to the Don about better rewards for the all-important button man who was first in the front line when trouble arose, but the Don had put him off. If Paulie had been making more money, he might have been able to resist the blandishments of the wily Turk, Sollozzo.

Clemenza finally narrowed down the list of candidates to three men. The first was an enforcer who worked with the colored policy bankers in Harlem, a big brawny brute of a man of great physical strength, a man with a great deal of personal charm who could get along with people and yet when necessary make them go in fear of him. But Clemenza scratched him off the list after considering his name for a half hour. This man got along too well with the black people, which hinted at some flaw of character. Also he would be too hard to replace in the position he now held.

The second name Clemenza considered and almost settled on was a hard-working chap who served faithfully and well in the organization. This man was the collector of delinquent accounts for Family-licensed shylocks in Manhattan. He had started off as a bookmaker's runner. But he was not quite yet ready for such an important promotion.

Finally he settled on Rocco Lampone. Lampone had served a short but impressive apprenticeship in the Family. During the war he had been wounded in Africa and been discharged in 1943. Because of the shortage of young men, Clemenza had taken him on even though Lampone was partially incapacitated by his injuries and walked with a pronounced limp. Clemenza had used him as a black-market contact in the garment center and with government employees controlling OPA food stamps. From that, Lampone had graduated to trouble-shooter for the whole operation. What Clemenza liked about him was his good judgment. He knew that there was no percentage in being tough about something that would only cost a heavy fine or six months in jail, small prices to pay for the enormous profits earned. He had the good sense to know that it was not an area for heavy threats but light ones. He kept the whole operation in a minor key, which was exactly what was needed.

Clemenza felt the relief of a conscientious administrator who has solved a knotty personnel problem. Yes, it would be Rocco Lampone who would assist. For Clemenza planned to handle this job himself, not only to help a new, inexperienced man "make his bones," but to settle a personal score with Paulie Gatto. Paulie had been his protégé, he had advanced Paulie over the heads of more deserving and more loyal people, he had helped Paulie "make his bones" and furthered his career in every way. Paulie had not only betrayed the Family, he had betrayed his *padrone*, Peter Clemenza. This lack of respect had to be repaid.

Everything else was arranged. Paulie Gatto had been instructed to pick him up at three in the afternoon, and to pick him up with his own car, nothing hot. Now Clemenza took up the telephone and dialed Rocco Lampone's number. He did not identify himself. He simply said, "Come to my house, I have an errand for you." He was pleased to note that despite the early hour, Lampone's voice was not sur-prised or dazed with sleep and he simply said, "OK." Good man. Clemenza added, "No rush, have your breakfast and lunch first be-fore you come see me. But not later than two in the afternoon."

There was another laconic OK on the other end and Clemenza hung up the phone. He had already alerted his people about replacing *caporegime* Tessio's people in the Corleone mall so that was done. He had capable subordinates and never interfered in a mechanical opera-tion of that kind.

He decided to wash his Cadillac. He loved the car. It gave him such a quiet peaceful ride, and its upholstery was so rich that he sometimes sat in it for an hour when the weather was good because it was more pleasant than sitting in the house. And it always helped him think when he was grooming the car. He remembered his father in Italy doing the same thing with donkeys.

Clemenza worked inside the heated garage, he hated cold. He ran over his plans. You had to be careful with Paulie, the man was like a rat, he could smell danger. And now of course despite being so tough he must be shitting in his pants because the old man was still alive. He'd be as skittish as a donkey with ants up his ass. But Clemenza was accustomed to these circumstances, usual in his work. First, he had to have a good excuse for Rocco to accompany them. Second, he had to have a plausible mission for the three of them to go on.

Of course, strictly speaking, this was not necessary. Paulie Gatto could be killed without any of these frills. He was locked in, he could not run away. But Clemenza felt strongly that it was important to keep good working habits and never give away a fraction of a percentage point. You never could tell what might happen and these matters were, after all, questions of life and death.

As he washed his baby-blue Cadillac, Peter Clemenza pondered and rehearsed his lines, the expressions of his face. He would be curt with Paulie, as if displeased with him. With a man so sensitive and suspicious as Gatto this would throw him off the track or at least leave him uncertain. Undue friendliness would make him wary. But of course the curtness must not be too angry. It had to be rather an absentminded sort of irritation. And why Lampone? Paulie would find that most alarming, especially since Lampone had to be in the rear seat. Paulie wouldn't like being helpless at the wheel with Lampone behind his head. Clemenza rubbed and polished the metal of his Cadillac furiously. It was going to be tricky. Very tricky. For a moment he debated whether to recruit another man but decided against it. Here he followed basic reasoning. In years to come a situation might arise where it might be profitable for one of his partners to testify against him. If there were just one accomplice it was one's word against the other. But the word of a second accomplice could swing the balance. No, they would stick to procedure.

What annoyed Clemenza was that the execution had to be "public." That is, the body was to be found. He would have much preferred having it disappear. (Usual burying grounds were the nearby ocean or the swamplands of New Jersey on land owned by friends of the Family or by other more complicated methods.) But it had to be public so that embryo traitors would be frightened and the enemy warned that the Corleone Family had by no means gone stupid or soft. Sollozzo would be made wary by this quick discovery of his spy. The Corleone Family would win back some of its prestige. It had been made to look foolish by the shooting of the old man.

Clemenza sighed. The Cadillac gleamed like a huge blue steel egg, and he was nowhere near the solving of his problem. Then the solution hit him, logical and to the point. It would explain Rocco Lampone, himself and Paulie being together and give them a mission of sufficient secrecy and importance.

He would tell Paulie that their job today was to find an apartment in case the Family decided to "go to the mattresses."

Whenever a war between the Families became bitterly intense, the opponents would set up headquarters in secret apartments where the "soldiers" could sleep on mattresses scattered through the rooms. This was not so much to keep their families out of danger, their wives and little children, since any attack on noncombatants was undreamed of. All parties were too vulnerable to similar retaliation. But it was always smarter to live in some secret place where your everyday movements could not be charted either by your opponents or by some police who might arbitrarily decide to meddle.

And so usually a trusted *caporegime* would be sent out to rent a secret apartment and fill it with mattresses. That apartment would be used as a sally port into the city when an offensive was mounted. It was natural for Clemenza to be sent on such an errand. It was natural for him to take Gatto and Lampone with him to arrange all the details, including the furnishing of the apartment. Also, Clemenza thought with a grin, Paulie Gatto had proved he was greedy and the first thought that would pop into his head was how much he could get from Sollozzo for this valuable intelligence.

Rocco Lampone arrived early and Clemenza explained what had to be done and what their roles would be. Lampone's face lit up with surprised gratitude and he thanked Clemenza respectfully for the promotion allowing him to serve the Family. Clemenza was sure he had done well. He clapped Lampone on the shoulder and said, "You'll get something better for your living after today. We'll talk about that later. You understand the Family now is occupied with more critical matters, more important things to do." Lampone made a gesture that said he would be patient, knowing his reward was certain.

Clemenza went to his den's safe and opened it. He took out a gun and gave it to Lampone. "Use this one," he said. "They can never trace it. Leave it in the car with Paulie. When this job is finished I want you to take your wife and children on a vacation to Florida. Use your own money now and I'll pay you back later. Relax, get the sun. Use the Family hotel in Miami Beach so I'll know where I can get you when I want."

Clemenza's wife knocked on the door of the den to tell them that Paulie Gatto had arrived. He was parked in the driveway. Clemenza led the way through the garage and Lampone followed him. When Clemenza got into the front seat with Gatto he merely grunted in greeting, an exasperated look on his face. He looked at the wrist watch as if he expected to find that Gatto was late.

The ferret-faced button man was watching him intently, looking for a clue. He flinched a little when Lampone got into the rear seat behind him and said, "Rocco, sit on the other side. A big guy like you blocks up my rear-view mirror." Lampone shifted dutifully so that he was sitting behind Clemenza, as if such a request was the most natural thing in the world.

Clemenza said sourly to Gatto, "Damn that Sonny, he's running scared. He's already thinking of going to the mattresses. We have to find a place on the West Side. Paulie, you and Rocco gotta staff and supply it until the word comes down for the rest of the soldiers to use it. You know a good location?"

As he had expected, Gatto's eyes became greedily interested. Paulie had swallowed the bait and because he was thinking how much the information was worth to Sollozzo, he was forgetting to think about whether he was in danger. Also, Lampone was acting his part perfectly, staring out the window in a disinterested, relaxed way. Clemenza congratulated himself on his choice.

Gatto shrugged. "I'd have to think about it," he said.

Clemenza grunted. "Drive while you think, I want to get to New York today."

Paulie was an expert driver and traffic going into the city was light at this time in the afternoon, so the early winter darkness was just beginning to fall when they arrived. There was no small talk in the car. Clemenza directed Paulie to drive up to the Washington Heights section. He checked a few apartment buildings and told him to park near Arthur Avenue and wait. He also left Rocco Lampone in the car. He went into the Vera Mario Restaurant and had a light dinner of veal and salad, nodding his hello's to some acquaintances. After an hour had gone by he walked the several blocks to where the car was parked and entered it. Gatto and Lampone were still waiting. "Shit," Clemenza said, "they want us back in Long Beach. They got some other job for us now. Sonny says we can let this one go until later. Rocco, you live in the city, can we drop you off?"

Rocco said quietly, "I have my car out at your place and my old lady needs it first thing in the morning."

"That's right," Clemenza said. "Then you have to come back with us, after all."

Again on the ride back to Long Beach nothing was said. On the stretch of road that led into the city, Clemenza said suddenly, "Paulie, pull over, I gotta take a leak." From working together so long, Gatto knew the fat *caporegime* had a weak bladder. He had often made such a request. Gatto pulled the car off the highway onto the soft earth that led to the swamp. Clemenza climbed out of the car and took a few steps into the bushes. He actually relieved himself. Then as he opened the door to get back into the car he took a quick look up and down the highway. There were no lights, the road was completely dark. "Go ahead," Clemenza said. A second later the interior of the car reverberated with the report of a gun. Paulie Gatto seemed to jump forward, his body flinging against the steering wheel and then slumping over to the seat. Clemenza had stepped back hastily to avoid being hit with fragments of skull bone and blood.

Rocco Lampone scrambled out of the back seat. He still held the gun and he threw it into the swamp. He and Clemenza walked hastily to a car parked nearby and got in. Lampone reached underneath the seat and found the key that had been left for them. He started the car and drove Clemenza to his home. Then instead of going back by the same route, he took the Jones Beach Causeway right on through to the town of Merrick and onto the Meadowbrook Parkway until he reached the Northern State Parkway. He rode that to the Long Island Expressway and then continued on to the Whitestone Bridge and through the Bronx to his home in Manhattan.

Chapter

✕✕✕✕✕✕✕✕✕✕✕✕✕✕✕✕✕✕✕✕✕

7

ON the night before the shooting of Don Corleone, his strongest and most loyal and most feared retainer prepared to meet with the enemy. Luca Brasi had made contact with the forces of Sollozzo several months before. He had done so on the orders of Don Corleone himself. He had done so by frequenting the nightclubs controlled by the Tattaglia Family and by taking up with one of their top call girls. In bed with this call girl he grumbled about how he was held down in the Corleone Family, how his worth was not recognized. After a week of this affair with the call girl, Luca was approached by Bruno Tattaglia, manager of the nightclub. Bruno was the youngest son, and ostensibly not connected with the Family business of prostitution. But his famous nightclub with its dancing line of long-stemmed beauties was the finishing school for many of the city hookers.

The first meeting was all above-board, Tattaglia offering him a job to work in the Family business as enforcer. The flirtation went on for nearly a month. Luca played his role of man infatuated with a young beautiful girl, Bruno Tattaglia the role of a businessman trying to recruit an able executive from a rival. At one such meeting, Luca pretended to be swayed, then said, "But one thing must be understood. I will never go against the Godfather. Don Corleone is a man I respect. I understand that he must put his sons before me in the Family business."

Bruno Tattaglia was one of the new generation with a barely hidden contempt for the old Moustache Petes like Luca Brasi, Don Corleone and even his own father. He was just a little too respectful. Now he said, "My father wouldn't expect you to do anything against the Corleones. Why should he? Everybody gets along with everybody else now, it's not like the old days. It's just that if you're looking for a new job, I can pass along the word to my father. There's always need for a man like you in our business. It's a hard business and it needs hard men to keep it running smooth. Let me know if you ever make up your mind."

Luca shrugged. "It's not so bad where I'm at." And so they left it.

The general idea had been to lead the Tattaglias to believe that he knew about the lucrative narcotics operation and that he wanted a piece of it free-lance. In that fashion he might hear something about Sollozzo's plans if the Turk had any, or whether he was getting ready to step on the toes of Don Corleone. After waiting for two months with nothing else happening, Luca reported to the Don that obviously Sollozzo was taking his defeat graciously. The Don had told him to keep trying but merely as a sideline, not to press it.

Luca had dropped into the nightclub the evening before Don Corleone's being shot. Almost immediately Bruno Tattaglia had come to his table and sat down.

"I have a friend who wants to talk to you," he said.

"Bring him over," Luca said. "I'll talk to any friend of yours."

"No," Bruno said. "He wants to see you in private."

"Who is he?" Luca asked.

"Just a friend of mine," Bruno Tattaglia said. "He wants to put a proposition to you. Can you meet him later on tonight?"

"Sure," Luca said. "What time and where?"

Tattaglia said softly, "The club closes at four in the morning. Why don't you meet in here while the waiters are cleaning up?"

They knew his habits, Luca thought, they must have been checking him out. He usually got up about three or four in the afternoon and had breakfast, then amused himself by gambling with cronies in the Family or had a girl. Sometimes he saw one of the midnight movies and then would drop in for a drink at one of the clubs. He never went to bed before dawn. So the suggestion of a four A.M. meeting was not as outlandish as it seemed.

"Sure, sure," he said. "I'll be back at four." He left the club and caught a cab to his furnished room on Tenth Avenue. He boarded with an Italian family to which he was distantly related. His two rooms were separated from the rest of their railroad flat by a special door. He liked the arrangement because it gave him some family life and also protection against surprise where he was most vulnerable.

The sly Turkish fox was going to show his bushy tail, Luca thought. If things went far enough, if Sollozzo committed himself tonight, maybe the whole thing could be wound up as a Christmas present for the Don. In his room, Luca unlocked the trunk beneath the bed and took out a bulletproof vest. It was heavy. He undressed and put it on over his woolen underwear, then put his shirt and jacket over it. He thought for a moment of calling the Don's house at Long Beach to tell him of this new development but he knew the Don never talked over the phone, to anyone, and the Don had given him this assignment in secret and so did not want anyone, not even Hagen or his eldest son, to know about it.

Luca always carried a gun. He had a license to carry a gun, probably the most expensive gun license ever issued anyplace, anytime. It had cost a total of ten thousand dollars but it would keep him out of jail if he was frisked by the cops. As a top executive operating official of the Family he rated the license. But tonight, just in case he could finish off the job, he wanted a "safe" gun. One that could not possibly be traced. But then thinking the matter over, he decided that he would just listen to the proposition tonight and report back to the Godfather, Don Corleone.

He made his way back to the club but he did not drink anymore. Instead he wandered out to 48th Street, where he had a leisurely late supper at Patsy's, his favorite Italian restaurant. When it was time for his appointment he drifted uptown to the club entrance. The doorman was no longer there when he went in. The hatcheck girl was gone. Only Bruno Tattaglia waited to greet him and lead him to the deserted bar at the side of the room. Before him he could see the desert of small tables with the polished yellow wood dance floor gleaming like a small diamond in the middle of them. In the shadows was the empty bandstand, out of it grew the skeleton metal stalk of a microphone.

Luca sat at the bar and Bruno Tattaglia went behind it. Luca refused the drink offered to him and lit a cigarette. It was possible that this would turn out to be something else, not the Turk. But then he saw Sollozzo emerge out of the shadows at the far end of the room.

Sollozzo shook his hand and sat at the bar next to him. Tattaglia put a glass in front of the Turk, who nodded his thanks. "Do you know who I am?" asked Sollozzo.

Luca nodded. He smiled grimly. The rats were being flushed out of their holes. It would be his pleasure to take care of this renegade Sicilian.

"Do you know what I am going to ask of you?" Sollozzo asked.

Luca shook his head.

"There's big business to be made," Sollozzo said. "I mean millions for everybody at the top level. On the first shipment I can guarantee you fifty thousand dollars. I'm talking about drugs. It's the coming thing."

Luca said, "Why come to me? You want me to talk to my Don?"

Sollozzo grimaced. "I've already talked to the Don. He wants no part of it. All right, I can do without him. But I need somebody strong to protect the operation physically. I understand you're not happy with your Family, you might make a switch."

Luca shrugged. "If the offer is good enough."

Sollozzo had been watching him intently and seemed to have come to a decision. "Think about my offer for a few days and then we'll talk again," he said. He put out his hand but Luca pretended not to see it and busied himself putting a cigarette in his mouth. Behind the bar, Bruno Tattaglia made a lighter appear magically and held it to Luca's cigarette. And then he did a strange thing. He dropped the lighter on the bar and grabbed Luca's right hand, holding it tight.

Luca reacted instantly, his body slipping off the bar stool and trying to twist away. But Sollozzo had grabbed his other hand at the wrist. Still, Luca was too strong for both of them and would have broken free except that a man stepped out of the shadows behind him and threw a thin silken cord around his neck. The cord pulled tight, choking off Luca's breath. His face became purple, the strength in his arms drained away. Tattaglia and Sollozzo held his hands easily now, and they stood there curiously childlike as the man behind Luca pulled the cord around Luca's neck tighter and tighter. Suddenly the floor was wet and slippery. Luca's sphincter, no longer under control, opened, the waste of his body spilled out. There was no strength in him anymore and his legs folded, his body sagged. Sollozzo and Tattaglia let his hands go and only the strangler stayed with the victim, sinking to his knees to follow Luca's falling body, drawing the cord so tight that it cut into the flesh of the neck and disappeared. Luca's eyes were bulging out of his head as if in the utmost surprise and this surprise was the only humanity remaining to him. He was dead.

"I don't want him found," Sollozzo said. "It's important that he not be found right now." He turned on his heel and left, disappearing back into the shadows.

Chapter

8

THE day after the shooting of Don Corleone was a busy time for the Family. Michael stayed by the phone relaying messages to Sonny. Tom Hagen was busy trying to find a mediator satisfactory to both parties so that a conference could be arranged with Sollozzo. The Turk had suddenly become cagey, perhaps he knew that the Family button men of Clemenza and Tessio were ranging far and wide over the city in an attempt to pick up his trail. But Sollozzo was sticking close to his hideout, as were all top members of the Tattaglia Family. This was expected by Sonny, an elementary precaution he knew the enemy was bound to take.

Clemenza was tied up with Paulie Gatto. Tessio had been given the assignment of trying to track down the whereabouts of Luca Brasi. Luca had not been home since the night before the shooting, a bad sign. But Sonny could not believe that Brasi had either turned traitor or had been taken by surprise.

Mama Corleone was staying in the city with friends of the Family so that she could be near the hospital. Carlo Rizzi, the son-in-law, had offered his services but had been told to take care of his own business that Don Corleone had set him up in, a lucrative bookmaking territory in the Italian section of Manhattan. Connie was staying with her mother in town so that she too could visit her father in the hospital.

Freddie was still under sedation in his own room of his parents' house. Sonny and Michael had paid him a visit and had been astonished at his paleness, his obvious illness. "Christ," Sonny said to Michael when they left Freddie's room, "he looks like he got plugged worse than the old man."

Michael shrugged. He had seen soldiers in the same condition on the battlefield. But he had never expected it to happen to Freddie. He remembered the middle brother as being physically the toughest one in the family when all of them were kids. But he had also been the most obedient son to his father. And yet everyone knew that the Don had given up on this middle son ever being important to the business. He wasn't quite smart enough, and failing that, not quite ruthless enough. He was too retiring a person, did not have enough force.

Late in the afternoon, Michael got a call from Johnny Fontane in Hollywood. Sonny took the phone. "Nah, Johnny, no use coming back here to see the Old Man. He's too sick and it would give you a lot of bad publicity, and I know the old man wouldn't like that. Wait until he's better and we can move him home, then come see him. OK, I'll give him your regards." Sonny hung up the phone. He turned to Michael and said, "That'll make Pop happy, that Johnny wanted to fly from California to see how he was."

Late that afternoon, Michael was called to the listed phone in the kitchen by one of Clemenza's men. It was Kay.

"Is your father all right?" she asked. Her voice was a little strained, a little unnatural. Michael knew that she couldn't quite believe what had happened, that his father really was what the newspapers called a gangster.

"He'll be OK," Michael said.

"Can I come with you when you visit him in the hospital?" Kay asked.

Michael laughed. She had remembered him telling her how important it was to do such things if you wanted to get along with the old Italians. "This is a special case," he said. "If the newspaper guys get a hold of your name and background you'll be on page three of the *Daily News*. Girl from old Yankee family mixed up with son of big Mafia chief. How would your parents like that?"

Kay said dryly, "My parents never read the *Daily News*." Again there was an awkward pause and then she said, "You're OK, aren't you, Mike, you're not in any danger?"

Mike laughed again. "I'm known as the sissy of the Corleone family. No threat. So they don't have to bother coming after me. No, it's all over, Kay, there won't be any more trouble. It was all sort of an accident anyway. I'll explain when I see you."

"When will that be?" she asked.

Michael pondered. "How about late tonight? We'll have a drink and supper in your hotel and then I'll go to the hospital and see my old man. I'm getting tired of hanging around here answering phones. OK? But don't tell anybody. I don't want newspaper photographers snapping pictures of us together. No kidding, Kay, it's damned embarrassing, especially for your parents."

"All right," Kay said. "I'll be waiting. Can I do any Christmas shopping for you? Or anything else?"

"No," Michael said. "Just be ready."

She gave a little excited laugh. "I'll be ready," she said. "Aren't I always?"

"Yes, you are," he said. "That's why you're my best girl."

"I love you," she said. "Can you say it?"

Michael looked at the four hoods sitting in the kitchen. "No," he said. "Tonight, OK?"

"OK," she said. He hung up.

Clemenza had finally come back from his day's work and was bustling around the kitchen cooking up a huge pot of tomato sauce. Michael nodded to him and went to the corner office where he found Hagen and Sonny waiting for him impatiently. "Is Clemenza out there?" Sonny asked.

Michael grinned. "He's cooking up spaghetti for the troops, just like the army."

Sonny said impatiently, "Tell him to cut out that crap and come on in here. I have more important things for him to do. Get Tessio in here with him."

In a few minutes they were all gathered in the office. Sonny said curtly to Clemenza, "You take care of him?"

Clemenza nodded. "You won't see him anymore."

With a slight electric shock, Michael realized they were talking about Paulie Gatto and that little Paulie was dead, murdered by that jolly wedding dancer, Clemenza.

Sonny asked Hagen, "You have any luck with Sollozzo?"

Hagen shook his head. "He seems to have cooled off on the negotiation idea. Anyway he doesn't seem to be too anxious. Or maybe he's just being very careful so that our button men won't nail him. Anyway I haven't been able to set up a top-notch go-between he'll trust. But he must know he has to negotiate now. He missed his chance when he let the old man get away from him."

Sonny said, "He's a smart guy, the smartest our Family ever came up against. Maybe he figured we're just stalling until the old man gets better or we can get a line on him."

Hagen shrugged. "Sure, he figures that. But he still has to negotiate. He has no choice. I'll get it set up tomorrow. That's certain."

One of Clemenza's men knocked on the office door and then came in. He said to Clemenza, "It just came over the radio, the cops found Paulie Gatto. Dead in his car."

Clemenza nodded and said to the man, "Don't worry about it." The button man gave his *caporegime* an astonished look, which was followed by a look of comprehension, before he went back to the kitchen.

The conference went on as if there had been no interruption. Sonny asked Hagen, "Any change in the Don's condition?"

Hagen shook his head. "He's OK but he won't be able to talk for another couple of days. He's all knocked out. Still recovering from the operation. Your mother spends most of the day with him, Connie too. There's cops all over the hospital and Tessio's men hang around too, just in case. In a couple of days he'll be all right and then we can see what he wants us to do. Meanwhile we have to keep Sollozzo from doing anything rash. That's why I want to start you talking deals with him."

Sonny grunted. "Until he does, I've got Clemenza and Tessio looking for him. Maybe we'll get lucky and solve the whole business."

"You won't get lucky," Hagen said. "Sollozzo is too smart." Hagen paused. "He knows once he comes to the table he'll have to go our way mostly. That's why he's stalling. I'm guessing he's trying to line up support from the other New York Families so that we won't go after him when the old man gives us the word."

Sonny frowned. "Why the hell should they do that?"

Hagen said patiently, "To avert a big war which hurts everybody and brings the papers and government into the act. Also, Sollozzo will give them a piece of the action. And you know how much dough there is in drugs. The Corleone Family doesn't need it, we have the gambling, which is the best business to have. But the other Families are hungry. Sollozzo is a proven man, they know he can make the operation go on a big scale. Alive he's money in their pockets, dead he's trouble."

Sonny's face was as Michael had never seen it. The heavy Cupid mouth and bronzed skin seemed gray. "I don't give a fuck what they want. They better not mess in this fight."

Clemenza and Tessio shifted uneasily in their chairs, infantry leaders who hear their general rave about storming an impregnable hill no matter what the cost. Hagen said a little impatiently, "Come on, Sonny, your father wouldn't like you thinking that way. You know what he always says, 'That's a waste.' Sure, we're not going to let anybody stop us if the old man says we go after Sollozzo. But this is not a personal thing, this is business. If we go after the Turk and the Families interfere, we'll negotiate the issue. If the Families see that we're determined to have Sollozzo, they'll let us. The Don will make concessions in other areas to square things. But don't go blood crazy on a thing like this. It's business. Even the shooting of your father was business, not personal. You should know that by now."

Sonny's eyes were still hard. "OK, I understand all that. Just so long as you understand that nobody stands in our way when we want Sollozzo."

Sonny turned to Tessio. "Any leads on Luca?"

Tessio shook his head. "None at all. Sollozzo must have snatched him."

Hagen said quietly, "Sollozzo wasn't worried about Luca, which struck me as funny. He's too smart not to worry about a guy like Luca. I think he maybe got him out of the picture, one way or the other."

Sonny muttered, "Christ, I hope Luca isn't fighting against us. That's the one thing I'd be afraid of. Clemenza, Tessio, how do you two guys figure it?"

Clemenza said slowly, "Anybody could go wrong, look at Paulie. But with Luca, he was a man who could only go one way. The Godfather was the only thing he believed in, the only man he feared. But not only that, Sonny, he respected your father as no one else respected him and the Godfather has earned respect from everyone. No, Luca would never betray us. And I find it hard to believe that a man like Sollozzo, no matter how cunning, could surprise Luca. He was a man who suspected everyone and everything. He was always ready for the worst. I think maybe he just went off someplace for a few days. We'll be hearing from him anytime now."

Sonny turned to Tessio. The Brooklyn *caporegime* shrugged. "Any man can turn traitor. Luca was very touchy. Maybe the Don offended him some way. That could be. I think though that Sollozzo gave him a little surprise. That fits in with what the *Consigliori* says. We should expect the worst."

Sonny said to all of them, "Sollozzo should get the word soon about Paulie Gatto. How will that affect him?"

Clemenza said grimly, "It will make him think. He will know the Corleone Family are not fools. He will realize that he was very lucky yesterday."

Sonny said sharply, "That wasn't luck. Sollozzo was planning that for weeks. They must have tailed the old man to his office every day and watched his routine. Then they bought Paulie off and maybe Luca. They snatched Tom right on the button. They did everything they wanted to do. They were unlucky, not lucky. Those button men they hired weren't good enough and the old man moved too quick. If they had killed him, I would have had to make a deal and Sollozzo would have won. For now. I would have waited maybe and got him five, ten years from now. But don't call him lucky, Pete, that's underrating him. And we've done that too much lately."

One of the button men brought a bowl of spaghetti in from the kitchen and then some plates, forks and wine. They ate as they talked. Michael watched in amazement. He didn't eat and neither did Tom, but Sonny, Clemenza and Tessio dug in, mopping up sauce with crusts of bread. It was almost comical. They continued their discussion.

Tessio didn't think that the loss of Paulie Gatto would upset Sollozzo, in fact he thought that the Turk might have anticipated it, indeed might have welcomed it. A useless mouth off the payroll. And he would not be frightened by it; after all, would they be in such a situation?

Michael spoke up diffidently. "I know I'm an amateur in this, but from everything you guys have said about Sollozzo, plus the fact that all of a sudden he's out of touch with Tom, I'd guess he has an ace up his sleeve. He might be ready to pull off something real tricky that would put him back on top. If we could figure out what that would be, we'd be in the driver's seat."

Sonny said reluctantly, "Yeah, I thought of that and the only thing

I can figure is Luca. The word is already out that he's to be brought here before he's allowed any of his old rights in the Family. The only other thing I can think of is that Sollozzo has made his deal with the Families in New York and we'll get the word tomorrow that they will be against us in a war. That we'll have to give the Turk his deal. Right, Tom?"

Hagen nodded. "That's what it looks like to me. And we can't move against that kind of opposition without your father. He's the only one who can stand against the Families. He has the political connections they always need and he can use them for trading. If he wants to badly enough."

Clemenza said a little arrogantly for a man whose top button man had recently betrayed him, "Sollozzo will never get near this house, Boss, you don't have to worry about that."

Sonny looked at him thoughtfully for a moment. Then he said to Tessio, "How about the hospital, your men got it covered?"

For the first time during the conference Tessio seemed to be absolutely sure of his ground. "Outside and inside," he said. "Right around the clock. The cops have it covered pretty good too. Detectives at the bedroom door waiting to question the old man. That's a laugh. The Don is still getting that stuff in the tubes, no food, so we don't have to worry about the kitchen, which would be something to worry about with those Turks, they believe in poison. They can't get at the Don, not in any way."

Sonny tilted back in his chair. "It wouldn't be me, they have to do business with me, they need the Family machine." He grinned at Michael. "I wonder if it's you? Maybe Sollozzo figures to snatch you and hold you for a hostage to make a deal."

Michael thought ruefully, there goes my date with Kay. Sonny wouldn't let him out of the house. But Hagen said impatiently, "No, he could have snatched Mike anytime if he wanted insurance. But everybody knows that Mike is not in the Family business. He's a civilian and if Sollozzo snatches him, then he loses all the other New York Families. Even the Tattaglias would have to help hunt him down. No, it's simple enough. Tomorrow we'll get a representative from all the Families who'll tell us we have to do business with the Turk. That's what he's waiting for. That's his ace in the hole."

Michael heaved a sigh of relief. "Good," he said. "I have to go into town tonight."

"Why?" Sonny asked sharply.

Michael grinned. "I figure I'll drop in to the hospital and visit the old man, see Mom and Connie. And I got some other things to do." Like the Don, Michael never told his real business and now he didn't want to tell Sonny he was seeing Kay Adams. There was no reason not to tell him, it was just habit.

There was a loud murmur of voices in the kitchen. Clemenza went out to see what was happening. When he came back he was holding Luca Brasi's bulletproof vest in his hands. Wrapped in the vest was a huge dead fish.

Clemenza said dryly, "The Turk has heard about his spy Paulie Gatto."

Tessio said just as dryly, "And now we know about Luca Brasi."

Sonny lit a cigar and took a shot of whiskey. Michael, bewildered, said, "What the hell does that fish mean?" It was Hagen the Irisher, the *Consigliori*, who answered him. "The fish means that Luca Brasi is sleeping on the bottom of the ocean," he said. "It's an old Sicilian message."

Chapter

9

WHEN Michael Corleone went into the city that night it was with a depressed spirit. He felt that he was being enmeshed in the Family business against his will and he resented Sonny using him even to answer the phone. He felt uncomfortable being on the inside of the Family councils as if he could be absolutely trusted with such secrets as murder. And now, going to see Kay, he felt guilty about her also. He had never been completely honest with her about his family. He had told her about them but always with little jokes and colorful anecdotes that made them seem more like adventurers in a Technicolor movie than what they really were. And now his father had been shot down in the street and his eldest brother was making plans for murder. That was putting it plainly and simply but that was never how he would tell it to Kay. He had already said his father being shot was more like an "accident" and that all the trouble was over. Hell, it looked like it was just beginning. Sonny and Tom were off-center on this guy Sollozzo, they were still underrating him, even though Sonny was smart enough to see the danger. Michael tried to think what the Turk might have up his sleeve. He was obviously a bold man, a clever man, a man of extraordinary force. You had to figure him to come up with a real surprise. But then Sonny and Tom and

Clemenza and Tessio were all agreed that everything was under control and they all had more experience than he did. He was the "civilian" in this war, Michael thought wryly. And they'd have to give him a hell of a lot better medals than he'd gotten in World War II to make him join this one.

Thinking this made him feel guilty about not feeling more sympathy for his father. His own father shot full of holes and yet in a curious way Michael, better than anyone else, understood when Tom had said it was just business, not personal. That his father had paid for the power he had wielded all his life, the respect he had extorted from all those around him.

What Michael wanted was out, out of all this, to lead his own life. But he couldn't cut loose from the family until the crisis was over. He had to help in a civilian capacity. With sudden clarity he realized that he was annoyed with the role assigned to him, that of the privileged noncombatant, the excused conscientious objector. That was why the word "civilian" kept popping into his skull in such an irritating way.

When he got to the hotel, Kay was waiting for him in the lobby. (A couple of Clemenza's people had driven him into town and dropped him off on a nearby corner after making sure they were not followed.)

They had dinner together and some drinks. "What time are you going to visit your father?" Kay asked.

Michael looked at his watch. "Visiting hours end at eight-thirty. I think I'll go after everybody has left. They'll let me up. He has a private room and his own nurses so I can just sit with him for a while. I don't think he can talk yet or even know if I'm there. But I have to show respect."

Kay said quietly, "I feel so sorry for your father, he seemed like such a nice man at the wedding. I can't believe the things the papers are printing about him. I'm sure most of it's not true."

Michael said politely, "I don't think so either." He was surprised to find himself so secretive with Kay. He loved her, he trusted her, but he would never tell her anything about his father or the Family. She was an outsider.

"What about you?" Kay asked. "Are you going to get mixed up in this gang war the papers are talking about so gleefully?"

Michael grinned, unbuttoned his jacket and held it wide open. "Look, no guns," he said. Kay laughed.

It was getting late and they went up to their room. She mixed a drink for both of them and sat on his lap as they drank. Beneath her dress she was all silk until his hand touched the glowing skin of her thigh. They fell back on the bed together and made love with all their clothes on, their mouths glued together. When they were finished they lay very still, feeling the heat of their bodies burning through their garments. Kay murmured, "Is that what you soldiers call a quickie?"

"Yeah," Michael said.

"It's not bad," Kay said in a judicious voice.

They dozed off until Michael suddenly started up anxiously and looked at his watch. "Damn," he said. "It's nearly ten. I have to get down to the hospital." He went to the bathroom to wash up and comb his hair. Kay came in after him and put her arms around his waist from behind. "When are we going to get married?" she asked.

"Whenever you say," Michael said. "As soon as this family thing quiets down and my old man gets better. I think you'd better explain things to your parents though."

"What should I explain?" Kay said quietly.

Michael ran the comb through his hair. "Just say that you've met a brave, handsome guy of Italian descent. Top marks at Dartmouth. Distinguished Service Cross during the war plus the Purple Heart. Honest. Hard-working. But his father is a Mafia chief who has to kill bad people, sometimes bribe high government officials and in his line of work gets shot full of holes himself. But that has nothing to do with his honest hard-working son. Do you think you can remember all that?"

Kay let go his body and leaned against the door of the bathroom. "Is he really?" she said. "Does he really?" She paused. "Kill people?"

Michael finished combing his hair. "I don't really know," he said. "Nobody really knows. But I wouldn't be surprised."

Before he went out the door she asked, "When will I see you again?"

Michael kissed her. "I want you to go home and think things over in that little hick town of yours," he said. "I don't want you to get mixed up in this business in any way. After the Christmas holidays I'll be back at school and we'll get together up in Hanover. OK?"

"OK," she said. She watched him go out the door, saw him wave before he stepped into the elevator. She had never felt so close to him, never so much in love and if someone had told her she would not see Michael again until three years passed, she would not have been able to bear the anguish of it.

When Michael got out of the cab in front of the French Hospital he was surprised to see that the street was completely deserted. When he entered the hospital he was even more surprised to find the lobby empty. Damn it, what the hell were Clemenza and Tessio doing? Sure, they never went to West Point but they knew enough about tactics to have outposts. A couple of their men should have been in the lobby at least.

Even the latest visitors had departed, it was almost ten-thirty at night. Michael was tense and alert now. He didn't bother to stop at the information desk, he already knew his father's room number up on the fourth floor. He took the self-service elevator. Oddly enough nobody stopped him until he reached the nurses' station on the fourth floor. But he strode right past her query and on to his father's room. There was no one outside the door. Where the hell were the two detectives who were supposed to be waiting around to guard and question the old man? Where the hell were Tessio and Clemenza's people? Could there be someone inside the room? But the door was open. Michael went in. There was a figure in the bed and by the December moonlight straining through the window Michael could see his father's face. Even now it was impassive, the chest heaved shallowly with his uneven breath. Tubes hung from steel gallows beside the bed and ran into his nose. On the floor was a glass jar receiving the poisons emptied from his stomach by other tubes. Michael stayed there for a few moments to make sure his father was all right, then backed out of the room.

He told the nurse, "My name is Michael Corleone, I just want to sit with my father. What happened to the detectives who were supposed to be guarding him?"

The nurse was a pretty young thing with a great deal of confidence in the power of her office. "Oh, your father just had too many visitors, it interfered with the hospital service," she said. "The police came and made them all leave about ten minutes ago. And then just five minutes ago I had to call the detectives to the phone for an emergency alarm from their headquarters, and then they left too. But don't worry, I look in on your father often and I can hear any sound from his room. That's why we leave the doors open."

"Thank you," Michael said. "I'll sit with him for a little while. OK?"

She smiled at him. "Just for a little bit and then I'm afraid you'll have to leave. It's the rules, you know."

Michael went back into his father's room. He took the phone from its cradle and got the hospital operator to give him the house in Long Beach, the phone in the corner office room. Sonny answered. Michael whispered, "Sonny, I'm down at the hospital, I came down late. Sonny, there's nobody here. None of Tessio's people. No detectives at the door. The old man was completely unprotected." His voice was trembling.

There was a long silence and then Sonny's voice came, low and impressed, "This is Sollozzo's move you were talking about."

Michael said, "That's what I figured too. But how did he get the cops to clear everybody out and where did they go? What happened to Tessio's men? Jesus Christ, has that bastard Sollozzo got the New York Police Department in his pocket too?"

"Take it easy, kid." Sonny's voice was soothing. "We got lucky again with you going to visit the hospital so late. Stay in the old man's room. Lock the door from the inside. I'll have some men there inside of fifteen minutes, soon as I make some calls. Just sit tight and don't panic. OK, kid?"

"I won't panic," Michael said. For the first time since it had all started he felt a furious anger rising in him, a cold hatred for his father's enemies.

He hung up the phone and rang the buzzer for the nurse. He decided to use his own judgment and disregard Sonny's orders. When the nurse came in he said, "I don't want you to get frightened, but we have to move my father right away. To another room or another floor. Can you disconnect all these tubes so we can wheel the bed out?"

The nurse said, "That's ridiculous. We have to get permission from the doctor."

Michael spoke very quickly. "You've read about my father in the papers. You've seen that there's no one here tonight to guard him. Now I've just gotten word some men will come into the hospital to kill him. Please believe me and help me." He could be extraordinarily persuasive when he wanted to be.

The nurse said, "We don't have to disconnect the tubes. We can wheel the stand with the bed."

"Do you have an empty room?" Michael whispered.

"At the end of the hall," the nurse said.

It was done in a matter of moments, very quickly and very efficiently. Then Michael said to the nurse, "Stay here with him until help comes. If you're outside at your station you might get hurt."

At that moment he heard his father's voice from the bed, hoarse but full of strength, "Michael, is it you? What happened, what is it?"

Michael leaned over the bed. He took his father's hand in his. "It's Mike," he said. "Don't be afraid. Now listen, don't make any noise at all, especially if somebody calls out your name. Some people want to kill you, understand? But I'm here so don't be afraid."

Don Corleone, still not fully conscious of what had happened to him the day before, in terrible pain, yet smiled benevolently on his youngest son, wanting to tell him, but it was too much effort, "Why should I be afraid now? Strange men have come to kill me ever since I was twelve years old."

Chapter

10

THE hospital was small and private with just one entrance. Michael looked through the window down into the street. There was a curved courtyard that had steps leading down into the street and the street was empty of cars. But whoever came into the hospital would have to come through that entrance. He knew he didn't have much time so he ran out of the room and down the four flights and through the wide doors of the ground floor entrance. Off to the side he saw the ambulance yard and there was no car there, no ambulances either.

Michael stood on the sidewalk outside the hospital and lit a cigarette. He unbuttoned his coat and stood in the light of a lamppost so that his features could be seen A young man was walking swiftly down from Ninth Avenue, a package under his arm. The young man wore a combat jacket and had a heavy shock of black hair. His face was familiar when he came under the lamplight but Michael could not place it. But the young man stopped in front of him and put out his hand, saying in a heavy Italian accent, "Don Michael, do you remember me? Enzo, the baker's helper to Nazorine the Paniterra; his son-in-law. Your father saved my life by getting the government to let me stay in America."

Michael shook his hand. He remembered him now.

Enzo went on, "I've come to pay my respects to your father. Will they let me into the hospital so late?"

Michael smiled and shook his head. "No, but thanks anyway. I'll tell the Don you came." A car came roaring down the street and Michael was instantly alert. He said to Enzo, "Leave here quickly. There may be trouble. You don't want to get involved with the police."

He saw the look of fear on the young Italian's face. Trouble with the police might mean being deported or refusal of citizenship. But the young man stood fast. He whispered in Italian, "If there's trouble I'll stay to help. I owe it to the Godfather."

Michael was touched. He was about to tell the young man to go away again, but then he thought, why not let him stay? Two men in front of the hospital might scare off any of Sollozzo's crew sent to do a job. One man almost certainly would not. He gave Enzo a cigarette and lit it for him. They both stood under the lamppost in the cold December night. The yellow panes of the hospital, bisected by the greens of Christmas decorations, twinkled down on them. They had almost finished their cigarettes when a long low black car turned into 30th Street from Ninth Avenue and cruised toward them, very close to the curb. It almost stopped. Michael peered to see their faces inside, his body flinching involuntarily. The car seemed about to stop, then speeded forward. Somebody had recognized him. Michael gave Enzo another cigarette and noticed that the baker's hands were shaking. To his surprise his own hands were steady.

They stayed in the street smoking for what was no more than ten minutes when suddenly the night air was split by a police siren. A patrol car made a screaming turn from Ninth Avenue and pulled up in front of the hospital. Two more squad cars followed right behind it. Suddenly the hospital entranceway was flooded with uniformed police and detectives. Michael heaved a sigh of relief. Good old Sonny must have gotten through right away. He moved forward to meet them.

Two huge, burly policemen grabbed his arms. Another frisked him. A massive police captain, gold braid on his cap, came up the steps, his men parting respectfully to leave a path. He was a vigorous man for his girth and despite the white hair that peeked out of his cap. His face was beefy red. He came up to Michael and said harshly, "I thought I got all you guinea hoods locked up. Who the hell are you and what are you doing here?"

One of the cops standing beside Michael said, "He's clean, Captain."

Michael didn't answer. He was studying this police captain, coldly searching his face, the metallic blue eyes. A detective in plain clothes said, "That's Michael Corleone, the Don's son."

Michael said quietly, "What happened to the detectives who were supposed to be guarding my father? Who pulled them off that detail?"

The police captain was choleric with rage. "You fucking hood, who the hell are you to tell me my business? I pulled them off. I don't give a shit how many dago gangsters kill each other. If it was up to me, I wouldn't lift a finger to keep your old man from getting knocked off. Now get the hell out of here. Get out of this street, you punk, and stay out of this hospital when it's not visiting hours."

Michael was still studying him intently. He was not angry at what this police captain was saying. His mind was racing furiously. Was it possible that Sollozzo had been in that first car and had seen him standing in front of the hospital? Was it possible that Sollozzo had then called this captain and said, "How come the Corleones' men are still around the hospital when I paid you to lock them up?" Was it possible that all had been carefully planned as Sonny had said? Everything fitted in. Still cool, he said to the captain, "I'm not leaving this hospital until you put guards around my father's room."

The captain didn't bother answering. He said to the detective standing beside him, "Phil, lock this punk up."

The detective said hesitantly, "The kid is clean, Captain. He's a war hero and he's never been mixed up in the rackets. The papers could make a stink."

The captain started to turn on the detective, his face red with fury. He roared out, "Goddamn it, I said lock him up."

Michael, still thinking clearly, not angry, said with deliberate malice, "How much is the Turk paying you to set my father up, Captain?"

The police captain turned to him. He said to the two burly patrolmen, "Hold him." Michael felt his arms pinned to his sides. He saw the captain's massive fist arching toward his face. He tried to weave away but the fist caught him high on the cheekbone. A grenade exploded in his skull. His mouth filled with blood and small hard bones that he realized were his teeth. He could feel the side of his head puff up as if it were filling with air. His legs were weightless and he would have fallen if the two policemen had not held him up. But he was still conscious. The plainclothes detective had stepped in front of him to keep the captain from hitting him again and was saying, "Jesus Christ, Captain, you really hurt him."

The captain said loudly, "I didn't touch him. He attacked me and he fell. Do you understand that? He resisted arrest."

Through a red haze Michael could see more cars pulling up to the curb. Men were getting out. One of them he recognized as Clemenza's lawyer, who was now speaking to the police captain, suavely and surely. "The Corleone Family has hired a firm of private detectives to guard Mr. Corleone. These men with me are licensed to carry firearms, Captain. If you arrest them, you'll have to appear before a judge in the morning and tell him why."

The lawyer glanced at Michael. "Do you want to prefer charges against whoever did this to you?" he asked.

Michael had trouble talking. His jaws wouldn't come together but he managed to mumble. "I slipped," he said. "I slipped and fell." He saw the captain give him a triumphant glance and he tried to answer that glance with a smile. At all costs he wanted to hide the delicious icy chilliness that controlled his brain, the surge of wintry cold hatred that pervaded his body. He wanted to give no warning to anyone in this world as to how he felt at this moment. As the Don would not. Then he felt himself carried into the hospital and he lost consciousness.

When he woke up in the morning he found that his jaw had been wired together and that four of his teeth along the left side of his mouth were missing. Hagen was sitting beside his bed.

"Did they drug me up?" Michael asked.

"Yeah," Hagen said. "They had to dig some bone fragments out of your gums and they figured it would be too painful. Besides you were practically out anyway."

"Is there anything else wrong with me?" Michael asked.

"No," Hagen said. "Sonny wants you out at the Long Beach house. Think you can make it?"

"Sure," Michael said. "Is the Don all right?"

Hagen flushed. "I think we've solved the problem now. We have a firm of private detectives and we have the whole area loaded. I'll tell you more when we get in the car."

Clemenza was driving, Michael and Hagen sat in the back. Michael's head throbbed. "So what the hell really happened last night, did you guys ever find out?"

Hagen spoke quietly. "Sonny has an inside man, that Detective Phillips who tried to protect you. He gave us the scoop. The police captain, McCluskey, is a guy who's been on the take very heavy ever since he's been a patrolman. Our Family has paid him quite a bit. And he's greedy and untrustworthy to do business with. But Sollozzo must have paid him a big price. McCluskey had all Tessio's men around and in the hospital arrested right after visiting hours. It didn't help that some of them were carrying guns. Then McCluskey pulled the official guard detectives off the Don's door. Claimed he needed them and that some other cops were supposed to go over and take their place but they got their assignments bollixed. Baloney. He was paid off to set the Don up. And Phillips said he's the kind of guy who'll try it again. Sollozzo must have given him a fortune for openers and promised him the moon to come."

"Was my getting hurt in the papers?"

"No," Hagen said. "We kept that quiet. Nobody wants that known. Not the cops. Not us."

"Good," Michael said. "Did that boy Enzo get away?"

"Yeah," Hagen said. "He was smarter than you. When the cops came he disappeared. He claims he stuck with you while Sollozzo's car went by. Is that true?"

"Yeah," Michael said. "He's a good kid."

"He'll be taken care of," Hagen said. "You feeling OK?" His face was concerned. "You look lousy."

"I'm OK," Michael said. "What was that police captain's name?"

"McCluskey," Hagen said. "By the way, it might make you feel better to know that the Corleone Family finally got up on the scoreboard. Bruno Tattaglia, four o'clock this morning."

Michael sat up. "How come? I thought we were supposed to sit tight."

Hagen shrugged. "After what happened at the hospital Sonny got hard. The button men are out all over New York and New Jersey. We made the list last night. I'm trying to hold Sonny in, Mike. Maybe you can talk to him. This whole business can still be settled without a major war."

"I'll talk to him," Michael said. "Is there a conference this morning?"

"Yeah," Hagen said. "Sollozzo finally got in touch and wants to sit down with us. A negotiator is arranging the details. That means we win. Sollozzo knows he's lost and he wants to get out with his life." Hagen paused. "Maybe he thought we were soft, ready to be taken, because we didn't strike back. Now with one of the Tattaglia sons dead he knows we mean business. He really took an awful gamble bucking the Don. By the way, we got the confirmation on Luca. They killed him the night before they shot your father. In Bruno's nightclub. Imagine that?"

Michael said, "No wonder they caught him off guard."

At the houses in Long Beach the entrance to the mall was blocked by a long black car parked across its mouth. Two men leaned against the hood of the car. The two houses on each side, Michael noticed, had opened windows on their upper floors. Christ, Sonny must really mean business.

Clemenza parked the car outside the mall and they walked inside it. The two guards were Clemenza's men and he gave them a frown of greeting that served as a salute. The men nodded their heads in acknowledgment. There were no smiles, no greetings. Clemenza led Hagen and Michael Corleone into the house.

The door was opened by another guard before they rang. He had obviously been watching from a window. They went to the corner office and found Sonny and Tessio waiting for them. Sonny came to Michael, took his younger brother's head in his hands and said kiddingly, "Beautiful. Beautiful." Michael knocked his hands away, and went to the desk and poured himself some scotch, hoping it would dull the ache in his wired jaw.

The five of them sat around the room but the atmosphere was different than their earlier meetings. Sonny was gayer, more cheerful, and Michael realized what that gaiety meant. There were no longer any doubts in his older brother's mind. He was committed and nothing would sway him. The attempt by Sollozzo the night before was the final straw. There could no longer be any question of a truce.

"We got a call from the negotiator while you were gone," Sonny said to Hagen. "The Turk wants a meeting now." Sonny laughed. "The balls on that son of a bitch," he said admiringly. "After he craps out last night he wants a meeting today or the next day. Meanwhile we're supposed just to lay back and take everything he dishes out. What fucking nerve."

Tom asked cautiously, "What did you answer?"

Sonny grinned. "I said sure, why not? Anytime he says, I'm in no hurry. I've got a hundred button men out on the street twenty-four hours a day. If Sollozzo shows one hair on his asshole he's dead. Let them take all the time they want."

Hagen said, "Was there a definite proposal?"

"Yeah," Sonny said. "He wants us to send Mike to meet him to hear his proposition. The negotiator guarantees Mike's safety. Sollozzo doesn't ask us to guarantee his safety, he knows he can't ask that. No point. So the meeting will be arranged on his side. His people will pick Mike up and take Mike to the meeting place. Mike will listen to Sollozzo and then they'll turn him loose. But the meeting place is secret. The promise is the deal will be so good we can't turn it down."

Hagen asked, "What about the Tattaglias? What will they do about Bruno?"

"That's part of the deal. The negotiator says the Tattaglia Family has agreed to go along with Sollozzo. They'll forget about Bruno Tattaglia. He pays for what they did to my father. One cancels out the other." Sonny laughed again. "The nervy bastards."

Hagen said cautiously, "We should hear what they have to say."

Sonny shook his head from side to side. "No, no, Consigliori, not this time." His voice held a faint trace of Italian accent. He was consciously mocking his father just to kid around. "No more meetings. No more discussions. No more Sollozzo tricks. When the negotiator gets in touch with us again for our answer I want you to give him one message. I want Sollozzo. If not, it's all-out war. We'll go to the mattresses and we'll put all the button men out on the street. Business will just have to suffer."

"The other Families won't stand for an all-out war," Hagen said. "It puts too much heat on everybody."

Sonny shrugged. "They have a simple solution. Give me Sollozzo. Or fight the Corleone Family." Sonny paused, then said roughly, "No more advice on how to patch it up, Tom. The decision is made. Your job is to help me win. Understand?"

Hagen bowed his head. He was deep in thought for a moment. Then he said, "I spoke to your contact in the police station. He says that Captain McCluskey is definitely on Sollozzo's payroll and for big

money. Not only that, but McCluskey is going to get a piece of the
drug operation. McCluskey has agreed to be Sollozzo's bodyguard.
The Turk doesn't poke his nose out of his hole without McCluskey.
When he meets Mike for the conference, McCluskey will be sitting
beside him. In civilian clothes but carrying his gun. Now what you
have to understand, Sonny, is that while Sollozzo is guarded like this,
he's invulnerable. Nobody has ever gunned down a New York police
captain and gotten away with it. The heat in this town would be
unbearable what with the newspapers, the whole police department,
the churches, everything. That would be disastrous. The Families
would be after you. The Corleone Family would become outcasts.
Even the old man's political protection would run for cover. So take
that into consideration."

Sonny shrugged. "McCluskey can't stay with the Turk forever.
We'll wait."

Tessio and Clemenza were puffing on their cigars uneasily, not
daring to speak, but sweating. It would be their skins that would go
on the line if the wrong decision was made.

Michael spoke for the first time. He asked Hagen, "Can the old man
be moved out of the hospital onto the mall here?"

Hagen shook his head. "That's the first thing I asked. Impossible.
He's in very bad shape. He'll pull through but he needs all kinds of
attention, maybe some more surgery. Impossible."

"Then you have to get Sollozzo right away," Michael said. "We
can't wait. The guy is too dangerous. He'll come up with some new
idea. Remember, the key is still that he gets rid of the old man. He
knows that. OK, he knows that now it's very tough so he's willing to
take defeat for his life. But if he's going to get killed anyway, he'll
have another crack at the Don. And with that police captain helping
him who knows what the hell might happen. We can't take that
chance. We have to get Sollozzo right away."

Sonny was scratching his chin thoughtfully. "You're right, kid," he
said. "You got right to the old nuts. We can't let Sollozzo get another
crack at the old man."

Hagen said quietly, "What about Captain McCluskey?"

Sonny turned to Michael with an odd little smile. "Yeah, kid, what
about that tough police captain?"

Michael said slowly, "OK, it's an extreme. But there are times
when the most extreme measures are justified. Let's think now that
we have to kill McCluskey. The way to do it would be to have him

heavily implicated so that it's not an honest police captain doing his duty but a crooked police official mixed up in the rackets who got what was coming to him, like any crook. We have newspaper people on our payroll we can give that story to with enough proof so that they can back it up. That should take some of the heat off. How does that sound?" Michael looked around deferentially to the others. Tessio and Clemenza had gloomy faces and refused to speak. Sonny said with the same odd smile, "Go on, kid, you're doing great. Out of the mouths of infants, as the Don always used to say. Go ahead, Mike, tell us more."

Hagen was smiling too a little and averting his head. Michael flushed. "Well, they want me to go to a conference with Sollozzo. It will be me, Sollozzo and McCluskey all on our own. Set up the meeting for two days from now, then get our informers to find out where the meeting will be held. Insist that it has to be a public place, that I'm not going to let them take me into any apartments or houses. Let it be a restaurant or a bar at the height of the dinner hour, something like that, so that I'll feel safe. They'll feel safe too. Even Sollozzo won't figure that we'll dare to gun the captain. They'll frisk me when I meet them so I'll have to be clean then, but figure out a way you can get a weapon to me while I'm meeting them. Then I'll take both of them."

All four heads turned and stared at him. Clemenza and Tessio were gravely astonished. Hagen looked a little sad but not surprised. He started to speak and thought better of it. But Sonny, his heavy Cupid's face twitching with mirth, suddenly broke out in loud roars of laughter. It was deep belly laughter, not faking. He was really breaking up. He pointed a finger at Michael, trying to speak through gasps of mirth. "You, the high-class college kid, you never wanted to get mixed up in the Family business. Now you wanta kill a police captain and the Turk just because you got your face smashed by McCluskey. You're taking it personal, it's just business and you're taking it personal. You wanta kill these two guys just because you got slapped in the face. It was all a lot of crap. All these years it was just a lot of crap."

Clemenza and Tessio, completely misunderstanding, thinking that Sonny was laughing at his young brother's bravado for making such an offer, were also smiling broadly and a little patronizingly at Michael. Only Hagen warily kept his face impassive.

Michael looked around at all of them, then stared at Sonny, who still couldn't stop laughing. "*You'll* take both of them?" Sonny said. "Hey, kid, they won't give you medals, they put you in the electric chair. You know that? This is no hero business, kid, you don't shoot people from a mile away. You shoot when you see the whites of their eyes like we got taught in school, remember? You gotta stand right next to them and blow their heads off and their brains get all over your nice Ivy League suit. How about that, kid, you wanta do that just because some dumb cop slapped you around?" He was still laughing.

Michael stood up. "You'd better stop laughing," he said. The change in him was so extraordinary that the smiles vanished from the faces of Clemenza and Tessio. Michael was not tall or heavily built but his presence seemed to radiate danger. In that moment he was a reincarnation of Don Corleone himself. His eyes had gone a pale tan and his face was bleached of color. He seemed at any moment about to fling himself on his older and stronger brother. There was no doubt that if he had had a weapon in his hands Sonny would have been in danger. Sonny stopped laughing, and Michael said to him in a cold deadly voice, "Don't you think I can do it, you son of a bitch?"

Sonny had got over his laughing fit. "I know you can do it," he said. "I wasn't laughing at what you said. I was just laughing at how funny things turn out. I always said you were the toughest one in the Family, tougher than the Don himself. You were the only one who could stand off the old man. I remember you when you were a kid. What a temper you had then. Hell, you even used to fight me and I was a lot older than you. And Freddie had to beat the shit out of you at least once a week. And now Sollozzo has you figured for the soft touch in the Family because you let McCluskey hit you without fighting back and you wouldn't get mixed up in the Family fights. He figures he got nothing to worry about if he meets you head to head. And McCluskey too, he's got you figured for a yellow guinea." Sonny paused and then said softly, "But you're a Corleone after all, you son of a bitch. And I was the only one who knew it. I've been sitting here waiting for the last three days, ever since the old man got shot, waiting for you to crack out of that Ivy League, war hero bullshit character you've been wearing. I've been waiting for you to become my right arm so we can kill those fucks that are trying to destroy our father and our Family. And all it took was a sock on the jaw. How do you like that?" Sonny made a comical gesture, a punch, and repeated, "How do you like that?"

The tension had relaxed in the room. Mike shook his head. "Sonny, I'm doing it because it's the only thing to do. I can't give Sollozzo another crack at the old man. I seem to be the only one who can get close enough to him. And I figured it out. I don't think you can get anybody else to knock off a police captain. Maybe you would do it, Sonny, but you have a wife and kids and you have to run the Family business until the old man is in shape. So that leaves me and Freddie. Freddie is in shock and out of action. Finally that leaves just me. It's all logic. The sock on the jaw had nothing to do with it."

Sonny came over and embraced him. "I don't give a damn what your reasons are, just so long as you're with us now. And I'll tell you another thing, you're right all the way. Tom, what's your say?"

Hagen shrugged. "The reasoning is solid. What makes it so is that I don't think the Turk is sincere about a deal. I think he'll still try to get at the Don. Anyway on his past performance that's how we have to figure him. So we try to get Sollozzo. We get him even if we have to get the police captain. But whoever does the job is going to get an awful lot of heat. Does it have to be Mike?"

Sonny said softly, "I could do it."

Hagen shook his head impatiently. "Sollozzo wouldn't let you get within a mile of him if he had ten police captains. And besides you're the acting head of the Family. You can't be risked." Hagen paused and said to Clemenza and Tessio, "Do either one of you have a top button man, someone really special, who would take on this job? He wouldn't have to worry about money for the rest of his life."

Clemenza spoke first. "Nobody that Sollozzo wouldn't know, he'd catch on right away. He'd catch on if me or Tessio went too."

Hagen said, "What about somebody really tough who hasn't made his rep yet, a good rookie?"

Both *caporegimes* shook their heads. Tessio smiled to take the sting out of his words and said, "That's like bringing a guy up from the minors to pitch the World Series."

Sonny broke in curtly, "It has to be Mike. For a million different reasons. Most important they got him down as faggy. And he can do the job, I guarantee that, and that's important because this is the only shot we'll get at that sneaky bastard Turk. So now we have to figure out the best way to back him up. Tom, Clemenza, Tessio, find out where Sollozzo will take him for the conference, I don't care how much it costs. When we find that out we can figure out how we can get a weapon into his hands. Clemenza, I want you to get him a really 'safe' gun out of your collection, the 'coldest' one you got. Impossible to trace. Try to make it short barrel with a lot of blasting power. It doesn't have to be accurate. He'll be right on top of them when he uses it. Mike, as soon as you've used the gun, drop it on the floor. Don't be caught with it on you. Clemenza, tape the barrel and the trigger with that special stuff you got so he won't leave prints. Remember, Mike, we can square everything, witnesses, and so forth, but if they catch you with the gun on you we can't square that. We'll have transportation and protection and then we'll make you disappear for a nice long vacation until the heat wears off. You'll be gone a long time, Mike, but I don't want you saying good-bye to your girl friend or even calling her. After it's all over and you're out of the country I'll send her word that you're OK. Those are orders." Sonny smiled at his brother. "Now stick with Clemenza and get used to handling the gun he picks out for you. Maybe even practice a little. We'll take care of everything else. Everything. OK, kid?"

Again Michael Corleone felt that delicious refreshing chilliness all over his body. He said to his brother, "You didn't have to give me that crap about not talking to my girl friend about something like this. What the hell did you think I was going to do, call her up to say good-bye?"

Sonny said hastily, "OK, but you're still a rookie so I spell things out. Forget it."

Michael said with a grin, "What the hell do you mean, a rookie? I listened to the old man just as hard as you did. How do you think I got so smart?" They both laughed.

Hagen poured drinks for everyone. He looked a little glum. The statesman forced to go to war, the lawyer forced to go to law. "Well, anyway now we know what we're going to do," he said.

Chapter

⬦⬦⬦⬦⬦⬦⬦⬦⬦⬦⬦⬦⬦⬦⬦⬦⬦⬦⬦⬦⬦⬦⬦⬦

11

CAPTAIN Mark McCluskey sat in his office fingering three envelopes bulging with betting slips. He was frowning and wishing he could decode the notations on the slips. It was very important that he do so. The envelopes were the betting slips that his raiding parties had picked up when they had hit one of the Corleone Family bookmakers the night before. Now the bookmaker would have to buy back the slips so that players couldn't claim winners and wipe him out.

It was very important for Captain McCluskey to decode the slips because he didn't want to get cheated when he sold the slips back to the bookmaker. If there was fifty grand worth of action, then maybe he could sell it back for five grand. But if there were a lot of heavy bets and the slips represented a hundred grand or maybe even two hundred grand, then the price should be considerably higher. McCluskey fiddled with the envelope and then decided to let the bookie sweat a little bit and make the first offer. That might tip off what the real price should be.

McCluskey looked at the station house clock on the wall of his office. It was time for him to pick up that greasy Turk, Sollozzo, and take him to wherever he was going to meet the Corleone Family. McCluskey went over to his wall locker and started to change into his civilian clothes. When he was finished he called his wife and told her he would not be home for supper that night, that he would be out on the job. He never confided in his wife on anything. She thought they lived the way they did on his policeman's salary. McCluskey grunted with amusement. His mother had thought the same thing but he had learned early. His father had shown him the ropes.

His father had been a police sergeant, and every week father and son had walked through the precinct and McCluskey Senior had introduced his six-year-old son to the storekeepers, saying, "And this is my little boy."

The storekeepers would shake his hand and compliment him extravagantly and ring open their cash registers to give the little boy a gift of five or ten dollars. At the end of the day, little Mark McCluskey would have all the pockets of his suit stuffed with paper money, would feel so proud that his father's friends liked him well enough to give him a present every month they saw him. Of course his father put the money in the bank for him, for his college education, and little Mark got at most a fifty-cent piece for himself.

Then when Mark got home and his policemen uncles asked him what he wanted to be when he grew up and he would lisp childishly, "A policeman," they would all laugh uproariously. And of course later on, though his father wanted him to go to college first, he went right from high school to studying for the police force.

He had been a good cop, a brave cop. The tough young punks terrorizing street corners fled when he approached and finally vanished from his beat altogether. He was a very tough cop and a very fair one. He never took his son around to the storekeepers to collect his money presents for ignoring garbage violations and parking violations; he took the money directly into his own hand, direct because he felt he earned it. He never ducked into a movie house or goofed off into restaurants when he was on foot patrol as some of the other cops did, especially on winter nights. He always made his rounds. He gave his stores a lot of protection, a lot of service. When winos and drunks filtered up from the Bowery to panhandle on his beat he got rid of them so roughly that they never came back. The tradespeople in his precinct appreciated it. And they showed their appreciation.

He also obeyed the system. The bookies in his precinct knew he would never make trouble to get an extra payoff for himself, that he was content for his share of the station house bag. His name was on the list with the others and he never tried to make extras. He was a fair cop who took only clean graft and his rise in the police department was steady if not spectacular.

During this time he was raising a large family of four sons, none of whom became policemen. They all went to Fordham University and since by that time Mark McCluskey was rising from sergeant to lieutenant and finally to captain, they lacked for nothing. It was at this time that McCluskey got the reputation for being a hard bargainer. The bookmakers in his district paid more protection money than the bookmakers in any other part of the city, but maybe that was because of the expense of putting four boys through college.

McCluskey himself felt there was nothing wrong with clean graft. Why the hell should his kids go to CCNY or a cheap Southern college just because the Police Department didn't pay its people enough money to live on and take care of their families properly with? He protected all these people with his life and his record showed his citations for gun duels with stickup men on his beat, strong-arm protection guys, would-be pimps. He had hammered them into the ground. He had kept his little corner of the city safe for ordinary people and he sure as hell was entitled to more than his lousy one C note a week. But he wasn't indignant about his low pay, he understood that everybody had to take care of themselves.

Bruno Tattaglia was an old friend of his. Bruno had gone to Fordham with one of his sons and then Bruno had opened his nightclub and whenever the McCluskey family spent an infrequent night on the town, they could enjoy the cabaret with liquor and dinner—on the house. On New Year's Eve they received engraved invitations to be guests of the management and always received one of the best tables. Bruno always made sure they were introduced to the celebrities who performed in his club, some of them famous singers and Hollywood stars. Of course sometimes he asked a little favor, like getting an employee with a record cleared for a cabaret work license, usually a pretty girl with a police dossier as a hustler or roller. McCluskey would be glad to oblige.

McCluskey made it a policy never to show that he understood what other people were up to. When Sollozzo had approached him with the proposition to leave old man Corleone uncovered in the hospital, McCluskey didn't ask why. He asked price. When Sollozzo said ten grand, McCluskey knew why. He did not hesitate. Corleone was one of the biggest Mafia men in the country with more political connections than Capone had ever had. Whoever knocked him off would be doing the country a big favor. McCluskey took the money in advance and did the job. When he received a call from Sollozzo that there were still two of Corleone's men in front of the hospital he had flown into a rage. He had locked up all of Tessio's men, he had pulled the detective guards off the door of Corleone's hospital room. And now, being a man of principle, he would have to give back the ten grand, money he had already earmarked to insure the education of his grandchildren. It was in that rage that he had gone to the hospital and struck Michael Corleone.

But it had all worked out for the best. He had met with Sollozzo in the Tattaglia nightclub and they had made an even better deal. Again McCluskey didn't ask questions, since he knew all the answers. He just made sure of his price. It never occurred to him that he himself could be in any danger. That anyone would consider even for a moment killing a New York City police captain was too fantastic. The toughest hood in the Mafia had to stand still if the lowliest patrolman decided to slap him around. There was absolutely no percentage in killing cops. Because then all of a sudden a lot of hoods were killed resisting arrest or escaping the scene of a crime, and who the hell was going to do anything about that?

McCluskey sighed and got ready to leave the station house. Problems, always problems. His wife's sister in Ireland had just died after many years of fighting cancer and that cancer had cost him a pretty penny. Now the funeral would cost him more. His own uncles and aunts in the old country needed a little help now and then to keep their potato farms and he sent the money to do the trick. He didn't begrudge it. And when he and his wife visited the old country they were treated like a king and queen. Maybe they would go again this summer now that the war was over and with all this extra money coming in. McCluskey told his patrolman clerk where he would be if he was needed. He did not feel it necessary to take any precautions. He could always claim Sollozzo was an informer he was meeting. Outside the station house he walked a few blocks and then caught a cab to the house where he would meet with Sollozzo.

It was Tom Hagen who had to make all the arrangements for Michael's leaving the country, his false passport, his seaman's card, his berth on an Italian freighter that would dock in a Sicilian port. Emissaries were sent that very day by plane to Sicily to prepare a hiding place with the Mafia chief in the hill country.

Sonny arranged for a car and an absolutely trustworthy driver to be waiting for Michael when he stepped out of the restaurant where the meeting would be held with Sollozzo. The driver would be Tessio himself, who had volunteered for the job. It would be a beat-up-looking car but with a fine motor. It would have phony license plates and the car itself would be untraceable. It had been saved for a special job requiring the best.

Michael spent the day with Clemenza, practicing with the small gun that would be gotten to him. It was a .22 filled with soft-nosed bullets that made pinpricks going in and left insulting gaping holes when they exited from the human body. He found that it was accurate up to five of his steps away from a target. After that the bullets might go anywhere. The trigger was tight but Clemenza worked on this with some tools so that it pulled easier. They decided to leave it noisy. They didn't want an innocent bystander misunderstanding the situation and interfering out of ignorant courage. The report of the gun would keep them away from Michael.

Clemenza kept instructing him during the training session. "Drop the gun as soon as you've finished using it. Just let your hand drop to your side and the gun slip out. Nobody will notice. Everybody will think you're still armed. They'll be staring at your face. Walk out of the place very quickly but don't run. Don't look anybody directly in the eye but don't look away from them either. Remember, they'll be scared of you, believe me, they'll be scared of you. Nobody will interfere. As soon as you're outside Tessio will be in the car waiting for you. Get in and leave the rest to him. Don't be worried about accidents. You'd be surprised how well these affairs go. Now put this hat on and let's see how you look." He clapped a gray fedora on Michael's head. Michael, who never wore a hat, grimaced. Clemenza reassured him. "It helps against identification, just in case. Mostly it gives witnesses an excuse to change their identification when we make them see the light. Remember, Mike, don't worry about prints. The butt and trigger are fixed with special tape. Don't touch any other part of the gun, remember that."

Michael said, "Has Sonny found out where Sollozzo is taking me?"

Clemenza shrugged. "Not yet. Sollozzo is being very careful. But don't worry about him harming you. The negotiator stays in our hands until you come back safe. If anything happens to you, the negotiator pays."

"Why the hell should he stick his neck out?" Michael asked.

"He gets a big fee," Clemenza said. "A small fortune. Also he is an important man in the Families. He knows Sollozzo can't let anything happen to him. Your life is not worth the negotiator's life to Sollozzo. Very simple. You'll be safe all right. We're the ones who catch hell afterwards."

"How bad will it be?" Michael asked.

"Very bad," Clemenza said. "It means an all-out war with the Tattaglia Family against the Corleone Family. Most of the others will line up with the Tattaglias. The Sanitation Department will be sweeping up a lot of dead bodies this winter." He shrugged. "These things have to happen once every ten years or so. It gets rid of the bad blood. And then if we let them push us around on the little things they wanta take over everything. You gotta stop them at the beginning. Like they shoulda stopped Hitler at Munich, they should never let him get away with that, they were just asking for big trouble when they let him get away with that."

Michael had heard his father say this same thing before, only in 1939 before the war actually started. If the Families had been running the State Department there would never have been World War II, he thought with a grin.

They drove back to the mall and to the Don's house, where Sonny still made his headquarters. Michael wondered how long Sonny could stay cooped up in the safe territory of the mall. Eventually he would have to venture out. They found Sonny taking a nap on the couch. On the coffee table was the remains of his late lunch, scraps of steak and bread crumbs and a half-empty bottle of whiskey.

His father's usually neat office was taking on the look of a badly kept furnished room. Michael shook his brother awake and said, "Why don't you stop living like a bum and get this place cleaned up."

Sonny yawned. "What the hell are you, inspecting the barracks? Mike, we haven't got the word yet where they plan to take you, those bastards Sollozzo and McCluskey. If we don't find that out, how the hell are we going to get the gun to you?"

"Can't I carry it on me?" Michael asked. "Maybe they won't frisk me and even if they do maybe they'll miss it if we're smart enough. And even if they find it—so what. They'll just take it off me and no harm done."

Sonny shook his head. "Nah," he said. "We have to make this a sure hit on that bastard Sollozzo. Remember, get him first if you possibly can. McCluskey is slower and dumber. You should have plenty of time to take him. Did Clemenza tell you to be sure to drop the gun?"

"A million times," Michael said.

Sonny got up from the sofa and stretched. "How does your jaw feel, kid?"

"Lousy," Michael said. The left side of his face ached except those parts that felt numb because of the drugged wire holding it together. He took the bottle of whiskey from the table and swigged directly from it. The pain eased.

Sonny said, "Easy, Mike, now is no time to get slowed up by booze."

Michael said, "Oh, Christ, Sonny, stop playing the big brother. I've been in combat against tougher guys than Sollozzo and under worse conditions. Where the hell are his mortars? Has he got air cover? Heavy artillery? Land mines? He's just a wise son of a bitch with a big-wheel cop sidekick. Once anybody makes up their mind to kill them there's no other problem. That's the hard part, making up your mind. They'll never know what hit them."

Tom Hagen came into the room. He greeted them with a nod and went directly to the falsely listed telephone. He called a few times and then shook his head at Sonny. "Not a whisper," he said. "Sollozzo is keeping it to himself as long as he can."

The phone rang. Sonny answered it and he held up a hand as if to signal for quiet though no one had spoken. He jotted some notes down on a pad, then said, "OK, he'll be there," and hung up the phone.

Sonny was laughing. "That son of a bitch Sollozzo, he really is something. Here's the deal. At eight tonight he and Captain McCluskey pick up Mike in front of Jack Dempsey's bar on Broadway. They go someplace to talk, and get this. Mike and Sollozzo talk in Italian so that the Irish cop don't know what the hell they are talking about. He even tells me, don't worry, he knows McCluskey doesn't know one word in Italian unless it's 'soldi' and he's checked you out, Mike, and knows you can understand Sicilian dialect."

Michael said dryly, "I'm pretty rusty but we won't talk long."

Tom Hagen said, "We don't let Mike go until we have the negotiator. Is that arranged?"

Clemenza nodded. "The negotiator is at my house playing pinochle with three of my men. They wait for a call from me before they let him go."

Sonny sank back in the leather armchair. "Now how the hell do we find out the meeting place? Tom, we've got informers with the Tattaglia Family, how come they haven't given us the word?"

Hagen shrugged. "Sollozzo is really damn smart. He's playing this close to the vest, so close that he's not using any men as a cover. He figures the captain will be enough and that security is more important than guns. He's right too. We'll have to put a tail on Mike and hope for the best."

Sonny shook his head. "Nah, anybody can lose a tail when they really want to. That's the first thing they'll check out."

By this time it was five in the afternoon. Sonny, with a worried look on his face, said, "Maybe we should just let Mike blast whoever is in the car when it tries to pick him up."

Hagen shook his head. "What if Sollozzo is not in the car? We've tipped our hand for nothing. Damn it, we have to find out where Sollozzo is taking him."

Clemenza put in, "Maybe we should start trying to figure why he's making it such a big secret."

Michael said impatiently, "Because it's the percentage. Why should he let us know anything if he can prevent it? Besides, he smells danger. He must be leery as hell even with that police captain for his shadow."

Hagen snapped his fingers. "That detective, that guy Phillips. Why don't you give him a ring, Sonny? Maybe he can find out where the hell the captain can be reached. It's worth a try. McCluskey won't give a damn who knows where he's going."

Sonny picked up the phone and dialed a number. He spoke softly into the phone, then hung up. "He'll call us back," Sonny said.

They waited for nearly another thirty minutes and then the phone rang. It was Phillips. Sonny jotted something down on his pad and then hung up. His face was taut. "I think we've got it," he said. "Captain McCluskey always has to leave word on where he can be reached. From eight to ten tonight he'll be at the Luna Azure up in the Bronx. Anybody know it?"

Tessio spoke confidently. "I do. It's perfect for us. A small family place with big booths where people can talk in private. Good food. Everybody minds their own business. Perfect." He leaned over Sonny's desk and arranged stubbed-out cigarettes into map figures. "This is the entrance. Mike, when you finish just walk out and turn left, then turn the corner. I'll spot you and put on my headlights and catch you on the fly. If you have any trouble, yell and I'll try to come in and get you out. Clemenza, you gotta work fast. Send somebody up there to plant the gun. They got an old-fashioned toilet with a space between the water container and the wall. Have your man tape the gun behind there. Mike, after they frisk you in the car and find you're clean, they won't be too worried about you. In the restaurant, wait a bit before you excuse yourself. No, better still, ask permission to go. Act a little in trouble first, very natural. They can't figure anything. But when you come out again, don't waste any time. Don't sit down again at the table, start blasting. And don't take chances. In the head, two shots apiece, and out as fast as your legs can travel."

Sonny had been listening judiciously. "I want somebody very good, very safe, to plant that gun," he told Clemenza. "I don't want my brother coming out of that toilet with just his dick in his hand."

Clemenza said emphatically, "The gun will be there."

"OK," Sonny said. "Everybody get rolling."

Tessio and Clemenza left. Tom Hagen said, "Sonny, should I drive Mike down to New York?"

"No," Sonny said. "I want you here. When Mike finishes, then our work begins and I'll need you. Have you got those newspaper guys lined up?"

Hagen nodded. "I'll be feeding them info as soon as things break."

Sonny got up and came to stand in front of Michael. He shook his hand. "OK, kid," he said, "you're on. I'll square it with Mom your not seeing her before you left. And I'll get a message to your girl friend when I think the time is right. OK?"

"OK," Mike said. "How long do you think before I can come back?"

"At least a year," Sonny said.

Tom Hagen put in, "The Don might be able to work faster than that, Mike, but don't count on it. The time element hinges on a lot of factors. How well we can plant stories with the newsmen. How much the Police Department wants to cover up. How violently the other Families react. There's going to be a hell of a lot of heat and trouble. That's the only thing we can be sure of."

Michael shook Hagen's hand. "Do your best," he said. "I don't want to do another three-year stretch away from home."

Hagen said gently, "It's not too late to back out, Mike, we can get somebody else, we can go back over our alternatives. Maybe it's not necessary to get rid of Sollozzo."

Michael laughed. "We can talk ourselves into any viewpoint," he said. "But we figured it right the first time. I've been riding the gravy train all my life, it's about time I paid my dues."

"You shouldn't let that broken jaw influence you," Hagen said. "McCluskey is a stupid man and it was business, not personal."

For the second time he saw Michael Corleone's face freeze into a mask that resembled uncannily the Don's. "Tom, don't let anybody kid you. It's all personal, every bit of business. Every piece of shit every man has to eat every day of his life is personal. They call it business. OK. But it's personal as hell. You know where I learned that from? The Don. My old man. The Godfather. If a bolt of lightning hit a friend of his the old man would take it personal. He took my going into the Marines personal. That's what makes him great. The Great Don. He takes everything personal. Like God. He knows every feather that falls from the tail of a sparrow or however the hell it goes. Right? And you know something? Accidents don't happen to people who take accidents as a personal insult. So I came late, OK, but I'm coming all the way. Damn right, I take that broken jaw personal; damn right, I take Sollozzo trying to kill my father personal." He laughed. "Tell the old man I learned it all from him and that I'm glad I had this chance to pay him back for all he did for me. He was a good father." He paused and then he said thoughtfully to Hagen, "You know, I can never remember him hitting me. Or Sonny. Or Freddie. And of course Connie, he wouldn't even yell at her. And tell me the truth, Tom, how many men do you figure the Don killed or had killed."

Tom Hagen turned away. "I'll tell you one thing you didn't learn from him: talking the way you're talking now. There are things that have to be done and you do them and you never talk about them. You don't try to justify them. They can't be justified. You just do them. Then you forget it."

Michael Corleone frowned. He said quietly, "As the *Consigliori*, you agree that it's dangerous to the Don and our Family to let Sollozzo live?"

"Yes," Hagen said.

"OK," Michael said. "Then I have to kill him."

Michael Corleone stood in front of Jack Dempsey's restaurant on Broadway and waited for his pickup. He looked at his watch. It said five minutes to eight. Sollozzo was going to be punctual. Michael had made sure he was there in plenty of time. He had been waiting fifteen minutes.

All during the ride from Long Beach into the city he had been trying to forget what he had said to Hagen. For if he believed what he said, then his life was set on an irrevocable course. And yet, could it be otherwise after tonight? He might be dead after tonight if he didn't stop all this crap, Michael thought grimly. He had to keep his mind on the business at hand. Sollozzo was no dummy and Mc-Cluskey was a very tough egg. He felt the ache in his wired jaw and welcomed the pain, it would keep him alert.

Broadway wasn't that crowded on this cold winter night, even though it was near theater time. Michael flinched as a long black car pulled up to the curb and the driver, leaning over, opened the front door and said, "Get in, Mike." He didn't know the driver, a young punk with slick black hair and an open shirt, but he got in. In the back seat were Captain McCluskey and Sollozzo.

Sollozzo reached a hand over the back of the seat and Michael shook it. The hand was firm, warm and dry. Sollozzo said, "I'm glad you came, Mike. I hope we can straighten everything out. All this is terrible, it's not the way I wanted things to happen at all. It should never have happened."

Michael Corleone said quietly, "I hope we can settle things tonight, I don't want my father bothered any more."

"He won't be," Sollozzo said sincerely. "I swear to you by my children he won't be. Just keep an open mind when we talk. I hope you're not a hothead like your brother Sonny. It's impossible to talk business with him."

Captain McCluskey grunted. "He's a good kid, he's all right." He leaned over to give Michael an affectionate pat on the shoulder. "I'm sorry about the other night, Mike. I'm getting too old for my job, too grouchy. I guess I'll have to retire pretty soon. Can't stand the aggravation, all day I get aggravation. You know how it is." Then with a doleful sigh, he gave Michael a thorough frisk for a weapon.

Michael saw a slight smile on the driver's lips. The car was going west with no apparent attempt to elude any trailers. It went up on to the West Side Highway, speeding in and out of traffic. Anyone following would have had to do the same. Then to Michael's dismay it took the exit for the George Washington Bridge, they were going over to New Jersey. Whoever had given Sonny the info on where the meeting was to be held had given him the wrong dope.

The car threaded through the bridge approaches and then was on it, leaving the blazing city behind. Michael kept his face impassive. Were they going to dump him into the swamps or was it just a last-minute change in meeting place by the wily Sollozzo? But when they were nearly all the way across, the driver gave the wheel a violent twist. The heavy automobile jumped into the air when it hit the divider and bounced over into the lanes going back to New York City. Both McCluskey and Sollozzo were looking back to see if anyone had tried doing the same thing. The driver was really hitting it back to New York and then they were off the bridge and going toward the East Bronx. They went through side streets with no cars behind them. By this time it was nearly nine o'clock. They had made sure there was no one on their tail. Sollozzo lit up a cigarette after offering his pack to McCluskey and Michael, both of whom refused. Sollozzo said to the driver, "Nice work. I'll remember it."

Ten minutes later the car pulled up in front of a restaurant in a small Italian neighborhood. There was no one on the streets and because of the lateness of the hour only a few people were still at dinner. Michael had been worried that the driver would come in with them, but he stayed outside with his car. The negotiator had not mentioned a driver, nobody had. Technically Sollozzo had broken the agreement by bringing him along. But Michael decided not to mention it, knowing they would think he would be afraid to mention it, afraid of ruining the chances for the success of the parley.

The three of them sat at the only round table, Sollozzo refusing a booth. There were only two other people in the restaurant. Michael wondered whether they were Sollozzo plants. But it didn't matter. Before they could interfere it would be all over.

McCluskey asked with real interest, "Is the Italian food good here?"

Sollozzo reassured him. "Try the veal, it's the finest in New York." The solitary waiter had brought a bottle of wine to the table and uncorked it. He poured three glasses full. Surprisingly McCluskey did not drink. "I must be the only Irishman who don't take the booze," he said. "I seen too many good people get in trouble because of the booze."

Sollozzo said placatingly to the captain, "I am going to talk Italian to Mike, not because I don't trust you but because I can't explain myself properly in English and I want to convince Mike that I mean well, that it's to everybody's advantage for us to come to an agreement tonight. Don't be insulted by this, it's not that I don't trust you."

Captain McCluskey gave them both an ironic grin. "Sure, you two go right ahead," he said. "I'll concentrate on my veal and spaghetti."

Sollozzo began speaking to Michael in rapid Sicilian. He said, "You must understand that what happened between me and your father was strictly a business matter. I have a great respect for Don Corleone and would beg for the opportunity to enter his service. But you must understand that your father is an old-fashioned man. He stands in the way of progress. The business I am in is the coming thing, the wave of the future, there are untold millions of dollars for everyone to make. But your father stands in the way because of certain unrealistic scruples. By doing this he imposes his will on men like myself. Yes, yes, I know, he says to me, 'Go ahead, it's your business,' but we both know that is unrealistic. We must tread on each other's corns. What he is really telling me is that I cannot operate my business. I am a man who respects himself and cannot let another man impose his will on me so what had to happen did happen. Let me say that I had the support, the silent support of all the New York Families. And the Tattaglia Family became my partners. If this quarrel continues, then the Corleone Family will stand alone against everyone. Perhaps if your father were well, it could be done. But the eldest son is not the man the Godfather is, no disrespect intended. And the Irish *Consigliori*, Hagen, is not the man Genco Abbandando was, God rest his soul. So I propose a peace, a truce. Let us cease all hostilities until your father is well again and can take part in these bargainings. The Tattaglia Family agrees, upon my persuasions and my indemnities, to forgo justice for their son Bruno. We will have peace. Meanwhile, I have to make a living and will do a little trading in my business. I do not ask your cooperation but I ask you, the Corleone Family, not to interfere. These are my proposals. I assume you have the authority to agree, to make a deal."

Michael said in Sicilian, "Tell me more about how you propose to start your business, exactly what part my Family has to play in it and what profit we can take from this business."

"You want the whole proposition in detail then?" Sollozzo asked.

Michael said gravely, "Most important of all I must have sure guarantees that no more attempts will be made on my father's life."

Sollozzo raised his hand expressively. "What guarantees can I give you? I'm the hunted one. I've missed my chance. You think too highly of me, my friend. I am not that clever."

Michael was sure now that the conference was only to gain a few days' time. That Sollozzo would make another attempt to kill the Don. What was beautiful was that the Turk was underrating him as a punk kid. Michael felt that strange delicious chill filling his body. He made his face look distressed. Sollozzo asked sharply, "What is it?"

Michael said with an embarrassed air, "The wine went right to my bladder. I've been holding it in. Is it all right if I go to the bathroom."

Sollozzo was searching his face intently with his dark eyes. He reached over and roughly thrust his hand in Michael's crotch, under it and around, searching for a weapon. Michael looked offended. McCluskey said curtly, "I frisked him. I've frisked thousands of young punks. He's clean."

Sollozzo didn't like it. For no reason at all he didn't like it. He glanced at the man sitting at a table opposite them and raised his eyebrows toward the door of the bathroom. The man gave a slight nod that he had checked it, that there was nobody inside. Sollozzo said reluctantly, "Don't take too long." He had marvelous antenna, he was nervous.

Michael got up and went into the bathroom. The urinal had a pink bar of soap in it secured by a wire net. He went into the booth. He really had to go, his bowels were loose. He did it very quickly, then reached behind the enamel water cabinet until his hand touched the small, blunt-nosed gun fastened with tape. He ripped the gun loose, remembering that Clemenza had said not to worry about leaving prints on the tape. He shoved the gun into his waistband and buttoned his jacket over it. He washed his hands and wet his hair. He wiped his prints off the faucet with his handkerchief. Then he left the toilet.

Sollozzo was sitting directly facing the door of the toilet, his dark eyes blazing with alertness. Michael gave a smile. "Now I can talk," he said with a sigh of relief.

Captain McCluskey was eating the plate of veal and spaghetti that had arrived. The man on the far wall had been stiff with attention, now he too relaxed visibly.

Michael sat down again. He remembered Clemenza had told him

not to do this, to come out of the toilet and blaze away. But either out of some warning instinct or sheer funk he had not done so. He had felt that if he had made one swift move he would have been cut down. Now he felt safe and he must have been scared because he was glad he was no longer standing on his legs. They had gone weak with trembling.

Sollozzo was leaning toward him. Michael, his belly covered by the table, unbuttoned his jacket and listened intently. He could not understand a word the man was saying. It was literally gibberish to him. His mind was so filled with pounding blood that no word registered. Underneath the table his right hand moved to the gun tucked into his waistband and he drew it free. At that moment the waiter came to take their order and Sollozzo turned his head to speak to the waiter. Michael thrust the table away from him with his left hand and his right hand shoved the gun almost against Sollozzo's head. The man's coordination was so acute that he had already begun to fling himself away at Michael's motion. But Michael, younger, his reflexes sharper, pulled the trigger. The bullet caught Sollozzo squarely between his eye and his ear and when it exited on the other side blasted out a huge gout of blood and skull fragments onto the petrified waiter's jacket. Instinctively Michael knew that one bullet was enough. Sollozzo had turned his head in that last moment and he had seen the light of life die in the man's eyes as clearly as a candle goes out.

Only one second had gone by as Michael pivoted to bring the gun to bear on McCluskey. The police captain was staring at Sollozzo with phlegmatic surprise, as if this had nothing to do with him. He did not seem to be aware of his own danger. His veal-covered fork was suspended in his hand and his eyes were just turning on Michael. And the expression on his face, in his eyes, held such confident outrage, as if now he expected Michael to surrender or to run away, that Michael smiled at him as he pulled the trigger. This shot was bad, not mortal. It caught McCluskey in his thick bull-like throat and he started to choke loudly as if he had swallowed too large a bite of the veal. Then the air seemed to fill with a fine mist of sprayed blood as he coughed it out of his shattered lungs. Very coolly, very deliberately, Michael fired the next shot through the top of his white-haired skull.

The air seemed to be full of pink mist. Michael swung toward the man sitting against the wall. This man had not made a move. He seemed paralyzed. Now he carefully showed his hands on top of the table and looked away. The waiter was staggering back toward the kitchen, an expression of horror on his face, staring at Michael in disbelief. Sollozzo was still in his chair, the side of his body propped up by the table. McCluskey, his heavy body pulling downward, had fallen off his chair onto the floor. Michael let the gun slip out of his hand so that it bounced off his body and made no noise. He saw that neither the man against the wall nor the waiter had noticed him dropping the gun. He strode the few steps toward the door and opened it. Sollozzo's car was parked at the curb still, but there was no sign of the driver. Michael turned left and around the corner. Head-lights flashed on and a battered sedan pulled up to him, the door swinging open. He jumped in and the car roared away. He saw that it was Tessio at the wheel, his trim features hard as marble.

"Did you do the job on Sollozzo?" Tessio asked.

For that moment Michael was struck by the idiom Tessio had used. It was always used in a sexual sense, to do the job on a woman meant seducing her. It was curious that Tessio used it now. "Both of them," Michael said.

"Sure?" Tessio asked.

"I saw their brains," Michael said.

There was a change of clothes for Michael in the car. Twenty minutes later he was on an Italian freighter slated for Sicily. Two hours later the freighter put out to sea and from his cabin Michael could see the lights of New York City burning like the fires of hell. He felt an enormous sense of relief. He was out of it now. The feeling was familiar and he remembered being taken off the beach of an island his Marine division had invaded. The battle had been still going on but he had received a slight wound and was being ferried back to a hospital ship. He had felt the same overpowering relief then that he felt now. All hell would break loose but he wouldn't be there.

On the day after the murder of Sollozzo and Captain McCluskey, the police captains and lieutenants in every station house in New York City sent out the word: there would be no more gambling, no more prostitution, no more deals of any kind until the murderer of Captain McCluskey was caught. Massive raids began all over the city. All unlawful business activities came to a standstill.

Later that day an emissary from the Families asked the Corleone

Family if they were prepared to give up the murderer. They were told that the affair did not concern them. That night a bomb exploded in the Corleone Family mall in Long Beach, thrown from a car that pulled up to the chain, then roared away. That night also two button men of the Corleone Family were killed as they peaceably ate their dinner in a small Italian restaurant in Greenwich Village. The Five Families War of 1946 had begun.

Book II

Chapter

><><><><><><><><><><><><><><><>

12

JOHNNY FONTANE waved a casual dismissal to the manservant and said, "See you in the morning, Billy." The colored butler bowed his way out of the huge dining room–living room with its view of the Pacific Ocean. It was a friendly–good-bye sort of bow, not a servant's bow, and given only because Johnny Fontane had company for dinner.

Johnny's company was a girl named Sharon Moore, a New York City Greenwich Village girl in Hollywood to try for a small part in a movie being produced by an old flame who had made the big time. She had visited the set while Johnny was acting in the Woltz movie. Johnny had found her young and fresh and charming and witty, and had asked her to come to his place for dinner that evening. His invitations to dinner were already famous and had the force of royalty and of course she said yes.

Sharon Moore obviously expected him to come on very strong because of his reputation, but Johnny hated the Hollywood "piece of meat" approach. He never slept with any girl unless there was something about her he really liked. Except, of course, sometimes when he was very drunk and found himself in bed with a girl he didn't even remember meeting or seeing before. And now that he was thirty-five years old, divorced once, estranged from his second wife, with maybe a thousand pubic scalps dangling from his belt, he simply wasn't that eager. But there was something about Sharon Moore that aroused affection in him and so he had invited her to dinner.

He never ate much but he knew young pretty girls ambitiously starved themselves for pretty clothes and were usually big eaters on a date so there was plenty of food on the table. There was also plenty of liquor; champagne in a bucket, scotch, rye, brandy and liqueurs on the sideboard. Johnny served the drinks and the plates of food already prepared. When they had finished eating he led her into the huge living room with its glass wall that looked out onto the Pacific. He put a stack of Ella Fitzgerald records on the hi-fi and settled on the couch with Sharon. He made a little small talk with her, found out about what she had been like as a kid, whether she had been a tomboy or boy crazy, whether she had been homely or pretty, lonely or gay. He always found these details touching, it always evoked the tenderness he needed to make love.

They nestled together on the sofa, very friendly, very comfortable. He kissed her on the lips, a cool friendly kiss, and when she kept it that way he left it that way. Outside the huge picture window he could see the dark blue sheet of the Pacific lying flat beneath the moonlight.

"How come you're not playing any of your records?" Sharon asked him. Her voice was teasing. Johnny smiled at her. He was amused by her teasing him. "I'm not that Hollywood," he said.

"Play some for me," she said. "Or sing for me. You know, like the movies. I'll bubble up and melt all over you just like those girls do on the screen."

Johnny laughed outright. When he had been younger, he had done just such things and the result had always been stagy, the girls trying to look sexy and melting, making their eyes swim with desire for an imagined fantasy camera. He would never dream of singing to a girl now; for one thing, he hadn't sung for months, he didn't trust his voice. For another thing, amateurs didn't realize how much professionals depended on technical help to sound as good as they did. He could have played his records but he felt the same shyness about hearing his youthful passionate voice as an aging, balding man running to fat feels about showing pictures of himself as a youth in the full bloom of manhood.

"My voice is out of shape," he said. "And honestly, I'm sick of hearing myself sing."

They both sipped their drinks. "I hear you're great in this picture," she said. "Is it true you did it for nothing?"

"Just a token payment," Johnny said.

He got up to give her a refill on her brandy glass, gave her a gold-monogrammed cigarette and flashed his lighter out to hold the light for her. She puffed on the cigarette and sipped her drink and he sat down beside her again. His glass had considerably more brandy in it than hers, he needed it to warm himself, to cheer himself, to charge himself up. His situation was the reverse of the lover's usual one. He had to get himself drunk instead of the girl. The girl was usually too willing where he was not. The last two years had been hell on his ego, and he used this simple way to restore it, sleeping with a young fresh girl for one night, taking her to dinner a few times, giving her an expensive present and then brushing her off in the nicest way possible so that her feelings wouldn't be hurt. And then they could always say they had had a thing with the great Johnny Fontane. It wasn't true love, but you couldn't knock it if the girl was beautiful and genuinely nice. He hated the hard, bitchy ones, the ones who screwed for him and then rushed off to tell their friends that they'd screwed the great Johnny Fontane, always adding that they'd had better. What amazed him more than anything else in his career were the complaisant husbands who almost told him to his face that they forgave their wives since it was allowed for even the most virtuous matron to be unfaithful with a great singing and movie star like Johnny Fontane. That really floored him.

He loved Ella Fitzgerald on records. He loved that kind of clean singing, that kind of clean phrasing. It was the only thing in life he really understood and he knew he understood it better than anyone else on earth. Now lying back on the couch, the brandy warming his throat, he felt a desire to sing, not music, but to phrase with the records, yet it was something impossible to do in front of a stranger. He put his free hand in Sharon's lap, sipping his drink from his other hand. Without any slyness but with the sensualness of a child seeking warmth, his hand in her lap pulled up the silk of her dress to show milky white thigh above the sheer netted gold of her stockings and as always, despite all the women, all the years, all the familiarity, Johnny felt the fluid sticky warmness flooding through his body at that sight.

The miracle still happened, and what would he do when that failed him as his voice had?

He was ready now. He put his drink down on the long inlaid cocktail table and turned his body toward her. He was very sure, very deliberate, and yet tender. There was nothing sly or lecherously lascivious in his caresses. He kissed her on the lips while his hands rose to her breasts. His hand fell to her warm thighs, the skin so silky to his touch. Her returning kiss was warm but not passionate and he preferred it that way right now. He hated girls who turned on all of a sudden as if their bodies were motors galvanized into erotic pumpings by the touching of a hairy switch.

Then he did something he always did, something that had never yet failed to arouse him. Delicately and as lightly as it was possible to do so and still feel something, he brushed the tip of his middle finger deep down between her thighs. Some girls never even felt that initial move toward lovemaking. Some were distracted by it, not sure it was a physical touch because at the same time he always kissed them deeply on the mouth. Still others seemed to suck in his finger or gobble it up with a pelvic thrust. And of course before he became famous, some girls had slapped his face. It was his whole technique and usually it served him well enough.

Sharon's reaction was unusual. She accepted it all, the touch, the kiss, then shifted her mouth off his, shifted her body ever so slightly back along the couch and picked up her drink. It was a cool but definite refusal. It happened sometimes. Rarely; but it happened. Johnny picked up his drink and lit a cigarette.

She was saying something very sweetly, very lightly. "It's not that I don't like you, Johnny, you're much nicer than I thought you'd be. And it's not because I'm not that kind of a girl. It's just that I have to be turned on to do it with a guy, you know what I mean?"

Johnny Fontane smiled at her. He still liked her. "And I don't turn you on?"

She was a little embarrassed. "Well, you know, when you were so great singing and all, I was still a little kid. I sort of just missed you I was the next generation. Honest, it's not that I'm goody-goody. I you were James Dean or somebody I grew up on, I'd have my pantic off in a second."

He didn't like her quite so much now. She was sweet, she was witty, she was intelligent. She hadn't fallen all over herself to screw for him or try to hustle him because his connections would help her in show biz. She was really a straight kid. But there was something else he recognized. It had happened a few times before. The girl who went on a date with her mind all made up not to go to bed with him, no matter how much she liked him, just so that she could tell her friends, and even more, herself, that she had turned down a chance to screw for the great Johnny Fontane. It was something he understood now that he was older and he wasn't angry. He just didn't like her quite that much and he had really liked her a lot.

And now that he didn't like her quite so much, he relaxed more. He sipped his drink and watched the Pacific Ocean. She said, "I hope you're not sore, Johnny. I guess I'm being square, I guess in Hollywood a girl's supposed to put out just as casually as kissing a beau good night. I just haven't been around long enough."

Johnny smiled at her and patted her cheek. His hand fell down to pull her skirt discreetly over her rounded silken knees. "I'm not sore," he said. "It's nice having an old-fashioned date." Not telling what he felt: the relief at not having to prove himself a great lover, not having to live up to his screened, godlike image. Not having to listen to the girl trying to react as if he really had lived up to that image, making more out of a very simple, routine piece of ass than it really was.

They had another drink, shared a few more cool kisses and then she decided to go. Johnny said politely, "Can I call you for dinner some night?"

She played it frank and honest to the end. "I know you don't want to waste your time and then get disappointed," she said. "Thanks for a wonderful evening. Someday I'll tell my children I had supper with the great Johnny Fontane all alone in his apartment."

He smiled at her. "And that you didn't give in," he said. They both laughed. "They'll never believe that," she said. And then Johnny, being a little phony in his turn, said, "I'll give it to you in writing, want me to?" She shook her head. He continued on. "Anybody doubts you, give me a buzz on the phone, I'll straighten them right out. I'll tell them how I chased you all around the apartment but you kept your honor. OK?"

He had, finally, been a little too cruel and he felt stricken at the hurt on her young face. She understood that he was telling her that he hadn't tried too hard. He had taken the sweetness of her victory away from her. Now she would feel that it had been her lack of charm or attractiveness that had made her the victor this night. And being the girl she was, when she told the story of how she resisted the great Johnny Fontane, she would always have to add with a wry little smile, "Of course, he didn't try very hard." So now taking pity on her, he said, "If you ever feel real down, give me a ring. OK? I don't have to shack up every girl I know."

"I will," she said. She went out the door.

He was left with a long evening before him. He could have used what Jack Woltz called the "meat factory," the stable of willing starlets, but he wanted human companionship. He wanted to talk like a human being. He thought of his first wife, Virginia. Now that the work on the picture was finished he would have more time for the kids. He wanted to become part of their life again. And he worried about Virginia too. She wasn't equipped to handle the Hollywood sharpies who might come after her just so that they could brag about having screwed Johnny Fontane's first wife. As far as he knew, nobody could say that yet. Everybody could say it about his second wife though, he thought wryly. He picked up the phone.

He recognized her voice immediately and that was not surprising. He had heard it the first time when he was ten years old and they had been in 4B together. "Hi, Ginny," he said, "you busy tonight? Can I come over for a little while?"

"All right," she said. "The kids are sleeping though; I don't want to wake them up."

"That's OK," he said. "I just wanted to talk to you."

Her voice hesitated slightly, then carefully controlled not to show any concern, she asked, "Is it anything serious, anything important?"

"No," Johnny said. "I finished the picture today and I thought maybe I could just see you and talk to you. Maybe I could take a look at the kids if you're sure they won't wake up."

"OK," she said. "I'm glad you got that part you wanted."

"Thanks," he said. "I'll see you in about a half hour."

When he got to what had been his home in Beverly Hills, Johnny Fontane sat in the car for a moment staring at the house. He remembered what his Godfather had said, that he could make his own life what he wanted. Great chance if you knew what you wanted. But what did he want?

His first wife was waiting for him at the door. She was pretty, petite and brunette, a nice Italian girl, the girl next door who would never fool around with another man and that had been important to him. Did he still want her, he asked himself, and the answer was no.

For one thing, he could no longer make love to her, their affection had grown too old. And there were some things, nothing to do with sex, she could never forgive him. But they were no longer enemies.

She made him coffee and served him homemade cookies in the living room. "Stretch out on the sofa," she said, "you look tired." He took off his jacket and his shoes and loosened his tie while she sat in the chair opposite him with a grave little smile on her face. "It's funny," she said.

"What's funny?" he asked her, sipping coffee and spilling some of it on his shirt.

"The great Johnny Fontane stuck without a date," she said.

"The great Johnny Fontane is lucky if he can even get it up anymore," he said.

It was unusual for him to be so direct. Ginny asked, "Is there something really the matter?"

Johnny grinned at her. "I had a date with a girl in my apartment and she brushed me off. And you know, I was relieved."

To his surprise he saw a look of anger pass over Ginny's face. "Don't worry about those little tramps," she said. "She must have thought that was the way to get you interested in her." And Johnny realized with amusement that Ginny was actually angry with the girl who had turned him down.

"Ah, what the hell," he said. "I'm tired of that stuff. I have to grow up sometime. And now that I can't sing anymore I guess I'll have a tough time with dames. I never got in on my looks, you know."

She said loyally, "You were always better looking than you photographed."

Johnny shook his head. "I'm getting fat and I'm getting bald. Hell, if this picture doesn't make me big again I better learn how to bake pizzas. Or maybe we'll put you in the movies, you look great."

She looked thirty-five. A good thirty-five, but thirty-five. And out here in Hollywood that might as well be a hundred. The young beautiful girls thronged through the city like lemmings, lasting one year, some two. Some of them so beautiful they could make a man's heart almost stop beating until they opened their mouths, until the greedy hopes for success clouded the loveliness of their eyes. Ordinary women could never hope to compete with them on a physical level. And you could talk all you wanted to about charm, about intelligence, about chic, about poise, the raw beauty of these girls overpowered everything else. Perhaps if there were not so many of them there might be a chance for an ordinary, nice-looking woman. And since Johnny Fontane could have all of them, or nearly all of them, Ginny knew that he was saying all this just to flatter her. He had always been nice that way. He had always been polite to women even at the height of his fame, paying them compliments, holding lights for their cigarettes, opening doors. And since all this was usually done for *him*, it made it even more impressive to the girls he went out with. And he did it with all girls, even the one-night stands, I-don't-know-your-name girls.

She smiled at him, a friendly smile. "You already made me, Johnny, remember? For twelve years. You don't have to give me your line."

He sighed and stretched out on the sofa. "No kidding, Ginny, you look good. I wish I looked that good."

She didn't answer him. She could see he was depressed. "Do you think the picture is OK? Will it do you some good?" she asked.

Johnny nodded. "Yeah. It could bring me all the way back. If I get the Academy thing and play my cards right, I can make it big again even without the singing. Then maybe I can give you and the kids more dough."

"We have more than enough," Ginny said.

"I wanta see more of the kids too," Johnny said. "I want to settle down a little bit. Why can't I come every Friday night for dinner here? I swear I'll never miss one Friday, I don't care how far away I am or how busy I am. And then whenever I can I'll spend weekends or maybe the kids can spend some part of their vacations with me."

Ginny put an ashtray on his chest. "It's OK with me," she said. "I never got married because I wanted you to keep being their father." She said this without any kind of emotion, but Johnny Fontane, staring up at the ceiling, knew she said it as an atonement for those other things, the cruel things she had once said to him when their marriage had broken up, when his career had started going down the drain.

"By the way, guess who called me," she said.

Johnny wouldn't play that game, he never did. "Who?" he asked.

Ginny said, "You could take at least one lousy guess." Johnny didn't answer. "Your Godfather," she said.

Johnny was really surprised. "He never talks to anybody on the phone. What did he say to you?"

"He told me to help you," Ginny said. "He said you could be as big as you ever were, that you were on your way back, but that you needed people to believe in you. I asked him why should I? And he said because you're the father of my children. He's such a sweet old guy and they tell such horrible stories about him."

Virginia hated phones and she had had all the extensions taken out except for the one in her bedroom and one in the kitchen. Now they could hear the kitchen phone ringing. She went to answer it. When she came back into the living room there was a look of surprise on her face. "It's for you, Johnny," she said. "It's Tom Hagen. He says it's important."

Johnny went into the kitchen and picked up the phone. "Yeah, Tom," he said.

Tom Hagen's voice was cool. "Johnny, the Godfather wants me to come out and see you and set some things up that can help you out now that the picture is finished. He wants me to catch the morning plane. Can you meet it in Los Angeles? I have to fly back to New York the same night so you won't have to worry about keeping your night free for me."

"Sure, Tom," Johnny said. "And don't worry about me losing a night. Stay over and relax a bit. I'll throw a party and you can meet some movie people." He always made that offer, he didn't want the folks from his old neighborhood to think he was ashamed of them.

"Thanks," Hagen said, "but I really have to catch the early morning plane back. OK, you'll meet the eleven-thirty A.M. out of New York?"

"Sure," Johnny said.

"Stay in your car," Hagen said. "Send one of your people to meet me when I get off the plane and bring me to you."

"Right," Johnny said.

He went back to the living room and Ginny looked at him inquiringly. "My Godfather has some plans for me, to help me out," Johnny said. "He got me the part in the movie, I don't know how. But I wish he'd stay out of the rest of it."

He went back onto the sofa. He felt very tired. Ginny said, "Why don't you sleep in the guest bedroom tonight instead of going home. You can have breakfast with the kids and you won't have to drive home so late. I hate to think of you all alone in that house of yours anyway. Don't you get lonely?"

"I don't stay home much," Johnny said.

She laughed and said, "Then you haven't changed much." She paused and then said, "Shall I fix up the other bedroom?"

Johnny said, "Why can't I sleep in your bedroom?"

She flushed. "No," she said. She smiled at him and he smiled back. They were still friends.

When Johnny woke up the next morning it was late, he could tell by the sun coming in through the drawn blinds. It never came in that way unless it was in the afternoon. He yelled, "Hey, Ginny, do I still rate breakfast?" And far away he heard her voice call, "Just a second."

And it was just a second. She must have had everything ready, hot in the oven, the tray waiting to be loaded, because as Johnny lit his first cigarette of the day, the door of the bedroom opened and his two small daughters came in wheeling the breakfast cart.

They were so beautiful it broke his heart. Their faces were shining and clear, their eyes alive with curiosity and the eager desire to run to him. They wore their hair braided old-fashioned in long pigtails and they wore old-fashioned frocks and white patent-leather shoes. They stood by the breakfast cart watching him as he stubbed out his cigarette and waited for him to call and hold his arms wide. Then they came running to him. He pressed his face between their two fresh fragrant cheeks and scraped them with his beard so that they shrieked. Ginny appeared in the bedroom door and wheeled the breakfast cart the rest of the way so that he could eat in bed. She sat beside him on the edge of the bed, pouring his coffee, buttering his toast. The two young daughters sat on the bedroom couch watching him. They were too old now for pillow fights or to be tossed around. They were already smoothing their mussed hair. Oh, Christ, he thought, pretty soon they'll be all grown up, Hollywood punks will be out after them.

He shared his toast and bacon with them as he ate, gave them sips of coffee. It was a habit left over from when he had been singing with the band and rarely ate with them so they liked to share his food when he had his odd-hour meals like afternoon breakfasts or morning suppers. The change-around in food delighted them—to eat steak and french fries at seven in the morning, bacon and eggs in the afternoon.

Only Ginny and a few of his close friends knew how much he idolized his daughters. That had been the worst thing about the divorce and leaving home. The one thing he had fought about, and for, was his position as a father to them. In a very sly way he had made Ginny understand he would not be pleased by her remarrying, not because he was jealous of her, but because he was jealous of his position as a father. He had arranged the money to be paid to her so it would be enormously to her advantage financially not to remarry. It was understood that she could have lovers as long as they were not introduced into her home life. But on this score he had absolute faith in her. She had always been amazingly shy and old-fashioned in sex. The Hollywood gigolos had batted zero when they started swarming around her, sniffing for the financial settlement and the favors they could get from her famous husband.

He had no fear that she expected a reconciliation because he had wanted to sleep with her the night before. Neither one of them wanted to renew their old marriage. She understood his hunger for beauty, his irresistible impulse toward young women far more beautiful than she. It was known that he always slept with his movie co-stars at least once. His boyish charm was irresistible to them, as their beauty was to him.

"You'll have to start getting dressed pretty soon," Ginny said. "Tom's plane will be getting in." She shooed the daughters out of the room.

"Yeah," Johnny said. "By the way, Ginny, you know I'm getting divorced? I'm gonna be a free man again."

She watched him getting dressed. He always kept fresh clothes at her house ever since they had come to their new arrangement after the wedding of Don Corleone's daughter. "Christmas is only two weeks away," she said. "Shall I plan on you being here?"

It was the first time he had even thought about the holidays. When his voice was in shape, holidays were lucrative singing dates but even then Christmas was sacred. If he missed this one, it would be the second one. Last year he had been courting his second wife in Spain, trying to get her to marry him.

"Yeah," he said. "Christmas Eve and Christmas." He didn't mention New Year's Eve. That would be one of the wild nights he needed every once in a while, to get drunk with his friends, and he didn't want a wife along then. He didn't feel guilty about it.

She helped him put on his jacket and brushed it off. He was always fastidiously neat. She could see him frowning because the shirt he had put on was not laundered to his taste, the cuff links, a pair he had not worn for some time, were a little too loud for the way he liked to dress now. She laughed softly and said, "Tom won't notice the difference."

The three women of the family walked him to the door and out on the driveway to his car. The two little girls held his hands, one on each side. His wife walked a little behind him. She was getting pleasure out of how happy he looked. When he reached his car he turned around and swung each girl in turn high up in the air and kissed her on the way down. Then he kissed his wife and got into the car. He never liked drawn-out good-byes.

Arrangements had been made by his PR man and aide. At his house a chauffeured car was waiting, a rented car. In it were the PR man and another member of his entourage. Johnny parked his car and hopped in and they were on their way to the airport. He waited inside the car while the PR man went out to meet Tom Hagen's plane. When Tom got into the car they shook hands and drove back to his house.

Finally he and Tom were alone in the living room. There was a coolness between them. Johnny had never forgiven Hagen for acting as a barrier to his getting in touch with the Don when the Don was angry with him, in those bad days before Connie's wedding. Hagen never made excuses for his actions. He could not. It was part of his job to act as a lightning rod for resentments which people were too awed to feel toward the Don himself though he had earned them.

"Your Godfather sent me out here to give you a hand on some things," Hagen said. "I wanted to get it out of the way before Christmas."

Johnny Fontane shrugged. "The picture is finished. The director was a square guy and treated me right. My scenes are too important to be left on the cutting-room floor just for Woltz to pay me off. He can't ruin a ten-million-dollar picture. So now everything depends on how good people think I am in the movie."

Hagen said cautiously, "Is winning this Academy Award so terribly important to an actor's career, or is it just the usual publicity crap that really doesn't mean anything one way or the other?" He paused and added hastily, "Except of course the glory, everybody likes glory."

Johnny Fontane grinned at him. "Except my Godfather. And you. No, Tom, it's not a lot of crap. An Academy Award can make an actor for ten years. He can get his pick of roles. The public goes to see him. It's not everything, but for an actor it's the most important thing in the business. I'm counting on winning it. Not because I'm such a great actor but because I'm known primarily as a singer and the part is foolproof. And I'm pretty good too, no kidding."

Tom Hagen shrugged and said, "Your Godfather tells me that the way things stand now, you don't have a chance of winning the award."

Johnny Fontane was angry. "What the hell are you talking about? The picture hasn't even been cut yet, much less shown. And the Don isn't even in the movie business. Why the hell did you fly the three thousand miles just to tell me that shit?" He was so shaken he was almost in tears.

Hagen said worriedly, "Johnny, I don't know a damn thing about all this movie stuff. Remember, I'm just a messenger boy for the Don. But we have discussed this whole business of yours many times. He worries about you, about your future. He feels you still need his help and he wants to settle your problem once and for all. That's why I'm here now, to get things rolling. But you have to start growing up, Johnny. You have to stop thinking about yourself as a singer or an actor. You've got to start thinking about yourself as a prime mover, as a guy with muscle."

Johnny Fontane laughed and filled his glass. "If I don't win that Oscar I'll have as much muscle as one of my daughters. My voice is gone; if I had that back I could make some moves. Oh, hell. How does my Godfather know I won't win it? OK, I believe he knows. He's never been wrong."

Hagen lit a thin cigar. "We got the word that Jack Woltz won't spend studio money to support your candidacy. In fact he's sent the word out to everybody who votes that he does not want you to win. But holding back the money for ads and all that may do it. He's also arranging to have one other guy get as much of the opposition votes as he can swing. He's using all sorts of bribes—jobs, money, broads, everything. And he's trying to do it without hurting the picture or hurting it as little as possible."

Johnny Fontane shrugged. He filled his glass with whiskey and downed it. "Then I'm dead."

Hagen was watching him with his mouth curled up with distaste. "Drinking won't help your voice," he said.

"Fuck you," Johnny said.

Hagen's face suddenly became smoothly impassive. Then he said, "OK, I'll keep this purely business."

Johnny Fontane put his drink down and went over to stand in front of Hagen. "I'm sorry I said that, Tom," he said. "Christ, I'm sorry. I'm taking it out on you because I wanta kill that bastard Jack Woltz and I'm afraid to tell off my Godfather. So I get sore at you." There were tears in his eyes. He threw the empty whiskey glass against the wall but so weakly that the heavy shot glass did not even shatter and rolled along the floor back to him so that he looked down at it in baffled fury. Then he laughed. "Jesus Christ," he said.

He walked over to the other side of the room and sat opposite Hagen. "You know, I had everything my own way for a long time. Then I divorced Ginny and everything started going sour. I lost my voice. My records stopped selling. I didn't get any more movie work. And then my Godfather got sore at me and wouldn't talk to me on the phone or see me when I came into New York. You were always the guy barring the path and I blamed you, but I knew you wouldn't do it without orders from the Don. But you can't get sore at him. It's like getting sore at God. So I curse you. But you've been right all along the line. And to show you I mean my apology I'm taking your advice. No more booze until I get my voice back. OK?"

The apology was sincere. Hagen forgot his anger. There must be something to this thirty-five-year-old boy or the Don would not be so fond of him. He said, "Forget it, Johnny." He was embarrassed at the depth of Johnny's feeling and embarrassed by the suspicion that it might have been inspired by fear, fear that he might turn the Don against him. And of course the Don could never be turned by anyone for any reason. His affection was mutable only by himself.

"Things aren't so bad," he told Johnny. "The Don says he can cancel out everything Woltz does against you. That you will almost certainly win the Award. But he feels that won't solve your problem. He wants to know if you have the brains and balls to become a producer on your own, make your own movies from top to bottom."

"How the hell is he going to get me the Award?" Johnny asked incredulously.

Hagen said sharply, "How do you find it so easy to believe that Woltz can finagle it and your Godfather can't? Now since it's necessary to get your faith for the other part of our deal I must tell you this. Just keep it to yourself. Your Godfather is a much more powerful man than Jack Woltz. And he is much more powerful in areas far more critical. How can he swing the Award? He controls, or controls the people who control, all the labor unions in the industry, all the people or nearly all the people who vote. Of course you have to be good, you have to be in contention on your own merits. And your Godfather has more brains than Jack Woltz. He doesn't go up to these people and put a gun to their heads and say, 'Vote for Johnny Fontane or you are out of a job.' He doesn't strong-arm where strong-arm doesn't work or leaves too many hard feelings. He'll make those people vote for you because they want to. But they won't want to unless he takes an interest. Now just take my word for it that he can get you the Award. And that if he doesn't do it, you won't get it."

"OK," Johnny said. "I believe you. And I have the balls and brains to be a producer but I don't have the money. No bank would finance me. It takes millions to support a movie."

Hagen said dryly, "When you get the Award, start making plans to produce three of your own movies. Hire the best people in the business, the best technicians, the best stars, whoever you need. Plan on three to five movies."

"You're crazy," Johnny said. "That many movies could mean twenty million bucks."

"When you need the money," Hagen said, "get in touch with me. I'll give you the name of the bank out here in California to ask for financing. Don't worry, they finance movies all the time. Just ask them for the money in the ordinary way, with the proper justifications, like a regular business deal. They will approve. But first you have to see me and tell me the figures and the plans. OK?"

Johnny was silent for a long time. Then he said quietly, "Is there anything else?"

Hagen smiled. "You mean, do you have to do any favors in return for a loan of twenty million dollars? Sure you will." He waited for Johnny to say something. "Nothing you wouldn't do anyway if the Don asked you to do it for him."

Johnny said, "The Don has to ask me himself if it's something serious, you know what I mean? I won't take your word or Sonny's for it."

Hagen was surprised by this good sense. Fontane had some brains after all. He had sense to know that the Don was too fond of him, and too smart, to ask him to do something foolishly dangerous, whereas Sonny might. He said to Johnny, "Let me reassure you on one thing.

Your Godfather has given me and Sonny strict instructions not to involve you in any way in anything that might get you bad publicity through our fault. And he will never do that himself. I guarantee you that any favor he asks of you, you will offer to do before he requests it. OK?"

Johnny smiled. "OK," he said.

Hagen said, "Also he has faith in you. He thinks you have brains and so he figures the bank will make money on the investment, which means he will make money on it. So it's really a business deal, never forget that. Don't go screwing around with the money. You may be his favorite godson but twenty million bucks is a lot of dough. He has to stick his neck out to make sure you get it."

"Tell him not to worry," Johnny said. "If a guy like Jack Woltz can be a big movie genius, anybody can."

"That's what your Godfather figures," Hagen said. "Can you have me driven back to the airport? I've said all I have to say. When you do start signing contracts for everything, hire your own lawyers, I won't be in on it. But I'd like to see everything before you sign, if that's OK with you. Also, you'll never have any labor troubles. That will cut costs on your pictures to some extent, so when the accountants lump some of that in, disregard those figures."

Johnny said cautiously, "Do I have to get your OK on anything else, scripts, stars, any of that?"

Hagen shook his head. "No," he said. "It may happen that the Don would object to something but he'll object to you direct if he does. But I can't imagine what that would be. Movies don't affect him at all, in any way, so he has no interest. And he doesn't believe in meddling, that I can tell you from experience."

"Good," Johnny said. "I'll drive you to the airport myself. And thank the Godfather for me. I'd call him up and thank him but he never comes to the phone. Why is that, by the way?"

Hagen shrugged. "He hardly ever talks on the phone. He doesn't want his voice recorded, even saying something perfectly innocent. He's afraid that they can splice the words together so that it sounds as if he says something else. I think that's what it is. Anyway his only worry is that someday he'll be framed by the authorities. So he doesn't want to give them an edge."

They got into Johnny's car and drove to the airport. Hagen was thinking that Johnny was a better guy than he figured. He'd already learned something, just his driving him personally to the airport proved that. The personal courtesy, something the Don himself always believed in. And the apology. That had been sincere. He had known Johnny a long time and he knew the apology would never be made out of fear. Johnny had always had guts. That's why he had always been in trouble, with his movie bosses and with his women. He was also one of the few people who was not afraid of the Don. Fontane and Michael were maybe the only two men Hagen knew of whom this could be said. So the apology was sincere, he would accept it as such. He and Johnny would have to see a lot of each other in the next few years. And Johnny would have to pass the next test, which would prove how smart he was. He would have to do something for the Don that the Don would never ask him to do or insist that he do as part of the agreement. Hagen wondered if Johnny Fontane was smart enough to figure out that part of the bargain.

After Johnny dropped Hagen off at the airport (Hagen insisted that Johnny not hang around for his plane with him) he drove back to Ginny's house. She was surprised to see him. But he wanted to stay at her place so that he would have time to think things out, to make his plans. He knew that what Hagen had told him was extremely important, that his whole life was being changed. He had once been a big star but now at the young age of thirty-five he was washed up. He didn't kid himself about that. Even if he won the Award as best actor, what the hell could it mean at the most? Nothing, if his voice didn't come back. He'd be just second-rate, with no real power, no real juice. Even that girl turning him down, she had been nice and smart and acting sort of hip, but would she have been so cool if he had really been at the top? Now with the Don backing him with dough he could be as big as anybody in Hollywood. He could be a king. Johnny smiled. Hell. He could even be a Don.

It would be nice living with Ginny again for a few weeks, maybe longer. He'd take the kids out every day, maybe have a few friends over. He'd stop drinking and smoking, really take care of himself. Maybe his voice would get strong again. If that happened and with the Don's money, he'd be unbeatable. He'd really be as close to an old-time king or emperor as it was possible to be in America. And it wouldn't depend on his voice holding up or how long the public cared about him as an actor. It would be an empire rooted in money and the most special, the most coveted kind of power.

Ginny had the guest bedroom made up for him. It was understood that he would not share her room, that they would not live as man and wife. They could never have that relationship again. And though the outside world of gossip columnists and movie fans gave the blame for the failure of their marriage solely to him, yet in a curious way, between the two of them, they both knew that she was even more to blame for their divorce.

When Johnny Fontane became the most popular singer and movie musical comedy star in motion pictures, it had never occurred to him to desert his wife and children. He was too Italian, still too old-style. Naturally he had been unfaithful. That had been impossible to avoid in his business and the temptations to which he was continually exposed. And despite being a skinny, delicate-looking guy, he had the wiry horniness of many small-boned Latin types. And women delighted him in their surprises. He loved going out with a demure sweet-faced virginal-looking girl and then uncapping her breasts to find them so unexpectedly slopingly full and rich, lewdly heavy in contrast to the cameo face. He loved to find sexual shyness and timidity in the sexy-looking girls who were all fake motion like a shifty basketball player, vamping as if they had slept with a hundred guys, and then when he got them alone having to battle for hours to get in and do the job and finding out they were virgins.

And all these Hollywood guys laughed at his fondness for virgins. They called it an old guinea taste, square, and look how long it took to make a virgin give you a blow job with all the aggravation and then they usually turned out to be a lousy piece of ass. But Johnny knew that it was how you handled a young girl. You had to come on to her the right way and then what could be greater than a girl who was tasting her first dick and loving it? Ah, it was so great breaking them in. It was so great having them wrap their legs around you. Their thighs were all different shapes, their asses were different, their skins were all different colors and shades of white and brown and tan and when he had slept with that young colored girl in Detroit, a good girl, not a hustler, the young daughter of a jazz singer on the same nightclub bill with him, she had been one of the sweetest things he had ever had. Her lips had really tasted like warm honey with pepper mixed in it, her dark brown skin was rich, creamy, and she had been as sweet as God had ever made any woman and she had been a virgin.

And the other guys were always talking about blow jobs this and other variations and he really didn't enjoy that stuff so much. He never liked a girl that much after they tried it that way, it just didn't satisfy him right. He and his second wife had finally not got along because she preferred the old sixty-nine too much to a point where she didn't want anything else and he had to fight to stick it in. She began making fun of him and calling him a square and the word got around that he made love like a kid. Maybe that was why that girl last night had turned him down. Well, the hell with it, she wouldn't be too great in the sack anyway. You could tell a girl who really liked to fuck and they were always the best. Especially the ones who hadn't been at it too long. What he really hated were the ones who had started screwing at twelve and were all fucked out by the time they were twenty and just going through the motions and some of them were the prettiest of all and could fake you out.

Ginny brought coffee and cake into his bedroom and put it on the long table in the sitting room part. He told her simply that Hagen was helping him put together the money credit for a producing package and she was excited about that. He would be important again. But she had no idea of how powerful Don Corleone really was so she didn't understand the significance of Hagen coming from New York. He told her Hagen was also helping with legal details.

When they had finished the coffee he told her he was going to work that night, and make phone calls and plans for the future. "Half of all this will be in the kids' names," he told her. She gave him a grateful smile and kissed him good night before she left his room.

There was a glass dish full of his favorite monogrammed cigarettes, a humidor with pencil-thin black Cuban cigars on his writing desk. Johnny tilted back and started making calls. His brain was really whirring along. He called the author of the book, the best-selling novel, on which his new film was based. The author was a guy his own age who had come up the hard way and was now a celebrity in the literary world. He had come out to Hollywood expecting to be treated like a wheel and, like most authors, had been treated like shit. Johnny had seen the humiliation of the author one night at the Brown Derby. The writer had been fixed up with a well-known bosomy starlet for a date on the town and a sure shack-up later. But while they were at dinner the starlet had deserted the famous author because a ratty-looking movie comic had waggled his finger at her. That had given the writer the right slant on just who was who in the

Hollywood pecking order. It didn't matter that his book had made him world famous. A starlet would prefer the crummiest, the rattiest, the phoniest movie wheel.

Now Johnny called the author at his New York home to thank him for the great part he had written in his book for him. He flattered the shit out of the guy. Then casually he asked him how he was doing on his next novel and what it was all about. He lit a cigar while the author told him about a specially interesting chapter and then finally said, "Gee, I'd like to read it when you're finished. How about sending me a copy? Maybe I can get you a good deal for it, better than you got with Woltz."

The eagerness in the author's voice told him that he had guessed right. Woltz had chiseled the guy, given him peanuts for the book. Johnny mentioned that he might be in New York right after the holidays and would the author want to come and have dinner with some of his friends. "I know a few good-looking broads," Johnny said jokingly. The author laughed and said OK.

Next Johnny called up the director and cameraman on the film he had just finished to thank them for having helped him in the film. He told them confidentially that he knew Woltz had been against him and he doubly appreciated their help and that if there was ever anything he could do for them they should just call.

Then he made the hardest call of all, the one to Jack Woltz. He thanked him for the part in the picture and told him how happy he would be to work for him anytime. He did this merely to throw Woltz off the track. He had always been very square, very straight. In a few days Woltz would find out about his maneuvering and be astounded by the treachery of this call, which was exactly what Johnny Fontane wanted him to feel.

After that he sat at the desk and puffed at his cigar. There was whiskey on a side table but he had made some sort of promise to himself and Hagen that he wouldn't drink. He shouldn't even be smoking. It was foolish; whatever was wrong with his voice probably wouldn't be helped by knocking off drinking and smoking. Not too much, but what the hell, it might help and he wanted all the percentages with him, now that he had a fighting chance.

Now with the house quiet, his divorced wife sleeping, his beloved daughters sleeping, he could think back to that terrible time in his life when he had deserted them. Deserted them for a whore tramp of a bitch who was his second wife. But even now he smiled at the thought of her, she was such a lovely broad in so many ways and, besides, the only thing that saved his life was the day that he had made up his mind never to hate a woman or, more specifically, the day he had decided he could not afford to hate his first wife and his daughters, his girl friends, his second wife, and the girl friends after that, right up to Sharon Moore brushing him off so that she could brag about refusing to screw for the great Johnny Fontane.

He had traveled with the band singing and then he had become a radio star and a star of the movie stage shows and then he had finally made it in the movies. And in all that time he had lived the way he wanted to, screwed the women he wanted to, but he had never let it affect his personal life. Then he had fallen for his soon-to-be second wife, Margot Ashton; he had gone absolutely crazy for her. His career had gone to hell, his voice had gone to hell, his family life had gone to hell. And there had come the day when he was left without anything.

The thing was, he had always been generous and fair. He had given his first wife everything he owned when he divorced her. He had made sure his two daughters would get a piece of everything he made, every record, every movie, every club date. And when he had been rich and famous he had refused his first wife nothing. He had helped out all her brothers and sisters, her father and mother, the girl friends she had gone to school with and their families. He had never been a stuck-up celebrity. He had sung at the weddings of his wife's two younger sisters, something he hated to do. He had never refused her anything except the complete surrender of his own personality.

And then when he had touched bottom, when he could no longer get movie work, when he could no longer sing, when his second wife had betrayed him, he had gone to spend a few days with Ginny and his daughters. He had more or less flung himself on her mercy one night because he felt so lousy. That day he had heard one of his recordings and he had sounded so terrible that he accused the sound technicians of sabotaging the record. Until finally he had become convinced that that was what his voice really sounded like. He had smashed the master record and refused to sing anymore. He was so ashamed that he had not sung a note except with Nino at Connie Corleone's wedding.

He had never forgotten the look on Ginny's face when she found out about all his misfortunes. It had passed over her face only for a second but that was enough for him never to forget it. It was a look of savage and joyful satisfaction. It was a look that could only make him believe that she had contemptuously hated him all these years. She quickly recovered and offered him cool but polite sympathy. He had pretended to accept it. During the next few days he had gone to see three of the girls he had liked the most over the years, girls he had remained friends with and sometimes still slept with in a comradely way, girls that he had done everything in his power to help, girls to whom he had given the equivalent of hundreds of thousands of dollars in gifts or job opportunities. On their faces he had caught that same fleeting look of savage satisfaction.

It was during that time that he knew he had to make a decision. He could become like a great many other men in Hollywood, successful producers, writers, directors, actors, who preyed on beautiful women with lustful hatred. He could use power and monetary favors grudgingly, always alert for treason, always believing that women would betray and desert him, adversaries to be bested. Or he could refuse to hate women and continue to believe in them.

He knew he could not afford *not* to love them, that something of his spirit would die if he did not continue to love women no matter how treacherous and unfaithful they were. It didn't matter that the women he loved most in the world were secretly glad to see him crushed, humiliated, by a wayward fortune; it did not matter that in the most awful way, not sexually, they had been unfaithful to him. He had no choice. He had to accept them. And so he made love to all of them, gave them presents, hid the hurt their enjoyment of his misfortunes gave him. He forgave them knowing he was being paid back for having lived in the utmost freedom from women and in the fullest flush of their flavor. But now he never felt guilty about being untrue to them. He never felt guilty about how he treated Ginny, insisting on remaining the sole father of his children, yet never even considering remarrying her, and letting her know that too. That was one thing he had salvaged out of his fall from the top. He had grown a thick skin about the hurts he gave women.

He was tired and ready for bed but one note of memory stuck with him: singing with Nino Valenti. And suddenly he knew what would please Don Corleone more than anything else. He picked up the phone and told the operator to get him New York. He called Sonny Corleone and asked him for Nino Valenti's number. Then he called Nino. Nino sounded a little drunk as usual.

"Hey, Nino, how'd you like to come out here and work for me," Johnny said. "I need a guy I can trust."

Nino, kidding around, said, "Gee, I don't know, Johnny, I got a good job on the truck, boffing housewives along my route, picking up a clear hundred-fifty every week. What you got to offer?"

"I can start you at five hundred and get you blind dates with movie stars, how's that?" Johnny said. "And maybe I'll let you sing at my parties."

"Yeah, OK, let me think about it." Nino said. "Let me talk it over with my lawyer and my accountant and my helper on the truck."

"Hey, no kidding around, Nino," Johnny said. "I need you out here. I want you to fly out tomorrow morning and sign a personal contract for five hundred a week for a year. Then if you steal one of my broads and I fire you, you pick up at least a year's salary. OK?"

There was a long pause. Nino's voice was sober. "Hey, Johnny, you kidding?"

Johnny said, "I'm serious, kid. Go to my agent's office in New York. They'll have your plane ticket and some cash. I'm gonna call them first thing in the morning. So you go up there in the afternoon. OK? Then I'll have somebody meet you at the plane and bring you out to the house."

Again there was a long pause and then Nino's voice, very subdued, uncertain, said, "OK, Johnny." He didn't sound drunk anymore.

Johnny hung up the phone and got ready for bed. He felt better than any time since he had smashed that master record.

Chapter

✠✠✠✠✠✠✠✠✠✠✠✠✠✠✠✠✠✠

13

JOHNNY FONTANE sat in the huge recording studio and figured costs on a yellow pad. Musicians were filing in, all of them friends he had known since he was a kid singer with the bands. The conductor, top man in the business of pop accompaniment and a man who had been kind to him when things went sour, was giving each musician bundles of music and verbal instructions. His name was Eddie Neils. He had taken on this recording as a favor to Johnny, though his schedule was crowded.

Nino Valenti was sitting at a piano fooling around nervously with the keys. He was also sipping from a huge glass of rye. Johnny didn't mind that. He knew Nino sang just as well drunk as sober and what they were doing today wouldn't require any real musicianship on Nino's part.

Eddie Neils had made special arrangements of some old Italian and Sicilian songs, and a special job on the duel-duet song that Nino and Johnny had sung at Connie Corleone's wedding. Johnny was making the record primarily because he knew that the Don loved such songs and it would be a perfect Christmas gift for him. He also had a hunch that the record would sell in the high numbers, not a million, of course. And he had figured out that helping Nino was how the Don wanted his payoff. Nino was, after all, another one of the Don's godchildren.

Johnny put his clipboard and yellow pad on the folding chair beside him and got up to stand beside the piano. He said, "Hey, *paisan*," and Nino glanced up and tried to smile. He looked a little sick. Johnny leaned over and rubbed his shoulder blades. "Relax, kid," he said. "Do a good job today and I'll fix you up with the best and most famous piece of ass in Hollywood."

Nino took a gulp of whiskey. "Who's that, Lassie?"

Johnny laughed. "No, Deanna Dunn. I guarantee the goods."

Nino was impressed but couldn't help saying with pseudo-hopefulness, "You can't get me Lassie?"

The orchestra swung into the opening song of the medley. Johnny Fontane listened intently. Eddie Neils would play all the songs through in their special arrangements. Then would come the first take for the record. As Johnny listened he made mental notes on exactly how he would handle each phrase, how he would come into each song. He knew his voice wouldn't last long, but Nino would be doing most of the singing, Johnny would be singing under him. Except of course in the duet-duel song. He would have to save himself for that.

He pulled Nino to his feet and they both stood by their microphones. Nino flubbed the opening, flubbed it again. His face was beginning to get red with embarrassment. Johnny kidded him, "Hey, you stalling for overtime?"

"I don't feel natural without my mandolin," Nino said.

Johnny thought that over for a moment. "Hold that glass of booze in your hand," he said.

It seemed to do the trick. Nino kept drinking from the glass as he sang but he was doing fine. Johnny sang easily, not straining, his voice merely dancing around Nino's main melody. There was no emotional satisfaction in this kind of singing but he was amazed at his own technical skill. Ten years of vocalizing had taught him something.

When they came to the duet-duel song that ended the record, Johnny let his voice go and when they finished his vocal chords ached. The musicians had been carried away by the last song, a rare thing for these calloused veterans. They hammered down their instruments and stamped their feet in approval as applause. The drummer gave them a ruffle of drums.

With stops and conferences they worked nearly four hours before they quit. Eddie Neils came over to Johnny and said quietly, "You sounded pretty good, kid. Maybe you're ready to do a record. I have a new song that's perfect for you."

Johnny shook his head. "Come on, Eddie, don't kid me. Besides in a couple of hours I'll be too hoarse to even talk. Do you think we'll have to fix up much of the stuff we did today?"

Eddie said thoughtfully, "Nino will have to come into the studio tomorrow. He made some mistakes. But he's much better than I thought he would be. As for your stuff, I'll have the sound engineers fix anything I don't like. OK?"

"OK," Johnny said. "When can I hear the pressing?"

"Tomorrow night," Eddie Neils said. "Your place?"

"Yeah," Johnny said. "Thanks, Eddie. See you tomorrow." He took Nino by the arm and walked out of the studio. They went to his house instead of Ginny's.

By this time it was late afternoon. Nino was still more than half-drunk. Johnny told him to get under the shower and then take a snooze. They had to be at a big party at eleven that night.

When Nino woke up, Johnny briefed him. "This party is a movie star Lonely Hearts Club," he said. "These broads tonight are dames you've seen in the movies as glamour queens millions of guys would give their right arms to screw. And the only reason they'll be at the party tonight is to find somebody to shack them up. Do you know why? Because they are hungry for it, they are just a little old. And just like every dame, they want it with a little bit of class."

"What's the matter with your voice?" Nino asked.

Johnny had been speaking almost in a whisper. "Everytime after I sing a little bit that happens. I won't be able to sing for a month now. But I'll get over the hoarseness in a couple of days."

Nino said thoughtfully, "Tough, huh?"

Johnny shrugged. "Listen, Nino, don't get too drunk tonight. You have to show these Hollywood broads that my *paisan* buddy ain't weak in the poop. You gotta come across. Remember, some of these dames are very powerful in movies, they can get you work. It doesn't hurt to be charming after you knock off a piece."

Nino was already pouring himself a drink. "I'm always charming," he said. He drained the glass. Grinning, he asked, "No kidding, can you really get me close to Deanna Dunn?"

"Don't be so anxious," Johnny said. "It's not going to be like you think."

The Hollywood Movie Star Lonely Hearts Club (so called by the young juvenile leads whose attendance was mandatory) met every Friday night at the palatial, studio-owned home of Roy McElroy, press agent or rather public relations counsel for the Woltz International Film Corporation. Actually, though it was McElroy's open house party, the idea had come from the practical brain of Jack Woltz himself. Some of his money-making movie stars were getting older now. Without the help of special lights and genius makeup men they looked their age. They were having problems. They had also become, to some extent, desensitized physically and mentally. They could no longer "fall in love." They could no longer assume the role of hunted women. They had been made too imperious; by money, by fame, by their former beauty. Woltz gave his parties so that it would be easier for them to pick up lovers, one-night stands, who, if they had the stuff, could graduate into full-time bed partners and so work their way upward. Since the action sometimes degenerated into brawls or sexual excess that led to trouble with the police, Woltz decided to hold the parties in the house of the public relations counselor, who would be right there to fix things up, pay off newsmen and police officers and keep everything quiet.

For certain virile young male actors on the studio payroll who had not yet achieved stardom or featured roles, attendance at the Friday night parties was a not always pleasant duty. This was explained by the fact that a new film yet to be released by the studio would be shown at the party. In fact that was the excuse for the party itself. People would say, "Let's go over to see what the new picture so and so made is like." And so it was put in a professional context.

Young female starlets were forbidden to attend the Friday night parties. Or rather discouraged. Most of them took the hint.

Screenings of the new movies took place at midnight and Johnny and Nino arrived at eleven. Roy McElroy proved to be, at first sight, an enormously likable man, well-groomed, beautifully dressed. He greeted Johnny Fontane with a surprised cry of delight. "What the hell are you doing here?" he said with genuine astonishment.

Johnny shook his hand. "I'm showing my country cousin the sights. Meet Nino."

McElroy shook hands with Nino and gazed at him appraisingly. "They'll eat him up alive," he said to Johnny. He led them to the rear patio.

The rear patio was really a series of huge rooms whose glass doors had been opened to a garden and pool. There were almost a hundred people milling around, all with drinks in their hands. The patio lighting was artfully arranged to flatter feminine faces and skin. These were women Nino had seen on the darkened movie screens when he had been a teenager. They had played their part in his erotic dreams of adolescence. But seeing them now in the flesh was like seeing them in some horrible makeup. Nothing could hide the tiredness of their spirit and their flesh; time had eroded their godhead. They posed and moved as charmingly as he remembered but they were like wax fruit, they could not lubricate his glands. Nino took two drinks, wandered to a table where he could stand next to a nest of bottles. Johnny moved with him. They drank together until behind them came the magic voice of Deanna Dunn.

Nino, like millions of other men, had that voice imprinted on his brain forever. Deanna Dunn had won two Academy Awards, had been in the biggest movie grosser made in Hollywood. On the screen she had a feline feminine charm that made her irresistible to all men. But the words she was saying had never been heard on the silver screen. "Johnny, you bastard, I had to go to my psychiatrist again because you gave me a one-night stand. How come you never came back for seconds?"

Johnny kissed her on her proffered cheek. "You wore me out for a month," he said. "I want you to meet my cousin Nino. A nice strong Italian boy. Maybe he can keep up with you."

Deanna Dunn turned to give Nino a cool look. "Does he like to watch previews?"

Johnny laughed. "I don't think he's ever had the chance. Why don't you break him in?"

Nino had to take a big drink when he was alone with Deanna Dunn. He was trying to be nonchalant but it was hard. Deanna Dunn had the upturned nose, the clean-cut classical features of the Anglo-Saxon beauty. And he knew her so well. He had seen her alone in a bedroom, heartbroken, weeping over her dead flier husband who had left her with fatherless children. He had seen her angry, hurt, humiliated, yet with a shining dignity when a caddish Clark Gable had

BOOK II · 185

taken advantage of her, then left her for a sexpot. (Deanna Dunn never played sexpots in the movies.) He had seen her flushed with requited love, writhing in the embrace of the man she adored and he had seen her die beautifully at least a half dozen times. He had seen her and heard her and dreamed about her and yet he was not prepared for the first thing she said to him alone.

"Johnny is one of the few men with balls in this town," she said. "The rest are all fags and sick morons who couldn't get it up with a broad if you pumped a truckload of Spanish fly into their scrotums." She took Nino by the hand and led him into a corner of the room, out of traffic and out of competition.

Then still coolly charming, she asked him about himself. He saw through her. He saw that she was playing the role of the rich society girl who is being kind to the stableboy or the chauffeur, but who in the movie would either discourage his amatory interest (if the part were played by Spencer Tracy), or throw up everything in her mad desire for him (if the part were played by Clark Gable). But it didn't matter. He found himself telling her about how he and Johnny had grown up together in New York, about how he and Johnny had sung together on little club dates. He found her marvelously sympathetic and interested. Once she asked casually, "Do you know how Johnny made that bastard Jack Woltz give him the part?" Nino froze and shook his head. She didn't pursue it.

The time had come to see the preview of a new Woltz movie. Deanna Dunn led Nino, her warm hand imprisoning his, to an interior room of the mansion that had no windows but was furnished with about fifty small two-person couches scattered around in such a way as to give each one a little island of semiprivacy.

Nino saw there was a small table beside the couch and on the table were an ice bowl, glasses and bottles of liquor plus a tray of cigarettes. He gave Deanna Dunn a cigarette, lit it and then mixed them both drinks. They didn't speak to each other. After a few minutes the lights went out.

He had been expecting something outrageous. After all, he had heard the legends of Hollywood depravity. But he was not quite prepared for Deanna Dunn's voracious plummet on his sexual organ without even a courteous and friendly word of preparation. He kept sipping his drink and watching the movie, but not tasting, not seeing. He was excited in a way he had never been before but part of it was because this woman servicing him in the dark had been the object of his adolescent dreams.

Yet in a way his masculinity was insulted. So when the world-famous Deanna Dunn was sated and had tidied him up, he very coolly fixed her a fresh drink in the darkness and lit her a fresh cigarette and said in the most relaxed voice imaginable, "This looks like a pretty good movie."

He felt her stiffen beside him on the couch. Could it be she was waiting for some sort of compliment? Nino poured his glass full from the nearest bottle his hand touched in the darkness. The hell with that. She'd treated him like a goddamn male whore. For some reason now he felt a cold anger at all these women. They watched the picture for another fifteen minutes. He leaned away from her so their bodies did not touch.

Finally she said in a low harsh whisper, "Don't be such a snotty punk, you liked it. You were as big as a house."

Nino sipped his drink and said in his natural off-hand manner, "That's the way it *always* is. You should see it when I get excited."

She laughed a little and kept quiet for the rest of the picture. Finally it was over and the lights went on. Nino took a look around. He could see there had been a ball here in the darkness though oddly enough he hadn't heard a thing. But some of the dames had that hard, shiny, bright-eyed look of women who had just been worked over real good. They sauntered out of the projection room. Deanna Dunn left him immediately to go over and talk to an older man Nino recognized as a famous featured player, only now, seeing the guy in person, he realized that he was a fag. He sipped his drink thoughtfully.

Johnny Fontane came up beside him and said, "Hi, old buddy, having a good time?"

Nino grinned. "I don't know. It's different. Now when I go back to the old neighborhood I can say Deanna Dunn had me."

Johnny laughed. "She can be better than that if she invites you home with her. Did she?"

Nino shook his head. "I got too interested in the movie," he said. But this time Johnny didn't laugh.

"Get serious, kid," he said. "A dame like that can do you a lot of good. And you used to boff anything. Man, sometimes I still get nightmares when I remember those ugly broads you used to bang."

Nino waved his glass drunkenly and said very loud, "Yeah, they were ugly but they were *women*." Deanna Dunn, in the corner, turned her head to look at them. Nino waved his glass at her in greeting.

Johnny Fontane sighed. "OK, you're just a guinea peasant."

"And I ain't gonna change," Nino said with his charmingly drunken smile.

Johnny understood him perfectly. He knew Nino was not as drunk as he pretended. He knew that Nino was only pretending so that he could say things which he felt were too rude to say to his new Hollywood *padrone* when sober. He put his arm around Nino's neck and said affectionately, "You wise guy bum, you know you got an ironclad contract for a year and you can say and do anything you want and I can't fire you."

"You can't fire me?" Nino said with drunken cunning.

"No," Johnny said.

"Then fuck you," Nino said.

For a moment Johnny was surprised into anger. He saw the careless grin on Nino's face. But in the past few years he must have gotten smarter, or his own descent from stardom had made him more sensitive. In that moment he understood Nino, why his boyhood singing partner had never become successful, why he was trying to destroy any chance of success now. That Nino was reacting away from all the prices of success, that in some way he felt insulted by everything that was being done for him.

Johnny took Nino by the arm and led him out of the house. Nino could barely walk now. Johnny was talking to him soothingly. "OK, kid, you just sing for me, I wanta make dough on you. I won't try to run your life. You do whatever you wanta do. OK, *paisan*? All you gotta do is sing for me and earn me money now that I can't sing anymore. You got that, old buddy?"

Nino straightened up. "I'll sing for you, Johnny," he said, his voice slurring so that he could barely be understood. "I'm a better singer than you now. I was always a better singer than you, you know that?"

Johnny stood there thinking; so that was it. He knew that when his voice was healthy Nino simply wasn't in the same league with him, never had been in those years they had sung together as kids. He saw Nino was waiting for an answer, weaving drunkenly in the

California moonlight. "Fuck you," he said gently, and they both laughed together like the old days when they had both been equally young.

When Johnny Fontane got word about the shooting of Don Corleone he not only worried about his Godfather, but also wondered whether the financing for his movie was still alive. He had wanted to go to New York to pay his respects to his Godfather in the hospital but he had been told not to get any bad publicity, that was the last thing Don Corleone would want. So he waited. A week later a messenger came from Tom Hagen. The financing was still on but for only one picture at a time.

Meanwhile Johnny let Nino go his own way in Hollywood and California, and Nino was doing all right with the young starlets. Sometimes Johnny called him up for a night out together but never leaned on him. When they talked about the Don getting shot, Nino said to Johnny, "You know, once I asked the Don for a job in his organization and he wouldn't give it to me. I was tired of driving a truck and I wanted to make a lot of dough. You know what he told me? He says every man has only one destiny and that my destiny was to be an artist. Meaning that I couldn't be a racket guy."

Johnny thought that one over. The Godfather must be just about the smartest guy in the world. He'd known immediately that Nino could never make a racket guy, would only get himself in trouble or get killed. Get killed with just one of his wisecracks. But how did the Don know that he would be an artist? Because, goddamn it, he figured that someday I'd help Nino. And how did he figure that? Because he would drop the word to me and I would try to show my gratitude. Of course he never asked me to do it. He just let me know it would make him happy if I did it. Johnny Fontane sighed. Now the Godfather was hurt, in trouble, and he could kiss the Academy Award good-bye with Woltz working against him and no help on his side. Only the Don had the personal contacts that could apply pressure and the Corleone Family had other things to think about. Johnny had offered to help, Hagen had given him a curt no.

Johnny was busy getting his own picture going. The author of the book he had starred in had finished his new novel and came west on Johnny's invitation, to talk it over without agents or studios getting into the act. The second book was perfect for what Johnny wanted. He wouldn't have to sing, it had a good gutsy story with plenty of dames and sex and it had a part that Johnny instantly recognized as tailor-made for Nino. The character talked like Nino, acted like him, even looked like him. It was uncanny. All Nino would have to do would be to get up on the screen and be himself.

Johnny worked fast. He found that he knew a lot more about production than he thought he did, but he hired an executive producer, a man who knew his stuff but had trouble finding work because of the blacklist. Johnny didn't take advantage but gave the man a fair contract. "I expect you to save me more dough this way," he told the man frankly.

So he was surprised when the executive producer came to him and told him the union rep had to be taken care of to the tune of fifty thousand dollars. There were a lot of problems dealing with overtime and hiring and the fifty thousand dollars would be well spent. Johnny debated whether the executive producer was hustling him and then said, "Send the union guy to me."

The union guy was Billy Goff. Johnny said to him, "I thought the union stuff was fixed by my friends. I was told not to worry about it. At all."

Goff said, "Who told you that?"

Johnny said, "You know goddamn well who told me. I won't say his name but if he tells me something that's it."

Goff said, "Things have changed. Your friend is in trouble and his word don't go this far west anymore."

Johnny shrugged. "See me in a couple of days. OK?"

Goff smiled. "Sure, Johnny," he said. "But calling in New York ain't going to help you."

But calling New York did help. Johnny spoke to Hagen at his office. Hagen told him bluntly not to pay. "Your Godfather will be sore as hell if you pay that bastard a dime," he told Johnny. "It will make the Don lose respect and right now he can't afford that."

"Can I talk to the Don?" Johnny asked. "Will you talk to him? I gotta get the picture rolling."

"Nobody can talk to the Don right now," Hagen said. "He's too sick. I'll talk to Sonny about fixing things up. But I'll make the decision on this. Don't pay that smart bastard a dime. If anything changes, I'll let you know."

Annoyed, Johnny hung up. Union trouble could add a fortune to making the film and screw up the works generally. For a moment he debated slipping Goff the fifty grand on the quiet. After all, the Don telling him something and Hagen telling him something and giving him orders were two different things. But he decided to wait for a few days.

By waiting he saved fifty thousand dollars. Two nights later, Goff was found shot to death in his home in Glendale. There was no more talk of union trouble. Johnny was a little shaken by the killing. It was the first time the long arm of the Don had struck such a lethal blow so close to him.

As the weeks went by and he became busier and busier with getting the script ready, casting the movie and working out production details, Johnny Fontane forgot about his voice, his not being able to sing. Yet when the Academy Award nominations came out and he found himself one of the candidates, he was depressed because he was not asked to sing one of the songs nominated for the Oscar at the ceremony that would be televised nationally. But he shrugged it off and kept working. He had no hope of winning the Academy Award now that his Godfather was no longer able to put pressure on, but getting the nomination had some value.

The record he and Nino had cut, the one of Italian songs, was selling much better than anything he had cut lately, but he knew that it was Nino's success more than his. He resigned himself to never being able to again sing professionally.

Once a week he had dinner with Ginny and the kids. No matter how hectic things got he never skipped that duty. But he didn't sleep with Ginny. Meanwhile his second wife had finagled a Mexican divorce and so he was a bachelor again. Oddly enough he was not that frantic to bang starlets who would have been easy meat. He was too snobbish really. He was hurt that none of the young stars, the actresses who were still on top, ever gave him a tumble. But it was good to work hard. Most nights he would go home alone, put his old records on the player, have a drink and hum along with them for a few bars. He had been good, damn good. He hadn't realized how good he was. Even aside from the special voice, which could have happened to anybody, he was good. He had been a real artist and never knew it, and never knew how much he loved it. He'd ruined his voice with booze and tobacco and broads just when he really knew what it was all about.

Sometimes Nino came over for a drink and listened with him and Johnny would say to him scornfully, "You guinea bastard, you never sang like that in your life." And Nino would give him that curiously charming smile and shake his head and say, "No, and I never will," in a sympathetic voice, as if he knew what Johnny was thinking.

Finally, a week before shooting the new picture, the Academy Award night rolled around. Johnny invited Nino to come along but Nino refused. Johnny said, "Buddy, I never asked you a favor, right? Do me a favor tonight and come with me. You're the only guy who'll really feel sorry for me if I don't win."

For one moment Nino looked startled. Then he said, "Sure, old buddy, I can make it." He paused for a moment and said, "If you don't win, forget it. Just get as drunk as you can get and I'll take care of you. Hell, I won't even drink myself tonight. How about that for being a buddy?"

"Man," Johnny Fontane said, "that's some buddy."

The Academy Award night came and Nino kept his promise. He came to Johnny's house dead sober and they left for the presentation theater together. Nino wondered why Johnny hadn't invited any of his girls or his ex-wives to the Award dinner. Especially Ginny. Didn't he think Ginny would root for him? Nino wished he could have just one drink, it looked like a long bad night.

Nino Valenti found the whole Academy Award affair a bore until the winner of the best male actor was announced. When he heard the words "Johnny Fontane," he found himself jumping into the air and applauding. Johnny reached out a hand for him to shake and Nino shook it. He knew his buddy needed human contact with someone he trusted and Nino felt an enormous sadness that Johnny didn't have anyone better than himself to touch in his moment of glory.

What followed was an absolute nightmare. Jack Woltz's picture had swept all the major awards and so the studio's party was swamped with newspaper people and all the on-the-make hustlers, male and female. Nino kept his promise to remain sober, and he tried to watch over Johnny. But the women of the party kept pulling Johnny Fontane into bedrooms for a little chat and Johnny kept getting drunker and drunker.

Meanwhile the woman who had won the award for the best actress was suffering the same fate but loving it more and handling it better. Nino turned her down, the only man at the party to do so.

Finally somebody had a great idea. The public mating of the two winners, everybody else at the party to be spectators in the stands.

The actress was stripped down and the other women started to undress Johnny Fontane. It was then that Nino, the only sober person there, grabbed the half-clothed Johnny and slung him over his shoulder and fought his way out of the house and to their car. As he drove Johnny home, Nino thought that if that was success, he didn't want it.

Book III

Chapter

><><><><><><><><><><><><><><><><><

14

THE Don was a real man at the age of twelve. Short, dark, slender, living in the strange Moorish-looking village of Corleone in Sicily, he had been born Vito Andolini, but when strange men came to kill the son of the man they had murdered, his mother sent the young boy to America to stay with friends. And in the new land he changed his name to Corleone to preserve some tie with his native village. It was one of the few gestures of sentiment he was ever to make.

In Sicily at the turn of the century the Mafia was the second government, far more powerful than the official one in Rome. Vito Corleone's father became involved in a feud with another villager who took his case to the Mafia. The father refused to knuckle under and in a public quarrel killed the local Mafia chief. A week later he himself was found dead, his body torn apart by *lupara* blasts. A month after the funeral Mafia gunmen came inquiring after the young boy, Vito. They had decided that he was too close to manhood, that he might try to avenge the death of his father in the years to come. The twelve-year-old Vito was hidden by relatives and shipped to America. There he was boarded with the Abbandandos, whose son Genco was later to become *Consigliori* to his Don.

Young Vito went to work in the Abbandando grocery store on

Ninth Avenue in New York's Hell's Kitchen. At the age of eighteen Vito married an Italian girl freshly arrived from Sicily, a girl of only sixteen but a skilled cook, a good housewife. They settled down in a tenement on Tenth Avenue, near 35th Street, only a few blocks from where Vito worked, and two years later were blessed with their first child, Santino, called by all his friends Sonny because of his devotion to his father.

In the neighborhood lived a man called Fanucci. He was a heavy-set, fierce-looking Italian who wore expensive light-colored suits and a cream-colored fedora. This man was reputed to be of the "Black Hand," an offshoot of the Mafia which extorted money from families and storekeepers by threat of physical violence. However, since most of the inhabitants of the neighborhood were violent themselves, Fanucci's threats of bodily harm were effective only with elderly couples without male children to defend them. Some of the store-keepers paid him trifling sums as a matter of convenience. However, Fanucci was also a scavenger on fellow criminals, people who illegally sold Italian lottery or ran gambling games in their homes. The Abbandando grocery gave him a small tribute, this despite the protests of young Genco, who told his father he would settle the Fanucci hash. His father forbade him. Vito Corleone observed all this without feeling in any way involved.

One day Fanucci was set upon by three young men who cut his throat from ear to ear, not deeply enough to kill him, but enough to frighten him and make him bleed a great deal. Vito saw Fanucci fleeing from his punishers, the circular slash flowing red. What he never forgot was Fanucci holding the cream-colored fedora under his chin to catch the dripping blood as he ran. As if he did not want his suit soiled or did not want to leave a shameful trail of carmine.

But this attack proved a blessing in disguise for Fanucci. The three young men were not murderers, merely tough young boys deter-mined to teach him a lesson and stop him from scavenging. Fanucci proved himself a murderer. A few weeks later the knife-wielder was shot to death and the families of the other two young men paid an indemnity to Fanucci to make him forswear his vengeance. After that the tributes became higher and Fanucci became a partner in the neighborhood gambling games. As for Vito Corleone, it was none of his affair. He forgot about it immediately.

During World War I, when imported olive oil became scarce,

Fanucci acquired a part-interest in the Abbandando grocery store by supplying it not only with oil, but imported Italian salami, hams and cheeses. He then moved a nephew into the store and Vito Corleone found himself out of a job.

By this time, the second child, Frederico, had arrived and Vito Corleone had four mouths to feed. Up to this time he had been a quiet, very contained young man who kept his thoughts to himself. The son of the grocery store owner, young Genco Abbandando, was his closest friend, and to the surprise of both of them, Vito reproached his friend for his father's deed. Genco, flushed with shame, vowed to Vito that he would not have to worry about food. That he, Genco, would steal food from the grocery to supply his friend's needs. This offer though was sternly refused by Vito as too shameful, a son stealing from his father.

The young Vito, however, felt a cold anger for the dreaded Fanucci. He never showed this anger in any way but bided his time. He worked in the railroad for a few months and then, when the war ended, work became slow and he could earn only a few days' pay a month. Also, most of the foremen were Irish and American and abused the workmen in the foulest language, which Vito always bore stone-faced as if he did not comprehend, though he understood English very well despite his accent.

One evening as Vito was having supper with his family there was a knock on the window that led to the open air shaft that separated them from the next building. When Vito pulled aside the curtain he saw to his astonishment one of the young men in the neighborhood, Peter Clemenza, leaning out from a window on the other side of the air shaft. He was extending a white-sheeted bundle.

"Hey, *paisan*," Clemenza said. "Hold these for me until I ask for them. Hurry up." Automatically Vito reached over the empty space of the air shaft and took the bundle. Clemenza's face was strained and urgent. He was in some sort of trouble and Vito's helping action was instinctive. But when he untied the bundle in his kitchen, there were five oily guns staining the white cloth. He put them in his bedroom closet and waited. He learned that Clemenza had been taken away by the police. They must have been knocking on his door when he handed the guns over the air shaft.

Vito never said a word to anyone and of course his terrified wife dared not open her lips even in gossip for fear her own husband would be sent to prison. Two days later Peter Clemenza reappeared in the neighborhood and asked Vito casually, "Do you have my goods still?"

Vito nodded. He was in the habit of talking little. Clemenza came up to his tenement flat and was given a glass of wine while Vito dug the bundle out of his bedroom closet.

Clemenza drank his wine, his heavy good-natured face alertly watching Vito. "Did you look inside?"

Vito, his face impassive, shook his head. "I'm not interested in things that don't concern me," he said.

They drank wine together the rest of the evening. They found each other congenial. Clemenza was a storyteller; Vito Corleone was a listener to storytellers. They became casual friends.

A few days later Clemenza asked the wife of Vito Corleone if she would like a fine rug for her living room floor. He took Vito with him to help carry the rug.

Clemenza led Vito to an apartment house with two marble pillars and a white marble stoop. He used a key to open the door and they were inside a plush apartment. Clemenza grunted, "Go on the other side of the room and help me roll it up."

The rug was a rich red wool. Vito Corleone was astonished by Clemenza's generosity. Together they rolled the rug into a pile and Clemenza took one end while Vito took the other. They lifted it and started carrying it toward the door.

At that moment the apartment bell rang. Clemenza immediately dropped the rug and strode to the window. He pulled the drape aside slightly and what he saw made him draw a gun from inside his jacket. It was only at that moment the astonished Vito Corleone realized that they were stealing the rug from some stranger's apartment.

The apartment bell rang again. Vito went up alongside Clemenza so that he too could see what was happening. At the door was a uniformed policeman. As they watched, the policeman gave the doorbell a final push, then shrugged and walked away down the marble steps and down the street.

Clemenza grunted in a satisfied way and said, "Come on, let's go." He picked up his end of the rug and Vito picked up the other end. The policeman had barely turned the corner before they were edging out the heavy oaken door and into the street with the rug between them. Thirty minutes later they were cutting the rug to fit the living room of Vito Corleone's apartment. They had enough left over for the bedroom. Clemenza was an expert workman and from the pockets of his wide, ill-fitting jacket (even then he liked to wear loose clothes though he was not so fat), he had the necessary carpet-cutting tools.

Time went on, things did not improve. The Corleone family could not eat the beautiful rug. Very well, there was no work, his wife and children must starve. Vito took some parcels of food from his friend Genco while he thought things out. Finally he was approached by Clemenza and Tessio, another young tough of the neighborhood. They were men who thought well of him, the way he carried himself, and they knew he was desperate. They proposed to him that he become one of their gang which specialized in hijacking trucks of silk dresses after those trucks were loaded up at the factory on 31st Street. There was no risk. The truck drivers were sensible working-men who at the sight of a gun flopped on the sidewalk like angels while the hijackers drove the truck away to be unloaded at a friend's warehouse. Some of the merchandise would be sold to an Italian wholesaler, part of the loot would be sold door-to-door in the Italian neighborhoods—Arthur Avenue in the Bronx, Mulberry Street, and the Chelsea district in Manhattan—all to poor Italian families looking for a bargain, whose daughters could never be able to afford such fine apparel. Clemenza and Tessio needed Vito to drive since they knew he chauffeured the Abbandando grocery store delivery truck. In 1919, skilled automobile drivers were at a premium.

Against his better judgment, Vito Corleone accepted their offer. The clinching argument was that he would clear at least a thousand dollars for his share of the job. But his young companions struck him as rash, the planning of the job haphazard, the distribution of the loot foolhardy. Their whole approach was too careless for his taste. But he thought them of good, sound character. Peter Clemenza, already burly, inspired a certain trust, and the lean saturnine Tessio inspired confidence.

The job itself went off without a hitch. Vito Corleone felt no fear, much to his astonishment, when his two comrades flashed guns and made the driver get out of the silk truck. He was also impressed with the coolness of Clemenza and Tessio. They didn't get excited but joked with the driver, told him if he was a good lad they'd send his wife a few dresses. Because Vito thought it stupid to peddle dresses himself and so gave his whole share of stock to the fence, he made only seven hundred dollars. But this was a considerable sum of money in 1919.

The next day on the street, Vito Corleone was stopped by the cream-suited, white-fedoraed Fanucci. Fanucci was a brutal-looking man and he had done nothing to disguise the circular scar that stretched in a white semicircle from ear to ear, looping under his chin. He had heavy black brows and coarse features which, when he smiled, were in some odd way amiable.

He spoke with a very thick Sicilian accent. "Ah, young fellow," he said to Vito. "People tell me you're rich. You and your two friends. But don't you think you've treated me a little shabbily? After all, this is my neighborhood and you should let me wet my beak." He used the Sicilian phrase of the Mafia, "Fari vagnari a pizzu." Pizzu means the beak of any small bird such as a canary. The phrase itself was a demand for part of the loot.

As was his habit, Vito Corleone did not answer. He understood the implication immediately and was waiting for a definite demand.

Fanucci smiled at him, showing gold teeth and stretching his noose-like scar tight around his face. He mopped his face with a handkerchief and unbuttoned his jacket for a moment as if to cool himself but really to show the gun he carried stuck in the waistband of his comfortably wide trousers. Then he sighed and said, "Give me five hundred dollars and I'll forget the insult. After all, young people don't know the courtesies due a man like myself."

Vito Corleone smiled at him and even as a young man still unblooded, there was something so chilling in his smile that Fanucci hesitated a moment before going on. "Otherwise the police will come to see you, your wife and children will be shamed and destitute. Of course if my information as to your gains is incorrect I'll dip my beak just a little. But no less than three hundred dollars. And don't try to deceive me."

For the first time Vito Corleone spoke. His voice was reasonable, showed no anger. It was courteous, as befitted a young man speaking to an older man of Fanucci's eminence. He said softly, "My two friends have my share of the money, I'll have to speak to them."

Fanucci was reassured. "You can tell your two friends that I expect them to let me wet my beak in the same manner. Don't be afraid to tell them," he added reassuringly. "Clemenza and I know each other well, he understands these things. Let yourself be guided by him. He has more experience in these matters."

Vito Corleone shrugged. He tried to look a little embarrassed. "Of course," he said. "You understand this is all new to me. Thank you for speaking to me as a godfather."

Fanucci was impressed. "You're a good fellow," he said. He took Vito's hand and clasped it in both of his hairy ones. "You have respect," he said. "A fine thing in the young. Next time speak to me first, eh? Perhaps I can help you in your plans."

In later years Vito Corleone understood that what had made him act in such a perfect, tactical way with Fanucci was the death of his own hot-tempered father who had been killed by the Mafia in Sicily. But at that time all he felt was an icy rage that this man planned to rob him of the money he had risked his life and freedom to earn. He had not been afraid. Indeed he thought, at that moment, that Fanucci was a crazy fool. From what he had seen of Clemenza, that burly Sicilian would sooner give up his life than a penny of his loot. After all, Clemenza had been ready to kill a policeman merely to steal a rug. And the slender Tessio had the deadly air of a viper.

But later that night, in Clemenza's tenement apartment across the air shaft, Vito Corleone received another lesson in the education he had just begun. Clemenza cursed, Tessio scowled, but then both men started talking about whether Fanucci would be satisfied with two hundred dollars. Tessio thought he might.

Clemenza was positive. "No, that scarface bastard must have found out what we made from the wholesaler who bought the dresses. Fanucci won't take a dime less than three hundred dollars. We'll have to pay."

Vito was astonished but was careful not to show his astonishment. "Why do we have to pay him? What can he do to the three of us? We're stronger than him. We have guns. Why do we have to hand over the money we earned?"

Clemenza explained patiently. "Fanucci has friends, real brutes. He has connections with the police. He'd like us to tell him our plans because he could set us up for the cops and earn their gratitude. Then they would owe him a favor. That's how he operates. And he has a license from Maranzalla himself to work this neighborhood." Maranzalla was a gangster often in the newspapers, reputed to be the leader of a criminal ring specializing in extortion, gambling and armed robbery.

Clemenza served wine that he had made himself. His wife, after putting a plate of salami, olives and a loaf of Italian bread on the table, went down to sit with her women cronies in front of the building, carrying her chair with her. She was a young Italian girl only a few years in the country and did not yet understand English.

Vito Corleone sat with his two friends and drank wine. He had never used his intelligence before as he was using it now. He was surprised at how clearly he could think. He recalled everything he knew about Fanucci. He remembered the day the man had had his throat cut and had run down the street holding his fedora under his chin to catch the dripping blood. He remembered the murder of the man who had wielded the knife and the other two having their sentences removed by paying an indemnity. And suddenly he was sure that Fanucci had no great connections, could not possibly have. Not a man who informed to the police. Not a man who allowed his vengeance to be bought off. A real *Mafioso* chief would have had the other two men killed also. No. Fanucci had got lucky and killed one man but had known he could not kill the other two after they were alerted. And so he had allowed himself to be paid. It was the personal brutal force of the man that allowed him to levy tribute on the shopkeepers, the gambling games that ran in the tenement apartments. But Vito Corleone knew of at least one gambling game that had never paid Fanucci tributes and nothing had ever happened to the man running it.

And so it was Fanucci alone. Or Fanucci with some gunmen hired for special jobs on a strictly cash basis. Which left Vito Corleone with another decision. The course his own life must take.

It was from this experience came his oft-repeated belief that every man has but one destiny. On that night he could have paid Fanucci the tribute and have become again a grocery clerk with perhaps his own grocery store in the years to come. But destiny had decided that he was to become a Don and had brought Fanucci to him to set him on his destined path.

When they finished the bottle of wine, Vito said cautiously to Clemenza and Tessio, "If you like, why not give me two hundred dollars each to pay to Fanucci? I guarantee he will accept that amount from me. Then leave everything in my hands. I'll settle this problem to your satisfaction."

At once Clemenza's eyes gleamed with suspicion. Vito said to him coldly, "I never lie to people I have accepted as my friends. Speak to Fanucci yourself tomorrow. Let him ask you for the money. But don't pay him. And don't in any way quarrel with him. Tell him you have to get the money and will give it to me to give him. Let him understand that you are willing to pay what he asks. Don't bargain. I'll quarrel over the price with him. There's no point making him angry with us if he's as dangerous a man as you say he is."

They left it at that. The next day Clemenza spoke with Fanucci to make sure that Vito was not making up the story. Then Clemenza came to Vito's apartment and gave him the two hundred dollars. He peered at Vito Corleone and said, "Fanucci told me nothing below three hundred dollars, how will you make him take less?"

Vito Corleone said reasonably, "Surely that's no concern of yours. Just remember that I've done you a service."

Tessio came later. Tessio was more reserved than Clemenza, sharper, more clever but with less force. He sensed something amiss, something not quite right. He was a little worried. He said to Vito Corleone, "Watch yourself with that bastard of a Black Hand, he's tricky as a priest. Do you want me to be here when you hand him the money, as a witness?"

Vito Corleone shook his head. He didn't even bother to answer. He merely said to Tessio, "Tell Fanucci I'll pay him the money here in my house at nine o'clock tonight. I'll have to give him a glass of wine and talk, reason with him to take the lesser sum."

Tessio shook his head. "You won't have much luck. Fanucci never retreats."

"I'll reason with him," Vito Corleone said. It was to become a famous phrase in the years to come. It was to become the warning rattle before a deadly strike. When he became a Don and asked opponents to sit down and reason with him, they understood it was the last chance to resolve an affair without bloodshed and murder.

Vito Corleone told his wife to take the two children, Sonny and Fredo, down into the street after supper and on no account to let them come up to the house until he gave her permission. She was to sit on guard at the tenement door. He had some private business with Fanucci that could not be interrupted. He saw the look of fear on her face and was angry. He said to her quietly, "Do you think you've married a fool?" She didn't answer. She did not answer because she was frightened, not of Fanucci now, but of her husband. He was changing visibly before her eyes, hour by hour, into a man who radiated some dangerous force. He had always been quiet, speaking little, but always gentle, always reasonable, which was extraordinary in a young Sicilian male. What she was seeing was the shedding of his protective coloration of a harmless nobody now that he was ready to start on his destiny. He had started late, he was twenty-five years old, but he was to start with a flourish.

Vito Corleone had decided to murder Fanucci. By doing so he would have an extra seven hundred dollars in his bankroll. The three hundred dollars he himself would have to pay the Black Hand terrorist and the two hundred dollars from Tessio and the two hundred dollars from Clemenza. If he did not kill Fanucci, he would have to pay the man seven hundred dollars cold cash. Fanucci alive was not worth seven hundred dollars to him. He would not pay seven hundred dollars to keep Fanucci alive. If Fanucci needed seven hundred dollars for an operation to save his life, he would not give Fanucci seven hundred dollars for the surgeon. He owed Fanucci no personal debt of gratitude, they were not blood relatives, he did not love Fanucci. Whyfore, then, should he give Fanucci seven hundred dollars?

And it followed inevitably, that since Fanucci wished to take seven hundred dollars from him by force, why should he not kill Fanucci? Surely the world could do without such a person.

There were of course some practical reasons. Fanucci might indeed have powerful friends who would seek vengeance. Fanucci himself was a dangerous man, not so easily killed. There were the police and the electric chair. But Vito Corleone had lived under a sentence of death since the murder of his father. As a boy of twelve he had fled his executioners and crossed the ocean into a strange land, taking a strange name. And years of quiet observation had convinced him that he had more intelligence and more courage than other men, though he had never had the opportunity to use that intelligence and courage.

And yet he hesitated before taking that first step toward his destiny. He even packed the seven hundred dollars in a single fold of bills and put the money in a convenient side pocket of his trousers. But he put the money in the left side of his trousers. In the right-hand pocket he put the gun Clemenza had given him to use in the hijacking of the silk truck.

Fanucci came promptly at nine in the evening. Vito Corleone set out a jug of homemade wine that Clemenza had given him.

Fanucci put his white fedora on the table beside the jug of wine. He unloosened his broad multiflowered tie, its tomato stains camouflaged by the bright patterns. The summer night was hot, the gaslight feeble. It was very quiet in the apartment. But Vito Corleone was icy.

To show his good faith he handed over the roll of bills and watched carefully as Fanucci, after counting it, took out a wide leather wallet and stuffed the money inside. Fanucci sipped his glass of wine and said, "You still owe me two hundred dollars." His heavy-browed face was expressionless.

Vito Corleone said in his cool reasonable voice, "I'm a little short, I've been out of work. Let me owe you the money for a few weeks."

This was a permissible gambit. Fanucci had the bulk of the money and would wait. He might even be persuaded to take nothing more or to wait a little longer. He chuckled over his wine and said, "Ah, you're a sharp young fellow. How is it I've never noticed you before? You're too quiet a chap for your own interest. I could find some work for you to do that would be very profitable."

Vito Corleone showed his interest with a polite nod and filled up the man's glass from the purple jug. But Fanucci thought better of what he was going to say and rose from his chair and shook Vito's hand. "Good night, young fellow," he said. "No hard feelings, eh? If I can ever do you a service let me know. You've done a good job for yourself tonight."

Vito let Fanucci go down the stairs and out the building. The street was thronged with witnesses to show that he had left the Corleone home safely. Vito watched from the window. He saw Fanucci turn the corner toward 11th Avenue and knew he was headed toward his apartment, probably to put away his loot before coming out on the streets again. Perhaps to put away his gun. Vito Corleone left his apartment and ran up the stairs to the roof. He traveled over the square block of roofs and descended down the steps of an empty loft building fire escape that left him in the back yard. He kicked the back door open and went through the front door. Across the street was Fanucci's tenement apartment house.

The village of tenements extended only as far west as Tenth Avenue. Eleventh Avenue was mostly warehouses and lofts rented by firms who shipped by New York Central Railroad and wanted access to the freight yards that honeycombed the area from Eleventh Avenue to the Hudson River. Fanucci's apartment house was one of the few left standing in this wilderness and was occupied mostly by bachelor trainmen, yard workers, and the cheapest prostitutes. These people did not sit in the street and gossip like honest Italians, they sat in beer taverns guzzling their pay. So Vito Corleone found it an easy matter to slip across the deserted Eleventh Avenue and into the vestibule of

Fanucci's apartment house. There he drew the gun he had never fired and waited for Fanucci.

He watched through the glass door of the vestibule, knowing Fanucci would come down from Tenth Avenue. Clemenza had showed him the safety on the gun and he had triggered it empty. But as a young boy in Sicily at the early age of nine, he had often gone hunting with his father, had often fired the heavy shotgun called the *lupara*. It was his skill with the *lupara* even as a small boy that had brought the sentence of death upon him by his father's murderers.

Now waiting in the darkened hallway, he saw the white blob of Fanucci crossing the street toward the doorway. Vito stepped back, shoulders pressed against the inner door that led to the stairs. He held his gun out to fire. His extended hand was only two paces from the outside door. The door swung in. Fanucci, white, broad, smelly, filled the square of light. Vito Corleone fired.

The opened door let some of the sound escape into the street, the rest of the gun's explosion shook the building. Fanucci was holding on to the sides of the door, trying to stand erect, trying to reach for his gun. The force of his struggle had torn the buttons off his jacket and made it swing loose. His gun was exposed but so was a spidery vein of red on the white shirtfront of his stomach. Very carefully, as if he were plunging a needle into a vein, Vito Corleone fired his second bullet into that red web.

Fanucci fell to his knees, propping the door open. He let out a terrible groan, the groan of a man in great physical distress that was almost comical. He kept giving these groans; Vito remembered hearing at least three of them before he put the gun against Fanucci's sweaty, suety cheek and fired into his brain. No more than five seconds had passed when Fanucci slumped into death, jamming the door open with his body.

Very carefully Vito took the wide wallet out of the dead man's jacket pocket and put it inside his shirt. Then he walked across the street into the loft building, through that into the yard and climbed the fire escape to the roof. From there he surveyed the street. Fanucci's body was still lying in the doorway but there was no sign of any other person. Two windows had gone up in the tenement and he could see dark heads poked out but since he could not see their features they had certainly not seen his. And such men would not give information to the police. Fanucci might lie there until dawn or until a patrolman making the rounds stumbled on his body. No person in that house would deliberately expose himself to police suspicion or questioning. They would lock their doors and pretend they had heard nothing.

He could take his time. He traveled over the rooftops to his own roof door and down to his own flat. He unlocked the door, went inside and then locked the door behind him. He rifled the dead man's wallet. Besides the seven hundred dollars he had given Fanucci there were only some singles and a five-dollar note.

Tucked inside the flap was an old five-dollar gold piece, probably a luck token. If Fanucci was a rich gangster, he certainly did not carry his wealth with him. This confirmed some of Vito's suspicions.

He knew he had to get rid of the wallet and the gun (knowing enough even then that he must leave the gold piece in the wallet). He went up on the roof again and traveled over a few ledges. He threw the wallet down one air shaft and then he emptied the gun of bullets and smashed its barrel against the roof ledge. The barrel wouldn't break. He reversed it in his hand and smashed the butt against the side of a chimney. The butt split into two halves. He smashed it again and the pistol broke into barrel and handle, two separate pieces. He used a separate air shaft for each. They made no sound when they struck the earth five stories below, but sank into the soft hill of garbage that had accumulated there. In the morning more garbage would be thrown out of the windows and, with luck, would cover everything. Vito returned to his apartment.

He was trembling a little but was absolutely under control. He changed his clothes and fearful that some blood might have splattered on them, he threw them into a metal tub his wife used for washing. He took lye and heavy brown laundry soap to soak the clothes and scrubbed them with the metal wash board beneath the sink. Then he scoured tub and sink with lye and soap. He found a bundle of newly washed clothes in the corner of the bedroom and mingled his own clothes with these. Then he put on a fresh shirt and trousers and went down to join his wife and children and neighbors in front of the tenement.

All these precautions proved to be unnecessary. The police, after discovering the dead body at dawn, never questioned Vito Corleone. Indeed he was astonished that they never learned about Fanucci's visit to his home on the night he was shot to death. He had counted on that for an alibi, Fanucci leaving the tenement alive. He only learned later that the police had been delighted with the murder of

Fanucci and not too anxious to pursue his killers. They had assumed it was another gang execution, and had questioned hoodlums with records in the rackets and a history of strong-arm. Since Vito had never been in trouble he never came into the picture.

But if he had outwitted the police, his partners were another matter. Pete Clemenza and Tessio avoided him for the next week, for the next two weeks, then they came to call on him one evening. They came with obvious respect. Vito Corleone greeted them with impassive courtesy and served them wine.

Clemenza spoke first. He said softly, "Nobody is collecting from the store owners on Ninth Avenue. Nobody is collecting from the card games and gambling in the neighborhood."

Vito Corleone gazed at both men steadily but did not reply. Tessio spoke. "We could take over Fanucci's customers. They would pay us."

Vito Corleone shrugged. "Why come to me? I have no interest in such things."

Clemenza laughed. Even in his youth, before growing his enormous belly, he had a fat man's laugh. He said now to Vito Corleone, "How about that gun I gave you for the truck job? Since you won't need it any more you can give it back to me."

Very slowly and deliberately Vito Corleone took a wad of bills out of his side pocket and peeled off five tens. "Here, I'll pay you. I threw the gun away after the truck job." He smiled at the two men.

At that time Vito Corleone did not know the effect of this smile. It was chilling because it attempted no menace. He smiled as if it was some private joke only he himself could appreciate. But since he smiled in that fashion only in affairs that were lethal, and since the joke was not really private and since his eyes did not smile, and since his outward character was usually so reasonable and quiet, the sudden unmasking of his true self was frightening.

Clemenza shook his head. "I don't want the money," he said. Vito pocketed the bills. He waited. They all understood each other. They knew he had killed Fanucci and though they never spoke about it to anyone the whole neighborhood, within a few weeks, also knew. Vito Corleone was treated as a "man of respect" by everyone. But he made no attempt to take over the Fanucci rackets and tributes.

What followed then was inevitable. One night Vito's wife brought a neighbor, a widow, to the flat. The woman was Italian and of unimpeachable character. She worked hard to keep a home for her fatherless children. Her sixteen-year-old son brought home his pay envelope sealed, to hand over to her in the old-country style; her seventeen-year-old daughter, a dressmaker, did the same. The whole family sewed buttons on cards at night at slave labor piece rates. The woman's name was Signora Colombo.

Vito Corleone's wife said, "The Signora has a favor to ask of you. She is having some trouble."

Vito Corleone expected to be asked for money, which he was ready to give. But it seemed that Mrs. Colombo owned a dog which her youngest son adored. The landlord had received complaints on the dog barking at night and had told Mrs. Colombo to get rid of it. She had pretended to do so. The landlord had found out that she had deceived him and had ordered her to vacate her apartment. She had promised this time to truly get rid of the dog and she had done so. But the landlord was so angry that he would not revoke his order. She had to get out or the police would be summoned to put her out. And her poor little boy had cried so when they had given the dog away to relatives who lived in Long Island. All for nothing, they would lose their home.

Vito Corleone asked her gently, "Why do you ask me to help you?"

Mrs. Colombo nodded toward his wife. "She told me to ask you."

He was surprised. His wife had never questioned him about the clothes he had washed the night he had murdered Fanucci. Had never asked him where all the money came from when he was not working. Even now her face was impassive. Vito said to Mrs. Colombo, "I can give you some money to help you move, is that what you want?"

The woman shook her head, she was in tears. "All my friends are here, all the girls I grew up with in Italy. How can I move to another neighborhood with strangers? I want you to speak to the landlord to let me stay."

Vito nodded. "It's done then. You won't have to move. I'll speak to him tomorrow morning."

His wife gave him a smile which he did not acknowledge, but he felt pleased. Mrs. Colombo looked a little uncertain. "You're sure he'll say yes, the landlord?" she asked.

"Signor Roberto?" Vito said in a surprised voice. "Of course he will. He's a good-hearted fellow. Once I explain how things are with you he'll take pity on your misfortunes. Now don't let it trouble you any more. Don't get so upset. Guard your health, for the sake of your children."

The landlord, Mr. Roberto, came to the neighborhood every day to check on the row of five tenements that he owned. He was a *padrone*, a man who sold Italian laborers just off the boat to the big corporations. With his profits he had bought the tenements one by one. An educated man from the North of Italy, he felt only contempt for these illiterate Southerners from Sicily and Naples who swarmed like vermin through his buildings, who threw garbage down the air shafts, who let cockroaches and rats eat away his walls without lifting a hand to preserve his property. He was not a bad man, he was a good husband and father, but constant worry about his investments, about the money he earned, about the inevitable expenses that came with being a man of property had worn his nerves to a frazzle so that he was in a constant state of irritation. When Vito Corleone stopped him on the street to ask for a word, Mr. Roberto was brusque. Not rude, since any one of these Southerners might stick a knife into you if rubbed the wrong way, though this young man looked like a quiet fellow.

"Signor Roberto," said Vito Corleone, "the friend of my wife, a poor widow with no man to protect her, tells me that for some reason she has been ordered to move from her apartment in your building. She is in despair. She has no money, she has no friends except those that live here. I told her that I would speak to you, that you are a reasonable man who acted out of some misunderstanding. She has gotten rid of the animal that caused all the trouble and so why shouldn't she stay? As one Italian to another, I ask you the favor."

Signor Roberto studied the young man in front of him. He saw a man of medium stature but strongly built, a peasant but not a bandit, though he so laughably dared to call himself an Italian. Roberto shrugged. "I have already rented the apartment to another family for higher rent," he said. "I cannot disappoint them for the sake of your friend."

Vito Corleone nodded in agreeable understanding. "How much more a month?" he asked.

"Five dollars," Mr. Roberto said. This was a lie. The railway flat, four dark rooms, rented for twelve dollars a month to the widow and he had not been able to get more than that from the new tenant.

Vito Corleone took a roll of bills out of his pocket and peeled off three tens. "Here is the six months' increase in advance. You needn't speak to her about it, she's a proud woman. See me again in another six months. But of course you'll let her keep her dog."

"Like hell," Mr. Roberto said. "And who the hell are you to give me orders. Watch your manners or you'll be out on your Sicilian ass in the street there."

Vito Corleone raised his hands in surprise. "I'm asking you a favor, only that. One never knows when one might need a friend, isn't that true? Here, take this money as a sign of my goodwill and make your own decision. I wouldn't dare to quarrel with it." He thrust the money into Mr. Roberto's hand. "Do me this little favor, just take the money and think things over. Tomorrow morning if you want to give me the money back by all means do so. If you want the woman out of your house, how can I stop you? It's your property, after all. If you don't want the dog in there, I can understand. I dislike animals myself." He patted Mr. Roberto on the shoulder. "Do me this service, eh? I won't forget it. Ask your friends in the neighborhood about me, they'll tell you I'm a man who believes in showing his gratitude."

But of course Mr. Roberto had already begun to understand. That evening he made inquiries about Vito Corleone. He did not wait until the next morning. He knocked on the Corleone door that very night, apologizing for the lateness of the hour and accepted a glass of wine from Signora Corleone. He assured Vito Corleone that it had all been a dreadful misunderstanding, that of course Signora Colombo could remain in the flat, of course she could keep her dog. Who were those miserable tenants to complain about noise from a poor animal when they paid such a low rent? At the finish he threw the thirty dollars Vito Corleone had given him on the table and said in the most sincere fashion, "Your good heart in helping this poor widow has shamed me and I wish to show that I, too, have some Christian charity. Her rent will remain what it was."

All concerned played this comedy prettily. Vito poured wine, called for cakes, wrung Mr. Roberto's hand and praised his warm heart. Mr. Roberto sighed and said that having made the acquaintance of such a man as Vito Corleone restored his faith in human nature. Finally they tore themselves away from each other. Mr. Roberto, his bones turned to jelly with fear at his narrow escape, caught the streetcar to his home in the Bronx and took to his bed. He did not reappear in his tenements for three days.

Vito Corleone was now a "man of respect" in the neighborhood. He was reputed to be a member of the Mafia of Sicily. One day a man who ran card games in a furnished room came to him and voluntarily paid him twenty dollars each week for his "friendship." He had only to visit the game once or twice a week to let the players understand they were under his protection.

Store owners who had problems with young hoodlums asked him to intercede. He did so and was properly rewarded. Soon he had the enormous income for that time and place of one hundred dollars a week. Since Clemenza and Tessio were his friends, his allies, he had to give them each part of the money, but this he did without being asked. Finally he decided to go into the olive oil importing business with his boyhood chum, Genco Abbandando. Genco would handle the business, the importing of the olive oil from Italy, the buying at the proper price, the storing in his father's warehouse. Genco had the experience for this part of the business. Clemenza and Tessio would be the salesmen. They would go to every Italian grocery store in Manhattan, then Brooklyn, then the Bronx, to persuade store owners to stock *Genco Pura* olive oil. (With typical modesty, Vito Corleone refused to name the brand after himself.) Vito of course would be the head of the firm since he was supplying most of the capital. He also would be called in on special cases, where store owners resisted the sales talks of Clemenza and Tessio. Then Vito Corleone would use his own formidable powers of persuasion.

For the next few years Vito Corleone lived that completely satisfying life of a small businessman wholly devoted to building up his commercial enterprise in a dynamic, expanding economy. He was a devoted father and husband but so busy he could spare his family little of his time. As *Genco Pura* olive oil grew to become the best-selling imported Italian oil in America, his organization mushroomed. Like any good businessman he came to understand the benefits of undercutting his rivals in price, barring them from distribution outlets by persuading store owners to stock less of their brands. Like any good businessman he aimed at holding a monopoly by forcing his rivals to abandon the field or by merging with his own company. However, since he had started off relatively helpless, economically, since he did not believe in advertising, relying on word of mouth, and since if truth be told, his olive oil was no better than his competitors', he could not use the common strangleholds of legitimate businessmen. He had to rely on the force of his own personality and his reputation as a "man of respect."

Even as a young man, Vito Corleone became known as a "man of reasonableness." He never uttered a threat. He always used logic that proved to be irresistible. He always made certain that the other fellow got his share of profit. Nobody lost. He did this, of course, by obvious means. Like many businessmen of genius he learned that free competition was wasteful, monopoly efficient. And so he simply set about achieving that efficient monopoly. There were some oil wholesalers in Brooklyn, men of fiery temper, headstrong, not amenable to reason, who refused to see, to recognize, the vision of Vito Corleone, even after he had explained everything to them with the utmost patience and detail. With these men Vito Corleone threw up his hands in despair and sent Tessio to Brooklyn to set up a headquarters and solve the problem. Warehouses were burned, truckloads of olive-green oil were dumped to form lakes in the cobbled waterfront streets. One rash man, an arrogant Milanese with more faith in the police than a saint has in Christ, actually went to the authorities with a complaint against his fellow Italians, breaking the ten-century-old law of *omerta*. But before the matter could progress any further the wholesaler disappeared, never to be seen again, leaving behind, deserted, his devoted wife and three children, who, God be thanked, were fully grown and capable of taking over his business and coming to terms with the *Genco Pura* Oil Company.

But great men are not born great, they grow great, and so it was with Vito Corleone. When Prohibition came to pass and alcohol forbidden to be sold, Vito Corleone made the final step from a quite ordinary, somewhat ruthless businessman to a great Don in the world of criminal enterprise. It did not happen in a day, it did not happen in a year, but by the end of the Prohibition period and the start of the Great Depression, Vito Corleone had become the Godfather, the Don, Don Corleone.

It started casually enough. By this time the *Genco Pura* Oil Company had a fleet of six delivery trucks. Through Clemenza, Vito Corleone was approached by a group of Italian bootleggers who smuggled alcohol and whiskey in from Canada. They needed trucks and deliverymen to distribute their produce over New York City. They needed deliverymen who were reliable, discreet and of a certain determination and force. They were willing to pay Vito Corleone for his trucks and for his men. The fee was so enormous that Vito Corleone cut back drastically on his oil business to use the trucks almost exclusively for the service of the bootlegger-smugglers. This despite the fact that these gentlemen had accompanied their offer with a silky threat. But even then Vito Corleone was so mature a man that he did not take insult at a threat or become angry and refuse a profitable offer because of it. He evaluated the threat, found it lacking in conviction, and lowered his opinion of his new partners because they had been so stupid to use threats where none were needed. This was useful information to be pondered at its proper time.

Again he prospered. But, more important, he acquired knowledge and contacts and experience. And he piled up good deeds as a banker piles up securities. For in the following years it became clear that Vito Corleone was not only a man of talent but, in his way, a genius.

He made himself the protector of the Italian families who set themselves up as small speakeasies in their homes, selling whiskey at fifteen cents a glass to bachelor laborers. He became godfather to Mrs. Colombo's youngest son when the lad made his confirmation and gave a handsome present of a twenty-dollar gold piece. Meanwhile, since it was inevitable that some of his trucks be stopped by the police, Genco Abbandando hired a fine lawyer with many contacts in the Police Department and the judiciary. A system of payoffs was set up and soon the Corleone organization had a sizable "sheet," the list of officials entitled to a monthly sum. When the lawyer tried to keep this list down, apologizing for the expense, Vito Corleone reassured him. "No, no," he said. "Get everyone on it even if they can't help us right now. I believe in friendship and I am willing to show my friendship first."

As time went by the Corleone empire became larger, more trucks were added, the "sheet" grew longer. Also the men working directly for Tessio and Clemenza grew in number. The whole thing was becoming unwieldy. Finally Vito Corleone worked out a system of organization. He gave Clemenza and Tessio each the title of *Caporegime*, or captain, and the men who worked beneath them the rank of soldier. He named Genco Abbandando his counselor, or *Consigliori*. He put layers of insulation between himself and any operational act. When he gave an order it was to Genco or to one of the *caporegimes* alone. Rarely did he have a witness to any order he gave any particular one of them. Then he split Tessio's group and made it responsible for Brooklyn. He also split Tessio off from Clemenza and made it clear over the years that he did not want the two men to associate even socially except when absolutely necessary. He explained this to the more intelligent Tessio, who caught his drift immediately, though Vito explained it as a security measure against the law. Tessio understood that Vito did not want his two *caporegimes* to have any opportunity to conspire against him and he also understood there was no ill will involved, merely a tactical precaution. In return Vito gave Tessio a free hand in Brooklyn while he kept Clemenza's Bronx fief very much under his thumb. Clemenza was the braver, more reckless, the crueler man despite his outward jollity, and needed a tighter rein.

The Great Depression increased the power of Vito Corleone. And indeed it was about that time he came to be called Don Corleone. Everywhere in the city, honest men begged for honest work in vain. Proud men demeaned themselves and their families to accept official charity from a contemptuous officialdom. But the men of Don Corleone walked the streets with their heads held high, their pockets stuffed with silver and paper money. With no fear of losing their jobs. And even Don Corleone, that most modest of men, could not help feeling a sense of pride. He was taking care of his world, his people. He had not failed those who depended on him and gave him the sweat of their brows, risked their freedom and their lives in his service. And when an employee of his was arrested and sent to prison by some mischance, that unfortunate man's family received a living allowance; and not a miserly, beggarly, begrudging pittance but the same amount the man earned when free.

This of course was not pure Christian charity. Not his best friends would have called Don Corleone a saint from heaven. There was some self-interest in this generosity. An employee sent to prison knew he had only to keep his mouth shut and his wife and children would be cared for. He knew that if he did not inform to the police a warm welcome would be his when he left prison. There would be a party waiting in his home, the best of food, homemade ravioli, wine, pastries, with all his friends and relatives gathered to rejoice in his freedom. And sometime during the night the *Consigliori*, Genco Abbandando, or perhaps even the Don himself, would drop by to pay his respects to such a stalwart, take a glass of wine in his honor, and leave a handsome present of money so that he could enjoy a week or two of leisure with his family before returning to his daily toil. Such was the infinite sympathy and understanding of Don Corleone.

It was at this time that the Don got the idea that he ran his world far better than his enemies ran the greater world which continually obstructed his path. And this feeling was nurtured by the poor people of the neighborhood who constantly came to him for help. To get on the home relief, to get a young boy a job or out of jail, to borrow a small sum of money desperately needed, to intervene with landlords who against all reason demanded rent from jobless tenants.

Don Vito Corleone helped them all. Not only that, he helped them with goodwill, with encouraging words to take the bitter sting out of the charity he gave them. It was only natural then that when these Italians were puzzled and confused on who to vote for to represent them in the state legislature, in the city offices, in the Congress, they should ask the advice of their friend Don Corleone, their Godfather. And so he became a political power to be consulted by practical party chiefs. He consolidated this power with a far-seeing statesmanlike intelligence; by helping brilliant boys from poor Italian families through college, boys who would later become lawyers, assistant district attorneys, and even judges. He planned for the future of his empire with all the foresight of a great national leader.

The repeal of Prohibition dealt this empire a crippling blow but again he had taken his precautions. In 1933 he sent emissaries to the man who controlled all the gambling activities of Manhattan, the crap games on the docks, the shylocking that went with it as hot dogs go with baseball games, the bookmaking on sports and horses, the illicit gambling houses that ran poker games, the policy or numbers racket of Harlem. This man's name was Salvatore Maranzano and he was one of the acknowledged *pezzonovante*, .90 calibers, or big shots of the New York underworld. The Corleone emissaries proposed to Maranzano an equal partnership beneficial to both parties. Vito Corleone with his organization, his police and political contacts, could give the Maranzano operations a stout umbrella and the new strength to expand into Brooklyn and the Bronx. But Maranzano was a shortsighted man and spurned the Corleone offer with contempt. The great Al Capone was Maranzano's friend and he had his own organization, his own men, plus a huge war chest. He would not brook this upstart whose reputation was more that of a Parliamentary debater than a true *Mafioso*. Maranzano's refusal touched off the great war of 1933 which was to change the whole structure of the underworld in New York City.

At first glance it seemed an uneven match. Salvatore Maranzano had a powerful organization with strong enforcers. He had a friendship with Capone in Chicago and could call on help in that quarter. He also had a good relationship with the Tattaglia Family, which controlled prostitution in the city and what there was of the thin drug traffic at that time. He also had political contacts with powerful business leaders who used his enforcers to terrorize the Jewish unionists in the garment center and the Italian anarchist syndicates in the building trades.

Against this, Don Corleone could throw two small but superbly organized *regimes* led by Clemenza and Tessio. His political and police contacts were negated by the business leaders who would support Maranzano. But in his favor was the enemy's lack of intelligence about his organization. The underworld did not know the true strength of his soldiers and even were deceived that Tessio in Brooklyn was a separate and independent operation.

And yet despite all this, it was an unequal battle until Vito Corleone evened out the odds with one master stroke.

Maranzano sent a call to Capone for his two best gunmen to come to New York to eliminate the upstart. The Corleone Family had friends and intelligence in Chicago who relayed the news that the two gunmen were arriving by train. Vito Corleone dispatched Luca Brasi to take care of them with instructions that would liberate the strange man's most savage instincts.

Brasi and his people, four of them, received the Chicago hoods at the railroad station. One of Brasi's men procured and drove a taxicab for the purpose and the station porter carrying the bags led the Capone men to this cab. When they got in, Brasi and another of his men crowded in after them, guns ready, and made the two Chicago boys lie on the floor. The cab drove to a warehouse near the docks that Brasi had prepared for them.

The two Capone men were bound hand and foot and small bath towels were stuffed into their mouths to keep them from crying out.

Then Brasi took an ax from its place against the wall and started hacking at one of the Capone men. He chopped the man's feet off, then the legs at the knees, then the thighs where they joined the torso. Brasi was an extremely powerful man but it took him many swings to accomplish his purpose. By that time of course the victim had given up the ghost and the floor of the warehouse was slippery with the hacked fragments of his flesh and the gouting of his blood. When Brasi turned to his second victim he found further effort unnecessary. The second Capone gunman out of sheer terror had, impossibly, swallowed the bath towel in his mouth and suffocated. The bath towel was found in the man's stomach when the police performed their autopsy to determine the cause of death.

A few days later in Chicago the Capones received a message from Vito Corleone. It was to this effect: "You know now how I deal with enemies. Why does a Neapolitan interfere in a quarrel between two Sicilians? If you wish me to consider you as a friend I owe you a service which I will pay on demand. A man like yourself must know how much more profitable it is to have a friend who, instead of calling on you for help, takes care of his own affairs and stands ever ready to help you in some future time of trouble. If you do not wish my friendship, so be it. But then I must tell you that the climate in this city is damp; unhealthy for Neapolitans, and you are advised never to visit it."

The arrogance of this letter was a calculated one. The Don held the Capones in small esteem as stupid, obvious cutthroats. His intelligence informed him that Capone had forfeited all political influence because of his public arrogance and the flaunting of his criminal wealth. The Don knew, in fact was positive, that without political influence, without the camouflage of society, Capone's world, and others like it, could be easily destroyed. He knew Capone was on the path to destruction. He also knew that Capone's influence did not extend beyond the boundaries of Chicago, terrible and all-prevading as that influence there might be.

The tactic was successful. Not so much because of its ferocity but because of the chilling swiftness, the quickness of the Don's reaction. If his intelligence was so good, any further moves would be fraught with danger. It was better, far wiser, to accept the offer of friendship with its implied payoff. The Capones sent back word that they would not interfere.

The odds were now equal. And Vito Corleone had earned an enormous amount of "respect" throughout the United States underworld with his humiliation of the Capones. For six months he outgeneraled Maranzano. He raided the crap games under that man's protection, located his biggest policy banker in Harlem and had him relieved of a day's play not only in money but in records. He engaged his enemies on all fronts. Even in the garment centers he sent Clemenza and his men to fight on the side of the unionists against the enforcers on the payroll of Maranzano and the owners of the dress firms. And on all fronts his superior intelligence and organization made him the victor. Clemenza's jolly ferocity, which Corleone employed judiciously, also helped turn the tide of battle. And then Don Corleone sent the held-back reserve of the Tessio *regime* after Maranzano himself.

By this time Maranzano had dispatched emissaries suing for a peace. Vito Corleone refused to see them, put them off on one pretext or another. The Maranzano soldiers were deserting their leader, not wishing to die in a losing cause. Bookmakers and shylocks were paying the Corleone organization their protection money. The war was all but over.

And then finally on New Year's Eve of 1933, Tessio got inside the defenses of Maranzano himself. The Maranzano lieutenants were anxious for a deal and agreed to lead their chief to the slaughter. They told him that a meeting had been arranged in a Brooklyn restaurant with Corleone and they accompanied Maranzano as his bodyguards. They left him sitting at a checkered table, morosely munching a piece of bread, and fled the restaurant as Tessio and four of his men entered. The execution was swift and sure. Maranzano, his mouth full of half-chewed bread, was riddled with bullets. The war was over.

The Maranzano empire was incorporated into the Corleone operation. Don Corleone set up a system of tribute, allowing all incumbents to remain in their bookmaking and policy number spots. As a bonus he had a foothold in the unions of the garment center which in later years was to prove extremely important. And now that he had settled his business affairs the Don found trouble at home.

Santino Corleone, Sonny, was sixteen years old and grown to an astonishing six feet with broad shoulders and a heavy face that was sensual but by no means effeminate. But where Fredo was a quiet boy, and Michael, of course, a toddler, Santino was constantly in trouble. He got into fights, did badly in school and, finally, Clemenza, who was the boy's godfather and had a duty to speak, came to Don Corleone one evening and informed him that his son had taken part in an armed robbery, a stupid affair which could have gone very badly. Sonny was obviously the ringleader, the two other boys in the robbery his followers.

It was one of the very few times that Vito Corleone lost his temper. Tom Hagen had been living in his home for three years and he asked Clemenza if the orphan boy had been involved. Clemenza shook his head. Don Corleone had a car sent to bring Santino to his offices in the *Genco Pura* Olive Oil Company.

For the first time, the Don met defeat. Alone with his son, he gave full vent to his rage, cursing the hulking Sonny in Sicilian dialect, a language so much more satisfying than any other for expressing rage. He ended up with a question. "What gave you the right to commit such an act? What made you wish to commit such an act?"

Sonny stood there, angry, refusing to answer. The Don said with contempt, "And so stupid. What did you earn for that night's work. Fifty dollars each? Twenty dollars? You risked your life for twenty dollars, eh?"

As if he had not heard these last words, Sonny said defiantly, "I saw you kill Fanucci."

The Don said, "Ahhh" and sank back in his chair. He waited.

Sonny said, "When Fanucci left the building, Mama said I could go up the house. I saw you go up the roof and I followed you. I saw everything you did. I stayed up there and I saw you throw away the wallet and the gun."

The Don sighed. "Well, then I can't talk to you about how you should behave. Don't you want to finish school, don't you want to be a lawyer? Lawyers can steal more money with a briefcase than a thousand men with guns and masks."

Sonny grinned at him and said slyly, "I want to enter the family business." When he saw that the Don's face remained impassive, that he did not laugh at the joke, he added hastily, "I can learn how to sell olive oil."

Still the Don did not answer. Finally he shrugged. "Every man has one destiny," he said. He did not add that the witnessing of Fanucci's murder had decided that of his son. He merely turned away and added quietly, "Come in tomorrow morning at nine o'clock. Genco will show you what to do."

But Genco Abbandando, with that shrewd insight that a *Consigliori* must have, realized the true wish of the Don and used Sonny mostly as a bodyguard for his father, a position in which he could also learn the subtleties of being a Don. And it brought out a professorial instinct in the Don himself, who often gave lectures on how to succeed for the benefit of his eldest son.

Besides his oft-repeated theory that a man has but one destiny, the Don constantly reproved Sonny for that young man's outbursts of temper. The Don considered a use of threats the most foolish kind of exposure; the unleashing of anger without forethought as the most dangerous indulgence. No one had ever heard the Don utter a naked threat, no one had ever seen him in an uncontrollable rage. It was unthinkable. And so he tried to teach Sonny his own disciplines. He claimed that there was no greater natural advantage in life than having an enemy overestimate your faults, unless it was to have a friend underestimate your virtues.

The *caporegime*, Clemenza, took Sonny in hand and taught him how to shoot and to wield a garrot. Sonny had no taste for the Italian rope, he was too Americanized. He preferred the simple, direct, impersonal Anglo-Saxon gun, which saddened Clemenza. But Sonny became a constant and welcome companion to his father, driving his car, helping him in little details. For the next two years he seemed like the usual son entering his father's business, not too bright, not too eager, content to hold down a soft job.

Meanwhile his boyhood chum and semiadopted brother Tom Hagen was going to college. Fredo was still in high school; Michael, the youngest brother, was in grammar school, and baby sister Connie was a toddling girl of four. The family had long since moved to an apartment house in the Bronx. Don Corleone was considering buying a house in Long Island, but he wanted to fit this in with other plans he was formulating.

Vito Corleone was a man with vision. All the great cities of America were being torn by underworld strife. Guerrilla wars by the dozen flared up, ambitious hoodlums trying to carve themselves a bit of empire; men like Corleone himself were trying to keep their borders and rackets secure. Don Corleone saw that the newspapers and government agencies were using these killings to get stricter and stricter laws, to use harsher police methods. He foresaw that public indignation might even lead to a suspension of democratic procedures which could be fatal to him and his people. His own empire, internally, was secure. He decided to bring peace to all the warring factions in New York City and then in the nation.

He had no illusions about the dangerousness of his mission. He spent the first year meeting with different chiefs of gangs in New York, laying the groundwork, sounding them out, proposing spheres of influence that would be honored by a loosely bound confederated council. But there were too many factions, too many special interests that conflicted. Agreement was impossible. Like other great rulers and lawgivers in history Don Corleone decided that order and peace were impossible until the number of reigning states had been reduced to a manageable number.

There were five or six "Families" too powerful to eliminate. But the rest, the neighborhood Black Hand terrorists, the free-lance shylocks, the strong-arm bookmakers operating without the proper, that is to say paid, protection of the legal authorities, would have to go. And so he mounted what was in effect a colonial war against these people and threw all the resources of the Corleone organization against them.

The pacification of the New York area took three years and had some unexpected rewards. At first it took the form of bad luck. A group of mad-dog Irish stickup artists the Don had marked for extermination almost carried the day with sheer Emerald Isle élan. By chance, and with suicidal bravery, one of these Irish gunmen pierced the Don's protective cordon and put a shot into his chest. The assassin was immediately riddled with bullets but the damage was done.

However this gave Santino Corleone his chance. With his father out of action, Sonny took command of a troop, his own *regime*, with the rank of *caporegime*, and like a young, untrumpeted Napoleon, showed a genius for city warfare. He also showed a merciless ruthlessness, the lack of which had been Don Corleone's only fault as a conqueror.

From 1935 to 1937 Sonny Corleone made a reputation as the most cunning and relentless executioner the underworld had yet known. Yet for sheer terror even he was eclipsed by the awesome man named Luca Brasi.

It was Brasi who went after the rest of the Irish gunmen and singlehandedly wiped them out. It was Brasi, operating alone when one of the six powerful families tried to interfere and become the protector of the independents, who assassinated the head of that family as a warning. Shortly after, the Don recovered from his wound and made peace with that particular family.

By 1937 peace and harmony reigned in New York City except for minor incidents, minor misunderstandings which were, of course, sometimes fatal.

As the rulers of ancient cities always kept an anxious eye on the barbarian tribes roving around their walls, so Don Corleone kept an eye on the affairs of the world outside his world. He noted the coming of Hitler, the fall of Spain, Germany's strong-arming of Britain at Munich. Unblinkered by that outside world, he saw clearly the coming global war and he understood the implications. His own world would be more impregnable than before. Not only that, fortunes could be made in time of war by alert, foresighted folk. But to do so peace must reign in his domain while war raged in the world outside.

Don Corleone carried his message through the United States. He conferred with compatriots in Los Angeles, San Francisco, Cleveland, Chicago, Philadelphia, Miami, and Boston. He was the underworld apostle of peace and, by 1939, more successful than any Pope, he had achieved a working agreement amongst the most powerful underworld organizations in the country. Like the Constitution of the United States this agreement respected fully the internal authority of each member in his state or city. The agreement covered only spheres of influence and an agreement to enforce peace in the underworld.

And so when World War II broke out in 1939, when the United States joined the conflict in 1941, the world of Don Vito Corleone was at peace, in order, fully prepared to reap the golden harvest on equal terms with all the other industries of a booming America. The Corleone Family had a hand in supplying black-market OPA food stamps, gasoline stamps, even travel priorities. It could help get war contracts and then help get black-market materials for those garment center clothing firms who were not given enough raw material because they did not have government contracts. He could even get all the young men in his organization, those eligible for Army draft, excused from fighting in the foreign war. He did this with the aid of doctors who advised what drugs had to be taken before physical examination, or by placing the men in draft-exempt positions in the war industries.

And so the Don could take pride in his rule. His world was safe for those who had sworn their loyalty to him; other men who believed in law and order were dying by the millions. The only fly in the ointment was that his own son, Michael Corleone, refused to be helped, insisted on volunteering to serve his own country. And to the Don's astonishment, so did a few of his other young men in the organization. One of the men, trying to explain this to his *caporegime*, said, "This country has been good to me." Upon this story being relayed to the Don he said angrily to the *caporegime*, "*I* have been good to him." It might have gone badly for these people but, as he had excused his son Michael, so must he excuse other young men who so misunderstood their duty to their Don and to themselves.

At the end of World War II Don Corleone knew that again his world would have to change its ways, that it would have to fit itself more snugly into the ways of the other, larger world. He believed he could do this with no loss of profit.

There was reason for this belief in his own experience. What had put him on the right track were two personal affairs. Early in his career the then-young Nazorine, only a baker's helper planning to get married, had come to him for assistance. He and his future bride, a good Italian girl, had saved their money and had paid the enormous sum of three hundred dollars to a wholesaler of furniture recommended to them. This wholesaler had let them pick out everything they wanted to furnish their tenement apartment. A fine sturdy bedroom set with two bureaus and lamps. Also the living room set of heavy stuffed sofa and stuffed armchairs, all covered with rich gold-threaded fabric. Nazorine and his fiancée had spent a happy day picking out what they wanted from the huge warehouse crowded with furniture. The wholesaler took their money, their three hundred dollars wrung from the sweat of their blood, and pocketed it and promised the furniture to be delivered within the week to the already rented flat.

The very next week however, the firm had gone into bankruptcy. The great warehouse stocked with furniture had been sealed shut and attached for payment of creditors. The wholesaler had disappeared to give other creditors time to unleash their anger on the empty air. Nazorine, one of these, went to his lawyer, who told him nothing could be done until the case was settled in court and all creditors satisfied. This might take three years and Nazorine would be lucky to get back ten cents on the dollar.

Vito Corleone listened to this story with amused disbelief. It was not possible that the law could allow such thievery. The wholesaler owned his own palatial home, an estate in Long Island, a luxurious automobile, and was sending his children to college. How could he keep the three hundred dollars of the poor baker Nazorine and not give him the furniture he had paid for? But, to make sure, Vito Corleone had Genco Abbandando check it out with the lawyers who represented the *Genco Pura* company.

They verified the story of Nazorine. The wholesaler had all his personal wealth in his wife's name. His furniture business was incorporated and he was not personally liable. True, he had shown bad faith by taking the money of Nazorine when he knew he was going to file bankruptcy but this was a common practice. Under law there was nothing to be done.

Of course the matter was easily adjusted. Don Corleone sent his *Consigliori*, Genco Abbandando, to speak to the wholesaler, and as was to be expected, that wide-awake businessman caught the drift immediately and arranged for Nazorine to get his furniture. But it was an interesting lesson for the young Vito Corleone.

The second incident had more far-reaching repercussions. In 1939, Don Corleone had decided to move his family out of the city. Like any other parent he wanted his children to go to better schools and mix with better companions. For his own personal reasons he wanted the anonymity of suburban life where his reputation was not known. He bought the mall property in Long Beach, which at that time had only four newly built houses but with plenty of room for more. Sonny was formally engaged to Sandra and would soon marry, one of the houses would be for him. One of the houses was for the Don. Another was for Genco Abbandando and his family. The other was kept vacant at the time.

A week after the mall was occupied, a group of three workmen came in all innocence with their truck. They claimed to be furnace inspectors for the town of Long Beach. One of the Don's young bodyguards let the men in and led them to the furnace in the basement. The Don, his wife and Sonny were in the garden taking their ease and enjoying the salty sea air.

Much to the Don's annoyance he was summoned into the house by his bodyguard. The three workmen, all big burly fellows, were grouped around the furnace. They had taken it apart, it was strewn around the cement basement floor. Their leader, an authoritative man, said to the Don in a gruff voice, "Your furnace is in lousy shape. If you want us to fix it and put it together again, it'll cost you one hundred fifty dollars for labor and parts and then we'll pass you for county inspection." He took out a red paper label. "We stamp this seal on it, see, then nobody from the county bothers you again."

The Don was amused. It had been a boring, quiet week in which he had had to neglect his business to take care of such family details moving to a new house entailed. In more broken English than his usual slight accent he asked, "If I don't pay you, what happens to my furnace?"

The leader of the three men shrugged. "We just leave the furnace the way it is now." He gestured at the metal parts strewn over the floor.

The Don said meekly, "Wait, I'll get you your money." Then he went out into the garden and said to Sonny, "Listen, there's some men working on the furnace, I don't understand what they want. Go in and take care of the matter." It was not simply a joke; he was considering making his son his *underboss*. This was one of the tests a business executive had to pass.

Sonny's solution did not altogether please his father. It was too direct, too lacking in Sicilian subtleness. He was the Club, not the Rapier. For as soon as Sonny heard the leader's demand he held the three men at gunpoint and had them thoroughly bastinadoed by the bodyguards. Then he made them put the furnace together again and tidy up the basement. He searched them and found that they actually were employed by a house-improvement firm with headquarters in Suffolk County. He learned the name of the man who owned the firm. Then he kicked the three men to their truck. "Don't let me see you in Long Beach again," he told them. "I'll have your balls hanging from your ears."

It was typical of the young Santino, before he became older and crueler, that he extended his protection to the community he lived in. Sonny paid a personal call to the home-improvement firm owner and told him not to send any of his men into the Long Beach area ever again. As soon as the Corleone Family set up their usual business liaison with the local police force they were informed of all such complaints and all crimes by professional criminals. In less than a year Long Beach became the most crime-free town of its size in the United States. Professional stickup artists and strong-arms received one warning not to ply their trade in the town. They were allowed one offense. When they committed a second they simply disappeared. The flimflam home-improvement gyp artists, the door-to-door con men were politely warned that they were not welcome in Long Beach. Those confident con men who disregarded the warning were beaten within an inch of their lives. Resident young punks who had no respect for law and proper authority were advised in the most fatherly fashion to run away from home. Long Beach became a model city.

What impressed the Don was the legal validity of these sales swindles. Clearly there was a place for a man of his talents in that other world which had been closed to him as an honest youth. He took appropriate steps to enter that world.

And so he lived happily on the mall in Long Beach, consolidating and enlarging his empire, until after the war was over, the Turk Sollozzo broke the peace and plunged the Don's world into its own war, and brought him to his hospital bed.

Book IV

Book IV

Chapter

✦✦✦✦✦✦✦✦✦✦✦✦✦✦✦✦✦✦✦✦✦✦✦✦✦

15

IN the New Hampshire village, every foreign phenomenon was properly noticed by housewives peering from windows, storekeepers lounging behind their doors. And so when the black automobile bearing New York license plates stopped in front of the Adams' home, every citizen knew about it in a matter of minutes.

Kay Adams, really a small-town girl despite her college education, was also peering from her bedroom window. She had been studying for her exams and preparing to go downstairs for lunch when she spotted the car coming up the street, and for some reason she was not surprised when it rolled to a halt in front of her lawn. Two men got out, big burly men who looked like gangsters in the movies to her eyes, and she flew down the stairs to be the first at the door. She was sure they came from Michael or his family and she didn't want them talking to her father and mother without any introduction. It wasn't that she was ashamed of any of Mike's friends, she thought; it was just that her mother and father were old-fashioned New England Yankees and wouldn't understand her even knowing such people.

She got to the door just as the bell rang and she called to her mother, "I'll get it." She opened the door and the two big men stood there. One reached inside his breast pocket like a gangster reaching for a gun and the move so surprised Kay that she let out a little gasp but the man had taken out a small leather case which he flapped open to show an identification card. "I'm Detective John Phillips from the New York Police Department," he said. He motioned to the other man, a dark-complexioned man with very thick, very black eyebrows. "This is my partner, Detective Siriani. Are you Miss Kay Adams?"

Kay nodded. Phillips said, "May we come in and talk to you for a few minutes. It's about Michael Corleone."

She stood aside to let them in. At that moment her father appeared in the small side hall that led to his study. "Kay, what is it?" he asked.

Her father was a gray-haired, slender, distinguished-looking man who not only was the pastor of the town Baptist church but had a reputation in religious circles as a scholar. Kay really didn't know her father well, he puzzled her, but she knew he loved her even if he gave the impression he found her uninteresting as a person. Though they had never been close, she trusted him. So she said simply, "These men are detectives from New York. They want to ask me questions about a boy I know."

Mr. Adams didn't seem surprised. "Why don't we go into my study?" he said.

Detective Phillips said gently, "We'd rather talk to your daughter alone, Mr. Adams."

Mr. Adams said courteously, "That depends on Kay, I think. My dear, would you rather speak to these gentlemen alone or would you prefer to have me present? Or perhaps your mother?"

Kay shook her head. "I'll talk to them alone."

Mr. Adams said to Phillips, "You can use my study. Will you stay for lunch?" The two men shook their heads. Kay led them into the study.

They rested uncomfortably on the edge of the couch as she sat in her father's big leather chair. Detective Phillips opened the conversation by saying, "Miss Adams, have you seen or heard from Michael Corleone at any time in the last three weeks?" The one question was enough to warn her. Three weeks ago she had read the Boston newspapers with their headlines about the killing of a New York police captain and a narcotics smuggler named Virgil Sollozzo. The newspaper had said it was part of the gang war involving the Corleone Family.

Kay shook her head. "No, the last time I saw him he was going to see his father in the hospital. That was perhaps a month ago."

The other detective said in a harsh voice, "We know all about that meeting. Have you seen or heard from him since then?"

"No," Kay said.

Detective Phillips said in a polite voice, "If you do have contact with him we'd like you to let us know. It's very important we get to talk to Michael Corleone. I must warn you that if you do have contact with him you may be getting involved in a very dangerous situation. If you help him in any way, you may get yourself in very serious trouble."

Kay sat up very straight in the chair. "Why shouldn't I help him?" she asked. "We're going to be married, married people help each other."

It was Detective Siriani who answered her. "If you help, you may be an accessory to murder. We're looking for your boy friend because he killed a police captain in New York plus an informer the police officer was contacting. We *know* Michael Corleone is the person who did the shooting."

Kay laughed. Her laughter was so unaffected, so incredulous, that the officers were impressed. "Mike wouldn't do anything like that," she said. "He never had anything to do with his family. When we went to his sister's wedding it was obvious that he was treated as an outsider, almost as much as I was. If he's hiding now it's just so that he won't get any publicity, so his name won't be dragged through all this. Mike is not a gangster. I know him better than you or anybody else can know him. He is too nice a man to do anything as despicable as murder. He is the most law-abiding person I know, and I've never known him to lie."

Detective Phillips asked gently, "How long have you known him?"

"Over a year," Kay said and was surprised when the two men smiled.

"I think there are a few things you should know," Detective Phillips said. "On the night he left you, he went to the hospital. When he came out he got into an argument with a police captain who had come to the hospital on official business. He assaulted that police officer but got the worst of it. In fact he got a broken jaw and lost some teeth. His friends took him out to the Corleone Family houses at Long Beach. The following night the police captain he had the fight with was gunned down and Michael Corleone disappeared.

Vanished. We have our contacts, our informers. They all point the finger at Michael Corleone but we have no evidence for a court of law. The waiter who witnessed the shooting doesn't recognize a picture of Mike but he may recognize him in person. And we have Sollozzo's driver, who refuses to talk, but we might make him talk if we have Michael Corleone in our hands. So we have all our people looking for him, the FBI is looking for him, everybody is looking for him. So far, no luck, so we thought you might be able to give us a lead."

Kay said coldly, "I don't believe a word of it." But she felt a bit sick knowing the part about Mike getting his jaw broken must be true. Not that that would make Mike commit murder.

"Will you let us know if Mike contacts you?" Phillips asked.

Kay shook her head. The other detective, Siriani, said roughly, "We know you two have been shacking up together. We have the hotel records and witnesses. If we let that information slip to the newspapers your father and mother would feel pretty lousy. Real respectable people like them wouldn't think much of a daughter shacking up with a gangster. If you don't come clean right now I'll call your old man in here and give it to him straight."

Kay looked at him with astonishment. Then she got up and went to the door of the study and opened it. She could see her father standing at the living-room window, sucking at his pipe. She called out, "Dad, can you join us?" He turned, smiled at her, and walked to the study. When he came through the door he put his arm around his daughter's waist and faced the detectives and said, "Yes, gentlemen?"

When they didn't answer, Kay said coolly to Detective Siriani, "Give it to him straight, officer."

Siriani flushed. "Mr. Adams, I'm telling you this for your daughter's good. She is mixed up with a hoodlum we have reason to believe committed a murder on a police officer. I'm just telling her she can get into serious trouble unless she cooperates with us. But she doesn't seem to realize how serious this whole matter is. Maybe you can talk to her."

"That is quite incredible," Mr. Adams said politely.

Siriani jutted his jaw. "Your daughter and Michael Corleone have been going out together for over a year. They have stayed overnight in hotels together registered as man and wife. Michael Corleone is wanted for questioning in the murder of a police officer. Your daughter refuses to give us any information that may help us. Those are the facts. You can call them incredible but I can back everything up."

"I don't doubt your word, sir," Mr. Adams said gently. "What I find incredible is that my daughter could be in serious trouble. Unless you're suggesting that she is a"—here his face became one of scholarly doubt—"a 'moll,' I believe it's called."

Kay looked at her father in astonishment. She knew he was being playful in his donnish way and she was surprised that he could take the whole affair so lightly.

Mr. Adams said firmly, "However, rest assured that if the young man shows his face here I shall immediately report his presence to the authorities. As will my daughter. Now, if you will forgive us, our lunch is growing cold."

He ushered the men out of the house with every courtesy and closed the door on their backs gently but firmly. He took Kay by the arm and led her toward the kitchen far in the rear of the house, "Come, my dear, your mother is waiting lunch for us."

By the time they reached the kitchen, Kay was weeping silently, out of relief from strain, at her father's unquestioning affection. In the kitchen her mother took no notice of her weeping, and Kay realized that her father must have told her about the two detectives. She sat down at her place and her mother served her silently. When all three were at the table her father said grace with bowed head.

Mrs. Adams was a short stout woman always neatly dressed, hair always set. Kay had never seen her in disarray. Her mother too had always been a little disinterested in her, holding her at arm's length. And she did so now. "Kay, stop being so dramatic. I'm sure it's all a great deal of fuss about nothing at all. After all, the boy was a Dartmouth boy, he couldn't possibly be mixed up in anything so sordid."

Kay looked up in surprise. "How did you know Mike went to Dartmouth?"

Her mother said complacently, "You young people are so mysterious, you think you're so clever. We've known about him all along, but of course we couldn't bring it up until you did."

"But how did you know?" Kay asked. She still couldn't face her father now that he knew about her and Mike sleeping together. So she didn't see the smile on his face when he said, "We opened your mail, of course."

Kay was horrified and angry. Now she could face him. What he had done was more shameful than her own sin. She could never believe it of him. "Father, you didn't, you couldn't have."

Mr. Adams smiled at her. "I debated which was the greater sin, opening your mail, or going in ignorance of some hazard my only child might be incurring. The choice was simple, and virtuous."

Mrs. Adams said between mouthfuls of boiled chicken, "After all, my dear, you are terribly innocent for your age. We had to be aware. And you never spoke about him."

For the first time Kay was grateful that Michael was never affectionate in his letters. She was grateful that her parents hadn't seen some of her letters. "I never told you about him because I thought you'd be horrified about his family."

"We were," Mr. Adams said cheerfully. "By the way, has Michael gotten in touch with you?"

Kay shook her head. "I don't believe he's guilty of anything."

She saw her parents exchange a glance over the table. Then Mr. Adams said gently, "If he's not guilty and he's vanished, then perhaps something else happened to him."

At first Kay didn't understand. Then she got up from the table and ran to her room.

Three days later Kay Adams got out of a taxi in front of the Corleone mall in Long Beach. She had phoned, she was expected. Tom Hagen met her at the door and she was disappointed that it was him. She knew he would tell her nothing.

In the living room he gave her a drink. She had seen a couple of other men lounging around the house but not Sonny. She asked Tom Hagen directly, "Do you know where Mike is? Do you know where I can get in touch with him?"

Hagen said smoothly, "We know he's all right but we don't know where he is right now. When he heard about that captain being shot he was afraid they'd accuse him. So he just decided to disappear. He told me he'd get in touch in a few months."

The story was not only false but meant to be seen through, he was giving her that much. "Did that captain really break his jaw?" Kay asked.

"I'm afraid that's true," Tom said. "But Mike was never a vindictive man. I'm sure that had nothing to do with what happened."

Kay opened her purse and took out a letter. "Will you deliver this to him if he gets in touch with you?"

Hagen shook his head. "If I accepted that letter and you told a court of law I accepted that letter, it might be interpreted as my having knowledge of his whereabouts. Why don't you just wait a bit? I'm sure Mike will get in touch."

She finished her drink and got up to leave. Hagen escorted her to the hall but as he opened the door, a woman came in from outside. A short, stout woman dressed in black. Kay recognized her as Michael's mother. She held out her hand and said, "How are you, Mrs. Corleone?"

The woman's small black eyes darted at her for a moment, then the wrinkled, leathery, olive-skinned face broke into a small curt smile of greeting that was yet in some curious way truly friendly. "Ah, you Mikey's little girl," Mrs. Corleone said. She had a heavy Italian accent, Kay could barely understand her. "You eat something?" Kay said no, meaning she didn't want anything to eat, but Mrs. Corleone turned furiously on Tom Hagen and berated him in Italian ending with, "You don't even give this poor girl coffee, you *disgrazia*." She took Kay by the hand, the old woman's hand surprisingly warm and alive, and led her into the kitchen. "You have coffee and eat something, then somebody drive you home. A nice girl like you, I don't want you to take the train." She made Kay sit down and bustled around the kitchen, tearing off her coat and hat and draping them over a chair. In a few seconds there was bread and cheese and salami on the table and coffee perking on the stove.

Kay said timidly, "I came to ask about Mike, I haven't heard from him. Mr. Hagen said nobody knows where he is, that he'll turn up in a little while."

Hagen spoke quickly, "That's all we can tell her now, Ma."

Mrs. Corleone gave him a look of withering contempt. "Now you gonna tell me what to do? My husband don't tell me what to do, God have mercy on him." She crossed herself.

"Is Mr. Corleone all right?" Kay asked.

"Fine," Mrs. Corleone said. "Fine. He's getting old, he's getting foolish to let something like that happen." She tapped her head disrespectfully. She poured the coffee and forced Kay to eat some bread and cheese.

After they drank their coffee Mrs. Corleone took one of Kay's hands in her two brown ones. She said quietly, "Mikey no gonna write you, you no gonna hear from Mikey. He hide two–three years.

Maybe more, maybe much more. You go home to your family and find a nice young fellow and get married."

Kay took the letter out of her purse. "Will you send this to him?"

The old lady took the letter and patted Kay on the cheek. "Sure, sure," she said. Hagen started to protest and she screamed at him in Italian. Then she led Kay to the door. There she kissed her on the cheek very quickly and said, "You forget about Mikey, he no the man for you anymore."

There was a car waiting for her with two men up front. They drove her all the way to her hotel in New York never saying a word. Neither did Kay. She was trying to get used to the fact that the young man she had loved was a cold-blooded murderer. And that she had been told by the most unimpeachable source: his mother.

Chapter

×◆×◆×◆×◆×◆×◆×◆×◆×◆×◆×

16

CARLO RIZZI was punk sore at the world. Once married into the Corleone Family, he'd been shunted aside with a small bookmaker's business on the Upper East Side of Manhattan. He'd counted on one of the houses in the mall on Long Beach, he knew the Don could move retainer families out when he pleased and he had been sure it would happen and he would be on the inside of everything. But the Don wasn't treating him right. The "Great Don," he thought with scorn. An old Moustache Pete who'd been caught out on the street by gunmen like any dumb small-time hood. He hoped the old bastard croaked. Sonny had been his friend once and if Sonny became the head of the Family maybe he'd get a break, get on the inside.

He watched his wife pour his coffee. Christ, what a mess she turned out to be. Five months of marriage and she was already spreading, besides blowing up. Real guinea broads all these Italians in the East.

He reached out and felt Connie's soft spreading buttocks. She smiled at him and he said contemptuously, "You got more ham than a hog." It pleased him to see the hurt look on her face, the tears springing into her eyes. She might be a daughter of the Great Don but she was his wife, she was his property now and he could treat her as he pleased. It made him feel powerful that one of the Corleones was his doormat.

He had started her off just right. She had tried to keep that purse full of money presents for herself and he had given her a nice black eye and taken the money from her. Never told her what he'd done with it, either. That might have really caused some trouble. Even now he felt just the slightest twinge of remorse. Christ, he'd blown nearly fifteen grand on the track and show girl bimbos.

He could feel Connie watching his back and so he flexed his muscles as he reached for the plate of sweet buns on the other side of the table. He'd just polished off ham and eggs but he was a big man and needed a big breakfast. He was pleased with the picture he knew he presented to his wife. Not the usual greasy dark guinzo husband but crew-cut blond, huge golden-haired forearms and broad shoulders and thin waist. And he knew he was physically stronger than any of those so-called hard guys that worked for the family. Guys like Clemenza, Tessio, Rocco Lampone, and that guy Paulie that somebody had knocked off. He wondered what the story was about that. Then for some reason he thought about Sonny. Man to man he could take Sonny, he thought, even though Sonny was a little bigger and a little heavier. But what scared him was Sonny's rep, though he himself had never seen Sonny anything but good-natured and kidding around. Yeah, Sonny was his buddy. Maybe with the old Don gone, things would open up.

He dawdled over his coffee. He hated this apartment. He was used to the bigger living quarters of the West and in a little while he would have to go crosstown to his "book" to run the noontime action. It was a Sunday, the heaviest action of the week what with baseball going already and the tail end of basketball and the night trotters starting up. Gradually he became aware of Connie bustling around behind him and he turned his head to watch her.

She was getting dressed up in the real New York City guinzo style that he hated. A silk flowered-pattern dress with belt, showy bracelet and earrings, flouncy sleeves. She looked twenty years older. "Where the hell are you going?" he asked.

She answered him coldly, "To see my father out in Long Beach. He still can't get out of bed and he needs company."

Carlo was curious. "Is Sonny still running the show?"

Connie gave him a bland look. "What show?"

He was furious. "You lousy little guinea bitch, don't talk to me like that or I'll beat that kid right out of your belly." She looked frightened and this enraged him even more. He sprang from his chair and slapped her across the face, the blow leaving a red welt. With quick precision he slapped her three more times. He saw her upper lip split bloody and puff up. That stopped him. He didn't want to leave a mark. She ran into the bedroom and slammed the door and he heard the key turning in the lock. He laughed and returned to his coffee.

He smoked until it was time for him to dress. He knocked on the door and said, "Open it up before I kick it in." There was no answer. "Come on, I gotta get dressed," he said in a loud voice. He could hear her getting up off the bed and coming toward the door, then the key turned in the lock. When he entered she had her back to him, walking back toward the bed, lying down on it with her face turned away to the wall.

He dressed quickly and then saw she was in her slip. He wanted her to go visit her father, he hoped she would bring back information. "What's the matter, a few slaps take all the energy out of you?" She was a lazy slut.

"I don't wanna go." Her voice was tearful, the words mumbled. He reached out impatiently and pulled her around to face him. And then he saw why she didn't want to go and thought maybe it was just as well.

He must have slapped her harder than he figured. Her left cheek was blown up, the cut upper lip ballooned grotesquely puffy and white beneath her nose. "OK," he said, "but I won't be home until late. Sunday is my busy day."

He left the apartment and found a parking ticket on his car, a fifteen-dollar green one. He put it in the glove compartment with the stack of others. He was in a good humor. Slapping the spoiled little bitch around always made him feel good. It dissolved some of the frustration he felt at being treated so badly by the Corleones.

The first time he had marked her up, he'd been a little worried. She had gone right out to Long Beach to complain to her mother and father and to show her black eye. He had really sweated it out. But when she came back she had been surprisingly meek, the dutiful little Italian wife. He had made it a point to be the perfect husband over the next few weeks, treating her well in every way, being lovey and nice with her, banging her every day, morning and night. Finally she had told him what had happened since she thought he would never act that way again.

She had found her parents coolly unsympathetic and curiously amused. Her mother had had a little sympathy and had even asked her father to speak to Carlo Rizzi. Her father had refused. "She is my daughter," he had said, "but now she belongs to her husband. He knows his duties. Even the King of Italy didn't dare to meddle with the relationship of husband and wife. Go home and learn how to behave so that he will not beat you."

Connie had said angrily to her father, "Did you ever hit your wife?" She was his favorite and could speak to him so impudently. He had answered, "She never gave me reason to beat her." And her mother had nodded and smiled.

She told them how her husband had taken the wedding present money and never told her what he did with it. Her father had shrugged and said, "I would have done the same if my wife had been as presumptuous as you."

And so she had returned home, a little bewildered, a little frightened. She had always been her father's favorite and she could not understand his coldness now.

But the Don had not been so unsympathetic as he pretended. He made inquiries and found out what Carlo Rizzi had done with the wedding present money. He had men assigned to Carlo Rizzi's bookmaking operation who would report to Hagen everything Rizzi did on the job. But the Don could not interfere. How expect a man to discharge his husbandly duties to a wife whose family he feared? It was an impossible situation and he dared not meddle. Then when Connie became pregnant he was convinced of the wisdom of his decision and felt he never could interfere though Connie complained to her mother about a few more beatings and the mother finally became concerned enough to mention it to the Don. Connie even hinted that she might want a divorce. For the first time in her life the Don was angry with her. "He is the father of your child. What can a child come to in this world if he has no father?" he said to Connie.

Learning all this, Carlo Rizzi grew confident. He was perfectly safe. In fact he bragged to his two "writers" on the book, Sally Rags and Coach, about how he bounced his wife around when she got snotty and saw their looks of respect that he had the guts to man-handle the daughter of the great Don Corleone.

But Rizzi would not have felt so safe if he had known that when Sonny Corleone learned of the beatings he had flown into a murderous rage and had been restrained only by the sternest and most imperious command of the Don himself, a command that even Sonny dared not disobey. Which was why Sonny avoided Rizzi, not trusting himself to control his temper.

So feeling perfectly safe on this beautiful Sunday morning, Carlo Rizzi sped crosstown on 96th Street to the East Side. He did not see Sonny's car coming the opposite way toward his house.

Sonny Corleone had left the protection of the mall and spent the night with Lucy Mancini in town. Now on the way home he was traveling with four bodyguards, two in front and two behind. He didn't need guards right beside him, he could take care of a single direct assault. The other men traveled in their own cars and had apartments on either side of Lucy's apartment. It was safe to visit her as long as he didn't do it too often. But now that he was in town he figured he would pick up his sister Connie and take her out to Long Beach. He knew Carlo would be working at his book and the cheap bastard wouldn't get her a car. So he'd give his sister a lift out.

He waited for the two men in front to go into the building and then followed them. He saw the two men in back pull up behind his car and get out to watch the streets. He kept his own eyes open. It was a million-to-one shot that the opposition even knew he was in town but he was always careful. He had learned that in the 1930's war.

He never used elevators. They were death traps. He climbed the eight flights to Connie's apartment, going fast. He knocked on her door. He had seen Carlo's car go by and knew she would be alone. There was no answer. He knocked again and then he heard his sister's voice, frightened, timid, asking, "Who is it?"

The fright in the voice stunned him. His kid sister had always been fresh and snotty, tough as anybody in the family. What the hell had happened to her? He said, "It's Sonny." The bolt inside slid back and the door opened and Connie was in his arms sobbing. He was so surprised he just stood there. He pushed her away from him and saw her swollen face and he understood what had happened.

He pulled away from her to run down the stairs and go after her husband. Rage flamed up in him, contorting his own face. Connie saw the rage and clung to him, not letting him go, making him come into the apartment. She was weeping out of terror now. She knew her older brother's temper and feared it. She had never complained to him about Carlo for that reason. Now she made him come into the apartment with her.

"It was my fault," she said. "I started a fight with him and I tried to hit him so he hit me. He really didn't try to hit me that hard. I walked into it."

Sonny's heavy Cupid face was under control. "You going to see the old man today?"

She didn't answer, so he added, "I thought you were, so I dropped over to give you a lift. I was in the city anyway."

She shook her head. "I don't want them to see me this way. I'll come next week."

"OK," Sonny said. He picked up her kitchen phone and dialed a number. "I'm getting a doctor to come over here and take a look at you and fix you up. In your condition you have to be careful. How many months before you have the kid?"

"Two months," Connie said. "Sonny, please don't do anything. Please don't."

Sonny laughed. His face was cruelly intent when he said, "Don't worry, I won't make your kid an orphan before he's born." He left the apartment after kissing her lightly on her uninjured cheek.

On East 112th Street a long line of cars were double-parked in front of a candy store that was the headquarters of Carlo Rizzi's book. On the sidewalk in front of the store, fathers played catch with small children they had taken for a Sunday morning ride and to keep them company as they placed their bets. When they saw Carlo Rizzi coming they stopped playing ball and bought their kids ice cream to keep them quiet. Then they started studying the newspapers that gave the starting pitchers, trying to pick out winning baseball bets for the day.

Carlo went into the large room in the back of the store. His two "writers," a small wiry man called Sally Rags and a big husky fellow called Coach, were already waiting for the action to start. They had their huge, lined pads in front of them ready to write down bets. On a wooden stand was a blackboard with the names of the sixteen big league baseball teams chalked on it, paired to show who was playing against who. Against each pairing was a blocked-out square to enter the odds.

Carlo asked Coach, "Is the store phone tapped today?"

Coach shook his head. "The tap is still off."

Carlo went to the wall phone and dialed a number. Sally Rags and Coach watched him impassively as he jotted down the "line," the odds on all the baseball games for that day. They watched him as he hung up the phone and walked over to the blackboard and chalked up the odds against each game. Though Carlo did not know it, they already gotten the line and were checking his work. In the first week in his job Carlo had made a mistake in transposing the odds onto the blackboard and had created that dream of all gamblers, a "middle." That is, by betting the odds with him and then betting against the same team with another bookmaker at the correct odds, the gambler could not lose. The only one who could lose was Carlo's book. That mistake had caused a six-thousand-dollar loss in the book for the week and confirmed the Don's judgment about his son-in-law. He had given the word that all of Carlo's work was to be checked.

Normally the highly placed members of the Corleone Family would never be concerned with such an operational detail. There was at least a five-layer insulation to their level. But since the book was being used as a testing ground for the son-in-law, it had been placed under the direct scrutiny of Tom Hagen, to whom a report was sent every day.

Now with the line posted, the gamblers were thronging into the back room of the candy store to jot down the odds on their newspapers next to the games printed there with probable pitchers. Some of them held their little children by the hand as they looked up at the blackboard. One guy who made big bets looked down at the little girl he was holding by the hand and said teasingly, "Who do you like today, Honey, Giants or the Pirates?" The little girl, fascinated by the colorful names, said, "Are Giants stronger than Pirates?" The father laughed.

A line began to form in front of the two writers. When a writer filled one of his sheets he tore it off, wrapped the money he had collected in it and handed it to Carlo. Carlo went out the back exit of the room and up a flight of steps to an apartment which housed the candy store owner's family. He called in the bets to his central exchange and put the money in a small wall safe that was hidden by an extended window drape. Then he went back down into the candy store after having first burned the bet sheet and flushed its ashes down the toilet bowl.

None of the Sunday games started before two P.M. because of the blue laws, so after the first crowd of bettors, family men who had to get their bets in and rush home to take their families to the beach, came the trickling of bachelor gamblers or the diehards who condemned their families to Sundays in the hot city apartments. These bachelor bettors were the big gamblers, they bet heavier and came back around four o'clock to bet the second games of doubleheaders. They were the ones who made Carlo's Sundays a full-time day with overtime, though some married men called in from the beach to try and recoup their losses.

By one-thirty the betting had trickled off so that Carlo and Sally Rags could go out and sit on the stoop beside the candy store and get some fresh air. They watched the stickball game the kids were having. A police car went by. They ignored it. This book had very heavy protection at the precinct and couldn't be touched on a local level. A raid would have to be ordered from the very top and even then a warning would come through in plenty of time.

Coach came out and sat beside them. They gossiped a while about baseball and women. Carlo said laughingly, "I had to bat my wife around again today, teach her who's boss."

Coach said casually, "She's knocked up pretty big now, ain't she?"

"Ahh, I just slapped her face a few times," Carlo said. "I didn't hurt her." He brooded for a moment. "She thinks she can boss me around, I don't stand for that."

There were still a few bettors hanging around shooting the breeze, talking baseball, some of them sitting on the steps above the two writers and Carlo. Suddenly the kids playing stickball in the street scattered. A car came screeching up the block and to a halt in front of the candy store. It stopped so abruptly that the tires screamed and before it had stopped, almost, a man came hurtling out of the driver's seat, moving so fast that everybody was paralyzed. The man was Sonny Corleone.

His heavy Cupid-featured face with its thick, curved mouth was an ugly mask of fury. In a split second he was at the stoop and had grabbed Carlo Rizzi by the throat. He pulled Carlo away from the others, trying to drag him into the street, but Carlo wrapped his huge muscular arms around the iron railings of the stoop and hung on. He cringed away, trying to hide his head and face in the hollow of his shoulders. His shirt ripped away in Sonny's hand.

What followed then was sickening. Sonny began beating the cowering Carlo with his fists, cursing him in a thick, rage-choked voice. Carlo, despite his tremendous physique, offered no resistance, gave no cry for mercy or protest. Coach and Sally Rags dared not interfere. They thought Sonny meant to kill his brother-in-law and had no desire to share his fate. The kids playing stickball gathered to curse the driver who had made them scatter, but now were watching with awestruck interest. They were tough kids but the sight of Sonny in his rage silenced them. Meanwhile another car had drawn up behind Sonny's and two of his bodyguards jumped out. When they saw what was happening they too dared not interfere. They stood alert, ready to protect their chief if any bystanders had the stupidity to try to help Carlo.

What made the sight sickening was Carlo's complete subjection, but it was perhaps this that saved his life. He clung to the iron railings with his hands so that Sonny could not drag him into the street and despite his obvious equal strength, still refused to fight back. He let the blows rain on his unprotected head and neck until Sonny's rage ebbed. Finally, his chest heaving, Sonny looked down at him and said, "You dirty bastard, you ever beat up my sister again I'll kill you."

These words released the tension. Because of course, if Sonny intended to kill the man he would never have uttered the threat. He uttered it in frustration because he could not carry it out. Carlo refused to look at Sonny. He kept his head down and his hands and arms entwined in the iron railing. He stayed that way until the car roared off and he heard Coach say in his curiously paternal voice, "OK, Carlo, come on into the store. Let's get out of sight."

It was only then that Carlo dared to get out of his crouch against the stone steps of the stoop and unlock his hands from the railing. Standing up, he could see the kids look at him with the staring, sickened faces of people who had witnessed the degradation of a fellow human being. He was a little dizzy but it was more from shock, the raw fear that had taken command of his body; he was not badly hurt despite the shower of heavy blows. He let Coach lead him by the arm into the back room of the candy store and put ice on his face, which, though it was not cut or bleeding, was lumpy with swelling bruises. The fear was subsiding now and the humiliation he had suffered made him sick to his stomach so that he had to throw up. Coach held his head over the sink, supported him as if he were drunk, then helped him upstairs to the apartment and made him lie down in one of the bedrooms. Carlo never noticed that Sally Rags had disappeared.

Sally Rags had walked down to Third Avenue and called Rocco Lampone to report what had happened. Rocco took the news calmly and in his turn called his *caporegime*, Pete Clemenza. Clemenza groaned and said, "Oh, Christ, that goddamn Sonny and his temper," but his finger had prudently clicked down on the hook so that Rocco never heard his remark.

Clemenza called the house in Long Beach and got Tom Hagen. Hagen was silent for a moment and then he said, "Send some of your people and cars out on the road to Long Beach as soon as you can, just in case Sonny gets held up by traffic or an accident. When he gets sore like that he doesn't know what the hell he's doing. Maybe some of our friends on the other side will hear he was in town. You never can tell."

Clemenza said doubtfully, "By the time I could get anybody on the road, Sonny will be home. That goes for the Tattaglias too."

"I know," Hagen said patiently. "But if something out of the ordinary happens, Sonny may be held up. Do the best you can, Pete."

Grudgingly Clemenza called Rocco Lampone and told him to get a few people and cars and cover the road to Long Beach. He himself went out to his beloved Cadillac and with three of the platoon of guards who now garrisoned his home, started over the Atlantic Beach Bridge, toward New York City.

One of the hangers-on around the candy store, a small bettor on the payroll of the Tattaglia Family as an informer, called the contact he had with his people. But the Tattaglia Family had not streamlined itself for the war, the contact still had to go all the way through the insulation layers before he finally got to the *caporegime* who contacted the Tattaglia chief. By that time Sonny Corleone was safely back in the mall, in his father's house, in Long Beach, about to face his father's wrath.

Chapter

✕✕✕✕✕✕✕✕✕✕✕✕✕✕✕✕✕✕✕✕✕✕✕✕

17

THE war of 1947 between the Corleone Family and the Five Families combined against them proved to be expensive for both sides. It was complicated by the police pressure put on everybody to solve the murder of Captain McCluskey. It was rare that operating officials of the Police Department ignored political muscle that protected gambling and vice operations, but in this case the politicians were as helpless as the general staff of a rampaging, looting army whose field officers refuse to follow orders.

This lack of protection did not hurt the Corleone Family as much as it did their opponents. The Corleone group depended on gambling for most of its income, and was hit expecially hard in its "numbers" or "policy" branch of operations. The runners who picked up the action were swept into police nets and usually given a medium shellacking before being booked. Even some of the "banks" were located and raided, with heavy financial loss. The "bankers," .90 calibers in their own right, complained to the *caporegimes*, who brought their complaints to the family council table. But there was nothing to be done. The bankers were told to go out of business. Local Negro free-lancers were allowed to take over the operation in Harlem, the richest territory, and they operated in such scattered fashion that the police found it hard to pin them down.

After the death of Captain McCluskey, some newspapers printed stories involving him with Sollozzo. They published proof that McCluskey had received large sums of money in cash, shortly before his death. These stories had been planted by Hagen, the information supplied by him. The Police Department refused to confirm or deny these stories, but they were taking effect. The police force got the word through informers, through police on the Family payroll, that McCluskey had been a rogue cop. Not that he had taken money or clean graft, there was no rank-and-file onus to that. But that he had taken the dirtiest of dirty money; murder and drugs money. And in the morality of policemen, this was unforgivable.

Hagen understood that the policeman believes in law and order in a curiously innocent way. He believed in it more than does the public he serves. Law and order is, after all, the magic from which he derives his power, individual power which he cherishes as nearly all men cherish individual power. And yet there is always the smoldering resentment against the public he serves. They are at the same time his ward and his prey. As wards they are ungrateful, abusive and demanding. As prey they are slippery and dangerous, full of guile. As soon as one is in the policeman's clutches the mechanism of the society the policeman defends marshals all its resources to cheat him of his prize. The fix is put in by politicians. Judges give lenient suspended sentences to the worst hoodlums. Governors of the States and the President of the United States himself give full pardons, assuming that respected lawyers have not already won his acquittal. After a time the cop learns. Why should he not collect the fees these hoodlums are paying? He needs it more. His children, why should they not go to college? Why shouldn't his wife shop in more expensive places? Why shouldn't he himself get the sun with a winter vacation in Florida? After all, he risks his life and that is no joke.

But usually he draws the line against accepting dirty graft. He will take money to let a bookmaker operate. He will take money from a man who hates getting parking tickets or speeding tickets. He will allow call girls and prostitutes to ply their trade; for a consideration. These are vices natural to man. But usually he will not take a payoff for drugs, armed robberies, rape, murder and other assorted perversions. In his mind these attack the very core of his personal authority and cannot be countenanced.

The murder of a police captain was comparable to regicide. But when it became known that McCluskey had been killed while in the company of a notorious narcotics peddler, when it became known that he was suspected of conspiracy to murder, the police desire for vengeance began to fade. Also, after all, there were still mortgage payments to be made, cars to be paid off, children to be launched into the world. Without their "sheet" money, policemen had to scramble to make ends meet. Unlicensed peddlers were good for lunch money. Parking ticket payoffs came to nickels and dimes. Some of the more desperate even began shaking down suspects (homosexuals, assaults and batteries) in the precinct squad rooms. Finally the brass relented. They raised the prices and let the Families operate. Once again the payoff sheet was typed up by the precinct bagman, listing every man assigned to the local station and what his cut was each month. Some semblance of social order was restored.

It had been Hagen's idea to use private detectives to guard Don Corleone's hospital room. These were, of course, supplemented by the much more formidable soldiers of Tessio's *regime*. But Sonny was not satisfied even with this. By the middle of February, when the Don could be moved without danger, he was taken by ambulance to his home in the mall. The house had been renovated so that his bedroom was now a hospital room with all equipment necessary for any emergency. Nurses specially recruited and checked had been hired for round-the-clock care, and Dr. Kennedy, with the payment of a huge fee, had been persuaded to become the physician in residence to this private hospital. At least until the Don would need only nursing care.

The mall itself was made impregnable. Button men were moved into the extra houses, the tenants sent on vacations to their native villages in Italy, all expenses paid.

Freddie Corleone had been sent to Las Vegas to recuperate and also to scout out the ground for a Family operation in the luxury hotel-gambling casino complex that was springing up. Las Vegas was part of the West Coast empire still neutral and the Don of that empire had guaranteed Freddie's safety there. The New York five Families had no desire to make more enemies by going into Vegas after Freddie Corleone. They had enough trouble on their hands in New York.

Dr. Kennedy had forbade any discussion of business in front of the Don. This edict was completely disregarded. The Don insisted on the council of war being held in his room. Sonny, Tom Hagen, Pete Clemenza and Tessio gathered there the very first night of his homecoming.

Don Corleone was too weak to speak much but he wished to listen and exercise veto powers. When it was explained that Freddie had been sent to Las Vegas to learn the gambling casino business, he nodded his head approvingly. When he learned that Bruno Tattaglia had been killed by Corleone button men he shook his head and sighed. But what distressed him most of all was learning that Michael had killed Sollozzo and Captain McCluskey and had then been forced to flee to Sicily. When he heard this he motioned them out and they continued the conference in the corner room that held the law library.

Sonny Corleone relaxed in the huge armchair behind the desk. "I think we'd better let the old man take it easy for a couple of weeks, until the doc says he can do business." He paused. "I'd like to have it going again before he gets better. We have the go-ahead from the cops to operate. The first thing is the policy banks in Harlem. The black boys up there had their fun, now we have to take it back. They screwed up the works but good, just like they usually do when they run things. A lot of their runners didn't pay off winners. They drive up in Cadillacs and tell their players they gotta wait for their dough or maybe just pay them half what they win. I don't want any runner looking rich to his players. I don't want them dressing too good. I don't want them driving new cars. I don't want them welching on paying a winner. And I don't want any free-lancers staying in business, they give us a bad name. Tom, let's get that project moving right away. Everything else will fall in line as soon as you send out the word that the lid is off."

Hagen said, "There are some very tough boys up in Harlem. They got a taste of the big money. They won't go back to being runners or sub-bankers again."

Sonny shrugged. "Just give their names to Clemenza. That's his job, straightening them out."

Clemenza said to Hagen, "No problem."

It was Tessio who brought up the most important question. "Once we start operating, the five Families start their raids. They'll hit our bankers in Harlem and our bookmakers on the East Side. They may even try to make things tough for the garment center outfits we service. This war is going to cost a lot of money."

"Maybe they won't," Sonny said. "They know we'll hit them right back. I've got peace feelers out and maybe we can settle everything by paying an indemnity for the Tattaglia kid."

Hagen said, "We're getting the cold shoulder on those negotiations. They lost a lot of dough the last few months and they blame us for it. With justice. I think what they want is for us to agree to come in on the narcotics trade, to use the Family influence politically. In other words, Sollozzo's deal minus Sollozzo. But they won't broach that until they've hurt us with some sort of combat action. Then after we've been softened up they figure we'll listen to a proposition on narcotics."

Sonny said curtly, "No deal on drugs. The Don said no and it's *no* until he changes it."

Hagen said briskly, "Then we're faced with a tactical problem. Our money is out in the open. Bookmaking and policy. We can be hit. But the Tattaglia Family has prostitution and call girls and the dock unions. How the hell are we going to hit them? The other Families are in some gambling. But most of them are in the construction trades, shylocking, controlling the unions, getting the government contracts. They get a lot from strong-arm and other stuff that involves innocent people. Their money isn't out in the street. The Tattaglia nightclub is too famous to touch, it would cause too much of a stink. And with the Don still out of action their political influence matches ours. So we've got a real problem here."

"It's my problem, Tom," Sonny said. "I'll find the answer. Keep the negotiation alive and follow through on the other stuff. Let's go back into business and see what happens. Then we'll take it from there. Clemenza and Tessio have plenty of soldiers, we can match the whole Five Families gun for gun if that's the way they want it. We'll just go to the mattresses."

There was no problem getting the free-lance Negro bankers out of business. The police were informed and cracked down. With a special effort. At that time it was not possible for a Negro to make a payoff to a high police or political official to keep such an operation going. This was due to racial prejudice and racial distrust more than anything else. But Harlem had always been considered a minor problem, and its settlement was expected.

The Five Families struck in an unexpected direction. Two powerful officials in the garment unions were killed, officials who were members of the Corleone Family. Then the Corleone Family shylocks were barred from the waterfront piers as were the Corleone Family bookmakers. The longshoremen's union locals had gone over to the Five Families. Corleone bookmakers all over the city were threatened to persuade them to change their allegiance. The biggest numbers banker in Harlem, an old friend and ally of the Corleone Family, was brutally murdered. There was no longer any option. Sonny told his *caporegimes* to go to the mattresses.

Two apartments were set up in the city and furnished with mattresses for the button men to sleep on, a refrigerator for food, and guns and ammunition. Clemenza staffed one apartment and Tessio the other. All Family bookmakers were given bodyguard teams. The policy bankers in Harlem, however, had gone over to the enemy and at the moment nothing could be done about that. All this cost the Corleone Family a great deal of money and very little was coming in. As the next few months went by, other things became obvious. The most important was that the Corleone Family had overmatched itself.

There were reasons for this. With the Don still too weak to take a part, a great deal of the Family's political strength was neutralized. Also, the last ten years of peace had seriously eroded the fighting qualities of the two *caporegimes*, Clemenza and Tessio. Clemenza was still a competent executioner and administrator but he no longer had the energy or the youthful strength to lead troops. Tessio had mellowed with age and was not ruthless enough. Tom Hagen, despite his abilities, was simply not suited to be a *Consigliori* in a time of war. His main fault was that he was not a Sicilian.

Sonny Corleone recognized these weaknesses in the Family's wartime posture but could not take any steps to remedy them. He was not the Don and only the Don could replace the *caporegimes* and the *Consigliori*. And the very act of replacement would make the situation more dangerous, might precipitate some treachery. At first, Sonny had thought of fighting a holding action until the Don could become well enough to take charge, but with the defection of the policy bankers, the terrorization of the bookmakers, the Family position was becoming precarious. He decided to strike back.

But he decided to strike right at the heart of the enemy. He planned the execution of the heads of the five Families in one grand tactical maneuver. To that purpose he put into effect an elaborate system of surveillance of these leaders. But after a week the enemy chiefs promptly dived underground and were seen no more in public.

The Five Families and the Corleone Empire were in stalemate.

Chapter

18

AMERIGO BONASERA lived only a few blocks from his undertaking establishment on Mulberry Street and so always went home for supper. Evenings he returned to his place of business, dutifully joining those mourners paying their respects to the dead who lay in state in his somber parlors.

He always resented the jokes made about his profession, the macabre technical details which were so unimportant. Of course none of his friends or family or neighbors would make such jokes. Any profession was worthy of respect to men who for centuries earned bread by the sweat of their brows.

Now at supper with his wife in their solidly furnished apartment, gilt statues of the Virgin Mary with their red-glassed candles flickering on the sideboard, Bonasera lit a Camel cigarette and took a relaxing glass of American whiskey. His wife brought steaming plates of soup to the table. The two of them were alone now; he had sent his daughter to live in Boston with her mother's sister, where she could forget her terrible experience and her injuries at the hands of the two ruffians Don Corleone had punished.

As they ate their soup his wife asked, "Are you going back to work tonight?"

Amerigo Bonasera nodded. His wife respected his work but did not understand it. She did not understand that the technical part of his profession was the least important. She thought, like most other people, that he was paid for his skill in making the dead look so lifelike in their coffins. And indeed his skill in this was legendary. But even more important, even more necessary was his physical presence at the wake. When the bereaved family came at night to receive their blood relatives and their friends beside the coffin of their loved one, they needed Amerigo Bonasera with them.

For he was a strict chaperone to death. His face always grave, yet strong and comforting, his voice unwavering, yet muted to a low register, he commanded the mourning ritual. He could quiet grief that was too unseemly, he could rebuke unruly children whose parents had not the heart to chastise. Never cloying in the tender of his condolences, yet never was he offhand. Once a family used Amerigo Bonasera to speed a loved one on, they came back to him again and again. And he never, never, deserted one of his clients on that terrible last night above ground.

Usually he allowed himself a little nap after supper. Then he washed and shaved afresh, talcum powder generously used to shroud the heavy black beard. A mouthwash always. He respectfully changed into fresh linen, white gleaming shirt, the black tie, a freshly pressed dark suit, dull black shoes and black socks. And yet the effect was comforting instead of somber. He also kept his hair dyed black, an unheard-of frivolity in an Italian male of his generation; but not out of vanity. Simply because his hair had turned a lively pepper and salt, a color which struck him as unseemly for his profession.

After he finished his soup, his wife placed a small steak before him with a few forkfuls of green spinach oozing yellow oil. He was a light eater. When he finished this he drank a cup of coffee and smoked another Camel cigarette. Over his coffee he thought about his poor daughter. She would never be the same. Her outward beauty had been restored but there was the look of a frightened animal in her eyes that had made him unable to bear the sight of her. And so they had sent her to live in Boston for a time. Time would heal her wounds. Pain and terror was not so final as death, as he well knew. His work made him an optimist.

He had just finished the coffee when his phone in the living room rang. His wife never answered it when he was home, so he got up and drained his cup and stubbed out his cigarette. As he walked to the phone he pulled off his tie and started to unbutton his shirt, getting ready for his little nap. Then he picked up the phone and said with quiet courtesy, "Hello."

The voice on the other end was harsh, strained. "This is Tom Hagen," it said. "I'm calling for Don Corleone, at his request."

Amerigo Bonasera felt the coffee churning sourly in his stomach, felt himself going a little sick. It was more than a year since he had put himself in the debt of the Don to avenge his daughter's honor and in that time the knowledge that he must pay that debt had receded. He had been so grateful seeing the bloody faces of those two ruffians that he would have done anything for the Don. But time erodes gratitude more quickly than it does beauty. Now Bonasera felt the sickness of a man faced with disaster. His voice faltered as he answered, "Yes, I understand. I'm listening."

He was surprised at the coldness in Hagen's voice. The *Consigliori* had always been a courteous man, though not Italian, but now he was being rudely brusque. "You owe the Don a service," Hagen said. "He has no doubt that you will repay him. That you will be happy to have this opportunity. In one hour, not before, perhaps later, he will be at your funeral parlor to ask for your help. Be there to greet him. Don't have any people who work for you there. Send them home. If you have any objections to this, speak now and I'll inform Don Corleone. He has other friends who can do him this service."

Amerigo Bonasera almost cried out in his fright, "How can you think I would refuse the Godfather? Of course I'll do anything he wishes. I haven't forgotten my debt. I'll go to my business immediately, at once."

Hagen's voice was gentler now, but there was something strange about it. "Thank you," he said. "The Don never doubted you. The question was mine. Oblige him tonight and you can always come to me in any trouble, you'll earn my personal friendship."

This frightened Amerigo Bonasera even more. He stuttered, "The Don himself is coming to me tonight?"

"Yes," Hagen said.

"Then he's completely recovered from his injuries, thank God," Bonasera said. His voice made it a question.

There was a pause at the other end of the phone, then Hagen's voice said very quietly, "Yes." There was a click and the phone went dead.

Bonasera was sweating. He went into the bedroom and changed his shirt and rinsed his mouth. But he didn't shave or use a fresh tie. He put on the same one he had used during the day. He called the funeral parlor and told his assistant to stay with the bereaved family using the front parlor that night. He himself would be busy in the laboratory working area of the building. When the assistant started asking questions Bonasera cut him off very curtly and told him to follow orders exactly.

He put on his suit jacket and his wife, still eating, looked up at him in surprise. "I have work to do," he said and she did not dare question him because of the look on his face. Bonasera went out of the house and walked the few blocks to his funeral parlor.

This building stood by itself on a large lot with a white picket fence running all around it. There was a narrow roadway leading from the street to the rear, just wide enough for ambulances and hearses. Bonasera unlocked the gate and left it open. Then he walked to the rear of the building and entered it through the wide door there. As he did so he could see mourners already entering the front door of the funeral parlor to pay their respects to the current corpse.

Many years ago when Bonasera had bought this building from an undertaker planning to retire, there had been a stoop of about ten steps that mourners had to mount before entering the funeral parlor. This had posed a problem. Old and crippled mourners determined to pay their respects had found the steps almost impossible to mount, so the former undertaker had used the freight elevator for these people, a small metal platform, that rose out of the ground beside the building. The elevator was for coffins and bodies. It would descend underground, then rise into the funeral parlor itself, so that a crippled mourner would find himself rising through the floor beside the coffin as other mourners moved their black chairs aside to let the elevator rise through the trapdoor. Then when the crippled or aged mourner had finished paying his respects, the elevator would again come up through the polished floor to take him down and out again.

Amerigo Bonasera had found this solution to the problem unseemly and penny-pinching. So he had had the front of the building remodeled, the stoop done away with and a slightly inclining walk put in its place. But of course the elevator was still used for coffins and corpses.

In the rear of the building, cut off from the funeral parlor and reception rooms by a massive soundproof door, was the business office, the embalming room, a storeroom for coffins, and a carefully locked closet holding chemicals and the awful tools of his trade. Bonasera went to the office, sat at his desk and lit up a Camel, one of the few times he had ever smoked in this building. Then he waited for Don Corleone.

He waited with a feeling of the utmost despair. For he had no doubt as to what services he would be called upon to perform. For the last year the Corleone Family had waged war against the five great Mafia Families of New York and the carnage had filled the newspapers. Many men on both sides had been killed. Now the Corleone Family had killed somebody so important that they wished to hide his body, make it disappear, and what better way than to have it officially buried by a registered undertaker? And Amerigo Bonasera had no illusions about the act he was to commit. He would be an accessory to murder. If it came out, he would spend years in jail. His daughter and wife would be disgraced, his good name, the respected name of Amerigo Bonasera, dragged through the bloody mud of the Mafia war.

He indulged himself by smoking another Camel. And then he thought of something even more terrifying. When the other Mafia Families found out that he had aided the Corleones they would treat him as an enemy. They would murder him. And now he cursed the day he had gone to the Godfather and begged for his vengeance. He cursed the day his wife and the wife of Don Corleone had become friends. He cursed his daughter and America and his own success. And then his optimism returned. It could all go well. Don Corleone was a clever man. Certainly everything had been arranged to keep the secret. He had only to keep his nerve. For of course the one thing more fatal than any other was to earn the Don's displeasure.

He heard tires on gravel. His practiced ear told him a car was coming through the narrow driveway and parking in the back yard. He opened the rear door to let them in. The huge fat man, Clemenza, entered, followed by two very rough-looking young fellows. They searched the rooms without saying a word to Bonasera, then Clemenza went out. The two young men remained with the undertaker.

A few moments later Bonasera recognized the sound of a heavy ambulance coming through the narrow driveway. Then Clemenza appeared in the doorway followed by two men carrying a stretcher. And Amerigo Bonasera's worst fears were realized. On the stretcher was a corpse swaddled in a gray blanket but with bare yellow feet sticking out the end.

Clemenza motioned the stretcher-bearers into the embalming room. And then from the blackness of the yard another man stepped into the lighted office room. It was Don Corleone.

The Don had lost weight during his illness and moved with a curious stiffness. He was holding his hat in his hands and his hair seemed thin over his massive skull. He looked older, more shrunken than when Bonasera had seen him at the wedding, but he still radiated power. Holding his hat against his chest, he said to Bonasera, "Well, old friend, are you ready to do me this service?"

Bonasera nodded. The Don followed the stretcher into the embalming room and Bonasera trailed after him. The corpse was on one of the guttered tables. Don Corleone made a tiny gesture with his hat and the other men left the room.

Bonasera whispered, "What do you wish me to do?"

Don Corleone was staring at the table. "I want you to use all your powers, all your skill, as you love me," he said. "I do not wish his mother to see him as he is." He went to the table and drew down the gray blanket. Amerigo Bonasera against all his will, against all his years of training and experience, let out a gasp of horror. On the embalming table was the bullet-smashed face of Sonny Corleone. The left eye drowned in blood had a star fracture in its lens. The bridge of his nose and left cheekbone were hammered into pulp.

For one fraction of a second the Don put out his hand to support himself against Bonasera's body. "See how they have massacred my son," he said.

Chapter

19

PERHAPS it was the stalemate that made Sonny Corleone embark on the bloody course of attrition that ended in his own death. Perhaps it was his dark violent nature given full rein. In any case, that spring and summer he mounted senseless raids on enemy auxiliaries. Tattaglia Family pimps were shot to death in Harlem, dock goons were massacred. Union officials who owed allegiance to the Five Families were warned to stay neutral, and when the Corleone bookmakers and shylocks were still barred from the docks, Sonny sent Clemenza and his *regime* to wreak havoc upon the long shore.

This slaughter was senseless because it could not affect the outcome of the war. Sonny was a brilliant tactician and won his brilliant victories. But what was needed was the strategical genius of Don Corleone. The whole thing degenerated into such a deadly guerrilla war that both sides found themselves losing a great deal of revenue and lives to no purpose. The Corleone Family was finally forced to close down some of its most profitable bookmaking stations, including the book given to son-in-law Carlo Rizzi for his living. Carlo took to drink and running with chorus girls and giving his wife Connie a hard time. Since his beating at the hands of Sonny he had not dared to hit his wife again but he had not slept with her. Connie had thrown herself at his feet and he had spurned her, as he thought, like a Roman, with exquisite patrician pleasure. He had sneered at her, "Go call your brother and tell him I won't screw you, maybe he'll beat me up until I get a hard on."

But he was in deadly fear of Sonny though they treated each other with cold politeness. Carlo had the sense to realize that Sonny would kill him, that Sonny was a man who could, with the naturalness of an animal, kill another man, while he himself would have to call up all his courage, all his will, to commit murder. It never occurred to Carlo that because of this he was a better man than Sonny Corleone, if such terms could be used; he envied Sonny his awesome savagery, a savagery which was now becoming a legend.

Tom Hagen, as the *Consigliori*, disapproved of Sonny's tactics and yet decided not to protest to the Don simply because the tactics, to some extent, worked. The Five Families seemed to be cowed, finally, as the attrition went on, and their counterblows weakened and finally ceased altogether. Hagen at first distrusted this seeming pacification of the enemy but Sonny was jubilant. "I'll pour it on," he told Hagen, "and then those bastards will come begging for a deal."

Sonny was worried about other things. His wife was giving him a hard time because the rumors had gotten to her that Lucy Mancini had bewitched her husband. And though she joked publicly about her Sonny's equipment and technique, he had stayed away from her too long and she missed him in her bed, and she was making life miserable for him with her nagging.

In addition to this Sonny was under the enormous strain of being a marked man. He had to be extraordinarily careful in all his movements and he knew that his visits to Lucy Mancini had been charted by the enemy. But here he took elaborate precautions since this was the traditional vulnerable spot. He was safe there. Though Lucy had not the slightest suspicion, she was watched twenty-four hours a day by men of the Santino *regime* and when an apartment became vacant on her floor it was immediately rented by one of the most reliable men of that *regime*.

The Don was recovering and would soon be able to resume command. At that time the tide of battle must swing to the Corleone Family. This Sonny was sure of. Meanwhile he would guard his Family's empire, earn the respect of his father, and, since the position was not hereditary to an absolute degree, cement his claim as heir to the Corleone Empire.

But the enemy was making its plans. They too had analyzed the situation and had come to the conclusion that the only way to stave off complete defeat was to kill Sonny Corleone. They understood the situation better now and felt it was possible to negotiate with the Don, known for his logical reasonableness. They had come to hate Sonny for his bloodthirstiness, which they considered barbaric. Also not good business sense. Nobody wanted the old days back again with all its turmoil and trouble.

One evening Connie Corleone received an anonymous phone call, a girl's voice, asking for Carlo. "Who is this?" Connie asked.

The girl on the other end giggled and said, "I'm a friend of Carlo's. I just wanted to tell him I can't see him tonight. I have to go out of town."

"You lousy bitch," Connie Corleone said. She screamed it again into the phone. "You lousy tramp bitch." There was a click on the other end.

Carlo had gone to the track for that afternoon and when he came home in the late evening he was sore at losing and half drunk from the bottle he always carried. As soon as he stepped into the door, Connie started screaming curses at him. He ignored her and went in to take a shower. When he came out he dried his naked body in front of her and started dolling up to go out.

Connie stood with hands on hips, her face pointy and white with rage. "You're not going any place," she said. "Your girl friend called and said she can't make it tonight. You lousy bastard, you have the nerve to give your whores my phone number. I'll kill you, you bastard." She rushed at him, kicking and scratching.

He held her off with one muscular forearm. "You're crazy," he said coldly. But she could see he was worried, as if he knew the crazy girl he was screwing would actually pull such a stunt. "She was kidding around, some nut," Carlo said.

Connie ducked around his arm and clawed at his face. She got a little bit of his cheek under her fingernails. With surprising patience he pushed her away. She noticed he was careful because of her pregnancy and that gave her the courage to feed her rage. She was also excited. Pretty soon she wouldn't be able to do anything, the doctor had said no sex for the last two months and she wanted it, before the last two months started. Yet her wish to inflict a physical injury on Carlo was very real too. She followed him into the bedroom.

She could see he was scared and that filled her with contemptuous delight. "You're staying home," she said, "you're not going out."

"OK, OK," he said. He was still undressed, only wearing his shorts. He liked to go around the house like that, he was proud of his V-shaped body, the golden skin. Connie looked at him hungrily. He tried to laugh. "You gonna give me something to eat at least?"

That mollified her, his calling on her duties, one of them at least. She was a good cook, she had learned that from her mother. She sauteed veal and peppers, preparing a mixed salad while the pan simmered. Meanwhile Carlo stretched out on his bed to read the next day's racing form. He had a water glass full of whiskey beside him which he kept sipping at.

Connie came into the bedroom. She stood in the doorway as if she could not come close to the bed without being invited. "The food is on the table," she said.

"I'm not hungry yet," he said, still reading the racing form.

"It's on the table," Connie said stubbornly.

"Stick it up your ass," Carlo said. He drank off the rest of the whiskey in the water glass, tilted the bottle to fill it again. He paid no more attention to her.

Connie went into the kitchen, picked up the plates filled with food and smashed them against the sink. The loud crashes brought Carlo in from the bedroom. He looked at the greasy veal and peppers splattered all over the kitchen walls and his finicky neatness was outraged. "You filthy guinea spoiled brat," he said venomously. "Clean that up right now or I'll kick the shit out of you."

"Like hell I will," Connie said. She held her hands like claws ready to scratch his bare chest to ribbons.

Carlo went back into the bedroom and when he came out he was holding his belt doubled in his hand. "Clean it up," he said and there was no mistaking the menace in his voice. She stood there not moving and he swung the belt against her heavily padded hips, the leather stinging but not really hurting. Connie retreated to the kitchen cabinets and her hand went into one of the drawers to haul out the long bread knife. She held it ready.

Carlo laughed. "Even the female Corleones are murderers," he said. He put the belt down on the kitchen table and advanced toward her. She tried a sudden lunge but her pregnant heavy body made her slow and he eluded the thrust she aimed at his groin in such deadly earnest. He disarmed her easily and then he started to slap her face with a slow medium-heavy stroke so as not to break the skin. He hit her again and again as she retreated around the kitchen table trying to escape him and he pursued her into the bedroom. She tried to bite his hand and he grabbed her by the hair to lift her head up. He slapped her face until she began to weep like a little girl, with pain and humiliation. Then he threw her contemptuously onto the bed. He drank from the bottle of whiskey still on the night table. He seemed very drunk now, his light blue eyes had a crazy glint in them and finally Connie was truly afraid.

Carlo straddled his legs apart and drank from the bottle. He reached down and grabbed a chunk of her pregnant heavy thigh in his hand. He squeezed very hard, hurting her and making her beg for mercy. "You're fat as a pig," he said with disgust and walked out of the bedroom.

Thoroughly frightened and cowed, she lay in the bed, not daring to see what her husband was doing in the other room. Finally she rose and went to the door to peer into the living room. Carlo had opened a fresh bottle of whiskey and was sprawled on the sofa. In a little while he would drink himself into sodden sleep and she could sneak into the kitchen and call her family in Long Beach. She would tell her mother to send someone out here to get her. She just hoped Sonny didn't answer the phone, she knew it would be best to talk to Tom Hagen or her mother.

It was nearly ten o'clock at night when the kitchen phone in Don Corleone's house rang. It was answered by one of the Don's body-guards who dutifully turned the phone over to Connie's mother. But Mrs. Corleone could hardly understand what her daughter was saying, the girl was hysterical yet trying to whisper so that her husband in the next room would not hear her. Also her face had become swollen because of the slaps, and her puffy lips thickened her speech. Mrs. Corleone made a sign to the bodyguard that he should call Sonny, who was in the living room with Tom Hagen.

Sonny came into the kitchen and took the phone from his mother. "Yeah, Connie," he said.

Connie was so frightened both of her husband and of what her brother would do that her speech became worse. She babbled, "Sonny, just send a car to bring me home, I'll tell you then, it's nothing, Sonny. Don't you come. Send Tom, please, Sonny. It's nothing, I just want to come home."

By this time Hagen had come into the room. The Don was already under a sedated sleep in the bedroom above and Hagen wanted to keep an eye on Sonny in all crises. The two interior bodyguards were also in the kitchen. Everybody was watching Sonny as he listened on the phone.

There was no question that the violence in Sonny Corleone's nature rose from some deep mysterious physical well. As they watched they could actually see the blood rushing to his heavily corded neck, could see the eyes film with hatred, the separate features of his face tightening, growing pinched, then his face took on the grayish hue of a sick man fighting off some sort of death, except that the adrenalin pumping through his body made his hands tremble. But his voice was controlled, pitched low, as he told his sister, "You wait there. You just wait there." He hung up the phone.

He stood there for a moment quite stunned with his own rage, then he said, "The fucking sonofabitch, the fucking sonofabitch." He ran out of the house.

Hagen knew the look on Sonny's face, all reasoning power had left him. At this moment Sonny was capable of anything. Hagen also knew that the ride into the city would cool Sonny off, make him more rational. But that rationality might make him even more dangerous, though the rationality would enable him to protect himself against the consequences of his rage. Hagen heard the car motor roaring into life and he said to the two bodyguards, "Go after him."

Then he went to the phone and made some calls. He arranged for some men of Sonny's *regime* living in the city to go up to Carlo Rizzi's apartment and get Carlo out of there. Other men would stay with Connie until Sonny arrived. He was taking a chance, thwarting Sonny, but he knew the Don would back him up. He was afraid that Sonny might kill Carlo in front of witnesses. He did not expect trouble from the enemy. The Five Families had been quiet too long and obviously were looking for peace of some kind.

By the time Sonny roared out of the mall in his Buick, he had already regained, partly, his senses. He noted the two bodyguards getting into a car to follow him and approved. He expected no danger, the Five Families had quit counterattacking, were not really fighting anymore. He had grabbed his jacket in the foyer and there was a gun in a secret dashboard compartment of the car, the car registered in the name of a member of his *regime*, so that he personally could not get into any legal trouble. But he did not anticipate needing any weapon. He did not even know what he was going to do with Carlo Rizzi.

Now that he had a chance to think, Sonny knew he could not kill the father of an unborn child, and that father his sister's husband. Not over a domestic spat. Except that it was not just a domestic spat. Carlo was a bad guy and Sonny felt responsible that his sister had met the bastard through him.

The paradox in Sonny's violent nature was that he could not hit a woman and had never done so. That he could not harm a child or anything helpless. When Carlo had refused to fight back against him that day, it had kept Sonny from killing him, complete submission disarmed his violence. As a boy, he had been truly tenderhearted. That he had become a murderer as a man was simply his destiny.

But he would settle this thing once and for all, Sonny thought, as he headed the Buick toward the causeway that would take him over the water from Long Beach to the parkways on the other side of Jones Beach. He always used this route when he went to New York. There was less traffic.

He decided he would send Connie home with the bodyguards and then he would have a session with his brother-in-law. What would happen after that he didn't know. If the bastard had really hurt Connie, he'd make a cripple out of the bastard. But the wind coming over the causeway, the salty freshness of the air, cooled his anger. He put the window down all the way.

He had taken the Jones Beach Causeway, as always, because it was usually deserted this time of night, at this time of year, and he could speed recklessly until he hit the parkways on the other side. And even there traffic would be light. The release of driving very fast would help dissipate what he knew was a dangerous tension. He had already left his bodyguards' car far behind.

The causeway was badly lit, there was not a single car. Far ahead he saw the white cone of the manned tollbooth. There were other tollbooths beside it but they were staffed only during the day, for heavier traffic. Sonny started braking the Buick and at the same time searched his pockets for change. He had none. He reached for his wallet, flipped it open with one hand and fingered out a bill. He came within the arcade of light and he saw to his mild surprise a car in the tollbooth slot blocking it, the driver obviously asking some sort of directions from the toll taker. Sonny honked his horn and the other car obediently rolled through to let his car slide into the slot.

Sonny handed the toll taker the dollar bill and waited for his change. He was in a hurry now to close the window. The Atlantic Ocean air had chilled the whole car. But the toll taker was fumbling with his change; the dumb son of a bitch actually dropped it. Head and body disappeared as the toll man stooped down in his booth to pick up the money.

At that moment Sonny noticed that the other car had not kept going but had parked a few feet ahead, still blocking his way. At that same moment his lateral vision caught sight of another man in the darkened tollbooth to his right. But he did not have time to think about that because two men came out of the car parked in front and walked toward him. The toll collector still had not appeared. And then in the fraction of a second before anything actually happened, Santino Corleone knew he was a dead man. And in that moment his mind was lucid, drained of all violence, as if the hidden fear finally real and present had purified him.

Even so, his huge body in a reflex for life, crashed against the Buick door, bursting its lock. The man in the darkened tollbooth opened fire and the shots caught Sonny Corleone in the head and neck as his massive frame spilled out of the car. The two men in front held up their guns now, the man in the darkened tollbooth cut his fire, and Sonny's body sprawled on the asphalt with the legs still partly inside. The two men each fired shots into Sonny's body, then kicked him in the face to disfigure his features even more, to show a mark made by a more personal human power.

Seconds afterward, all four men, the three actual assassins and the bogus toll collector, were in their car and speeding toward the Meadowbrook Parkway on the other side of Jones Beach. Their pursuit was blocked by Sonny's car and body in the tollgate slot but when Sonny's bodyguards pulled up a few minutes later and saw his body lying there, they had no intention to pursue. They swung their car around in a huge arc and returned to Long Beach. At the first public phone off the causeway one of them hopped out and called Tom Hagen. He was very curt and very brisk. "Sonny's dead, they got him at the Jones Beach toll."

Hagen's voice was perfectly calm. "OK," he said. "Go to Clemenza's house and tell him to come here right away. He'll tell you what to do."

Hagen had taken the call in the kitchen, with Mama Corleone bustling around preparing a snack for the arrival of her daughter. He had kept his composure and the old woman had not noticed anything amiss. Not that she could not have, if she wanted to, but in her life with the Don she had learned it was far wiser *not* to perceive. That if it was necessary to know something painful, it would be told to her soon enough. And if it was a pain that could be spared her, she could do without. She was quite content not to share the pain of her men, after all did they share the pain of women? Impassively she boiled her coffee and set the table with food. In her experience pain and fear did not dull physical hunger; in her experience the taking of food dulled pain. She would have been outraged if a doctor had tried to sedate her with a drug, but coffee and a crust of bread were another matter; she came, of course, from a more primitive culture.

And so she let Tom Hagen escape to his corner conference room and once in that room, Hagen began to tremble so violently he had to sit down with his legs squeezed together, his head hunched into his contracted shoulders, hands clasped together between his knees as if he were praying to the devil.

He was, he knew now, no fit *Consigliori* for a Family at war. He had been fooled, faked out, by the Five Families and their seeming timidity. They had remained quiet, laying their terrible ambush. They had planned and waited, holding their bloody hands no matter what provocation they had been given. They had waited to land one terrible blow. And they had. Old Genco Abbandando would never have fallen for it, he would have smelled a rat, he would have smoked them out, tripled his precautions. And through all this Hagen felt his grief. Sonny had been his true brother, his savior; his hero when they had been boys together. Sonny had never been mean or bullying with him, had always treated him with affection, had taken him in his arms when Sollozzo had turned him loose. Sonny's joy at that reunion had been real. That he had grown up to be a cruel and violent and bloody man was, for Hagen, not relevant.

He had walked out of the kitchen because he knew he could never tell Mama Corleone about her son's death. He had never thought of her as his mother as he thought of the Don as his father and Sonny as his brother. His affection for her was like his affection for Freddie and Michael and Connie. The affection for someone who has been kind but not loving. But he could not tell her. In a few short months she had lost all her sons; Freddie exiled to Nevada. Michael hiding for his life in Sicily, and now Santino dead. Which of the three had she loved most of all? She had never shown.

It was no more than a few minutes. Hagen got control of himself again and picked up the phone. He called Connie's number. It rang for a long time before Connie answered in a whisper.

Hagen spoke to her gently. "Connie, this is Tom. Wake your husband up, I have to talk to him."

Connie said in a low frightened voice, "Tom, is Sonny coming here?"

"No," Hagen said. "Sonny's not coming there. Don't worry about that. Just wake Carlo up and tell him it's very important I speak to him."

Connie's voice was weepy. "Tom, he beat me up, I'm afraid he'll hurt me again if he knows I called home."

Hagen said gently, "He won't. He'll talk to me and I'll straighten him out. Everything will be OK. Tell him it's very important, very, very important he come to the phone. OK?"

It was almost five minutes before Carlo's voice came over the phone, a voice half slurred by whiskey and sleep. Hagen spoke sharply to make him alert.

"Listen, Carlo," he said, "I'm going to tell you something very shocking. Now prepare yourself because when I tell it to you I want you to answer me very casually as if it's less than it is. I told Connie it was important so you have to give her a story. Tell her the Family has decided to move you both to one of the houses in the mall and to give you a big job. That the Don has finally decided to give you a chance in the hope of making your home life better. You got that?"

There was a hopeful note in Carlo's voice as he answered, "Yeah, OK."

Hagen went on, "In a few minutes a couple of my men are going to knock on your door to take you away with them. Tell them I want them to call me first. Just tell them that. Don't say anything else. I'll instruct them to leave you there with Connie. OK?"

"Yeah, yeah, I got it," Carlo said. His voice was excited. The tension in Hagen's voice seemed to have finally alerted him that the news coming up was going to be really important.

Hagen gave it to him straight. "They killed Sonny tonight. Don't say anything. Connie called him while you were asleep and he was on his way over there, but I don't want her to know that, even if she guesses it, I don't want her to know it for sure. She'll start thinking it's all her fault. Now I want you to stay with her tonight and not tell her anything. I want you to make up with her. I want you to be the perfect loving husband. And I want you to stay that way until she has her baby at least. Tomorrow morning somebody, maybe you, maybe the Don, maybe her mother, will tell Connie that her brother got killed. And I want you by her side. Do me this favor and I'll take care of you in the times to come. You got that?"

Carlo's voice was a little shaky. "Sure, Tom, sure. Listen, me and you always got along. I'm grateful. Understand?"

"Yeah," Hagen said. "Nobody will blame your fight with Connie for causing this, don't worry about that. I'll take care of that." He paused and softly, encouragingly, "Go ahead now, take care of Connie." He broke the connection.

He had learned never to make a threat, the Don had taught him that, but Carlo had gotten the message all right: he was a hair away from death.

Hagen made another call to Tessio, telling him to come to the mall in Long Beach immediately. He didn't say why and Tessio did not ask. Hagen sighed. Now would come the part he dreaded.

He would have to waken the Don from his drugged slumber. He would have to tell the man he most loved in the world that he had failed him, that he had failed to guard his domain and the life of his eldest son. He would have to tell the Don everything was lost unless the sick man himself could enter the battle. For Hagen did not delude himself. Only the great Don himself could snatch even a stalemate from this terrible defeat. Hagen didn't even bother checking with Don Corleone's doctors, it would be to no purpose. No matter what the doctors ordered, even if they told him that the Don could not rise from his sickbed on pain of death, he must tell his adopted father and then follow him. And of course there was no question about what the Don would do. The opinions of medical men were irrelevant now, everything was irrelevant now. The Don must be told and he must either take command or order Hagen to surrender the Corleone power to the Five Families.

And yet with all his heart, Hagen dreaded the next hour. He tried to prepare his own manner. He would have to be in all ways strict with his own guilt. To reproach himself would only add to the Don's burden. To show his own grief would only sharpen the grief of the Don. To point out his own shortcomings as a wartime *Consigliori*, would only make the Don reproach himself for his own bad judgment for picking such a man for such an important post.

He must, Hagen knew, tell the news, present his analysis of what

must be done to rectify the situation and then keep silent. His reactions thereafter must be the reactions invited by his Don. If the
Don wanted him to show guilt, he would show guilt; if the Don
invited grief, he would lay bare his genuine sorrow.

Hagen lifted his head at the sound of motors, cars rolling up onto
the mall. The *caporegimes* were arriving. He would brief them first
and then he would go up and wake Don Corleone. He got up and
went to the liquor cabinet by the desk and took out a glass and bottle.
He stood there for a moment so unnerved he could not pour the
liquid from bottle to glass. Behind him, he heard the door to the room
close softly and, turning, he saw, fully dressed for the first time since
he had been shot, Don Corleone.

The Don walked across the room to his huge leather armchair and
sat down. He walked a little stiffly, his clothes hung a little loosely on
his frame but to Hagen's eyes he looked the same as always. It was
almost as if by his will alone the Don had discarded all external
evidence of his still weakened frame. His face was sternly set with all
its old force and strength. He sat straight in the armchair and he said
to Hagen, "Give me a drop of anisette."

Hagen switched bottles and poured them both a portion of the
fiery, licorice-tasting alcohol. It was peasant, homemade stuff, much
stronger than that sold in stores, the gift of an old friend who every
year presented the Don with a small truckload.

"My wife was weeping before she fell asleep," Don Corleone said.
"Outside my window I saw my *caporegimes* coming to the house and
it is midnight. So, *Consigliori* of mine, I think you should tell your
Don what everyone knows."

Hagen said quietly, "I didn't tell Mama anything. I was about to
come up and wake you and tell you the news myself. In another
moment I would have come to waken you."

Don Corleone said impassively, "But you needed a drink first."

"Yes," Hagen said.

"You've had your drink," the Don said. "You can tell me now."
There was just the faintest hint of reproach for Hagen's weakness.

"They shot Sonny on the causeway," Hagen said. "He's dead."

Don Corleone blinked. For just the fraction of a second the wall of
his will disintegrated and the draining of his physical strength was
plain on his face. Then he recovered.

He clasped his hands in front of him on top of the desk and looked directly into Hagen's eyes. "Tell me everything that happened," he said. He held up one of his hands. "No, wait until Clemenza and Tessio arrive so you won't have to tell it all again."

It was only a few moments later that the two *caporegimes* were escorted into the room by a bodyguard. They saw at once that the Don knew about his son's death because the Don stood up to receive them. They embraced him as old comrades were permitted to do. They all had a drink of anisette which Hagen poured them before he told them the story of that night.

Don Corleone asked only one question at the end. "Is it certain my son is dead?"

Clemenza answered. "Yes," he said. "The bodyguards were of Santino's *regime* but picked by me. I questioned them when they came to my house. They saw his body in the light of the tollhouse. He could not live with the wounds they saw. They place their lives in forfeit for what they say."

Don Corleone accepted this final verdict without any sign of emotion except for a few moments of silence. Then he said, "None of you are to concern yourselves with this affair. None of you are to commit any acts of vengeance, none of you are to make any inquiries to track down the murderers of my son without my express command. There will be no further acts of war against the Five Families without my express and personal wish. Our Family will cease all business operations and cease to protect any of our business operations until after my son's funeral. Then we will meet here again and decide what must be done. Tonight we must do what we can for Santino, we must bury him as a Christian. I will have friends of mine arrange things with the police and all other proper authorities. Clemenza, you will remain with me at all times as my bodyguard, you and the men of your *regime*. Tessio, you will guard all other members of my Family. Tom, I want you to call Amerigo Bonasera and tell him I will need his services at some time during this night. To wait for me at his establishment. It may be an hour, two hours, three hours. Do you all understand that?"

The three men nodded. Don Corleone said, "Clemenza, get some men and cars and wait for me. I will be ready in a few minutes. Tom, you did well. In the morning I want Constanzia with her mother. Make arrangements for her and her husband to live in the mall. Have Sandra's friends, the women, go to her house to stay with her. My wife will go there also when I have spoken with her. My wife will tell her the misfortune and the women will arrange for the church to say their masses and prayers for his soul."

The Don got up from his leather armchair. The other men rose with him and Clemenza and Tessio embraced him again. Hagen held the door open for the Don, who paused to look at him for a moment. Then the Don put his hand on Hagen's cheek, embraced him quickly, and said, in Italian, "You've been a good son. You comfort me." Telling Hagen that he had acted properly in this terrible time. The Don went up to his bedroom to speak to his wife. It was then that Hagen made the call to Amerigo Bonasera for the undertaker to redeem the favor he owed to the Corleones.

Book V

Chapter

><×××××××××××××××××××××××××××<

20

THE death of Santino Corleone sent shock waves through the underworld of the nation. And when it became known that Don Corleone had risen from his sick bed to take charge of the Family affairs, when spies at the funeral reported that the Don seemed to be fully recovered, the heads of the Five Families made frantic efforts to prepare a defense against the bloody retaliatory war that was sure to follow. Nobody made the mistake of assuming that Don Corleone could be held cheaply because of his past misfortunes. He was a man who had made only a few mistakes in his career and had learned from every one of them.

Only Hagen guessed the Don's real intentions and was not surprised when emissaries were sent to the Five Families to propose a peace. Not only to propose a peace but a meeting of all the Families in the city and with invitations to Families all over the United States to attend. Since the New York Families were the most powerful in the country, it was understood that their welfare affected the welfare of the country as a whole.

At first there were suspicions. Was Don Corleone preparing a trap? Was he trying to throw his enemies off their guard? Was he attempting to prepare a wholesale massacre to avenge his son? But Don

Corleone soon made it clear that he was sincere. Not only did he involve all the Families in the country in this meeting, but made no move to put his own people on a war footing or to enlist allies. And then he took the final irrevocable step that established the authenticity of these intentions and assured the safety of the grand council to be assembled. He called on the services of the Bocchicchio Family.

The Bocchicchio Family was unique in that, once a particularly ferocious branch of the Mafia in Sicily, it had become an instrument of peace in America. Once a group of men who earned their living by a savage determination, they now earned their living in what perhaps could be called a saintly fashion. The Bocchicchios' one asset was a closely knit structure of blood relationships, a family loyalty severe even for a society where family loyalty came before loyalty to a wife.

The Bocchicchio Family, extending out to third cousins, had once numbered nearly two hundred when they ruled the particular economy of a small section of southern Sicily. The income for the entire family then came from four or five flour mills, by no means owned communally, but assuring labor and bread and a minimal security for all Family members. This was enough, with intermarriages, for them to present a common front against their enemies.

No competing mill, no dam that would create a water supply to their competitors or ruin their own selling of water, was allowed to be built in their corner of Sicily. A powerful landowning baron once tried to erect his own mill strictly for his personal use. The mill was burned down. He called on the *carabineri* and higher authorities, who arrested three of the Bocchicchio Family. Even before the trial the manor house of the baron was torched. The indictment and accusations were withdrawn. A few months later one of the highest functionaries in the Italian government arrived in Sicily and tried to solve the chronic water shortage of that island by proposing a huge dam. Engineers arrived from Rome to do surveys while watched by grim natives, members of the Bocchicchio clan. Police flooded the area, housed in a specially built barracks.

It looked like nothing could stop the dam from being built and supplies and equipment had actually been unloaded in Palermo. That was as far as they got. The Bocchicchios had contacted fellow Mafia chiefs and extracted agreements for their aid. The heavy equipment was sabotaged, the lighter equipment stolen. Mafia deputies in the Italian Parliament launched a bureaucratic counterattack against the planners. This went on for several years and in that time Mussolini came to power. The dictator decreed that the dam must be built. It was not. The dictator had known that the Mafia would be a threat to his regime, forming what amounted to a separate authority from his own. He gave full powers to a high police official, who promptly solved the problem by throwing everybody into jail or deporting them to penal work islands. In a few short years he had broken the power of the Mafia, simply by arbitrarily arresting anyone even suspected of being a *mafioso*. And so also brought ruin to a great many innocent families.

The Bocchicchios had been rash enough to resort to force against this unlimited power. Half of the men were killed in armed combat, the other half deported to penal island colonies. There were only a handful left when arrangements were made for them to emigrate to America via the clandestine underground route of jumping ship through Canada. There were almost twenty immigrants and they settled in a small town not far from New York City, in the Hudson Valley, where by starting at the very bottom they worked their way up to owning a garbage hauling firm and their own trucks. They became prosperous because they had no competition. They had no competition because competitors found their trucks burned and sabotaged. One persistent fellow who undercut prices was found buried in the garbage he had picked up during the day, smothered to death.

But as the men married, to Sicilian girls, needless to say, children came, and the garbage business though providing a living, was not really enough to pay for the finer things America had to offer. And so, as a diversification, the Bocchicchio Family became negotiators and hostages in the peace efforts of warring Mafia families.

A strain of stupidity ran through the Bocchicchio clan, or perhaps they were just primitive. In any case they recognized their limitations and knew they could not compete with other Mafia families in the struggle to organize and control more sophisticated business structures like prostitution, gambling, dope and public fraud. They were straight-from-the-shoulder people who could offer a gift to an ordinary patrolman but did not know how to approach a political bagman. They had only two assets. Their honor and their ferocity.

A Bocchicchio never lied, never committed an act of treachery. Such behavior was too complicated. Also, a Bocchicchio never forgot an injury and never left it unavenged no matter what the cost. And so by accident they stumbled into what would prove to be their most lucrative profession.

When warring families wanted to make peace and arrange a parley, the Bocchicchio clan was contacted. The head of the clan would handle the initial negotiations and arrange for the necessary hostages. For instance, when Michael had gone to meet Sollozzo, a Bocchicchio had been left with the Corleone Family as surety for Michael's safety, the service paid for by Sollozzo. If Michael were killed by Sollozzo, then the Bocchicchio male hostage held by the Corleone Family would be killed by the Corleones. In this case the Bocchicchios would take their vengeance on Sollozzo as the cause of their clansman's death. Since the Bocchicchios were so primitive, they never let anything, any kind of punishment, stand in their way of vengeance. They would give up their own lives and there was no protection against them if they were betrayed. A Bocchicchio hostage was gilt-edged insurance.

And so now when Don Corleone employed the Bocchicchios as negotiators and arranged for them to supply hostages for all the Families to come to the peace meeting, there could be no question as to his sincerity. There could be no question of treachery. The meeting would be safe as a wedding.

Hostages given, the meeting took place in the director's conference room of a small commercial bank whose president was indebted to Don Corleone and indeed some of whose stock belonged to Don Corleone though it was in the president's name. The president always treasured that moment when he had offered to give Don Corleone a written document proving his ownership of the shares, to preclude any treachery. Don Corleone had been horrified. "I would trust you with my whole fortune," he told the president. "I would trust you with my life and the welfare of my children. It is inconceivable to me that you would ever trick me or otherwise betray me. My whole world, all my faith in my judgment of human character would collapse. Of course I have my own written records so that if something should happen to me my heirs would know that you hold something in trust for them. But I know that even if I were not here in this world to guard the interests of my children, you would be faithful to their needs."

The president of the bank, though not Sicilian, was a man of tender sensibilities. He understood the Don perfectly. Now the Godfather's request was the president's command and so on a Saturday afternoon, the executive suite of the bank, the conference room with its deep leather chairs, its absolute privacy, was made available to the Families.

Security at the bank was taken over by a small army of hand-picked men wearing bank guard uniforms. At ten o'clock on a Saturday morning the conference room began to fill up. Besides the Five Families of New York, there were representatives from ten other Families across the country, with the exception of Chicago, that black sheep of their world. They had given up trying to civilize Chicago, and they saw no point in including those mad dogs in this important conference.

A bar had been set up and a small buffet. Each representative to the conference had been allowed one aide. Most of the Dons had brought their *Consiglioris* as aides so there were comparatively few young men in the room. Tom Hagen was one of those young men and the only one who was not Sicilian. He was an object of curiosity, a freak.

Hagen knew his manners. He did not speak, he did not smile. He waited on his boss, Don Corleone, with all the respect of a favorite earl waiting on his king; bringing him a cold drink, lighting his cigar, positioning his ashtray; with respect but no obsequiousness.

Hagen was the only one in that room who knew the identity of the portraits hanging on the dark paneled walls. They were mostly portraits of fabulous financial figures done in rich oils. One was of Secretary of the Treasury Hamilton. Hagen could not help thinking that Hamilton might have approved of this peace meeting being held in a banking institution. Nothing was more calming, more conducive to pure reason, than the atmosphere of money.

The arrival time had been staggered for between nine-thirty to ten A.M. Don Corleone, in a sense the host since he had initiated the peace talks, had been the first to arrive; one of his many virtues was punctuality. The next to arrive was Carlo Tramonti, who had made the southern part of the United States his territory. He was an impressively handsome middle-aged man, tall for a Sicilian, with a very deep sunburn, exquisitely tailored and barbered. He did not look Italian, he looked more like one of those pictures in the magazines of millionaire fishermen lolling on their yachts. The Tramonti Family earned its livelihood from gambling, and no one meeting their Don would ever guess with what ferocity he had won his empire.

Emigrating from Sicily as a small boy, he had settled in Florida and grown to manhood there, employed by the American syndicate of

Southern small-town politicians who controlled gambling. These were very tough men backed up by very tough police officials and they never suspected that they could be overthrown by such a greenhorn immigrant. They were unprepared for his ferocity and could not match it simply because the rewards being fought over were not, to their minds, worth so much bloodshed. Tramonti won over the police with bigger shares of the gross; he exterminated those redneck hooligans who ran their operation with such a complete lack of imagination. It was Tramonti who opened ties with Cuba and the Batista regime and eventually poured money into the pleasure resorts of Havana gambling houses, whorehouses, to lure gamblers from the American mainland. Tramonti was now a millionaire many times over and owned one of the most luxurious hotels in Miami Beach.

When he came into the conference room followed by his aide, an equally sunburned *Consigliori*, Tramonti embraced Don Corleone, made a face of sympathy to show he sorrowed for the dead son.

Other Dons were arriving. They all knew each other, they had met over the years, either socially or when in the pursuit of their businesses. They had always showed each other professional courtesies and in their younger, leaner days had done each other little services. The second Don to arrive was Joseph Zaluchi from Detroit. The Zaluchi Family, under appropriate disguises and covers, owned one of the horse-racing tracks in the Detroit area. They also owned a good part of the gambling. Zaluchi was a moon-faced, amiable-looking man who lived in a one-hundred-thousand-dollar house in the fashionable Grosse Point section of Detroit. One of his sons had married into an old, well-known American family. Zaluchi, like Don Corleone, was sophisticated. Detroit had the lowest incidence of physical violence of any of the cities controlled by the Families; there had been only two executions in the last three years in that city. He disapproved of traffic in drugs.

Zaluchi had brought his *Consigliori* with him and both men came to Don Corleone to embrace him. Zaluchi had a booming American voice with only the slightest trace of an accent. He was conservatively dressed, very businessman, and with a hearty goodwill to match. He said to Don Corleone, "Only your voice could have brought me here." Don Corleone bowed his head in thanks. He could count on Zaluchi for support.

The next two Dons to arrive were from the West Coast, motoring from there in the same car since they worked together closely in any case. They were Frank Falcone and Anthony Molinari and both were younger than any of the other men who would come to the meeting; in their early forties. They were dressed a little more informally than the others, there was a touch of Hollywood in their style and they were a little more friendly than necessary. Frank Falcone controlled the movie unions and the gambling at the studios plus a complex of pipeline prostitution that supplied girls to the whorehouses of the states in the Far West. It was not in the realm of possibility for any Don to become "show biz" but Falcone had just a touch. His fellow Dons distrusted him accordingly.

Anthony Molinari controlled the waterfronts of San Francisco and was preeminent in the empire of sports gambling. He came of Italian fishermen stock and owned the best San Francisco sea food restaurant, in which he took such pride that the legend had it he lost money on the enterprise by giving too good value for the prices charged. He had the impassive face of the professional gambler and it was known that he also had something to do with dope smuggling over the Mexican border and from the ships plying the lanes of the oriental oceans. Their aides were young, powerfully built men, obviously not counselors but bodyguards, though they would not dare to carry arms to this meeting. It was general knowledge that these bodyguards knew karate, a fact that amused the other Dons but did not alarm them in the slightest, no more than if the California Dons had come wearing amulets blessed by the Pope. Though it must be noted that some of these men were religious and believed in God.

Next arrived the representative from the Family in Boston. This was the only Don who did not have the respect of his fellows. He was known as a man who did not do right by his "people," who cheated them unmercifully. This could be forgiven, each man measures his own greed. What could not be forgiven was that he could not keep order in his empire. The Boston area had too many murders, too many petty wars for power, too many unsupported free-lance activities; it flouted the law too brazenly. If the Chicago Mafia were savages, then the Boston people were *gavoones*, or uncouth louts; ruffians. The Boston Don's name was Domenick Panza. He was short, squat; as one Don put it, he looked like a thief.

The Cleveland syndicate, perhaps the most powerful of the strictly gambling operations in the United States, was represented by a sensitive-looking elderly man with gaunt features and snow-white hair. He was known, of course not to his face, as "the Jew" because he had surrounded himself with Jewish assistants rather than Sicilians. It was even rumored that he would have named a Jew as his *Consigliori* if he had dared. In any case, as Don Corleone's Family was known as the Irish Gang because of Hagen's membership, so Don Vincent Forlenza's Family was known as the Jewish Family with somewhat more accuracy. But he ran an extremely efficient organization and he was not known ever to have fainted at the sight of blood, despite his sensitive features. He ruled with an iron hand in a velvet political glove.

The representatives of the Five Families of New York were the last to arrive and Tom Hagen was struck by how much more imposing, impressive, these five men were than the out-of-towners, the hicks. For one thing, the five New York Dons were in the old Sicilian tradition, they were "men with a belly" meaning, figuratively, power and courage; and literally, physical flesh, as if the two went together, as indeed they seemed to have done in Sicily. The five New York Dons were stout, corpulent men with massive leonine heads, features on a large scale, fleshy imperial noses, thick mouths, heavy folded cheeks. They were not too well tailored or barbered; they had the look of no-nonsense busy men without vanity.

There was Anthony Stracci, who controlled the New Jersey area and the shipping on the West Side docks of Manhattan. He ran the gambling in Jersey and was very strong with the Democratic political machine. He had a fleet of freight hauling trucks that made him a fortune primarily because his trucks could travel with a heavy overload and not be stopped and fined by highway weight inspectors. These trucks helped ruin the highways and then his road-building firm, with lucrative state contracts, repaired the damage wrought. It was the kind of operation that would warm any man's heart, business of itself creating more business. Stracci, too, was old-fashioned and never dealt in prostitution, but because his business was on the waterfront it was impossible for him not to be involved in the drug-smuggling traffic. Of the five New York Families opposing the Corleones his was the least powerful but the most well disposed.

The Family that controlled upper New York State, that arranged smuggling of Italian immigrants from Canada, all upstate gambling and exercised veto power on state licensing of racing tracks, was headed by Ottilio Cuneo. This was a completely disarming man with the face of a jolly round peasant baker, whose legitimate activity was one of the big milk companies. Cuneo was one of those men who loved children and carried a pocket full of sweets in the hopes of being able to pleasure one of his many grandchildren or the small offspring of his associates. He wore a round fedora with the brim turned down all the way round like a woman's sun hat, which broadened his already moon-shaped face into the very mask of joviality. He was one of the few Dons who had never been arrested and whose true activities had never even been suspected. So much so that he had served on civic committees and had been voted as "Businessman of the Year for the State of New York" by the Chamber of Commerce.

The closest ally to the Tattaglia Family was Don Emilio Barzini. He had some of the gambling in Brooklyn and some in Queens. He had some prostitution. He had strong-arm. He completely controlled Staten Island. He had some of the sports betting in the Bronx and Westchester. He was in narcotics. He had close ties to Cleveland and the West Coast and he was one of the few men shrewd enough to be interested in Las Vegas and Reno, the open cities of Nevada. He also had interests in Miami Beach and Cuba. After the Corleone Family, his was perhaps the strongest in New York and therefore in the country. His influence reached even to Sicily. His hand was in every unlawful pie. He was even rumored to have a toehold in Wall Street. He had supported the Tattaglia Family with money and influence since the start of the war. It was his ambition to supplant Don Corleone as the most powerful and respected Mafia leader in the country and to take over part of the Corleone empire. He was a man much like Don Corleone, but more modern, more sophisticated, more businesslike. He could never be called an old Moustache Pete and he had the confidence of the newer, younger, brasher leaders on their way up. He was a man of great personal force in a cold way, with none of Don Corleone's warmth and he was perhaps at this moment the most "respected" man in the group.

The last to arrive was Don Phillip Tattaglia, the head of the Tattaglia Family that had directly challenged the Corleone power by supporting Sollozzo, and had so nearly succeeded. And yet curiously enough he was held in a slight contempt by the others. For one thing, it was known that he had allowed himself to be dominated by Sollozzo, had in fact been led by the nose by that fine Turkish hand. He was held responsible for all this commotion, this uproar that had so affected the conduct of everyday business by the New York Families. Also he was a sixty-year-old dandy and woman-chaser. And he had ample opportunity to indulge his weakness.

For the Tattaglia Family dealt in women. Its main business was prostitution. It also controlled most of the nightclubs in the United States and could place any talent anywhere in the country. Phillip Tattaglia was not above using strong-arm to get control of promising singers and comics and muscling in on record firms. But prostitution was the main source of the Family income.

His personality was unpleasant to these men. He was a whiner, always complaining of the costs in his Family business. Laundry bills, all those towels, ate up the profits (but he owned the laundry firm that did the work). The girls were lazy and unstable, running off, committing suicide. The pimps were treacherous and dishonest and without a shred of loyalty. Good help was hard to find. Young lads of Sicilian blood turned up their noses at such work, considered it beneath their honor to traffic and abuse women; those rascals who would slit a throat with a song on their lips and the cross of an Easter palm in the lapel of their jackets. So Phillip Tattaglia would rant on to audiences unsympathetic and contemptuous. His biggest howl was reserved for authorities who had it in their power to issue and cancel liquor licenses for his nightclubs and cabarets. He swore he had made more millionaires than Wall Street with the money he had paid those thieving guardians of official seals.

In a curious way his almost victorious war against the Corleone Family had not won him the respect it deserved. They knew his strength had come first from Sollozzo and then from the Barzini Family. Also the fact that with the advantage of surprise he had not won complete victory was evidence against him. If he had been more efficient, all this trouble could have been avoided. The death of Don Corleone would have meant the end of the war.

It was proper, since they had both lost sons in their war against each other, that Don Corleone and Phillip Tattaglia should acknowledge each other's presence only with a formal nod. Don Corleone was the object of attention, the other men studying him to see what mark of weakness had been left on him by his wounds and defeats. The puzzling factor was why Don Corleone had sued for peace after the death of his favorite son. It was an acknowledgment of defeat and would almost surely lead to a lessening of his power. But they would soon know.

There were greetings, there were drinks to be served and almost another half hour went by before Don Corleone took his seat at the polished walnut table. Unobtrusively, Hagen sat in the chair slightly to the Don's left and behind him. This was the signal for the other Dons to make their way to the table. Their aides sat behind them, the *Consiglioris* up close so that they could offer any advice when needed.

Don Corleone was the first to speak and he spoke as if nothing had happened. As if he had not been grievously wounded and his eldest son slain, his empire in a shambles, his personal family scattered, Freddie in the West and under the protection of the Molinari Family and Michael secreted in the wastelands of Sicily. He spoke naturally, in Sicilian dialect.

"I want to thank you all for coming," he said. "I consider it a service done to me personally and I am in the debt of each and every one of you. And so I will say at the beginning that I am here not to quarrel or convince, but only to reason and as a reasonable man do everything possible for us all to part friends here too. I give my word on that, and some of you who know me well know I do not give my word lightly. Ah, well, let's get down to business. We are all honorable men here, we don't have to give each other assurances as if we were lawyers."

He paused. None of the others spoke. Some were smoking cigars, others sipping their drinks. All of these men were good listeners, patient men. They had one other thing in common. They were those rarities, men who had refused to accept the rule of organized society, men who refused the dominion of other men. There was no force, no mortal man who could bend them to their will unless they wished it. They were men who guarded their free will with wiles and murder. Their wills could be subverted only by death. Or the utmost reasonableness.

Don Corleone sighed. "How did things ever go so far?" he asked rhetorically. "Well, no matter. A lot of foolishness has come to pass. It was so unfortunate, so unnecessary. But let me tell what happened, as I see it."

He paused to see if someone would object to his telling his side of the story.

"Thank God my health has been restored and maybe I can help set this affair aright. Perhaps my son was too rash, too headstrong, I don't say no to that. Anyway let me just say that Sollozzo came to me with a business affair in which he asked me for my money and my influence. He said he had the interest of the Tattaglia Family. The affair involved drugs, in which I have no interest. I'm a quiet man and such endeavors are too lively for my taste. I explained this to Sollozzo, with all respect for him and the Tattaglia Family. I gave him my 'no' with all courtesy. I told him his business would not interfere with mine, that I had no objection to his earning his living in this fashion. He took it ill and brought misfortune down on all our heads. Well, that's life. Everyone here could tell his own tale of sorrow. That's not to my purpose."

Don Corleone paused and motioned to Hagen for a cold drink, which Hagen swiftly furnished him. Don Corleone wet his mouth. "I'm willing to make the peace," he said. "Tattaglia has lost a son, I have lost a son. We are quits. What would the world come to if people kept carrying grudges against all reason? That has been the cross of Sicily, where men are so busy with vendettas they have no time to earn bread for their families. It's foolishness. So I say now, let things be as they were before. I have not taken any steps to learn who betrayed and killed my son. Given peace, I will not do so. I have a son who cannot come home and I must receive assurances that when I arrange matters so that he can return safely that there will be no interference, no danger from the authorities. Once that's settled maybe we can talk about other matters that interest us and do ourselves, all of us, a profitable service today." Corleone gestured expressively, submissively, with his hands. "That is all I want."

It was very well done. It was the Don Corleone of old. Reasonable. Pliant. Soft-spoken. But every man there had noted that he had claimed good health, which meant he was a man not to be held cheaply despite the misfortunes of the Corleone Family. It was noted that he had said the discussion of other business was useless until the peace he asked for was given. It was noted that he had asked for the old status quo, that he would lose nothing despite his having got the worst of it over the past year.

However, it was Emilio Barzini who answered Don Corleone, not Tattaglia. He was curt and to the point without being rude or insulting.

"That is all true enough," Barzini said. "But there's a little more. Don Corleone is too modest. The fact is that Sollozzo and the Tattaglias could not go into their new business without the assistance of Don Corleone. In fact, his disapproval injured them. That's not his fault of course. The fact remains that judges and politicians who would accept favors from Don Corleone, even on drugs, would not allow themselves to be influenced by anybody else when it came to narcotics. Sollozzo couldn't operate if he didn't have some insurance of his people being treated gently. We all know that. We would all be poor men otherwise. And now that they have increased the penalties the judges and the prosecuting attorneys drive a hard bargain when one of our people get in trouble with narcotics. Even a Sicilian sentenced to twenty years might break the *omerta* and talk his brains out. That can't happen. Don Corleone controls all that apparatus. His refusal to let us use it is not the act of a friend. He takes the bread out of the mouths of our families. Times have changed, it's not like the old days where everyone can go his own way. If Corleone has all the judges in New York, then he must share them or let us others use them. Certainly he can present a bill for such services, we're not communists, after all. But he has to let us draw water from the well. It's that simple."

When Barzini had finished talking there was a silence. The lines were now drawn, there could be no return to the old status quo. What was more important was that Barzini by speaking out was saying that if peace was not made he would openly join the Tattaglia in their war against the Corleone. And he had scored a telling point. Their lives and their fortunes depended upon their doing each other services, the denial of a favor asked by a friend was an act of aggression. Favors were not asked lightly and so could not be lightly refused.

Don Corleone finally spoke to answer. "My friends," he said, "I didn't refuse out of spite. You all know me. When have I ever refused an accommodation? That's simply not in my nature. But I had to refuse this time. Why? Because I think this drug business will destroy us in the years to come. There is too much strong feeling about such traffic in this country. It's not like whiskey or gambling or even women which most people want and is forbidden them by the *pezzonovante* of the church and the government. But drugs are dangerous for everyone connected with them. It could jeopardize all other business. And let me say I'm flattered by the belief that I am so powerful with the judges and law officials, I wish it were true. I do have some influence but many of the people who respect my counsel might lose this respect if drugs become involved in our relationship. They are afraid to be involved in such business and they have strong feelings about it. Even policemen who help us in gambling and other things would refuse to help us in drugs. So to ask me to perform a service in these matters is to ask me to do a disservice to myself. But I'm willing to do even that if all of you think it proper in order to adjust other matters."

When Don Carleone had finished speaking the room became much more relaxed with more whisperings and cross talk. He had conceded the important point. He would offer his protection to any organized business venture in drugs. He was, in effect, agreeing almost entirely to Sollozzo's original proposal if that proposal was endorsed by the national group gathered here. It was understood that he would never participate in the operational phase, nor would he invest his money. He would merely use his protective influence with the legal apparatus. But this was a formidable concession.

The Don of Los Angeles, Frank Falcone, spoke to answer. "There's no way of stopping our people from going into that business. They go in on their own and they get in trouble. There's too much money in it to resist. So it's more dangerous if we don't go in. At least if we control it we can cover it better, organize it better, make sure it causes less trouble. Being in it is not so bad, there has to be control, there has to be protection, there has to be organization, we can't have everybody running around doing just what they please like a bunch of anarchists."

The Don of Detroit, more friendly to Corleone than any of the others, also now spoke against his friend's position, in the interest of reasonableness. "I don't believe in drugs," he said. "For years I paid my people extra so they wouldn't do that kind of business. But it didn't matter, it didn't help. Somebody comes to them and says, 'I have powders, if you put up the three-, four-thousand-dollar investment we can make fifty thousand distributing.' Who can resist such a profit? And they are so busy with their little side business they neglect the work I pay them to do. There's more money in drugs. It's getting bigger all the time. There's no way to stop it so we have to control the business and keep it respectable. I don't want any of it near schools, I don't want any of it sold to children. That is an *infamita*. In my city I would try to keep the traffic in the dark people, the colored. They are the best customers, the least troublesome and they are animals anyway. They have no respect for their wives or their families or for themselves. Let them lose their souls with drugs. But something has to be done, we just can't let people do as they please and make trouble for everyone."

This speech of the Detroit Don was received with loud murmurs of approval. He had hit the nail on the head. You couldn't even pay people to stay out of the drug traffic. As for his remarks about children, that was his well-known sensibility, his tenderheartedness speaking. After all, who would sell drugs to children? Where would children get the money? As for his remarks about the coloreds, that was not even heard. The Negroes were considered of absolutely no account, of no force whatsoever. That they had allowed society to grind them into the dust proved them of no account and his mentioning them in any way proved that the Don of Detroit had a mind that always wavered toward irrelevancies.

All the Dons spoke. All of them deplored the traffic in drugs as a bad thing that would cause trouble but agreed there was no way to control it. There was, simply, too much money to be made in the business, therefore it followed that there would be men who would dare anything to dabble in it. That was human nature.

It was finally agreed. Drug traffic would be permitted and Don Corleone must give it some legal protection in the East. It was understood that the Barzini and Tattaglia Families would do most of the large-scale operations. With this out of the way the conference was able to move on to other matters of a wider interest. There were many complex problems to be solved. It was agreed that Las Vegas and Miami were to be open cities where any of the Families could operate. They all recognized that these were the cities of the future. It was also agreed that no violence would be permitted in these cities and that petty criminals of all types were to be discouraged. It was agreed that in momentous affairs, in executions that were necessary but might cause too much of a public outcry, the execution must be approved by this council. It was agreed that button men and other soldiers were to be restrained from violent crimes and acts of vengeance against each other on personal matters. It was agreed that Families would do each other services when requested, such as providing executioners, technical assistance in pursuing certain courses of action such as bribing jurors, which in some instances could be vital. These discussions, informal, colloquial and on a high level, took time and were broken by lunch and drinks from the buffet bar.

Finally Don Barzini sought to bring the meeting to an end. "That's the whole matter then," he said. "We have the peace and let me pay my respects to Don Corleone, whom we all have known over the years as a man of his word. If there are any more differences we can meet again, we need not become foolish again. On my part the road is new and fresh. I'm glad this is all settled."

Only Phillip Tattaglia was a little worried still. The murder of Santino Corleone made him the most vulnerable person in this group if war broke out again. He spoke at length for the first time.

"I've agreed to everything here, I'm willing to forget my own misfortune. But I would like to hear some strict assurances from Corleone. Will he attempt any individual vengeance? When time goes by and his position perhaps becomes stronger, will he forget that we have sworn our friendship? How am I to know that in three or four years he won't feel that he's been ill served, forced against his will to this agreement and so free to break it? Will we have to guard against each other all the time? Or can we truly go in peace with peace of mind? Would Corleone give us all his assurances as I now give mine?"

It was then that Don Corleone gave the speech that would be long remembered, and that reaffirmed his position as the most far-seeing statesman among them, so full of common sense, so direct from the heart; and to the heart of the matter. In it he coined a phrase that was to become as famous in its way as Churchill's Iron Curtain, though not public knowledge until more than ten years later.

For the first time he stood up to address the council. He was short and a little thin from his "illness," perhaps his sixty years showed a bit more but there was no question that he had regained all his former strength, and had all his wits.

"What manner of men are we then, if we do not have our reason," he said. "We are all no better than beasts in a jungle if that were the case. But we have reason, we can reason with each other and we can reason with ourselves. To what purpose would I start all these troubles again, the violence and the turmoil? My son is dead and that is a misfortune and I must bear it, not make the innocent world around me suffer with me. And so I say, I give my honor, that I will never seek vengeance, I will never seek knowledge of the deeds that have been done in the past. I will leave here with a pure heart.

"Let me say that we must always look to our interests. We are all men who have refused to be fools, who have refused to be puppets dancing on a string pulled by the men on high. We have been fortunate here in this country. Already most of our children have found a better life. Some of you have sons who are professors, scientists, musicians, and you are fortunate. Perhaps your grandchildren will become the new *pezzonovanti*. None of us here want to see our children follow in our footsteps, it's too hard a life. They can be as others, their position and security won by our courage. I have grandchildren now and I hope their children may someday, who knows, be a governor, a President, nothing's impossible here in America. But we have to progress with the times. The time is past for guns and killings and massacres. We have to be cunning like the business people, there's more money in it and it's better for our children and our grandchildren.

"As for our own deeds, we are not responsible to the .90 calibers, the *pezzonovantis* who take it upon themselves to decide what we shall do with our lives, who declare wars they wish us to fight in to protect what they own. Who is to say we should obey the laws they make for their own interest and to our hurt? And who are they then to meddle when we look after our own interests? *Sonna cosa nostra,*" Don Corleone said, "these are our own affairs. We will manage our world for ourselves because it is our world, *cosa nostra.* And so we have to stick together to guard against outside meddlers. Otherwise they will put the ring in our nose as they have put the ring in the nose of all the millions of Neapolitans and other Italians in this country.

"For this reason I forgo my vengeance for my dead son, for the common good. I swear now that as long as I am responsible for the actions of my Family there will not be one finger lifted against any man here without just cause and utmost provocation. I am willing to sacrifice my commercial interests for the common good. This is my word, this is my honor, there are those of you here who know I have never betrayed either.

"But I have a selfish interest. My youngest son had to flee, accused of Sollozzo's murder and that of a police captain. I must now make arrangements so that he can come home with safety, cleared of all those false charges. That is my affair and I will make those arrangements. I must find the real culprits perhaps, or perhaps I must convince the authorities of his innocence, perhaps the witnesses and informants will recant their lies. But again I say that this is my affair and I believe I will be able to bring my son home.

"But let me say this. I am a superstitious man, a ridiculous failing but I must confess it here. And so if some unlucky accident should befall my youngest son, if some police officer should accidentally shoot him, if he should hang himself in his cell, if new witnesses appear to testify to his guilt, my superstition will make me feel that it was the result of the ill will still borne me by some people here. Let me go further. If my son is struck by a bolt of lightning I will blame some of the people here. If his plane should fall into the sea or his ship sink beneath the waves of the ocean, if he should catch a mortal fever, if his automobile should be struck by a train, such is my superstition that I would blame the ill will felt by people here. Gentlemen, that ill will, that bad luck, I could never forgive. But aside from that let me swear by the souls of my grandchildren that I will never break the peace we have made. After all, are we or are we not better men than those *pezzonovanti* who have killed countless millions of men in our lifetimes?"

With this Don Corleone stepped from his place and went down the table to where Don Phillip Tattaglia was sitting. Tattaglia rose to greet him and the two men embraced, kissing each other's cheeks. The other Dons in the room applauded and rose to shake hands with everybody in sight and to congratulate Don Corleone and Don Tattaglia on their new friendship. It was not perhaps the warmest friendship in the world, they would not send each other Christmas gift greetings, but they would not murder each other. That was friendship enough in this world, all that was needed.

Since his son Freddie was under the protection of the Molinari Family in the West, Don Corleone lingered with the San Francisco Don after the meeting to thank him. Molinari said enough for Don Corleone to gather that Freddie had found his niche out there, was happy and had become something of a ladies' man. He had a genius for running a hotel, it seemed. Don Corleone shook his head in wonder, as many fathers do when told of undreamed-of talents in their children. Wasn't it true that sometimes the greatest misfortunes brought unforeseen rewards? They both agreed that this was so. Meanwhile Corleone made it clear to the San Francisco Don that he was in his debt for the great service done in protecting Freddie. He let it be known that his influence would be exerted so that the important racing wires would always be available to his people no matter what changes occurred in the power structure in the years to come, an important guarantee since the struggle over this facility was a constant open wound complicated by the fact that the Chicago people had their heavy hand in it. But Don Corleone was not without influence even in that land of barbarians and so his promise was a gift of gold.

It was evening before Don Corleone, Tom Hagen and the body-guard-chauffeur, who happened to be Rocco Lampone, arrived at the mall in Long Beach. When they went into the house the Don said to Hagen, "Our driver, that man Lampone, keep an eye on him. He's a fellow worth something better I think." Hagen wondered at this remark. Lampone had not said a word all day, had not even glanced at the two men in the back seat. He had opened the door for the Don, the car had been in front of the bank when they emerged, he had done everything correctly but no more than any well-trained chauffeur might do. Evidently the Don's eye had seen something he had not seen.

The Don dismissed Hagen and told him to come back to the house after supper. But to take his time and rest a little since they would put in a long night of discussion. He also told Hagen to have Clemenza and Tessio present. They should come at ten P.M., not before. Hagen was to brief Clemenza and Tessio on what had happened at the meeting that afternoon.

At ten the Don was waiting for the three men in his office, the corner room of the house with its law library and special phone. There was a tray with whiskey bottles, ice and soda water. The Don gave his instructions.

"We made the peace this afternoon," he said. "I gave my word and my honor and that should be enough for all of you. But our friends are not so trustworthy so let's all be on our guard still. We don't want any more nasty little surprises." The Don turned to Hagen. "You've let the Bocchicchio hostages go?"

Hagen nodded. "I called Clemenza as soon as I got home."

Corleone turned to the massive Clemenza. The *caporegime* nodded. "I released them. Tell me, Godfather, is it possible for a Sicilian to be as dumb as the Bocchicchios pretend to be?"

Don Corleone smiled a little. "They are clever enough to make a good living. Why is it so necessary to be more clever than that? It's not the Bocchicchios who cause the troubles of this world. But it's true, they haven't got the Sicilian head."

They were all in a relaxed mood, now that the war was over. Don Corleone himself mixed drinks and brought one to each man. The Don sipped his carefully and lit up a cigar.

"I want nothing set forth to discover what happened to Sonny, that's done with and to be forgotten. I want all cooperation with the other Families even if they become a little greedy and we don't get our proper share in things. I want nothing to break this peace no matter what the provocation until we've found a way to bring Michael home. And I want that to be first thing on your minds. Remember this, when he comes back he must come back in absolute safety. I don't mean from the Tattaglias or the Barzinis. What I'm concerned about are the police. Sure, we can get rid of the real evidence against him; that waiter won't testify, nor that spectator or gunman or whatever he was. The real evidence is the least of our worries since we know about it. What we have to worry about is the police framing false evidence because their informers have assured them that Michael Corleone is the man who killed their captain. Very well. We have to demand that the Five Families do everything in their power to correct this belief of the police. All their informers who work with the police must come up with new stories. I think after my speech this afternoooon they will understand it is to their interest to do so. But that's not enough. We have to come up with something special so Michael won't ever have to worry about that again. Otherwise there's no point in him coming back to this country. So let's all think about that. That's the most important matter.

"Now, any man should be allowed one foolishness in his life. I have had mine. I want all the land around the mall bought, the houses bought. I don't want any man able to look out his window into my garden even if it's a mile away. I want a fence around the mall and I want the mall to be on full protection all the time. I want a gate in that fence. In short, I wish now to live in a fortress. Let me say to you now that I will never go into the city to work again. I will be semiretired. I feel an urge to work in the garden, to make a little wine when the grapes are in season. I want to live in my house. The only time I'll leave is to go on a little vacation or to see someone on important business and then I want all precautions taken. Now don't take this amiss. I'm not preparing anything. I'm being prudent, I've always been a prudent man, there is nothing I find so little to my taste as carelessness in life. Women and children can afford to be careless, men cannot. Be leisurely in all these things, no frantic preparations to alarm our friends. It can be done in such a way as to seem natural.

"Now I'm going to leave things more and more up to each of you three. I want the Santino *regime* disbanded and the men placed in your *regimes*. That should reassure our friends and show that I mean peace. Tom, I want you to put together a group of men who will go to Las Vegas and give me a full report on what is going on out there. Tell me about Fredo, what is really happening out there, I hear I wouldn't recognize my own son. It seems he's a cook now, that he amuses himself with young girls more than a grown man should. Well, he was always too serious when he was young and he was never the man for Family business. But let's find out what really can be done out there."

Hagen said quietly, "Should we send your son-in-law? After all, Carlo is a native of Nevada, he knows his way around."

Don Corleone shook his head. "No, my wife is lonely here without any of her children. I want Constanzia and her husband moved into one of the houses on the mall. I want Carlo given a responsible job, maybe I've been too harsh on him, and"—Don Corleone made a grimace—"I'm short of sons. Take him out of the gambling and put him in with the unions where he can do some paper work and a lot of talking. He's a good talker." There was the tiniest note of contempt in the Don's voice.

Hagen nodded. "OK, Clemenza and I will go over all the people and put together a group to do the Vegas job. Do you want me to call Freddie home for a few days?"

The Don shook his head. He said cruelly, "What for? My wife can still cook our meals. Let him stay out there." The three men shifted uneasily in their seats. They had not realized Freddie was in such severe disfavor with his father and they suspected it must be because of something they did not know.

Don Corleone sighed. "I hope to grow some good green peppers and tomatoes in the garden this year, more than we can eat. I'll make you presents of them. I want a little peace, a little quiet and tranquillity for my old age. Well, that's all. Have another drink if you like."

It was a dismissal. The men rose. Hagen accompanied Clemenza and Tessio to their cars and arranged meetings with them to thrash out the operational details that would accomplish the stated desires of their Don. Then he went back into the house where he knew Don Corleone would be waiting for him.

The Don had taken off his jacket and tie and was lying down on the couch. His stern face was relaxed into lines of fatigue. He waved Hagen into a chair and said, "Well, *Consigliori*, do you disapprove of any of my deeds today?"

Hagen took his time answering. "No," he said. "But I don't find it consistent, nor true to your nature. You say you don't want to find out how Santino was killed or want vengeance for it. I don't believe that. You gave your word for peace and so you'll keep the peace but I can't believe you will give your enemies the victory they seem to have won today. You've construeted a magnificent riddle that I can't solve, so how can I approve or disapprove?"

A look of content came over the Don's face. "Well, you know me better than anyone else. Even though you're not a Sicilian, I made you one. Everything you say is true, but there's a solution and you'll comprehend it before it spins out to the end. You agree everyone has to take my word and I'll keep my word. And I want my orders obeyed exactly. But, Tom, the most important thing is we have to get Michael home as soon as possible. Make that first in your mind and in your work. Explore all the legal alleys, I don't care how much money you have to spend. It has to be foolproof when he comes home. Consult the best lawyers on criminal law. I'll give you the names of some judges who will give you a private audience. Until that time we have to guard against all treacheries."

Hagen said, "Like you, I'm not worried so much about the real evidence as the evidence they will manufacture. Also some police friend may kill Michael after he's arrested. They may kill him in his cell or have one of the prisoners do it. As I see it, we can't even afford to have him arrested or accused."

Don Corleone sighed. "I know, I know. That's the difficulty. But we can't take too long. There are troubles in Sicily. The young fellows over there don't listen to their elders anymore and a lot of the men deported from America are just too much for the old-fashioned Dons to handle. Michael could get caught in between. I've taken some precautions against that and he's still got a good cover but that cover won't last forever. That's one of the reasons I had to make the peace. Barzini has friends in Sicily and they were beginning to sniff Michael's trail. That gives you one of the answers to your riddle. I had to make the peace to insure my son's safety. There was nothing else to do."

Hagen didn't bother asking the Don how he had gotten this information. He was not even surprised, and it was true that this solved part of the riddle. "When I meet with Tattaglia's people to firm up the details, should I insist that all his drug middlemen be clean? The judges will be a little skittish about giving light sentences to a man with a record."

Don Corleone shrugged. "They should be smart enough to figure that out themselves. Mention it, don't insist. We'll do our best but if they use a real snowbird and he gets caught, we won't lift a finger. We'll just tell them nothing can be done. But Barzini is a man who will know that without being told. You notice how he never committed himself in this affair. One might never have known he was in any way concerned. That is a man who doesn't get caught on the losing side."

Hagen was startled. "You mean he was behind Sollozzo and Tattaglia all the time?"

Don Corleone sighed. "Tattaglia is a pimp. He could never have outfought Santino. That's why I don't have to know about what happened. It's enough to know that Barzini had a hand in it."

Hagen let this sink in. The Don was giving him clues but there was something very important left out. Hagen knew what it was but he knew it was not his place to ask. He said good night and turned to go. The Don had a last word for him.

"Remember, use all your wits for a plan to bring Michael home," the Don said. "And one other thing. Arrange with the telephone man so that every month I get a list of all the telephone calls, made and received, by Clemenza and Tessio. I suspect them of nothing. I would swear they would never betray me. But there's no harm in knowing any little thing that may help us before the event."

Hagen nodded and went out. He wondered if the Don was keeping a check on him also in some way and then was ashamed of his suspicion. But now he was sure that in the subtle and complex mind of the Godfather a far-ranging plan of action was being initiated that made the day's happenings no more than a tactical retreat. And there was that one dark fact that no one mentioned, that he himself had not dared to ask, that Don Corleone ignored. All pointed to a day of reckoning in the future.

Chapter

※※※※※※※※※

21

BUT it was to be nearly another year before Don Corleone could arrange for his son Michael to be smuggled back into the United States. During that time the whole Family racked their brains for suitable schemes. Even Carlo Rizzi was listened to now that he was living in the mall with Connie. (During that time they had a second child, a boy.) But none of the schemes met with the Don's approval.

Finally it was the Bocchicchio Family who through a misfortune of its own solved the problem. There was one Bocchicchio, a young cousin of no more than twenty-five years of age, named Felix, who was born in America and with more brains than anyone in the clan had ever had before. He had refused to be drawn into the Family garbage hauling business and married a nice American girl of English stock to further his split from the clan. He went to school at night, to become a lawyer, and worked during the day as a civil service post office clerk. During that time he had three children but his wife was a prudent manager and they lived on his salary until he got his law degree.

Now Felix Bocchicchio, like many young men, thought that having struggled to complete his education and master the tools of his profession, his virtue would automatically be rewarded and he would earn a decent living. This proved not to be the case. Still proud, he refused all help from his clan. But a lawyer friend of his, a young man well connected and with a budding career in a big law firm, talked Felix into doing him a little favor. It was very complicated, seemingly legal, and had to do with a bankruptcy fraud. It was a million-to-one shot against its being found out. Felix Bocchicchio took the chance. Since the fraud involved using the legal skills he had learned in a university, it seemed not so reprehensible, and, in an odd way, not even criminal.

To make a foolish story short, the fraud was discovered. The lawyer friend refused to help Felix in any manner, refused to even answer his telephone calls. The two principals in the fraud, shrewd middle-aged businessmen who furiously blamed Felix Bocchicchio's legal clumsiness for the plan going awry, pleaded guilty and cooperated with the state, naming Felix Bocchicchio as the ringleader of the fraud and claiming he had used threats of violence to control their business and force them to cooperate with him in his fraudulent schemes. Testimony was given that linked Felix with uncles and cousins in the Bocchicchio clan who had criminal records for strong-arm, and this evidence was damning. The two businessmen got off with suspended sentences. Felix Bocchicchio was given a sentence of one to five years and served three of them. The clan did not ask help from any of the Families or Don Corleone because Felix had refused to ask their help and had to be taught a lesson: that mercy comes only from the Family, that the Family is more loyal and more to be trusted than society.

In any case, Felix Bocchicchio was released from prison after serving three years, went home and kissed his wife and three children and lived peacefully for a year, and then showed that he was of the Bocchicchio clan after all. Without any attempt to conceal his guilt, he procured a weapon, a pistol, and shot his lawyer friend to death. He then searched out the two businessmen and calmly shot them both through the head as they came out of a luncheonette. He left the bodies lying in the street and went into the luncheonette and ordered a cup of coffee which he drank while he waited for the police to come and arrest him.

His trial was swift and his judgment merciless. A member of the criminal underworld had cold-bloodedly murdered state witnesses who had sent him to the prison he richly deserved. It was a flagrant flouting of society and for once the public, the press, the structure of society and even soft-headed and soft-hearted humanitarians were united in their desire to see Felix Bocchicchio in the electric chair. The governor of the state would no more grant him clemency than the officials of the pound spare a mad dog, which was the phrase of one of the governor's closest political aides. The Bocchicchio clan of course would spend whatever money was needed for appeals to higher courts, they were proud of him now, but the conclusion was certain. After the legal folderol, which might take a little time, Felix Bocchicchio would die in the electric chair.

It was Hagen who brought this case to the attention of the Don at the request of one of the Bocchicchios who hoped that something could be done for the young man. Don Corleone curtly refused. He was not a magician. People asked him the impossible. But the next day the Don called Hagen into his office and had him go over the case in the most intimate detail. When Hagen was finished, Don Corleone told him to summon the head of the Bocchicchio clan to the mall for a meeting.

What happened next had the simplicity of genius. Don Corleone guaranteed to the head of the Bocchicchio clan that the wife and children of Felix Bocchicchio would be rewarded with a handsome pension. The money for this would be handed over to the Bocchicchio clan immediately. In turn, Felix must confess to the murder of Sollozzo and the police captain McCluskey.

There were many details to be arranged. Felix Bocchicchio would have to confess convincingly, that is, he would have to know some of the true details to confess to. Also he must implicate the police captain in narcotics. Then the waiter at the Luna Restaurant must be persuaded to identify Felix Bocchicchio as the murderer. This would take some courage, as the description would change radically, Felix Bocchicchio being much shorter and heavier. But Don Corleone would attend to that. Also since the condemned man had been a great believer in higher education and a college graduate, he would want his children to go to college. And so a sum of money would have to be paid by Don Corleone that would take care of the children's college. Then the Bocchicchio clan had to be reassured that there was no hope for clemency on the original murders. The new confession of course would seal the man's already almost certain doom.

Everything was arranged, the money paid and suitable contact made with the condemned man so that he could be instructed and advised. Finally the plan was sprung and the confession made headlines in all the newspapers. The whole thing was a huge success. But Don Corleone, cautious as always, waited until Felix Bocchicchio was actually executed four months later before finally giving the command that Michael Corleone could return home.

Chapter

22

LUCY MANCINI, a year after Sonny's death, still missed him terribly, grieved for him more fiercely than any lover in any romance. And her dreams were not the insipid dreams of a schoolgirl, her longings not the longings of a devoted wife. She was not rendered desolate by the loss of her "life's companion," or miss him because of his stalwart character. She held no fond remembrances of sentimental gifts, of girlish hero worship, his smile, the amused glint of his eyes when she said something endearing or witty.

No. She missed him for the more important reason that he had been the only man in the world who could make her body achieve the act of love. And, in her youth and innocence, she still believed that he was the only man who could possibly do so.

Now a year later she sunned herself in the balmy Nevada air. At her feet the slender, blond young man was playing with her toes. They were at the side of the hotel pool for the Sunday afternoon and despite the people all around them his hand was sliding up her bare thigh.

"Oh, Jules, stop," Lucy said. "I thought doctors at least weren't as silly as other men."

Jules grinned at her. "I'm a Las Vegas doctor." He tickled the inside of her thigh and was amazed how just a little thing like that could excite her so powerfully. It showed on her face though she tried to hide it. She was really a very primitive, innocent girl. Then why couldn't he make her come across? He had to figure that one out and never mind the crap about a lost love that could never be replaced. This was living tissue here under his hand and living tissue required other living tissue. Dr. Jules Segal decided he would make the big push tonight at his apartment. He'd wanted to make her come across without any trickery but if trickery there had to be, he was the man for it. All in the interests of science of course. And, besides, this poor kid was dying for it.

"Jules, stop, please stop," Lucy said. Her voice was trembling.

Jules was immediately contrite. "OK, honey," he said. He put his head in her lap and using her soft thighs as a pillow, he took a little nap. He was amused at her squirming, the heat that registered from her loins and when she put her hand on his head to smooth his hair, he grasped her wrist playfully and held it loverlike but really to feel her pulse. It was galloping. He'd get her tonight and he'd solve the mystery, what the hell ever it was. Fully confident, Dr. Jules Segal fell asleep.

Lucy watched the people around the pool. She could never have imagined her life would change so in less than two years. She never regretted her "foolishness" at Connie Corleone's wedding. It was the most wonderful thing that had ever happened to her and she lived it over and over again in her dreams. As she lived over and over again the months that followed.

Sonny had visited her once a week, sometimes more, never less. The days before she saw him again her body was in torment. Their passion for each other was of the most elementary kind, undiluted by poetry or any form of intellectualism. It was love of the coarsest nature, a fleshly love, a love of tissue for opposing tissue.

When Sonny called to tell her he was coming she made certain there was enough liquor in the apartment and enough food for supper and breakfast because usually he would not leave until late the next morning. He wanted his fill of her as she wanted her fill of him. He had his own key and when he came in the door she would fly into his massive arms. They would both be brutally direct, brutally primitive. During their first kiss they would be fumbling at each other's clothing and he would be lifting her in the air, and she would be wrapping her legs around his huge thighs. They would be making love standing up in the foyer of her apartment as if they had to repeat their first act of love together, and then he would carry her so to the bedroom.

They would lie in bed making love. They would live together in the apartment for sixteen hours, completely naked. She would cook for him, enormous meals. Sometimes he would get phone calls obviously about business but she never even listened to the words. She would be too busy toying with his body, fondling it, kissing it, burying her mouth in it. Sometimes when he got up to get a drink and he walked by her, she couldn't help reaching out to touch his naked body, hold him, make love to him as if those special parts of his body were a plaything, a specially constructed, intricate but innocent toy revealing its known, but still surprising ecstasies. At first she had been ashamed of these excesses on her part but soon saw that they pleased her lover, that her complete sensual enslavement to his body flattered him. In all this there was an animal innocence. They were happy together.

When Sonny's father was gunned down in the street, she understood for the first time that her lover might be in danger. Alone in her apartment, she did not weep, she wailed aloud, an animal wailing. When Sonny did not come to see her for almost three weeks she subsisted on sleeping pills, liquor and her own anguish. The pain she felt was physical pain, her body ached. When he finally did come she held on to his body at almost every moment. After that he came at least once a week until he was killed.

She learned of his death through the newspaper accounts and that very same night she took a massive overdose of sleeping pills. For some reason, instead of killing, the pills made her so ill that she staggered out into the hall of her apartment and collapsed in front of the elevator door where she was found and taken to the hospital. Her relationship to Sonny was not generally known so her case received only a few inches in the tabloid newspapers.

It was while she was in the hospital that Tom Hagen came to see her and console her. It was Tom Hagen who arranged a job for her in Las Vegas working in the hotel run by Sonny's brother Freddie. It was Tom Hagen who told her that she would receive an annuity from the Corleone Family, that Sonny had made provisions for her. He had asked her if she was pregnant, as if that were the reason for her taking the pills and she had told him no. He asked her if Sonny had come to see her that fatal night or had called that he would come to see her and she told him no, that Sonny had not called. That she was always home waiting for him when she finished working. And she had told Hagen the truth. "He's the only man I could ever love," she said. "I can't love anybody else." She saw him smile a little but he also looked surprised. "Do you find that so unbelievable?" she asked. "Wasn't he the one who brought you home when you were a kid?"

"He was a different person," Hagen said, "he grew up to be a different kind of man."

"Not to me," Lucy said. "Maybe to everybody else, but not to me." She was still too weak to explain how Sonny had never been anything but gentle with her. He'd never been angry with her, never even irritable or nervous.

Hagen made all the arrangements for her to move to Las Vegas. A rented apartment was waiting, he took her to the airport himself and he made her promise that if she ever felt lonely or if things didn't go right, she would call him and he would help her in any way he could.

Before she got on the plane she asked him hesitantly, "Does Sonny's father know what you're doing?"

Hagen smiled, "I'm acting for him as well as myself. He's old-fashioned in these things and he would never go against the legal wife of his son. But he feels that you were just a young girl and Sonny should have known better. And your taking all those pills shook everybody up." He didn't explain how incredible it was to a man like the Don that any person should try suicide.

Now, after nearly eighteen months in Las Vegas, she was surprised to find herself almost happy. Some nights she dreamed about Sonny and lying awake before dawn continued her dream with her own caresses until she could sleep again. She had not had a man since. But the life in Vegas agreed with her. She went swimming in the hotel pools, sailed on Lake Mead and drove through the desert on her day off. She became thinner and this improved her figure. She was still voluptuous but more in the American than the old Italian style. She worked in the public relations section of the hotel as a receptionist and had nothing to do with Freddie though when he saw her he would stop and chat a little. She was surprised at the change in Freddie. He had become a ladies' man, dressed beautifully, and seemed to have a real flair for running a gambling resort. He controlled the hotel side, something not usually done by casino owners.

With the long, very hot summer seasons, or perhaps his more active sex life, he too had become thinner and Hollywood tailoring made him look almost debonair in a deadly sort of way.

It was after six months that Tom Hagen came out to see how she was doing. She had been receiving a check for six hundred dollars a month, every month, in addition to her salary. Hagen explained that this money had to be shown as coming from some place and asked her to sign complete powers of attorney so that he could channel the money properly. He also told her that as a matter of form she would be listed as owner of five "points" in the hotel in which she worked. She would have to go through all the legal formalities required by the Nevada laws but everything would be taken care of for her and her own personal inconvenience would be at a minimum. However she was not to discuss this arrangement with anyone without his consent. She would be protected legally in every way and her money every month would be assured. If the authorities or any law-enforcement agencies ever questioned her, she was to simply refer them to her lawyer and she would not be bothered any further.

Lucy agreed. She understood what was happening but had no objections to how she was being used. It seemed a reasonable favor. But when Hagen asked her to keep her eyes open around the hotel, keep an eye on Freddie and on Freddie's boss, the man who owned and operated the hotel, as a major stockholder, she said to him, "Oh, Tom, you don't want me to spy on *Freddie?*"

Hagen smiled. "His father worries about Freddie. He's in fast company with Moe Greene and we just want to make sure he doesn't get into any trouble." He didn't bother to explain to her that the Don had backed the building of this hotel in the desert of Las Vegas not only to supply a haven for his son, but to get a foot in the door for bigger operations.

It was shortly after this interview that Dr. Jules Segal came to work as the hotel house physician. He was very thin, very handsome and charming and seemed very young to be a doctor, at least to Lucy. She met him when a lump grew above her wrist on her forearm. She worried about it for a few days, then one morning went to the doctor's suite of offices in the hotel. Two of the show girls from the chorus line were in the waiting room, gossiping with each other. They had the blond peach-colored prettiness Lucy always envied. They looked angelic. But one of the girls was saying, "I swear if I have another dose I'm giving up dancing."

When Dr. Jules Segal opened his office door to motion one of the show girls inside, Lucy was tempted to leave, and if it had been something more personal and serious she would have. Dr. Segal was wearing slacks and an open shirt. The horn-rimmed glasses helped and his quiet reserved manner, but the impression he gave was an informal one, and like many basically old-fashioned people, Lucy didn't believe that medicine and informality mixed.

When she finally got into his office there was something so reassuring in his manner that all her misgivings fled. He spoke hardly at all and yet he was not brusque, and he took his time. When she asked him what the lump was he patiently explained that it was a quite common fibrous growth that could in no way be malignant or a cause for serious concern. He picked up a heavy medical book and said, "Hold out your arm."

She held out her arms tentatively. He smiled at her for the first time. "I'm going to cheat myself out of a surgical fee," he said. "I'll just smash it with this book and it will flatten out. It may pop up again but if I remove it surgically, you'll be out of money and have to wear bandages and all that. OK?"

She smiled at him. For some reason she had an absolute trust in him. "OK," she said. In the next instant she let out a yell as he brought down the heavy medical volume on her forearm. The lump had flattened out, almost.

"Did it hurt that much?" he asked.

"No," she said. She watched him completing her case history card. "Is that all?"

He nodded, not paying any more attention to her. She left.

A week later he saw her in the coffee shop and sat next to her at the counter. "How's the arm?" he asked.

She smiled at him. "Fine," she said. "You're pretty unorthodox but you're pretty good."

He grinned at her. "You don't know how unorthodox I am. And I didn't know how rich you were. The Vegas *Sun* just published the list of point owners in the hotel and Lucy Mancini has a big ten points. I could have made a fortune on that little bump."

She didn't answer him, suddenly reminded of Hagen's warnings. He grinned again. "Don't worry, I know the score, you're just one of the dummies, Vegas is full of them. How about seeing one of the shows with me tonight and I'll buy you dinner. I'll even buy you some roulette chips."

She was a little doubtful. He urged her. Finally she said, "I'd like to come but I'm afraid you might be disappointed by how the night ends. I'm not really a swinger like most of the girls here in Vegas."

"That's why I asked you," Jules said cheerfully. "I've prescribed a night's rest for myself."

Lucy smiled at him and said a little sadly, "Is it that obvious?" He shook his head and she said, "OK, supper then, but I'll buy my own roulette chips."

They went to the supper show and Jules kept her amused by describing different types of bare thighs and breasts in medical terms; but without sneering, all in good humor. Afterward they played roulette together at the same wheel and won over a hundred dollars. Still later they drove up to Boulder Dam in the moonlight and he tried to make love to her but when she resisted after a few kisses he knew that she really meant no and stopped. Again he took his defeat with great good humor. "I told you I wouldn't," Lucy said with half-guilty reproach.

"You would have been awfully insulted if I didn't even try," Jules said. And she had to laugh because it was true.

The next few months they became best friends. It wasn't love because they didn't make love, Lucy wouldn't let him. She could see he was puzzled by her refusal but not hurt the way most men would be and that made her trust him even more. She found out that beneath his professional doctor's exterior he was wildly fun-loving and reckless. On weekends he drove a souped-up MG in the California races. When he took a vacation he went down into the interior of Mexico, the real wild country, he told her, where strangers were murdered for their shoes and life was as primitive as a thousand years ago. Quite accidentally she learned that he was a surgeon and had been connected with a famous hospital in New York.

All this made her more puzzled than ever at his having taken the job at the hotel. When she asked him about it, Jules said, "You tell me your dark secret and I'll tell you mine."

She blushed and let the matter drop. Jules didn't pursue it either and their relationship continued, a warm friendship that she counted on more than she realized.

Now, sitting at the side of the pool with Jules' blond head in her lap, she felt an overwhelming tenderness for him. Her loins ached and without realizing it her fingers sensuously stroked the skin of his neck. He seemed to be sleeping, not noticing, and she became excited just by the feel of him against her. Suddenly he raised his head from her lap and stood up. He took her by the hand and led her over the grass on to the cement walk. She followed him dutifully even when he led her into one of the cottages that held his private apartment. When they were inside he fixed them both big drinks. After the blazing sun and her own sensuous thoughts the drink went to her head and made her dizzy. Then Jules had his arms around her and their bodies, naked except for scanty bathing suits, were pressed against each other. Lucy was murmuring, "Don't," but there was no conviction in her voice and Jules paid no attention to her. He quickly stripped her bathing bra off so that he could fondle her heavy breasts, kissed them and then stripped off her bathing trunks and as he did so kept kissing her body, her rounded belly and the insides of her thighs. He stood up, struggling out of his own bathing shorts and embracing her, and then, naked in each other's arms, they were lying on his bed and she could feel him entering her and it was enough, just the slight touch, for her to reach her climax and then in the second afterward she could read in the motions of his body, his surprise. She felt the overwhelming shame she had felt before she knew Sonny, but Jules was twisting her body over the edge of the bed, positioning her legs a certain way and she let him control her limbs and her body, and then he was entering her again and kissing her and this time she could feel him but more important she could tell that he was feeling something too and coming to his climax.

When he rolled off her body, Lucy huddled into one corner of the bed and began to cry. She felt so ashamed. And then she was shockingly surprised to hear Jules laugh softly and say, "You poor benighted Eye-talian girl, so that's why you kept refusing me all these months? You dope." He said "you dope" with such friendly affection that she turned toward him and he took her naked body against his saying, "You are medieval, you are positively medieval." But the voice was soothingly comforting as she continued to weep.

Jules lit a cigarette and put it in her mouth so that she choked on the smoke and had to stop crying. "Now listen to me," he said, "if you had had a decent modern raising with a family culture that was part of the twentieth century your problem would have been solved years ago. Now let me tell you what your problem is: it's not the equivalent of being ugly, of having bad skin and squinty eyes that facial surgery really doesn't solve. Your problem is like having a wart or a mole on your chin, or an improperly formed ear. Stop thinking of it in sexual terms. Stop thinking in your head that you have a big box no man can love because it won't give his penis the necessary friction. What you have is a pelvic malformation and what we surgeons call a weakening of the pelvic floor. It usually comes after child-bearing but it can be simply bad bone structure. It's a common condition and many women live a life of misery because of it when a simple operation could fix them up. Some women even commit suicide because of it. But I never figured you for that condition because you have such a beautiful body. I thought it was psychological, since I know your story, you told it to me often enough, you and Sonny. But let me give you a thorough physical examination and I can tell you just exactly how much work will have to be done. Now go in and take a shower."

Lucy went in and took her shower. Patiently and over her protests, Jules made her lie on the bed, legs spread apart. He had an extra doctor's bag in his apartment and it was open. He also had a small glass-topped table by the bed which held some other instruments. He was all business now, examining her, sticking his fingers inside her and moving them around. She was beginning to feel humiliated when he kissed her on the navel and said, almost absentmindedly, "First time I've enjoyed my work." Then he flipped her over and thrust a finger in her rectum, feeling around, but his other hand was stroking her neck affectionately. When he was finished he turned her right side up again, kissed her tenderly on the mouth and said, "Baby, I'm going to build you a whole new thing down there, and then I'll try it out personally. It will be a medical first, I'll be able to write a paper on it for the official journals."

Jules did everything with such good-humored affection, he so obviously cared for her, that Lucy got over her shame and embarrassment. He even had the medical textbook down off its shelf to show her a case like her own and the surgical procedure to correct it. She found herself quite interested.

"It's a health thing too," Jules said. "If you don't get it corrected you're going to have a hell of a lot of trouble later on with your whole plumbing system. The structure becomes progressively weaker unless it's corrected by surgery. It's a damn shame that old-fashioned prudery keeps a lot of doctors from properly diagnosing and correcting the situation, and a lot of women from complaining about it."

"Don't talk about it, please don't talk about it," Lucy said.

He could see that she was still to some extent ashamed of her secret, embarrassed by her "ugly defect." Though to his medically trained mind this seemed the height of silliness, he was sensitive enough to identify with her. It also put him on the right track to making her feel better.

"OK, I know your secret so now I'll tell you mine," he said. "You always ask me what I'm doing here in this town, one of the youngest and most brilliant surgeons in the East." He was mocking some newspaper reports about himself. "The truth is that I'm an abortionist, which in itself is not so bad, so is half the medical profession; but I got caught. I had a friend, a doctor named Kennedy, we interned together, and he's a really straight guy but he said he'd help me. I understand Tom Hagen had told him if he ever needed help on anything the Corleone Family was indebted to him. So he spoke to Hagen. The next thing I know the charges were dropped, but the Medical Association and the Eastern establishment had me blacklisted. So the Corleone Family got me this job out here. I make a good living. I do a job that has to be done. These show girls are always getting knocked up and aborting them is the easiest thing in the world if they come to me right away. I curette 'em like you scrape a frying pan. Freddie Corleone is a real terror. By my count he's knocked up fifteen girls while I've been here. I've seriously considered giving him a father-to-son talk about sex. Especially since I've had to treat him three times for clap and once for syphilis. Freddie is the original bareback rider."

Jules stopped talking. He had been deliberately indiscreet, something he never did, so that Lucy would know that other people, including someone she knew and feared a little like Freddie Corleone, also had shameful secrets.

"Think of it as a piece of elastic in your body that has lost its elasticity," Jules said. "By cutting out a piece, you make it tighter, snappier."

"I'll think about it," Lucy said, but she was sure she was going to go through with it, she trusted Jules absolutely. Then she thought of something else. "How much will it cost?"

Jules frowned. "I haven't the facilities here for surgery like that and I'm not the expert at it. But I have a friend in Los Angeles who's the best in the field and has facilities at the best hospital. In fact he tightens up all the movie stars, when those dames find out that getting their faces and breasts lifted isn't the whole answer to making a man love them. He owes me a few favors so it won't cost anything. I do his abortions for him. Listen, if it weren't unethical I'd tell you the names of some of the movie sex queens who have had the operation."

She was immediately curious. "Oh, come on, tell me," she said. "Come on." It would be a delicious piece of gossip and one of the things about Jules was that she could show her feminine love of gossip without him making fun of it.

"I'll tell you if you have dinner with me and spend the night with me," Jules said. "We have a lot of lost time to make up for because of your silliness."

Lucy felt an overwhelming affection to him for being so kind and she was able to say, "You don't have to sleep with me, you know you won't enjoy it the way I am now."

Jules burst out laughing. "You dope, you incredible dope. Didn't you ever hear of any other way of making love, far more ancient, far more civilized. Are you really that innocent?"

"Oh that," she said.

"Oh that," he mimicked her. "Nice girls don't do that, manly men don't do that. Even in the year 1948. Well, baby, I can take you to the house of a little old lady right here in Las Vegas who was the youngest madam of the most popular whorehouse in the wild west days, back in 1880, I think it was. She likes to talk about the old days. You know what she told me? That those gunslingers, those manly, virile, straight-shooting cowboys would always ask the girls for a 'French,' what we doctors call fellatio, what you call 'oh that.' Did you ever think of doing 'oh that' with your beloved Sonny?"

For the first time she truly surprised him. She turned on him with what he could think of only as a Mona Lisa smile (his scientific mind immediately darting off on a tangent, could this be the solving of that centuries-old mystery?) and said quietly, "I did everything with Sonny." It was the first time she had ever admitted anything like that to anyone.

Two weeks later Jules Segal stood in the operating room of the Los Angeles hospital and watched his friend Dr. Frederick Kellner perform the specialty. Before Lucy was put under anesthesia, Jules leaned over and whispered, "I told him you were my special girl so he's going to put in some real tight walls." But the preliminary pill had already made her dopey and she didn't laugh or smile. His teasing remark did take away some of the terror of the operation.

Dr. Kellner made his incision with the confidence of a pool shark making an easy shot. The technique of any operation to strengthen the pelvic floor required the accomplishment of two objectives. The musculofibrous pelvic sling had to be shortened so that the slack was taken up. And of course the vaginal opening, the weak spot itself in the pelvic floor, had to be brought forward, brought under the pubic arch and so relieved from the line of direct pressure above. Repairing the pelvic sling was called perincorrhaphy. Suturing the vaginal wall was called colporrhaphy.

Jules saw that Dr. Kellner was working carefully now, the big danger in the cutting was going too deep and hitting the rectum. It was a fairly uncomplicated case, Jules had studied all the X rays and tests. Nothing should go wrong except that in surgery something could always go wrong.

Kellner was working on the diaphragm sling, the T forceps held the vaginal flap, and exposing the ani muscle and the fasci which formed its sheath. Kellner's gauze-covered fingers were pushing aside loose connective tissue. Jules kept his eyes on the vaginal wall for the appearance of the veins, the telltale danger signal of injuring the rectum. But old Kellner knew his stuff. He was building a new snatch as easily as a carpenter nails together two-by-four studs.

Kellner was trimming away the excess vaginal wall using the fastening-down stitch to close the "bite" taken out of the tissue of the redundant angle, insuring that no troublesome projections would form. Kellner was trying to insert three fingers into the narrowed opening of the lumen, then two. He just managed to get two fingers in, probing deeply and for a moment he looked up at Jules and his china-blue eyes over the gauze mask twinkled as though asking if that was narrow enough. Then he was busy again with his sutures.

It was all over. They wheeled Lucy out to the recovery room and Jules talked to Kellner. Kellner was cheerful, the best sign that everything had gone well. "No complications at all, my boy," he told Jules. "Nothing growing in there, very simple case. She has wonderful body tone, unusual in these cases and now she's in first-class shape for fun and games. I envy you, my boy. Of course you'll have to wait a little while but then I guarantee you'll like my work."

Jules laughed. "You're a true Pygmalion, Doctor. Really, you were marvelous."

Dr. Kellner grunted. "That's all child's play, like your abortions. If society would only be realistic, people like you and I, really talented people, could do important work and leave this stuff for the hacks.

By the way, I'll be sending you a girl next week, a very nice girl, they seem to be the ones who always get in trouble. That will make us all square for this job today."

Jules shook his hand. "Thanks, Doctor. Come out yourself sometime and I'll see that you get all the courtesies of the house."

Kellner gave him a wry smile. "I gamble every day, I don't need your roulette wheels and crap tables. I knock heads with fate too often as it is. You're going to waste out there, Jules. Another couple of years and you can forget about serious surgery. You won't be up to it." He turned away.

Jules knew it was not meant as a reproach but as a warning. Yet it took the heart out of him anyway. Since Lucy wouldn't be out of the recovery room for at least twelve hours, he went out on the town and got drunk. Part of the getting drunk was his feeling of relief that everything had worked out so well with Lucy.

The next morning when he went to the hospital to visit her he was surprised to find two men at her bedside and flowers all over the room. Lucy was propped up on pillows, her face radiant. Jules was surprised because Lucy had broken with her family and had told him not to notify them unless something went wrong. Of course Freddie Corleone knew she was in the hospital for a minor operation; that had been necessary so that they both could get time off, and Freddie had told Jules that the hotel would pick up all the bills for Lucy.

Lucy was introducing them and one of the men Jules recognized instantly. The famous Johnny Fontane. The other was a big, muscular, snotty-looking Italian guy whose name was Nino Valenti. They both shook hands with Jules and then paid no further attention to him. They were kidding Lucy, talking about the old neighborhood in New York, about people and events Jules had no way of sharing. So he said to Lucy, "I'll drop by later, I have to see Dr. Kellner anyway."

But Johnny Fontane was turning the charm on him. "Hey, buddy, we have to leave ourselves, you keep Lucy company. Take good care of her, Doc." Jules noticed a peculiar hoarseness in Johnny Fontane's voice and remembered suddenly that the man hadn't sung in public for over a year now, that he had won the Academy Award for his acting. Could the man's voice have changed so late in life and the papers keeping it a secret, everybody keeping it a secret? Jules loved inside gossip and he kept listening to Fontane's voice in an attempt to diagnose the trouble. It could be simple strain, or too much booze and cigarettes or even too much women. The voice had an ugly timbre to it, he could never be called the sweet crooner anymore.

"You sound like you have a cold," Jules said to Johnny Fontane.

Fontane said politely, "Just strain, I tried to sing last night. I guess I just can't accept the fact that my voice changed, getting old you know." He gave Jules a what-the-hell grin.

Jules said casually, "Didn't you get a doctor to look at it? Maybe it's something that can be fixed."

Fontane was not so charming now. He gave Jules a long cool look. "That's the first thing I did nearly two years ago. Best specialists. My own doctor who's supposed to be the top guy out here in California. They told me to get a lot of rest. Nothing wrong, just getting older. A man's voice changes when he gets older."

Fontane ignored him after that, paying attention to Lucy, charming her as he charmed all women. Jules kept listening to the voice. There had to be a growth on those vocal chords. But then why the hell hadn't the specialists spotted it? Was it malignant and inoperable? Then there was other stuff.

He interrupted Fontane to ask, "When was the last time you got examined by a specialist?"

Fontane was obviously irritated but trying to be polite for Lucy's sake. "About eighteen months ago," he said.

"Does your own doctor take a look once in a while?" Jules asked.

"Sure he does," Johnny Fontane said irritably. "He gives me a codeine spray and checks me out. He told me it's just my voice aging, that all the drinking and smoking and other stuff. Maybe you know more than he does?"

Jules asked, "What's his name?"

Fontane said with just a faint flicker of pride, "Tucker, Dr. James Tucker. What do you think of him?"

The name was familiar, linked to famous movie stars, female, and to an expensive health farm.

"He's a sharp dresser," Jules said with a grin.

Fontane was angry now. "You think you're a better doctor than he is?"

Jules laughed. "Are you a better singer than Carmen Lombardo?" He was surprised to see Nino Valenti break up in laughter, banging his head on his chair. The joke hadn't been that good. Then on the wings of those guffaws he caught the smell of bourbon and knew that even this early in the morning Mr. Valenti, whoever the hell he was, was at least half drunk.

Fontane was grinning at his friend. "Hey, you're supposed to be laughing at my jokes, not his." Meanwhile Lucy stretched out her hand to Jules and drew him to her bedside.

"He looks like a bum but he's a brilliant surgeon," Lucy told them. "If he says he's better than Dr. Tucker then he's better than Dr. Tucker. You listen to him, Johnny."

The nurse came in and told them they would have to leave. The resident was going to do some work on Lucy and needed privacy. Jules was amused to see Lucy turn her head away so when Johnny Fontane and Nino Valenti kissed her they would hit her cheek instead of her mouth, but they seemed to expect it. She let Jules kiss her on the mouth and whispered, "Come back this afternoon, please?" He nodded.

Out in the corridor, Valenti asked him, "What was the operation for? Anything serious?"

Jules shook his head. "Just a little female plumbing. Absolutely routine, please believe me. I'm more concerned than you are, I hope to marry the girl."

They were looking at him appraisingly so he asked, "How did you find out she was in the hospital?"

"Freddie called us and asked us to look in," Fontane said. "We all grew up in the same neighborhood. Lucy was maid of honor when Freddie's sister got married."

"Oh," Jules said. He didn't let on that he knew the whole story, perhaps because they were so cagey about protecting Lucy and her affair with Sonny.

As they walked down the corridor, Jules said to Fontane, "I have visiting doctor's privileges here, why don't you let me have a look at your throat?"

Fontane shook his head. "I'm in a hurry."

Nino Valenti said, "That's a million-dollar throat, he can't have cheap doctors looking down it." Jules saw Valenti was grinning at him, obviously on his side.

Jules said cheerfully, "I'm no cheap doctor. I was the brightest young surgeon and diagnostician on the East Coast until they got me on an abortion rap."

As he had known it would, that made them take him seriously. By admitting his crime he inspired belief in his claim of high competence. Valenti recovered first. "If Johnny can't use you, I got a girl friend I want you to look at, not at her throat though."

Fontane said to him nervously, "How long will you take?"

"Ten minutes," Jules said. It was a lie but he believed in telling lies to people. Truth telling and medicine just didn't go together except in dire emergencies, if then.

"OK," Fontane said. His voice was darker, hoarser, with fright.

Jules recruited a nurse and a consulting room. It didn't have everything he needed but there was enough. In less than ten minutes he knew there was a growth on the vocal chords, that was easy. Tucker, that incompetent sartorial son of a bitch of a Hollywood phony, should have been able to spot it. Christ, maybe the guy didn't even have a license and if he did it should be taken away from him. Jules didn't pay any attention to the two men now. He picked up the phone and asked for the throat man at the hospital to come down. Then he swung around and said to Nino Valenti, "I think it might be a long wait for you, you'd better leave."

Fontane stared at him in utter disbelief. "You son of a bitch, you think you're going to keep me here? You think you're going to fuck around with my throat?"

Jules, with more pleasure than he would have thought possible, gave it to him straight between the eyes. "You can do whatever you like," he said. "You've got a growth of some sort on your vocal chords, in your larynx. If you stay here the next few hours, we can nail it down, whether it's malignant or nonmalignant. We can make a decision for surgery or treatment. I can give you the whole story. I can give you the name of the top specialist in America and we can have him out here on the plane tonight, with your money that is, and if I think it necessary. But you can walk out of here and see your quack buddy or sweat while you decide to see another doctor, or get referred to somebody incompetent. Then if it's malignant and gets big enough they'll cut out your whole larynx or you'll die. Or you can just sweat. Stick here with me and we can get it all squared away in a few hours. You got anything more important to do?"

Valenti said, "Let's stick around, Johnny, what the hell. I'll go down the hall and call the studio. I won't tell them anything, just that we're held up. Then I'll come back here and keep you company."

It proved to be a very long afternoon but a rewarding one. The diagnosis of the staff throat man was perfectly sound as far as Jules could see after the X rays and swab analysis. Halfway through,

Johnny Fontane, his mouth soaked with iodine, retching over the roll of gauze stuck in his mouth, tried to quit. Nino Valenti grabbed him by the shoulders and slammed him back into the chair. When it was all over Jules grinned at Fontane and said, "Warts."

Fontane didn't grasp it. Jules said again, "Just some warts. We'll slice them right off like skin off baloney. In a few months you'll be OK."

Valenti let out a yell but Fontane was still frowning. "How about singing afterward, how will it affect my singing?"

Jules shrugged. "On that there's no guarantee. But since you can't sing now what's the difference?"

Fontane looked at him with distaste. "Kid, you don't know what the hell you're talking about. You act like you're giving me good news when what you're telling me is maybe I won't sing anymore. Is that right, maybe I won't sing anymore?"

Finally Jules was disgusted. He'd operated as a real doctor and it had been a pleasure. He had done this bastard a real favor and he was acting as if he'd been done dirt. Jules said coldly, "Listen, Mr. Fontane, I'm a doctor of medicine and you can call me Doctor, not kid. And I did give you very good news. When I brought you down here I was certain that you had a malignant growth in your larynx which would entail cutting out your whole voice box. Or which could kill you. I was worried that I might have to tell you that you were a dead man. And I was so delighted when I could say the word 'warts.' Because your singing gave me so much pleasure, helped me seduce girls when I was younger and you're a real artist. But also you're a very spoiled guy. Do you think because you're Johnny Fontane you can't get cancer? Or a brain tumor that's inoperable? Or a failure of the heart? Do you think you're never going to die? Well, it's not all sweet music and if you want to see real trouble take a walk through this hospital and you'll sing a love song about warts. So just stop the crap and get on with what you have to do. Your Adolphe Menjou medical man can get you the proper surgeon but if he tries to get into the operating room I suggest you have him arrested for attempted murder."

Jules started to walk out of the room when Valenti said, "Attaboy, Doc, that's telling him."

Jules whirled around and said, "Do you always get looped before noontime?"

Valenti said, "Sure," and grinned at him and with such good humor that Jules said more gently than he had meant to, "You have to figure you'll be dead in five years if you keep that up."

Valenti was lumbering up to him with little dancing steps. He threw his arms around Jules, his breath stank of bourbon. He was laughing very hard. "Five years?" he asked still laughing. "Is it going to take *that long?*"

A month after her operation Lucy Mancini sat beside the Vegas hotel pool, one hand holding a cocktail, the other hand stroking Jules' head, which lay in her lap.

"You don't have to build up your courage," Jules said teasingly. "I have champagne waiting in our suite."

"Are you sure it's OK so soon?" Lucy asked.

"I'm the doctor," Jules said. "Tonight's the big night. Do you realize I'll be the first surgeon in medical history who tried out the results of his "medical first" operation? You know, the Before and After. I'm going to enjoy writing it up for the journals. Let's see, 'while the Before was distinctly pleasurable for psychological reasons and the sophistication of the surgeon-instructor, the post-operative coitus was extremely rewarding strictly for its neurological"—he stopped talking because Lucy had yanked on his hair hard enough for him to yell with pain.

She smiled down at him. "If you're not satisfied tonight I can really say it's your fault," she said.

"I guarantee my work. I planned it even though I just let old Kellner do the manual labor," Jules said. "Now let's just rest up, we have a long night of research ahead."

When they went up to their suite—they were living together now—Lucy found a surprise waiting: a gourmet supper and next to her champagne glass, a jeweler's box with a huge diamond engagement ring inside it.

"That shows you how much confidence I have in my work," Jules said. "Now let's see you earn it."

He was very tender, very gentle with her. She was a little scary at first, her flesh jumping away from his touch but then, reassured, she felt her body building up to a passion she had never known. and when they were done the first time and Jules whispered, "I do good work," she whispered back, "Oh, yes, you do; yes, you do." And they both laughed to each other as they started making love again.

Book VI

Chapter

23

AFTER five months of exile in Sicily, Michael Corleone came finally to understand his father's character and his destiny. He came to understand men like Luca Brasi, the ruthless *caporegime* Clemenza, his mother's resignation and acceptance of her role. For in Sicily he saw what they would have been if they had chosen *not* to struggle against their fate. He understood why the Don always said, "A man has only one destiny." He came to understand the contempt for authority and legal government, the hatred for any man who broke *omerta*, the law of silence.

Dressed in old clothes and a billed cap, Michael had been transported from the ship docked at Palermo to the interior of the Sicilian island, to the very heart of a province controlled by the Mafia, where the local *capo-mafioso* was greatly indebted to his father for some past service. The province held the town of Corleone, whose name the Don had taken when he emigrated to America so long ago. But there were no longer any of the Don's relatives alive. The women had died of old age. All the men had been killed in vendettas or had also emigrated, either to America, Brazil or to some other province on the Italian mainland. He was to learn later that this small poverty-stricken town had the highest murder rate of any place in the world.

Michael was installed as a guest in the home of a bachelor uncle of the *capo-mafioso*. The uncle, in his seventies, was also the doctor for the district. The *capo-mafioso* was a man in his late fifties named Don Tommasino and he operated as the *gabbellotto* for a huge estate belonging to one of Sicily's most noble families. The *gabbellotto*, a sort of overseer to the estates of the rich, also guaranteed that the poor would not try to claim land not being cultivated, would not try to encroach in any way on the estate, by poaching or trying to farm it as squatters. In short, the *gabbellotto* was a *mafioso* who for a certain sum of money protected the real estate of the rich from all claims made on it by the poor, legal or illegal. When any poor peasant tried to implement the law which permitted him to buy uncultivated land, the *gabbellotto* frightened him off with threats of bodily harm or death. It was that simple.

Don Tommasino also controlled the water rights in the area and vetoed the local building of any new dams by the Roman government. Such dams would ruin the lucrative business of selling water from the artesian wells he controlled, make water too cheap, ruin the whole important water economy so laboriously built up over hundreds of years. However, Don Tommasino was an old-fashioned Mafia chief and would have nothing to do with dope traffic or prostitution. In this Don Tommasino was at odds with the new breed of Mafia leaders springing up in big cities like Palermo, new men who, influenced by American gangsters deported to Italy, had no such scruples.

The Mafia chief was an extremely portly man, a "man with a belly," literally as well as in the figurative sense that meant a man able to inspire fear in his fellow men. Under his protection, Michael had nothing to fear, yet it was considered necessary to keep the fugitive's identity a secret. And so Michael was restricted to the walled estate of Dr. Taza, the Don's uncle.

Dr. Taza was tall for a Sicilian, almost six feet, and had ruddy cheeks and snow-white hair. Though in his seventies, he went every week to Palermo to pay his respects to the younger prostitutes of that city, the younger the better. Dr. Taza's other vice was reading. He read everything and talked about what he read to his fellow townsmen, patients who were illiterate peasants, the estate shepherds, and this gave him a local reputation for foolishness. What did books have to do with them?

In the evenings Dr. Taza, Don Tommasino and Michael sat in the huge garden populated with those marble statues that on this island seemed to grow out of the garden as magically as the black heady grapes. Dr. Taza loved to tell stories about the Mafia and its exploits over the centuries and in Michael Corleone he had a fascinated listener. There were times when even Don Tommasino would be carried away by the balmy air, the fruity, intoxicating wine, the elegant and quiet comfort of the garden, and tell a story from his own practical experience. The doctor was the legend, the Don the reality.

In this antique garden, Michael Corleone learned about the roots from which his father grew. That the word "Mafia" had originally meant place of refuge. Then it became the name for the secret organization that sprang up to fight against the rulers that had crushed the country and its people for centuries. Sicily was a land that had been more cruelly raped than any other in history. The Inquisition had tortured rich and poor alike. The landowning barons and the princes of the Catholic Church exercised absolute power over the shepherds and farmers. The police were the instruments of their power and so identified with them that to be called a policeman is the foulest insult one Sicilian can hurl at another.

Faced with the savagery of this absolute power, the suffering people learned never to betray their anger and their hatred for fear of being crushed. They learned never to make themselves vulnerable by uttering any sort of threat since giving such a warning insured a quick reprisal. They learned that society was their enemy and so when they sought redress for their wrongs they went to the rebel underground, the Mafia. And the Mafia cemented its power by originating the law of silence, the *omerta*. In the countryside of Sicily a stranger asking directions to the nearest town will not even receive the courtesy of an answer. And the greatest crime any member of the Mafia could commit would be to tell the police the name of the man who had just shot him or done him any kind of injury. *Omerta* became the religion of the people. A woman whose husband has been murdered would not tell the police the name of her husband's murderer, not even of her child's murderer, her daughter's raper.

Justice had never been forthcoming from the authorities and so the people had always gone to the Robin Hood Mafia. And to some extent the Mafia still fulfilled this role. People turned to their local *capo-mafioso* for help in every emergency. He was their social worker, their district captain ready with a basket of food and a job, their protector.

But what Dr. Taza did not add, what Michael learned on his own in the months that followed, was that the Mafia in Sicily had become the illegal arm of the rich and even the auxiliary police of the legal and political structure. It had become a degenerate capitalist structure, anti-communist, anti-liberal, placing its own taxes on every form of business endeavor no matter how small.

Michael Corleone understood for the first time why men like his father chose to become thieves and murderers rather than members of the legal society. The poverty and fear and degradation were too awful to be acceptable to any man of spirit. And in America some emigrating Sicilians had assumed there would be an equally cruel authority.

Dr. Taza offered to take Michael into Palermo with him on his weekly visit to the bordello but Michael refused. His flight to Sicily had prevented him from getting proper medical treatment for his smashed jaw and he now carried a memento from Captain McCluskey on the left side of his face. The bones had knitted badly, throwing his profile askew, giving him the appearance of depravity when viewed from that side. He had always been vain about his looks and this upset him more than he thought possible. The pain that came and went he didn't mind at all, Dr. Taza gave him some pills that deadened it. Taza offered to treat his face but Michael refused. He had been there long enough to learn that Dr. Taza was perhaps the worst physician in Sicily. Dr. Taza read everything but his medical literature, which he admitted he could not understand. He had passed his medical exams through the good offices of the most important Mafia chief in Sicily who had made a special trip to Palermo to confer with Taza's professors about what grades they should give him. And this too showed how the Mafia in Sicily was cancerous to the society it inhabited. Merit meant nothing. Talent meant nothing. Work meant nothing. The Mafia Godfather gave you your profession as a gift.

Michael had plenty of time to think things out. During the day he took walks in the countryside, always accompanied by two of the shepherds attached to Don Tommasino's estate. The shepherds of the island were often recruited to act as the Mafia's hired killers and did their job simply to earn money to live. Michael thought about his father's organization. If it continued to prosper it would grow into what had happened here on this island, so cancerous that it would destroy the whole country. Sicily was already a land of ghosts, its men emigrating to every other country on earth to be able to earn their bread, or simply to escape being murdered for exercising their political and economic freedoms.

On his long walks the most striking thing in Michael's eyes was the magnificent beauty of the country; he walked through the orange orchards that formed shady deep caverns through the countryside with their ancient conduits splashing water out of the fanged mouths of great snake stones carved before Christ. Houses built like ancient Roman villas, with huge marble portals and great vaulted rooms, falling into ruins or inhabited by stray sheep. On the horizon the bony hills shone like picked bleached bones piled high. Gardens and fields, sparkly green, decorated the desert landscape like bright emerald necklaces. And sometimes he walked as far as the town of Corleone, its eighteen thousand people strung out in dwellings that pitted the side of the nearest mountain, the mean hovels built out of black rock quarried from that mountain. In the last year there had been over sixty murders in Corleone and it seemed that death shadowed the town. Further on, the wood of Ficuzza broke the savage monotony of arable plain.

His two shepherd bodyguards always carried their *luparas* with them when accompanying Michael on his walks. The deadly Sicilian shotgun was the favorite weapon of the Mafia. Indeed the police chief sent by Mussolini to clean the Mafia out of Sicily had, as one of his first steps, ordered all stone walls in Sicily to be knocked down to not more than three feet in height so that murderers with their *luparas* could not use the walls as ambush points for their assassinations. This didn't help much and the police minister solved his problem by arresting and deporting to penal colonies any male suspected of being a *mafioso*.

When the island of Sicily was liberated by the Allied Armies, the American military government officials believed that anyone imprisoned by the Fascist regime was a democrat and many of these *mafiosi* were appointed as mayors of villages or interpreters to the military government. This good fortune enabled the Mafia to reconstitute itself and become more formidable than ever before.

The long walks, a bottle of strong wine at night with a heavy plate of pasta and meat, enabled Michael to sleep. There were books in Italian in Dr. Taza's library and though Michael spoke dialect Italian and had taken some college courses in Italian, his reading of these books took a great deal of effort and time. His speech became almost accentless and, though he could never pass as a native of the district, it would be believed that he was one of those strange Italians from the far north of Italy bordering the Swiss and Germans.

The distortion of the left side of his face made him more native. It was the kind of disfigurement common in Sicily because of the lack of medical care. The little injury that cannot be patched up simply for lack of money. Many children, many men, bore disfigurements that in America would have been repaired by minor surgery or sophisticated medical treatments.

Michael often thought of Kay, of her smile, her body, and always felt a twinge of conscience at leaving her so brutally without a word of farewell. Oddly enough his conscience was never troubled by the two men he had murdered; Sollozzo had tried to kill his father, Captain McCluskey had disfigured him for life.

Dr. Taza always kept after him about getting surgery done for his lopsided face, especially when Michael asked him for pain-killing drugs, the pain getting worse as time went on, and more frequent. Taza explained that there was a facial nerve below the eye from which radiated a whole complex of nerves. Indeed, this was the favorite spot for Mafia torturers, who searched it out on the cheeks of their victims with the needle-fine point of an ice pick. That particular nerve in Michael's face had been injured or perhaps there was a splinter of bone lanced into it. Simple surgery in a Palermo hospital would permanently relieve the pain.

Michael refused. When the doctor asked why, Michael grinned and said, "It's something from home."

And he really didn't mind the pain, which was more an ache, a small throbbing in his skull, like a motored apparatus running in liquid to purify it.

It was nearly seven months of leisurely rustic living before Michael felt real boredom. At about this time Don Tommasino became very busy and was seldom seen at the villa. He was having his troubles with the "new Mafia" springing up in Palermo, young men who were making a fortune out of the postwar construction boom in that city. With this wealth they were trying to encroach on the country fiefs of old-time Mafia leaders whom they contemptuously labeled Moustache Petes. Don Tommasino was kept busy defending his domain. And so Michael was deprived of the old man's company and had to be content with Dr. Taza's stories, which were beginning to repeat themselves.

One morning Michael decided to take a long hike to the mountains beyond Corleone. He was, naturally, accompanied by the two shepherd bodyguards. This was not really a protection against enemies of the Corleone Family. It was simply too dangerous for anyone not a native to go wandering about by himself. It was dangerous enough for a native. The region was loaded with bandits, with Mafia partisans fighting against each other and endangering everybody else in the process. He might also be mistaken for a *pagliaio* thief.

A *pagliaio* is a straw-thatched hut erected in the fields to house farming tools and to provide shelter for the agricultural laborers so that they will not have to carry them on the long walk from their homes in the village. In Sicily the peasant does not live on the land he cultivates. It is too dangerous and any arable land, if he owns it, is too precious. Rather, he lives in his village and at sunrise begins his voyage out to work in distant fields, a commuter on foot. A worker who arrived at his *pagliaio* and found it looted was an injured man indeed. The bread was taken out of his mouth for that day. The Mafia, after the law proved helpless, took this interest of the peasant under its protection and solved the problem in typical fashion. It hunted down and slaughtered all *pagliaio* thieves. It was inevitable that some innocents suffered. It was possible that if Michael wandered past a *pagliaio* that had just been looted he might be adjudged the criminal unless he had somebody to vouch for him.

So on one sunny morning he started hiking across the fields followed by his two faithful shepherds. One of them was a plain simple fellow, almost moronic, silent as the dead and with a face as impassive as an Indian. He had the wiry small build of the typical Sicilian before they ran to the fat of middle age. His name was Calo.

The other shepherd was more outgoing, younger, and had seen something of the world. Mostly oceans, since he had been a sailor in the Italian navy during the war and had just had time enough to get himself tattooed before his ship was sunk and he was captured by the British. But the tattoo made him a famous man in his village. Sicilians do not often let themselves be tattooed, they do not have the opportunity nor the inclination. (The shepherd, Fabrizzio, had done so primarily to cover a splotchy red birthmark on his belly.) And yet the Mafia market carts had gaily painted scenes on their sides, beautifully primitive paintings done with loving care. In any case, Fabrizzio, back in his native village, was not too proud of that tattoo on his chest, though it showed a subject dear to the Sicilian "honor," a husband stabbing a naked man and woman entwined together on the hairy floor of his belly. Fabrizzio would joke with Michael and ask questions about America, for of course it was impossible to keep them in the dark about his true nationality. Still, they did not know exactly who he was except that he was in hiding and there could be no babbling about him. Fabrizzio sometimes brought Michael a fresh cheese still sweating the milk that formed it.

They walked along dusty country roads passing donkeys pulling gaily painted carts. The land was filled with pink flowers, orange orchards, groves of almond and olive trees, all blooming. That had been one of the surprises. Michael had expected a barren land because of the legendary poverty of Sicilians. And yet he had found it a land of gushing plenty, carpeted with flowers scented by lemon blossoms. It was so beautiful that he wondered how its people could bear to leave it. How terrible man had been to his fellow man could be measured by the great exodus from what seemed to be a Garden of Eden.

He had planned to walk to the coastal village of Mazara, and then take a bus back to Corleone in the evening, and so tire himself out and be able to sleep. The two shepherds wore rucksacks filled with bread and cheese they could eat on the way. They carried their *luparas* quite openly as if out for a day's hunting.

It was a most beautiful morning. Michael felt as he had felt when as a child he had gone out early on a summer day to play ball. Then each day had been freshly washed, freshly painted. And so it was now. Sicily was carpeted in gaudy flowers, the scent of orange and lemon blossoms so heavy that even with his facial injury which pressed on the sinuses, he could smell it.

The smashing on the left side of his face had completely healed but the bone had formed improperly and the pressure on his sinuses made his left eye hurt. It also made his nose run continually, he filled up handkerchiefs with mucus and often blew his nose out onto the ground as the local peasants did, a habit that had disgusted him when he was a boy and had seen old Italians, disdaining handkerchiefs as English foppery, blow out their noses in the asphalt gutters.

His face too felt "heavy." Dr. Taza had told him that this was due to the pressure on his sinuses caused by the badly healed fracture. Dr. Taza called it an eggshell fracture of the zygoma; that if it had been treated before the bones knitted, it could have been easily remedied by a minor surgical procedure using an instrument like a spoon to push out the bone to its proper shape. Now, however, said the doctor, he would have to check into a Palermo hospital and undergo a major procedure called maxillo-facial surgery where the bone would be broken again. That was enough for Michael. He refused. And yet more than the pain, more than the nose dripping, he was bothered by the feeling of heaviness in his face.

He never reached the coast that day. After going about fifteen miles he and his shepherds stopped in the cool green watery shade of an orange grove to eat lunch and drink their wine. Fabrizzio was chattering about how he would someday get to America. After drinking and eating they lolled in the shade and Fabrizzio unbuttoned his shirt and contracted his stomach muscles to make the tattoo come alive. The naked couple on his chest writhed in a lover's agony and the dagger thrust by the husband quivered in their transfixed flesh. It amused them. It was while this was going on that Michael was hit with what Sicilians call "the thunderbolt."

Beyond the orange grove lay the green ribboned fields of a baronial estate. Down the road from the grove was a villa so Roman it looked as if it had been dug up from the ruins of Pompeii. It was a little palace with a huge marble portico and fluted Grecian columns and through those columns came a bevy of village girls flanked by two stout matrons clad in black. They were from the village and had obviously fulfilled their ancient duty to the local baron by cleaning his villa and otherwise preparing it for his winter sojourn. Now they were going into the fields to pick the flowers with which they would fill the rooms. They were gathering the pink *sulla*, purple wisteria, mixing them with orange and lemon blossoms. The girls, not seeing the men resting in the orange grove, came closer and closer.

They were dressed in cheap gaily printed frocks that clung to their bodies. They were still in their teens but with the full womanliness sun-drenched flesh ripened into so quickly. Three or four of them started chasing one girl, chasing her toward the grove. The girl being chased held a bunch of huge purple grapes in her left hand and with her right hand was picking grapes off the cluster and throwing them at her pursuers. She had a crown of ringleted hair as purple-black as the grapes and her body seemed to be bursting out of its skin.

Just short of the grove she poised, startled, her eyes having caught the alien color of the men's shirts. She stood there up on her toes poised like a deer to run. She was very close now, close enough for the men to see every feature of her face.

She was all ovals—oval-shaped eyes, the bones of her face, the

contour of her brow. Her skin was an exquisite dark creaminess and
her eyes, enormous, dark violet or brown but dark with long heavy
lashes shadowed her lovely face. Her mouth was rich without being
gross, sweet without being weak and dyed dark red with the juice of
the grapes. She was so incredibly lovely that Fabrizzio murmured,
"Jesus Christ, take my soul, I'm dying," as a joke, but the words came
out a little too hoarsely. As if she had heard him, the girl came down
off her toes and whirled away from them and fled back to her pursuers. Her haunches moved like an animal's beneath the tight print of
her dress; as pagan and as innocently lustful. When she reached her
friends she whirled around again and her face was like a dark hollow
against the field of bright flowers. She extended an arm, the hand full
of grapes pointed toward the grove. The girls fled laughing, with the
black-clad, stout matrons scolding them on.

As for Michael Corleone, he found himself standing, his heart
pounding in his chest; he felt a little dizzy. The blood was surging
through his body, through all its extremities and pounding against the
tips of his fingers, the tips of his toes. All the perfumes of the island
came rushing in on the wind, orange, lemon blossoms, grapes, flowers.
It seemed as if his body had sprung away from him out of himself.
And then he heard the two shepherds laughing.

"You got hit by the thunderbolt, eh?" Fabrizzio said, clapping him
on the shoulder. Even Calo became friendly, patting him on the arm
and saying, "Easy, man, easy," but with affection. As if Michael had
been hit by a car. Fabrizzio handed him a wine bottle and Michael
took a long slug. It cleared his head.

"What the hell are you damn sheep lovers talking about?" he said.

Both men laughed. Calo, his honest face filled with the utmost
seriousness, said, "You can't hide the thunderbolt. When it hits you,
everybody can see it. Christ, man, don't be ashamed of it, some men
pray for the thunderbolt. You're a lucky fellow."

Michael wasn't too pleased about his emotions being so easily read.
But this was the first time in his life such a thing had happened to
him. It was nothing like his adolescent crushes, it was nothing like the
love he'd had for Kay, a love based as much on her sweetness, her
intelligence and the polarity of the fair and dark. This was an
overwhelming desire for possession, this was an inerasible printing of
the girl's face on his brain and he knew she would haunt his memory
every day of his life if he did not possess her. His life had become
simplified, focused on one point, everything else was unworthy of

even a moment's attention. During his exile he had always thought of Kay, though he felt they could never again be lovers or even friends. He was, after all was said, a murderer, a *mafioso* who had "made his bones." But now Kay was wiped completely out of his consciousness.

Fabrizzio said briskly, "I'll go to the village, we'll find out about her. Who knows, she may be more available than we think. There's only one cure for the thunderbolt, eh, Calo?"

The other shepherd nodded his head gravely. Michael didn't say anything. He followed the two shepherds as they started down the road to the nearby village into which the flock of girls had disappeared.

The village was grouped around the usual central square with its fountain. But it was on a main route so there were some stores, wine shops and one little café with three tables out on a small terrace. The shepherds sat at one of the tables and Michael joined them. There was no sign of the girls, not a trace. The village seemed deserted except for small boys and a meandering donkey.

The proprietor of the café came to serve them. He was a short, burly man, almost dwarfish but he greeted them cheerfully and set a dish of chickpeas at their table. "You're strangers here," he said, "so let me advise you. Try my wine. The grapes come from my own farm and it's made by my sons themselves. They mix it with oranges and lemons. It's the best wine in Italy."

They let him bring the wine in a jug and it was even better than he claimed, dark purple and as powerful as a brandy. Fabrizzio said to the café proprietor, "You know all the girls here, I'll bet. We saw some beauties coming down the road, one in particular got our friend here hit with the thunderbolt." He motioned to Michael.

The café owner looked at Michael with new interest. The cracked face had seemed quite ordinary to him before, not worth a second glance. But a man hit with the thunderbolt was another matter. "You had better bring a few bottles home with you, my friend," he said. "You'll need help in getting to sleep tonight."

Michael asked the man, "Do you know a girl with her hair all curly? Very creamy skin, very big eyes, very dark eyes. Do you know a girl like that in the village?"

The café owner said curtly, "No. I don't know any girl like that." He vanished from the terrace into his café.

The three men drank their wine slowly, finished off the jug and called for more. The owner did not reappear. Fabrizzio went into the café after him. When Fabrizzio came out he grimaced and said to Michael, "Just as I thought, it's his daughter we were talking about and now he's in the back boiling up his blood to do us a mischief. I think we'd better start walking toward Corleone."

Despite his months on the island Michael still could not get used to the Sicilian touchiness on matters of sex, and this was extreme even for a Sicilian. But the two shepherds seemed to take it as a matter of course. They were waiting for him to leave. Fabrizzio said, "The old bastard mentioned he has two sons, big tough lads that he has only to whistle up. Let's get going."

Michael gave him a cold stare. Up to now he had been a quiet, gentle young man, a typical American, except that since he was hiding in Sicily he must have done something manly. This was the first time the shepherds had seen the Corleone stare. Don Tommasino, knowing Michael's true identity and deed, had always been wary of him, treating him as a fellow "man of respect." But these unsophisticated sheep herders had come to their own opinion of Michael, and not a wise one. The cold look, Michael's rigid white face, his anger that came off him like cold smoke off ice, sobered their laughter and snuffed out their familiar friendliness.

When he saw he had their proper, respectful attention Michael said to them, "Get that man out here to me."

They didn't hesitate. They shouldered their *luparas* and went into the dark coolness of the café. A few seconds later they reappeared with the café owner between them. The stubby man looked in no way frightened but his anger had a certain wariness about it.

Michael leaned back in his chair and studied the man for a moment. Then he said very quietly, "I understand I've offended you by talking about your daughter. I offer you my apologies, I'm a stranger in this country, I don't know the customs that well. Let me say this. I meant no disrespect to you or her."

The shepherd bodyguards were impressed. Michael's voice had never sounded like this before when speaking to them. There was command and authority in it though he was making an apology. The café owner shrugged, more wary still, knowing he was not dealing with some farmboy. "Who are you and what do you want from my daughter?"

Without even hesitating Michael said, "I am an American hiding in Sicily, from the police of my country. My name is Michael. You can inform the police and make your fortune but then your daughter would lose a father rather than gain a husband. In any case I want to meet your daughter. With your permission and under the supervision of your family. With all decorum. With all respect. I'm an honorable man and I don't think of dishonoring your daughter. I want to meet her, talk to her and then if it hits us both right we'll marry. If not, you'll never see me again. She may find me unsympathetic after all, and no man can remedy that. But when the proper time comes I'll tell you everything about me that a wife's father should know."

All three men were looking at him with amazement. Fabrizzio whispered in awe, "It's the real thunderbolt." The café owner, for the first time, didn't look so confident, or contemptuous; his anger was not so sure. Finally he asked, "Are you a friend of the friends?"

Since the word Mafia could never be uttered aloud by the ordinary Sicilian, this was as close as the café owner could come to asking if Michael was a member of the Mafia. It was the usual way of asking if someone belonged but it was ordinarily not addressed to the person directly concerned.

"No," Michael said. "I'm a stranger in this country."

The café owner gave him another look, the smashed left side of his face, the long legs rare in Sicily. He took a look at the two shepherds carrying their *luparas* quite openly without fear and remembered how they had come into his café and told him their *padrone* wanted to talk to him. The café owner had snarled that he wanted the son of a bitch out of his terrace and one of the shepherds had said, "Take my word, it's best you go out and speak to him yourself." And something had made him come out. Now something made him realize that it would be best to show this stranger some courtesy. He said grudgingly, "Come Sunday afternoon. My name is Vitelli and my house is up there on the hill, above the village. But come here to the café and I'll take you up."

Fabrizzio started to say something but Michael gave him one look and the shepherd's tongue froze in his mouth. This was not lost on Vitelli. So when Michael stood up and stretched out his hand, the café owner took it and smiled. He would make some inquiries and if the answers were wrong he could always greet Michael with his two sons bearing their own shotguns. The café owner was not without his contacts among the "friends of the friends." But something told him this was one of those wild strokes of good fortune that Sicilians always believed in, something told him that his daughter's beauty would make her fortune and her family secure. And it was just as well. Some of the local youths were already beginning to buzz around and this stranger with his broken face could do the necessary job of scaring them off. Vitelli, to show his goodwill, sent the strangers off with a bottle of his best and coldest wine. He noticed that one of the shepherds paid the bill. This impressed him even more, made it clear that Michael was the superior of the two men who accompanied him.

Michael was no longer interested in his hike. They found a garage and hired a car and driver to take them back to Corleone, and some time before supper, Dr. Taza must have been informed by the shepherds of what had happened. That evening, sitting in the garden, Dr. Taza said to Don Tommasino, "Our friend got hit by the thunderbolt today."

Don Tommasino did not seem surprised. He grunted. "I wish some of those young fellows in Palermo would get a thunderbolt, maybe I could get some peace." He was talking about the new-style Mafia chiefs rising in the big cities of Palermo and challenging the power of old-regime stalwarts like himself.

Michael said to Tommasino, "I want you to tell those two sheep herders to leave me alone Sunday. I'm going to go to this girl's family for dinner and I don't want them hanging around."

Don Tommasino shook his head. "I'm responsible to your father for you, don't ask me that. Another thing, I hear you've even talked marriage. I can't allow that until I've sent somebody to speak to your father."

Michael Corleone was very careful, this was after all a man of respect. "Don Tommasino, you know my father. He's a man who goes deaf when somebody says the word no to him. And he doesn't get his hearing back until they answer him with a yes. Well, he has heard my no many times. I understand about the two guards, I don't want to cause you trouble, they can come with me Sunday, but if I want to marry I'll marry. Surely if I don't permit my own father to interfere with my personal life it would be an insult to him to allow you to do so."

The *capo-mafioso* sighed. "Well, then, marriage it will have to be. I know your thunderbolt. She's a good girl from a respectable family. You can't dishonor them without the father trying to kill you, and then you'll have to shed blood. Besides, I know the family well, I can't allow it to happen."

Michael said, "She may not be able to stand the sight of me, and she's a very young girl, she'll think me old." He saw the two men smiling at him. "I'll need some money for presents and I think I'll need a car."

The Don nodded. "Fabrizzio will take care of everything, he's a clever boy, they taught him mechanics in the navy. I'll give you some money in the morning and I'll let your father know what's happening. That I must do."

Michael said to Dr. Taza, "Have you got anything that can dry up this damn snot always coming out of my nose? I can't have that girl seeing me wiping it all the time."

Dr. Taza said, "I'll coat it with a drug before you have to see her. It makes your flesh a little numb but, don't worry, you won't be kissing her for a while yet." Both doctor and Don smiled at this witticism.

By Sunday, Michael had an Alfa Romeo, battered but serviceable. He had also made a bus trip to Palermo to buy presents for the girl and her family. He had learned that the girl's name was Apollonia and every night he thought of her lovely face and her lovely name. He had to drink a good deal of wine to get some sleep and orders were given to the old women servants in the house to leave a chilled bottle at his bedside. He drank it empty every night.

On Sunday, to the tolling of church bells that covered all of Sicily, he drove the Alfa Romeo to the village and parked it just outside the café. Calo and Fabrizzio were in the back seat with their *luparas* and Michael told them they were to wait in the café, they were not to come to the house. The café was closed but Vitelli was there waiting for them, leaning against the railing of his empty terrace.

They shook hands all around and Michael took the three packages, the presents, and trudged up the hill with Vitelli to his home. This proved to be larger than the usual village hut, the Vitellis were not poverty-stricken.

Inside the house was familiar with statues of the Madonna entombed in glass, votive lights flickering redly at their feet. The two sons were waiting, also dressed in their Sunday black. They were two sturdy young men just out of their teens but looking older because of their hard work on the farm. The mother was a vigorous woman, as stout as her husband. There was no sign of the girl.

After the introductions, which Michael did not even hear, they sat in the room that might possibly have been a living room or just as easily the formal dining room. It was cluttered with all kinds of furniture and not very large but for Sicily it was middle-class splendor.

Michael gave Signor Vitelli and Signora Vitelli their presents. For the father it was a gold cigar-cutter, for the mother a bolt of the finest cloth purchasable in Palermo. He still had one package for the girl. His presents were received with reserved thanks. The gifts were a little too premature, he should not have given anything until his second visit.

The father said to him, in man-to-man country fashion, "Don't think we're so of no account to welcome strangers into our house so easily. But Don Tommasino vouched for you personally and nobody in this province would ever doubt the word of that good man. And so we make you welcome. But I must tell you that if your intentions are serious about my daughter, we will have to know a little more about you and your family. You can understand, your family is from this country."

Michael nodded and said politely, "I will tell you anything you wish to know anytime."

Signor Vitelli held up a hand. "I'm not a nosy man. Let's see if it's necessary first. Right now you're welcome in my house as a friend of Don Tommasino."

Despite the drug painted inside his nose, Michael actually smelled the girl's presence in the room. He turned and she was standing in the arched doorway that led to the back of the house. The smell was of fresh flowers and lemon blossoms but she wore nothing in her hair of jet black curls, nothing on her plain severe black dress, obviously her Sunday best. She gave him a quick glance and a tiny smile before she cast her eyes down demurely and sat down next to her mother.

Again Michael felt that shortness of breath, that flooding through his body of something that was not so much desire as an insane possessiveness. He understood for the first time the classical jealousy of the Italian male. He was at that moment ready to kill anyone who touched this girl, who tried to claim her, take her away from him. He wanted to own her as wildly as a miser wants to own gold coins, as hungrily as a sharecropper wants to own his own land. Nothing was going to stop him from owning this girl, possessing her, locking her in a house and keeping her prisoner only for himself. He didn't want anyone even to see her. When she turned to smile at one of her brothers Michael gave that young man a murderous look without even realizing it. The family could see it was a classical case of the "thunderbolt" and they were reassured. This young man would be putty in their daughter's hands until they were married. After that of course things would change but it wouldn't matter.

Michael had bought himself some new clothes in Palermo and was no longer the roughly dressed peasant, and it was obvious to the family that he was a Don of some kind. His smashed face did not make him as evil-looking as he believed; because his other profile was so handsome it made the disfigurement interesting even. And in any case this was a land where to be called disfigured you had to compete with a host of men who had suffered extreme physical misfortune.

Michael looked directly at the girl, the lovely ovals of her face. Her lips now he could see were almost blue so dark was the blood pulsating in them. He said, not daring to speak her name, "I saw you by the orange groves the other day. When you ran away. I hope I didn't frighten you?"

The girl raised her eyes to him for just a fraction. She shook her head. But the loveliness of those eyes had made Michael look away. The mother said tartly, "Apollonia, speak to the poor fellow, he's come miles to see you," but the girl's long jet lashes remained closed like wings over her eyes. Michael handed her the present wrapped in gold paper and the girl put it in her lap. The father said, "Open it, girl," but her hands did not move. Her hands were small and brown, an urchin's hands. The mother reached over and opened the package impatiently, yet careful not to tear the precious paper. The red velvet jeweler's box gave her pause, she had never held such a thing in her hands and didn't know how to spring its catch. But she got it open on pure instinct and then took out the present.

It was a heavy gold chain to be worn as a necklace, and it awed them not only because of its obvious value but because a gift of gold in this society was also a statement of the most serious intentions. It was no less than a proposal of matrimony, or rather the signal that there was the intention to propose matrimony. They could no longer doubt the seriousness of this stranger. And they could not doubt his substance.

Apollonia still had not touched her present. Her mother held it up for her to see and she raised those long lashes for a moment and then she looked directly at Michael, her doelike brown eyes grave, and said, "Grazia." It was the first time he had heard her voice.

It had all the velvety softness of youth and shyness and it set Michael's ears ringing. He kept looking away from her and talking to the father and mother simply because looking at her confused him so much. But he noticed that despite the conservative looseness of her dress her body almost shone through the cloth with sheer sensuality. And he noticed the darkening of her skin blushing, the dark creamy skin, going darker with the blood surging to her face.

Finally Michael rose to go and the family rose too. They said their good-byes formally, the girl at last confronting him as they shook hands, and he felt the shock of her skin on his skin, her skin warm and rough, peasant skin. The father walked down the hill with him to his car and invited him to Sunday dinner the next week. Michael nodded but he knew he couldn't wait a week to see the girl again.

He didn't. The next day, without his shepherds, he drove to the village and sat on the garden terrace of the café to chat with her father. Signor Vitelli took pity on him and sent for his wife and daughter to come down to the café to join them. This meeting was less awkward. The girl Apollonia was less shy, and spoke more. She was dressed in her everyday print frock which suited her coloring much better.

The next day the same thing happened. Only this time Apollonia was wearing the gold chain he had given her. He smiled at her then, knowing that this was a signal to him. He walked with her up the hill, her mother close behind them. But it was impossible for the two young people to keep their bodies from brushing against each other and once Apollonia stumbled and fell against him so that he had to hold her and her body so warm and alive in his hands started a deep wave of blood rising in his body. They could not see the mother behind them smiling because her daughter was a mountain goat and had not stumbled on this path since she was an infant in diapers. And smiling because this was the only way this young man was going to get his hands on her daughter until the marriage.

This went on for two weeks. Michael brought her presents every time he came and gradually she became less shy. But they could never meet without a chaperone being present. She was just a village girl, barely literate, with no idea of the world, but she had a freshness, an eagerness for life that, with help of the language barrier, made her seem interesting. Everything went very swiftly at Michael's request. And because the girl was not only fascinated by him but knew he must be rich, a wedding date was set for the Sunday two weeks away.

Now Don Tommasino took a hand. He had received word from

America that Michael was not subject to orders but that all elementary precautions should be taken. So Don Tommasino appointed himself the parent of the bridegroom to insure the presence of his own bodyguards. Calo and Fabrizzio were also members of the wedding party from Corleone as was Dr. Taza. The bride and groom would live in Dr. Taza's villa surrounded by its stone wall.

The wedding was the usual peasant one. The villagers stood in the streets and threw flowers as the bridal party, principals and guests, went on foot from the church to the bride's home. The wedding procession pelted the neighbors with sugar-coated almonds, the traditional wedding candies, and with candies left over made sugary white mountains on the bride's wedding bed, in this case only a symbolic one since the first night would be spent in the villa outside Corleone. The wedding feast went on until midnight but bride and groom would leave before that in the Alfa Romeo. When that time came Michael was surprised to find that the mother was coming with them to the Corleone villa at the request of the bride. The father explained: the girl was young, a virgin, a little frightened, she would need someone to talk to on the morning following her bridal night; to put her on the right track if things went wrong. These matters could sometimes get very tricky. Michael saw Apollonia looking at him with doubt in her huge doe-brown eyes. He smiled at her and nodded.

And so it came about that they drove back to the villa outside Corleone with the mother-in-law in the car. But the older woman immediately put her head together with the servants of Dr. Taza, gave her daughter a hug and a kiss and disappeared from the scene. Michael and his bride were allowed to go to their huge bedroom alone.

Apollonia was still wearing her bridal costume with a cloak thrown over it. Her trunk and case had been brought up to the room from the car. On a small table was a bottle of wine and a plate of small wedding cakes. The huge canopied bed was never out of their vision. The young girl in the center of the room waited for Michael to make the first move.

And now that he had her alone, now that he legally possessed her, now that there was no barrier to his enjoying that body and face he had dreamed about every night, Michael could not bring himself to approach her. He watched as she took off the bridal shawl and draped it over a chair, and placed the bridal crown on the small dressing table. That table had an array of perfumes and creams that Michael had had sent from Palermo. The girl tallied them with her eyes for a moment.

Michael turned off the lights, thinking the girl was waiting for some darkness to shield her body while she undressed. But the Sicilian moon came through the unshuttered windows, bright as gold, and Michael went to close the shutters but not all the way, the room would be too warm.

The girl was still standing by the table and so Michael went out of the room and down the hall to the bathroom. He and Dr. Taza and Don Tommasino had taken a glass of wine together in the garden while the women had prepared themselves for bed. He had expected to find Apollonia in her nightgown when he returned, already between the covers. He was surprised that the mother had not done this service for her daughter. Maybe Apollonia had wanted him to help her to undress. But he was certain she was too shy, too innocent for such forward behavior.

Coming back into the bedroom, he found it completely dark, someone had closed the shutters all the way. He groped his way toward the bed and could make out the shape of Apollonia's body lying under the covers, her back to him, her body curved away from him and huddled up. He undressed and slipped naked beneath the sheets. He stretched out one hand and touched silky naked skin. She had not put on her gown and this boldness delighted him. Slowly, carefully, he put one hand on her shoulder and pressed her body gently so that she would turn to him. She turned slowly and his hand touched her breast, soft, full and then she was in his arms so quickly that their bodies came together in one line of silken electricity and he finally had his arms around her, was kissing her warm mouth deeply, was crushing her body and breasts against him and then rolling his body on top of hers.

Her flesh and hair, taut silk, now she was all eagerness, surging against him wildly in a virginal erotic frenzy. When he entered her she gave a little gasp and was still for just a second and then in a powerful forward thrust of her pelvis she locked her satiny legs around his hips. When they came to the end they were locked together so fiercely, straining against each other so violently, that falling away from each other was like the tremble before death.

That night and the weeks that followed, Michael Corleone came to understand the premium put on virginity by socially primitive people. It was a period of sensuality that he had never before experienced, a sensuality mixed with a feeling of masculine power. Apollonia in those first days became almost his slave. Given trust, given affection, a young full-blooded girl aroused from virginity to erotic awareness was as delicious as an exactly ripe fruit.

She on her part brightened up the rather gloomy masculine atmosphere of the villa. She had packed her mother off the very next day after her bridal night and presided at the communal table with bright girlish charm. Don Tommasino dined with them every night and Dr. Taza told all his old stories as they drank wine in the garden full of statues garlanded with blood-red flowers, and so the evenings passed pleasantly enough. At night in their bedroom the newly married couple spent hours of feverish lovemaking. Michael could not get enough of Apollonia's beautifully sculpted body, her honey-colored skin, her huge brown eyes glowing with passion. She had a wonderfully fresh smell, a fleshly smell perfumed by her sex yet almost sweet and unbearably aphrodisiacal. Her virginal passion matched his nuptial lust and often it was dawn when they fell into an exhausted slumber. Sometimes, spent but not yet ready for sleep, Michael sat on the window ledge and stared at Apollonia's naked body while she slept. Her face too was lovely in repose, a perfect face he had seen before only in art books of painted Italian Madonnas who by no stretch of the artist's skill could be thought virginal.

In the first week of their marriage they went on picnics and small trips in the Alfa Romeo. But then Don Tommasino took Michael aside and explained that the marriage had made his presence and identity common knowledge in that part of Sicily and precautions had to be taken against the enemies of the Corleone Family, whose long arms also stretched to this island refuge. Don Tommasino put armed guards around his villa and the two shepherds, Calo and Fabrizzio, were fixtures inside the walls. So Michael and his wife had to remain on the villa grounds. Michael passed the time by teaching Apollonia to read and write English and to drive the car along the inner walls of the villa. About this time Don Tommasino seemed to be preoccupied and poor company, he was still having trouble with the new Mafia in the town of Palermo, Dr. Taza said.

One night in the garden an old village woman who worked in the house as a servant brought a dish of fresh olives and then turned to Michael and said, "Is it true what everybody is saying that you are the son of Don Corleone in New York City, the Godfather?"

Michael saw Don Tommasino shaking his head in disgust at the general knowledge of their secret. But the old crone was looking at him in so concerned a fashion, as if it was important for her to know the truth, that Michael nodded. "Do you know my father?" he asked.

The woman's name was Filomena and her face was as wrinkled and brown as a walnut, her brown-stained teeth showing through the shell of her flesh. For the first time since he had been in the villa she smiled at him. "The Godfather saved my life once," she said, "and my brains too." She made a gesture toward her head.

She obviously wanted to say something else so Michael smiled to encourage her. She asked almost fearfully, "Is it true that Luca Brasi is dead?"

Michael nodded again and was surprised at the look of release on the old woman's face. Filomena crossed herself and said, "God forgive me, but may his soul roast in hell for eternity."

Michael remembered his old curiosity about Brasi, and had the sudden intuition that this woman knew the story Hagen and Sonny had refused to tell him. He poured the woman a glass of wine and made her sit down. "Tell me about my father and Luca Brasi," he said gently. "I know some of it, but how did they become friends and why was Brasi so devoted to my father? Don't be afraid, come tell me."

Filomena's wrinkled face, her raisin-black eyes, turned to Don Tommasino, who in some way signaled his permission. And so Filomena passed the evening for them by telling her story.

Thirty years before, Filomena had been a midwife in New York City, on Tenth Avenue, servicing the Italian colony. The women were always pregnant and she prospered. She taught doctors a few things when they tried to interfere in a difficult birth. Her husband was then a prosperous grocery store owner, dead now poor soul, she blessed him, though he had been a card player and wencher who never thought to put aside for hard times. In any event one cursed night thirty years ago when all honest people were long in their beds, there came a knocking on Filomena's door. She was by no means frightened, it was the quiet hour babes prudently chose to enter safely into this sinful world, and so she dressed and opened the door. Outside it was Luca Brasi whose reputation even then was fearsome. It was known also that he was a bachelor. And so Filomena was immediately frightened. She thought he had come to do her husband harm, that perhaps her husband had foolishly refused Brasi some small favor.

But Brasi had come on the usual errand. He told Filomena that there was a woman about to give birth, that the house was out of the neighborhood some distance away and that she was to come with him. Filomena immediately sensed something amiss. Brasi's brutal face looked almost like that of a madman that night, he was obviously in the grip of some demon. She tried to protest that she attended only women whose history she knew but he shoved a handful of green dollars in her hand and ordered her roughly to come along with him. She was too frightened to refuse.

In the street was a Ford, its driver of the same feather as Luca Brasi. The drive was no more than thirty minutes to a small frame house in Long Island City right over the bridge. A two-family house but obviously now tenanted only by Brasi and his gang. For there were some other ruffians in the kitchen playing cards and drinking. Brasi took Filomena up the stairs to a bedroom. In the bed was a young pretty girl who looked Irish, her face painted, her hair red; and with a belly swollen like a sow. The poor girl was so frightened. When she saw Brasi she turned her head away in terror, yes terror, and indeed the look of hatred on Brasi's evil face was the most frightening thing she had ever seen in her life. (Here Filomena crossed herself again.)

To make a long story short, Brasi left the room. Two of his men assisted the midwife and the baby was born, the mother was exhausted and went into a deep sleep. Brasi was summoned and Filomena, who had wrapped the newborn child in an extra blanket, extended the bundle to him and said, "If you're the father, take her. My work is finished."

Brasi glared at her, malevolent, insanity stamped on his face. "Yes, I'm the father," he said. "But I don't want any of that race to live. Take it down to the basement and throw it into the furnace."

For a moment Filomena thought she had not understood him properly. She was puzzled by his use of the word "race." Did he mean because the girl was not Italian? Or did he mean because the girl was obviously of the lowest type; a whore in short? Or did he mean that anything springing from his loins he forbade to live. And then she was sure he was making a brutal joke. She said shortly, "It's your child, do what you want." And she tried to hand him the bundle.

At this time the exhausted mother awoke and turned on her side to face them. She was just in time to see Brasi thrust violently at the bundle, crushing the newborn infant against Filomena's chest. She called out weakly, "Luc, Luc, I'm sorry," and Brasi turned to face her.

It was terrible, Filomena said now. So terrible. They were like two mad animals. They were not human. The hatred they bore each other blazed through the room. Nothing else, not even the newborn infant, existed for them at that moment. And yet there was a strange passion. A bloody, demonical lust so unnatural you knew they were damned forever. Then Luca Brasi turned back to Filomena and said harshly, "Do what I tell you, I'll make you rich."

Filomena could not speak in her terror. She shook her head. Finally she managed to whisper, "You do it, you're the father, do it if you like." But Brasi didn't answer. Instead he drew a knife from inside his shirt. "I'll cut your throat," he said.

She must have gone into shock then because the next thing she remembered they were all standing in the basement of the house in front of a square iron furnace. Filomena was still holding the blanketed baby, which had not made a sound. (Maybe if it had cried, maybe if I had been shrewd enough to pinch it, Filomena said, that monster would have shown mercy.)

One of the men must have opened the furnace door, the fire now was visible. And then she was alone with Brasi in that basement with its sweating pipes, its mousy odor. Brasi had his knife out again. And there could be no doubting that he would kill her. There were the flames, there were Brasi's eyes. His face was the gargoyle of the devil, it was not human, it was not sane. He pushed her toward the open furnace door.

At this point Filomena fell silent. She folded her bony hands in her lap and looked directly at Michael. He knew what she wanted, how she wanted to tell him, without using her voice. He asked gently, "Did you do it?" She nodded.

It was only after another glass of wine and crossing herself and muttering a prayer that she continued her story. She was given a bundle of money and driven home. She understood that if she uttered a word about what had happened she would be killed. But two days later Brasi murdered the young Irish girl, the mother of the infant, and was arrested by the police. Filomena, frightened out of her wits, went to the Godfather and told her story. He ordered her to keep silent, that he would attend to everything. At that time Brasi did not work for Don Corleone.

Before Don Corleone could set matters aright, Luca Brasi tried to commit suicide in his cell, hacking at his throat with a piece of glass. He was transferred to the prison hospital and by the time he recovered Don Corleone had arranged everything. The police did not have a case they could prove in court and Luca Brasi was released.

Though Don Corleone assured Filomena that she had nothing to fear from either Luca Brasi or the police, she had no peace. Her nerves were shattered and she could no longer work at her profession. Finally she persuaded her husband to sell the grocery store and they returned to Italy. Her husband was a good man, had been told everything and understood. But he was a weak man and in Italy squandered the fortune they had both slaved in America to earn. And so after he died she had become a servant. So Filomena ended her story. She had another glass of wine and said to Michael, "I bless the name of your father. He always sent me money when I asked, he saved me from Brasi. Tell him I say a prayer for his soul every night and that he shouldn't fear dying."

After she had left, Michael asked Don Tommasino, "Is her story true?" The *capo-mafioso* nodded. And Michael thought, no wonder nobody had wanted to tell him the story. Some story. Some Luca.

The next morning Michael wanted to discuss the whole thing with Don Tommasino but learned that the old man had been called to Palermo by an urgent message delivered by a courier. That evening Don Tommasino returned and took Michael aside. News had come from America, he said. News that it grieved him to tell. Santino Corleone had been killed.

Chapter

✕✕✕✕✕✕✕✕✕✕✕✕✕✕✕✕✕✕✕

24

THE Sicilian sun, early-morning lemon-colored, filled Michael's bedroom. He awoke and, feeling Apollonia's satiny body against his own sleep-warm skin, made her come awake with love. When they were done, even all the months of complete possession could not stop him from marveling at her beauty and her passion.

She left the bedroom to wash and dress in the bathroom down the hall. Michael, still naked, the morning sun refreshing his body, lit a cigarette and relaxed on the bed. This was the last morning they would spend in this house and the villa. Don Tommasino had arranged for him to be transferred to another town on the southern coast of Sicily. Apollonia, in the first month of pregnancy, wanted to visit with her family for a few weeks and would join him at the new hiding place after the visit.

The night before, Don Tommasino had sat with Michael in the garden after Apollonia had gone to bed. The Don had been worried and tired, and admitted that he was concerned about Michael's safety. "Your marriage brought you into sight," he told Michael. "I'm surprised your father hasn't made arrangements for you to go someplace else. In any case I'm having my own troubles with the young Turks in Palermo. I've offered some fair arrangements so that they can wet their beaks more than they deserve, but those scum want everything. I can't understand their attitude. They've tried a few little tricks but I'm not so easy to kill. They must know I'm too strong for them to hold me so cheaply. But that's the trouble with young people, no matter how talented. They don't reason things out and they want all the water in the well."

And then Don Tommasino had told Michael that the two shepherds, Fabrizzio and Calo, would go with him as bodyguards in the Alfa Romeo. Don Tommasino would say his good-byes tonight since he would be off early in the morning, at dawn, to see to his affairs in Palermo. Also, Michael was not to tell Dr. Taza about the move, since the doctor planned to spend the evening in Palermo and might blab.

Michael had known Don Tommasino was in trouble. Armed guards patrolled the walls of the villa at night and a few faithful shepherds with their *luparas* were always in the house. Don Tommasino himself went heavily armed and a personal bodyguard attended him at all times.

The morning sun was now too strong. Michael stubbed out his cigarette and put on work pants, work shirt and the peaked cap most Sicilian men wore. Still barefooted, he leaned out his bedroom window and saw Fabrizzio sitting in one of the garden chairs. Fabrizzio was lazily combing his thick dark hair, his *lupara* was carelessly thrown across the garden table. Michael whistled and Fabrizzio looked up to his window.

"Get the car," Michael called down to him. "I'll be leaving in five minutes. Where's Calo?"

Fabrizzio stood up. His shirt was open, exposing the blue and red lines of the tattoo on his chest. "Calo is having a cup of coffee in the kitchen," Fabrizzio said. "Is your wife coming with you?"

Michael squinted down at him. It occurred to him that Fabrizzio had been following Apollonia too much with his eyes the last few weeks. Not that he would dare ever to make an advance toward the wife of a friend of the Don's. In Sicily there was no surer road to death. Michael said coldly, "No, she's going home to her family first, she'll join us in a few days." He watched Fabrizzio hurry into the stone hut that served as a garage for the Alfa Romeo.

Michael went down the hall to wash. Apollonia was gone. She was most likely in the kitchen preparing his breakfast with her own hands to wash out the guilt she felt because she wanted to see her family one more time before going so far away to the other end of Sicily. Don

Tommasino would arrange transportation for her to where Michael would be.

Down in the kitchen the old woman Filomena brought him his coffee and shyly bid him a good-bye. "I'll remember you to my father," Michael said and she nodded.

Calo came into the kitchen and said to Michael, "The car's outside, shall I get your bag?"

"No, I'll get it," Michael said. "Where's Apolla?"

Calo's face broke into an amused grin. "She's sitting in the driver's seat of the car, dying to step on the gas. She'll be a real American woman before she gets to America." It was unheard of for one of the peasant women in Sicily to attempt driving a car. But Michael sometimes let Apollonia guide the Alfa Romeo around the inside of the villa walls, always beside her however because she sometimes stepped on the gas when she meant to step on the brake.

Michael said to Calo, "Get Fabrizzio and wait for me in the car." He went out of the kitchen and ran up the stairs to the bedroom. His bag was already packed. Before picking it up he looked out the window and saw the car parked in front of the portico steps rather than the kitchen entrance. Apollonia was sitting in the car, her hands on the wheel like a child playing. Calo was just putting the lunch basket in the rear seat. And then Michael was annoyed to see Fabrizzio disappearing through the gates of the villa on some errand outside. What the hell was he doing? He saw Fabrizzio take a look over his shoulder, a look that was somehow furtive. He'd have to straighten that damn shepherd out. Michael went down the stairs and decided to go through the kitchen to see Filomena again and give her a final farewell. He asked the old woman, "Is Dr. Taza still sleeping?"

Filomena's wrinkled face was sly. "Old roosters can't greet the sun. The doctor went to Palermo last night."

Michael laughed. He went out the kitchen entrance and the smell of lemon blossoms penetrated even his sinus-filled nose. He saw Apollonia wave to him from the car just ten paces up the villa's driveway and then he realized she was motioning him to stay where he was, that she meant to drive the car to where he stood. Calo stood grinning beside the car, his *lupara* dangling in his hand. But there was still no sign of Fabrizzio. At that moment, without any conscious reasoning process, everything came together in his mind, and Michael shouted to the girl, "No! No!" But his shout was drowned in the roar of the tremendous explosion as Apollonia switched on the ignition.

The kitchen door shattered into fragments and Michael was hurled along the wall of the villa for a good ten feet. Stones tumbling from the villa roof hit him on the shoulders and one glanced off his skull as he was lying on the ground. He was conscious just long enough to see that nothing remained of the Alfa Romeo but its four wheels and the steel shafts which held them together.

He came to consciousness in a room that seemed very dark and heard voices that were so low that they were pure sound rather than words. Out of animal instinct he tried to pretend he was still unconscious but the voices stopped and someone was leaning from a chair close to his bed and the voice was distinct now, saying, "Well, he's with us finally." A lamp went on, its light like white fire on his eyeballs and Michael turned his head. It felt very heavy, numb. And then he could see the face over his bed was that of Dr. Taza.

"Let me look at you a minute and I'll put the light out," Dr. Taza said gently. He was busy shining a small pencil flashlight into Michael's eyes. "You'll be all right," Dr. Taza said and turned to someone else in the room. "You can speak to him."

It was Don Tommasino sitting on a chair near his bed, Michael could see him clearly now. Don Tommasino was saying, "Michael, Michael, can I talk to you? Do you want to rest?"

It was easier to raise a hand to make a gesture and Michael did so and Don Tommasino said, "Did Fabrizzio bring the car from the garage?"

Michael, without knowing he did so, smiled. It was in some strange way, a chilling smile, of assent. Don Tommasino said, "Fabrizzio has vanished. Listen to me, Michael. You've been unconscious for nearly a week. Do you understand? Everybody thinks you're dead, so you're safe now, they've stopped looking for you. I've sent messages to your father and he's sent back instructions. It won't be long now, you'll be back in America. Meanwhile you'll rest here quietly. You're safe up in the mountains, in a special farmhouse I own. The Palermo people have made their peace with me now that you're supposed to be dead, so it was you they were after all the time. They wanted to kill you while making people think it was me they were after. That's something you should know. As for everything else, leave it all to me. You recover your strength and be tranquil."

Michael was remembering everything now. He knew his wife was dead, that Calo was dead. He thought of the old woman in the kitchen. He couldn't remember if she had come outside with him. He whispered, "Filomena?" Don Tommasino said quietly, "She wasn't hurt, just a bloody nose from the blast. Don't worry about her."

Michael said, "Fabrizzio. Let your shepherds know that the one who gives me Fabrizzio will own the finest pastures in Sicily."

Both men seemed to sigh with relief. Don Tommasino lifted a glass from a nearby table and drank from it an amber fluid that jolted his head up. Dr. Taza sat on the bed and said almost absently, "You know, you're a widower. That's rare in Sicily." As if the distinction might comfort him.

Michael motioned to Don Tommasino to lean closer. The Don sat on the bed and bent his head. "Tell my father to get me home," Michael said. "Tell my father I wish to be his son."

But it was to be another month before Michael recovered from his injuries and another two months after that before all the necessary papers and arrangements were ready. Then he was flown from Palermo to Rome and from Rome to New York. In all that time no trace had been found of Fabrizzio.

Book VII

Chapter

25

WHEN Kay Adams received her college degree, she took a job teaching grade school in her New Hampshire hometown. The first six months after Michael vanished she made weekly telephone calls to his mother asking about him. Mrs. Corleone was always friendly and always wound up saying, "You a very very nice girl. You forget about Mikey and find a nice husband." Kay was not offended at her bluntness and understood that the mother spoke out of concern for her as a young girl in an impossible situation.

When her first school term ended, she decided to go to New York to buy some decent clothes and see some old college girl friends. She thought also about looking for some sort of interesting job in New York. She had lived like a spinster for almost two years, reading and teaching, refusing dates, refusing to go out at all, even though she had given up making calls to Long Beach. She knew she couldn't keep that up, she was becoming irritable and unhappy. But she had always believed Michael would write her or send her a message of some sort. That he had not done so humiliated her, it saddened her that he was so distrustful even of her.

She took an early train and was checked into her hotel by mid-afternoon. Her girl friends worked and she didn't want to bother them at their jobs, she planned to call them at night. And she didn't really feel like going shopping after the exhausting train trip. Being alone in the hotel room, remembering all the times she and Michael had used hotel rooms to make love, gave her a feeling of desolation. It was that more than anything else that gave her the idea of calling Michael's mother out in Long Beach.

The phone was answered by a rough masculine voice with a typical, to her, New York accent. Kay asked to speak to Mrs. Corleone. There was a few minutes' silence and then Kay heard the heavily accented voice asking who it was.

Kay was a little embarrassed now. "This is Kay Adams, Mrs. Corleone," she said. "Do you remember me?"

"Sure, sure, I remember you," Mrs. Corleone said. "How come you no call up no more? You get a married?"

"Oh, no," Kay said. "I've been busy." She was surprised at the mother obviously being annoyed that she had stopped calling. "Have you heard anything from Michael? Is he all right?"

There was silence at the other end of the phone and then Mrs. Corleone's voice came strong. "Mikey is a home. He no call you up? He no see you?"

Kay felt her stomach go weak from shock and a humiliating desire to weep. Her voice broke a little when she asked, "How long has he been home?"

Mrs. Corleone said, "Six months."

"Oh, I see," Kay said. And she did. She felt hot waves of shame that Michael's mother knew he was treating her so cheaply. And then she was angry. Angry at Michael, at his mother, angry at all foreigners, Italians who didn't have the common courtesy to keep up a decent show of friendship even if a love affair was over. Didn't Michael know she would be concerned for him as a friend even if he no longer wanted her for a bed companion, even if he no longer wanted to marry her? Did he think she was one of those poor benighted Italian girls who would commit suicide or make a scene after giving up her virginity and then being thrown over? But she kept her voice as cool as possible. "I see, thank you very much," she said. "I'm glad Michael is home again and all right. I just wanted to know. I won't call you again."

Mrs. Corleone's voice came impatiently over the phone as if she had heard nothing that Kay had said. "You wanta see Mikey, you come out here now. Give him a nice surprise. You take a taxi, and I tell the man at the gate to pay the taxi for you. You tell the taxi man he get two times his clock, otherwise he no come way out the Long Beach. But don't you pay. My husband's man at the gate pay the taxi."

"I couldn't do that, Mrs. Corleone," Kay said coldly. "If Michael wanted to see me, he would have called me at home before this. Obviously he doesn't want to resume our relationship."

Mrs. Corleone's voice came briskly over the phone. "You a very nice girl, you gotta nice legs, but you no gotta much brains." She chuckled. "You come out to see *me*, not Mikey. I wanta talk to you. You come right now. An' no pay the taxi. I wait for you." The phone clicked. Mrs. Corleone had hung up.

Kay could have called back and said she wasn't coming but she knew she had to see Michael, to talk to him, even if it was just polite talk. If he was home now, openly, that meant he was no longer in trouble, he could live normally. She jumped off the bed and started to get ready to see him. She took a great deal of care with her makeup and dress. When she was ready to leave she stared at her reflection in the mirror. Was she better-looking than when Michael had disappeared? Or would he find her unattractively older? Her figure had become more womanly, her hips rounder, her breasts fuller, Italians liked that supposedly, though Michael had always said he loved her being so thin. It didn't matter really, Michael obviously didn't want anything to do with her anymore, otherwise he most certainly would have called in the six months he had been home.

The taxi she hailed refused to take her to Long Beach until she gave him a pretty smile and told him she would pay double the meter. It was nearly an hour's ride and the mall in Long Beach had changed since she last saw it. There were iron fences around it and an iron gate barred the mall entrance. A man wearing slacks and a white jacket over a red shirt opened the gate, poked his head into the cab to read the meter and gave the cab driver some bills. Then when Kay saw the driver was not protesting and was happy with the money paid, she got out and walked across the mall to the central house.

Mrs. Corleone herself opened the door and greeted Kay with a warm embrace that surprised her. Then she surveyed Kay with an appraising eye. "You a beautiful girl," she said flatly. "I have stupid sons." She pulled Kay inside the door and led her to the kitchen, where a platter of food was already set out and a pot of coffee perked on the stove. "Michael comes home pretty soon," she said. "You surprise him."

They sat down together and the old woman forced Kay to eat, meanwhile asking questions with great curiosity. She was delighted that Kay was a schoolteacher and that she had come to New York to visit old girl friends and that Kay was only twenty-four years old. She kept nodding her head as if all the facts accorded with some private specifications in her mind. Kay was so nervous that she just answered the questions, never saying anything else.

She saw him first through the kitchen window. A car pulled up in front of the house and two other men got out. Then Michael. He straightened up to talk with one of the other men. His profile, the left one, was exposed to her view. It was cracked, indented, like the plastic face of a doll that a child has wantonly kicked. In a curious way it did not mar his handsomeness in her eyes but moved her to tears. She saw him put a snow-white handkerchief to his mouth and nose and hold it there for a moment while he turned away to come into the house.

She heard the door open and his footsteps in the hall turning into the kitchen and then he was in the open space, seeing her and his mother. He seemed impassive, and then he smiled ever so slightly, the broken half of his face halting the widening of his mouth. And Kay, who had meant just to say "Hello, how are you," in the coolest possible way, slipped out of her seat to run into his arms, bury her face against his shoulder. He kissed her wet cheek and held her until she finished weeping and then he walked her out to his car, waved his bodyguard away and drove off with her beside him, she repairing her makeup by simply wiping what was left of it away with her handkerchief.

"I never meant to do that," Kay said. "It's just that nobody told me how badly they hurt you."

Michael laughed and touched the broken side of his face. "You mean this? That's nothing. Just gives me sinus trouble. Now that I'm home I'll probably get it fixed. I couldn't write you or anything," Michael said. "You have to understand that before anything else."

"OK," she said.

"I've got a place in the city," Michael said. "Is it all right if we go there or should it be dinner and drinks at a restaurant?"

"I'm not hungry," Kay said.

They drove toward New York in silence for a while. "Did you get your degree?" Michael asked.

"Yes," Kay said. "I'm teaching grade school in my hometown now.

Did they find the man who really killed the policeman, is that why you were able to come home?"

For a moment Michael didn't answer. "Yes, they did," he said. "It was in all the New York papers. Didn't you read about it?"

Kay laughed with the relief of him denying he was a murderer. "We only get the New York *Times* up in our town," she said. "I guess it was buried back in page eighty-nine. If I'd read about it I'd have called your mother sooner." She paused and then said, "It's funny, the way your mother used to talk, I almost believed you had done it. And just before you came, while we were drinking coffee, she told me about that crazy man who confessed."

Michael said, "Maybe my mother did believe it at first."

"Your own mother?" Kay asked.

Michael grinned. "Mothers are like cops. They always believe the worst."

Michael parked the car in a garage on Mulberry Street where the owner seemed to know him. He took Kay around the corner to what looked like a fairly decrepit brownstone house which fitted into the rundown neighborhood. Michael had a key to the front door and when they went inside Kay saw that it was as expensively and comfortably furnished as a millionaire's town house. Michael led her to the upstairs apartment which consisted of an enormous living room, a huge kitchen and door that led to the bedroom. In one corner of the living room was a bar and Michael mixed them both a drink. They sat on a sofa together and Michael said quietly, "We might as well go into the bedroom." Kay took a long pull from her drink and smiled at him. "Yes," she said.

For Kay the lovemaking was almost like it had been before except that Michael was rougher, more direct, not as tender as he had been. As if he were on guard against her. But she didn't want to complain. It would wear off. In a funny way, men were more sensitive in a situation like this, she thought. She had found making love to Michael after a two-year absence the most natural thing in the world. It was as if he had never been away.

"You could have written me, you could have trusted me," she said, nestling against his body. "I would have practiced the New England *omerta*. Yankees are pretty closemouthed too, you know."

Michael laughed softly in the darkness. "I never figured you to be waiting," he said. "I never figured you to wait after what happened."

Kay said quickly, "I never believed you killed those two men.

Except maybe when your mother seemed to think so. But I never believed it in my heart. I know you too well."

She could hear Michael give a sigh. "It doesn't matter whether I did or not," he said. "You have to understand that."

Kay was a little stunned by the coldness in his voice. She said, "So just tell me now, did you or didn't you?"

Michael sat up on his pillow and in the darkness a light flared as he got a cigarette going. "If I asked you to marry me, would I have to answer that question first before you'd give me an answer to mine?"

Kay said, "I don't care, I love you, I don't care. If you loved me you wouldn't be afraid to tell me the truth. You wouldn't be afraid I might tell the police. That's it, isn't it? You're really a gangster then, isn't that so? But I really don't care. What I care about is that you obviously don't love me. You didn't even call me up when you got back home."

Michael was puffing on his cigarette and some burning ashes fell on Kay's bare back. She flinched a little and said jokingly, "Stop torturing me, I won't talk."

Michael didn't laugh. His voice sounded absentminded. "You know, when I came home I wasn't that glad when I saw my family, my father, my mother, my sister Connie, and Tom. It was nice but I didn't really give a damn. Then I came home tonight and saw you in the kitchen and I was glad. Is that what you mean by love?"

"That's close enough for me," Kay said.

They made love again for a while. Michael was more tender this time. And then he went out to get them both a drink. When he came back he sat on an armchair facing the bed. "Let's get serious," he said. "How do you feel about marrying me?" Kay smiled at him and motioned him into the bed. Michael smiled back at her. "Be serious," he said. "I can't tell you about anything that happened. I'm working for my father now. I'm being trained to take over the family olive oil business. But you know my family has enemies, my father has enemies. You might be a very young widow, there's a chance, not much of a one, but it could happen. And I won't be telling you what happened at the office every day. I won't be telling you anything about my business. You'll be my wife but you won't be my partner in life, as I think they say. Not an equal partner. That can't be."

Kay sat up in bed. She switched on a huge lamp standing on the night table and then she lit a cigarette. She leaned back on the pillows and said quietly, "You're telling me you're a gangster, isn't that it?

You're telling me that you're responsible for people being killed and other sundry crimes related to murder. And that I'm not ever to ask about that part of your life, not even to think about it. Just like in the horror movies when the monster asks the beautiful girl to marry him." Michael grinned, the cracked part of his face turned toward her, and Kay said in contrition, "Oh, Mike, I don't even notice that stupid thing, I swear I don't."

"I know," Michael said laughing. "I like having it now except that it makes the snot drip out of my nose."

"You said be serious," Kay went on. "If we get married what kind of a life am I supposed to lead? Like your mother, like an Italian housewife with just the kids and home to take care of? And what about if something happens? I suppose you could wind up in jail someday."

"No, that's not possible," Michael said. "Killed, yes; jail, no."

Kay laughed at this confidence, it was a laugh that had a funny mixture of pride with its amusement. "But how can you say that?" she said. "Really."

Michael sighed. "These are all the things I can't talk to you about, I don't want to talk to you about."

Kay was silent for a long time. "Why do you want me to marry you after never calling me all these months? Am I so good in bed?"

Michael nodded gravely. "Sure," he said. "But I'm getting it for nothing so why should I marry you for that? Look, I don't want an answer now. We're going to keep seeing each other. You can talk it over with your parents. I hear your father is a real tough guy in his own way. Listen to his advice."

"You haven't answered why, why you want to marry me," Kay said.

Michael took a white handkerchief from the drawer of the night table and held it to his nose. He blew into it and then wiped. "There's the best reason for not marrying me," he said. "How would that be having a guy around who always has to blow his nose?"

Kay said impatiently, "Come on, be serious, I asked you a question."

Michael held the handkerchief in his hand. "OK," he said, "this one time. You are the only person I felt any affection for, that I care about. I didn't call you because it never occurred to me that you'd still be interested in me after everything that's happened. Sure, I could have chased you, I could have conned you, but I didn't want to do that. Now here's something I'll trust you with and I don't want you to repeat it even to your father. If everything goes right, the Corleone Family will be completely legitimate in about five years. Some very tricky things have to be done to make that possible. That's when you may become a wealthy widow. Now what do I want you for? Well, because I want you and I want a family. I want kids; it's time. And I don't want those kids to be influenced by me the way I was influenced by my father. I don't mean my father deliberately influenced me. He never did. He never even wanted me in the family business. He wanted me to become a professor or a doctor, something like that. But things went bad and I had to fight for my Family. I had to fight because I love and admire my father. I never knew a man more worthy of respect. He was a good husband and a good father and a good friend to people who were not so fortunate in life. There's another side to him, but that's not relevant to me as his son. Anyway I don't want that to happen to my kids. I want them to be influenced by you. I want them to grow up to be All-American kids, real All-American, the whole works. Maybe they or their grandchildren will go into politics." Michael grinned. "Maybe one of them will be President of the United States. Why the hell not? In my history course at Dartmouth we did some background on all the Presidents and they had fathers and grandfathers who were lucky they didn't get hanged. But I'll settle for my kids being doctors or musicians or teachers. They'll never be in the Family business. By the time they are that old I'll be retired anyway. And you and I will be part of some country club crowd, the good simple life of well-to-do Americans. How does that strike you for a proposition?"

"Marvelous," Kay said. "But you sort of skipped over the widow part."

"There's not much chance of that. I just mentioned it to give a fair presentation." Michael patted his nose with the handkerchief.

"I can't believe it, I can't believe you're a man like that, you're just not," Kay said. Her face had a bewildered look. "I just don't understand the whole thing, how it could possibly be."

"Well, I'm not giving any more explanations," Michael said gently. "You know, you don't have to think about any of this stuff, it has nothing to do with you really, or with our life together if we get married."

Kay shook her head. "How can you want to marry me, how can you hint that you love me, you never say the word but you just now said you loved your father, you never said you loved me, how could you if you distrust me so much you can't tell me about the most important things in your life? How can you want to have a wife you can't trust? Your father trusts your mother. I know that."

"Sure," Michael said. "But that doesn't mean he tells her everything. And, you know, he has reason to trust her. Not because they got married and she's his wife. But she bore him four children in times when it was not that safe to bear children. She nursed and guarded him when people shot him. She believed in him. He was always her first loyalty for forty years. After you do that maybe I'll tell you a few things you really don't want to hear."

"Will we have to live in the mall?" Kay asked.

Michael nodded. "We'll have our own house, it won't be so bad. My parents don't meddle. Our lives will be our own. But until everything gets straightened out, I have to live in the mall."

"Because it's dangerous for you to live outside it," Kay said.

For the first time since she had come to know him, she saw Michael angry. It was cold chilling anger that was not externalized in any gesture or change in voice. It was a coldness that came off him like death and Kay knew that it was this coldness that would make her decide not to marry him if she so decided.

"The trouble is all that damn trash in the movies and the newspapers," Michael said. "You've got the wrong idea of my father and the Corleone Family. I'll make a final explanation and this one will be really final. My father is a businessman trying to provide for his wife and children and those friends he might need someday in a time of trouble. He doesn't accept the rules of the society we live in because those rules would have condemned him to a life not suitable to a man like himself, a man of extraordinary force and character. What you have to understand is that he considers himself the equal of all those great men like Presidents and Prime Ministers and Supreme Court Justices and Governors of the States. He refuses to accept their will over his own. He refuses to live by rules set up by others, rules which condemn him to a defeated life. But his ultimate aim is to enter that society with a certain power since society doesn't really protect its members who do not have their own individual power. In the meantime he operates on a code of ethics he considers far superior to the legal structures of society."

Kay was looking at him incredulously. "But that's ridiculous," she said. "What if everybody felt the same way? How could society ever function, we'd be back in the times of the cavemen. Mike, you don't believe what you're saying, do you?"

Michael grinned at her. "I'm just telling you what my father believes. I just want you to understand that whatever else he is, he's not irresponsible, or at least not in the society which he has created. He's not a crazy machine-gunning mobster as you seem to think. He's a responsible man in his own way."

"And what do you believe?" Kay asked quietly.

Michael shrugged. "I believe in my family," he said. "I believe in you and the family we may have. I don't trust society to protect us, I have no intention of placing my fate in the hands of men whose only qualification is that they managed to con a block of people to vote for them. But that's for now. My father's time is done. The things he did can no longer be done except with a great deal of risk. Whether we like it or not the Corleone Family has to join that society. But when they do I'd like us to join it with plenty of our own power; that is, money and ownership of other valuables. I'd like to make my children as secure as possible before they join that general destiny."

"But you volunteered to fight for your country, you were a war hero," Kay said. "What happened to make you change?"

Michael said, "This is really getting us no place. But maybe I'm just one of those real old-fashioned conservatives they grow up in your hometown. I take care of myself, individual. Governments really don't do much for their people, that's what it comes down to, but that's not it really. All I can say, I have to help my father, I have to be on his side. And you have to make your decision about being on my side." He smiled at her. "I guess getting married was a bad idea."

Kay patted the bed. "I don't know about marrying, but I've gone without a man for two years and I'm not letting you off so easy now. Come on in here."

When they were in bed together, the light out, she whispered to him, "Do you believe me about not having a man since you left?"

"I believe you," Michael said.

"Did you?" she whispered in a softer voice.

"Yes," Michael said. He felt her stiffen a little. "But not in the last six months." It was true. Kay was the first woman he had made love to since the death of Apollonia.

Chapter

26

THE garish suite overlooked the fake fairyland grounds in the rear of the hotel; transplanted palm trees lit up by climbers of orange lights, two huge swimming pools shimmering dark blue by the light of the desert stars. On the horizon were the sand and stone mountains that ringed Las Vegas nestling in its neon valley. Johnny Fontane let the heavy, richly embroidered gray drape fall and turned back to the room.

A special detail of four men, a pit boss, a dealer, extra relief man, and a cocktail waitress in her scanty nightclub costume were getting things ready for private action. Nino Valenti was lying on the sofa in the living room part of the suite, a water glass of whiskey in his hand. He watched the people from the casino setting up the blackjack table with the proper six padded chairs around its horseshoe outer rim. "That's great, that's great," he said in a slurred voice that was not quite drunken. "Johnny, come on and gamble with me against these bastards. I got the luck. We'll beat their crullers in."

Johnny sat on a footstool opposite the couch. "You know I don't gamble," he said. "How you feeling, Nino?"

Nino Valenti grinned at him. "Great. I got broads coming up at midnight, then some supper, then back to the blackjack table. You know I got the house beat for almost fifty grand and they've been grinding me for a week?"

"Yeah," Johnny Fontane said. "Who do you want to leave it to when you croak?"

Nino drained his glass empty. "Johnny, where the h ll did you get your rep as a swinger? You're a deadhead, Johnny. Christ, the tourists in this town have more fun than you do."

Johnny said, "Yeah. You want a lift to that blackjack table?"

Nino struggled erect on the sofa and planted his feet firmly on the rug. "I can make it," he said. He let the glass slip to the floor and got up and walked quite steadily to where the blackjack table had been set up. The dealer was ready. The pit boss stood behind the dealer watching. The relief dealer sat on a chair away from the table. The cocktail waitress sat on another chair in a line of vision so that she could see any of Nino Valenti's gestures.

Nino rapped on the green baize with his knuckles. "Chips," he said.

The pit boss took a pad from his pocket and filled out a slip and put it in front of Nino with a small fountain pen. "Here you are, Mr. Valenti," he said. "The usual five thousand to start." Nino scrawled his signature on the bottom of the slip and the pit boss put it in his pocket. He nodded to the dealer.

The dealer with incredibly deft fingers took stacks of black and gold one-hundred-dollar chips from the built-in racks before him. In not more than five seconds Nino had five even stacks of one-hundred-dollar chips before him, each stack had ten chips.

There were six squares a little larger than playing card shapes etched in white on the green baize, each square placed to correspond to where a player would sit. Now Nino was placing bets on three of these squares, single chips, and so playing three hands each for a hundred dollars. He refused to take a hit on all three hands because the dealer had a six up, a bust card, and the dealer did bust. Nino raked in his chips and turned to Johnny Fontane. "That's how to start the night, huh, Johnny?"

Johnny smiled. It was unusual for a gambler like Nino to have to sign a chit while gambling. A word was usually good enough for the high rollers. Maybe they were afraid Nino wouldn't remember his take-out because of his drinking. They didn't know that Nino remembered everything.

Nino kept winning and after the third round lifted a finger at the cocktail waitress. She went to the bar at the end of the room and brought him his usual rye in a water glass. Nino took the drink, switched it to his other hand so he could put an arm around the waitress. "Sit with me, honey, play a few hands; bring me luck."

The cocktail waitress was a very beautiful girl, but Johnny could see she was all cold hustle, no real personality, though she worked at it. She was giving Nino a big smile but her tongue was hanging out for one of those black and gold chips. What the hell, Johnny thought, why shouldn't she get some of it? He just regretted that Nino wasn't getting something better for his money.

Nino let the waitress play his hands for a few rounds and then gave her one of the chips and a pat on the behind to send her away from the table. Johnny motioned to her to bring him a drink. She did so but she did it as if she were playing the most dramatic moment in the most dramatic movie ever made. She turned all her charm on the great Johnny Fontane. She made her eyes sparkle with invitation, her walk was the sexiest walk ever walked, her mouth was very slightly parted as if she were ready to bite the nearest object of her obvious passion. She resembled nothing so much as a female animal in heat, but it was a deliberate act. Johnny Fontane thought, oh, Christ, one of them. It was the most popular approach of women who wanted to take him to bed. It only worked when he was very drunk and he wasn't drunk now. He gave the girl one of his famous grins and said, "Thank you, honey." The girl looked at him and parted her lips in a thank-you smile, her eyes went all smoky, her body tensed with the torso leaning slightly back from the long tapering legs in their mesh stockings. An enormous tension seemed to be building up in her body, her breasts seemed to grow fuller and swell burstingly against her thin scantily cut blouse. Then her whole body gave a slight quiver that almost let off a sexual twang. The whole impression was one of a woman having an orgasm simply because Johnny Fontane had smiled at her and said, "Thank you, honey." It was very well done. It was done better than Johnny had ever seen it done before. But by now he knew it was fake. And the odds were always good that the broads who did it were a lousy lay.

He watched her go back to her chair and nursed his drink slowly. He didn't want to see that little trick again. He wasn't in the mood for it tonight.

It was an hour before Nino Valenti began to go. He started leaning first, wavered back, and then plunged off the chair straight to the

floor. But the pit boss and the relief dealer had been alerted by the
first weave and caught him before he hit the ground. They lifted him
and carried him through the parted drapes that led to the bedroom of
the suite.

Johnny kept watching as the cocktail waitress helped the other two
men undress Nino and shove him under the bed covers. The pit boss
was counting Nino's chips and making a note on his pad of chits, then
guarding the table with its dealer's chips. Johnny said to him, "How
long has that been going on?"

The pit boss shrugged. "He went early tonight. The first time we
got the house doc and he fixed Mr. Valenti up with something and
gave him some sort of a lecture. Then Nino told us that we shouldn't
call the doc when that happened, just put him to bed and he'd be OK
in the morning. So that's what we do. He's pretty lucky, he was a
winner again tonight, almost three grand."

Johnny Fontane said, "Well, let's get the house doc up here tonight, OK? Page the casino floor if you have to."

It was almost fifteen minutes before Jules Segal came into the suite.
Johnny noted with irritation that this guy never looked like a doctor.
Tonight he was wearing a blue loose-knit polo shirt with white trim,
some sort of white suede shoes and no socks. He looked funny as hell
carrying the traditional black doctor's bag.

Johnny said, "You oughta figure out a way to carry your stuff in a
cut-down golf bag."

Jules grinned understandingly, "Yeah, this medical school carryall
is a real drag. Scares the hell out of people. They should change the
color anyway."

He went over to where Nino was lying in bed. As he opened his
bag he said to Johnny, "Thanks for that check you sent me as a
consultant. It was excessive. I didn't do that much."

"Like hell you didn't," Johnny said. "Anyway, forget that, that
was a long time ago. What's with Nino?"

Jules was making a quick examination of heartbeat, pulse and blood
pressure. He took a needle out of his bag and shoved it casually into
Nino's arm and pressed the plunger. Nino's sleeping face lost its waxy
paleness, color came into the cheeks, as if the blood had started
pumping faster.

"Very simple diagnosis," Jules said briskly. "I had a chance to
examine him and run some tests when he first came here and fainted.
I had him moved to the hospital before he regained consciousness.

He's got diabetes, mild adult stabile, which is no problem if you take care of it with medication and diet and so forth. He insists on ignoring it. Also he is firmly determined to drink himself to death. His liver is going and his brain will go. Right now he's in a mild diabetic coma. My advice is to have him put away."

Johnny felt a sense of relief. It couldn't be too serious, all Nino had to do was take care of himself. "You mean in one of those joints where they dry you out?" Johnny asked.

Jules went over to the bar in the far corner of the room and made himself a drink. "No," he said. "I mean committed. You know, the crazy house."

"Don't be funny," Johnny said.

"I'm not joking," Jules said. "I'm not up on all the psychiatric jazz but I know something about it, part of my trade. Your friend Nino can be put back into fairly good shape unless the liver damage has gone too far, which we can't know until an autopsy really. But the real disease is in his head. In essence he doesn't care if he dies, maybe he even wants to kill himself. Until that is cured there's no hope for him. That's why I say, have him committed and then he can undergo the necessary psychiatric treatment."

There was a knock on the door and Johnny went to answer it. It was Lucy Mancini. She came into Johnny's arms and kissed him. "Oh, Johnny, it's so good to see you," she said.

"It's been a long time," Johnny Fontane said. He noticed that Lucy had changed. She had gotten much slimmer, her clothes were a hell of a lot better and she wore them better. Her hair style fitted her face in a sort of boyish cut. She looked younger and better than he had ever seen her and the thought crossed his mind that she could keep him company here in Vegas. It would be a pleasure hanging out with a real broad. But before he could turn on the charm he remembered she was the doc's girl. So it was out. He made his smile just friendly and said, "What are you doing coming to Nino's apartment at night, eh?"

She punched him in the shoulder. "I heard Nino was sick and that Jules came up. I just wanted to see if I could help. Nino's OK, isn't he?"

"Sure," Johnny said. "He'll be fine."

Jules Segal had sprawled out on the couch. "Like hell he is," Jules said. "I suggest we all sit here and wait for Nino to come to. And then we all talk him into committing himself. Lucy, he likes you, maybe you can help. Johnny, if you're a real friend of his you'll go along. Otherwise old Nino's liver will shortly be exhibit A in some university medical lab."

Johnny was offended by the doctor's flippant attitude. Who the hell did he think he was? He started to say so but Nino's voice came from the bed, "Hey, old buddy, how about a drink?"

Nino was sitting up in bed. He grinned at Lucy and said, "Hey, baby, come to old Nino." He held his arms wide open. Lucy sat on the edge of the bed and gave him a hug. Oddly enough Nino didn't look bad at all now, almost normal.

Nino snapped his fingers. "Come on, Johnny, gimmee a drink. The night's young yet. Where the hell's my blackjack table?"

Jules took a long slug from his own glass and said to Nino, "You can't have a drink. Your doctor forbids it."

Nino scowled. "Screw my doctor." Then a play-acting look of contrition came on his face. "Hey, Julie, that's you. You're my doctor, right? I don't mean you, old buddy. Johnny, get me a drink or I get up out of bed and get it myself."

Johnny shrugged and moved toward the bar. Jules said indifferently, "I'm saying he shouldn't have it."

Johnny knew why Jules irritated him. The doctor's voice was always cool, the words never stressed no matter how dire, the voice always low and controlled. If he gave a warning the warning was in the words alone, the voice itself was neutral, as if uncaring. It was this that made Johnny sore enough to bring Nino his water glass of whiskey. Before he handed it over he said to Jules, "This won't kill him, right?"

"No, it won't kill him," Jules said calmly. Lucy gave him an anxious glance, started to say something, then kept still. Meanwhile Nino had taken the whiskey and poured it down his throat.

Johnny was smiling down at Nino; they had shown the punk doctor. Suddenly Nino gasped, his face seemed to turn blue, he couldn't catch his breath and was choking for air. His body leaped upward like a fish, his face was gorged with blood, his eyes bulging. Jules appeared on the other side of the bed facing Johnny and Lucy. He took Nino by the neck and held him still and plunged the needle into the shoulder near where it joined the neck. Nino went limp in his hands, the heaves of his body subsided, and after a moment he slumped down back onto his pillow. His eyes closed in sleep.

Johnny, Lucy and Jules went back into the living room part of the suite and sat around the huge solid coffee table. Lucy picked up one of the aquamarine phones and ordered coffee and some food to be sent up. Johnny had gone over to the bar and mixed himself a drink.

"Did you know he would have that reaction from the whiskey?" Johnny asked.

Jules shrugged. "I was pretty sure he would."

Johnny said sharply, "Then why didn't you warn me?"

"I warned you," Jules said.

"You didn't warn me right," Johnny said with cold anger. "You are really one hell of a doctor. You don't give a shit. You tell me to get Nino in a crazy house, you don't bother to use a nice word like sanitorium. You really like to stick it to people, right?"

Lucy was staring down in her lap. Jules kept smiling at Fontane. "Nothing was going to stop you from giving Nino that drink. You had to show you didn't have to accept my warnings, my orders. Remember when you offered me a job as your personal physician after that throat business? I turned you down because I knew we could never get along. A doctor thinks he's God, he's the high priest in modern society, that's one of his rewards. But you would never treat me that way. I'd be a flunky God to you. Like those doctors you guys have in Hollywood. Where do you get those people from anyway? Christ, don't they know anything or don't they just care? They must know what's happening to Nino but they just give him all kinds of drugs to keep him going. They wear those silk suits and they kiss your ass because you're a power movie man and so you think they are great doctors. Show biz, docs, you gotta have heart? Right? But they don't give a fuck if you live or die. Well, my little hobby, unforgivable as it is, is to keep people alive. I let you give Nino that drink to show you what could happen to him." Jules leaned toward Johnny Fontane, his voice still calm, unemotional. "Your friend is almost terminal. Do you understand that? He hasn't got a chance without therapy and strict medical care. His blood pressure and diabetes and bad habits can cause a cerebral hemorrhage in this very next instant. His brain will blow itself apart. Is that vivid enough for you? Sure, I said crazy house. I want you to understand what's needed. Or you won't make a move. I'll put it to you straight. You can save your buddy's life by having him committed. Otherwise kiss him good-bye."

Lucy murmured, "Jules, darling, Jules, don't be so tough. Just tell him."

Jules stood up. His usual cool was gone, Johnny Fontane noticed with satisfaction. His voice too had lost its quiet unaccented monotone.

"Do you think this is the first time I've had to talk to people like you in a situation like this?" Jules said. "I did it every day. Lucy says don't be so tough, but she doesn't know what she's talking about. You know, I used to tell people, 'don't eat so much or you'll die, don't smoke so much or you'll die, don't work so much or you'll die, don't drink so much or you'll die.' Nobody listens. You know why? Because I don't say, 'You will die tomorrow.' Well, I can tell you that Nino may very well die tomorrow."

Jules went over to the bar and mixed himself another drink. "How about it, Johnny, are you going to get Nino committed?"

Johnny said, "I don't know."

Jules took a quick drink at the bar and filled his glass again. "You know, it's a funny thing, you can smoke yourself to death, drink yourself to death, work yourself to death and even eat yourself to death. But that's all acceptable. The only thing you can't do medically is screw yourself to death and yet that's where they put all the obstacles." He paused to finish his drink. "But even that's trouble, for women anyway. I used to have women who weren't supposed to have any more babies. 'It's dangerous,' I'd tell them. 'You could die,' I'd tell them. And a month later they pop in, their faces all rosy, and say, 'Doctor, I think I'm pregnant,' and sure enough they'd kill the rabbit. 'But it's *dangerous*,' I'd tell them. My voice used to have expression in those days. And they'd smile at me and say, 'But my husband and I are very strict Catholic,' they'd say."

There was a knock on the door and two waiters wheeled in a cart covered with food and silver service coffeepots. They took a portable table from the bottom of the cart and set it up. Then Johnny dismissed them.

They sat at the table and ate the hot sandwiches Lucy had ordered and drank the coffee. Johnny leaned back and lit up a cigarette. "So you save lives. How come you became an abortionist?"

Lucy spoke up for the first time. "He wanted to help girls in trouble, girls who might commit suicide or do something dangerous to get rid of the baby."

Jules smiled at her and sighed. "It's not that simple. I became a surgeon finally. I've got the good hands, as ballplayers say. But I was so good I scared myself silly. I'd open up some poor bastard's belly and know he was going to die. I'd operate and know that the cancer or tumor would come back but I'd send them off home with a smile and a lot of bullshit. Some poor broad comes in and I slice off one tit. A year later she's back and I slice off the other tit. A year after that, I scoop out her insides like you scoop the seeds out of a cantaloupe. After all that she dies anyway. Meanwhile husbands keep calling up and asking, 'What do the tests show? What do the tests show?'

"So I hired an extra secretary to take all those calls. I saw the patient only when she was fully prepared for examination, tests or operation. I spent the minimum possible time with the victim because I was, after all, a busy man. And then finally I'd let the husband talk to me for two minutes. 'It's terminal,' I'd say. And they could never hear that last word. They understood what it meant but they never heard it. I thought at first that unconsciously I was dropping my voice on the last word, so I consciously said it louder. But still they never heard it. One guy even said, 'What the hell do you mean, it's germinal?' " Jules started to laugh. "Germinal, terminal, what the hell. I started to do abortions. Nice and easy, everybody happy, like washing the dishes and leaving a clean sink. That was my class. I loved it, I loved being an abortionist. I don't believe that a two-month fetus is a human being so no problems there. I was helping young girls and married women who were in trouble, I was making good money. I was out of the front lines. When I got caught I felt like a deserter that has been hauled in. But I was lucky, a friend pulled some strings and got me off but now the big hospitals won't let me operate. So here I am. Giving good advice again which is being ignored just like in the old days."

"I'm not ignoring it," Johnny Fontane said. "I'm thinking it over."

Lucy finally changed the subject. "What are you doing in Vegas, Johnny? Relaxing from your duties as big-time Hollywood wheel or working?"

Johnny shook his head. "Mike Corleone wants to see me and have a talk. He's flying in tonight with Tom Hagen. Tom said they'll be seeing you, Lucy. You know what it's all about?"

Lucy shook her head. "We're all having dinner together tomorrow night. Freddie too. I think it might have something to do with the hotel. The casino has been dropping money lately, which shouldn't be. The Don might want Mike to check it out."

"I hear Mike finally got his face fixed," Johnny said.

Lucy laughed. "I guess Kay talked him into it. He wouldn't do it when they were married. I wonder why? It looked so awful and made his nose drip. He should have had it done sooner." She paused for a moment. "Jules was called in by the Corleone Family for that operation. They used him as a consultant and an observer."

Johnny nodded and said dryly, "I recommended him for it."

"Oh," Lucy said. "Anyway, Mike said he wanted to do something for Jules. That's why he's having us to dinner tomorrow night."

Jules said musingly, "He didn't trust anybody. He warned me to keep track of what everybody did. It was fairly straight, ordinary surgery. Any competent man could do it."

There was a sound from the bedroom of the suite and they looked toward the drapes. Nino had become conscious again. Johnny went and sat on the bed. Jules and Lucy went over to the foot of the bed. Nino gave them a wan grin. "OK, I'll stop being a wise guy. I feel really lousy. Johnny, remember about a year ago, what happened when we were with those two broads down in Palm Springs? I swear to you I wasn't jealous about what happened. I was glad. You believe me, Johnny?"

Johnny said reassuringly, "Sure, Nino, I believe you."

Lucy and Jules looked at each other. From everything they had heard and knew about Johnny Fontane it seemed impossible that he would take a girl away from a close friend like Nino. And why was Nino saying he wasn't jealous a year after it happened? The same thought crossed both their minds, that Nino was drinking himself to death romantically because a girl had left him to go with Johnny Fontane.

Jules checked Nino again. "I'll get a nurse to be in the room with you tonight," Jules said. "You really have to stay in bed for a couple of days. No kidding."

Nino smiled. "OK, Doc, just don't make the nurse too pretty."

Jules made a call for the nurse and then he and Lucy left. Johnny sat in a chair near the bed to wait for the nurse. Nino was falling asleep again, an exhausted look on his face. Johnny thought about what he had said, about not being jealous about what had happened over a year ago with those two broads down in Palm Springs. The thought had never entered his head that Nino might be jealous.

A year ago Johnny Fontane had sat in his plush office, the office of the movie company he headed, and felt as lousy as he had ever felt in his life. Which was surprising because the first movie he had produced, with himself as star and Nino in a featured part, was making tons of money. Everything had worked. Everybody had done their job. The picture was brought in under budget. Everybody was going to make a fortune out of it and Jack Woltz was losing ten years of his life. Now Johnny had two more pictures in production, one starring himself, one starring Nino. Nino was great on the screen as one of those charming, dopey lover-boys that women loved to shove between their tits. Little boy lost. Everything he touched made money, it was rolling in. The Godfather was getting his percentage through the bank, and that made Johnny feel really good. He had justified his Godfather's faith. But today that wasn't helping much.

And now that he was a successful independent movie producer he had as much power, maybe more, than he had ever had as a singer. Beautiful broads fell all over him just like before, though for a more commercial reason. He had his own plane, he lived more lavishly even, with the special tax benefits a businessman had that artists didn't get. Then what the hell was bothering him?

He knew what it was. The front of his head hurt, his nasal passages hurt, his throat itched. The only way he could scratch and relieve that itch was by singing and he was afraid to even try. He had called Jules Segal about it, when it would be safe to try to sing and Jules had said anytime he felt like it. So he'd tried and sounded so hoarse and lousy he'd given up. And his throat would hurt like hell the next day, hurt in a different way than before the warts had been taken off. Hurt worse, burning. He was afraid to keep singing, afraid that he'd lose his voice forever, or ruin it.

And if he couldn't sing, what the hell was the use of everything else? Everything else was just bullshit. Singing was the only thing he really knew. Maybe he knew more about singing and his kind of music than anybody else in the world. He was that good, he realized now. All those years had made him a real pro. Nobody could tell him the right and the wrong, he didn't have to ask anybody. He knew. What a waste, what a damn waste.

It was a Friday and he decided to spend the weekend with Virginia and the kids. He called her up as he always did to tell her he was coming. Really to give her a chance to say no. She never said no. Not in all the years they had been divorced. Because she would never say no to a meeting of her daughters and their father. What a broad, Johnny thought. He'd been lucky with Virginia. And though he knew he cared more about her than any other woman he knew it was impossible for them ever to live together sexually. Maybe when they were sixty-five, like when you retire, they'd retire together, retire from everything.

But reality shattered these thoughts when he arrived there and found Virginia was feeling a little grouchy herself and the two girls not that crazy to see him because they had been promised a weekend visit with some girl friends on a California ranch where they could ride horses.

He told Virginia to send the girls off to the ranch and kissed them good-bye with an amused smile. He understood them so well. What kid wouldn't rather go riding horses on a ranch than hang around with a grouchy father who picked his own spots as a father. He said to Virginia, "I'll have a few drinks and then I'll shove off too."

"All right," she said. She was having one of her bad days, rare, but recognizable. It wasn't too easy for her leading this kind of life.

She saw him taking an extra large drink. "What are you cheering yourself up for?" Virginia asked. "Everything is going so beautifully for you. I never dreamed you had it in you to be such a good businessman."

Johnny smiled at her. "It's not so hard," he said. At the same time he was thinking, so that's what was wrong. He understood women and he understood now that Virginia was down because she thought he was having everything his own way. Women really hated seeing their men doing too well. It irritated them. It made them less sure of the hold they exerted over them through affection, sexual custom or marriage ties. So more to cheer her up than voice his own complaints, Johnny said, "What the hell difference does it make if I can't sing."

Virginia's voice was annoyed. "Oh, Johnny, you're not a kid anymore. You're over thirty-five. Why do you keep worrying about that silly singing stuff? You make more money as a producer anyhow."

Johnny looked at her curiously and said, "I'm a singer. I love to sing. What's being old got to do with that?"

Virginia was impatient. "I never liked your singing anyway. Now that you've shown you can make movies, I'm glad you can't sing anymore."

They were both surprised when Johnny said with fury, "That's a fucking lousy thing to say." He was shaken. How could Virginia feel like that, how could she dislike him so much?

Virginia smiled at his being hurt and because it was so outrageous that he should be angry at her she said, "How do you think I felt when all those girls came running after you because of the way you sang? How would you feel if I went ass-naked down the street to get men running after me? That's what your singing was and I used to wish you'd lose your voice and could never sing again. But that was before we got divorced."

Johnny finished his drink. "You don't understand a thing. Not a damn thing." He went into the kitchen and dialed Nino's number. He quickly arranged for them both to go down to Palm Springs for the weekend and gave Nino the number of a girl to call, a real fresh young beauty he'd been meaning to get around to. "She'll have a friend for you," Johnny said. "I'll be at your place in an hour."

Virginia gave him a cool good-bye when he left. He didn't give a damn, it was one of the few times he was angry with her. The hell with it, he'd just tear loose for the weekend and get all the poison out of his system.

Sure enough, everything was fine down in Palm Springs. Johnny used his own house down there, it was always kept open and staffed this time of year. The two girls were young enough to be great fun and not too rapacious for some kind of favor. Some people came over to keep them company at the pool until suppertime. Nino went to his room with his girl to get ready for supper and a quick bang while he was still warm from the sun. Johnny wasn't in the mood, so he sent his girl, a short bandbox blonde named Tina, up to shower by herself. He never could make love to another woman after he'd had a fight with Virginia.

He went into the glass-walled patio living room that held a piano. When singing with the band he had fooled around with the piano just for laughs, so he could pick out a song in a fake moonlight-soft ballad style. He sat down now and hummed along a bit with the piano, very softly, muttering a few words but not really singing. Before he knew it Tina was in the living room making him a drink and sitting beside him at the piano. He played a few tunes and she hummed with him. He left her at the piano and went up to take his shower. In the shower he sang short phrases, more like speaking. He got dressed and went back down. Tina was still alone; Nino was really working his girl over or getting drunk.

Johnny sat down at the piano again while Tina wandered off outside to watch the pool. He started singing one of his old songs. There was no burning in his throat. The tones were coming out muted but with proper body. He looked at the patio. Tina was still out there, the glass door was closed, she wouldn't hear him. For some reason he didn't want anybody to hear him. He started off fresh on an old ballad that was his favorite. He sang full out as if he were singing in public, letting himself go, waiting for the familiar burning rasp in his throat but there was none. He listened to his voice, it was different somehow, but he liked it. It was darker, it was a man's voice, not a kid's, rich he thought, dark rich. He finished the song easing up and sat there at the piano thinking about it.

Behind him Nino said, "Not bad, old buddy, not bad at all."

Johnny swiveled his body around. Nino was standing in the doorway, alone. His girl wasn't with him. Johnny was relieved. He didn't mind Nino hearing him.

"Yeah," Johnny said. "Let's get rid of those two broads. Send them home."

Nino said, "You send them home. They're nice kids, I'm not gonna hurt their feelings. Besides I just banged mine twice. How would it look if I sent her away without even giving her dinner?"

The hell with it, Johnny thought. Let the girls listen even if he sounded lousy. He called up a band leader he knew in Palm Springs and asked him to send over a mandolin for Nino. The band leader protested, "Hell, nobody plays a mandolin in California." Johnny yelled, "Just get one."

The house was loaded with recording equipment and Johnny had the two girls work the turn-off and volumes. After they had dinner, Johnny went to work. He had Nino playing the mandolin as accompaniment and sang all his old songs. He sang them all the way out, not nursing his voice at all. His throat was fine, he felt that he could sing forever. In the months he had not been able to sing he had often thought about singing, planned out how he would phrase lyrics differently now than as a kid. He had sung the songs in his head with more sophisticated variations of emphasis. Now he was doing it for real. Sometimes it would go wrong in the actual singing, stuff that had sounded good when he heard it just in his head didn't work out when he tried it really singing out loud. OUT LOUD, he thought. He wasn't listening to himself now, he was concentrating on performing. He fumbled a little on timing but that was OK, just rusty. He had a metronome in his head that would never fail him. Just a little practice was all he needed.

Finally he stopped singing. Tina came over to him with eyes shining and gave him a long kiss. "Now I know why Mother goes to all your movies," she said. It was the wrong thing to say at any time except this. Johnny and Nino laughed.

They played the feedback and now Johnny could really listen to himself. His voice had changed, changed a hell of a lot but was still unquestionably the voice of Johnny Fontane. It had become much richer and darker as he had noticed before but there was also the quality of a man singing rather than a boy. The voice had more true emotion, more character. And the technical part of his singing was far superior to anything he had ever done. It was nothing less than masterful. And if he was that good now, rusty as hell, how good would he be when he got in shape again? Johnny grinned at Nino. "Is that as good as I think it is?"

Nino looked at his happy face thoughtfully. "It's very damn good," he said. "But let's see how you sing tomorrow."

Johnny was hurt that Nino should be so downbeat. "You son of a bitch, you know you can't sing like that. Don't worry about tomorrow. I feel great." But he didn't sing any more that night. He and Nino took the girls to a party and Tina spent the night in his bed but he wasn't much good there. The girl was a little disappointed. But what the hell, you couldn't do everything all in one day, Johnny thought.

He woke up in the morning with a sense of apprehension, with a vague terror that he had dreamed his voice had come back. Then when he was sure it was not a dream he got scared that his voice would be shot again. He went to the window and hummed a bit, then he went down to the living room still in his pajamas. He picked out a tune on the piano and after a while tried singing with it. He sang mutedly but there was no pain, no hoarseness in his throat, so he turned it on. The chords were true and rich, he didn't have to force it at all. Easy, easy, just pouring out. Johnny realized that the bad time was over, he had it all now. And it didn't matter a damn if he fell on his face with movies, it didn't matter if he couldn't get it up with Tina the night before, it didn't matter that Virginia would hate him being able to sing again. For a moment he had just one regret. If only his voice had come back to him while trying to sing for his daughters, how lovely that would have been. That would have been so lovely.

The hotel nurse had come into the room wheeling a cart loaded with medication. Johnny got up and stared down at Nino, who was sleeping or maybe dying. He knew Nino wasn't jealous of his getting his voice back. He understood that Nino was only jealous because he was *so happy* about getting his voice back. That he cared so much about singing. For what was very obvious now was that Nino Valenti didn't care enough about anything to make him want to stay alive.

Chapter

27

MICHAEL CORLEONE arrived late in the evening and, by his own order, was not met at the airport. Only two men accompanied him: Tom Hagen and a new bodyguard, named Albert Neri.

The most lavish suite of rooms in the hotel had been set aside for Michael and his party. Already waiting in that suite were the people it would be necessary for Michael to see.

Freddie greeted his brother with a warm embrace. Freddie was much stouter, more benevolent-looking, *cheerful*, and far more dandified. He wore an exquisitely tailored gray silk suit and accessories to match. His hair was razor cut and arranged as carefully as a movie star's, his face glowed with perfect barbering and his hands were manicured. He was an altogether different man than the one who had been shipped out of New York four years before.

He leaned back and surveyed Michael fondly. "You look a hell of a lot better now that you got your face fixed. Your wife finally talked you into it, huh? How is Kay? When she gonna come out and visit us out here?"

Michael smiled at his brother. "You're looking pretty good too. Kay would have come out this time, but she's carrying another kid and she has the baby to look after. Besides this is business, Freddie, I have to fly back tomorrow night or the morning after."

"You have to eat something first," Freddie said. "We've got a great chef in the hotel, you'll get the best food you ever ate. Go take your shower and change and everything will be set up right here. I have all the people you want to see lined up, they'll be waiting around for when you're ready, I just have to call them."

Michael said pleasantly, "Let's save Moe Greene to the end, OK? Ask Johnny Fontane and Nino up to eat with us. And Lucy and her doctor friend. We can talk while we eat." He turned to Hagen. "Anybody you want to add to that, Tom?"

Hagen shook his head. Freddie had greeted him much less affectionately than Michael, but Hagen understood. Freddie was on his father's shit list and Freddie naturally blamed the *Consigliori* for not straightening things out. Hagen would gladly have done so, but he didn't know why Freddie was in his father's bad graces. The Don did not give voice to specific grievances. He just made his displeasure felt.

It was after midnight before they gathered around the special dinner table set up in Michael's suite. Lucy kissed Michael and didn't comment on his face looking so much better after the operation. Jules Segal boldly studied the repaired cheekbone and said to Michael, "A good job. It's knitted nicely. Is the sinus OK?"

"Fine," Michael said. "Thanks for helping out."

Dinner focused on Michael as they ate. They all noted his resemblance in speech and manner to the Don. In some curious way he inspired the same respect, the same awe, and yet he was perfectly natural, at pains to put everyone at their ease. Hagen as usual remained in the background. The new man they did not know; Albert Neri was also very quiet and unobtrusive. He had claimed he was not hungry and sat in an armchair close to the door reading a local newspaper.

After they had had a few drinks and food, the waiters were dismissed. Michael spoke to Johnny Fontane. "Hear your voice is back as good as ever, you got all your old fans back. Congratulations."

"Thanks," Johnny said. He was curious about exactly why Michael wanted to see him. What favor would he be asked?

Michael addressed them all in general. "The Corleone Family is thinking of moving out here to Vegas. Selling out all our interests in the olive oil business and settling here. The Don and Hagen and myself have talked it over and we think here is where the future is for the Family. That doesn't mean right now or next year. It may take two, three, even four years to get things squared away. But that's the general plan. Some friends of ours own a good percentage of this hotel and casino so that will be our foundation. Moe Greene will sell us his interest so it can be wholly owned by friends of the Family.

Freddie's moon face was anxious. "Mike, you sure about Moe Greene selling? He never mentioned it to me and he loves the business. I really don't think he'll sell."

Michael said quietly, "I'll make him an offer he can't refuse."

The words were said in an ordinary voice, yet the effect was chilling, perhaps because it was a favorite phrase of the Don's. Michael turned to Johnny Fontane. "The Don is counting on you to help us get started. It's been explained to us that entertainment will be the big factor in drawing gamblers. We hope you'll sign a contract to appear five times a year for maybe a week-long engagement. We hope your friends in movies do the same. You've done them a lot of favors, now you can call them in."

"Sure," Johnny said. "I'll do anything for my Godfather, you know that, Mike." But there was just the faint shadow of doubt in his voice.

Michael smiled and said, "You won't lose money on the deal and neither will your friends. You get points in the hotel, and if there's somebody else you think important enough, they get some points too. Maybe you don't believe me, so let me say I'm speaking the Don's words."

Johnny said hurriedly, "I believe you, Mike. But there's ten more hotels and casinos being built on the Strip right now. When you come in, the market may be glutted, you may be too late with all that competition already there."

Tom Hagen spoke up. "The Corleone Family has friends who are financing three of those hotels." Johnny understood immediately that he meant the Corleone Family owned the three hotels, with their casinos. And that there would be plenty of points to give out.

"I'll start working on it," Johnny said.

Michael turned to Lucy and Jules Segal. "I owe you," he said to Jules. "I hear you want to go back to cutting people up and that hospitals won't let you use their facilities because of that old abortion business. I have to know from you, is that what you want?"

Jules smiled. "I guess so. But you don't know the medical setup.

Whatever power you have doesn't mean anything to them. I'm afraid you can't help me in that."

Michael nodded absentmindedly. "Sure, you're right. But some friends of mine, pretty well-known people, are going to build a big hospital for Las Vegas. The town will need it the way it's growing and the way it's projected to grow. Maybe they'll let you into the operating room if it's put to them right. Hell, how many surgeons as good as you can they get to come out to this desert? Or any half as good? We'll be doing the hospital a favor. So stick around. I hear you and Lucy are going to get married?"

Jules shrugged. "When I see that I have any future."

Lucy said wryly, "Mike, if you don't build that hospital, I'll die an old maid."

They all laughed. All except Jules. He said to Michael, "If I took a job like that there couldn't be any strings attached."

Michael said coldly, "No strings. I just owe you and I want to even out."

Lucy said gently, "Mike, don't get sore."

Michael smiled at her. "I'm not sore." He turned to Jules. "That was a dumb thing for you to say. The Corleone Family has pulled some strings for you. Do you think I'm so stupid I'd ask you to do things you'd hate to do? But if I did, so what? Who the hell else ever lifted a finger to help you when you were in trouble? When I heard you wanted to get back to being a real surgeon, I took a lot of time to find out if I could help. I can. I'm not asking you for anything. But at least you can consider our relationship friendly, and I assume you would do for me what you'd do for any good friend. That's my string. But you can refuse it."

Tom Hagen lowered his head and smiled. Not even the Don himself could have done it any better.

Jules was flushing. "Mike, I didn't mean it that way at all. I'm very grateful to you and your father. Forget I said it."

Michael nodded and said, "Fine. Until the hospital gets built and opens up you'll be medical director for the four hotels. Get yourself a staff. Your money goes up too, but you can discuss that with Tom at a later time. And Lucy, I want you to do something more important. Maybe coordinate all the shops that will be opening up in the hotel arcades. On the financial side. Or maybe hiring the girls we need to work in the casinos, something like that. So if Jules doesn't marry you, you can be a rich old maid."

Freddie had been puffing on his cigar angrily. Michael turned to him and said gently, "I'm just the errand boy for the Don, Freddie. What he wants you to do he'll tell you himself, naturally, but I'm sure it will be something big enough to make you happy. Everybody tells us what a great job you've been doing out here."

"Then why is he sore at me?" Freddie asked plaintively. "Just because the casino has been losing money? I don't control that end, Moe Greene does. What the hell does the old man want from me?"

"Don't worry about it," Michael said. He turned to Johnny Fontane. "Where's Nino? I was looking forward to seeing him again."

Johnny shrugged. "Nino is pretty sick. A nurse is taking care of him in his room. But the doc here says he should be committed, that he's trying to kill himself. Nino!"

Michael said thoughtfully, really surprised, "Nino was always a real good guy. I never knew him to do anything lousy, say anything to put anybody down. He never gave a damn about anything. Except the booze."

"Yeah," Johnny said. "The money is rolling in, he could get a lot of work, singing or in the movies. He gets fifty grand a picture now and he blows it. He doesn't give a damn about being famous. All the years we've been buddies I've never known him to do anything creepy. And the son of a bitch is drinking himself to death."

Jules was about to say something when there was a knock on the door of the suite. He was surprised when the man in the armchair, the man nearest the door, did not answer it but kept reading the newspaper. It was Hagen who went to open it. And was almost brushed aside when Moe Greene came striding into the room followed by his two bodyguards.

Moe Greene was a handsome hood who had made his rep as a Murder Incorporated executioner in Brooklyn. He had branched out into gambling and gone west to seek his fortune, had been the first person to see the possibilities of Las Vegas and built one of the first hotel casinos on the Strip. He still had murderous tantrums and was feared by everyone in the hotel, not excluding Freddie, Lucy and Jules Segal. They always stayed out of his way whenever possible.

His handsome face was grim now. He said to Michael Corleone, "I've been waiting around to talk to you, Mike. I got a lot of things to do tomorrow so I figured I'd catch you tonight. How about it?"

Michael Corleone looked at him with what seemed to be friendly astonishment. "Sure," he said. He motioned in Hagen's direction. "Get Mr. Greene a drink, Tom."

Jules noticed that the man called Albert Neri was studying Moe Greene intently, not paying any attention to the bodyguards who were leaning against the door. He knew there was no chance of any violence, not in Vegas itself. That was strictly forbidden as fatal to the whole project of making Vegas the legal sanctuary of American gamblers.

Moe Greene said to his bodyguards, "Draw some chips for all these people so that they can gamble on the house." He obviously meant Jules, Lucy, Johnny Fontane and Michael's bodyguard, Albert Neri.

Michael Corleone nodded agreeably. "That's a good idea." It was only then that Neri got out of his chair and prepared to follow the others out.

After the good-byes were said, there were Freddie, Tom Hagen, Moe Greene and Michael Corleone left in the room.

Greene put his drink down on the table and said with barely controlled fury, "What's this I hear the Corleone Family is going to buy me out? I'll buy *you* out. You don't buy me out."

Michael said reasonably, "Your casino has been losing money against all the odds. There's something wrong with the way you operate. Maybe we can do better."

Greene laughed harshly. "You goddamn Dagos, I do you a favor and take Freddie in when you're having a bad time and now you push me out. That's what you think. I don't get pushed out by nobody and I got friends that will back me up."

Michael was still quietly reasonable. "You took Freddie in because the Corleone Family gave you a big chunk of money to finish furnishing your hotel. And bankroll your casino. And because the Molinari Family on the Coast guaranteed his safety and gave you some service for taking him in. The Corleone Family and you are evened out. I don't know what you're getting sore about. We'll buy your share at any reasonable price you name, what's wrong with that? What's unfair about that? With your casino losing money we're doing you a favor."

Greene shook his head. "The Corleone Family don't have that much muscle anymore. The Godfather is sick. You're getting chased out of New York by the other Families and you think you can find easier pickings here. I'll give you some advice, Mike, don't try."

Michael said softly, "Is that why you thought you could slap Freddie around in public?"

Tom Hagen, startled, turned his attention to Freddie. Freddie Corleone's face was getting red. "Ah, Mike, that wasn't anything. Moe didn't mean anything. He flies off the handle sometimes, but me and him are good friends. Right, Moe?"

Greene was wary. "Yeah, sure. Sometimes I got to kick asses to make this place run right. I got sore at Freddie because he was banging all the cocktail waitresses and letting them goof off on the job. We had a little argument and I straightened him out."

Michael's face was impassive when he said to his brother, "You straightened out, Freddie?"

Freddie stared sullenly at his younger brother. He didn't answer. Greene laughed and said, "The son of a bitch was taking them to bed two at a time, the old sandwich job. Freddie, I gotta admit you really put it to those broads. Nobody else could make them happy after you got through with them."

Hagen saw that this had caught Michael by surprise. They looked at each other. This was perhaps the real reason the Don was displeased with Freddie. The Don was straitlaced about sex. He would consider such cavorting by his son Freddie, two girls at a time, as degeneracy. Allowing himself to be physically humiliated by a man like Moe Greene would decrease respect for the Corleone Family. That too would be part of the reason for being in his father's bad books.

Michael rising from his chair, said, in a tone of dismissal, "I have to get back to New York tomorrow, so think about your price."

Greene said savagely, "You son of a bitch, you think you can just brush me off like that? I killed more men than you before I could jerk off. I'll fly to New York and talk to the Don himself. I'll make him an offer."

Freddie said nervously to Tom Hagen, "Tom, you're the *Consigliori*, you can talk to the Don and advise him."

It was then that Michael turned the full chilly blast of his personality on the two Vegas men. "The Don has sort of semiretired," he said. "I'm running the Family business now. And I've removed Tom from the *Consigliori* spot. He'll be strictly my lawyer here in Vegas. He'll be moving out with his family in a couple of months to get all the legal work started. So anything you have to say, say it to me."

Nobody answered. Michael said formally, "Freddie, you're my older brother, I have respect for you. But don't ever take sides with anybody against the Family again. I won't even mention it to the Don." He turned to Moe Greene. "Don't insult people who are trying to help you. You'd do better to use your energy to find out why the casino is losing money. The Corleone Family has big dough invested here and we're not getting our money's worth, but I still didn't come here and abuse you. I offer a helping hand. Well, if you prefer to spit on that helping hand, that's your business. I can't say any more."

He had not once raised his voice but his words had a sobering effect on both Greene and Freddie. Michael stared at both of them, moving away from the table to indicate that he expected them both to leave. Hagen went to the door and opened it. Both men left without saying good night.

The next morning Michael Corleone got the message from Moe Greene: he would not sell his share of the hotel at any price. It was Freddie who delivered the message. Michael shrugged and said to his brother, "I want to see Nino before I go back to New York."

In Nino's suite they found Johnny Fontane sitting on the couch eating breakfast. Jules was examining Nino behind the closed drapes of the bedroom. Finally the drapes were drawn back.

Michael was shocked at how Nino looked. The man was visibly disintegrating. The eyes were dazed, the mouth loose, all the muscles of his face slack. Michael sat on his bedside and said, "Nino, it's good to catch up with you. The Don always asks about you."

Nino grinned, it was the old grin. "Tell him I'm dying. Tell him show business is more dangerous than the olive oil business."

"You'll be OK," Michael said. "If there's anything bothering you that the Family can help, just tell me."

Nino shook his head. "There's nothing," he said. "Nothing."

Michael chatted for a few more moments and then left. Freddie accompanied him and his party to the airport, but at Michael's request didn't hang around for departure time. As they boarded the plane with Tom Hagen and Al Neri, Michael turned to Neri and said, "Did you make him good?"

Neri tapped his forehead. "I got Moe Greene mugged and numbered up here."

Chapter

×××××××××××××××××××××××××××××××××

28

ON the plane ride back to New York, Michael Corleone relaxed and tried to sleep. It was useless. The most terrible period of his life was approaching, perhaps even a fatal time. It could no longer be put off. Everything was in readiness, all precautions had been taken, two years of precautions. There could be no further delay. Last week when the Don had formally announced his retirement to the *caporegimes* and other members of the Corleone Family, Michael knew that this was his father's way of telling him the time was ripe.

It was almost three years now since he had returned home and over two years since he had married Kay. The three years had been spent in learning the Family business. He had put in long hours with Tom Hagen, long hours with the Don. He was amazed at how wealthy and powerful the Corleone Family truly was. It owned tremendously valuable real estate in midtown New York, whole office buildings. It owned, through fronts, partnerships in two Wall Street brokerage houses, pieces of banks on Long Island, partnerships in some garment center firms, all this in addition to its illegal operations in gambling.

The most interesting thing Michael Corleone learned, in going back over past transactions of the Corleone Family, was that the Family had received some protection income shortly after the war from a group of music record counterfeiters. The counterfeiters duplicated and sold phonograph records of famous artists, packaging everything so skillfully they were never caught. Naturally on the records they sold to stores the artists and original production company received not a penny. Michael Corleone noticed that Johnny Fontane had lost a lot of money owing to this counterfeiting because at that time, just before he lost his voice, his records were the most popular in the country.

He asked Tom Hagen about it. Why did the Don allow the counterfeiters to cheat his godson? Hagen shrugged. Business was business. Besides, Johnny was in the Don's bad graces, Johnny having divorced his childhood sweetheart to marry Margot Ashton. This had displeased the Don greatly.

"How come these guys stopped their operation?" Michael asked. "The cops got on to them?"

Hagen shook his head. "The Don withdrew his protection. That was right after Connie's wedding."

It was a pattern he was to see often, the Don helping those in misfortune whose misfortune he had partly created. Not perhaps out of cunning or planning but because of his variety of interests or perhaps because of the nature of the universe, the interlinking of good and evil, natural of itself.

Michael had married Kay up in New England, a quiet wedding, with only her family and a few of her friends present. Then they had moved into one of the houses on the mall in Long Beach. Michael was surprised at how well Kay got along with her parents and the other people living on the mall. And of course she had gotten pregnant right away, like a good, old-style Italian wife was supposed to, and that helped. The second kid on the way in two years was just icing.

Kay would be waiting for him at the airport, she always came to meet him, she was always so glad when he came back from a trip. And he was too. Except now. For the end of this trip meant that he finally had to take the action he had been groomed for over the last three years. The Don would be waiting for him. The *caporegimes* would be waiting for him. And he, Michael Corleone, would have to give the orders, make the decisions which would decide his and his Family's fate.

Every morning when Kay Adams Corleone got up to take care of the baby's early feeding, she saw Mama Corleone, the Don's wife, being driven away from the mall by one of the bodyguards, to return an hour later. Kay soon learned that her mother-in-law went to church every single morning. Often on her return, the old woman stopped by for morning coffee and to see her new grandchild.

Mama Corleone always started off by asking Kay why she didn't think of becoming a Catholic, ignoring the fact that Kay's child had already been baptized a Protestant. So Kay felt it was proper to ask the old woman why she went to church every morning, whether that was a necessary part of being a Catholic.

As if she thought that this might have stopped Kay from converting the old woman said, "Oh, no, no, some Catholics only go to church on Easter and Christmas. You go when you feel like going."

Kay laughed. "Then why do you go every single morning?"

In a completely natural way, Mama Corleone said, "I go for my husband," she pointed down toward the floor, "so he don't go down there." She paused. "I say prayers for his soul every day so he go up there." She pointed heavenward. She said this with an impish smile, as if she were subverting her husband's will in some way, or as if it were a losing cause. It was said jokingly almost, in her grim, Italian, old crone fashion. And as always when her husband was not present, there was an attitude of disrespect to the great Don.

"How is your husband feeling?" Kay asked politely.

Mama Corleone shrugged. "He's not the same man since they shot him. He lets Michael do all the work, he just plays the fool with his garden, his peppers, his tomatoes. As if he were some peasant still. But men are always like that."

Later in the morning Connie Corleone would walk across the mall with her two children to pay Kay a visit and chat. Kay liked Connie, her vivaciousness, her obvious fondness for her brother Michael. Connie had taught Kay how to cook some Italian dishes but sometimes brought her own more expert concoctions over for Michael to taste.

Now this morning as she usually did, she asked Kay what Michael thought of her husband, Carlo. Did Michael really like Carlo, as he seemed to? Carlo had always had a little trouble with the Family but now over the last years he had straightened out. He was really doing well in the labor union but he had to work so hard, such long hours. Carlo really liked Michael, Connie always said. But then, everybody liked Michael, just as everybody liked her father. Michael was the

Don all over again. It was the best thing that Michael was going to run the Family olive oil business.

Kay had observed before that when Connie spoke about her husband in relation to the Family, she was always nervously eager for some word of approval for Carlo. Kay would have been stupid if she had not noticed the almost terrified concern Connie had for whether Michael liked Carlo or not. One night she spoke to Michael about it and mentioned the fact that nobody ever spoke about Sonny Corleone, nobody even referred to him, at least not in her presence. Kay had once tried to express her condolences to the Don and his wife and had been listened to with almost rude silence and then ignored. She had tried to get Connie talking about her older brother without success.

Sonny's wife, Sandra, had taken her children and moved to Florida, where her own parents now lived. Certain financial arrangements had been made so that she and her children could live comfortably, but Sonny had left no estate.

Michael reluctantly explained what had happened the night Sonny was killed. That Carlo had beaten his wife and Connie had called the mall and Sonny had taken the call and rushed out in a blind rage. So naturally Connie and Carlo were always nervous that the rest of the Family blamed her for indirectly causing Sonny's death. Or blamed her husband, Carlo. But this wasn't the case. The proof was that they had given Connie and Carlo a house in the mall itself and promoted Carlo to an important job in the labor union setup. And Carlo had straightened out, stopped drinking, stopped whoring, stopped trying to be a wise guy. The Family was pleased with his work and attitude for the last two years. Nobody blamed him for what had happened.

"Then why don't you invite them over some evening and you can reassure your sister?" Kay said. "The poor thing is always so nervous about what you think of her husband. Tell her. And tell her to put those silly worries out of her head."

"I can't do that," Michael said. "We don't talk about those things in our family."

"Do you want me to tell her what you've told me?" Kay said.

She was puzzled because he took such a long time thinking over a suggestion that was obviously the proper thing to do. Finally he said, "I don't think you should, Kay. I don't think it will do any good. She'll worry anyway. It's something nobody can do anything about."

Kay was amazed. She realized that Michael was always a little colder to his sister Connie than he was to anyone else, despite Connie's affection. "Surely you don't blame Connie for Sonny being killed?" she said.

Michael sighed. "Of course not," he said. "She's my kid sister and I'm very fond of her. I feel sorry for her. Carlo straightened out, but he's really the wrong kind of husband. It's just one of those things. Let's forget about it."

It was not in Kay's nature to nag; she let it drop. Also she had learned that Michael was not a man to push, that he could become coldly disagreeable. She knew she was the only person in the world who could bend his will, but she also knew that to do it too often would be to destroy that power. And living with him the last two years had made her love him more.

She loved him because he was always fair. An odd thing. But he always was fair to everybody around him, never arbitrary even in little things. She had observed that he was now a very powerful man, people came to the house to confer with him and ask favors, treating him with deference and respect but one thing had endeared him to her above everything else.

Ever since Michael had come back from Sicily with his broken face, everybody in the Family had tried to get him to undergo corrective surgery. Michael's mother was after him constantly; one Sunday dinner with all the Corleones gathered on the mall she shouted at Michael, "You look like a gangster in the movies, get your face fixed for the sake of Jesus Christ and your poor wife. And so your nose will stop running like a drunken Irish."

The Don, at the head of the table, watching everything, said to Kay, "Does it bother you?"

Kay shook her head. The Don said to his wife, "He's out of your hands, it's no concern of yours." The old woman immediately held her peace. Not that she feared her husband but because it would have been disrespectful to dispute him in such a matter before the others.

But Connie, the Don's favorite, came in from the kitchen, where she was cooking the Sunday dinner, her face flushed from the stove, and said, "I think he should get his face fixed. He was the most handsome one in the family before he got hurt. Come on, Mike, say you'll do it."

Michael looked at her in an absentminded fashion. It seemed as if he really and truly had not heard anything said. He didn't answer.

Connie came to stand beside her father. "Make him do it," she said to the Don. Her two hands rested affectionately on his shoulders and she rubbed his neck. She was the only one who was ever so familiar with the Don. Her affection for her father was touching. It was trusting, like a little girl's. The Don patted one of her hands and said, "We're all starving here. Put the spaghetti on the table and then chatter."

Connie turned to her husband and said, "Carlo, you tell Mike to get his face fixed. Maybe he'll listen to you." Her voice implied that Michael and Carlo Rizzi had some friendly relationship over and above anyone else's.

Carlo, handsomely sunburned, blond hair neatly cut and combed, sipped at his glass of homemade wine and said, "Nobody can tell Mike what to do." Carlo had become a different man since moving into the mall. He knew his place in the Family and kept to it.

There was something that Kay didn't understand in all this, something that didn't quite meet the eye. As a woman she could see that Connie was deliberately charming her father, though it was beautifully done and even sincere. Yet it was not spontaneous. Carlo's reply had been a manly knuckling of his forehead. Michael had absolutely ignored everything.

Kay didn't care about her husband's disfigurement but she worried about his sinus trouble which sprang from it. Surgery repair of the face would cure the sinus also. For that reason she wanted Michael to enter the hospital and get the necessary work done. But she understood that in a curious way he desired his disfigurement. She was sure that the Don understood this too.

But after Kay gave birth to her first child, she was surprised by Michael asking her, "Do you want me to get my face fixed?"

Kay nodded. "You know how kids are, your son will feel bad about your face when he gets old enough to understand it's not normal. I just don't want our child to see it. I don't mind at all, honestly, Michael."

"OK." He smiled at her. "I'll do it."

He waited until she was home from the hospital and then made all the necessary arrangements. The operation was successful. The cheek indentation was now just barely noticeable.

Everybody in the Family was delighted, but Connie more so than anyone. She visited Michael every day in the hospital, dragging Carlo along. When Michael came home, she gave him a big hug and a kiss and looked at him admiringly and said, "Now you're my handsome brother again."

Only the Don was unimpressed, shrugging his shoulders and remarking, "What's the difference?"

But Kay was grateful. She knew that Michael had done it against all his own inclinations. Had done it because she had asked him to, and that she was the only person in the world who could make him act against his own nature.

On the afternoon of Michael's return from Vegas, Rocco Lampone drove the limousine to the mall to pick up Kay so that she could meet her husband at the airport. She always met her husband when he arrived from out of town, mostly because she felt lonely without him, living as she did in the fortified mall.

She saw him come off the plane with Tom Hagen and the new man he had working for him, Albert Neri. Kay didn't care much for Neri, he reminded her of Luca Brasi in his quiet ferociousness. She saw Neri drop behind Michael and off to the side, saw his quick penetrating glance as his eyes swept over everybody nearby. It was Neri who first spotted Kay and touched Michael's shoulder to make him look in the proper direction.

Kay ran into her husband's arms and he quickly kissed her and let her go. He and Tom Hagen and Kay got into the limousine and Albert Neri vanished. Kay did not notice that Neri had gotten into another car with two other men and that this car rode behind the limousine until it reached Long Beach.

Kay never asked Michael how his business had gone. Even such polite questions were understood to be awkward, not that he wouldn't give her an equally polite answer, but it would remind them both of the forbidden territory their marriage could never include. Kay didn't mind anymore. But when Michael told her he would have to spend the evening with his father to tell him about the Vegas trip, she couldn't help making a little frown of disappointment.

"I'm sorry," Michael said. "Tomorrow night we'll go into New York and see a show and have dinner, OK?" He patted her stomach, she was almost seven months pregnant. "After the kid comes you'll be tied down again. Hell, you're more Italian than Yankee. Two kids in two years."

Kay said tartly, "And you're more Yankee than Italian. Your first evening home and you spend it on business." But she smiled at him when she said it. "You won't be home late?"

"Before midnight," Michael said. "Don't wait up for me if you feel tired."

"I'll wait up," Kay said.

At the meeting that night, in the corner room library of Don Corleone's house, were the Don himself, Michael, Tom Hagen, Carlo Rizzi, and the two *caporegimes*, Clemenza and Tessio.

The atmosphere of the meeting was by no means so congenial as in former days. Ever since Don Corleone had announced his semiretirement and Michael's take-over of the Family business, there had been some strain. Succession in control of such an enterprise as the Family was by no means hereditary. In any other Family powerful *caporegimes* such as Clemenza and Tessio might have succeeded to the position of Don. Or at least they might have been allowed to split off and form their own Family.

Then, too, ever since Don Corleone had made the peace with the Five Families, the strength of the Corleone Family had declined. The Barzini Family was now indisputably the most powerful one in the New York area; allied as they were to the Tattaglias, they now held the position the Corleone Family had once held. Also they were slyly whittling down the power of the Corleone Family, muscling into their gambling areas, testing the Corleones' reactions and, finding them weak, establishing their own bookmakers.

The Barzinis and Tattaglias were delighted with the Don's retirement. Michael, formidable as he might prove to be, could never hope to equal the Don in cunning and influence for at least another decade. The Corleone Family was definitely in a decline.

It had, of course, suffered serious misfortunes. Freddie had proved to be nothing more than an innkeeper and lady's man, the idiom for lady's man untranslatable but connoting a greedy infant always at its mother's nipple—in short, unmanly. Sonny's death too, had been a disaster. Sonny had been a man to be feared, not to be taken lightly. Of course he had made a mistake in sending his younger brother, Michael, to kill the Turk and the police captain. Though necessary in a tactical sense, as a long-term strategy it proved to be a serious error. It had forced the Don, eventually, to rise from his sickbed. It had deprived Michael of two years of valuable experience and training under his father's tutelage. And of course an Irish as a *Consigliori* had been the only foolishness the Don had ever perpetrated. No Irish man could hope to equal a Sicilian for cunning. So went the opinion of all the Families and they were naturally more respectful to the Barzini-Tattaglia alliance than to the Corleones. Their opinion of Michael was that he was not equal to Sonny in force though more intelligent certainly, but not as intelligent as his father. A mediocre successor and a man not to be feared too greatly.

Also, though the Don was generally admired for his statesmanship in making the peace, the fact that he had not avenged Sonny's murder lost the Family a great deal of respect. It was recognized that such statesmanship sprang out of weakness.

All this was known to the men sitting in the room and perhaps even believed by a few. Carlo Rizzi liked Michael but did not fear him as he had feared Sonny. Clemenza, too, though he gave Michael credit for a bravura performance with the Turk and the police captain, could not help thinking Michael too soft to be a Don. Clemenza had hoped to be given permission to form his own Family, to have his own empire split away from the Corleone. But the Don had indicated that this was not to be and Clemenza respected the Don too much to disobey. Unless of course the whole situation became intolerable.

Tessio had a better opinion of Michael. He sensed something else in the young man: a force cleverly kept hidden, a man jealously guarding his true strength from public gaze, following the Don's precept that a friend should always underestimate your virtues and an enemy overestimate your faults.

The Don himself and Tom Hagen were of course under no illusions about Michael. The Don would never have retired if he had not had absolute faith in his son's ability to retrieve the Family position. Hagen had been Michael's teacher for the last two years and was amazed at how quickly Michael grasped all the intricacies of the Family business. Truly his father's son.

Clemenza and Tessio were annoyed with Michael because he had reduced the strength of their *regimes* and had never reconstituted Sonny's *regime*. The Corleone Family, in effect, had now only two fighting divisions with less personnel than formerly. Clemenza and Tessio considered this suicidal, especially with the Barzini-Tattaglia encroachments on their empires. So now they were hopeful these errors might be corrected at this extraordinary meeting convened by the Don.

Michael started off by telling them about his trip to Vegas and Moe

Greene's refusing the offer to buy him out. "But we'll make him an offer he can't refuse," Michael said. "You already know the Corleone Family plans to move its operations West. We'll have four of the hotel casinos on the Strip. But it can't be right away. We need time to get things straightened out." He spoke directly to Clemenza. "Pete, you and Tessio, I want you to go along with me for a year without questioning and without reservations. At the end of that year, both of you can split off from the Corleone Family and be your own bosses, have your own Families. Of course it goes without saying we'd maintain our friendship, I wouldn't insult you and your respect for my father by thinking otherwise for a minute. But up until that time I want you just to follow my lead and don't worry. There are negotiations going on that will solve problems that you think are not solvable. So just be a little patient."

Tessio spoke up. "If Moe Greene wanted to talk to your father, why not let him? The Don could always persuade anybody, there was never anyone who could stand up to his reasonableness."

The Don answered this directly. "I've retired. Michael would lose respect if I interfered. And besides that's a man I'd rather not talk to."

Tessio remembered the stories he'd heard about Moe Greene slapping Freddie Corleone around one night in the Vegas hotel. He began to smell a rat. He leaned back. Moe Greene was a dead man, he thought. The Corleone Family *did not wish* to persuade him.

Carlo Rizzi spoke up. "Is the Corleone Family going to stop operating in New York altogether?"

Michael nodded. "We're selling the olive oil business. Everything we can, we turn over to Tessio and Clemenza. But, Carlo, I don't want you to worry about your job. You grew up in Nevada, you know the state, you know the people. I'm counting on you being my right-hand man when we make our move out there."

Carlo leaned back, his face flushed with gratification. His time was coming, he would move in the constellations of power.

Michael went on. "Tom Hagen is no longer the *Consigliori*. He's going to be our lawyer in Vegas. In about two months he'll move out there permanently with his family. Strictly as a lawyer. Nobody goes to him with any other business as of now, this minute. He's a lawyer and that's all. No reflection on Tom. That's the way I want it. Besides, if I ever need any advice, who's a better counselor than my father?" They all laughed. But they had gotten the message despite the joke. Tom Hagen was out; he no longer held any power. They all took their fleeting glances to check Hagen's reaction but his face was impassive.

Clemenza spoke up in his fat man's wheeze. "Then in a year's time we're on our own, is that it?"

"Maybe less," Michael said courteously. "Of course you can always remain part of the Family, that's your choice. But most of our strength will be out West and maybe you'd do better organized on your own."

Tessio said quietly, "In that case I think you should give us permission to recruit new men for our *regimes*. Those Barzini bastards keep chiseling in on my territory. I think maybe it would be wise to teach them a little lesson in manners."

Michael shook his head. "No. No good. Just stay still. All that stuff will be negotiated, everything will be straightened out before we leave."

Tessio was not to be so easily satisfied. He spoke to the Don directly, taking a chance on incurring Michael's ill will. "Forgive me, Godfather, let our years of friendship be my excuse. But I think you and your son are all wrong with this Nevada business. How can you hope for success there without your strength here to back you up? The two go hand in hand. And with you gone from here the Barzini and the Tattaglia will be too strong for us. Me and Pete will have trouble, we'll come under their thumb sooner or later. And Barzini is a man not to my taste. I say the Corleone Family has to make its move from strength, not from weakness. We should build up our *regimes* and take back our lost territories in Staten Island at least."

The Don shook his head. "I made the peace, remember, I can't go back on my word."

Tessio refused to be silenced. "Everybody knows Barzini gave you provocation since then. And besides, if Michael is the new chief of the Corleone Family, what's to stop him from taking any action he sees fit? Your word doesn't strictly bind him."

Michael broke in sharply. He said to Tessio, very much the chief now, "There are things being negotiated which will answer your questions and resolve your doubts. If my word isn't enough for you, ask your Don."

But Tessio understood he had finally gone too far. If he dared to question the Don he would make Michael his enemy. So he shrugged and said, "I spoke for the good of the Family, not for myself. I can take care of myself."

Michael gave him a friendly smile. "Tessio, I never doubt you in any way. I never did. But trust in me. Of course I'm not equal to you and Pete in these things, but after all I've my father to guide me. I won't do too badly, we'll all come out fine."

The meeting was over. The big news was that Clemenza and Tessio would be permitted to form their own Families from their *regimes*. Tessio would have his gambling and docks in Brooklyn, Clemenza the gambling in Manhattan and the Family contacts in the racing tracks of Long Island.

The two *caporegimes* left not quite satisfied, still a little uneasy. Carlo Rizzi lingered hoping that the time had come when he finally would be treated as one of the family, but he quickly saw that Michael was not of that mind. He left the Don, Tom Hagen and Michael alone in the corner library room. Albert Neri ushered him out of the house and Carlo noticed that Neri stood in the doorway watching him walk across the floodlit mall.

In the library the three men had relaxed as only people can who have lived years together in the same house, in the same family. Michael served some anisette to the Don and scotch to Tom Hagen. He took a drink for himself, which he rarely did.

Tom Hagen spoke up first. "Mike, why are you cutting me out of the action?"

Michael seemed surprised. "You'll be my number one man in Vegas. We'll be legitimate all the way and you're the legal man. What can be more important than that?"

Hagen smiled a little sadly. "I'm not talking about that. I'm talking about Rocco Lampone building a secret *regime* without my knowledge. I'm talking about you dealing direct with Neri rather than through me or a *caporegime*. Unless of course you don't know what Lampone's doing."

Michael said softly, "How did you find out about Lampone's *regime?*"

Hagen shrugged. "Don't worry, there's no leak, nobody else knows. But in my position I can see what's happening. You gave Lampone his own living, you gave him a lot of freedom. So he needs people to help him in his little empire. But everybody he recruits has to be reported to me. And I notice everybody he puts on the payroll is a little too good for that particular job, is getting a little more money than that particular exercise is worth. You picked the right man when you picked Lampone, by the way. He's operating perfectly."

Michael grimaced. "Not so damn perfect if you noticed. Anyway the Don picked Lampone."

"OK," Tom said, "so why am I cut out of the action?"

Michael faced him and without flinching gave it to him straight. "Tom, you're not a wartime *Consigliori*. Things may get tough with this move we're trying to make and we may have to fight. And I want to get you out of the line of fire too, just in case."

Hagen's face reddened. If the Don had told him the same thing, he would have accepted it humbly. But where the hell did Mike come off making such a snap judgment?

"OK," he said, "but I happen to agree with Tessio. I think you're going about this all wrong. You're making the move out of weakness, not strength. That's always bad. Barzini is like a wolf, and if he tears you limb from limb, the other Families won't come rushing to help the Corleones."

The Don finally spoke. "Tom, it's not just Michael. I advised him on these matters. There are things that may have to be done that I don't want in any way to be responsible for. That is my wish, not Michael's. I never thought you were a bad *Consigliori*, I thought Santino a bad Don, may his soul rest in peace. He had a good heart, but he wasn't the right man to head the Family when I had my little misfortune. And who would have thought that Fredo would become a lackey of women? So don't feel badly. Michael has all my confidence as you do. For reasons which you can't know, you must have no part in what may happen. By the way, I told Michael that Lampone's secret *regime* would not escape your eye. So that shows I have faith in you."

Michael laughed. "I honestly didn't think you'd pick that up, Tom."

Hagen knew he was being mollified. "Maybe I can help," he said.

Michael shook his head decisively. "You're out, Tom."

Tom finished his drink and before he left he gave Michael a mild reproof. "You're nearly as good as your father," he told Michael. "But there's one thing you still have to learn."

"What's that?" Michael said politely.

"How to say no," Hagen answered.

Michael nodded gravely. "You're right," he said. "I'll remember that."

When Hagen had left, Michael said jokingly to his father, "So you've taught me everything else. Tell me how to say no to people in a way they'll like."

The Don moved to sit behind the big desk. "You cannot say 'no' to the people you love, not often. That's the secret. And then when you do, it has to sound like a 'yes.' Or you have to make them say 'no.' You have to take time and trouble. But I'm old-fashioned, you're the new modern generation, don't listen to me."

Michael laughed. "Right. You agree about Tom being out, though, don't you?"

The Don nodded. "He can't be involved in this."

Michael said quietly, "I think it's time for me to tell you that what I'm going to do is not purely out of vengeance for Apollonia and Sonny. It's the right thing to do. Tessio and Tom are right about the Barzinis."

Don Corleone nodded. "Revenge is a dish that tastes best when it is cold," he said. "I would not have made that peace but that I knew you would never come home alive otherwise. I'm surprised, though, that Barzini still made a last try at you. Maybe it was arranged before the peace talk and he couldn't stop it. Are you sure they were not after Don Tommasino?"

Michael said, "That's the way it was supposed to look. And it would have been perfect, even you would never have suspected. Except that I came out alive. I saw Fabrizzio going through the gate, running away. And of course I've checked it all out since I've been back."

"Have they found that shepherd?" the Don asked.

"I found him," Michael said. "I found him a year ago. He's got his own little pizza place up in Buffalo. New name, phony passport and identification. He's doing very well is Fabrizzio the shepherd."

The Don nodded. "So it's to no purpose to wait any longer. When will you start?"

Michael said, "I want to wait until after Kay has the baby. Just in case something goes wrong. And I want Tom settled in Vegas so he won't be concerned in the affair. I think a year from now."

"You've prepared for everything?" the Don asked. He did not look at Michael when he said this.

Michael said gently, "You have no part. You're not responsible. I take all responsibility. I would refuse to let you even veto. If you tried to do that now, I would leave the Family and go my own way. You're not responsible."

The Don was silent for a long time and then he sighed. He said, "So be it. Maybe that's why I retired, maybe that's why I've turned everything over to you. I've done my share in life, I haven't got the heart anymore. And there are some duties the best of men can't assume. That's it then."

During that year Kay Adams Corleone was delivered of a second child, another boy. She delivered easily, without any trouble whatsoever, and was welcomed back to the mall like a royal princess. Connie Corleone presented the baby with a silk layette handmade in Italy, enormously expensive and beautiful. She told Kay, "Carlo found it. He shopped all over New York to get something extra special after I couldn't find anything I really liked." Kay smiled her thanks, understood immediately that she was to tell Michael this fine tale. She was on her way to becoming a Sicilian.

Also during that year, Nino Valenti died of a cerebral hemorrhage. His death made the front pages of the tabloids because the movie Johnny Fontane had featured him in had opened a few weeks before and was a smash hit, establishing Nino as a major star. The papers mentioned that Johnny Fontane was handling the funeral arrangements, that the funeral would be private, only family and close friends to attend. One sensational story even claimed that in an interview Johnny Fontane had blamed himself for his friend's death, that he should have forced his friend to place himself under medical care, but the reporter made it sound like the usual self-reproach of the sensitive but innocent bystander to a tragedy. Johnny Fontane had made his childhood friend, Nino Valenti, a movie star and what more could a friend do?

No member of the Corleone Family attended the California funeral except Freddie. Lucy and Jules Segal attended. The Don himself had wanted to go to California but had suffered a slight heart attack, which kept him in his bed for a month. He sent a huge floral wreath instead. Albert Neri was also sent West as the official representative of the Family.

Two days after Nino's funeral, Moe Greene was shot to death in the Hollywood home of his movie-star mistress; Albert Neri did not reappear in New York until almost a month later. He had taken his vacation in the Caribbean and returned to duty tanned almost black.

Michael Corleone welcomed him with a smile and a few words of praise, which included the information that Neri would from then on receive an extra "living," the Family income from an East Side "book" considered especially rich. Neri was content, satisfied that he lived in a world that properly rewarded a man who did his duty.

Chapter

xxxxxxxxxxxxxxxxxxxxxxxxxxx

29

MICHAEL CORLEONE had taken precautions against every eventuality. His planning was faultless, his security impeccable. He was patient, hoping to use the full year to prepare. But he was not to get his necessary year because fate itself took a stand against him, and in the most surprising fashion. For it was the Godfather, the great Don himself, who failed Michael Corleone.

On one sunny Sunday morning, while the women were at church, Don Vito Corleone dressed in his gardening uniform: baggy gray trousers, a faded blue shirt, battered dirty-brown fedora decorated by a stained gray silk hatband. The Don had gained considerable weight in his few years and worked on his tomato vines, he said, for the sake of his health. But he deceived no one.

The truth was, he loved tending his garden; he loved the sight of it early on a morning. It brought back his childhood in Sicily sixty years ago, brought it back without the terror, the sorrow of his own father's death. Now the beans in their rows grew little white flowers on top; strong green stalks of scallion fenced everything in. At the foot of the garden a spouted barrel stood guard. It was filled with liquidy cow manure, the finest garden fertilizer. Also in that lower part of the garden were the square wooden frames he had built with his own hands, the sticks cross-tied with thick white string. Over these frames crawled the tomato vines.

The Don hastened to water his garden. It must be done before the sun waxed too hot and turned the water into a prism of fire that could burn his lettuce leaves like paper. Sun was more important than water, water also was important; but the two, imprudently mixed, could cause great misfortune.

The Don moved through his garden hunting for ants. If ants were present, it meant that lice were in his vegetables and the ants were going after the lice and he would have to spray.

He had watered just in time. The sun was becoming hot and the Don thought, "Prudence. Prudence." But there were just a few more plants to be supported by sticks and he bent down again. He would go back into the house when he finished this last row.

Quite suddenly it felt as if the sun had come down very close to his head. The air was filled with dancing golden specks. Michael's oldest boy came running through the garden toward where the Don knelt and the boy was enveloped by a yellow shield of blinding light. But the Don was not to be tricked, he was too old a hand. Death hid behind that flaming yellow shield ready to pounce out on him and the Don with a wave of his hand warned the boy away from his presence. Just in time. The sledgehammer blow inside his chest made him choke for air. The Don pitched forward into the earth.

The boy raced away to call his father. Michael Corleone and some men at the mall gate ran to the garden and found the Don lying prone, clutching handfuls of earth. They lifted the Don up and carried him to the shade of his stone-flagged patio. Michael knelt beside his father, holding his hand, while the other men called for an ambulance and doctor.

With a great effort the Don opened his eyes to see his son once more. The massive heart attack had turned his ruddy face almost blue. He was in extremis. He smelled the garden, the yellow shield of light smote his eyes, and he whispered, "Life is so beautiful."

He was spared the sight of his women's tears, dying before they came back from church, dying before the ambulance arrived, or the doctor. He died surrounded by men, holding the hand of the son he had most loved.

The funeral was royal. The Five Families sent their Dons and *caporegimes*, as did the Tessio and Clemenza Families. Johnny Fontane made the tabloid headlines by attending the funeral despite the advice of Michael not to appear. Fontane gave a statement to the newspapers that Vito Corleone was his Godfather and the finest man he had ever known and that he was honored to be permitted to pay his last respects to such a man and didn't give a damn who knew it.

The wake was held in the house of the mall, in the old-fashioned style. Amerigo Bonasera had never done finer work, had discharged all obligations, by preparing his old friend and Godfather as lovingly as a mother prepares a bride for her wedding. Everyone commented on how not even death itself had been able to erase the nobility and the dignity of the great Don's countenance and such remarks made Amerigo Bonasera fill with knowing pride, a curious sense of power. Only he knew what a terrible massacre death had perpetrated on the Don's appearance.

All the old friends and servitors came. Nazorine, his wife, his daughter and her husband and their children, Lucy Mancini came with Freddie from Las Vegas. Tom Hagen and his wife and children, the Dons from San Francisco and Los Angeles, Boston and Cleveland. Rocco Lampone and Albert Neri were pallbearers with Clemenza and Tessio and, of course, the sons of the Don. The mall and all its houses were filled with floral wreaths.

Outside the gates of the mall were the newspapermen and photographers and a small truck that was known to contain FBI men with their movie cameras recording this epic. Some newspapermen who tried to crash the funeral inside found that the gate and fence were manned with security guards who demanded identification and an invitation card. And though they were treated with the utmost courtesy, refreshment sent out to them, they were not permitted inside. They tried to speak with some of the people coming out but were met with stony stares and not a syllable.

Michael Corleone spent most of the day in the corner library room with Kay, Tom Hagen and Freddie. People were ushered in to see him, to offer their condolences. Michael received them with all courtesy even when some of them addressed him as Godfather or Don Michael, only Kay noticing his lips tighten with displeasure.

Clemenza and Tessio came to join this inner circle and Michael personally served them with a drink. There was some gossip of business. Michael informed them that the mall and all its houses were to be sold to a development and construction company. At an enormous profit, still another proof of the great Don's genius.

They all understood that now the whole empire would be in the West. That the Corleone Family would liquidate its power in New York. Such action had been awaiting the retirement or death of the Don.

It was nearly ten years since there had been such a celebration of people in this house, nearly ten years since the wedding of Constanzia Corleone and Carlo Rizzi, so somebody said. Michael walked to the window that looked out on the garden. That long time ago he had sat in the garden with Kay never dreaming that so curious a destiny was to be his. And his father dying had said, "Life is so beautiful." Michael could never remember his father ever having uttered a word about death, as if the Don respected death too much to philosophize about it.

It was time for the cemetery. It was time to bury the great Don. Michael linked his arm with Kay's and went out into the garden to join the host of mourners. Behind him came the *caporegimes* followed by their soldiers and then all the humble people the Godfather had blessed during his lifetime. The baker Nazorine, the widow Colombo and her sons and all the countless others of his world he had ruled so firmly but justly. There were even some who had been his enemies, come to do him honor.

Michael observed all this with a tight, polite smile. He was not impressed. Yet, he thought, if I can die saying, "Life is so beautiful," then nothing else is important. If I can believe in myself that much, nothing else matters. He would follow his father. He would care for his children, his family, his world. But his children would grow in a different world. They would be doctors, artists, scientists. Governors. Presidents. Anything at all. He would see to it that they joined the general family of humanity, but he, as a powerful and prudent parent would most certainly keep a wary eye on that general family.

On the morning after the funeral, all the most important officials of the Corleone Family assembled on the mall. Shortly before noon they were admitted into the empty house of the Don. Michael Corleone received them.

They almost filled the corner library room. There were the two *caporegimes*, Clemenza and Tessio; Rocco Lampone, with his reasonable, competent air; Carlo Rizzi, very quiet, very much knowing his place; Tom Hagen forsaking his strictly legal role to rally around in this crisis; Albert Neri trying to stay physically close to Michael, lighting his new Don's cigarette, mixing his drink, all to show an unswerving loyalty despite the recent disaster to the Corleone Family.

The death of the Don was a great misfortune for the Family. Without him it seemed that half their strength was gone and almost all their bargaining power against the Barzini-Tattaglia alliance. Everyone in the room knew this and they waited for what Michael would say. In their eyes he was not yet the new Don; he had not earned the position or the title. If the Godfather had lived, he might have assured his son's succession; now it was by no means certain.

Michael waited until Neri had served drinks. Then he said quietly, "I just want to tell everybody here that I understand how they feel. I know you all respected my father, but now you have to worry about yourselves and your families. Some of you wonder how what happened is going to affect the planning we've done and the promises I made. Well, the answer to that is: nothing. Everything goes on as before."

Clemenza shook his great shaggy buffalo head. His hair was an iron gray and his features more deeply embedded in added layers of fat, were unpleasant. "The Barzinis and Tattaglias are going to move in on us real hard, Mike. You gotta fight or have a 'sit-down' with them." Everyone in the room noticed that Clemenza had not used a formal form of address to Michael, much less the title of Don.

"Let's wait and see what happens," Michael said. "Let them break the peace first."

Tessio spoke up in his soft voice. "They already have Mike. They opened up two 'books' in Brooklyn this morning. I got the word from the police captain who runs the protection list at the station house. In a month I won't have a place to hang my hat in all Brooklyn."

Michael stared at him thoughtfully. "Have you done anything about it?"

Tessio shook his small, ferretlike head. "No," he said. "I didn't want to give you any problems."

"Good," Michael said. "Just sit tight. And I guess that's what I want to say to all of you. Just sit tight. Don't react to any provocation. Give me a few weeks to straighten things out, to see which way the wind is going to blow. Then I'll make the best deal I can for everybody here. Then we'll have a final meeting and make some final decisions."

He ignored their surprise and Albert Neri started ushering them out. Michael said sharply, "Tom, stick around a few minutes."

Hagen went to the window that faced the mall. He waited until he saw the *caporegimes* and Carlo Rizzo and Rocco Lampore being shepherded through the guarded gate by Neri. Then he turned to Michael and said, "Have you got all the political connections wired into you?"

Michael shook his head regretfully. "Not all. I needed about four more months. The Don and I were working on it. But I've got all the judges, we did that first, and some of the more important people in Congress. And the big party boys here in New York were no problem, of course. The Corleone Family is a lot stronger than anybody thinks, but I hoped to make it foolproof." He smiled at Hagen. "I guess you've figured everything out by now."

Hagen nodded. "It wasn't hard. Except why you wanted me out of the action. But I put on my Sicilian hat and I finally figured that too."

Michael laughed. "The old man said you would. But that's a luxury I can't afford anymore. I need you here. At least for the next few weeks. You better phone Vegas and talk to your wife. Just tell her a few weeks."

Hagen said musingly, "How do you think they'll come at you?"

Michael sighed. "The Don instructed me. Through somebody close. Barzini will set me up through somebody close that, supposedly, I won't suspect."

Hagen smiled at him. "Somebody like me."

Michael smiled back. "You're Irish, they won't trust you."

"I'm German-American," Hagen said.

"To them that's Irish," Michael said. "They won't go to you and they won't go to Neri because Neri was a cop. Plus both of you are *too close* to me. They can't take that gamble. Rocco Lampone isn't close enough. No, it will be Clemenza, Tessio or Carlo Rizzi."

Hagen said softly, "I'm betting it's Carlo."

"We'll see," Michael said. "It won't be long."

It was the next morning, while Hagen and Michael were having breakfast together. Michael took a phone call in the library, and when he came back to the kitchen, he said to Hagen, "It's all set up. I'm going to meet Barzini a week from now. To make a new peace now that the Don is dead." Michael laughed.

Hagen asked, "Who phoned you, who made the contact?" They both knew that whoever in the Corleone Family had made the contact had turned traitor.

Michael gave Hagen a sad regretful smile. "Tessio," he said.

They ate the rest of their breakfast in silence. Over coffee Hagen shook his head. "I could have sworn it would have been Carlo or maybe Clemenza. I never figured Tessio. He's the best of the lot."

"He's the most intelligent," Michael said. "And he did what seems to him to be the smart thing. He sets me up for the hit by Barzini and inherits the Corleone Family. He sticks with me and he gets wiped out; he's figuring I can't win."

Hagen paused before he asked reluctantly, "How right is he figuring?"

Michael shrugged. "It looks bad. But my father was the only one who understood that political connections and power are worth ten *regimes*. I think I've got most of my father's political power in my hands now, but I'm the only one who really knows that." He smiled at Hagen, a reassuring smile. "I'll make them call me Don. But I feel lousy about Tessio."

Hagen said, "Have you agreed to the meeting with Barzini?"

"Yeah," Michael said. "A week from tonight. In Brooklyn, on Tessio's ground where I'll be safe." He laughed again.

Hagen said, "Be careful before then."

For the first time Michael was cold with Hagen. "I don't need a *Consigliori* to give me that kind of advice," he said.

During the week preceding the peace meeting between the Corleone and Barzini Families, Michael showed Hagen just how careful he could be. He never set foot outside the mall and never received anyone without Neri beside him. There was only one annoying complication. Connie and Carl's oldest boy was to receive his Confirmation in the Catholic Church and Kay asked Michael to be the Godfather. Michael refused.

"I don't often beg you," Kay said. "Please do this just for me. Connie wants it so much. And so does Carl. It's very important to them. Please, Michael."

She could see he was angry with her for insisting and expected him to refuse. So she was surprised when he nodded and said, "OK. But I can't leave the mall. Tell them to arrange for the priest to confirm the kid here. I'll pay whatever it costs. If they run into trouble with the church people, Hagen will straighten it out."

And so the day before the meeting with the Barzini Family, Michael Corleone stood Godfather to the son of Carlo and Connie Rizzi. He presented the boy with an extremely expensive wristwatch and gold band. There was a small party in Carlo's house, to which were invited the *caporegimes*, Hagen, Lampone and everyone who lived on the mall, including, of course, the Don's widow. Connie was so overcome with emotion that she hugged and kissed her brother and Kay all during the evening. And even Carlo Rizzi became sentimental, wringing Michael's hand and calling him Godfather at every excuse—old country style. Michael himself had never been so affable, so outgoing. Connie whispered to Kay, "I think Carlo and Mike are going to be real friends now. Something like this always bring people together."

Kay squeezed her sister-in-law's arm. "I'm *so* glad," she said.

Book VIII

Chapter

30

ALBERT NERI sat in his Bronx apartment and carefully brushed the blue serge of his old policeman's uniform. He unpinned the badge and set it on the table to be polished. The regulation holster and gun were draped over a chair. This old routine of detail made him happy in some strange way, one of the few times he had felt happy since his wife had left him, nearly two years ago.

He had married Rita when she was a high school kid and he was a rookie policeman. She was shy, dark-haired, from a straitlaced Italian family who never let her stay out later than ten o'clock at night. Neri was completely in love with her, her innocence, her virtue, as well as her dark prettiness.

At first Rita Neri was fascinated by her husband. He was immensely strong and she could see people were afraid of him because of that strength and his unbending attitude toward what was right and wrong. He was rarely tactful. If he disagreed with a group's attitude or an individual's opinion, he kept his mouth shut or brutally spoke his contradiction. He never gave a polite agreement. He also had a true Sicilian temper and his rages could be awesome. But he was never angry with his wife.

Neri in the space of five years became one of the most feared policemen on the New York City force. Also one of the most honest. But he had his own ways of enforcing the law. He hated punks and when he saw a bunch of young rowdies making a disturbance on a street corner at night, disturbing passersby, he took quick and decisive action. He employed a physical strength that was truly extraordinary, which he himself did not fully appreciate.

One night in Central Park West he jumped out of the patrol car and lined up six punks in black silk jackets. His partner remained in the driver's seat, not wanting to get involved, knowing Neri. The six boys, all in their late teens, had been stopping people and asking them for cigarettes in a youthfully menacing way but not doing anyone any real physical harm. They had also teased girls going by with a sexual gesture more French than American.

Neri lined them up against the stone wall that closed off Central Park from Eighth Avenue. It was twilight, but Neri carried his favorite weapon, a huge flashlight. He never bothered drawing his gun; it was never necessary. His face when he was angry was so brutally menacing, combined with his uniform, that the usual punks were cowed. These were no exception.

Neri asked the first youth in the black silk jacket, "What's your name?" The kid answered with an Irish name. Neri told him, "Get off the street. I see you again tonight, I'll crucify you." He motioned with his flashlight and the youth walked quickly away. Neri followed the same procedure with the next two boys. He let them walk off. But the fourth boy gave an Italian name and smiled at Neri as if to claim some sort of kinship. Neri was unmistakably of Italian descent. Neri looked at this youth for a moment and asked superfluously, "You Italian?" The boy grinned confidently.

Neri hit him a stunning blow on the forehead with his flashlight. The boy dropped to his knees. The skin and flesh of his forehead had cracked open and blood poured down his face. But it was strictly a flesh wound. Neri said to him harshly, "You son of a bitch, you're a disgrace to the Italians. You give us all a bad name. Get on your feet." He gave the youth a kick in the side, not gentle, not too hard. "Get home and stay off the street. Don't ever let me catch you wearing that jacket again either. I'll send you to the hospital. Now get home. You're lucky I'm not your father."

Neri didn't bother with the other two punks. He just booted their asses down the Avenue, telling them he didn't want them on the street that night.

In such encounters all was done so quickly that there was no time for a crowd to gather or for someone to protest his actions. Neri would get into the patrol car and his partner would zoom it away. Of course once in a while there would be a real hard case who wanted to fight and might even pull a knife. These were truly unfortunate people. Neri would, with awesome, quick ferocity, beat them bloody and throw them into the patrol car. They would be put under arrest and charged with assaulting an officer. But usually their case would have to wait until they were discharged from the hospital.

Eventually Neri was transferred to the beat that held the United Nations building area, mainly because he had not shown his precinct sergeant the proper respect. The United Nations people with their diplomatic immunity parked their limousines all over the streets without regard to police regulations. Neri complained to the precinct and was told not to make waves, to just ignore it. But one night there was a whole side street that was impassable because of the carelessly parked autos. It was after midnight, so Neri took his huge flashlight from the patrol car and went down the street smashing windshields to smithereens. It was not easy, even for high-ranking diplomats, to get the windshields repaired in less than a few days. Protests poured into the police precinct station house demanding protection against this vandalism. After a week of windshield smashing the truth gradually hit somebody about what was actually happening and Albert Neri was transferred to Harlem.

One Sunday shortly afterward, Neri took his wife to visit his widowed sister in Brooklyn. Albert Neri had the fierce protective affection for his sister common to all Sicilians and he always visited her at least once every couple of months to make sure she was all right. She was much older than he was and had a son who was twenty. This son, Thomas, without a father's hand, was giving trouble. He had gotten into a few minor scrapes, was running a little wild. Neri had once used his contacts on the police force to keep the youth from being charged with larceny. On that occasion he had kept his anger in check but had given his nephew warning. "Tommy, you make my sister cry over you and I'll straighten you out myself." It was intended as a friendly pally-uncle warning, not really as a threat. But even though Tommy was the toughest kid in that tough Brooklyn neighborhood, he was afraid of his Uncle Al.

On this particular visit Tommy had come in very late Saturday night and was still sleeping in his room. His mother went to wake him, telling him to get dressed so that he could eat Sunday dinner with his uncle and aunt. The boy's voice came harshly through the partly opened door, "I don't give a shit, let me sleep," and his mother came back out into the kitchen smiling apologetically.

So they had to eat their dinner without him. Neri asked his sister if Tommy was giving her any real trouble and she shook her head.

Neri and his wife were about to leave when Tommy finally got up. He barely grumbled a hello and went into the kitchen. Finally he yelled in to his mother, "Hey, Ma, how about cooking me something to eat?" But it was not a request. It was the spoiled complaint of an indulged child.

His mother said shrilly, "Get up when it's dinnertime and then you can eat. I'm not going to cook again for you."

It was the sort of little ugly scene that was fairly commonplace, but Tommy still a little irritable from his slumber made a mistake. "Ah, fuck you and your nagging, I'll go out and eat." As soon as he said it he regretted it.

His Uncle Al was on him like a cat on a mouse. Not so much for the insult to his sister this particular day but because it was obvious that he often talked to his mother in such a fashion when they were alone. Tommy never dared say such a thing in front of her brother. This particular Sunday he had just been careless. To his misfortune.

Before the frightened eyes of the two women, Al Neri gave his nephew a merciless, careful, physical beating. At first the youth made an attempt at self-defense but soon gave that up and begged for mercy. Neri slapped his face until the lips were swollen and bloody. He rocked the kid's head back and slammed him against the wall. He punched him in the stomach, then got him prone on the floor and slapped his face into the carpet. He told the two women to wait and made Tommy go down the street and get into his car. There he put the fear of God into him. "If my sister ever tells me you talk like that to her again, this beating will seem like kisses from a broad," he told Tommy. "I want to see you straighten out. Now go up the house and tell my wife I'm waiting for her."

It was two months after this that Al Neri got back from a late shift on the force and found his wife had left him. She had packed all her clothes and gone back to her family. Her father told him that Rita was afraid of him, that she was afraid to live with him because of his temper. Al was stunned with disbelief. He had never struck his wife, never threatened her in any way, had never felt anything but affection for her. But he was so bewildered by her action that he decided to let a few days go by before he went over to her family's house to talk to her.

It was unfortunate that the next night he ran into trouble on his shift. His car answered a call in Harlem, a report of a deadly assault. As usual Neri jumped out of the patrol car while it was still rolling to a stop. It was after midnight and he was carrying his huge flashlight. It was easy spotting the trouble. There was a crowd gathered outside a tenement doorway. One Negro woman said to Neri, "There's a man in there cutting a little girl."

Neri went into the hallway. There was an open door at the far end with light streaming out and he could hear moaning. Still handling the flashlight, he went down the hall and through the open doorway.

He almost fell over two bodies stretched out on the floor. One was a Negro woman of about twenty-five. The other was a Negro girl of no more than twelve. Both were bloody from razor cuts on their faces and bodies. In the living room Neri saw the man who was responsible. He knew him well.

The man was Wax Baines, a notorious pimp, dope pusher and strong-arm artist. His eyes were popping from drugs now, the bloody knife he held in his hand wavered. Neri had arrested him two weeks before for severely assaulting one of his whores in the street. Baines had told him, "Hey, man, this none of your business." And Neri's partner had also said something about letting the niggers cut each other up if they wanted to, but Neri had hauled Baines into the station house. Baines was bailed out the very next day.

Neri had never much liked Negroes, and working in Harlem had made him like them even less. They all were on drugs or booze while they let their women work or peddle ass. He didn't have any use for any of the bastards. So Baines' brazen breaking of the law infuriated him. And the sight of the little girl all cut up with the razor sickened him. Quite coolly, in his own mind, he decided not to bring Baines in.

But witnesses were already crowding into the apartment behind him, some people who lived in the building and his partner from the patrol car.

Neri ordered Baines, "Drop your knife, you're under arrest."

Baines laughed. "Man, you gotta use your gun to arrest me." He held his knife up. "Or maybe you want this."

Neri moved very quickly, so his partner would not have time to draw a gun. The Negro stabbed with his knife, but Neri's extraordinary reflexes enabled him to catch the thrust with his left palm. With his right hand he swung the flashlight in a short vicious arc. The blow caught Baines on the side of the head and made his knees buckle comically like a drunk's. The knife dropped from his hand. He was quite helpless. So Neri's second blow was inexcusable, as the police departmental hearing and his criminal trial later proved with the help of the testimony of witnesses and his fellow policeman. Neri brought the flashlight down on the top of Baines' skull in an incredibly powerful blow which shattered the glass of the flashlight; the enamel shield and the bulb itself popping out and flying across the room. The heavy aluminum barrel of the flashlight tube bent and only the batteries inside prevented it from doubling on itself. One awed onlooker, a Negro man who lived in the tenement and later testified against Neri, said, "Man, that's a hard-headed nigger."

But Baines' head was not quite hard enough. The blow caved in his skull. He died two hours later in the Harlem Hospital.

Albert Neri was the only one surprised when he was brought up on departmental charges for using excessive force. He was suspended and criminal charges were brought against him. He was indicted for manslaughter, convicted and sentenced to from one to ten years in prison. By this time he was so filled with a baffled rage and hatred of all society that he didn't give a damn. That they dared to judge him a criminal! That they dared to send him to prison for killing an animal like that pimp-nigger! That they didn't give a damn for the woman and little girl who had been carved up, disfigured for life, and still in the hospital.

He did not fear prison. He felt that because of his having been a policeman and especially because of the nature of his offense, he would be well taken care of. Several of his buddy officers had already assured him they would speak to friends. Only his wife's father, a shrewd old-style Italian who owned a fish market in the Bronx, realized that a man like Albert Neri had little chance of surviving a year in prison. One of his fellow inmates might kill him; if not, he was almost certain to kill one of them. Out of guilt that his daughter had deserted a fine husband for some womanly foolishness, Neri's father-in-law used his contacts with the Corleone Family (he paid protection money to one of i. representatives and supplied the Corleone itself with the finest fish available, as a gift), he petitioned for their intercession.

The Corleone Family knew about Albert Neri. He was something of a legend as a legitimately tough cop; he had made a certain reputation as a man not to be held lightly, as a man who could inspire fear out of his own person regardless of the uniform and the sanctioned gun he wore. The Corleone Family was always interested in such men. The fact that he was a policeman did not mean too much. Many young men started down a false path to their true destiny. Time and fortune usually set them aright.

It was Pete Clemenza, with his fine nose for good personnel, who brought the Neri affair to Tom Hagen's attention. Hagen studied the copy of the official police dossier and listened to Clemenza. He said, "Maybe we have another Luca Brasi here."

Clemenza nodded his head vigorously. Though he was very fat, his face had none of the usual stout man's benignity. "My thinking exactly. Mike should look into this himself."

And so it was that before Albert Neri was transferred from the temporary jail to what would have been his permanent residence upstate, he was informed that the judge had reconsidered his case on the basis of new information and affidavits submitted by high police officials. His sentence was suspended and he was released.

Albert Neri was no fool and his father-in-law no shrinking violet. Neri learned what had happened and paid his debt to the father-in-law by agreeing to get a divorce from Rita. Then he made a trip out to Long Beach to thank his benefactor. Arrangements had been made beforehand, of course. Michael received him in his library.

Neri stated his thanks in formal tones and was surprised and gratified by the warmth with which Michael received his thanks.

"Hell, I couldn't let them do that to a fellow Sicilian," Michael said. "They should have given you a goddamn medal. But those damn politicians don't give a shit about anything except pressure groups. Listen, I would never have stepped into the picture if I hadn't checked everything out and saw what a raw deal you got. One of my people talked to your sister and she told us how you were always worried about her and her kid, how you straightened the kid out, kept him from going bad. Your father-in-law says you're the finest fellow in the world. That's rare." Tactfully Michael did not mention anything about Neri's wife having left him.

They chatted for a while. Neri had always been a taciturn man, but he found himself opening up to Michael Corleone. Michael was only about five years his senior, but Neri spoke to him as if he were much older, older enough to be his father.

Finally Michael said, "There's no sense getting you out of jail and then just leaving you high and dry. I can arrange some work for you. I have interests out in Las Vegas, with your experience you could be a hotel security man. Or if there's some little business you'd like to go into, I can put a word in with the banks to advance you a loan for capital."

Neri was overcome with grateful embarrassment. He proudly refused and then added, "I have to stay under the jurisdiction of the court anyway with the suspended sentence."

Michael said briskly, "That's all crap detail, I can fix that. Forget about that supervision and just so the banks won't get choosy I'll have your yellow sheet pulled."

The yellow sheet was a police record of criminal offenses committed by any individual. It was usually submitted to a judge when he was considering what sentence to give a convicted criminal. Neri had been long enough on the police force to know that many hoodlums going up for sentencing had been treated leniently by the judge because a clean yellow sheet had been submitted by the bribed Police Records Department. So he was not too surprised that Michael Corleone could do such a thing; he was, however, surprised that such trouble would be taken on his account.

"If I need help, I'll get in touch," Neri said.

"Good, good," Michael said. He looked at his watch and Neri took this for his dismissal. He rose to go. Again he was surprised.

"Lunchtime," Michael said. "Come on and eat with me and my family. My father said he'd like to meet you. We'll walk over to his house. My mother should have some fried peppers and eggs and sausages. Real Sicilian style."

That afternoon was the most agreeable Albert Neri had spent since he was a small boy, since the days before his parents had died when he was only fifteen. Don Corleone was at his most amiable and was delighted when he discovered that Neri's parents had originally come from a small village only a few minutes from his own. The talk was good, the food was delicious, the wine robustly red. Neri was struck by the thought that he was finally with his own true people. He understood that he was only a casual guest but he knew he could find a permanent place and be happy in such a world.

Michael and the Don walked him out to his car. The Don shook his hand and said, "You're a fine fellow. My son Michael here, I've been teaching him the olive oil business, I'm getting old, I want to retire. And he comes to me and he says he wants to interfere in your little affair. I tell him to just learn about the olive oil. But he won't leave me alone. He says, here is this fine fellow, a Sicilian and they are doing this dirty trick to him. He kept on, he gave me no peace until I interested myself in it. I tell you this to tell you that he was right. Now that I've met you, I'm glad we took the trouble. So if we can do anything further for you, just ask the favor. Understand? We're at your service." (Remembering the Don's kindness, Neri wished the great man was still alive to see the service that would be done this day.)

It took Neri less than three days to make up his mind. He understood he was being courted but understood more. That the Corleone Family approved that act of his which society condemned and had punished him for. The Corleone Family valued him, society did not. He understood that he would be happier in the world the Corleones had created than in the world outside. And he understood that the Corleone Family was the more powerful, within its narrower limits.

He visited Michael again and put his cards on the table. He did not want to work in Vegas but he would take a job with the Family in New York. He made his loyalty clear. Michael was touched, Neri could see that. It was arranged. But Michael insisted that Neri take a vacation first, down in Miami at the Family hotel there, all expenses paid and a month's salary in advance so he could have the necessary cash to enjoy himself properly.

That vacation was Neri's first taste of luxury. People at the hotel took special care of him, saying, "Ah, you're a friend of Michael Corleone." The word had been passed along. He was given one of the plush suites, not the grudging small room a poor relation might be fobbed off with. The man running the nightclub in the hotel fixed him up with some beautiful girls. When Neri got back to New York he had a slightly different view on life in general.

He was put in the Clemenza *regime* and tested carefully by that masterful personnel man. Certain precautions had to be taken. He had, after all, once been a policeman. But Neri's natural ferocity overcame whatever scruples he might have had at being on the other side of the fence. In less than a year he had "made his bones." He could never turn back.

Clemenza sang his praises. Neri was a wonder, the new Luca Brasi.

He would be better than Luca, Clemenza bragged. After all, Neri was his discovery. Physically the man was a marvel. His reflexes and coordination such that he could have been another Joe DiMaggio. Clemenza also knew that Neri was not a man to be controlled by someone like himself. Neri was made directly responsible to Michael Corleone, with Tom Hagen as the necessary buffer. He was a "special" and as such commanded a high salary but did not have his own living, a bookmaking or strong-arm operation. It was obvious that his respect for Michael Corleone was enormous and one day Hagen said jokingly to Michael, "Well now you've got your Luca."

Michael nodded. He had brought it off. Albert Neri was his man to the death. And of course it was a trick learned from the Don himself. While learning the business, undergoing the long days of tutelage by his father, Michael had one time asked, "How come you used a guy like Luca Brasi? An animal like that?"

The Don had proceeded to instruct him. "There are men in this world," he said, "who go about demanding to be killed. You must have noticed them. They quarrel in gambling games, they jump out of their automobiles in a rage if someone so much as scratches their fender, they humiliate and bully people whose capabilities they do not know. I have seen a man, a fool, deliberately infuriate a group of dangerous men, and he himself without any resources. These are people who wander through the world shouting, 'Kill me. Kill me.' And there is always somebody ready to oblige them. We read about it in the newspapers every day. Such people of course do a great deal of harm to others also.

"Luca Brasi was such a man. But he was such an extraordinary man that for a long time nobody could kill him. Most of these people are of no concern to ourselves but a Brasi is a powerful weapon to be used. The trick is that since he does not fear death and indeed looks for it, then the trick is to make yourself the only person in the world that he truly desires *not* to kill him. He has only that one fear, not of death, but that *you* may be the one to kill him. He is yours then."

It was one of the most valuable lessons given by the Don before he died, and Michael had used it to make Neri his Luca Brasi.

And now, finally, Albert Neri, alone in his Bronx apartment, was going to put on his police uniform again. He brushed it carefully. Polishing the holster would be next. And his policeman's cap too, the visor had to be cleaned, the stout black shoes shined. Neri worked with a will. He had found his place in the world, Michael Corleone had placed his absolute trust in him, and today he would not fail that trust.

Chapter

31

ON that same day two limousines parked on the Long Beach mall. One of the big cars waited to take Connie Corleone, her mother, her husband and her two children, to the airport. The Carlo Rizzi family was to take a vacation in Las Vegas in preparation for their permanent move to that city. Michael had given Carlo the order, over Connie's protests. Michael had not bothered to explain that he wanted everyone out of the mall before the Corleone-Barzini Families' meeting. Indeed the meeting itself was top secret. The only ones who knew about it were the *capos* of the Family.

The other limousine was for Kay and her children, who were being driven up to New Hampshire for a visit with her parents. Michael would have to stay in the mall; he had affairs too pressing to leave.

The night before Michael had also sent word to Carlo Rizzi that he would require his presence on the mall for a few days, that he could join his wife and children later that week. Connie had been furious. She had tried to get Michael on the phone, but he had gone into the city. Now her eyes were searching the mall for him, but he was closeted with Tom Hagen and not to be disturbed. Connie kissed Carlo good-bye when he put her in the limousine. "If you don't come out there in two days, I'll come back to get you," she threatened him.

He gave her a polite husbandly smile of sexual complicity. "I'll be there," he said.

She hung out the window. "What do you think Michael wants you for?" she asked. Her worried frown made her look old and unattractive.

Carlo shrugged. "He's been promising me a big deal. Maybe that's what he wants to talk about. That's what he hinted anyway." Carlo did not know of the meeting scheduled with the Barzini Family for that night.

Connie said eagerly, "Really, Carlo?"

Carlo nodded at her reassuringly. The limousine moved off through the gates of the mall.

It was only after the first limousine had left that Michael appeared to say good-bye to Kay and his own two children. Carlo also came over and wished Kay a good trip and a good vacation. Finally the second limousine pulled away and went through the gate.

Michael said, "I'm sorry I had to keep you here, Carlo. It won't be more than a couple of days."

Carlo said quickly, "I don't mind at all."

"Good," Michael said. "Just stay by your phone and I'll call you when I'm ready for you. I have to get some other dope before. OK?"

"Sure, Mike, sure," Carlo said. He went into his own house, made a phone call to the mistress he was discreetly keeping in Westbury, promising he would try to get to her late that night. Then he got set with a bottle of rye and waited. He waited a long time. Cars started coming through the gate shortly after noontime. He saw Clemenza get out of one, and then a little later Tessio came out of another. Both of them were admitted to Michael's house by one of the bodyguards. Clemenza left after a few hours, but Tessio did not reappear.

Carlo took a breath of fresh air around the mall, not more than ten minutes. He was familiar with all the guards who pulled duty on the mall, was even friendly with some of them. He thought he might gossip a bit to pass the time. But to his surprise none of the guards today were men he knew. They were all strangers to him. Even more surprising, the man in charge at the gate was Rocco Lampone, and Carlo knew that Rocco was of too high a rank in the Family to be pulling such menial duty unless something extraordinary was afoot.

Rocco gave him a friendly smile and hello. Carlo was wary. Rocco said, "Hey, I thought you were going on vacation with the Don?"

Carlo shrugged. "Mike wanted me to stick around for a couple of days. He has something for me to do."

"Yeah," Rocco Lampone said. "Me too. Then he tells me to keep a check on the gate. Well, what the hell, he's the boss." His tone implied that Michael was not the man his father was; a bit derogatory.

Carlo ignored the tone. "Mike knows what he's doing," he said. Rocco accepted the rebuke in silence. Carlo said so long and walked back to the house. Something was up, but Rocco didn't know what it was.

Michael stood in the window of his living room and watched Carlo strolling around the mall. Hagen brought him a drink, strong brandy. Michael sipped at it gratefully. Behind him, Hagen said, gently, "Mike, you have to start moving. It's time."

Michael sighed. "I wish it weren't so soon. I wish the old man had lasted a little longer."

"Nothing will go wrong," Hagen said. "If I didn't tumble, then nobody did. You set it up real good."

Michael turned away from the window. "The old man planned a lot of it. I never realized how smart he was. But I guess you know."

"Nobody like him." Hagen said. "But this is beautiful. This is the best. So you can't be too bad either."

"Let's see what happens," Michael said. "Are Tessio and Clemenza on the mall?"

Hagen nodded. Michael finished the brandy in his glass. "Send Clemenza in to me. I'll instruct him personally. I don't want to see Tessio at all. Just tell him I'll be ready to go to the Barzini meeting with him in about a half hour. Clemenza's people will take care of him after that."

Hagen said in a noncommittal voice, "There's no way to let Tessio off the hook?"

"No way," Michael said.

Upstate in the city of Buffalo, a small pizza parlor on a side street was doing a rush trade. As the lunch hours passed, business finally slackened off and the counterman took his round tin tray with its few leftover slices out of the window and put it on the shelf of the huge brick oven. He peeked into the oven at a pie baking there. The cheese had not yet started to bubble. When he turned back to the counter that enabled him to serve people in the street, there was a young, tough-looking man standing there. The man said, "Gimme a slice."

The pizza counterman took his wooden shovel and scooped one of the cold slices into the oven to warm it up. The customer, instead of waiting outside, decided to come through the door and be served. The store was empty now. The counterman opened the oven and took out the hot slice and served it on a paper plate. But the customer, instead of giving the money for it, was staring at him intently.

"I hear you got a great tattoo on your chest," the customer said. "I can see the top of it over your shirt, how about letting me see the rest of it?"

The counterman froze. He seemed to be paralyzed.

"Open your shirt," the customer said.

The counterman shook his head. "I got no tattoo," he said in heavily accented English. "That's the man who works at night."

The customer laughed. It was an unpleasant laugh, harsh, strained. "Come on, unbutton your shirt, let me see."

The counterman started backing toward the rear of the store, aiming to edge around the huge oven. But the customer raised his hand above the counter. There was a gun in it. He fired. The bullet caught the counterman in the chest and hurled him against the oven. The customer fired into his body again and the counterman slumped to the floor. The customer came around the serving shelf, reached down and ripped the buttons off the shirt. The chest was covered with blood, but the tattoo was visible, the intertwined lovers and the knife transfixing them. The counterman raised one of his arms feebly as if to protect himself. The gunman said, "Fabrizzio, Michael Corleone sends you his regards." He extended the gun so that it was only a few inches from the counterman's skull and pulled the trigger. Then he walked out of the store. At the curb a car was waiting for him with its door open. He jumped in and the car sped off.

Rocco Lampone answered the phone installed on one of the iron pillars of the gate. He heard someone saying, "Your package is ready," and the click as the caller hung up. Rocco got into his car and drove out of the mall. He crossed the Jones Beach Causeway, the same causeway on which Sonny Corleone had been killed, and drove out to the railroad station of Wantagh. He parked his car there. Another car was waiting for him with two men in it. They drove to a motel ten minutes farther out on Sunrise Highway and turned into its courtyard. Rocco Lampone, leaving his two men in the car, went to one of the little chalet-type bungalows. One kick sent its door flying off its hinges and Rocco sprang into the room.

Phillip Tattaglia, seventy years old and naked as a baby, stood over a bed on which lay a young girl. Phillip Tattaglia's thick head of hair was jet black, but the plumage of his crotch was steel gray. His body had the soft plumpness of a bird. Rocco pumped four bullets into him, all in the belly. Then he turned and ran back to the car. The two men dropped him off in the Wantagh station. He picked up his car and drove back to the mall. He went in to see Michael Corleone for a moment and then came out and took up his position at the gate.

Albert Neri, alone in his apartment, finished getting his uniform ready. Slowly he put it on, trousers, shirt, tie and jacket, holster and gunbelt. He had turned in his gun when he was suspended from the force, but, through some administrative oversight they had not made him give up his shield. Clemenza had supplied him with a new .38 Police Special that could not be traced. Neri broke it down, oiled it, checked the hammer, put it together again, clicked the trigger. He loaded the cylinders and was set to go.

He put the policeman's cap in a heavy paper bag and then put a civilian overcoat on to cover his uniform. He checked his watch. Fifteen minutes before the car would be waiting for him downstairs. He spent the fifteen minutes checking himself in the mirror. There was no question. He looked like a real cop.

The car was waiting with two of Rocco Lampone's men in front. Neri got into the back seat. As the car started downtown, after they had left the neighborhood of his apartment, he shrugged off the civilian overcoat and left it on the floor of the car. He ripped open the paper bag and put the police officer's cap on his head.

At 55th Street and Fifth Avenue the car pulled over to the curb and Neri got out. He started walking down the avenue. He had a queer feeling being back in uniform, patrolling the streets as he had done so many times. There were crowds of people. He walked downtown until he was in front of Rockefeller Center, across the way from St. Patrick's Cathedral. On his side of Fifth Avenue he spotted the limousine he was looking for. It was parked, nakedly alone between a whole string of red NO PARKING and NO STANDING signs. Neri slowed his pace. He was too early. He stopped to write something in his summons book and then kept walking. He was abreast of the limousine. He tapped its fender with his nightstick. The driver looked up in surprise. Neri pointed to the NO STANDING sign with his stick and motioned the driver to move his car. The driver turned his head away.

Neri walked out into the street so that he was standing by the driver's open window. The driver was a tough-looking hood, just the kind he loved to break up. Neri said with deliberate insultingness, "OK, wise guy, you want me to stick a summons up your ass or do you wanta get moving?"

The driver said impassively, "You better check with your precinct. Just give me the ticket if it'll make you feel happy."

"Get the hell out of here," Neri said, "or I'll drag you out of that car and break your ass."

The driver made a ten-dollar bill appear by some sort of magic, folded it into a little square using just one hand, and tried to shove it inside Neri's blouse. Neri moved back onto the sidewalk and crooked his finger at the driver. The driver came out of the car.

"Let me see your license and registration," Neri said. He had been hoping to get the driver to go around the block but there was no hope for that now. Out of the corner of his eye, Neri saw three short, heavyset men coming down the steps of the Plaza building, coming down toward the street. It was Barzini himself and his two bodyguards, on their way to meet Michael Corleone. Even as he saw this, one of the bodyguards peeled off to come ahead and see what was wrong with Barzini's car.

This man asked the driver, "What's up?"

The driver said curtly, "I'm getting a ticket, no sweat. This guy must be new in the precinct."

At that moment Barzini came up with his other bodyguard. He growled, "What the hell is wrong now?"

Neri finished writing in his summons book and gave the driver back his registration and license. Then he put his summons book back in his hip pocket and with the forward motion of his hand drew the .38 Special.

He put three bullets in Barzini's barrel chest before the other three men unfroze enough to dive for cover. By that time Neri had darted into the crowd and around the corner where the car was waiting for him. The car sped up to Ninth Avenue and turned downtown. Near Chelsea Park, Neri, who had discarded the cap and put on the overcoat and changed clothing, transferred to another car that was waiting for him. He had left the gun and the police uniform in the other car. It would be gotten rid of. An hour later he was safely in the mall on Long Beach and talking to Michael Corleone.

Tessio was waiting in the kitchen of the old Don's house and was sipping at a cup of coffee when Tom Hagen came for him. "Mike is ready for you now," Hagen said. "You better make your call to Barzini and tell him to start on his way."

Tessio rose and went to the wall phone. He dialed Barzini's office in New York and said curtly, "We're on our way to Brooklyn." He hung up and smiled at Hagen. "I hope Mike can get us a good deal tonight."

Hagen said gravely, "I'm sure he will." He escorted Tessio out of the kitchen and onto the mall. They walked toward Michael's house. At the door they were stopped by one of the bodyguards. "The boss says he'll come in a separate car. He says for you two to go on ahead."

Tessio frowned and turned to Hagen. "Hell, he can't do that; that screws up all my arrangements."

At that moment three more bodyguards materialized around them. Hagen said gently, "I can't go with you either, Tessio."

The ferret-faced *caporegime* understood everything in a flash of a second. And accepted it. There was a moment of physical weakness, and then he recovered. He said to Hagen, "Tell Mike it was business, I always liked him."

Hagen nodded. "He understands that."

Tessio paused for a moment and then said softly, "Tom, can you get me off the hook? For old times' sake?"

Hagen shook his head. "I can't," he said.

He watched Tessio being surrounded by bodyguards and led into a waiting car. He felt a little sick. Tessio had been the best soldier in the Corleone Family; the old Don had relied on him more than any other man with the exception of Luca Brasi. It was too bad that so intelligent a man had made such a fatal error in judgment so late in life.

Carlo Rizzi, still waiting for his interview with Michael, became jittery with all the arrivals and departures. Obviously something big was going on and it looked as if he were going to be left out. Impatiently he called Michael on the phone. One of the house bodyguards answered, went to get Michael, and came back with the message that Michael wanted him to sit tight, that he would get to him soon.

Carlo called up his mistress again and told her he was sure he would be able to take her to a late supper and spend the night. Michael had said he would call him soon, whatever he had planned couldn't take more than an hour or two. Then it would take him about forty minutes to drive to Westbury. It could be done. He promised her he would do it and sweet-talked her into not being sore. When he hung up he decided to get properly dressed so as to save time afterward. He had just slipped into a fresh shirt when there was a knock on the door. He reasoned quickly that Mike had tried to get him on the phone and had kept getting a busy signal so had simply sent a messenger to call him. Carlo went to the door and opened it. He felt his whole body go weak with a terrible sickening fear. Standing in the doorway was Michael Corleone, his face the face of that death Carlo Rizzi saw often in his dreams.

Behind Michael Corleone were Hagen and Rocco Lampone. They looked grave, like people who had come with the utmost reluctance to give a friend bad news. The three of them entered the house and Carlo Rizzi led them into the living room. Recovered from his first shock, he thought that he had suffered an attack of nerves. Michael's words made him really sick, physically nauseous.

"You have to answer for Santino," Michael said.

Carlo didn't answer, pretended not to understand. Hagen and Lampone had split away to opposite walls of the room. He and Michael faced each other.

"You fingered Sonny for the Barzini people," Michael said, his voice flat. "That little farce you played out with my sister, did Barzini kid you that would fool a Corleone?"

Carlo Rizzi spoke out of his terrible fear, without dignity, without any kind of pride. "I swear I'm innocent. I swear on the head of my children I'm innocent. Mike, don't do this to me, please, Mike, don't do this to me."

Michael said quietly, "Barzini is dead. So is Phillip Tattaglia. I want to square all the Family accounts tonight. So don't tell me you're innocent. It would be better for you to admit what you did."

Hagen and Lampone stared at Michael with astonishment. They were thinking that Michael was not yet the man his father was. Why try to get this traitor to admit guilt? That guilt was already proven as much as such a thing could be proven. The answer was obvious.

Michael still was not that confident of his right, still feared being unjust, still worried about that fraction of an uncertainty that only a confession by Carlo Rizzi could erase.

There was still no answer. Michael said almost kindly, "Don't be so frightened. Do you think I'd make my sister a widow? Do you think I'd make my nephews fatherless? After all I'm Godfather to one of your kids. No, your punishment will be that you won't be allowed any work with the Family. I'm putting you on a plane to Vegas to join your wife and kids and then I want you to stay there. I'll send Connie an allowance. That's all. But don't keep saying you're innocent, don't insult my intelligence and make me angry. Who approached you, Tattaglia or Barzini?"

Carlo Rizzi in his anguished hope for life, in the sweet flooding relief that he was not going to be killed, murmured, "Barzini."

"Good, good," Michael said softly. He beckoned with his right hand. "I want you to leave now. There's a car waiting to take you to the airport."

Carlo went out the door first, the other three men very close to him. It was night now, but the mall as usual was bright with floodlights. A car pulled up. Carlo saw it was his own car. He didn't recognize the driver. There was someone sitting in the back but on the far side. Lampone opened the front door and motioned to Carlo to get in. Michael said, "I'll call your wife and tell her you're on your way down." Carlo got into the car. His silk shirt was soaked with sweat.

The car pulled away, moving swiftly toward the gate. Carlo started to turn his head to see if he knew the man sitting behind him. At that moment, Clemenza, as cunningly and daintily as a little girl slipping a ribbon over the head of a kitten, threw his garrot around Carlo Rizzi's neck. The smooth rope cut into the skin with Clemenza's powerful yanking throttle, Carlo Rizzi's body went leaping into the air like a fish on a line, but Clemenza held him fast, tightening the garrot until the body went slack. Suddenly there was a foul odor in the air of the car. Carlo's body, sphincter released by approaching death, had voided itself. Clemenza kept the garrot tight for another few minutes to make sure, then released the rope and put it back in his pocket. He relaxed himself against the seat cushions as Carlo's body slumped against the door. After a few moments Clemenza rolled the window down to let out the stink.

The victory of the Corleone Family was complete. During that same twenty-four-hour period Clemenza and Lampone turned loose their *regimes* and punished the infiltrators of the Corleone domains. Neri was sent to take command of the Tessio *regime*. Barzini book-makers were put out of business; two of the highest-ranking Barzini enforcers were shot to death as they were peaceably picking their teeth over dinner in an Italian restaurant on Mulberry Street. A notorious fixer of trotting races was also killed as he returned home from a winning night at the track. Two of the biggest shylocks on the waterfront disappeared, to be found months later in the New Jersey swamps.

With this one savage attack, Michael Corleone made his reputation and restored the Corleone Family to its primary place in the New York Families. He was respected not only for his tactical brilliance but because some of the most important *caporegimes* in both the Barzini and Tattaglia Families immediately went over to his side.

It would have been a perfect triumph for Michael Corleone except for an exhibition of hysteria by his sister Connie.

Connie had flown home with her mother, the children left in Vegas. She had restrained her widow's grief until the limousine pulled into the mall. Then, before she could be restrained by her mother, she ran across the cobbled street to Michael Corleone's house. She burst through the door and found Michael and Kay in the living room. Kay started to go to her, to comfort her and take her in her arms in a sisterly embrace but stopped short when Connie started screaming at her brother, screaming curses and reproaches. "You lousy bastard," she shrieked. "You killed my husband. You waited until our father died and nobody could stop you and you killed him. You killed him. You blamed him about Sonny, you always did, everybody did. But you never thought about me. You never gave a damn about me. What am I going to do now, what am I going to do?" She was wailing. Two of Michael's bodyguards had come up behind her and were waiting for orders from him. But he just stood there impassively and waited for his sister to finish.

Kay said in a shocked voice, "Connie, you're upset, don't say such things."

Connie had recovered from her hysteria. Her voice held a deadly venom. "Why do you think he was always so cold to me? Why do you think he kept Carlo here on the mall? All the time he knew he was going to kill my husband. But he didn't dare while my father was alive. My father would have stopped him. He knew that. He was just waiting. And then he stood Godfather to our child just to throw us off the track. The coldhearted bastard. You think you know your husband? Do you know how many men he had killed with my Carlo? Just read the papers. Barzini and Tattaglia and the others. My brother had them killed."

She had worked herself into hysteria again. She tried to spit in Michael's face but she had no saliva.

"Get her home and get her a doctor," Michael said. The two guards immediately grabbed Connie's arms and pulled her out of the house.

Kay was still shocked, still horrified. She said to her husband, "What made her say all those things, Michael, what makes her believe that?"

Michael shrugged. "She's hysterical."

Kay looked into his eyes. "Michael, it's not true, please say it's not true."

Michael shook his head wearily. "Of course it's not. Just believe me, this one time I'm letting you ask about my affairs, and I'm giving you an answer. It is not true." He had never been more convincing. He looked directly into her eyes. He was using all the mutual trust they had built up in their married life to make her believe him. And she could not doubt any longer. She smiled at him ruefully and came into his arms for a kiss.

"We both need a drink," she said. She went into the kitchen for ice and while there heard the front door open. She went out of the kitchen and saw Clemenza, Neri and Rocco Lampone come in with the bodyguards. Michael had his back to her, but she moved so that she could see him in profile. At that moment Clemenza addressed her husband, greeting him formally.

"Don Michael," Clemenza said.

Kay could see how Michael stood to receive their homage. He reminded her of statues in Rome, statues of those Roman emperors of antiquity, who, by divine right, held the power of life and death over their fellow men. One hand was on his hip, the profile of his face showed a cold proud power, his body was carelessly, arrogantly at ease, weight resting on one foot slightly behind the other. The caporegimes stood before him. In that moment Kay knew that everything Connie had accused Michael of was true. She went back into the kitchen and wept.

Book IX

Chapter

⬥⬥⬥⬥⬥⬥⬥⬥⬥⬥⬥⬥⬥⬥⬥⬥⬥⬥

32

THE bloody victory of the Corleone Family was not complete until a year of delicate political maneuvering established Michael Corleone as the most powerful Family chief in the United States. For twelve months, Michael divided his time equally between his headquarters at the Long Beach mall and his new home in Las Vegas. But at the end of that year he decided to close out the New York operation and sell the houses and the mall property. For that purpose he brought his whole family East on a last visit. They would stay a month, wind up business, Kay would do the personal family's packing and shipping of household goods. There were a million other minor details.

Now the Corleone Family was unchallengeable, and Clemenza had his own Family. Rocco Lampone was the Corleone *caporegime*. In Nevada, Albert Neri was head of all security for the Family-controlled hotels. Hagen too, was part of Michael's Western Family.

Time helped heal the old wounds. Connie Corleone was reconciled to her brother Michael. Indeed not more than a week after her terrible accusations she apologized to Michael for what she had said and assured Kay that there had been no truth in her words, that it had been only a young widow's hysteria.

Connie Corleone easily found a new husband; in fact, she did not wait the year of respect before filling her bed again with a fine young fellow who had come to work for the Corleone Family as a male secretary. A boy from a reliable Italian family but graduated from the top business college in America. Naturally his marriage to the sister of the Don made his future assured.

Kay Adams Corleone had delighted her in-laws by taking instruction in the Catholic religion and joining that faith. Her two boys were also, naturally, being brought up in that church, as was required. Michael himself had not been too pleased by this development. He would have preferred the children to be Protestant, it was more American.

To her surprise, Kay came to love living in Nevada. She loved the scenery, the hills and canyons of garishly red rock, the burning deserts, the unexpected and blessedly refreshing lakes, even the heat. Her two boys rode their own ponies. She had real servants, not bodyguards. And Michael lived a more normal life. He owned a construction business; he joined the businessmen's clubs and civic committees; he had a healthy interest in local politics without interfering publicly. It was a good life. Kay was happy that they were closing down their New York house and that Las Vegas would be truly their permanent home. She hated coming back to New York. And so on this last trip she had arranged all the packing and shipping of goods with the utmost efficiency and speed, and now on the final day she felt that same urgency to leave that longtime patients feel when it is time to be discharged from the hospital.

On that final day, Kay Adams Corleone woke at dawn. She could hear the roar of the truck motors outside on the mall. The trucks that would empty all the houses of furniture. The Corleone Family would be flying back to Las Vegas in the afternoon, including Mama Corleone.

When Kay came out of the bathroom, Michael was propped up on his pillow smoking a cigarette. "Why the hell do you have to go to church *every* morning?" he said. "I don't mind Sundays, but why the hell during the week? You're as bad as my mother." He reached over in the darkness and switched on the tablelight.

Kay sat at the edge of the bed to pull on her stockings. "You know how converted Catholics are," she said. "They take it more seriously."

Michael reached over to touch her thigh, on the warm skin where the top of her nylon hose ended. "Don't," she said. "I'm taking Communion this morning."

He didn't try to hold her when she got up from the bed. He said, smiling slightly, "If you're such a strict Catholic, how come you let the kids duck going to church so much?"

She felt uncomfortable and she was wary. He was studying her with what she thought of privately as his "Don's" eye. "They have plenty of time," she said. "When we get back home, I'll make them attend more."

She kissed him good-bye before she left. Outside the house the air was already getting warm. The summer sun rising in the east was red. Kay walked to where her car was parked near the gates of the mall. Mama Corleone, dressed in her widow black, was already sitting in it, waiting for her. It had become a set routine, early Mass, every morning, together.

Kay kissed the old woman's wrinkled cheek, then got behind the wheel. Mama Corleone asked suspiciously, "You eata breakfast?"

"No," Kay said.

The old woman nodded her head approvingly. Kay had once forgotten that it was forbidden to take food from midnight on before receiving Holy Communion. That had been a long time ago, but Mama Corleone never trusted her after that and always checked. "You feel all right?" the old woman asked.

"Yes," Kay said.

The church was small and desolate in the early morning sunlight. Its stained-glass windows shielded the interior from heat, it would be cool there, a place to rest. Kay helped her mother-in-law up the white stone steps and then let her go before her. The old woman preferred a pew up front, close to the altar. Kay waited on the steps for an extra minute. She was always reluctant at this last moment, always a little fearful.

Finally she entered the cool darkness. She took the holy water on her fingertips and made the sign of the cross, fleetingly touched her wet fingertips to her parched lips. Candles flickered redly before the saints, the Christ on his cross. Kay genuflected before entering her row and then knelt on the hard wooden rail of the pew to wait for her call to Communion. She bowed her head as if she were praying, but she was not quite ready for that.

It was only here in these dim, vaulted churches that she allowed herself to think about her husband's other life. About that terrible night a year ago when he had deliberately used all their trust and love in each other to make her believe his lie that he had not killed his sister's husband.

She had left him because of that lie, not because of the deed. The next morning she had taken the children away with her to her parents' house in New Hampshire. Without a word to anyone, without really knowing what action she meant to take. Michael had immediately understood. He had called her the first day and then left her alone. It was a week before the limousine from New York pulled up in front of her house with Tom Hagen.

She had spent a long terrible afternoon with Tom Hagen, the most terrible afternoon of her life. They had gone for a walk in the woods outside her little town and Hagen had not been gentle.

Kay had made the mistake of trying to be cruelly flippant, a role to which she was not suited. "Did Mike send you up here to threaten me?" she asked. "I expected to see some of the 'boys' get out of the car with their machine guns to make me go back."

For the first time since she had known him, she saw Hagen angry. He said harshly, "That's the worst kind of juvenile crap I've ever heard. I never expected that from a woman like you. Come on, Kay."

"All right," she said.

They walked along the green country road. Hagen asked quietly, "Why did you run away?"

Kay said, "Because Michael lied to me. Because he made a fool of me when he stood Godfather to Connie's boy. He betrayed me. I can't love a man like that. I can't live with it. I can't let him be father to my children."

"I don't know what you're talking about," Hagen said.

She turned on him with now-justified rage. "I mean that he killed his sister's husband. Do you understand that?" She paused for a moment. "And he lied to me."

They walked on for a long time in silence. Finally Hagen said, "You have no way of really knowing that's all true. But just for the sake of argument let's assume that it's true. I'm not saying it is, remember. But what if I gave you what might be some justification for what he did. Or rather some possible justifications?"

Kay looked at him scornfully. "That's the first time I've seen the lawyer side of you, Tom. It's not your best side."

Hagen grinned. "OK. Just hear me out. What if Carlo had put Sonny on the spot, fingered him. What if Carlo beating up Connie that time was a deliberate plot to get Sonny out in the open, that they knew he would take the route over the Jones Beach Causeway? What if Carlo had been paid to help get Sonny killed? Then what?"

Kay didn't answer. Hagen went on. "And what if the Don, a great man, couldn't bring himself to do what he had to do, avenge his son's death by killing his daughter's husband? What if that, finally, was too much for him, and he made Michael his successor, knowing that Michael would take that load off his shoulders, would take that guilt?"

"It was all over with," Kay said, tears springing into her eyes. "Everybody was happy. Why couldn't Carlo be forgiven? Why couldn't everything go on and everybody forget?"

She had led across a meadow to a tree-shaded brook. Hagen sank down on the grass and sighed. He looked around, sighed again and said, "In this world you could do it."

Kay said. "He's not the man I married."

Hagen laughed shortly. "If he were, he'd be dead now. You'd be a widow now. You'd have no problem."

Kay blazed out at him. "What the hell does that mean? Come on, Tom, speak out straight once in your life. I know Michael can't, but you're not Sicilian, you can tell a woman the truth, you can treat her like an equal, a fellow human being."

There was another long silence. Hagen shook his head. "You've got Mike wrong. You're mad because he lied to you. Well, he warned you never to ask him about business. You're mad because he was Godfather to Carlo's boy. But you made him do that. Actually it was the right move for him to make if he was going to take action against Carlo. The classical tactical move to win the victim's trust." Hagen gave her a grim smile. "Is that straight enough talk for you?" But Kay had bowed her head.

Hagen went on. "I'll give you some more straight talk. After the Don died, Mike was set up to be killed. Do you know who set him up? Tessio, So Tessio had to be killed. Carlo had to be killed. Because treachery can't be forgiven. Michael could have forgiven it, but people never forgive themselves and so they would always be dangerous. Michael really liked Tessio. He loves his sister. But he would be shirking his duty to you and his children, to his whole family, to me and my family, if he let Tessio and Carlo go free. They would have been a danger to us all, all our lives."

Kay had been listening to this with tears running down her face. "Is that what Michael sent you up here to tell me?"

Hagen looked at her in genuine surprise. "No," he said. "He told me to tell you you could have everything you want and do everything you want as long as you take good care of the kids." Hagen smiled. "He said to tell you that you're his Don. That's just a joke."

Kay put her hand on Hagen's arm. "He didn't order you to tell me all the other things?"

Hagen hesitated a moment as if debating whether to tell her a final truth. "You still don't understand," he said. "If you told Michael what I've told you today, I'm a dead man." He paused again. "You and the children are the only people on this earth he couldn't harm."

It was a long five minutes after that Kay rose from the grass and they started walking back to the house. When they were almost there, Kay said to Hagen, "After supper, can you drive me and the kids to New York in your car?"

"That's what I came for," Hagen said.

A week after she returned to Michael she went to a priest for instruction to become a Catholic.

From the innermost recess of the church the bell tolled for repentance. As she had been taught to do, Kay struck her breast lightly with her clenched hand, the stroke of repentance. The bell tolled again and there was the shuffling of feet as the communicants left their seats to go to the altar rail. Kay rose to join them. She knelt at the altar and from the depths of the church the bell tolled again. With her closed hand she struck her heart once more. The priest was before her. She tilted back her head and opened her mouth to receive the papery thin wafer. This was the most terrible moment of all. Until it melted away and she could swallow and she could do what she came to do.

Washed clean of sin, a favored supplicant, she bowed her head and folded her hands over the altar rail. She shifted her body to make her weight less punishing to her knees.

She emptied her mind of all thought of herself, of her children, of all anger, of all rebellion, of all questions. Then with a profound and deeply willed desire to believe, to be heard, as she had done every day since the murder of Carlo Rizzi, she said the necessary prayers for the soul of Michael Corleone.

MARIO
PUZO

THE
LAST
DON

For

Virginia Altman
Domenick Cleri

PROLOGUE

Quogue
1965

ON PALM SUNDAY, one year after the Great War against the Santadio, Don Domenico Clericuzio celebrated the christening of two infants of his own blood and made the most important decision of his life. He invited the greatest Family chiefs in America, as well as Alfred Gronevelt, the owner of the Xanadu Hotel in Vegas, and David Redfellow, who had built up a vast drug empire in the United States. All his partners to some degree.

Now the most powerful Mafia Family head in America, Don Clericuzio planned to relinquish that power, on the surface. It was time to play a different hand; obvious power was too dangerous. But the relinquishing of power was dangerous in itself. He had to do it with the most skillful benignity and with personal goodwill. And he had to do it on his own base.

The Clericuzio estate in Quogue comprised twenty acres surrounded by a ten-foot-high redbrick wall armed by barbed wire and electronic sensors. It held, besides the mansion, the homes for his three sons as well as twenty small homes for trusted Family retainers.

Before the arrival of the guests, the Don and his sons sat around the white wrought-iron table in the trellised garden at the back of the mansion. The oldest, Giorgio, was tall, with a small, fierce mustache and the lanky frame of an English gentleman, which he adorned with tailored clothes. He was twenty-seven, saturnine, with savage wit and closed face. The Don informed Giorgio that he, Giorgio, would be applying to the Wharton School of Business. There he would learn all the intricacies of stealing money while staying within the law.

Giorgio did not question his father; this was a royal edict, not an invitation to discussion. He nodded obedience.

The Don addressed his nephew, Joseph "Pippi" De Lena, next. The Don loved Pippi as much as he did his sons, for in addition to blood—Pippi being his dead sister's son—Pippi was the great general who had conquered the savage Santadio.

"You will go and live permanently in Vegas," he said. "You will look after our interest in the Xanadu Hotel. Now that our Family is retiring from operations, there will not be much work here to do. However you will remain the Family Hammer."

He saw Pippi was not happy, that he must give reasons. "Your wife, Nalene, cannot live in the atmosphere of the Family, she cannot live in the Bronx Enclave. She is too different. She cannot be accepted by them. You must build your life away from us." Which was all true, but the Don had another reason. Pippi was the great hero general of the Clericuzio Family, and if he continued to be "Mayor" of the Bronx Enclave, he would be too powerful for the sons of the Don when the Don no longer lived.

"You will be my *Bruglione* in the West," he told Pippi. "You will become rich. But there is important work to do."

He handed Pippi the deed to a house in Las Vegas. The Don then turned to his youngest son, Vincent, a man of twenty-five. He was the shortest of the children, but built like a stone door. He was spare in speech, and he had a soft heart. He had learned all the classic peasant Italian dishes at his mother's knee, and it was he who had wept so bitterly at his mother's dying young.

The Don smiled at him. "I am about to decide your destiny," he said, "and set you on your true path. You will open the finest restaurant in New York. Spare no expense. I want you to show the French what real food is all about." Pippi and the other sons laughed, even Vincent smiled. The Don smiled at him. "You will go to the best cooking school in Europe for a year."

Vincent, though pleased, growled, "What can they teach me?"

The Don gave him a stern look. "Your pastries could be better," he said. "But the main purpose is to learn the finances of running such an enterprise. Who knows, someday you may own a chain of restaurants. Giorgio will give you the money."

The Don turned finally to Petie. Petie was the second and the most cheerful of his sons. He was affable, at twenty-six no more than a boy, but the Don knew he was a throwback to the Sicilian Clericuzio.

"Petie," the Don said, "Now that Pippi is in the West, you will be Mayor of the Bronx Enclave. You will supply all the soldiers for the Family. But also, I have bought you a construction company business, a large one. You will repair the skyscrapers of New York, you will build state police barracks, you will pave the city streets. That business is assured but I expect you to make it a great company. Your soldiers can have legitimate employment and you will make a great deal of money. First you will serve an apprenticeship under the man who now owns it. But remember, your primary duty is to supply and command soldiers of the Family." He turned to Giorgio.

"Giorgio," the Don said, "You will be my successor. You and Vinnie will no longer take part in that necessary part of the Family which invites danger, except when it is absolutely necessary. We must look ahead. Your children, my children, and little Dante and Croccifixio must never grow up in this world. We are rich, we no longer have to risk our lives to earn our daily bread. Our Family will now serve only as financial advisors to all the other Families. We will serve as their political support, mediate their quarrels. But to do this we must have cards to play. We must have an army. And we must protect everyone's money, for which they will let us wet our beaks."

He paused. "Twenty, thirty years from now, we will all disappear into the lawful world and enjoy our wealth without fear. Those two infants we are baptizing today will never have to commit our sins and take our risks."

"Then why keep the Bronx Enclave?" Giorgio asked.

"We hope someday to be saints," the Don said, "But not martyrs."

An hour later Don Clericuzio stood on the balcony of his mansion and watched the festivities below.

The huge lawn, carpeted with picnic tables crowned with winglike green umbrellas, was filled with the two hundred guests, many of them soldiers from the Bronx Enclave. Christenings were usually joyful affairs, but this one was subdued.

The victory over the Santadio had cost the Clericuzio dearly. The Don had lost his most dearly beloved son, Silvio. His daughter Rose Marie had lost her husband.

Now he watched the crowds of people mulling around the several long tables filled with crystal urns of deep red wine, bright white tureens of soups, pastas of every kind, platters laden with a variety of sliced meats and cheese, and crispy fresh breads of all sizes and shapes. He allowed himself to be soothed by the soft music of the small band playing in the background.

Directly in the center of the circle of picnic tables, the Don saw the two baby carriages with their blue blankets. How brave the two babies were, they had not flinched when struck with Holy Water. Beside them were the two mothers, Rose Marie and Nalene De Lena, Pippi's wife. He could see the babies' faces, so unmarked by life, Dante Clericuzio and Croccifixio De Lena. He was responsible for ensuring that these two children would never have to suffer to earn a living. If he succeeded, they would enter the regular society of the world. It was curious, he thought, that there was no man in the crowd paying homage to the infants.

He saw Vincent, usually dour with a face like granite, feeding some small children from the hot dog cart he had built for the feast. It resembled the New York street hot dog carts, except that it was bigger, it had a brighter umbrella, and Vincent gave out better food. He wore a clean white apron, and he made his hot dogs with sauerkraut and mustard, with red onions and hot sauce. Each small child had to give him a kiss on the cheek for a hot dog. Vincent was the most tenderhearted of his sons, despite his rough exterior.

On the boccie court, he saw Petie, playing with Pippi De Lena, Virginio Ballazzo, and Alfred Gronevelt. Petie was a practical joker, which the Don disapproved of; it always seemed a dangerous business to him. Even now Petie was disrupting the game with his tricks as one of the boccie balls flew into pieces after the first hit.

Virginio Ballazzo was the Don's underboss, an executive officer in the Clericuzio Family. He was a high-spirited man and was pretending to chase Petie, who was pretending to run. This struck the Don as ironic. He knew his son Petie was a natural-born assassin, and that the playful Ballazzo had a certain reputation in his own right.

But neither of them was a match for Pippi.

The Don could see the women in the crowd glancing at Pippi. Except for the two mothers, Rose Marie and Nalene. He was such a fine-looking man. As tall as the Don himself, a rugged strong body, a brutally handsome face. Many of the men were observing him also, some of them his soldiers from the Bronx Enclave. Observing his air of command, the litheness of his body in action, knowing his legend, *The Hammer,* the best of the "Qualified Men."

David Redfellow, young, rosy-cheeked, the most powerful drug dealer in America, was pinching the cheeks of the two infants in their carriages. Finally, Alfred Gronevelt, still clad in his jacket and tie, was obviously ill at ease at playing a strange game. Gronevelt was the same age as the Don himself, near sixty.

Today Don Clericuzio would change all their lives, he hoped for the better.

Giorgio came to the balcony to summon him to the first meeting of the day. The ten Mafia chiefs were assembling in the den of the house for the meeting. Giorgio had already briefed them as to Don Clericuzio's proposal. The christening was an excellent cover for the meeting, but they had no real social ties with the Clericuzio and wanted to be on their way as soon as possible.

The den of the Clericuzio was a windowless room with heavy furniture and a wet bar. All ten men looked somber as they sat around the large dark marble conference table. They each in turn greeted Don Clericuzio and then waited expectantly to hear what he had to say.

Don Clericuzio summoned his sons, Vincent and Petie, his executive officer, Ballazzo, and Pippi De Lena to join the meeting. When they arrived, Giorgio, cold and sardonic, made a brief introductory remark.

Don Clericuzio surveyed the faces of the men before him, the most powerful men in the illegal society that functioned to supply the solutions to the true needs of the people.

"My son Giorgio has briefed you on how everything will work," he said. "My proposal is this. I retire from all my interests with the exception of gambling. My New York activities I give to my old friend Virginio Ballazzo. He will form his own Family and be independent of the Clericuzio. In the rest of the country I yield all of my interests in the unions, transportation, alcohol, tobacco, and drugs to your Families. All my access to the law will be available. What I ask in return is that you let me handle your earnings. They will be safely held and available to you. You will not have to worry about the Government tracking down the money. For it I ask only a five percent commission."

This was a dream deal for the ten men. They were thankful that the Clericuzio were retreating when the Family could just as well have gone forward to control or destroy their empires.

Vincent walked around the table and poured each of them some wine. The men held their glasses up and toasted the Don's retirement.

After the Mafia dons made their ceremonious farewells, David Redfellow was escorted into the den by Petie. He sat in the leather armchair opposite the Don, and Vincent served him a glass of wine. Redfellow stood out from the other men not only because of his long hair but because he wore a diamond earring and a denim jacket with his clean, pressed jeans. He had Scandinavian blood. He was blond with clear blue eyes and always had a cheerful expression and a casual wit.

The Don owed a great debt of gratitude to David Redfellow. It was he who proved that lawful authorities could be bribed on drugs.

"David," Don Clericuzio said, "You are retiring from the drug business. I have something better for you."

Redfellow did not object. "Why now?" he asked the Don.

"Number one," the Don said, "the government is devoting too much time and trouble to the business. You would have to live with anxiety the rest of your life. More importantly, it has become too dangerous. My son Petie and his soldiers have served as your bodyguards. I can no longer permit that. The Colombians are too wild, too foolhardy, too violent. Let them have the drug business. You will retire to Europe. I will arrange for your protection there. You can keep yourself busy by buying a bank in Italy and you will live in Rome. We will do a lot of business there."

"Great," Redfellow said. "I don't speak Italian and I know nothing of banking."

"You will learn both," Don Clericuzio said. "And you will live a happy life in Rome. Or you can stay here if you wish, but then you will no longer have my support, Petie will no longer guard your life. Choose as you like."

"Who will take over my business?" Redfellow asked. "Do I get a buyout?"

"The Colombians will take over your business," the Don said. "That cannot be prevented, that is the tide of history. But the government will make their life misery. Now, yes or no?"

Redfellow thought it over and then laughed. "Tell me how to get started."

"Giorgio will take you to Rome and introduce you to my people there," the Don said. "And through the years he will advise you."

The Don embraced him. "Thank you for listening to my advice. We will still be partners in Europe and believe me, it will be a good life for you."

When David Redfellow left, the Don sent Giorgio to summon Alfred Gronevelt to the den. As the owner of the Xanadu Hotel in Vegas, Gronevelt had been under the protection of the now defunct Santadio Family.

"Mr. Gronevelt," the Don said. "You will continue to run the Hotel under my protection. You need have no fear for yourself or your property. You will keep your fifty-one percent of the Hotel. I will own the forty-nine percent formerly owned by the Santadio and be represented by the same legal identity. Are you agreeable?"

Gronevelt was a man of great dignity and great physical presence, despite his age. He said carefully, "If I stay, I must run the Hotel with the same authority. Otherwise I will sell you my percentage."

"Sell a gold mine?" the Don said incredulously. "No, no. Don't fear me. I'm a businessman above all. If the Santadio had been more temperate, all those terrible things would never have happened. Now they no longer exist. But you and I are reasonable men. My delegates get the Santadio points. And Joseph De Lena, Pippi, gets all the consideration due him. He will be my *Bruglione* in the West at a salary of one hundred thousand a year paid by your hotel in any manner you see fit. And if you have trouble of any kind with anyone, you go to him. And in your business, you always have trouble."

Gronevelt, a tall, spare man, seemed calm enough. "Why do you favor me? You have other and more profitable options."

Don Domenico said gravely, "Because you are a genius in what you do. Everyone in Las Vegas says so. And to prove my esteem I give you something in return."

Gronevelt smiled at this. "You've given me quite enough. My hotel. What else can be as important?"

The Don beamed at him benevolently, for though he was always a serious man, he delighted in surprising people with his power. "You can name the next appointment to the Nevada Gaming Commission," the Don said. "There is a vacancy."

Gronevelt for one of the few times in his life was surprised, and also impressed. Most of all he was elated, as he saw a future for his hotel that he had not even dreamed of. "If you can do that," Gronevelt said, "we will all be very rich in the coming years."

"It is done," the Don said. "Now you can go out and enjoy yourself."

Gronevelt said, "I'll be getting back to Vegas. I don't think it's wise to let everyone know I'm a guest here."

The Don nodded. "Petie, have someone drive Mr. Gronevelt to New York."

Now, besides the Don, only his sons, Pippi De Lena, and Virginio Ballazzo were left in the room. They looked slightly stunned. Only Giorgio had been his confidant. The others had not known the Don's plans.

Ballazzo was young for a *Bruglione*, only a few years older than Pippi. He had control over unions, garment center transportation, and some drugs. Don Domenico informed him that from now on he was to operate independently of the Clericuzio. He had only to pay a tribute of 10 percent. Otherwise, he had complete control over his operations.

Virginio Ballazzo was overcome by this largesse. He was usually an ebullient man who expressed his thanks or complaints with brio, but now he was too overcome with gratitude to do anything but embrace the Don.

"Of that ten percent, five will be reserved by me for your old age or misfortune," the Don told Ballazzo. "Now forgive me, but people change, they have faulty memories, gratitude for past generosities fades. Let me remind you to be accurate in your accountings." He paused for a moment. "After all, I am not the tax people, I cannot charge you those terrible interests and penalties."

Ballazzo understood. With Don Domenico, punishment was always swift and sure. There was not even a warning. And the punishment was always death. After all, how else could one deal with an enemy?

Don Clericuzio dismissed Ballazzo, but when the Don escorted Pippi to the door, he paused for a moment, then pulled Pippi close to him and whispered in his ear, "Remember, you and I have a secret. You must keep it a secret forever. I never gave you the order."

On the lawn outside the mansion, Rose Marie Clericuzio waited to speak to Pippi De Lena. She was a very young and very pretty widow, but black did not suit her. Mourning for her husband and brother suppressed the natural vivacity so necessary to her particular kind of looks. Her large brown eyes were too dark, her olive skin too sallow. Only her newly baptized blue-ribboned son, Dante, resting in her arms, gave her a splash of color. All through this day she had maintained a curious distance from her father, Don Clericuzio, and her three brothers, Giorgio, Vincent, and Petie. But now she was waiting to confront Pippi De Lena.

They were cousins, Pippi ten years older, and when she was a teenager, she had been madly in love with him. But Pippi was always paternal, always off-putting. Though a man famous for his weakness of the flesh, he had been too prudent to indulge that weakness with the daughter of his Don.

"Hello Pippi," she said. "Congratulations."

Pippi smiled with a charm that made his brutal looks attractive. He bent down to kiss the infant's forehead, noticing with surprise that the hair, which still held the faint smell of incense from the church, was thick for a child so young.

"Dante Clericuzio, a beautiful name," he said.

It was not so innocent a compliment. Rose Marie had taken back her maiden name for herself and her fatherless child. The Don had convinced her to do this with an impeccable logic, but still she felt a certain guilt.

Out of this guilt, Rose Marie said, "How did you convince your Protestant wife to have a Catholic ceremony and such a religious name?"

Pippi smiled at her. "My wife loves me and wants to please me."

And it was true, Rose Marie thought. Pippi's wife loved him because she did not know him. Not as she herself had known him and once loved him. "You named your son Croccifixio," Rose Marie said. "You could have pleased her at least with an American name."

"I named him after your grandfather, to please your father," Pippi said.

"As we all must," Rose Marie said. But her bitterness was masked by her smile, her bones structured in such a way that a smile appeared naturally on her face and gave her an air of sweetness that took the sting out of anything she said. She paused now, faltering. "Thank you for saving my life."

Pippi stared at her blankly for a moment, surprised, slightly apprehensive. Then he said softly, "You were never in any danger," and he put his arm around her shoulder. "Believe me," he said. "Don't think about these things. Forget everything. We have happy lives ahead of us. Just forget the past."

Rose Marie dipped her head to kiss her infant but really to hide her face from Pippi. "I understand everything," she said, knowing that he would repeat the conversation to her father and her brothers. "I have made peace with it." She wanted her family to know that she loved them still and that she was content her infant had been received into the Family, sanctified now by Holy Water, and saved from everlasting Hell.

At that moment Virginio Ballazzo gathered Rose Marie and Pippi up and swept them to the center of the lawn. Don Domenico Clericuzio emerged from the mansion, followed by his three sons.

Men in formal dress, women in gowns, infants in satin, the Clericuzio Family formed a half circle for the photographer. The crowd of guests clapped and shouted congratulations, and the moment was frozen: the moment of peace, of victory, and of love.

Later the picture was enlarged and framed and hung in the Don's study room, next to the last portrait of his son Silvio, killed in the war against the Santadio.

The Don watched the rest of the party festivities from the balcony of his bedroom.

Rose Marie wheeled her baby carriage past the bowlers, and Pippi's wife, Nalene, slim, tall, and elegant, came along the lawn carrying her infant, Croccifixio, in her arms. She put the child in the same carriage with Dante, and the two women gazed down lovingly.

The Don felt a surge of joy that these two infants would grow up sheltered and safe and would never know the price that had been paid for their happy destiny.

Then the Don saw Petie slip a baby bottle of milk into the carriage and everyone laughed as the two babies fought for it. Rose Marie raised her son Dante from the carriage, and the Don remembered her as she was just a few short years before. The Don sighed. There is nothing so beautiful as a woman in love, nor so heartbreaking as when she is made a widow, he thought with regret.

Rose Marie was the child he had most loved, she had been so radiant, so full of cheer. But Rose Marie had changed. The loss of her brother and her husband was too great. Yet, in the Don's experience, true lovers would always love again and widows grew tired of black weeds. And now she had an infant to cherish.

The Don looked back on his life and marveled it had come to such glorious fruition. Certainly he had made monstrous decisions to achieve power and wealth, but he felt little regret. And it all had been necessary and proved correct. Let other men groan over their sins,

Don Clericuzio accepted them and placed his faith in the God he knew would forgive him.

Now Pippi was playing boccie with three soldiers from the Bronx Enclave, men older than him, who had solid business shops in the Enclave, but who were in awe of Pippi. Pippi with his usual high spirits and skill was still the center of attention. He was a legend, he had played boccie against the Santadio.

Pippi was exuberant, shouting with joy when his ball jostled the opposing ball away from the target bowl. What a man Pippi was, the Don thought. A faithful soldier, a warm companion. Strong and quick, cunning and withholding.

His dear friend Virginio Ballazzo had appeared on the boccie court, the only man who could rival Pippi's skill. Ballazzo gave a great flourish as he let his ball go, and there was a loud cheer as he made the successful hit. He raised his hand to the balcony in triumph, and the Don clapped. He felt a sense of pride that such men flowered and prospered under his rule, as had all the people who had gathered together on this Palm Sunday in Quogue. And that his foresight would protect them in the difficult years to come.

What the Don could not foresee were the seeds of evil in as yet unformed human minds.

BOOK I

Hollywood
Las Vegas
1990

CHAPTER 1

BOZ SKANNET'S RED CAP of hair was sprayed by the lemon-colored sunlight of California spring. His taut, muscular body throbbed to enter a great battle. His whole being was elated that his deed would be seen by more than a billion people all over the world.

In the elastic waistband of Skannet's tennis slacks was a small pistol, concealed by the zippered jacket pulled down to his crotch. That white jacket blazed with vertical red lightning bolts. A blue-dotted scarlet bandana bound his hair.

In his right hand he held a huge, silvery Evian bottle. Boz Skannet presented himself perfectly to the showbiz world he was about to enter.

That world was a huge crowd in front of the Dorothy Chandler Pavilion in Los Angeles, a crowd awaiting the arrival of movie stars to the Academy Awards ceremony. Specially erected grandstands held the spectators, the street itself was filled with TV cameras and reporters who would send iconic images all over the world. Tonight people would see their great movie stars in the flesh, shed of their manufactured mythic skins, subject to real-life losing and winning.

Uniformed security guards with shiny brown batons tucked neatly in holsters formed a perimeter to keep the spectators in check.

Boz Skannet didn't worry about them. He was bigger, faster, and tougher than those men, and he had the element of surprise. He was wary of the TV reporters and cameramen who fearlessly staked out territory to intercept the celebrities. But they would be more eager to record than prevent.

A white limousine pulled up to the entrance of the Pavilion, and Skannet saw Athena Aquitane, "the most beautiful woman in the world," according to various magazines. As she emerged, the crowd pressed against the barriers shouting her name. Cameras surrounded her and charged her beauty to the far corners of the earth. She waved.

Skannet vaulted over the grandstand fence. He zigzagged through the traffic barriers, saw the brown shirts of the security guards start to converge, the pattern familiar. They didn't have the right angle. He slipped past them as easily as he had the tacklers on the football field years before. And he arrived at exactly the right second. There was Athena talking into the microphone, head tilted to show her best side to the cameras. Three men were standing beside her. Skannet made sure that the camera had him, and then he threw the liquid from the bottle into Athena Aquitane's face.

He shouted, "Here's some acid, you bitch." Then he looked directly into the camera, his face composed, serious, and dignified. "She deserved it," he said. He was covered by a wave of brown-shirted men with their batons at the ready. He knelt on the ground.

At the last moment Athena Aquitane had seen his face. She heard his shout and turned her head so that the liquid struck her cheek and ear.

A billion TV people saw it all. The lovely face of Athena, the silvery liquid on her cheek, the shock and the horror, the recognition when she saw her attacker; a look of true fear that for a second destroyed all her imperious beauty.

The one billion people around the world watched as the police dragged Skannet off. He looked like a movie star himself as he raised his shackled hands in a victory salute, only to collapse as an enraged police officer, finding the gun in his waistband, gave him a short, terrible blow to the kidney.

Athena Aquitane, still reeling from shock, automatically brushed the liquid from her cheek. She felt no burning. The liquid drops on her hand began to dissolve. People were crashing all around her, to protect her, to carry her away.

She pulled loose and said to them calmly, "It's only water." She licked the drops off her hand to be sure. Then she tried to smile. "Typical of my husband," she said.

Athena, showing the great courage that helped make her a legend, walked quickly into the Pavilion of the Academy Awards. When she won the Oscar for best actress, the audience rose and clapped for what seemed like forever.

In the chilled penthouse suite of the Xanadu Casino Hotel of Las Vegas, the eighty-five-year-old owner lay dying. But on this spring day, he thought he could hear, from sixteen floors below, an ivory ball clacking through red and black slots of roulette wheels, the distant surf of crapshooters hoarsely imploring tumbling dice, the whirring of thousands of slot machines devouring silver coins.

Alfred Gronevelt was as happy as any man could be while dying. He had spent nearly ninety years as a hustler, dilettante pimp, gambler, accessory to murder, political fixer, and finally as the strict but kindly lord of the Xanadu Casino Hotel. For fear of betrayal, he had never fully loved any human being, but he had been kind to many. He felt no regrets. Now, he looked forward to the tiny little treats left in his life. Like his afternoon journey through the Casino.

Croccifixio "Cross" De Lena, his right-hand man for the last five years, came into the bedroom and said, "Ready Alfred?" And Gronevelt smiled at him and nodded.

Cross picked him up and put him in the wheelchair, the nurse tucked the old man in blankets, the male attendant took his post to wheel. The nurse handed Cross a pillbox and opened the door of the penthouse. She would remain behind. Gronevelt could not abide her on these afternoon jaunts.

The wheelchair rolled easily over the false green turf of the penthouse garden and entered the special express elevator that descended the sixteen floors to the Casino.

Gronevelt sat straight in his chair, looking right and left. This was his pleasure, to see men and women who battled against him with the odds forever on his side. The wheelchair made a leisurely tour through the blackjack and roulette area, the baccarat pit, the jungle of crap tables. The gamblers barely noticed the old man in the wheelchair, his alert eyes, the bemused smile on his skeletal face.

Wheelchair gamblers were common in Vegas. They thought fate owed them some debt of luck for their misfortune.

Finally the chair rolled into the coffee shop/dining room. The attendant deposited him at their reserved booth and then retired to another table to await their signal to leave.

Gronevelt could see through the glass wall to the huge swimming pool, the water burning a hot blue in the Nevada sun, young women with small children studding its surface like colored toys. He felt a tiny rush of pleasure that all this was his creation.

"Alfred, eat a little something," Cross De Lena said.

Gronevelt smiled at him. He loved the way Cross looked, the man was so handsome in a way that appealed to both men and women, and he was one of the few people that Gronevelt had almost trusted during his lifetime.

"I love this business," Gronevelt said. "Cross, you'll inherit my points in the Hotel and I know you'll have to deal with our partners in New York. But never leave Xanadu."

Cross patted the old man's hand, all gristle beneath the skin. "I won't," he said.

Gronevelt felt the glass wall baking the sunlight into his blood. "Cross," he said, "I've taught you everything. We've done some hard things, really hard to do. Never look back. You know percentages work in different ways. Do as many good deeds as you can. That pays off too. I'm not talking about falling in love or indulging in hatred. Those are very bad percentage moves."

They sipped coffee together. Gronevelt ate only a flaky strudel pastry. Cross had orange juice with his coffee.

"One thing," Gronevelt said, "Don't ever give a Villa to anyone who doesn't make a million drop. Never forget that. The Villas are legendary. They are very important."

Cross patted Gronevelt's hand, let his hand rest on the old man's. His affection was genuine. In some ways he loved Gronevelt more than his father.

"Don't worry," Cross said. "The Villas are sacred. Anything else?"

Gronevelt's eyes were opaque, cataracts dimming their old fire. "Be careful," he said, "Always be very careful."

"I will," Cross said. And then, to distract the old man from his coming death, he said, "When are you going to tell me about the great Santadio War? You worked with them then. Nobody ever talks about it."

Gronevelt gave an old man's sigh, barely a whisper, almost emotionless. "I know time's getting short," he said. "But I can't talk to you yet. Ask your father."

"I've asked Pippi," Cross said, "But he won't talk."

"What's past is past," Gronevelt said. "Never go back. Not for excuses. Not for justification, not for happiness. You are what you are, the world is what it is."

Back in the penthouse suite, the nurse gave Gronevelt his afternoon bath and took his vital signs. She frowned and Gronevelt said, "It's only the percentages."

That night he slept fitfully, and as dawn broke he told the nurse to help him to the balcony. She settled him in the huge chair and wrapped him in blankets. Then she sat beside him and took his hand to check his pulse. When she tried to take her hand back, Gronevelt continued to hold it. She permitted it and they both watched the sun rise above the desert.

The sun was a red ball that turned the air from blue-black to dark orange. Gronevelt could see the tennis courts, the golf course, the swimming pool, the seven Villas gleaming like Versailles and all flying the Xanadu Hotel flag: forest green field with white doves. And beyond, the desert of endless sand.

I created all this, Gronevelt thought. I built pleasure domes in a wasteland. And I made myself a happy life. Out of nothing. I tried to be as good a man as possible in this world. Should I be judged? His mind wandered back to his childhood, he and his chums, fourteen-year-old philosophers, discussing God and moral values as boys did then.

"If you could have a million dollars by pushing a button and killing a million Chinamen," his chum said triumphantly, as if posing some great, impossible moral riddle, "would you do it?" And after a long discussion they all agreed they would not. Except Gronevelt.

And now he thought, he had been right. Not because of his successful life but because that great riddle could not even be posed anymore. It was no longer a dilemma. You could pose it only one way.

"Would you push the button to kill ten million Chinamen"—why Chinamen?—"for a thousand dollars?" That was now the question.

The world was turning crimson with light, and Gronevelt squeezed his nurse's hand to keep his balance. He could look directly into the sun, his cataracts a shield. He drowsily thought of certain women he had known and loved and certain actions he had taken. And of men he had to defeat pitilessly, and the mercies he had shown. He thought of Cross as a son and pitied him and all of the Santadio and the Clericuzio. And he was happy he was leaving it all behind. After all, was it better to live a happy life or a moral life? And did you have to be a Chinaman to decide?

That last confusion destroyed his mind utterly. The nurse, holding his hand, felt it grow cold, the muscles tense. She leaned over and checked his vital signs. There was no doubt he was no more.

Cross De Lena, heir and successor, arranged the state funeral of Gronevelt. All the luminaries of Las Vegas, all the top gamblers, all of Gronevelt's women friends, all the staff of the Hotel, had to be invited and notified. For Alfred Gronevelt had been the acknowledged genius of gambling in Las Vegas.

He had spurred and contributed funds to build the churches of all denominations, for as he often said, "People who believe in religion and gamble deserve some reward for their faith." He had forbidden the building of slums, he had built first-rate hospitals and top-notch schools. Always, he claimed, as a matter of self-interest. He despised Atlantic City, where under the guidance of the state they pocketed all the money and did nothing for the social infrastructure.

Gronevelt had led the way in convincing the public that gambling was not a sordid vice but a middle-class source of entertainment, as normal as golf or baseball. He had made gambling a respectable industry in America. All of Las Vegas wanted to honor him.

Cross put aside his own personal emotions. He felt a deep sense of loss; there had been a genuine bond of affection between them throughout his whole life. And now Cross owned fifty-one percent of the Hotel Xanadu. Worth at least $500 million.

He knew his life must change. Being so much more powerful and rich, there would have to be more danger. His relationship with Don Clericuzio and his Family would become more delicate, in that he was now their partner in an enormous enterprise.

The first call Cross made was to Quogue, where he spoke to Giorgio, who gave him certain instructions. Giorgio told him that none of the Family would attend the funeral except Pippi. Also, Dante would be on the next flight out to complete the mission already discussed, but he was not to attend the funeral. The fact that Cross now owned half the Hotel was not mentioned.

There was a message from his sister, Claudia, but when he called, he got her answering service. There was another message from Ernest Vail. He liked Vail and was carrying fifty grand of his markers, but Vail would have to wait until after the funeral.

There was also a message from his father, Pippi, who was a lifelong friend of Gronevelt. And whose advice he needed on how to conduct his future life. How would his father react to his new status, his new wealth? That would be as ticklish a problem as dealing with the Clericuzio, who would have to adjust to the fact that their *Bruglione* in the West was so powerful and wealthy in his own right.

That the Don himself would be fair, Cross had no doubt; that his own father would support him was almost a given. But the Don's children, Giorgio, Vincent, and Petie, how would they react, and the grandson, Dante? He and Dante had been enemies since they were baptized together in the Don's private chapel. It was a running joke in the Family.

And now Dante would be arriving in Vegas to do the "job" on Big Tim the Rustler. That bothered Cross because he had a perverse fondness for Big Tim. But his fate had been decided by the Don himself, and Cross worried about how Dante would do the job.

The funeral for Alfred Gronevelt was the grandest ever seen in Las Vegas, a tribute to genius. His body lay in state in the Protestant church his money had built, which combined the grandness of

European cathedrals with brown slanting walls from Native American culture. And with famed Vegas practicality, a huge parking lot, decorated with Native American motifs rather than European religious.

The choir that sang the praises of the Lord and recommended Gronevelt to Heaven was from the university where he had endowed three chairs in the humanities.

Hundreds of mourners who had graduated from college because of scholarships Gronevelt had funded looked truly grieved. Some of the crowd were high rollers who had lost fortunes to the Hotel and seemed mildly cheered that at last they had triumphed over Gronevelt. Women, on their own, some middle-aged, wept silently. There were representatives from the Jewish synagogues and Catholic churches he had helped to build.

It would have been against everything Gronevelt believed in to shut down his casino, but there were those managers and croupiers who were not on the day shift. Even some recipients of the Villas made their appearance and were accorded special respect by Cross and Pippi.

The governor of the state of Nevada, Walter Wavven, attended the funeral, escorted by the mayor. The Strip itself was cordoned off so that the long procession of silver hearses, black limos, and mourners on foot could follow the body to the cemetery and Alfred Gronevelt could pass through, for the last time, the world he had created.

That night the citizen visitors of Vegas gave Gronevelt the final tribute he would have most loved. They gambled with a frenzy that set a new record for the "Drop," except of course for New Year's Eve. They buried their money with his body to show their respect.

At the end of that day, Cross De Lena prepared to begin his new life.

That night, sitting alone in her beach house in the Malibu Colony, Athena Aquitane tried to decide what to do. The breeze from the ocean coming through the open doors made her shiver as she sat on the couch thinking.

It is hard to imagine a world-famous movie star as she was when she was a child. Hard to imagine her going through the process of becoming a woman. A movie star's charisma is so powerful that it seems as if their adult images as heroes, as beauties, had sprung full grown out of the head of Zeus. They never had a history of bed-wetting, never had acne, never had an ugly face to grow out of, never had the shrinking shyness and nerdiness of adolescence, never mas-turbated, never begged for love, never were at the mercy of fate. It was very hard, now, for Athena even to remember such a person.

Athena thought that she had been born as one of the luckiest peo-ple on earth. Everything came to her naturally. She had a wonderful father and mother, who recognized her gifts and nurtured them. They adored her physical beauty but did everything in their power to educate her mind. Her father tutored her in sports, her mother in lit-erature and the arts. She could never remember a time in her child-hood that she had been unhappy. Until she was seventeen years old.

She fell in love with Boz Skannet, who was four years older, a re-gional football star at his college. His family owned the biggest bank in Houston. Boz was almost as handsome as Athena was beautiful, plus he was funny, he was charming, he adored her. Their two per-fect bodies came together like magnets, nerve endings high voltage, flesh all silk and milk. They entered a special heaven and to ensure that this would last forever, they married.

Within a few short months Athena became pregnant, yet with her usual bodily perfection, she gained very little weight; she never felt sick and enjoyed the idea of having a baby. So she continued going to college, studying drama, and playing golf and tennis. Boz could overpower her in tennis, but she beat him easily in golf.

Boz went to work in his father's bank. Once she had the baby, a little girl that she'd named Bethany, Athena continued going to school, since Boz had enough money to hire a nanny and a maid. Marriage made Athena even more hungry for knowledge. She read voraciously, especially plays. She was delighted by Pirandello, dis-mayed by Strindberg; she wept over Tennessee Williams. She grew more vibrant, her intelligence framed her physical beauty by giving it dignity that beauty sometimes does not have. It was not surprising that many men, young and old, fell in love with her. Boz Skannet's friends envied him having such a wife. Athena prided herself in her perfection, until in later years she found that this very perfection irritated many people, including friends and lovers.

Boz joked that it was like a Rolls that he had to park in the street every night. He was intelligent enough to know that his wife was destined for greater things, to know that she was extraordinary. And he could see very clearly that he was fated to lose her, as he had lost his own dreams. There had been no war to prove his courage, though he knew himself to be fearless. He knew he had charm and good looks but no particular talent. He was not interested in amassing a huge fortune.

He was jealous of Athena's gifts, her certainty of her place in her world.

So Boz Skannet went forward to meet his fate. He drank to excess, he seduced his colleague's wives, and at his father's bank, he initiated shady transactions. He became proud of his cunning, as any man does of a newly acquired skill, and used it to hide his growing hatred of his wife. For was it not heroic to hate one so beautiful and perfect as Athena?

Boz's health was extraordinary despite debauch. He clung to it. He worked out in the gym, took boxing lessons. He loved the physicality of the ring, where he could smash his fist into a human face; the cunning of switching from jab to hook; the stoicism of receiving punishment. He loved hunting, the killing of game. He loved the seduction of naïve women, the schematism of romance.

Then with his newfound cunning he thought of a way out. He and Athena would have more children. Four, five, six. That would bring them together again. That would stop her from leaping up and away from him. But by that time Athena could see this for what it was and said no. She said more. "If you want children, have them with the other women you're screwing."

It was the first time that she had spoken coarsely to him. He was not surprised that she knew of his unfaithfulness, he had not attempted to hide it. In fact, that was his cunning. Then it would be he who had driven her away, not she who had left.

Athena observed what was happening to Boz, but she was too young and too intent on her own life to give it the necessary attention. It was only when Boz turned cruel that Athena, at twenty years of age, found the steel in her character, an impatience with stupidity.

Boz started playing those clever games of men who hate women. And it seemed to Athena that he was actually going insane.

He always picked up their dry cleaning on his way home from work, because as he often said, "Honey, your time is more valuable than mine. You have all your special classes in music and drama besides your degree work." He thought she would not detect his spiteful reproach because of the offhand tone of his voice.

One day Boz came home carrying an armload of her dresses while she was taking a bath. He looked down at her, all gold hair and white skin, rounded breasts and buttocks decorated with foamy soap. His voice thick, he said, "How would you like it if I threw this shit right into the tub with you?" But instead, he hung the clothes in the closet, helped her out of the water, and rubbed her dry with rosy pink towels. Then he made love to her. A few weeks later the scene was repeated. But this time he threw the clothes in the water.

One night he threatened to break all the dishes at dinner but did not. A week later, he smashed everything in the kitchen. He always apologized after these instances. Always tried to make love afterward. But now Athena refused him and they slept in separate bedrooms.

Another night at dinner Boz held up his fist and said, "Your face is too perfect. Maybe if I broke your nose, it would have more character, like Marlon Brando."

She ran into the kitchen, and he followed her. She was terribly frightened and picked up a knife. Boz laughed and said, "That's the one thing you can't do." And he was right. He easily took the knife away from her. "I was only kidding," he said. "You're only fault is you have no sense of humor."

Athena, at twenty, could have turned to her parents for help, but she did not, nor did she confide in friends. Instead she carefully thought things out, she trusted her intelligence. She saw that she would never finish college, the situation was too dangerous. She knew the authorities could not protect her. She considered briefly a campaign to make Boz truly love her again so that he would be the old Boz, but now she had such a physical aversion to him that she couldn't stand even the thought of him touching her, and she knew that she would never be able to give a convincing performance of love, though that option appealed to her dramatic sense.

What Boz did that finally forced her hand and made her certain she had to leave didn't have to do with her, it concerned Bethany.

He often tossed their one-year-old daughter into the air playfully and then pretended he was not going to catch her, only doing so with a last-minute lunge. But once he let the infant bounce, accidentally it seemed, on the sofa. And then finally one day he quite deliberately let the little girl fall to the floor. Athena gasped with horror and rushed to pick the baby up, to hold her, to comfort her. She stayed awake all night sitting beside the crib of the infant to be certain she was all right. Bethany had a fearful lump on her head. Boz tearfully apologized and promised he would no longer tease in such a fashion. But Athena had come to a decision.

The next day she cleared out her checking account and her savings account. She made intricate travel arrangements so that her movements could not be followed. Two days later, when Boz came home from work, she and the baby had disappeared.

Six months later Athena surfaced in Los Angeles, without a baby, and started her career. She easily got a mid-level agent and worked in small theater groups. She starred in a play at the Mark Taper Forum that led to small parts in small movies, and then was cast in a supporting role in an A movie. In her next picture she became a Bankable Star, and Boz Skannet reentered her life.

She bought him off for the next three years, but she wasn't surprised by what he did at the Academy. An old trick. This time just a little joke . . . but the next time, that bottle would be full of acid.

"There's a big flap at the Studio," Molly Flanders told Claudia De Lena that morning. "A problem with Athena Aquitane. Because of the attack at the Academy Awards, they're worried she won't go back to work on her picture. And Bantz wants you at the Studio. They want you to talk to Athena."

Claudia had come to Molly's office with Ernest Vail. "I'll call her as soon as we finish here," Claudia said. "She can't be serious."

Molly Flanders was an entertainment lawyer, and in a town of fearsome people she was the most feared litigator in the motion picture business. She absolutely loved fighting in the courtroom, and she nearly always won because she was a great actress and had a superb grasp of the law.

Before getting into entertainment law, she had been the premier defense attorney in the state of California. She had saved twenty murderers from the gas chamber. The worst any of these clients had to suffer was a few years for different degrees of manslaughter. But then her nerves had given way and she had switched to entertainment law. She often said it was less bloody and it had greater and more witty villains.

Now she represented A-picture directors, Bankable Stars, topnotch screenwriters. And on the morning after the Academy Awards, one of her favorite clients, Claudia De Lena, was in her office. With her was her screenwriting partner of the moment, a once famous novelist, Ernest Vail.

Claudia De Lena was an old friend, and though one of the least important of Flanders's clients, the most intimate. So when Claudia asked her to take on Vail, she agreed. Now she regretted it. Vail had come with a problem that even she couldn't solve. Also, he was a man she could feel no affection for, though she usually learned to like even her murder clients. Which made her feel a little guilty about giving him bad news.

"Ernest," she said, "I went over all the contracts, all the legal papers. And there is no point in your continuing to sue LoddStone Studios. The only way you can get the rights back is to croak before your copyright expires. Which means sometime in the next five years."

A decade before, Ernest Vail had been the most famous novelist in America, praised by critics, read by a vast public. One novel had a franchise character LoddStone had exploited. They bought the rights, made the picture, and achieved an enormous success. Two sequels also made a fortune in profit. The Studio had on its drawing board four more sequels. Unfortunately for Vail his first contract had given all the rights to the characters and title to the Studio, on all planets in the universe, in all forms of entertainment, discovered and undiscovered. The standard contract for novelists who had not yet amassed clout in movies.

Ernest Vail was a man who always had a grim, sour expression on his face. For which he had good reason. The critics still acclaimed his books, but the public no longer read them. Also, despite his talent, he had made a mess of his life. During the last twenty years his wife had left, taking their three children with her. On the one book that had become a successful movie, he had made a one-time score, but the Studio would make hundreds of millions over the years.

"Explain that to me," Vail said.

"The contracts are foolproof," Molly said. "The Studio owns your characters. There's only one loophole. Copyright law states that when you die all rights to your works revert to your heirs."

For the first time Vail smiled. "Redemption," he said.

Claudia asked, "What kind of money are we talking about?"

"On a fair deal," Molly said, "five percent of gross. Figure they get five more pictures out of it and they are not disasters, total rentals, a billion worldwide, so we're talking around thirty or forty million." She paused for a moment and smiled sardonically. "If you were dead, I could get your heirs a much better deal. We'd really have a gun to their heads."

Vail said, "Call the people at LoddStone. I want a meeting. I'll convince them that if they don't cut me in, I'll kill myself."

"They won't believe you," Molly said.

"Then I'll do it," Vail said.

"Talk sense," Claudia said amiably. "Ernest, you're only fifty-six years old. That's too young to die for money. For principle, for the good of your country, for love, sure. But not for money."

"I have to provide for my wife and kids," Vail said.

"Your ex-wife," Molly said. "And for Christ's sake, you've been married twice since."

"I'm talking about my real wife," Vail said. "The one who had my kids."

Molly understood why everybody in Hollywood disliked him. She said, "The Studio won't give you what you want. They know you won't kill yourself, and they won't be bluffed by a writer. If you were a Bankable Star, maybe. An A director, maybe. But never a writer. You're just shit in this business. Sorry, Claudia."

Claudia said, "Ernest knows that and I know that. If everybody in this town wasn't scared to death of a blank piece of paper, they'd get rid of us entirely. But can't you do something?"

Molly sighed and put in a call to Eli Marrion. She had enough clout to get through to Bobby Bantz, the president of LoddStone.

Claudia and Vail had a drink together afterward in the Polo Lounge. Vail said reflectively, "Big woman, Molly. Big women are easier to seduce. And they're much nicer in bed than small women. Ever notice?"

Not for the first time Claudia wondered why she was so fond of Vail. Not many people were. But she had loved Vail's novels, still did. "You're full of shit," she said.

Vail said, "I meant big women are sweeter. They bring you breakfast in bed, they do little things for you. Feminine things."

Claudia shrugged.

Vail said, "Big women are good-hearted. One brought me home from a party one night and really didn't know what to do with me. She looked around the bedroom exactly like my mother used to look around her kitchen when there was nothing in the house to eat and she was figuring out how to throw a meal together. She was wondering, how the hell we were going to have a good time with the materials at hand."

They sipped their drinks. As always, Claudia warmed to him when he was so disarming. "You know how Molly and I became friends?" Claudia said. "She was defending some guy who had murdered his girlfriend and she needed some good dialogue for him to use in the courtroom. I wrote the scene just as if it were a movie, and her client got manslaughter. I think I wrote the dialogue and the plot-line for three other cases before we stopped."

"I hate Hollywood," Vail said.

"You just hate Hollywood because LoddStone Studios screwed you on your book," Claudia said.

"Not just that," Vail said. "I'm like one of those old civilizations like the Aztecs, the Chinese empires, the Native American Indians, who were destroyed by a people with more sophisticated technology. I'm a real writer, I write novels to appeal to the mind. That kind of writing is a very backward technology. It can't stand up against movies. Movies have cameras, they have sets, they have music and they have these great faces. How can a writer conjure that up with just words? And movies have narrowed the field of battle. They don't have to conquer the brain, only the heart."

"Fuck you, I'm not a writer," Claudia said. "A screenwriter is not a writer? You just say that because you're not good at it."

Vail patted her on the shoulder. "I'm not putting you down," he said. "I'm not even putting down film as an art. I'm just defining."

"It's a lucky thing I love your books," Claudia said. "It's no wonder nobody out here likes you."

Vail smiled amiably. "No, no," he said. "They don't dislike me. They just have contempt for me. But when my estate gets the rights to my characters back on my death, they'll have respect."

"You're not serious," Claudia said.

"I think I am," Vail said. "It's a very tempting prospect. Suicide. Is it politically incorrect these days?"

"Oh shit," Claudia said. She wrapped her arm around Vail's neck. "The fight is just beginning," she said. "I'm sure they'll listen when I ask for your points. Okay?"

Vail smiled at her. "No hurry," he said. "It will take me at least six months just to figure out how to do myself in. I hate violence."

Claudia realized suddenly that Vail was serious. She was sur-prised at the panic she felt at the thought of his death. It was not that she loved him, though they had been lovers briefly. It was not even that she was fond of him. It was the thought that the beautiful books he had written were to him less powerful than money. That his art could be defeated by such a contemptible foe as money. Out of that panic she said, "If worse comes to worst, we'll go to Vegas and see my brother, Cross. He likes you. He'll do something."

Vail laughed. "He doesn't like me that much."

Claudia said, "He has a good heart. I know my brother."

"No, you don't," Vail said.

Athena had come home from the Dorothy Chandler Pavilion the night of the Academy Awards without celebrating and had gone right to bed. She tossed and turned for hours, but she couldn't sleep. Every muscle in her body felt taut. I won't let him do this again, she thought. Not again. I won't live in terror again.

She made herself a cup of tea and tried to drink it, but when she saw the small tremor in her hand, she became impatient, walked outside, and stood on the balcony looking into the dark night sky. She stood for hours, but her heart still raced in terror.

She dressed. In white shorts and tennis shoes. And as the red sun began to show itself over the horizon, she ran. She ran faster and faster along the beach, trying to stay on the hard wet sand, trying to follow the coastline as the cold water washed over her feet. She had to clear her head. She couldn't let Boz beat her. She had worked too hard and too long. And he would kill her, she never doubted that. But first he would play with her, torment her, finally he would disfigure her, he would make her ugly, thinking it would make her his again. She felt her own fury beating in her throat, and then the cool wind spraying ocean water in her face. No, no!

She thought about the Studio, they'd be frantic, they'd threaten her. But it was money, not her, they were concerned about. She thought about her friend Claudia, how this could have been her big break, and she felt sad. She thought about all the others, but she knew she couldn't afford the luxury of compassion. Boz was crazy, and people who weren't crazy would try to reason with him. He was smart enough to make them think they could win, but she knew better. She couldn't take the chance. She couldn't allow herself to take that chance. . . .

By the time she reached the large black boulders that meant the north beach ended, she was completely out of breath. She sat, trying to slow her heart down. She looked up when she heard the caw of seagulls as they swept down and seemed to glide along the water. Her eyes filled, but she pulled herself back with determination. She swallowed past the lump in her throat. And for the first time in a long time she wished her parents weren't so far away. Some part of her felt like a small child and wished desperately to run home to safety, to someone who could put their arms around her and just make everything better. She smiled at herself then, a crooked, wry smile, remembering when she really believed that was possible. Now, she was so loved by everyone, so admired, so adored . . . and so what? She felt more empty than she thought any human was capable of feeling, more lonely. Sometimes when she found herself passing an ordinary woman with her husband and children, a woman living an ordinary life, she felt such longing. Stop! she told herself. Think. It's up to you. Come up with a plan and carry it through. It's not only your life that depends on you. . . .

It was midmorning before she walked back home. And she walked with her head held high and her eyes staring straight ahead: She knew what she had to do.

Boz Skannet was kept in custody overnight. His lawyer organized a press conference when he was released. Skannet told reporters that he was married to Athena Aquitane, though he had not seen her for ten years, and that what he had done was just a practical joke. The liquid was only water. He predicted that Athena would not press charges, intimating he possessed a terrible secret about her. In this he proved correct. No charges were filed.

That day Athena Aquitane informed LoddStone Studios, the studio making one of the most costly pictures in movie history, that she would not return to work on that film. Because of the attack made on her, she feared for her life.

Without her, the film, a historical epic called *Messalina*, could not be completed. The fifty million dollars invested would be a total loss. It also meant that because of this no major studio would ever dare cast Athena Aquitane in a movie again.

LoddStone Studios released a statement that their star had suffered extreme exhaustion but that in a month she would be recovered enough to resume shooting.

CHAPTER 2

⟐

LODDSTONE STUDIOS WAS the most powerful movie-making entity in Hollywood, but Athena Aquitane's refusal to go back to work was a costly treachery. It was rare that mere "Talent" could deal such a damaging blow, but *Messalina* was the Studio "Locomotive" for the Christmas season, the big picture that would power all the Studio's releases through the long, hard winter.

It happened that the next Sunday was the date of the annual Festival of Brotherhood charity party, held at the Beverly Hills estate of Eli Marrion, major shareholder and chairman of LoddStone Studios.

Far back in the canyons above Beverly Hills, Eli Marrion's huge mansion was a showplace of twenty rooms, but the oddity of it was that it had only one bedchamber. Eli Marrion never liked anyone sleeping in his house. There were guest bungalows, of course, along with two tennis courts and a large swimming pool. Six of the rooms were devoted to his large collection of paintings.

Five hundred of the most eminent people in Hollywood were invited to this charity festival with an admission fee of one thousand dollars per person. There were bars and buffet tents and dancing tents spread over the grounds, and there was a band. But the house itself was off-limits. Toilet facilities were provided by portable units in gaily decorated, wittily designed tents.

The mansion, the guest bungalows, the tennis courts, and the swimming pool were roped off and barred by security men. None of the guests were offended by this, Eli Marrion was too lofty a personage for offense to be taken.

But as guests frolicked on the lawns, gossiping and dancing for an obligatory three hours, Marrion was in the huge conference room of the mansion with a group of people most concerned with the completion of the film *Messalina*.

Eli Marrion dominated this gathering. His body was eighty years old but so cleverly disguised you took it for no more than sixty. His gray hair was perfectly cut and tinted to silver, his dark suit broadened his shoulders, added flesh to his bones, insulated his pipe-thin shanks. Mahogany shoes anchored him to earth. A white shirt was vertically cut with a rose-colored tie that pinked his grayish pallor. But his rule over LoddStone Studios was absolute only when he wanted it to be. There were times when it was more prudent to let mere mortals exercise their free will.

Athena Aquitane's refusal to complete a film in progress was a problem serious enough to command even Marrion's attention. *Messalina*, a hundred-million-dollar production, the studio Locomotive, with video, TV, cable and foreign rights presold to cover the cost, was a golden treasure that was about to sink like an old Spanish galleon, never to be retrieved.

And there was Athena herself. At the age of thirty, a great star, already signed to do another blockbuster for LoddStone. A true Talent, of which there was nothing more valuable. Marrion adored Talent.

But Talent was like dynamite, it could be dangerous and you had to control it. You did that with love, with cajolery in its most abject form, you showered it with worldly goods. You became a father, a mother, a brother, a sister, even a lover. No sacrifice was too great. But there came a time when you could not be weak, when indeed you must be merciless.

So now in this room with Marrion were the people to enforce his will. Bobby Bantz, Skippy Deere, Melo Stuart, and Dita Tommey.

Eli Marrion, facing them in this familiar conference room, twenty million dollars worth of paintings, tables, chairs, and rugs, the crystal goblets and jugs totaling at least a half million more, could feel his bones crumbling within. Each day he was astonished how difficult it was to present himself to the world as the all-powerful figure he was presumed to be.

Mornings were no longer refreshing, it was fatiguing to shave, to knot his tie, to button the buttons on his shirt. More dangerous was the mental weakness. This took the form of pity for people less powerful than himself. Now he was using Bobby Bantz more, giving him more power. After all, the man was thirty years younger and was his closest friend, loyal to him for so long.

Bantz was president and chief executive officer of the Studio. For over thirty years, Bantz had been Marrion's hatchet man, and through the years they had become very close, like father and son, as it is said. They suited each other. After the age of seventy, Marrion had become too tenderhearted to do the things that absolutely had to be done.

It was Bantz who took over from movie directors after their artistic cut and made their films acceptable to audiences. It was Bantz who disputed percentages of directors, stars, and writers and made them either go to court to collect or settle for somewhat less. It was Bantz who negotiated very tough contracts with Talent. Especially writers.

Bantz refused to give even the standard lip service to writers. It was true you needed a script to start, but Bantz believed that you lived and died by casting. Star power. Directors were important because they could steal you blind. Producers, no slouches when it came to thievery, were necessary for the manic energy that started a movie.

But writers? All they had to do was make that initial tracing on blank white paper. You hired another dozen to work it over. Then the producer shaped the plot. The director invented Business (sometimes a whole new picture), and then the stars came up with inspired bits of dialogue. Then there was the Creative Staff of the Studio who, in long, carefully thought out memos, gave writers insights, plot ideas, and wish lists. Bantz had seen many a million-dollar script from a big-shot screenwriter paid a million dollars, only to find when the picture was finished it contained not a single plot incident or word of dialogue of the writer's. Sure, Eli had a soft spot for writers, but that was because they were so easy to screw on their contracts.

Marrion and Bantz had traveled the world together selling movies to film festivals and market centers, to London and Paris and Cannes, to Tokyo and Singapore. They had decided the fate of young artists. They had ruled an empire together, as Emperor and chief vassal.

Eli Marrion and Bobby Bantz agreed that Talent, those who wrote, acted in, and directed movies, were the most ungrateful people in the world. Oh, those hopeful pure artists could be so engaging, so grateful for their chance, so accommodating when they were fighting their way up, but how they could change after achieving fame. Honey-making bees turned into angry hornets. It was only natural that Marrion and Bantz kept a staff of twenty lawyers to throw a net over them.

Why were they always so much trouble? So unhappy? There was no doubt about it, people who pursued money rather than art had longer careers, got more pleasure in life, were much better and more socially valuable people than those artists who tried to show the divine spark in human beings. Too bad you couldn't make a movie about that. That money was more healing than art and love. But the public would never buy it.

Bobby Bantz had gathered them all up from the festival going on outside the mansion. The only Talent there was the director of *Messalina,* a woman named Dita Tommey, in the "A" class and known as the best with female stars, which in Hollywood today meant not homosexual but feminist. The fact that she was also a lesbian was irrelevant to all these men in the conference room. Dita Tommey brought in her pictures under budget, her pictures made money, and her liaisons with females caused far less trouble on a picture than a male director screwing his actresses did. Lesbian lovers of the famous were docile.

Eli Marrion sat at the head of the conference table and let Bantz lead the discussion.

Bantz said, "Dita, tell us exactly how we stand on the picture and what your thoughts are on solving the situation. Hell, I don't even understand the problem."

Tommey was short and very compact and always spoke to the point. She said, "Athena is scared to death. She is not coming back to work unless you geniuses come up with something that can erase that fear. If she doesn't come back, you guys are out fifty million bucks. The picture cannot be finished without her." She paused for a moment. "I've shot around her in the past week, so I've saved you money there."

"This fucking picture," Bantz said. "I never wanted to make it."

This provoked other men in the room; the producer, Skippy Deere, said, "Fuck you, Bobby," and Melo Stuart, Athena Aquitane's agent, said, "Bullshit."

In truth, *Messalina* had been enthusiastically supported by everyone. It had received one of the easiest "green lights" in history.

Messalina told the story of the Roman Empire under the Emperor Claudius from a feminist point of view. History, written by males, painted the Empress Messalina as a corrupt and murderous harlot, who one night took on the whole population of Rome in sexual debauch. But in the movie creating her life almost two thousand years later, she was revealed as a tragic heroine, an Antigone, another Medea. A woman who, using the only weapons available to her, tried to change a world in which men were so dominant that they treated the female sex, half the human race, as if they were slaves.

It was a great concept—rampant sex acts in full color and a highly relevant and popular theme—but it needed a perfect package to make the whole thing credible. First Claudia De Lena wrote a script that was witty and had a strong story line. Dita Tommey as director was a pragmatic and politically correct choice. She had a dry intelligence and was a proven director. Athena Aquitane was perfect as *Messalina* and had completely dominated the picture so far. She had the beauty of face and body, and the genius of her acting made everything plausible. More important, she was one of the three female Bankable Stars in the world. Claudia, with her own offbeat genius, had even given her a scene in which Messalina, seduced by the growing Christian legends, saved martyrs from the sure death of the amphitheater. When Tommey read the scene she said to Claudia, "Hey, there's a limit."

Claudia grinned at her and said, "Not in the movies."

Skippy Deere said, "We have to shut down the picture until we get Athena back to work. That will cost a hundred fifty grand a day. The situation is this. We've spent fifty million. We're halfway through, we can't write Athena out and we can't double her. So if she doesn't come back, we scrap the picture."

"We can't scrap it," Bantz said. "Insurance doesn't cover a star refusing to work. Drop her out of a plane, then insurance pays. Melo, it's your job to get her back. You're responsible."

Melo Stuart said, "I'm her agent but I can only have so much influence on a woman like her. Let me tell you this. She is genuinely frightened. This is not one of your temperamental things. She's scared. but she's an intelligent woman, so she must have a reason. This is a very dangerous, a very delicate, situation."

Bantz said, "If she torpedoes a hundred-million-dollar movie, she can never work again, did you tell her that?"

"She knows," Stuart said.

Bantz asked, "Who's the best person to talk sense into her? Skippy, you tried and failed. Melo, you did. Dita, I know you did your best. I even tried."

Tommey said to Bantz, "You don't count, Bobby. She detests you."

Bantz said sharply, "Sure, some people don't like my style but they listen to me."

Tommey said kindly, "Bobby, none of the Talent likes you, but Athena doesn't like you personally."

"I gave her the role that made her a star," Bantz said.

Melo Stuart said calmly, "She was born a star. You were lucky to get her."

Bantz said, "Dita, you're her friend. It's your job to get her back to work."

"Athena is not my friend," Tommey said. "She is a colleague who respects me because after I tried to make her, I desisted gracefully when I failed. Not like you, Bobby. You kept trying for years."

Bantz said amiably, "Dita, who the hell is she not to fuck us? Eli, you have to lay down the law."

All attention was fixed on the old man, who seemed bored. Eli Marrion was so thin that one male star had joked he should wear an eraser on his skull, but this was more malicious than apt. Marrion had a comparatively huge head and the broad gorilla face of a much heavier man, a broad nose, thick mouth, yet his face was curiously benign, somewhat gentle, some even said handsome. But his eyes gave him away, they were cold gray and radiated intelligence and an absolute concentration that daunted most people. It was perhaps for this reason that he insisted that everyone call him by his first name.

Marrion spoke in an emotionless voice. "If Athena won't listen to you people, she won't listen to me. My position of authority won't impress her. Which makes it all the more puzzling that she is so frightened over such a senseless attack by such a foolish man. Can't we buy our way out of this?"

"We will try," Bantz said. "But it makes no difference to Athena. She doesn't trust him."

Skippy Deere, the producer, said, "And we tried muscle. I got some friends in the police department to lean on him, but he's tough. His family has money and political connections and he's crazy in the bargain."

Stuart said, "Exactly how much does the Studio lose if it closes down the picture? I'll do my best to let you recoup on future packages."

There was a problem about letting Melo Stuart know the extent of the damages; as Athena's agent, it would give him too much leverage. Marrion did not answer but nodded to Bobby Bantz.

Bantz was reluctant, but spoke. "Actual money spent, fifty million. Okay, we can eat fifty million. But we have to give back the foreign sales money, the video money, and there's no Locomotive for Christmas. That can cost us another . . ." He paused, not willing to give that figure, "and then if we add the profits that we lose . . . shit, two hundred million dollars. You'd have to give us a break on a lot of packages, Melo."

Stuart smiled, thinking he would have to jack up his price for Athena. "But actually, in real cash put out, you only lose fifty," he said.

When Marrion spoke his voice had lost its gentleness. "Melo," he said, "How much will it cost us to get your client back to work?" They knew what had happened. Marrion had decided to act as if this was just a scam.

Stuart read the message. How much are you going to stick us up for on this little scheme? This was an attack on his integrity but he had no intention of getting on his high horse. Not with Marrion. If it had been Bantz, he would have been wrathfully indignant.

Stuart was a very powerful man in the movie world. He didn't have to kiss even Marrion's ass. He controlled a stable of five A directors, not strictly Bankable but very powerful indeed; two male Bankable Stars; and one female Bankable Star, Athena. Which meant he had three people who could assure a green light for any movie. But still it was not wise to anger Marrion. Stuart had become powerful by avoiding such dangers. Certainly this was a great situation for a stickup but not really. This was a rare time when straightforwardness could pay off.

Melo Stuart's greatest asset was his sincerity, he truly believed in what he sold, and he had believed in Athena's talent even ten years before, when she was an unknown. He believed in her now. But what if he could change her mind and bring her back before the cameras? Surely that was worth something, surely that option should not be closed off.

"This is not about money," Stuart said with passion. He felt a rapture for his own sincerity. "You could offer Athena an extra million and she would not go back. You must solve the problem of this so-called long-absent husband."

There was an ominous silence. Everybody paid attention. A sum of money had been mentioned. Was it an opening wedge?

Skippy Deere said, "She won't take money."

Dita Tommey shrugged. She didn't believe Stuart for a moment. But it wouldn't be her money. Bantz simply glared at Stuart, who coolly kept looking at Marrion.

Marrion analyzed Stuart's remark correctly. Athena would not come back for money. Talent was never so cunning. He decided to wrap up the meeting.

He said, "Melo, explain very carefully to your client, if she does not come back in one month's time the Studio abandons the picture and takes the loss. Then we sue her for everything she owns. She must know she can't work again for a major American studio afterwards." He smiled around the table. "What the hell, it's only fifty million."

They all knew he was serious, that he had lost his patience. Dita Tommey panicked, the picture meant more to her than anyone. It was her baby. If it succeeded she would be among those directors who would be Bankable. Her OK could get a green light. Out of her panic, she said, "Get Claudia De Lena to talk to her. She's one of Athena's closest friends."

Bobby Bantz said contemptuously, "I don't know what's worse, a star fucking somebody below the line or being friends with a writer."

At this Marrion again lost his patience. "Bobby, don't bring irrelevancies into a business discussion. Have Claudia talk to her. But let's wrap this thing up one way or another. We have other pictures to make."

But the next day a check for five million dollars arrived at Lodd-Stone Studios. It was from Athena Aquitane. She had returned the advance money she had been paid to do *Messalina*.

Now it was in the hands of the lawyers.

In just fifteen years Andrew Pollard had built the Pacific Ocean Security Company into the most prestigious protection organization on the West Coast. Starting in a suite of hotel rooms, he now owned a four-story building in Santa Monica with over fifty permanent HQ staff, five hundred investigators and guards under freelance contracts, plus a floating reserve group who worked for him a good part of the year.

Pacific Ocean Security provided services for the very rich and very famous. It protected the homes of movie magnates with armed personnel and electronic devices. It provided bodyguards for stars and producers. It supplied uniformed men to control the crowds at great media events such as the Academy Awards. It did investigative work in delicate matters such as providing counterintelligence to ward off would-be blackmailers.

Andrew Pollard became successful because he was a stickler for details. He planted ARMED RESPONSE signs on the grounds of his rich clients' houses that flashed in the night with an explosion of red light, plus he had patrols in the neighborhoods of the walled-in mansions. Careful in picking his personnel, he paid high enough wages so that they worried about being fired. He could afford to be generous. His clients were the richest people in the country and paid accordingly. He was also clever enough to work closely with the Los Angeles Police Department, top and bottom. He was a business friend of Jim Losey, the legendary detective, who was a hero to the rank and file. But most important, he had the backing of the Clericuzio Family.

Fifteen years before, while still a young police officer, still a little careless, he had been entrapped by the Internal Affairs Unit of the New York City Police Department. It was small graft, almost impossible to avoid. But he had stood fast and refused to inform on his superiors who were involved. The Clericuzio Family underlings observed this and set in motion a series of judicial moves so that Andrew Pollard was given a deal: Resign from the New York Police Department and escape punishment.

Pollard migrated to Los Angeles with his wife and child, and the Family gave him the money to set up his Pacific Ocean Security Company. Then the Family sent out word that Pollard's clients were not to be molested, their houses could not be burglarized, their persons were not to be mugged, their jewelry was not to be stolen and if stolen in error must be returned. It was for this reason that the flaming ARMED RESPONSE signs also flashed the name of the protection agency.

Andrew Pollard's success was almost magical, the mansions under his protection were never touched. His bodyguards were as nearly well trained as FBI men, so the company was never sued for inside jobs, sexual harassment of their employers, or child molesting, all of which happened in the world of security. There were a few cases of attempted blackmail, and there were some guards who sold intimate secrets to the scandal sheets, but that was unavoidable. All in all, Pollard ran a clean, efficient operation.

His company had computer access to confidential information about people in all walks of life. And it was only natural that when the Clericuzio Family needed data, it would be supplied. Pollard earned a good living and he was grateful to the Family. Plus the fact that every once in a while there was a job he could not ask his guards to do, and he would then make application to the western *Bruglione* for some help in the way of strong-arm.

There were slyer predators for whom Los Angeles and Hollywood were like some Edenesque jungle, teeming with victims. There were the movie executives lured into blackmailers' honey traps, the closeted movie stars, sadomasochistic directors, pedophile producers, all frightened their secrets would get out. Pollard was noted for dealing with these cases with finesse and discretion. He could negotiate the lowest possible payment and ensure that there would be no second dip.

Bobby Bantz summoned Andrew Pollard to his office the day after the Academy Awards. "I want all the info you can get on this Boz Skannet character," he told Pollard. "I want all the background on Athena Aquitane. For a major star, we know very little about her. I also want you to make a deal with Skannet. We need Athena for another three to six months on the picture, so structure a deal with Skannet so that he goes far away. Offer him twenty grand a month but you can go as high as a hundred."

Pollard said quietly, "And after he can do what he wants?"

"Then it's a job for the authorities," Bantz said. "You have to be very careful, Andrew. This guy has a powerful family. The movie industry cannot be accused of any off-color tactics, it might ruin the picture and hurt the Studio. So just make the deal. Plus we are using your firm for her personal security."

"And if he doesn't go for the deal?" Pollard asked.

"Then you have to guard her day and night," Bantz said. "Until the picture is done."

"I could lean on him just a little," Pollard said. "In a legal way of course. I'm not suggesting anything."

"He's too well connected," Bantz said. "The police authorities are leery of him. Even Jim Losey, who's such a good buddy of Skippy

Deere, won't use any muscle. Aside from public relations, the Studio could be sued for enormous amounts of money. I'm not saying you should treat him like a delicate flower but . . ."

Pollard got the message. A little rough stuff to scare the guy but pay him what he wanted. "I'll need contracts," he said.

Bantz took an envelope from his desk drawer. "He signs three copies and there's a check in there for fifty thousand dollars as a down payment. The figures in the contract are open, you can fill it in when you make the deal."

As he went out Bantz said after him, "Your people didn't help at the Academy Awards. They were sleeping on their fucking feet."

Pollard did not take offense. This was vintage Bantz.

"Those were just crowd-control guards," he said. "Don't worry, I'll put my top crew around Miss Aquitane."

In twenty-four hours Pacific Ocean Security computers had everything on Boz Skannet. He was thirty-four years old, a graduate of Texas A&M, where he had been Conference All-Star running back and then gone on to one season of professional football. His father owned a bank in Houston, but more important, his uncle ran the Republican political machine in Texas and was a close personal friend of the president. Mixed into all of this was a lot of money.

Boz Skannet was a piece of work in and of himself. As a vice president in his father's bank, he had narrowly escaped indictment in an oil lease scam. He had been arrested for assault six times. In one case he had beaten two police officers so severely they had to be hospitalized. Skannet was never prosecuted because he paid damages to the officers. There was a sexual harassment charge settled out of court. Before all this he had been married at twenty-one to Athena and had become the father of a baby girl the next year. The child was named Bethany. At age twenty, his wife disappeared with their daughter.

All this gave Andrew Pollard a picture. This was a bad guy. A guy who carried a grudge against his wife for ten years, a guy who fought armed police officers and was tough enough to send them to the hospital. The chances of scaring such a guy were nil. Pay him the money, get the contract signed, and stay the hell out of it.

Pollard called Jim Losey, who was handling the Skannet case for the Los Angeles PD. Pollard was in awe of Losey, who was the cop he would have liked to become. They had a working relationship. Losey received a handsome gift every Christmas from Pacific Ocean Security. Now Pollard wanted the police dope, wanted to know everything Losey had on the case.

"Jim," Pollard said, "Can you send me an info sheet on Boz Skannet? I need his address in L.A. and I'd like to know more about him."

"Sure," Losey said. "But the charges against him have been dropped. What are you in this for?"

"Protection job," Pollard said. "How dangerous is this guy?"

"He's fucking crazy," Losey said. "Tell your bodyguard team that if he gets close they should start shooting."

"You'd arrest me," Pollard said, laughing. "It's against the law."

"Yeah," Losey said, "I'd have to. What a fucking joke."

Boz Skannet was staying in a modest hotel on Ocean Avenue in Santa Monica, which worried Andrew Pollard because it was only a fifteen-minute drive to Athena's house in Malibu Colony. He ordered a four-man team to guard Athena's house and put a two-man team into Skannet's hotel. Then he arranged to meet with Skannet that afternoon.

Pollard took three of his biggest and toughest men with him. With a guy like Skannet you never knew what might happen.

Skannet let them into his hotel suite. He was affable, greeted them with a smile, but did not offer any refreshment. Curiously enough, he was wearing a tie, shirt, and jacket, perhaps to show that after all he was still a banker. Pollard introduced himself and his three bodyguards, all three showing their Pacific Ocean Security IDs. Skannet grinned at them and said, "You guys are sure big. I'll bet a hundred bucks I can kick the shit out of any one of you in a fair fight."

The three bodyguards, well-trained men, gave him small acknowledging smiles, but Pollard deliberately took offense. A calculated umbrage. "We're here to do business, Mr. Skannet," he said. "Not to endure threats. LoddStone Studios is prepared to pay you fifty thousand down right now and twenty thousand a month for eight months. All you have to do is leave Los Angeles." Pollard took the contracts and the big green-and-white check out of his briefcase.

Skannet studied them. "Very simple contract," he said. "I don't even need a lawyer. But it's also very simple money. I was thinking a hundred grand in front and fifty thousand a month."

"Too much," Pollard said. "We have a judge's restraining order against you. You get within a block of Athena and you go to jail. We have security around Athena twenty-four hours a day. And I've set up surveillance teams to keep track of your movements. So for you this is found money."

"I should have come to California sooner," Skannet said. "The streets are paved with gold. Why pay me anything?"

"The studio wants to reassure Miss Aquitane," Pollard said.

"She really is that big a star," Skannet said musingly. "Well, she was always special. And to think I used to fuck her five times a day." He grinned at the three men. "And brainy in the bargain."

Pollard looked at the man with curiosity. The guy was handsome as the rugged Marlboro man in the cigarette ads, except that his skin was red with sun and booze and his body build was bulkier. He had that charming drawl of the South, which was both humorous and dangerous. A lot of women fell in love with such men. In New York there had been some cops with the same kind of looks, and they had scored like bandits. You sent them out on murder cases and in a week they were consoling the widows. Jim Losey was a cop like that, come to think of it. Pollard had never been so lucky.

"Let's just talk business," Pollard said. He wanted Skannet to sign the contract and take the check in front of the witnesses, then maybe later if they had to, the Studio could make a case for extortion.

Skannet sat down at the table. "Have you got a pen?" he asked.

Pollard took his pen out of the briefcase and filled out the figures of twenty thousand a month. Skannet noted him doing so and said cheerfully, "So, I could have gotten more." Then he signed the three copies. "When do I have to leave L.A.?"

"This very night," Pollard said. "I'll take you to your plane."

"No thanks," Skannet said. "I think I'll drive to Las Vegas and gamble with this check."

"I'll be watching," Pollard said. Now was the time he felt he should show some muscle. "Let me warn you, if you show up in Los Angeles again, I'll have you arrested for extortion."

Skannet's red face brimmed with glee. "I'd love that," he said. "I'll be as famous as Athena."

That night the surveillance team reported that Boz Skannet had left but only to move into the Beverly Hills Hotel, and that he had deposited the fifty-thousand-dollar check in an account he had at the Bank of America. This indicated a number of things to Pollard. That Skannet had influence, because he had gotten into the Beverly Hills Hotel, and that he didn't give a shit about the deal he had made. Pollard reported this to Bobby Bantz and asked for instructions. Bantz told him to keep his mouth shut. The contract had been shown to Athena to reassure her and persuade her to go back to work. He did not tell Pollard she had laughed in their faces.

"You can stop the check," Pollard said.

"No," Bantz said, "he cashes it and we got him in court on fraud, extortion, whatever. I just don't want Athena to know he's still in town."

"I'll double the security on her," Pollard said. "But if he's crazy, if he really wants to harm her, that won't help."

"He's a bluffer," Bantz said. "He didn't do it the first time, why would he do anything now?"

"I'll tell you why," Pollard said. "We burglarized his room. Guess what we found? A container of real acid."

"Oh shit," Bantz said. "Can you tell the cops? Jim Losey maybe."

Pollard said, "Having acid is not a crime. Burglary is. Skannet can put me in jail."

"You never told me anything," Bantz said. "We never had this conversation. And forget what you know."

"Sure Mr. Bantz," Pollard said. "I won't even bill you for the information."

"Thanks a lot," Bantz said sarcastically. "Keep in touch."

. . .

Claudia was briefed by Skippy Deere. And instructed as was proper to their roles as producer and writer on a picture.

"You have to absolutely kiss Athena's ass," Deere said. "You have to grovel, you have to cry, you have to have a nervous breakdown. You have to remind her of everything you've ever done for her as an intimate and true friend and as a fellow professional. You must get Athena back on the picture."

Claudia was used to Skippy. "Why me?" she said coolly. "You're the producer, Dita is the director, Bantz is president of LoddStone. You guys go kiss her ass. You've had more practice than me."

"Because it was your project all the way," Deere said. "You wrote the original screenplay on spec, you got me and you got Athena. If the project fails, your name will always be associated with that failure."

When Deere left and she was alone in her office, Claudia knew Deere was right. In her desperation she thought of her brother, Cross. He was the only one who could help her, help make the problem of Boz disappear. She hated the thought of trading on her friendship with Athena, and knew Athena might refuse her but Cross never would. He never had.

She put in a call to the Xanadu Hotel in Vegas, but she was told that Cross would be in Quogue and would not be back until the next day. This brought back all the childhood memories she always tried to forget. She would never call her brother in Quogue. She never would voluntarily have anything to do with the Clericuzio again. She never wanted to remember her childhood again, never to think of her father or any of the Clericuzio.

BOOK II

The Clericuzio and Pippi De Lena

CHAPTER 3

⊞

THE CLERICUZIO FAMILY legend of ferocity had been established more than a hundred years ago in Sicily. There the Clericuzio had waged a twenty-year war with a rival family over the ownership of a piece of forest. The patriarch of the opposing clan, Don Pietro Forlenza, was on his deathbed, having survived eighty-five years of strife only to suffer a stroke, which his doctor predicted would end his life within a week. A member of the Clericuzio penetrated the sick man's bedchamber and stabbed him to death, shouting that the old man did not deserve a peaceful death.

Don Domenico Clericuzio often told this old story of murder to show how foolish were the old-fashioned ways, to point out that ferocity without selection was mere braggadocio. Ferocity was too precious a weapon to waste, it must always have an important purpose.

And indeed he had the proof, for it was ferocity that led the Clericuzio Family in Sicily to destruction. When Mussolini and his Fascists came to absolute power in Italy, they understood that the Mafia had to be destroyed. They did it by suspending due process of law and by using irresistible armed force. The Mafia was broken at the cost of thousands of innocent people going to jail or exile with them.

Only the Clericuzio clan had the courage to oppose Fascist decrees with force. They murdered the local Fascist prefect, they attacked Fascist garrisons. Most infuriating of all, when Mussolini gave a speech in Palermo they stole his prized bowler hat and umbrella imported from England. It was this peasant humor and contempt, which made a laughingstock of Mussolini in Sicily, that finally led to their ruin. There was a massive concentration of armed forces in their province. Five hundred members of the Clericuzio clan were killed outright. Another five hundred were exiled to the arid islands in the Mediterranean that served as penal colonies. Only the very heart of the Clericuzio survived, and the family shipped young Domenico Clericuzio to America. Where, proving that blood will tell, Don Domenico built his own empire, with far more cunning and foresight than his ancestors had shown in Sicily. But he always remembered that a lawless state was the great enemy. And so he loved America.

Early on he had been told the famous maxim of American justice, that it was better that a hundred guilty men go free than that one innocent man be punished. Struck almost dumb by the beauty of the concept, he became an ardent patriot. America was his country. He would never leave America.

Inspired by this, Don Domenico built the Clericuzio empire in America more solidly than the clan had in Sicily. He ensured his friendship to all political and judicial institutions with great gifts of cash. He did not rely on one or two streams of income but diversified in the finest tradition of American business enterprise. There was the construction industry, the garbage disposal industry, the different modes of transportation. But the great river of cash came from gambling, which was his love, in contrast to the income from drugs which, though most profitable, he distrusted. So in later years it was only in gambling that he allowed the Clericuzio Family to be involved operationally. The rest wetted the Clericuzio beak with a tithe of 5 percent.

After twenty-five years the Don's plan and the dream was coming true. Gambling was now respectable and, more important, increasingly legal. There were the ever-burgeoning state lotteries, those swindles perpetrated by the government on its citizens. The prizes stretched over twenty years, which, in effect, amounted to the state never paying the money at all, just the interest on the money withheld. And then that was taxed in the bargain. What a joke. Don Domenico knew the details, because his Family owned one of the management companies that ran the lottery for several states at a very good fee.

But the Don was banking on the day when gambling on sports would become legal in all the United States as it was now legal only in Nevada. He knew this from the tithe he collected on illegal gambling. Profits on the Super Bowl football game alone, if gambling became legal, would come to a billion dollars, in just one day. The World Series with its seven games would yield equal profit. College football, hockey, basketball, all rich streams. Then there would be intricate, tantalizing lotteries on sports events, legal gold mines. The Don knew he would not live to see that glorious day, but what a world it would be for his children. The Clericuzio would be the equal of the Renaissance princes. They would become the patrons of art, advisors and leaders of government, respectable in history books. A trailing cloak of gold would brush out its origins. All his descendants, his followers, his true friends, would be secure forever. Certainly the Don had the vision of a civilized society, the world, as this great tree shedding the fruit that must feed and shelter humanity. But in the roots of this great tree would be the immortal python of the Clericuzio, sucking nourishment from a source that could never fail.

If the Clericuzio Family was the Holy Church for the many Mafia empires scattered over the United States, then the head of the Family, Don Domenico Clericuzio, was the Pope, admired not only for his intelligence but for his strength.

Don Clericuzio was also revered for the strict moral code he enforced in his Family. Every man, woman, and child was completely responsible for his actions, no matter the stress, the remorse, or the hard circumstances. Actions defined a man; words were a fart in the wind. He disdained all social sciences, all psychology. He was a devout Catholic: payment for sins in this world, forgiveness in the next. Every debt had to be paid, and he was strict in his judgment in this world.

As in his loyalty. The creatures of his blood first; his God second (did he not have his own chapel in the house?); and third, his obligation to all the subjects in the domain of the Clericuzio Family.

As for the society, the government—patriot though he was—never entered the equation. Don Clericuzio had been born in Sicily, where society and the government were the enemy. His concept of free will was very clear. You could will yourself as a slave to earn your daily bread without dignity or hope, or you earned your bread as a man who commanded respect. Your Family was your society, your God was your punisher, and your followers protected you. To those on earth you owed a duty: that they would have bread to put in their mouths, respect from the world, and a shield from the punishment of other men.

The Don had not built his empire so that his children and his grandchildren would someday recede into a mass of helpless humanity. He built and kept building power so that the Family name and fortune would survive as long as the Church itself. What greater purpose could a man have in this world than to earn his daily bread, then in the next world to present himself to a forgiving deity? As for his fellow man and their faulty structures of society, they could all swim to the bottom of the ocean.

Don Domenico led his Family to the very heights of power. He did so with a Borgia-like cruelty and a Machiavellian subtleness, plus solid American business know-how. But above all with a patriarchal love for his followers. Virtue was rewarded. Injuries avenged. A livelihood guaranteed.

Finally, as the Don had planned, the Clericuzio reached such a height that it no longer took part in the usual operations of criminal activity except in the most dire circumstance. The other Mafia Families served chiefly as executive Barons, or *Brugliones*, who when in trouble went to the Clericuzio hat in hand. In Italian the words *"Bruglione"* and "baron" rhyme, however in the Italian dialect *"Bruglione"* means someone who fumbles the smallest tasks. It was Don Domenico's wit, sparked by the Barons' constant pleas for help, that changed the word "baron" to *Bruglione*. The Clericuzio made peace between them, sprang them from jail, hid their illegal gains in Europe, arranged foolproof ways for them to smuggle their drugs into America, used its influence with judges and different government regulators, both federal and state. Help with municipalities was usually not required. If a local *Bruglione* could not influence the city he lived in, he was not worth his salt.

The economic genius of Don Clericuzio's oldest son, Giorgio, cemented the Family power. Like some divine laundress he washed the great spouts of black money that a modern civilization spews from its guts. It was Giorgio who always tried to moderate his father's ferocity. Above all, Giorgio strove to keep the Clericuzio Family out of the glare of public notice. So the Family existed, even to the authorities, like some sort of UFO. There were random sightings, rumors, tales of horror and benignity. There were mentions in FBI and police department files, but there were no newspaper stories, not even in those publications that gloried in depicting the exploits of various other Mafia Families who, through carelessness and ego, came to misfortune.

Not that the Clericuzio Family was a toothless tiger. Giorgio's two younger brothers, Vincent and Petie, though not as clever as Giorgio, had almost the Don's ferocity. And they had a pool of enforcers who lived in an enclave of the Bronx that had always been Italian. This enclave of forty square blocks could have been used in a film of Old Italy. There were no bearded Hasidic Jews, blacks, Asians, or bohemian elements in the population, nor did any of these own a business establishment there. There was not one Chinese restaurant. The Clericuzio owned or controlled all real estate in the area. Of course some of the Italian families' progeny sprouted long hair and were guitar-playing rebels, but these teenagers were shipped to relatives in California. Every year, new, carefully screened immigrants from Sicily arrived to repopulate. The Bronx Enclave, surrounded by areas with the highest crime rate in the world, was singularly free of evil-doing.

Pippi De Lena had risen from Mayor of the Bronx Enclave to *Bruglione* of the Las Vegas area for the Clericuzio Family. But he remained directly under the rule of the Clericuzio, who still needed his special talent.

Pippi was the very essence of what was called *Qualificato*, that is, a Qualified Man. He had started early, making his "bones" at the age of seventeen, and what had made the deed even more impressive was he had done so with the garrote. For in America, young men in their callow pride disdained the rope. Also, he was very strong physically, of good height and with intimidating bulk. He was, of course, expert with firearms and explosives. All this aside, he was a charming man because of his zest for life; he had a geniality that put men at ease, and women appreciated his gallantry, which was half rustic Sicilian and half movie American. Though he took his work very seriously, he believed that life was to be enjoyed.

He did have his little weaknesses. He drank heartily, he gambled always, he was excessively fond of women. He was not as merciless as could be wished by the Don, perhaps because Pippi enjoyed too much the social company of other people. But all these weaknesses somehow made him more potent as a weapon. He was a man who used his vices to drain poison out of his body rather than to saturate it.

It helped his career, of course, that he was the nephew of the Don. He was of the blood, and that was important when Pippi broke the family tradition.

No man can live his life without making mistakes. Pippi De Lena, at the age of twenty-eight, married for love, and to compound that error he chose as a wife a completely inappropriate woman for a Qualified Man.

Her name was Nalene Jessup, and she danced in the show at the Las Vegas Xanadu Hotel. Pippi always proudly pointed out that she was not a showgirl who presented herself in the front line with her tits and ass showing, she was a *dancer*. Nalene was also an intellectual, by Vegas standards. She was bookish, took an interest in politics, and since her roots were in the particularly WASP culture of Sacramento, California, had old-fashioned values.

They were complete opposites. Pippi had no intellectual interests, he rarely read, listened to music, or attended movies or theater. Pippi had the face of a bull, Nalene the face of a flower. Pippi was extroverted, full of charm, yet he exuded danger. Nalene was so gentle in nature that not one of her fellow showgirls and dancers had ever been able to pick a fight with her, as they often did with each other to pass the time.

The only thing Pippi and Nalene had in common was dancing. For Pippi De Lena, the feared Clericuzio Hammer, was a veritable idiot savant when he stepped onto the ballroom floor. This was the poetry he could not read, the medieval gallantry of Holy Knights, the tenderness, the exquisite refinement of sex, the only time he reached out to something he could not understand.

For Nalene Jessup, it was a glimpse into his innermost soul. When they danced together for hours before making love, it made their sex ethereal, a true communication between kindred souls. He talked to her when they danced, alone in her apartment, or on the dance floors of the Vegas hotels.

He was a good storyteller with good stories to tell. He expressed his adoration of her in a flattering and witty way. He had an overwhelming masculine presence, which he laid at her feet as a slave, and he listened. He was proud and interested when she talked of books, the theater, the duties of democracy to lift up the downtrodden, the rights of blacks, the liberation of South Africa, the duty to feed the unfortunate poor of the Third World. Pippi was thrilled by these sentiments. They were exotic to him.

It helped that they suited each other sexually, that their opposites attracted each other. It was helpful to their love that Pippi saw the true Nalene but that Nalene did not see the real Pippi. What she saw was a man who adored her, who showered gifts upon her, who listened to her dreams.

They married a week after they met. Nalene was only eighteen, she knew no better. Pippi was twenty-eight and truly in love. He, too, was brought up with old-fashioned values, certainly from different poles, and they both wanted a family. Nalene was already an orphan, and Pippi was reluctant to include the Clericuzio in his newfound rapture. Also, he knew they would not approve. Better to face them with the deed and work things out gradually. They were wed in a Vegas chapel.

But here was another lapse in judgment. Don Clericuzio approved that Pippi married. As he often said, "A man's primary duty in life is to earn his own living," but to what purpose if he did not have a wife and children? The Don took umbrage that he had not been consulted, that the wedding had not been celebrated as part of the Clericuzio Family. After all, Pippi had Clericuzio blood.

The Don peevishly commented, "They can dance to the bottom of the ocean together," but nevertheless he sent lavish wedding presents. A huge Buick, the ownership of a collection agency that yielded the princely income for that time of one hundred thousand dollars a year; a promotion. Pippi De Lena would continue to serve the Clericuzio Family as one of its closely affiliated *Brugliones* in the West, but he was banished from the Bronx Enclave, for how could this alien wife live in harmony with the faithful. She was as foreign to them as the Muslims, the blacks, the Hasidim, and the Asians who were banned. So in essence, though Pippi remained the Clericuzio Hammer, though he was a local Baron, he lost some influence in the palace in Quogue.

The best man at the little civil ceremony of marriage was Alfred Gronevelt, owner of the Xanadu Hotel. He gave a small dinner party afterward, where bride and groom danced the night away. In the years following, Gronevelt and Pippi De Lena developed a close and loyal friendship.

The marriage lasted long enough to produce two children: a son and a daughter. The eldest, christened Croccifixio but always called Cross, at age ten was the physical image of his mother, with a graceful body and an almost effeminately handsome face. Yet he had the physical strength and superb coordination of his father. The younger, Claudia, at the age of nine, was the image of her father, blunt features only saved from ugliness by the freshness and innocence of childhood, yet without her father's gifts. But she had her mother's love of books, music, and theater, and her mother's gentleness of spirit. It was only natural that Cross and Pippi were close to each other, and that Claudia was closer to her mother, Nalene.

In the eleven years before the De Lena family broke apart, things went very well. Pippi established himself in Vegas as the *Bruglione,* the Collector for the Xanadu Hotel, and he still served as Hammer to the Clericuzio. He became rich, he lived a good life, though by the

Don's edict not an ostentatious one. He drank, he gambled, he danced with his wife, he played with his children and tried to prepare them for their entry into adulthood.

Pippi had learned in his own dangerous life to look far ahead. It was one of the reasons for his success. Early on he saw past Cross as a child to Cross as a man. He wanted that future man to be his ally. Or perhaps he wanted at least one human being close he could fully trust.

And so he trained Cross, taught him all the tricks of gambling, took him to dinner with Gronevelt so that he could hear stories of all the different ways a casino could be scammed. Gronevelt always opened up by saying, "Every night, millions of men lie awake figuring out how to cheat my casino."

Pippi took Cross hunting, taught him how to skin and gut animals, made him know the smell of blood, see his hands red with it. He made Cross take boxing lessons so that he could feel pain, taught him the use and care of guns but drew the line at teaching him the garrote; that was after all an indulgence of his own and not really useful in these modern days. Plus there could be no way of explaining such a rope to the boy's mother.

The Clericuzio Family owned a huge hunting lodge in the mountains of Nevada, and Pippi used it for his family's vacations. He took the children hunting while Nalene studied her books in the warmth of the lodge. On the hunt Cross easily shot wolves and deer and even some mountain lions and bears, which revealed that Cross was capable, that he had a good aptitude for guns, was always careful with them, always calm in danger, never flinched when he reached into the bloody guts, the slimy intestines. Dissecting limbs and heads, dressing the kill, he was never squeamish.

Claudia displayed no such virtues. She flinched at the sound of a gun and threw up while skinning a deer. After a few trips she refused to leave the lodge and spent time with her mother reading or walking along a nearby brook. Claudia refused even to fish, she could not bear to put the hard steel hook into the soft center of a worm.

Pippi concentrated on his son. He briefed the boy on basic behavior. Never show anger at a slight, tell nothing of yourself. Earn respect from everyone by deeds, not words. Respect the members of your blood family. Gambling was recreation, not a way to earn a living. Love your father, your mother, your sister, but beware of loving any other woman than your wife. And a wife was a woman who bore your children. And once that happened to you, your life was forfeit to give them their daily bread.

Cross was such a good pupil that his father doted on him. And he loved that Cross looked so much like Nalene, that he had her grace, that he was a replica of her without the intellectual gifts that were now destroying the marriage.

Pippi had never believed in the Don's dream that all of the younger children would disappear into legitimate society; he did not even believe it to be the best course of action. He acknowledged the old man's genius, but this was the romantic side of the great Don. After all, fathers wanted their sons to work with them, to be like them; blood was blood, that never changed.

And in this Pippi proved himself to be right. Despite all of Don Clericuzio's planning, even his own grandson, Dante, proved to be resistant to the grand design. Dante had grown to be a throwback to the Sicilian blood, thirsting for power, strongwilled. He never feared breaking the laws of society and of God.

When Cross was seven and Claudia six, Cross, aggressive by nature, fell into the habit of punching Claudia in the stomach, even in front of their father. Claudia cried for help. Pippi, as the parent, could resolve the problem in different ways. He could order Cross to stop, and if Cross did not, he could pick him up by the scruff of the neck and dangle him in midair, which he often did. Or he could order Claudia to fight back. Or he could cuff Cross against the wall, which he had done once or twice. But one time, perhaps because he had just had dinner and was feeling lazy, or more likely because Nalene always argued when he used force on the children, he lit up his cigar calmly and said to Cross, "Every time you hit your sister, I give her a dollar." As Cross continued punching his sister, Pippi rained dollar bills on the gleeful Claudia. Cross finally stopped in frustration.

Pippi swamped his wife with gifts, but they were gifts a master gives to his slave. They were bribes to disguise her servitude. Expensive gifts: diamond rings, fur coats, trips to Europe. He bought her a vacation house in Sacramento because she hated Vegas. When he gave her a Bentley, he wore a chauffeur's uniform to deliver it to her. Just before the end of their marriage, he gave her an antique ring certified as part of the Borgia collection. The only thing he restricted was her use of credit cards, she had to pay them out of her household allowance. Pippi never used them.

He was liberal in other ways. Nalene had complete physical freedom, Pippi was not a jealous Italian husband. Though he would not travel abroad except on business, he allowed Nalene to go to Europe with her women friends, because she so desperately wanted to see the museums in London, the ballet in Paris, the opera in Italy.

There were times that Nalene wondered about his lack of jealousy, but over the years she came to realize that no man in their circle would dare pay court to her.

On this marriage Don Clericuzio had commented sarcastically, "Do they think they can dance all their lives?"

The answer proved to be no. Nalene was not a good enough dancer to rise to the top, her legs paradoxically too long. She was of too serious a temperament to be a party girl. All this had made her settle for marriage. And she was happy for the first four years. She took care of the children, she attended classes at the University of Nevada and read voraciously.

But Pippi no longer was interested in the state of the environment, had no concern about the problems of whining blacks who couldn't even learn to steal without getting caught, and as far as the Native Americans, whoever they were, they could drown them at the bottom of the ocean. Discussions of books or music were completely beyond his horizon. And Nalene's demand that he never strike their children left him bewildered. Young children were animals; how could you make them behave in a civilized way without flinging them against a wall? He was always careful never to hurt them.

So in the fourth year of their marriage, Pippi took on mistresses. One in Las Vegas, one in Los Angeles, and one in New York. Nalene retaliated by getting her teaching degree.

They tried hard. They loved their children and made their lives pleasant. Nalene spent long hours with them reading and singing and dancing. The marriage was held together by Pippi's good humor. His vitality and animal exuberance somehow smoothed over the troubles of man and wife. The two children loved their mother and looked up to their father: the mother because she was so sweet and gentle, beautiful and full of natural affection; the father because he was strong.

Both parents were excellent teachers. From their mother, the children learned the social graces, good manners, dancing, how to dress, grooming. Their father taught the ways of the world, how to protect themselves from physical harm, how to gamble and train their bodies in athletics. They never resented their father for being physically rough with them, mainly because he did so only as discipline, never got angry when he did so, and then never held a grudge.

Cross was fearless but could bend. Claudia did not have her brother's physical courage but had a certain stubbornness. It helped that there was never any lack of money.

As the years went on, Nalene observed certain things. At first very small. When Pippi taught the children how to play cards—poker, blackjack, gin—he would stack the deck and clean them out of their allowance money, then at the end he would give them a glorious streak of luck so that they could fall asleep flushed with victory. What was curious was that Claudia as a child loved gambling far more than Cross. Later Pippi would demonstrate how he had cheated them. Nalene was angry, she felt he was playing with their lives as he played with hers. Pippi explained it was part of their education. She said it was not education but corruption. He said he wanted to prepare them for the reality of life, she wanted to prepare them for the beauty of life.

Pippi always had too much cash in his wallet, as suspicious a circumstance in the eyes of a wife as in the eyes of the tax collector. It was true that Pippi owned a thriving business, the Collection Agency, but they lived on too rich a scale for such a small operation.

When the family took vacations in the East and moved in the social circles of the Clericuzio Family, Nalene could not miss the respect with which Pippi was treated. She observed how careful men were with him, the deference, the long meetings the men held in private.

There were other little things. Pippi had to travel on business at least once a month. She never knew any of the details of his travel, and he never talked about his trips. He was legally licensed to carry a firearm, which was logical for a man whose business it was to collect large sums of money. He was very careful. Nalene and the children never had access to the weapon, he kept the bullets locked in separate cases.

As the years went by, Pippi took more trips, Nalene spent more time in her home with the children. Pippi and Nalene grew more apart sexually, and since Pippi was more tender and understanding in lust, they grew further and further apart.

It is impossible for a man to hide his true nature over a period of years from someone close to him. Nalene saw that Pippi was a man completely devoted to his own appetites, that he was violent in nature though never violent to her. That he was secretive, though he pretended openness. That though he was amiable, he was dangerous.

He had small personal follies that sometimes were endearing. For instance, other people had to enjoy what he enjoyed. Once they had taken a couple to dinner to an Italian restaurant. The couple did not particularly care for Italian food and ate sparingly. When Pippi observed this he could not finish his meal.

Sometimes he talked about his work at the Collection Agency. Nearly all the major hotels in Vegas were his clients, he collected delinquent gambling markers from customers who refused to pay up. He insisted to Nalene that force was never used, only a special kind of persuasion. It was a matter of honor that people pay their debts, everybody was responsible for their actions, and it offended him that men of substance did not always meet their obligations. Doctors, lawyers, heads of corporations, accepted the complimentary services of the hotel and then reneged on their side of the bargain. But they were easy to collect from. You went to their offices and made a loud fuss so that their clients and colleagues could hear. You made a scene, never a threat, called them deadbeats, degenerate gamblers who neglected their professions to wallow in vice.

Small business men were tougher, nickel-and-dime guys who tried to settle for a penny on a dollar. Then there were the clever ones who wrote checks that bounced and then claimed there had been a mistake. A favorite trick. They gave you a check for ten thousand when they only had eight thousand in their account. But Pippi had access to bank information, so he would merely deposit the extra two thousand to the man's account and then draw out the whole ten thousand. Pippi would laugh delightedly when he explained such coups to Nalene.

But the most important part of his job, Pippi explained to Nalene, was convincing a gambler not only to pay his debt but to keep gambling. Even a busted gambler had value. He worked. He earned money. So you simply had to postpone his debt, urge him to gamble in your casino without credit, and pay off his debt whenever he won.

One night Pippi told Nalene a story he thought enormously funny. That day he had been working in his Collection Agency office, which was in a small shopping mall near the Xanadu Hotel, when he heard gunfire in the street outside. He ran out just in time to see two masked armed men escaping from a neighboring jewelry shop. Without thinking Pippi drew his gun and fired at the men. They jumped into a waiting car and escaped. A few minutes later the police arrived, and after interrogating everyone, they arrested Pippi. Certainly they knew his gun was licensed, but by firing it he had committed a crime of "reckless endangerment." Alfred Gronevelt had gone down to the police station to bail him out.

"Why the hell did I do that?" Pippi asked. "Alfred said it was just the hunter in me. But I'll never understand. Me, shooting at robbers? Me, protecting society? And then they lock me up. They lock *me* up."

But these little revelations into his character were to some extent a clever ruse on Pippi's part, so that Nalene could glimpse part of his character without penetrating to the true secret. What made her finally decide on divorce was Pippi De Lena's arrest for murder. . . .

Danny Fuberta owned a New York travel agency that he had bought with his earnings as a loan shark under the protection of the now extinct Santadio Family. But he earned most of his livelihood as a Vegas junket master.

A junket master signed an exclusive contract with a Vegas hotel to transport vacationing gamblers into their clutches. Danny Fuberta chartered a 747 jet every month and recruited approximately two hundred customers to fly on it to the Xanadu Hotel. For a flat rate of a thousand dollars, the customer got a free round-trip flight from New York to Vegas, free booze and food in the air, free hotel rooms, free food and drink in the hotel. Fuberta always had a long waiting list for these junkets, and he picked his customers carefully. They had to be people with well-paying jobs, though not necessarily legal ones, and they had to gamble in the casino at least four hours every day. And, of course, where possible they had to establish credit at the Cashier's cage in the Hotel Xanadu.

One of Fuberta's greatest assets was his friendship with scam artists, bank robbers, drug dealers, cigarette smugglers, garment center hustlers, and other lowlifes who made handsome livings in the cesspools of New York. These men were prime customers. After all, they lived lives of great stress, they needed a relaxing vacation. They earned huge sums of black money, in cash, and they loved to gamble.

For every junket plane filled with two hundred customers that Danny Fuberta delivered to the Xanadu, he received a flat fee of twenty thousand dollars. Sometimes he received a bonus when the Xanadu customers lost heavily. All this in addition to the initial package charge provided him with a handsome monthly income. Unfortunately, Fuberta also had a weakness for gambling. And there came a time when his bills outpaced his income.

A resourceful man, Fuberta soon thought of a way to make himself solvent again. One of his duties as junket master was to certify the casino credit to be advanced to the junket customer.

Fuberta recruited a band of extremely competent armed robbers. With them Fuberta hatched a plan to steal $800,000 from the Xanadu Hotel.

Fuberta supplied the four men with false credentials identifying them as garment center owners with huge credit ratings, the particulars culled from his agency files. On the basis of these credentials, he certified them for the two-hundred-grand credit limit. Then he put them on the junket.

"Oh, they all had a picnic," Gronevelt said later.

During the two-day stay, Fuberta and his gang ran up huge room service bills, treated the beautiful chorus girls to dinner, signed for presents at the gift shop, but that was the least of it. They drew black chips from the casino, signed their markers.

They split into two teams. One team bet against the dice, the other team bet with the dice. In that way all they could lose was the percentage or break out even. So they drew a million dollars' worth of chips from the casino signing markers, which Fuberta later turned into cash. They looked like they were gambling furiously but were really treading water. In all this they created a great flurry of action. They fancied themselves actors, they implored the dice, they scowled when they lost, cheered when they won. At the end of the day they gave their chips to Fuberta to cash and signed markers to draw fresh chips from the cage. When the comedy ended two days later, the syndicate was $800,000 richer, they had been happy consumers of another twenty thousand in goodies, but they had a million dollars in markers in the cage.

Danny Fuberta, as the mastermind, got four hundred grand, and the four armed robbers were well satisfied with their share, especially when Fuberta promised them another shot. What could be better, a long weekend in the grand hotel, free food and booze, beautiful girls. And a hundred grand to boot. It was certainly better than robbing a bank where you risked your life.

Gronevelt uncovered the scam the very next day. The daily reports showed the markers high even for Fuberta's junket. The Drop at the table, the record of money kept after the night's play, was a figure too low for the amount of money wagered. Gronevelt called for the videotape from the "Eye in the Sky" surveillance camera. He didn't have to watch more than ten minutes before he understood the whole operation and know that the million dollars of markers was so much cigarette paper, the identities false.

His reaction was one of impatience. He had suffered countless scams over the years, but this one was so stupid. And he liked Danny Fuberta; the man had earned many dollars for the Xanadu. He knew what Fuberta would claim: that he, too, had been deceived by the false IDs, that he, too, was an innocent victim.

Gronevelt was annoyed by the incompetence of his Casino personnel. The Stick at the crap table should have caught on, and certainly the Box man should have picked up the cross-betting. It was not that clever a trick. But people went soft with good times, and Vegas was no exception. He thought regretfully that he would have to fire the Stick and the Box man, at least send them back to spinning a roulette wheel. But one thing he could not duck. He would have to turn the whole matter of Danny Fuberta over to the Clericuzio.

First he summoned Pippi De Lena to the hotel and showed him the documents and the film of the Eye in the Sky. Pippi knew Fuberta but not the other four men, so Gronevelt had snapshots made from isolated video stills and gave them to Pippi.

Pippi shook his head. "How the hell did Danny think he could get away with this? I thought he was a smart hustler."

"He's a gambler," Gronevelt said. "They believe their cards are always winning cards." He paused for a moment. "Danny will convince you he's not in on this. But remember, he had to certify that they were good for the money. He'll say he did it on the basis of their ID. A junket master has to certify that they are who they are. He had to know."

Pippi smiled and patted him on the back. "Don't worry, he won't convince me." They both laughed. It didn't matter if Danny Fuberta was guilty. He was responsible for his mistakes.

Pippi flew to New York the next day. To present the case to the Clericuzio Family in Quogue.

After passing through the guarded gates, he drove up the long paved road that cut through a long plateau of grass, its wall armed with barbed wire and electronics. There was a guard at the door of the mansion. And this was in a time of peace.

Giorgio greeted him, and he was led through the mansion into the garden at the rear. In the garden were tomato and cucumber plants, lettuce, and even melons, all framed by large-leafed fig trees. The Don had no use for flowers.

MARIO PUZO • 72

The Family was seated at the round wooden table eating an early lunch. There was the Don, glowing with health despite his near seventy years, visibly drinking in the fig-perfumed air of his garden. He was feeding his ten-year-old grandson, Dante, who was handsome but imperious for a boy the same age as Cross. Pippi always had the urge to give him a smack. The Don was putty in the hands of his grandson; he wiped his mouth, crooned endearments. Vincent and Petie looked sour. The meeting could not start until the kid finished eating and was led away by his mother, Rose Marie. Don Domenico beamed at him as the boy walked away. Then he turned to Pippi.

"Ah, my *Martèllo*," he said. "What do you think of Fuberta, that rascal? We gave him a living and he grows greedy at our expense."

Giorgio said placatingly, "If he repays, he could still be a money-maker for us." The only valid plea for mercy.

"It's not a small sum of money," the Don said. "We must have it back. Pippi, what do you think?"

Pippi shrugged. "I can try. But these are people who don't save for a rainy day."

Vincent, who hated small talk, said, "Let's see the photos." Pippi produced the pictures and Vincent and Petie studied the four armed robbers. Then Vincent said, "Me and Petie know them."

"Good," Pippi said. "Then you can straighten out those four guys. What do you want me to do with Fuberta?"

The Don said, "They have shown contempt for us. Who do they think we are? Some helpless fools who have to go to the police? Vincent, Petie, you help Pippi. I want the money back and these *mascalzoni* punished." They understood. Pippi was to be in charge. The sentence on the five men was death.

The Don left them for his walk in the garden.

Giorgio sighed. "The old man is too tough for the times we live in. This is more risk than the whole thing is worth."

"Not if Vinnie and Pete handle the four hoods," Pippi said. "That OK with you, Vince?"

Vincent said, "Giorgio, you'll have to talk to the old man. Those four won't have the money. We have to make a deal. They go out and earn and pay us back and they're home free. If we bury them, no money."

Vincent was a realistic enforcer who never let the lust for blood overcome more practical solutions.

"OK, I can sell Pop that," Giorgio said. "They were just helpers. But he won't let Fuberta off."

"The junket masters have to get the message," Pippi said.

"Cousin Pippi," Giorgio said smiling, "what bonus do you expect on this?"

Pippi hated when Giorgio called him cousin. Vincent and Petie called him cousin out of affection, but Giorgio only did so when in negotiation.

"For Fuberta it's my duty," Pippi said. "You gave me the Collection Agency and I get wages from the Xanadu. But getting the money back is hard so I should get a percentage. Just as Vince and Petie if they get some from the hoods."

"That's fair," Giorgio said. "But this is not like collecting markers. You can't expect fifty percent."

"No, no," Pippi said, "just let me wet my beak."

They all laughed at the old Sicilian idiom. Petie said, "Giorgio, don't be cheap. You don't want to chisel me and Vincent." Petie now ran the Bronx Enclave, chief of the Enforcers, and he was always promoting the idea that the button men should get more money. He would split his share with his men.

"You guys are greedy," Giorgio said with a smile. "But I'll recommend twenty percent to the old man." Pippi knew that meant it would be fifteen or ten. It was an old story with Giorgio.

"How about we pool it?" Vince said to Pippi. Meaning the three of them would share whatever money was recovered no matter from whom. It was meant as a friendly gesture. There was a far better chance of recovering money from people who were to live than people who were to die. Vincent understood Pippi's value.

"Sure, Vince," Pippi said. "I'd appreciate that."

He saw Dante walking hand and hand with the Don far off at the edge of the garden. He heard Giorgio say, "Isn't it amazing how Dante and my father get along? My father was never that friendly to me. They whisper to each other all the time. Well, the old man is so smart, the kid will learn."

Pippi saw that the boy had his face turned up to the Don. The two looked as if they shared a terrible secret that would give them dominion over Heaven and Earth. Later Pippi would believe that this vision put on him the evil eye, and triggered his misfortune.

Pippi De Lena had gained his reputation over the years by his careful planning. He was not just some rampaging gorilla but a skilled technician. As such he relied on psychological strategy to help in the physical execution of a job. With Danny Fuberta there were three problems. First of all he had to get the money back. Second, he had to coordinate carefully with Vincent and Petie Clericuzio. (That part was easy. Vincent and Petie were extremely efficient in their work. In two days they tracked down the hoods, forced a confession, and arranged for compensation.) Then third, he had to kill Danny Fuberta.

It was easy for Pippi to run into Fuberta accidentally, to turn on his charm and insist the man be his guest for lunch at a Chinese restaurant on the East Side. Fuberta knew Pippi was a collector for the Xanadu, they had necessarily done business over the years, but Pippi seemed so delighted to run into him in New York that Fuberta could not refuse.

Pippi played it in a very low key. He waited until they had ordered and then he said, "Gronevelt told me about the scam. You know you have a responsibility for those guys being certified for credit."

Fuberta swore his innocence, and Pippi gave him a big grin and slapped him on the shoulder in a comradely way. "Come on Danny," he said, "Gronevelt has the tapes, and your four buddies already fessed up. You're in big trouble but I can square things if you give back the money. Maybe I can even keep you in the junket business."

To back up his statement, he took out the four photos of the hoods. "These are your boys," he said, "and right now they are spilling out their guts. Laying all the shit on you. They told us about the split. So if you come up with your four hundred grand, you're clear."

Fuberta said, "Sure, I know these boys, but they're tough guys, they wouldn't talk."

"It's the Clericuzio who are asking," Pippi said.

"Oh shit," Danny said. "I didn't know they had the Hotel."

"Now you know," Pippi said. "If they don't get the money back, you're in big trouble."

"I should just walk out of here," Fuberta said.

"No, no," Pippi said. "Stick around, the Peking duck is great. Look, this can be straightened out, it's no big deal. Everybody tries to scam once in awhile, right? Just get the money back."

"I don't have a dime," Fuberta said.

For the first time Pippi showed some irritation. "You have to show a little respect," Pippi said. "Give a hundred thousand back and we'll take your marker for the other three hundred."

Fuberta thought it over as he munched a fried dumpling. "I can give you fifty," he said.

"That's good, that's very good," Pippi said. "You can pay off the rest by not taking your fee for running junkets to the Hotel. Is that fair?"

"I guess," Fuberta said.

"Don't worry any more, enjoy the food," Pippi said. He rolled some duck into a pancake, anointed it with black sweet sauce, and handed it to Fuberta. "This is terrific, Danny," he said. "Eat. Then we do business."

They ate chocolate ice cream for dessert and made arrangements for Pippi to pick up the fifty grand at Fuberta's travel agency after working hours. Pippi grabbed the lunch check, paying cash. "Danny," he said, "you notice how chocolate ice cream in a Chinese restaurant has so much cocoa? The best. You know what I think? The first Chinese restaurant in America got the recipe wrong and the ones that came after just copied that first wrong recipe. Great. Great chocolate ice cream."

But Danny Fuberta had not hustled for the forty-eight years of his life without being able to read the signs. After leaving Pippi he dived underground, sending a message that he was traveling to collect the money he owed the Xanadu Hotel. Pippi was not surprised. Fuberta was only using tactics common in such cases. He had disappeared so that he could negotiate in safety. Which meant he had no money and there would be no bonus unless Vincent and Petie collected on their end.

Pippi drew some men from the Bronx Enclave to scour the city. The word was put out that Danny Fuberta was wanted by the Clericuzio. A week went by, and Pippi became more and more irritated. He should have known that Fuberta would only be alerted by the demand for repayment. That Fuberta had figured out that fifty grand would not be enough, if he even had fifty grand.

After another week, Pippi became impatient, so that when the break came he moved more daringly than was prudent.

Danny Fuberta surfaced in a small restaurant on the Upper West Side. The owner, a Clericuzio soldier, made a quick call. Pippi arrived just as Fuberta was leaving the restaurant and, to Pippi's surprise, drew a gun. Fuberta was a hustler, had no experience in strong-arm. So when he fired, the shot was wide. Pippi put five bullets in him.

There were a few unfortunate things about this scene. One, there were eyewitnesses. Two, a patrol car arrived before Pippi could make his getaway. Three, Pippi had made no preparation for a shooting, he had meant to talk Fuberta into a secure location. Four, though a case could be made for self-defense, some witnesses said that Pippi shot first. It came down to the old truism that you were more in danger with the law when you were innocent than when you were guilty. Also, Pippi had a silencer on his gun, in preparation for his final friendly chat with Fuberta.

It helped matters that Pippi reacted perfectly to the disastrous arrival of the patrol car. He did not try to shoot his way out but followed the guidelines. The Clericuzio had a strict injunction: Never fire at an officer of the law. Pippi did not. He dropped his gun to the pavement, then kicked it away. He submitted peacefully to arrest and denied completely any connection with the dead man lying just a few feet away.

Such contingencies were foreseen and planned against. After all, no matter how much care was taken, there was always the malignancy of fate. Pippi now seemed to be drowning in a typhoon of ill fortune, but he knew he had only to let himself relax, that he could count on the Clericuzio Family to tow him to shore.

First there were the high-priced defense lawyers who would get him out on bail. Then there were the judges and prosecutors who could be persuaded to become stalwart in the defense of fair play, the witnesses whose memory could be made to fail, the staunchly independent American jurors who if given the slightest encouragement would refuse to convict in order to foil authority. A soldier of the Clericuzio Family did not have to shoot his way out of trouble like some mad dog.

But for the first time in his long service to the Family, Pippi De Lena had to stand trial in a court of law. And the usual legal strategy was that his wife and children must attend the trial. The jurors must know that on their decision rested the happiness of this innocent family. Twelve men and women tried and true had to harden their hearts. "Reasonable doubt" was a godsend to a juror wrung by pity.

During the trial, the police officers testified they had not seen Pippi with the gun or kicking it. Three of the eyewitnesses could not identify the defendant, the other two were so adamant in their identification of Pippi that they alienated jury and judge. The Clericuzio soldier who owned the restaurant testified that he had followed Danny Fuberta out of the restaurant because the man had not paid his check, that he had witnessed the shooting, and that the shooter definitely was not Pippi De Lena, the defendant.

Pippi had worn gloves at the time of the shooting, which was why there were no prints on the gun. Medical evidence was given for the defense that Pippi De Lena suffered from intermittent skin rashes, mysterious and incurable, and that the wearing of gloves had been recommended.

As maximum insurance a juror had been bribed. After all, Pippi was a high executive in the Family. But this final precaution had not been needed. Pippi was acquitted and deemed forever innocent in the eyes of the law.

But not by his wife, Nalene De Lena. Six months after the trial, Nalene told Pippi they must divorce.

There is a cost for those who live on a high level of tension. Physical parts of the body wear down. Excessive eating and drinking tax the liver and heart. Sleep is criminally evasive, the mind does not respond to beauty and will not invest in trust. Pippi and Nalene both suffered from this. She could not bear him in her bed, and he could not enjoy a partner who did not share his enjoyment. She could not hide the horror of knowing he was a murderer. He felt an enormous amount of relief that he did not any longer have to hide his true self from her.

"OK, we'll divorce," Pippi said to Nalene. "But I'm not losing my kids."

"I know who you are now," Nalene said. "I won't see you again and I will not have my children living with you."

This surprised Pippi. Nalene had never been forceful or outspoken. And it surprised him that she dared to speak to him, Pippi De Lena, in such a fashion. But women were always reckless. He then considered his own position. He was not equipped to bring up children. Cross was eleven and Claudia was ten, and he recognized the fact that, despite his closeness with Cross, both children loved their mother more than they did him.

He wanted to be fair to his wife. After all, he had received from her what he wanted, a family, children, a bedrock to his life, which every man needed. Who knew what he would have become if it had not been for her?

"Let's reason this out," he said. "Let's split without any bad feelings." He turned on the charm. "What the hell, we've had a good twelve years. We've had some happy times. And we have two wonderful kids, thanks to you." He paused, surprised again by her stern face. "Come on Nalene, I've been a good father, my kids like me. And I'll help you in whatever you want to do. Naturally you can keep the house here in Vegas. And I can get you one of the shops in the Xanadu. Dresses, jewelry, antiques. You'll earn your two hundred grand a year. And we can sort of share the kids."

Nalene said, "I hate Las Vegas. I always did. I have my teaching degree and a job in Sacramento. I've already enrolled the children in school up there."

It was at that moment that Pippi, with a sense of astonishment, realized that she was an opponent, she was dangerous. It was a concept completely foreign to him. Women, in his frame of reference, were never dangerous. Not a wife, not a mistress, not an aunt, not the wife of a friend, not even the daughter of the Don, Rose Marie. Pippi had always lived in a world where women could not be an enemy. Suddenly he felt that rage, that flow of energy, that he could feel toward men.

Out of that he said, "I'm not going to Sacramento to see my kids." He always became angry when someone rejected his charm, refused his friendship. Anyone who refused to be reasonable with Pippi De Lena was courting disaster. Once he decided on confrontation, Pippi took it to the limit. Also, he was astonished that his wife had already made plans.

"You said you know who I am," Pippi said. "So be very careful. You can move to Sacramento, you can move to the bottom of the ocean for all I care. But you take only one of my children with you. The other stays with me."

Nalene looked at him coolly. "The court will decide that," she said. "I think you should get a lawyer to talk to my lawyer." She almost laughed in his face when she saw his astonishment.

"You have a lawyer?" Pippi said. "You're taking me to the law?" Then he began to laugh. His laughter seemed to carry him away. He was almost hysterical.

It was strange to see a man who for twelve years had been a supplicating lover, a beggar for her flesh, her protection from the cruelties of the world, turn into a dangerous and threatening beast. At that moment she finally understood why other men had treated him with such respect, why they feared him. Now his ugly charm had none of that geniality that was so disarming. Oddly, she was not so much frightened as she was hurt that his love for her could so easily vanish. After all, for twelve years they had cradled each other's flesh, laughed together, danced together, and nurtured their children together, and now his gratitude for the gifts she had given him counted for nothing.

Pippi said to her coldly, "I don't care what you decide. I don't care what a judge decides. Be reasonable and I'll be reasonable. Be tough and you won't have anything."

For the first time she was terrified of all the things she loved; his powerful body, his large, heavy-boned hands, the irregular, blunt features she had always thought manly, that other people called ugly. All through their marriage, he had been more courtier than husband, had never raised his voice to her, had never even made a mild joke at her expense, had never scolded when she ran up bills. And it was true he had been a good father, only rough with the kids when they did not show respect for their mother.

She felt faint, but Pippi's face became more distinct, as though framed in some shadow. Extra flesh padded his cheeks, the very slight cleft in his chin seemed to be filled in with a tiny dot of black putty. His thick eyebrows had spears of white in them, but the hair on his massive skull was black, each strand as thick as horsehair. His eyes, usually so merry, were now a merciless flat tan.

"I thought you loved me," Nalene said. "How can you frighten me so?" She began to weep.

This disarmed Pippi. "Listen to me," he said. "Don't listen to your lawyer. You go to court, let's say I lose all the way down the line. You're still not going to get both kids. Nalene, don't make me be tough, I don't want to be. I understand you don't want to live with me anymore. I always thought I was so lucky to have you as long as I did. I want you to be happy. You'll get far more from me than you'll get from any court judge. But I'm getting old, I don't want to live without a family."

For one of the few times in her life Nalene could not resist malice. "You have the Clericuzio," she said.

"So I have," Pippi said. "You should remember that. But the important thing is, I don't want to be alone in my old age."

"Millions of men are," Nalene said. "And women too."

"Because they're helpless," Pippi said. "Strangers decide their lives. Other people veto their existence. I don't let anyone do that."

Nalene said scornfully, "You veto them?"

"That's right," Pippi said. He smiled down at her. "That's exactly right."

"You can visit them all you want," Nalene said. "But they both have to live with me."

At that he turned his back and said quietly, "Do what you want."

Nalene said, "Wait." Pippi turned to her. She saw on his face something so terrible in its soulless ferocity that she murmured, "If one of them wants to go with you, then OK."

Pippi suddenly became exuberant, as if the problem were resolved. "That's great," he said. "Your kid can visit me in Vegas and my kid can visit you in Sacramento. That's perfect. Let's settle it tonight."

Nalene made a last effort. "Forty is not old," she said. "You can start another family."

Pippi shook his head. "Never," he said. "You're the only woman who ever had the Indian sign on me. I married late and I know I'll never marry again. You're lucky I'm smart enough to know I can't keep you, and I'm smart enough to know I can't start over again."

"That's true," Nalene said. "You can't make me love you again."

"But I could kill you," Pippi said. He was smiling at her. As if it were a joke.

She looked into his eyes and believed him. She realized this was the source of his power, that when he made a threat people believed him. She summoned her last reserve of courage.

"Remember," she said, "if they both want to stay with me, you have to let them go."

"They love their father," Pippi said. "One of them will stay here with their old man."

That evening after dinner, the house iced with air conditioning, the desert heat outside too strong, the situation was explained to Cross, eleven years old, and Claudia, ten. Neither seemed surprised. Cross, as handsome as his mother was beautiful, already had the inner steeliness of his father, and his wariness. He was also completely without fear. He spoke up instantly. "I'm staying with Mom," he said.

Claudia was frightened by the choice. With a small child's cunning, she said, "I'm staying with Cross."

Pippi was surprised. Cross was closer to him than to Nalene. Cross was the one who came hunting with him, Cross liked to play cards with him, to golf and box. Cross had no interest in his mother's obsession with books and music. It was Cross who came down to the Collection Agency to keep him company when he had to catch up on paperwork on Saturday. In fact he had been sure that Cross would be the one he would get to keep. It was Cross he was hoping for.

He was tickled by Claudia's cunning answer. The kid was smart. But Claudia looked too much like himself, he didn't want to look at an ugly mug so much like his every day. And it was logical that Claudia go with her mother. Claudia loved the same things Nalene did. What the hell would he do with Claudia?

Pippi studied his two children. He was proud of them. They knew their mother was the weaker of the two parents, and they were sticking up for her. And he noticed that Nalene, with her theatrical instinct, had prepared cleverly for the occasion. She was dressed severely in black trousers and a black pullover, her golden hair was bound severely with a thin black headband, her face framed into a narrow, heartbreaking white oval. He was conscious of his own brutal appearance as it must appear to small children.

He turned on his charm. "All I'm asking is for one of you to keep me company," he said. "You can see each other as much as you want. Right Nalene? You kids don't want me living here in Vegas all alone."

The two children looked at him sternly. He turned to Nalene. "You have to help," he said. "You have to choose." And then he thought angrily, Why do I give a shit?

Nalene said, "You promised that if they both wanted to go with me, they could."

"Let's talk this out," Pippi said. His feelings were not hurt—he knew his children loved him, but they loved their mother more. He found that natural. It did not mean they had made the right choice.

Nalene said scornfully, "There's nothing to talk about. You promised."

Pippi did not know how terrible he looked to the other three. Did not know how cold his eyes became. He thought he had controlled his voice when he spoke, he thought he spoke reasonably.

"You've got to make a choice. I promise that if it doesn't work out, you can have your own way. But I have to have a chance."

Nalene shook her head. "You're ridiculous," she said. "We'll go to court."

At that moment Pippi made up his mind what he had to do. "It doesn't matter. You can have your way. But think about this. Think about our life together. Think about who you are and who I am. I beg of you to be reasonable. To think about all our futures. Cross is like me, Claudia is like you. Cross would be better off with me, Claudia would be better off with you. That's the way it is." He paused for a moment. "Isn't it enough for you to know they both love you better than me? That they would miss you more than they would me?" The last phrase hung in the air. He did not want the children to understand what he was saying.

But Nalene understood. Out of terror, she reached out and pulled Claudia close to her. At that moment Claudia looked at her brother beseechingly and said, "Cross . . ."

Cross had an impassive beauty of face. His body moved gracefully. Suddenly he was standing beside his father. "I'll go with you, Dad," he said. And Pippi took his hand gratefully.

Nalene was weeping now. "Cross, you'll visit me often, as much as you want. You'll have a special bedroom in Sacramento. Nobody else will use it." It was, finally, a betrayal.

Pippi almost bounded into the air with exuberance. It was such a weight lifted from his soul that he would not have to do what he had for one instant decided to do. "We have to celebrate," he said. "Even when we divorce, we'll be two happy families instead of one happy family. And live happily forever after." The others stared at him stony faced. "Well, what the hell, we'll try," he said.

Claudia never visited her brother and father in Vegas after the first two years. Cross went every year to Sacramento to visit Nalene and Claudia, but by his fifteenth year the visits dwindled to the Christmas holidays.

The two different parents were two different poles in life. Claudia and her mother became more and more alike. Claudia loved school; she loved books, the theater, films; she reveled in her mother's love. And Nalene found in Claudia her father's high spiritedness, his charm. She loved her plainness, which had none of the brutality of her father. They were happy together.

Claudia finished college and went to live in Los Angeles to try her hand in the film business. Nalene was sorry to see her go, but she had built up a satisfactory life with friends in Sacramento and had become an assistant principal at one of the public high schools.

Cross and Pippi had also become a happy family, but in a far different way. Pippi weighed the facts. Cross was an exceptional athlete in high school but an indifferent student. He had no interest in college. And although he had extraordinarily good looks, he was not excessively interested in women.

Cross enjoyed life with his father. Indeed, no matter how ugly the decision that had been made, it seemed to have turned out to be the right one. Indeed two happy families, but not together. Pippi proved to be as good a parent to Cross as Nalene was to Claudia, that is, he made Cross in his image.

Cross loved the workings of the Xanadu Hotel, the manipulation of customers, the fight against scam artists. And Cross did have a normal appetite for the showgirls; after all, Pippi must not judge his son by himself. Pippi decided that Cross would have to join the Family. Pippi believed the Don's oft-repeated words, "The most important thing in life is to earn your bread."

Pippi took Cross in as a partner in the Collection Agency. He brought him to the Xanadu Hotel for dinner with Gronevelt and maneuvered so that Gronevelt would take an interest in his son's welfare. He made Cross one of the foursome in his golf games with high-rolling gamblers at the Xanadu, always pairing Cross against himself. Cross, at the age of seventeen, had that particular virtue of the golf hustler, he played much better on a particular hole where the bets were high. Cross and his partner usually won. Pippi accepted these defeats with good grace; though they cost him money, they earned his son an enormous amount of goodwill.

He took Cross to New York for the social occasions of the Clericuzio Family: all holidays—particularly the Fourth of July, which the Clericuzio Family celebrated with great patriotic fervor; all the Clericuzio weddings, and funerals. After all, Cross was their first cousin, he had the blood of Don Clericuzio running in his veins.

When Pippi made his once-a-week foray at the tables of the Xanadu to win his eight-thousand-dollar weekly retainer with his special dealer, Cross sat watching. Pippi instructed him in the percentages of all forms of gambling. He taught him the management of the gambling bankroll, never to play when he felt unwell, never to play for more than two hours a day, never to play more than three days a week, never to bet heavily when he was on a losing streak, and always to ride a winning streak with a cautious intensity.

It did not seem unnatural to Pippi that a father should let his son see the ugliness of the real world. As the junior partner in the Collection Agency, it was very necessary for Cross to have such knowledge. For the collections were sometimes not as benign as Pippi had described to Nalene.

On a few of the more difficult collections, Cross showed no signs of abhorrence. He was yet too young and too pretty to inspire fear, but his body looked strong enough to enforce any orders Pippi might give.

Finally Pippi, to test his son, sent him out on a particularly tough case, where only persuasion, not force, could be used. The sending of Cross was in itself a signal that the collection would not be pressed, a sign of goodwill to the debtor. The debtor, a very small Mafia *Bruglione* in the northern corner of California, owed a hundred grand to the Xanadu. It was not a big enough matter to involve the Clericuzio name, things had to be handled on a lower level, the velvet glove rather than the iron fist.

Cross caught the Mafia Baron at a bad time. The man, Falco, listened to the reasoned approach made by Cross, then took out a gun and held it to the young man's throat. "Another word out of you and I'll shoot out your fucking tonsils," Falco said.

Cross, to his own surprise, felt no fear. "Settle for fifty grand," he said, "You wouldn't want to kill me for a lousy fifty grand? My father wouldn't like it."

"Who's your father?" Falco asked, his gun still steady.

Cross said, "Pippi De Lena, and he's going to shoot me anyway for settling for fifty grand."

Falco laughed and put his gun away. "OK, tell them I'll pay the next time I come to Vegas."

Cross said, "Just call me when you come in. I'll give you your usual comp RFB."

Falco had recognized Pippi's name, but there had also been something in Cross's face that had stopped him. The lack of fear, the coolness of his response, the little joke. All of this smacked of someone whose friends would avenge him. But the incident persuaded Cross to carry a weapon and a bodyguard on his future collections.

Pippi celebrated his courage with a vacation for both of them at the Xanadu. Gronevelt gave them two good suites and a purse of black chips for Cross.

At this time Gronevelt was eighty years old, white-haired, but his tall body was vigorous and still supple. He also had a pedagogical streak. He delighted in instructing Cross. When he handed him the purse of black chips, he said, "You can't win so I'll get these back. Now listen to me, you have one chance. My hotel has other diversions. A great golf course, gamblers from Japan come here to play on it. We have gourmet restaurants and wonderful girlie shows in our theater with the greatest stars from film and music. We have tennis courts and swimming pools. We have a special tour plane that can fly you over the Grand Canyon. All free. So there's no excuse that the five grand you have in that purse should be lost. Don't gamble."

On that three-day vacation, Cross followed Gronevelt's advice. Every morning he golfed with Gronevelt, his father, and a high roller staying at the Hotel. The betting was always substantial but never outrageous. Gronevelt noted with approval that Cross was at his best when the stakes were highest. "Nerves of steel, nerves of steel," Gronevelt said admiringly to Pippi.

But what Gronevelt approved of most was the kid's good judgment, his intelligence, his knowing the proper thing to do without being told. On the last morning, the high roller playing with them was in a sullen mood and with good reason. A skillful and ardent gambler, tremendously wealthy from a lucrative string of porn houses, he had lost nearly $500,000 the night before. It was not so much the money itself that bothered him as the fact that he had lost control in the middle of a streak of bad luck and had tried to press himself out of it; the mistake of a callow gambler.

That morning when Gronevelt proposed the moderate stake of fifty dollars a hole, he sneered and said, "Alfred, with what you took off me last night, you could afford a grand a hole."

Gronevelt was offended by this. His early-morning golf was a social occasion; linking it to the business of the Hotel was bad manners. But with his usual courtesy he said, "Of course. I'll even give you Pippi as your partner. I'll play with Cross."

They played. The porn house magnate shot well. So did Pippi. So did Gronevelt. Only Cross failed. He played the worst game of golf the others had ever seen. He hooked his drives, he dived into the bunkers, his ball sailed into the little pond (built on the Nevada desert at enormous expense), his nerve broke completely when he putted. The porn-house magnate, five thousand dollars richer, his ego restored, insisted on them sharing breakfast.

Cross said, "Sorry I let you down, Mr. Gronevelt."

Gronevelt looked at him gravely and said, "Someday, with your father's permission, you'll have to come work for me."

Cross, over the years, had observed closely the relationship between his father and Gronevelt. They were good friends, had dinner together once a week, and Pippi always deferred to Gronevelt in a very obvious way, which he did not do even with the Clericuzio. Gronevelt in his turn didn't seem to fear Pippi yet gave him every courtesy of the Xanadu, except a Villa. Plus Cross had caught on to Pippi's winning eight thousand dollars every week at the Hotel. Cross then made the connection. The Clericuzio and Alfred Gronevelt were partners in the Xanadu Hotel.

And Cross was aware that Gronevelt had some special interest in him, showed him extra consideration. As witness the gift of black chips on this vacation. And there had been many other kindnesses. Cross had total comp at the Xanadu for himself and his friends. When Cross graduated from high school, Gronevelt's present had been a convertible. From the time he was seventeen, Gronevelt had introduced him to the showgirls of the Hotel with obvious affection, to give him some weight. And Cross, over the years, came to know that Gronevelt himself, old as he was, often had women to his penthouse suite for dinner, and from the gossip of the girls, Gronevelt was a catch. He never had a serious love affair, but he was so extraordinarily generous with his gifts that the women were in awe of him. Any woman who stayed in his favor for a month became rich.

Once in one of their teacher and pupil talks, as Gronevelt instructed him in the lore of running a great casino hotel like the Xanadu, Cross dared to ask him about women in the context of employee relations.

Gronevelt smiled at him. "I leave the women in the shows to the entertainment director. The other women I treat exactly as if they were men. But if you're asking advice about your love life, I must tell you this. An intelligent, reasonable man in most cases has nothing to fear from women. You must beware of two things. Number one and most dangerous: the damsel in distress. Two: a woman who has more ambition than you do. Now don't think I'm heartless, I can make the same case for women, but that's not to our purpose. I was lucky, I loved the Xanadu more than anything else in the world. But I must tell you I regret not having any children."

"You seem to live the perfect life," Cross said.

"You think so?" Gronevelt said. "Well, I pay the price."

At the mansion in Quogue, a great fuss was made over Cross by the females of the Clericuzio Family. At the age of twenty he was in the full flower of youthful maleness—handsome, graceful, strong, and for his age, surprisingly courtly. The Family made jokes, not entirely free from Sicilian peasant malice, that thank God he looked like his mother and not his father.

On Easter Sunday, while more than a hundred relatives were celebrating Christ's resurrection, the final piece of the puzzle about his father was made clear to Cross by his cousin Dante.

In the vast walled garden of the Family mansion, Cross saw a beautiful young girl holding court with a group of young men. He watched his father go over to the buffet table for a platter of grilled sausage and make a friendly remark to the girl's group. He saw the girl visibly shrinking away from Pippi. Women usually liked his father; his ugliness, his good humor and high spirits disarmed them.

Dante had also observed this. "Beautiful girl," he said, smiling. "Let's go over and say hello."

He made the introductions. "Lila," he said, "this is our cousin Cross."

Lila was their age but not yet fully developed as a woman; she had the slightly imperfect beauty of adolescence. Her hair was the color of honey, her skin glowed as if refreshed from some inner stream, but her mouth was too vulnerable, as if not fully formed. She wore a white angora sweater that turned her skin to gold. Cross fell in love with her for that moment.

But when he tried to speak to her, Lila ignored him and walked to the sanctuary of matrons at another table.

Cross said a little sheepishly to Dante, "I guess she doesn't like my looks." Dante smiled at him wickedly.

Dante had turned into a curious young man with enormous vitality and a sharp, cunning face. He had the coarse black hair of the Clericuzio, which he kept confined underneath a curious Renaissance-style cap. He was very short, no more than five feet and a few inches, but he had an enormous confidence, perhaps because he was the favorite of the old Don. He carried with him always the air of malice. Now he said to Cross, "Her last name is Anacosta."

Cross remembered the name. A year before the Anacosta Family had suffered a tragedy. The head of the family and his oldest son had been shot to death in a Miami hotel room. But Dante was looking at Cross, waiting for some sort of answer. Cross made his face impassive. "So?" he said.

Dante said, "You work for your father, right?"

"Sure," Cross said.

"And you try to date Lila?" Dante said. "You're sick." He laughed.

Cross knew this was danger of some kind. He remained silent. Dante went on, "Don't you know what your father does?"

"He collects money," Cross said.

Dante shook his head. "You have to know. Your Dad takes people out for the Family. He's their number one Hammer."

It seemed to Cross that all the mysteries of his life were blown away on a sorcerer's wind. Everything was very clear. His mother's disgust of his father, the respect shown Pippi by his friends and the Clericuzio Family, his father's mysterious disappearances for weeks at a time, the weapon he always carried, sly little jokes he had not understood. He remembered his father's trial for murder, dismissed from his childhood memories in some curious way the night his father had taken his hand. Then, a sudden warmth for his father, a feeling that he must protect him in some way now that he was so naked.

But over all this Cross felt a terrible anger that Dante had dared to tell him this truth.

He said to Dante, "No, I don't know that. And you don't know that. Nobody knows that." He almost said, And you can go fuck yourself you little creep, but instead he smiled at Dante and said, "Where the hell did you get that fuckin' hat?"

Virginio Ballazzo was organizing the children's Easter egg hunt with the panache of a born clown. He gathered the children around him, beautiful flowers in Easter garb, their tiny faces like petals, skin like eggshells, hats beribboned with pink, and their faces rosy with excitement. Ballazo gave each of them a straw basket and a fond kiss and then shouted to them, "Go!" The children scattered.

Virginio Ballazzo himself was a treat to look at, his suits made in London, his shoes in Italy, shirts in France, his hair cut by a Michelangelo of Manhattan. Life had been good to Virginio and had blessed him with a daughter almost as beautiful as the children.

Lucille, called Ceil, was eighteen years old and on this day served as her father's assistant. As she handed out baskets, the men on the lawn whistled to themselves over her beauty. She was in shorts and an open white blouse. Her skin was dark with an undertone of rich cream. Her black hair was twisted around her head like a crown, and so she stood a youthful queen created by superb health, youth, and the genuine happiness that high spirits can give.

Now out of the corner of her eye she could see Cross and Dante quarreling, and she saw that for a moment Cross had suffered a crushing blow, his mouth crumpling.

She had one basket left on her arm, and she walked over to where Dante and Cross were standing. "Which one of you wants to hunt for eggs?" she asked, her smile flashing with good humor. She held out the basket.

The two of them looked at her with dazed admiration. The late-morning light turned her skin to gold, her eyes danced in delight. The white blouse swelled invitingly and yet so virginally, her round thighs milky white.

At that moment, one of the little girls began to scream. They all looked toward her. The child had found a huge egg, as big as a bowling ball and painted with vivid reds and blues. The child had been struggling to put it in her basket, her beautiful white straw hat askew, her face wide-eyed with astonishment and resolution. But the egg broke and a small bird flew out, which is what made the child scream.

Petie ran across the lawn and scooped up the young child to comfort her. It was one of his practical jokes, and the crowd laughed.

The little girl carefully straightened her hat, then shouted in a treble voice, "You tricked me," and slapped Petie in the face. The crowd roared with laughter as she ran away from Petie, who was still pleading for forgiveness. He caught her up in his arms and gave her a jeweled Easter Egg dangling from a gold chain. The little girl took it and gave him a kiss.

Ceil took Cross by the hand and led him to the tennis court, which was a hundred yards from the mansion. They sat in the three-walled tennis hut, its exposed side away from the festivities, so they could have privacy.

Dante watched them go with a sense of humiliation. He was very conscious that Cross was more attractive, and he felt snubbed. Yet he felt proud to have such a handsome cousin. To his surprise he found himself holding the basket, so he shrugged and joined the Easter egg hunt.

Hidden in the tennis shack, Ceil took Cross's face in her hands and kissed him on the lips. They were tender, brushing kisses. But when he put his hands under her blouse, she pushed him away. She had a brilliant smile on her face. "I wanted to kiss you since I was ten years old," she said. "And today was such a perfect day."

Cross was aroused by her kisses but only said, "Why?"

"Because you're so beautiful and so perfect," Ceil said. "Nothing is wrong on a day like today." She slipped her hand into his. "Don't we have wonderful families?" she said. Then abruptly she asked, "Why did you stay with your father?"

"It was just the way it worked out," Cross said.

"And did you just have a fight with Dante?" Ceil asked. "He's such a creep."

"Dante is OK," Cross said. "We were just kidding around. He's just a practical joker like my Uncle Petie."

"Dante is too rough," Ceil said, then kissed Cross again. She held his hands tight. "My father is making so much money, he's buying a house in Kentucky and a 1920 Rolls-Royce. He has three antique cars now and he's going to buy horses in Kentucky. Why don't you come over tomorrow and see the cars? You always loved my mother's cooking."

"I have to go back to Vegas tomorrow," Cross said. "I work in the Xanadu now."

Ceil gave his hand a tug. "I hate Vegas," she said. "I think it's a disgusting city."

"I think it's great," Cross said, smiling. "Why do you hate it if you've never been there?"

"Because people throw away hard-earned money," Ceil said with youthful indignation. "Thank God my father doesn't gamble. And all those sleazy showgirls."

Cross laughed. "I wouldn't know," he said. "I just run the golf course. I've never seen the inside of the casino."

She knew he was making fun of her, but she said, "If I invite you to visit me at college when I go away, will you come?"

"Sure," Cross said. In this game he was far more experienced than she was. And he felt a tenderness about her innocence, her holding of his hands, her ignorance of her father and the Family's true purpose. He understood that she was just staking out a tentative claim, the lovely weather, the explosion of celebration in her body of womanhood, and he was touched by the sweet, unsexy kisses.

"We better go back to the party," he said, and they strolled hand in hand to the picnic area. Her father, Virginio, was the first to notice them and rubbed one finger against another and said, "Shame, shame," gleefully. Then he embraced them both. It was a day Cross always remembered for its innocence, the young children chastely clad in white to announce the resurrection, and because he finally understood who his father was.

When Pippi and Cross went back to Vegas, things were different between them. Pippi obviously knew that the secret was out, and he paid Cross some attentions of extra affection. Cross was surprised that his feeling toward his father had not changed, that he still loved him. He could not imagine a life without his father, without the Clericuzio Family, without Gronevelt and the Xanadu Hotel. This was the life he had to lead, and he was not unhappy to lead it. But there began to build up in him an impatience. Another step had to be taken.

BOOK III

Claudia De Lena
Athena Aquitane

CHAPTER 4

CLAUDIA DE LENA drove from her apartment on the Pacific Palisades toward Athena's Malibu house and pondered what she would say to persuade Athena to come back to work on *Messalina*.

It was as important to her as it was to the Studio. *Messalina* was her first truly original script; her other work had been adaptations of novels, rewrites or doctoring of other scripts, or collaborations.

Also, she was a coproducer of *Messalina,* which gave her a power she had never previously enjoyed. Plus an adjusted gross of the profits. She would see some really big money. And she could then take the next step, to producer-writer. She was perhaps the only person west of the Mississippi who did not want to direct; that required a cruelty in human relationships that she could not tolerate.

Claudia's relationship with Athena was a true intimacy, not the professional friendship of fellow workers in the movie industry. Athena would know how much the picture meant to her career. Athena was intelligent. What really puzzled Claudia was Athena's fear of Boz Skannet. Athena had never been afraid of anything or anyone.

Well, one thing she would accomplish. She would find out exactly why Athena was so fearful, and then she could help. And certainly, she had to save Athena from ruining her own career. After all, who knew more about the intricacies and traps of the movie business than she did?

Claudia De Lena dreamed of a life as a writer in New York. She was not discouraged when, at the age of twenty-one, her first novel was turned down by twenty publishers. Instead, she decided to move to Los Angeles and try her hand at movie scripts.

Because she was witty and vivacious and talented, she soon made many friends in Los Angeles. She enrolled in a movie-script writing course at UCLA and met a young man whose father was a famous plastic surgeon. She and the young man became lovers, and he was bewitched by her body and intelligence. He revised her status from comradely bed partner to "serious relationship." He brought her home to his family for dinner. His father, the plastic surgeon, was enchanted by her. After dinner the surgeon put his hands around her face.

"It's unfair that a girl like you is not as pretty as you should be," he said. "Don't take offense, it's a perfectly natural misfortune. And it's my business. I can fix it if you let me."

Claudia was not offended, but she was indignant. "Why the hell should I be pretty? What good does that do me?" she said with a smile. "I'm pretty enough for your son."

"All the good in the world," the surgeon said. "And when I get through with you, you'll be too good for my son. You are a sweet and intelligent girl, but looks are power. Do you really want to spend the rest of your life standing around while men flock to good-looking women who have not one tenth of your intelligence? And you have to sit around like a dummy because your nose is too thick and you have a chin like a Mafia hood." As he said this he patted her cheek and said gently, "It won't take much doing. You have beautiful eyes and a beautiful mouth. And your figure is good enough for a movie star."

Claudia flinched away from him. She knew she resembled her father; the Mafia hood remark had touched a nerve.

"It doesn't matter," she said. "I can't pay your fee."

"Another thing," the surgeon said "I know the movie business. I have prolonged the careers of stars male and female. Now when the day comes for you to pitch a movie at a studio, your looks will play an important part. That may seem unfair to you. I know you're talented. But that's the movie world. Just think of it as a professional move, not some male-female thing. Though of course it is." He saw that she still hesitated. "I'll do it without a fee," he said. "I'll do it for you and for my son. Even though I fear that once you're as pretty as I think you will be, he will lose a girlfriend."

Claudia had always known she was not pretty, now the memory of her father preferring Cross came back to her. If she had been pretty, would her destiny have been changed? For the first time she took a good look at the surgeon. He was a handsome man, his eyes were gentle as if he understood everything she was feeling. She laughed. "Okay," she said. "Turn me into Cinderella."

The surgeon didn't have to do that much. He thinned her nose, rounded her chin, and scaled her skin. When Claudia reentered the world, she was a handsome, proud-looking woman with a perfect nose, a commanding presence, perhaps not quite pretty but somehow even more attractive.

The professional results were magical. Claudia, despite her youth, obtained a personal interview with Melo Stuart, who became her agent. He got her minor rewrites on scripts and invited her to parties where she met producers, directors, and stars. They were enchanted by her. In the next five years, despite her youth, she was ranked as a Class A writer on A films. In her personal life the effect was equally magical. The surgeon had been right. His son could not meet the competition. Claudia had a string of sexual conquests—some really submissions—that would have made a film star proud.

Claudia loved the movie business. She loved working with other writers, she loved arguing with producers, cajoling directors: the first with how to save money doing the script a certain way, the other with how a script could be done on the highest artistic level. She was in awe of actresses and actors, how they were attuned to her words, making them sound better and more touching. She loved the magic of the set, which most people found boring, she enjoyed the camaraderie of the crew and had no compunction about screwing "below the line." She was thrilled with the whole process of opening a movie and watching its success or failure. She believed in movies as a great art form, and when called in to do a rewrite, she fancied herself a healer and did not look to make changes solely to get screen credit. At the age of twenty-five she had an enormous reputation and friendships with many stars, the closest one being with Athena Aquitane.

What was more of a surprise to her was her ebullient sexuality. Going to bed with a man she liked was as natural to her as any act of friendship. She never did it for advantage, she was too talented; she sometimes joked that stars slept with her to get her next script.

Her first adventure had been with the surgeon himself, who proved to be much more charming and adept than his son. Perhaps enchanted by his own handiwork, he offered to set her up in an apartment with a weekly allowance, not only for the sex but for the enjoyment of her company. Claudia refused good-humoredly and said, "I thought there was no fee."

"You've already paid the fee," he said. "But I hope we can see each other now and then."

"Of course," Claudia said.

What she found extraordinary in herself was that she could make love to so many different kinds of men, of varying ages, types, and looks. And enjoy all of it. She was like an aspiring gourmet, who explored all sorts of strange delicacies. She played mentor with budding actors and screenwriters, but that was not the role she liked. She wanted to learn. And she found older men far more interesting.

On a memorable day, she had a one-night stand with the great Eli Marrion himself. She enjoyed it, but it was not truly successful.

They met at a LoddStone Studio party, and Marrion was intrigued with her because she was not afraid of him and made some penetrating and disparaging remarks on the Studio's latest blockbuster production. Also, Marrion had heard her repel Bobby Bantz's amorous advances with a witty remark that left no ill feelings.

Eli Marrion had given up sex the last few years. It was more work than fun, since he was nearly impotent. When he invited Claudia to come with him to the Beverly Hills bungalow owned by LoddStone, he assumed that she accepted because of his power. He had no idea that it was her sexual curiosity. What would it be like to go to bed with so powerful a man who was so old? That would not have been enough, but in addition she found Marrion attractive despite his age. His gorilla-like face could actually turn handsome when he smiled, which he did when he told her that everyone called him Eli, including his grandchildren. His intelligence and his natural charm intrigued her because she had heard about his ruthlessness. It would be interesting.

In the bedroom of the downstairs apartment of the Beverly Hills Hotel bungalow, she observed with amusement that he was shy. Claudia rejected any coyness, she helped him undress, and while he folded his clothes over a stuffed chair, she got herself naked, gave him a hug, and followed him beneath the bedcovers. Marrion tried to joke, "When King Solomon was dying, they sent virgins to his bed to keep him warm."

"Well, then, I'm not going to help you much," Claudia said. She kissed him and fondled him. His lips were pleasantly warm. His skin had a dryness and waxiness that was not distasteful. She had been surprised by his tinyness when he shed his clothing and shoes, and she considered for a moment what a three-thousand-dollar suit could do for a man in power. But his smallness with the huge head was also endearing. She was not at all put off. After ten minutes of fondling and kissing (the great Marrion kissed with the innocence of a child), they both realized that he was now fully impotent. Marrion thought, This is the last time I will ever be in bed with a woman. He sighed and relaxed as she cradled him in her arms.

"Okay, Eli," Claudia said. "Now I'll tell you in detail why your movie is lousy from a money standpoint and an artistic one." Still gently fondling him, she delivered a penetrating analysis of the script, the director, and the actors. "It's not that it's just a bad movie," Claudia said. "It's an unwatchable movie. Because it has no story sense and so all you have is some fucking director giving you a slide show of what he thinks is a story. And the actors just go through the motions because they know it's bullshit."

Marrion listened to her with a benign smile. He felt very comfortable. He realized that an essential part of his life was over, finished by an approaching death. That he would never again make love to a woman, or even try, was not humiliating. He knew Claudia would not talk about this night, and if she did, what would it matter? He still retained his worldly power. He could still change the destinies of thousands, as long as he remained alive. And now he was interested in her analysis of the film.

"You don't understand," he said. "I can bring a picture into existence but I can't execute the picture. You're quite right, I will never hire that director again. The Talent doesn't lose money, I do. But Talent has to take the blame. My question is, Will a movie make money? If it becomes a work of art, that's just a happy accident."

As they spoke, Marrion got out of bed and began to dress. Claudia hated it when men put on their clothes, they were so much more difficult to talk to. Marrion, to her, was infinitely more lovable naked, strange as that seemed; his spindly legs, his meager body, his huge head, all made her feel an affectionate pity. Oddly enough, his penis, flaccid, was bigger than that of most men in a similar state. She made a mental note to ask her surgeon about that. Did a penis grow larger as it grew more useless?

Now she saw how fatiguing it was for Marrion to button his shirt and put in his cuff links. She jumped out of bed to help him.

Marrion studied her nakedness. Her body was better than many of the stars he had gone to bed with, but he felt no mental flicker and the cells of his body did not react to her beauty. And he did not really feel regret or sadness.

Claudia helped put on his trousers, button his shirt, put in the cuff links. She straightened his maroon tie and brushed back his gray hair with her fingers. He slipped on his suit jacket and there he stood, all his visible power restored. She kissed him and said, "I had a good time."

Marrion was studying her as though she were some sort of opponent. Then he smiled his famous smile that erased the ugliness of his features. He accepted the fact that she was truly innocent, that she had a good heart, and he believed that it was because of her youth. It was just too bad that the world she lived in would change her.

"Well, at least I can feed you," Marrion said. He picked up the phone to call room service.

Claudia was hungry. She polished off a soup, duck with vegetables, and then a huge bowl of strawberry ice cream. Marrion ate very little but did his share in polishing off the bottle of wine. They talked about movies and books, and Claudia learned to her astonishment that Marrion was a far better reader than she was.

"I would have loved to be a writer," Marrion said. "I love writing, books give me so much pleasure. But you know I've rarely met a writer I could like personally, even when I adore their books. Ernest Vail for instance. He writes beautiful books but he's such a pain in the ass in real life. How can that be?"

"Because writers are not their books," Claudia said. "Their books are the distillation of the very best that is in them. They're like a ton of rocks that you have to crush to get a little diamond, if that's what you do to get a diamond."

"You know Ernest Vail?" Marrion asked. Claudia appreciated that he said this without a trace of salaciousness. He must have known about her love affair with Vail. "Now, I love his writing but I can't stand him personally. And he has a grudge against the Studio that is insane."

Claudia patted his hand, a familiarity that was permissible since she had seen him naked. "All the Talent has a grudge against the Studio," she said. "It's not personal. And besides, you're not exactly a sweetheart in business relationships. I may be the only writer in town who really likes you." They both laughed.

Before they parted, Marrion said to Claudia, "Any time you have a problem, please call." It was a message that he would not wish to pursue their personal relationship.

Claudia understood. "I'll never take advantage of that offer," she said. "And if you have trouble with a script, you can call me. Free advice but you have to pay my deal price if I have to write." Telling him that professionally he would need her more than she would need him. Which of course was not true but told him that she had her own faith in her talent. They parted friends.

On the Pacific Coast Highway, traffic was slow. Claudia looked to her left to see the sparkling ocean and marveled at how few people were on the beach. How different from Long Island, where she had visited when she was younger. Above her head she could see the hang gliders sailing just over the power lines and onto the beach. On her right side she saw a crowd around a sound truck and huge cameras. Somebody was shooting a movie. How she loved the Pacific Coast Highway. And how Ernest Vail had hated it. He said driving on that highway was like catching a ferry to Hell. . . .

Claudia De Lena first met Vail when she was hired to work on the movie script of his bestselling novel. She had always loved his books, his sentences were so graceful, they flowed into each other like musical notes. He understood life and the tragedies of character. He had a novelty of invention that always delighted her as fairy stories had enchanted her in her childhood. So she had been thrilled to meet him. But the reality of Ernest Vail was another thing entirely.

Vail was then in his early fifties. His physical presence had none of the grace of his prose. He was short and heavy and had a bald spot that he didn't bother to hide. He may have understood and loved the characters in his books, but he was totally ignorant of the niceties of everyday life. This was perhaps one of his charms, his childlike innocence. It was only when she got to know him better that Claudia discovered that beneath this innocence was an offbeat intelligence that could be enjoyed. He could be witty as a child is unconsciously witty, and he had a child's fragile egotism.

Ernest Vail seemed to be the happiest man in the world at that breakfast at the Polo Lounge. His novels had earned him a solid critical reputation and good but unimportant money. Then this latest book had broken through and become an enormous bestseller and was now being made into a movie by LoddStone Studios. Vail had written the script, and now Bobby Bantz and Skippy Deere were telling him how wonderful it was. And to Claudia's astonishment, Vail was swallowing their praise like some starlet headed for the casting couch. What the hell did Vail think Claudia was doing at this meeting? What dismayed her was that this was the same Bantz and Deere who had the day before told her that the script was a "piece of shit." Not being cruel or even pejorative. A Piece of Shit was simply something that didn't quite work.

Claudia was not put off by Vail's homeliness, after all she herself had been homely until she blossomed into handsomeness under the surgeon's knife. She was even somewhat charmed by his credulity and his enthusiasm.

Bantz said, "Ernest, we're bringing in Claudia to help you. She's a great technician, the best in the business, and she'll make it a real movie. I smell a big hit. And remember—you have ten percent of the net."

Claudia could see Vail swallow the hook. The poor bastard didn't even know that 10 percent of the net was 10 percent of nothing.

Vail seemed to be genuinely grateful for help. He said, "Sure, I can learn from her. Writing scripts is a lot more fun than writing books but it's new to me."

Skippy Deere said reassuringly, "Ernest, you have a natural flair. You can get a lot of work out here. And you can get rich on this picture, especially if it's a hit and especially if it wins the Academy."

Claudia studied the men. Two pricks and a dope, not an unusual trio in Hollywood. But then she had not been any smarter. Hadn't Skippy Deere screwed her, literally and figuratively? Yet she couldn't help admiring Skippy. He seemed so absolutely sincere.

Claudia knew the project was already in serious trouble and that the incomparable Benny Sly was working behind her and that Sly was turning Vail's intellectual hero into a franchise by writing him into a James Bond—Sherlock Holmes—Casanova. There would be nothing left of Vail's book but the bare bones.

It was out of this pity that Claudia agreed to have dinner with Vail that night to plan how they would work on the screenplay together. One of the tricks in collaboration was to stave off any romantic involvement, and she did this by presenting herself as unattractively as possible in work sessions. Romance was always distracting to her when writing.

To her astonishment the two months they spent working led to an enduring friendship. When they were both fired from the project on the same day, they went to Vegas together. Claudia had always loved gambling, and Vail had the same vice. In Vegas she introduced him to her brother Cross and was surprised that the two men hit it off. There was absolutely no basis for their friendship that she could see.

Ernest was an intellectual who had no interest in sports or golf. Cross hadn't read a book for years. She asked Ernest about this.

"He's a listener and I'm a talker," he said. Which struck Claudia as being not a real explanation.

She asked Cross; though he was her brother, he was the greater mystery. Cross pondered the question. Finally he said, "You don't have to keep an eye on him, he doesn't want anything." And as soon as Cross said it, she knew it was true. To her it was an astonishing revelation. Ernest Vail, to his misfortune, was a man who had no hidden agendas.

Her affair with Ernest Vail was different. Though he was a world-renowned novelist, he had no power in Hollywood. Also, he had no social gifts; indeed, he inspired antagonism. His articles in magazines addressed sensitive national issues and were always politically incorrect, but ironically this angered both sides. He jeered at the American democratic process; writing about feminism, he declared that women would always be subjugated by men until they became physically equal, and advised feminists to set up paramilitary training groups. On racial problems, he wrote an essay on language in which he insisted the blacks should call themselves "coloreds" because "black" was used in so many pejorative ways—black thoughts, black as hell, black countenance—and that the word always had a negative connotation except when used in the phrase "simple black dress."

But then he enraged both sides when he maintained that all Mediterranean races be designated as "colored." Including Italians, Spaniards, Greeks, et cetera.

When he wrote about class, he claimed that people with a great deal of money had to be cruel and defensive, and that the poor ought to become criminals since they had to fight laws written by the rich to protect their money. He wrote that all welfare was simply a necessary bribe to keep the poor from starting a revolution. About religion, he wrote that it should be prescribed like medication.

Unfortunately nobody could ever figure out whether he was joking or serious. None of these eccentricities ever appeared in his novels, so a reading of his works gave no insights.

But when Claudia worked with him on the screenplay of his best-selling novel, they established a close relationship. He was a devoted pupil, he gave her all the deference, and she on her part appreciated his somewhat sour jokes, his seriousness about social conditions. She was struck by his carelessness about money in practice and his concern about money in the abstract; his pure dumbness about how the world worked in terms of power, especially Hollywood. They got along so well that she asked him to read her novel. She was flattered when he came to the studio the next day with notes on his reading.

The novel had finally been published on the strength of her success as a screenwriter and the arm twisting of her agent, Melo Stuart. It had received a few reviews of faint praise and some derisive ones merely because she was a screenwriter. But Claudia still loved her book. It did not sell, nor did anyone purchase the movie rights. But it was in print. She inscribed one to Vail: "To America's greatest living novelist." It didn't help.

"You're a very lucky girl," Vail said. "You're not a novelist, you're a screenwriter. You will never be a novelist." Then without malice or derision he spent the next thirty minutes trying to strip her novel bare and showing her that it was a piece of nonsense, that it had no structure, no depth, no resonance in characterization, and that even her dialogue, her strong point, was terrible, witty without point. It was a brutal assassination but carried out with such logic that Claudia had to recognize its truth.

He ended up with what he thought was a kindness. "It's a very good book for an eighteen-year-old woman," Vail said. "All the faults I've mentioned can be repaired by experience, simply by getting older. But there's one thing you can never repair. You have no language."

At this Claudia, though crushed, took offense. Some of the reviewers had praised the lyrical quality of the writing. "You're wrong on that," she said. "I tried to write perfect sentences. And the thing I admire most in your books is the poetry of your language."

For the first time Vail smiled. "Thank you," he said. "I wasn't trying to be poetic. My language sprang out of the emotion of the characters. Your language, your poetry in this book is imposed. It's completely false."

Claudia burst into tears. "Who the fuck are *you*?" she said. "How can you say something so terribly destructive. How can you be so fucking positive?"

Vail seemed amused. "Hey, you can write publishable books and starve to death. But why, when you're a genius screenwriter? As for my being so positive, this is the only thing I know, but I know it absolutely. Or I'm wrong."

Claudia said, "You're not wrong but you are a sadistic prick."

Vail eyed her warily. "You're gifted," he said. "You have a great ear for movie dialogue, you're expert in story line. You really understand movies. Why would you want to be a blacksmith instead of an automobile mechanic? You are a movie person, you are not a novelist."

Claudia looked at him with wide-eyed wonder. "You don't even know how insulting you are."

"Sure I do," Vail said. "But it's for your own good."

"I can't believe you're the same person who wrote your books," she said venomously. "Nobody could believe you wrote them."

At this Vail broke into a delighted cackle. "That's true," he said. "Isn't that wonderful?"

All through the next week he was formal with her while they worked on the script. He assumed their friendship was over. Finally Claudia said to him, "Ernest, don't be so stiff. I forgive you. I even believe you're right. But why did you have to be so brutal? I even thought you were making one of those male power moves. You know, humiliate me then push me into bed. But I know you're too dumb for that. For Christ's sake, give a little sugar with your medicine."

Vail shrugged. "I have only one thing going for me," he said. "If I'm not honest about those things then I'm nothing. Also, I was brutal because I'm really very fond of you. You don't know how rare you are."

Claudia said smilingly, "Because of my talent, my wit, or my beauty?"

Vail waved his hand dismissively. "No, no," he said. "Because you are blessed, a very happy person. No tragedy will ever bring you down. That is very rare."

Claudia thought about it. "You know," she said, "there's something vaguely insulting about that. Does that mean I'm basically stupid?" She paused for a moment. "It's considered more sensitive to be melancholy."

"Right," Vail said. "I'm melancholy and so I'm more sensitive than you?" They both laughed and then she was hugging him.

"Thank you for being honest," she said.

"Don't get too cocky," Vail said. "Like my mother always said, 'Life is like a box of hand grenades, you never know what will blow you to kingdom come.' "

Claudia was laughing when she said, "Christ, do you always have to sound the note of doom? You'll never be a movie writer and that line shows it."

"But it's more truthful," Vail said.

Before they finished their collaboration on the script, Claudia dragged him into bed. She was fond enough of him that she wanted to see him with his clothes off so they could really talk, really exchange confidences.

As a lover Vail was far more enthusiastic than he was expert. He was also more grateful than most men. Best of all, he loved to talk after sex, his nakedness did not inhibit his lecturing, his intemperate judgments. And Claudia loved his nakedness. With his clothes off he seemed to have a monkey's agility and impetuousness, and he was very hairy: a matted chest, patches of furry hair on his back. Also, he was as greedy as a monkey, clutching her naked body as if she were a fruit hanging from a tree. His appetite amused Claudia. She relished the inherent comedy of sex. And she loved that he was famous all over the world, that she had seen him on TV and thought him a little pompous on literature, the grievous moral state of the world, so dignified clutching the pipe he rarely smoked and looking very professorial in his tweed jacket with sewn-leather elbow patches. But he was far more amusing in bed than on TV; he did not have an actor's projection.

There was never any talk of true love, of a "relationship." Claudia had no need for it and Vail had only a literary sense of the term. They both accepted that he was thirty years the elder and, aside from that, no bargain really except for his fame. They had nothing in common except literature, perhaps the worst basis for establishing a marriage, they agreed.

But she loved arguing with him about movies. Vail insisted that moving pictures were not art, that they were a regression to the primitive paintings found in lost caves. That film had no language, and since the progression of the human species depended on language, it was merely a regressive, minor art.

Claudia said, "So painting is not an art, Bach and Beethoven are not art, Michelangelo is not art. You're talking bullshit." And then she realized he was teasing her, that he enjoyed provoking her, though prudently only after sex.

By the time they were both fired from the script, they were really close friends. And before Vail went back to New York, he gave Claudia a tiny, lopsided ring with four different colored jewels. It didn't look expensive but it was a valuable antique that he spent a lot of time looking for. She always wore it thereafter. It became in her mind a lucky talisman.

But when he left, their sexual relationship was over. When and if he ever returned to L.A. she would be in the middle of another affair. And he recognized that their sex had been more friendship than passion.

Her farewell gift to him was a thorough education in the ways of Hollywood. She explained to him that their script was being rewritten by the great Benny Sly, the legendary rewriter of scripts, who had even been mentioned for a special Academy Award for rewrites. And that Benny Sly specialized in turning uncommercial stories into one-hundred-million-dollar blockbusters. Undoubtedly he would turn Vail's book into a movie that Vail would hate but that would surely make a lot of money.

Vail shrugged. "That's okay," he said. "I have ten percent of the net profits. I'll be rich."

Claudia looked at him with exasperation. "Net?" she cried out. "Do you buy Confederate money too? You'll never see a penny no matter how much the movie makes. LoddStone has a genius for making money disappear. Listen, I had net on five pictures that made a ton of money and I never saw a penny. You won't either."

Vail shrugged again. He did not seem to care, which made his actions in the years to follow even more puzzling.

Claudia's next affair made her remember Ernest saying life was like a box of hand grenades. For the first time, despite her intelligence, she fell guardedly in love with a completely unsuitable man. He was a young "genius" director. After that she fell deeply and unguardedly in love with a man who most women in the world would have fallen in love with. Equally unsuitable.

The initial flush of ego that she could attract such primary alpha males was quickly dampened by how they treated her.

The director, an unlikable ferret of a man only a few years older than she, had made three offbeat movies that not only were critical successes but had made a goodly sum of money. Every studio wanted a relationship with him. LoddStone Studios gave him a three-picture deal and also gave him Claudia to rewrite the script he was planning to shoot.

One of the elements of the director's genius was that he had a clear vision of what he wanted. At first he condescended to Claudia because she was a woman and a writer, both inferior in the power structure of Hollywood. They quarreled immediately.

He asked her to write a scene she felt did not belong to the structure of the plot. On its own Claudia recognized that the scene would be a flashy bit that would be just a show-off scene for the director.

"I can't write that scene," Claudia said. "It does nothing for the story. It's just action and camera."

The director said curtly. "That's why they're movies. Just do it the way we discussed it."

"I don't want to waste your time and mine," Claudia said. "Just go write with your fucking camera."

The director didn't waste time even getting angry. "You're fired," he said. "Off the picture." He clapped his hands.

But Skippy Deere and Bobby Bantz made them reconcile, which was only possible because the director had become intrigued by her stubbornness. The picture was a success, and Claudia had to admit this was more because of the director's talent as a moviemaker than hers as a writer. Quite simply she had not been able to see the director's vision. They fell into bed almost by accident, but the director proved to be a disappointment. He refused to be naked, he made love with his shirt on. But still Claudia had dreams of the two of them making great movies together. One of the great director-writer teams of all time. She was quite willing to be the subordinate partner, to make her talent serve his genius. They would create great art together and become a legend. The affair lasted a month, until Claudia finished her "spec" script of *Messalina* and showed it to him. He read it and tossed it aside. "A piece of feminist bullshit with tits and ass," he said. "You're a clever girl but it's not a picture I want to waste a year of my life making."

"It's only a first draft," Claudia said.

"Jesus, I hate people taking advantage of a personal relationship to get a movie made," the director said.

In that moment Claudia fell completely out of love with him. She was outraged. "I don't have to fuck you to make a movie," she said.

"Of course you don't," the director said. "You're talented and you have your reputation of being one of the great pieces of ass in the movie business."

Now Claudia was horrified. She never gossiped about her sexual partners. And she hated his tone, as if women were somehow shameful for doing what men did.

Claudia said to him, "You have talent, but a man who fucks with his shirt on has a worse reputation. And at least I never got laid by promising someone a screen test."

That was the end of their relationship, and it had started her thinking of Dita Tommey as the director. She decided that only a woman could do justice to her script.

Well, what the hell, Claudia thought. The bastard never got totally naked and he didn't like to talk after sex. He was truly a genius in film but he had no language. And for a genius he was a truly uninteresting man, except when he talked movies.

Now Claudia was approaching the great curve of the Pacific Coast Highway that showed the ocean as a great mirror by reflecting the cliffs to her right. It was her favorite spot in the world, natural beauty that always thrilled her. It was only ten minutes to the Malibu Colony, where Athena lived. Claudia tried to formulate her plea: to save the movie, to make Athena return. She remembered that at different times in their lives they had had the same lover, and she felt a flush of pride that the man who had loved Athena could love her.

The sun was at its most brilliant now. It polished the waves of the Pacific into huge diamonds. Claudia braked suddenly. She thought one of the gliders was coming down in front of her car. She could see the glider, a young girl with one tit hanging out of her blouse, give a demure wave as she sailed onto the beach. Why were they allowed, why didn't the police appear? She shook her head and pressed the gas pedal. Traffic was loosening and the highway swerved so that she could no longer see the ocean, though in a half mile it would reappear. Like true love, Claudia thought smilingly. True love in her life always reappeared.

When she truly fell in love, it was a painful but educational experience. And it was not really her fault, for the man was Steve Stalling, a Bankable Star and idol of women all over the world. He had a fearful masculine beauty, genuine charm, and an enormous vivacity that was fueled by the prudent use of cocaine. He also had great talent as an actor. More than anything else, he was a Don Juan. He screwed everything in sight—on location in Africa, in a small town in the American West, in Bombay, Singapore, Tokyo, London, Rome, Paris. He did this in the spirit of a gentleman giving alms to the poor, an act of Christian charity. There was never any question of a relationship, no more than a beggar would be invited to a benefactor's dinner party. He was so enchanted by Claudia that the affair lasted twenty-seven days.

It was a humiliating twenty-seven days for Claudia despite the pleasure. Steve Stallings was an irresistible lover, with the help of cocaine. He was more comfortable being naked than even Claudia. The fact that he had a perfectly proportioned body helped. Often Claudia caught him inspecting himself in the mirror in much the same way as a woman adjusting her hat.

Claudia knew she was just a lesser concubine. When they had dates he would always call her to say he would be an hour late and then would arrive six hours later. Sometimes he would cancel altogether. She was only his fallback position for the night. Also, when they made love he would always insist she use cocaine with him, which was fun but turned her brain into such mush she could not work the next few days, and what she did write, she distrusted. She realized that she was becoming what she detested more than anything else in the world: a woman whose whole life depended on the whims of a man.

She was humiliated by the fact that she was his fourth or fifth choice, but she didn't really blame him. She blamed herself. After all, at this point in his fame Steve Stallings could have almost any woman in America and he had chosen her. Stallings would grow old and less beautiful, he would become less famous and use more and more cocaine. He had to cash in during his prime. She was in love and, for one of the few times in her life, terribly unhappy.

So on the twenty-seventh day when Stallings called to say he would be an hour late, she told him, "Don't bother, Steve, I'm leaving your geisha house."

There was a pause, and when he answered he did not seem surprised. "We part friends I hope," he said. "I really enjoy your company."

"Sure," Claudia said and hung up. For the first time she did not want to remain friends at the end of an affair. What really bothered her was her lack of intelligence. It was obvious that all his behavior was a trick to make her go away, that it had taken her too long to take the hint. It was mortifying. How could she have been so dumb? She wept, but in a week she found she did not miss being in love at all. Her time was her own and she could work. It was a pleasure to get back to her writing with a head clear of cocaine and true love.

After her director genius of a lover had rejected her script, Claudia worked furiously for six months on the rewrite.

Claudia De Lena wrote her original screenplay of *Messalina* as a witty propaganda piece for feminism. But after five years in the movie business she knew that any message had to be coated with more basic ingredients, such as greed, sex, murder, and a belief in humanity. She knew she had to write great parts not only for her first choice, Athena Aquitane, but for at least three other female stars in lesser roles. Good female roles were so scarce that the script would attract top-name stars. And then, absolutely essential, the great villain—charming, ruthless, handsome, and witty. Here she drew on memories of her father.

Claudia at first wanted to approach a female independent producer with clout, but most studio heads who could green-light a picture were males. They would love the script but they would worry it would turn into too overt a propaganda piece with a female producer and a female director. They would want at least one male hand in there somewhere. Claudia had already decided that Dita Tommey would direct.

Tommey would certainly accept because it would be a megabudget film. Such a film if successful would put her in the Bankable class. Even if it failed it would enhance her reputation. A huge budget film that failed was sometimes more prestigious for a director than a small budget picture that made money.

Another reason was that Dita Tommey loved women exclusively and this picture would give her access to four beautiful famous women.

Claudia wanted Tommey because they had worked together on a picture a few years ago and it had been a good experience. She was very direct, very witty, very talented. Also she was not a "writer killer" director, who called in friends to rewrite and share credit. She never filed for writing credit on a film unless she contributed her fair share, and she was not a sexual harasser as were some directors and stars. Though the term "sexual harassment" could not really be used in the movie business, where the selling of sex appeal was part of the job.

Claudia made sure she sent the script to Skippy Deere on a Friday, he only read scripts carefully on weekends. She sent it to him because, despite his betrayals, he was the best producer in town. And because she could never let go completely on an old relationship. It worked. She got a call from him on Sunday morning. He wanted her to have lunch with him that very day.

Claudia threw her computer into her Mercedes and dressed to work: blue denim man's shirt, faded blue jeans, and slip-on sneakers. She tied her hair back with a red scarf.

She took Ocean Avenue in Santa Monica. In the Palisades Park that separated Ocean Avenue from Pacific Coast Highway, she saw the homeless men and women of Santa Monica gathering for their Sunday brunch. Volunteer social workers brought their food and drink to them every Sunday in the fresh air of the park at wooden tables and benches. Claudia always took this route to watch them, to remind herself of that other world where people did not have Mercedeses and swimming pools and did not shop on Rodeo Drive. In the early years she often volunteered to serve food in the park, now she just sent a check to the church that fed them. It had become too painful to go from one world to the other, it blunted her desire to succeed. She could not avoid watching the men, so shabbily dressed, their lives in ruins, yet some of them curiously dignified. To live so without hope seemed to her an extraordinary thing, and yet it was just a question of money, that money she earned so easily writing movie scripts. What she earned in six months was more money than these men saw in their entire lives.

At Skippy Deere's mansion in the Beverly Hills canyons, Claudia was led by the housekeeper to the swimming pool, with its bright blue-and-yellow cabanas. Deere was seated in a cushioned lounge chair. Beside him was the small marble table that held his phone and a stack of scripts. He was wearing his red-framed reading glasses that he only used at home. In his hand was a tall frosted glass of Evian water.

He sprang up and embraced her. "Claudia," he said, "we have business to do fast."

She was judging his voice. She could usually tell the reaction to her scripts by the tones of voices. There was the carefully modulated praise that meant a definite "no." Then there was the joyful, enthusiastic voice that expressed an unrestrained admiration and was almost always followed by at least three reasons why the script could not be bought; another studio was doing the same subject, the proper cast could not be assembled, the studios would not touch the subject matter. But Deere's voice was that of the determined business man latching onto a good thing. He was talking money and controls. That meant "Yes."

"This could be a very big picture," he told Claudia. "Very, very big. In fact it can't be small. I know what you're doing, you're a very clever girl, but I have to sell a studio on the sex. Of course I'll sell it to the female stars on feminism. The male star we can get if you soften him a little, give him more moments as a good guy. Now I know you want to be an associate producer on this, but I call the shots. You can have your say, I'm open to reason."

"I want to have my say on the director," Claudia said.

"You, the studio, and the stars," Deere said, laughing.

"I don't sell it unless I get approval of the director," Claudia said.

"Okay," Deere said. "So first tell the studio you want to direct, then back down, and they'll be so relieved that they'll give you the approval." He paused for a moment. "Who do you have in mind?"

"Dita Tommey," Claudia said.

"Good. Clever," Deere said. "Female stars love her. The Studio too. She brings everything in on budget, she doesn't live off the picture. But you and I do the casting before we bring her on."

"Who will you bring it to?" Claudia asked.

"LoddStone," Deere said. "They go with me pretty much so we won't have to fight too much about casting and directors. Claudia, you've written a perfect script. Witty, exciting, with a great point of view on early feminism and that's hot today. And sex. You justify Messalina and all women. I'll talk to Melo and Molly Flanders about your deal and she can talk to Business Affairs at LoddStone."

"You son of a bitch," Claudia said. "You've already talked to LoddStone?"

"Last night," Skippy Deere said with a grin. "I brought the script over to them and they gave me the green light if I can put everything together. And listen, Claudia, don't shit me. I know you've got Athena in your pocket on this, that's why you're being so tough." He paused for a moment. "That's what I told LoddStone. Now let's go to work."

That had been the beginning of the great project. She could not let it go down the drain now.

. . .

Claudia was approaching the traffic light where she would have to take a left turn onto the side road that would lead her to the Colony. For the first time, she felt a sense of panic. Athena was so strong-willed, as stars must be, that she would never change her mind. No matter; if Athena refused, she would fly to Vegas and ask her brother Cross to help. He had never failed her. Not when they were growing up, not when she went to live with her mother, not when their mother died.

Claudia had a memory of the great festive occasions at the Clericuzio mansion on Long Island. A setting from a Grimm's fairy tale, mansion enclosed by walls, she and Cross playing among the fig trees. There were two groups of boys ranging from eight to twelve years old. The opposing group was led by Dante Clericuzio, grandson of the old Don who had stationed himself at an upstairs window like a dragon.

Dante was an aggressive boy who loved to fight, who loved to be a general, and the only boy who dared to challenge her brother, Cross, in physical combat. Dante had Claudia on the ground, hitting her, trying to beat her into submission, when Cross appeared. Then Dante and Cross had fought. What had struck Claudia then was how confident Cross had been in the face of Dante's ferocity. And Cross won easily.

And so Claudia could not understand her mother's choice. How could she not love Cross more? Cross was so much more worthy. Proving his worth by electing to go with his father. And Claudia never doubted that Cross had wanted to stay with his mother and her.

In the years that followed the disruption, the family still maintained a relationship of sorts. Claudia came to know, by conversations, by the body language of the people around them, that her brother Cross had to some degree achieved their father's eminence. The affection between her and her brother remained constant, though they were now completely different. She realized that Cross was part of the Clericuzio Family, she was not.

Two years after Claudia moved to L.A., when she was twenty-three, her mother, Nalene, was diagnosed with cancer. Cross, then working with Gronevelt at the Xanadu after making his bones for the Clericuzio, came to spend the last two weeks with them in Sacramento. Cross hired nurses around the clock and a cook and housekeeper. The three of them lived together for the first time since the breakup of the family. Nalene forbade Pippi to visit her.

The cancer had affected Nalene's eyesight, so Claudia read to her constantly, from magazines, from newspapers and books. Cross went out to do the shopping. Sometimes he had to fly to Vegas for an afternoon to take care of Hotel business, but he always returned at evening.

During the night, Cross and Claudia would take turns holding their mother's hand, comforting her. And though she was heavily medicated, she continually pressed their hands. Sometimes she hallucinated and thought her two children were little again. One terrible night she wept and begged forgiveness of Cross for what she had done to him. Cross had to hold her in his arms and reassure her that everything had turned out for the best.

During the long evenings when their mother was deep into a drugged sleep, Cross and Claudia told each other the details of their lives.

Cross explained that he had sold the Collection Agency and left the Clericuzio Family, though they had used their influence to get him his job at the Xanadu Hotel. He hinted at his power and told Claudia that she was welcome at the Hotel anytime, RFB—room, food, and beverage free. Claudia asked how he could do that and Cross told her with just a touch of pride, "I have the Pencil."

Claudia found that pride comical and a little sad.

Claudia seemingly felt their mother's death far more strongly than Cross, but the experience had brought them together again. They regained their childhood intimacy. Claudia frequently went to Vegas over the years and met Gronevelt and observed the close relationship the old man had with her brother. During these years Claudia saw that Cross had a certain kind of power, but that he never linked his power with the Clericuzio Family. Since Claudia had severed all ties with the Family and never attended the funerals, weddings, and christenings, she didn't know that Cross still was part of the Family social structure. And Cross never spoke of it to her. She rarely saw her father. He had no interest in her.

New Year's Eve was the biggest event in Vegas; people all over the country flocked there, but Cross always had a suite for Claudia. Claudia was not a big gambler, but one New Year's Eve she got carried away. She had brought an aspiring actor with her and was trying to impress him. She lost control and signed fifty thousand dollars in markers. Cross had come down to the suite with the markers in his hand, and there was a curious look on his face. Claudia recognized it when he spoke. It was his father's face.

"Claudia," Cross said, "I thought you were smarter than me. What the hell is this?"

Claudia felt a little sheepish. Cross had often warned her to gamble only for small stakes. Also to never increase her bets when she was losing. And to spend no more than two or three hours gambling every day, because the length of time spent gambling was the greatest trap. Claudia had violated all his advice. . . .

She said, "Cross, give me a couple of weeks and I'll pay it off."

She was surprised by her brother's reaction. "I'll kill you before I let you pay off these markers." Very deliberately he tore up the slips of paper and put them in his pocket. He said, "Look, I invite you down here because I want to see you, not to take your money. Get this through your head, you cannot win. It has nothing to do with luck. Two and two make four."

"Okay, okay," Claudia said.

"I don't mind having to tear up these markers, but I hate your being dumb," Cross said.

They had left it at that, but Claudia wondered. Did Cross have that much power? Would Gronevelt approve or would he even know about this?

There had been other such incidents, but one of the most chilling involved a woman named Loretta Lang.

Loretta had been a singing and dancing star in the Xanadu Follies show. She had an abundance of verve and a natural humorous perkiness that charmed Claudia. Cross introduced them after the show.

Loretta Lang was as charming in person as she was on the stage. But Claudia noticed that Cross was not as charmed, in fact seemed a little irritated by her vivacity.

On Claudia's next visit, she brought along Melo Stuart for an evening in Vegas where they could catch the Follies show. Melo had come merely to indulge Claudia, not expecting much. He watched appraisingly and then told Claudia, "This girl has a real shot. Not singing or dancing, but she's a natural comic. A female with that is gold."

Backstage to meet Loretta, Melo put on his game face and said, "Loretta, I loved you. Loved you. Understand? Can you come to L.A. next week? I'll arrange to have you on film to show to a studio friend of mine. But first you have to sign a contract with my agency. You know I have to put in a lot of work before I make any money. That's the business, but remember I love you."

Loretta threw her arms around Melo. There was no witty mocking of devotion here, Claudia noted. A date was set and the three of them had dinner together to celebrate, before Melo caught his early morning plane back to L.A.

During supper Loretta confessed that she was already under an airtight contract with an agency that specialized in nightclub entertainment. A contract with three years to run. Melo assured Loretta that everything could be ironed out.

But things could not be ironed out. Loretta's showbiz agency insisted on controlling her career for the next three years. Loretta frantic, astonished Claudia by asking her to appeal to her brother, Cross.

"What the hell can Cross do?" Claudia asked.

Loretta said, "He has a lot of clout in this town. He can get a deal I can live with. Please?"

When Claudia went up to the penthouse suite on the roof of the Hotel and presented the problem to Cross, her brother looked at her with disgust. He shook his head.

"What the hell's the big deal?" Claudia asked. "Just put the word in, that's all I'm asking."

"You are dumb," Cross said. "I've seen dozens of dames like her. They ride friends like you up to the top and then you're history."

"So what?" Claudia said. "She's really talented. This could change her whole life for the better."

Cross shook his head again. "Don't ask me to do this," he said.

"Why not?" Claudia asked. She was used to asking people favors for other people, it was part of the movie business.

"Because once I get in to it, I have to succeed," Cross said.

"I'm not expecting you to succeed, I'm just asking you to do your best," Claudia said. "At least then I can tell Loretta we tried."

Cross laughed. "You really are dumb," he said. "Okay, tell Loretta and her agency to come and see me tomorrow. Ten A.M. sharp. And you might as well be there too."

At the meeting the next morning, Claudia met Loretta's showbiz agent for the first time. His name was Tolly Nevans, and he was dressed in the casual Vegas style, modified by the seriousness of the meeting. That is, he wore a blue blazer over a collarless white shirt and blue denim pants.

"Cross, a pleasure to see you again," Tolly Nevans said.

"We've met?" Cross asked. He never had handled the business details of the Follies show personally.

"A long time ago," Nevans said smoothly. "When Loretta opened her first time at the Xanadu."

Claudia noted the difference between the L.A. agents who dealt with big-time film talent and Tolly Nevans, who managed the much smaller-time world of nightclub entertainment. Nevans was a little more nervous, his physical appearance not so overpowering. He did not have the complete confidence of Melo Stuart.

Loretta pecked Cross on the cheek but did not say anything to him. Indeed she showed none of her usual vivacity. She sat next to Claudia, who sensed Loretta's tension.

Cross was in a golf outfit, white slacks, a white T-shirt, and white sneakers. He wore a blue baseball cap on his head. He offered drinks from the wet bar but they all refused. Then he said quietly, "Let's get this business settled. Loretta?"

Her voice trembled. "Tolly wants to keep his percentage of everything I earn. That includes any movie work. But the L.A. agency naturally wants their full percentage of any movie work they get me. I can't pay two percentages. And then Tolly wants to call the shots on anything I do. The L.A. people won't stand for that and neither will I."

Nevans shrugged. "We have a contract. We just want her to live up to that contract."

Loretta said, "But then my film agent won't sign me up."

Cross said, "It seems simple to me. Loretta, you just buy your way out of the contract."

Nevans said, "Loretta is a great performer, she makes a lot of money for us. We've always promoted her, we always believed in her talent. We've invested a lot of money. We can't just let her go now when she's paying off."

Cross said, "Loretta, buy him out."

Loretta almost wailed, "I can't pay two percentages. It's too cruel."

Claudia tried to control the smile on her face. But Cross did not. Nevans looked hurt.

Finally Cross said, "Claudia, go get your golf gear. I want you to shoot nine holes with me. I'll meet you downstairs at the Cashier's cage when I'm finished here."

Claudia had wondered at Cross being dressed for the meeting in such a cavalier way. As if he were not taking it seriously. It had offended her and she knew it offended Loretta. But it had reassured Tolly. The man had not proposed any compromise. So Claudia said to Cross, "I'll stick around, I want to see Solomon at work."

Cross could never get angry at his sister. He laughed and she smiled back at him. Then Cross turned to Nevans. "I see you're not bending. And I think you're right. How about a percentage of her movie earnings for one year? But you have to relinquish control or it won't work."

Loretta burst in angrily, "I'm not giving him that."

Nevans said, "And that's not what I want. The percentage is okay but what if we have a great booking for you and you're tied up in a movie? We lose money."

Cross sighed and said almost sadly, "Tolly, I want you to let this girl out of her contract. It is a request. Our hotel does a lot of business with you. Do me a favor."

For the first time Nevans seemed alarmed. He said in almost a pleading tone, "I'd love to do you this favor, Cross, but I have to check with my partners at the Agency." He paused for a moment. "Maybe I can arrange a buyout."

"No," Cross said. "I'm asking a favor. No buyout. And I want your answer now so I can go out and enjoy my golf game." He paused. "Just say yes or no."

Claudia was shocked by this abruptness. Cross was not threatening or intimidating as far as she could see. In fact he seemed to be giving up the whole affair, as if he had lost interest. But Claudia could see that Nevans was shaken.

What Nevans replied was surprising. "But that's unfair," he said. He shot a reproachful glance at Loretta, she lowered her eyes.

Cross pulled his baseball cap sideways in a swaggering manner. "It's just a request," he said. "You can refuse me. It's up to you."

"No, no," Nevans said. "I just didn't know you felt so strongly, that you were such good friends."

Suddenly Claudia saw an amazing change in her brother. Cross leaned over and gave Tolly Nevans a half hug of affection. His smile warmed his face. That bastard is handsome, she thought. And then Cross said in a voice full of gratitude, "Tolly, I won't forget this. Look, you have carte blanche here at the Xanadu for any new talent you want to showcase, third billing at the least. I'll even arrange to have a special night at the Follies with all the talent from you and on that night, I want you and your partners to have dinner with me at the hotel. Call me anytime and I'll leave word you get through. Direct. Okay?"

Claudia realized two things. Cross had deliberately shown his power. And that Cross had been careful to recompense Nevans to some degree but only after he had knuckled under, not before. Tolly Nevans would have his special night, would bask in power for that one night.

Claudia realized further that Cross had allowed her to see that power to show his love for her and that that love had a material force. And she saw in his beautifully planed face, in that beauty she had envied from childhood, of the sensual lips, the perfect nose, the oval eyes, all slightly hardening as if turning into the marble of ancient statues.

. . .

Claudia turned off the Pacific Coast Highway and drove to the gate of the Malibu Colony. She loved the Colony, the houses right on the beach, the ocean sparkling in front of them, and far off on the water, she saw again the reflections of the mountains behind them. She parked the car in front of Athena's house.

Boz Skannet was lying on the public beach south of the Malibu Colony fence. That fence of plain wire mesh ran down the beach for about ten steps into the water. But this fence was only a formal barrier. If you went out far enough, you could swim around it.

Boz was scouting for his next attack on Athena. Today would be a probing foray and so he had driven out to the public beach, bathing suit covered with a T-shirt and tennis slacks. His beach bag, really a tennis bag, held the vial of acid wrapped in towels.

From his spot on the beach he could look through the mesh fence at Athena's house. He could see the two private security guards on the beach. They were armed. If the back was covered, certainly the front of the house was covered. He didn't mind hurting the guards but he didn't want to make it seem like a madman slaughtering a whole bunch of people. That would detract from his justified destruction of Athena.

Boz Skannet took off his slacks and T-shirt and stretched out on his blanket, staring over the sand and the blue sheet of the Pacific Ocean beyond. The warmth of the sun made him drowsy. He thought of Athena.

In college he had heard a professor lecturing on Emerson's essays and quoting, "Beauty is its own excuse." Was it Emerson, was it Beauty? But he had thought of Athena.

It is so rare to find a human being so beautiful in physical form and so virtuous in other parts of her nature. And so he thought of Thena. Everybody had called her Thena in those days of her girlhood.

He had loved her so much in his youth that he lived in a dream of happiness that she loved him. He could not believe that life could be so sweet. And little by little everything had been tarnished with decay.

How did she dare to be so perfect? How did she dare to be so demanding of love? How did she dare to make so many people love her? Didn't she know how dangerous that would be?

And Boz wondered at himself. Why had his own love turned to hate? It was simple really. Because he knew he could not possess her to the end of their lives; that one day he must lose her. That one day she would lie down with other men, that one day she would disappear from his Heaven. And never think of him again.

He felt the sun's warmth move off his face and opened his eyes. Looming above him was a very large, well-dressed man who was carrying a folding chair. Boz recognized him. It was Jim Losey, the detective who had interrogated him after he threw the water in Thena's face.

Boz squinted up at him. "What a coincidence, both of us swimming on the same beach. What the fuck do you want?"

Losey unfolded the chair and sat on it. "My ex-wife gave me this chair. I was interrogating and arresting so many surfers she said I might as well be comfortable." He looked down at Boz Skannet almost kindly. "I just wanted to ask you a few questions. One, what are you doing so close to Miss Aquitane's house? You're violating the judge's restraining order."

"I'm on a public beach, there's a fence in between us, and I'm in a bathing suit. Do I look like I'm harassing her?" Boz said.

Losey had a sympathetic smile on his face. "Hey, look," he said, "if I was married to that broad, I couldn't stay away from her either. How about if I take a look in your beach bag?"

Boz put the beach bag beneath his head. "No," he said. "Unless you have a warrant."

Losey gave him a friendly smile. "Don't make me arrest you," he said. "Or just beat the shit out of you and take the bag."

This aroused Boz. He stood up, he offered the bag to Losey, but then he held it away from him. "Try and take it," he said.

Jim Losey was startled. In his own estimation he had never met anybody tougher than himself. In any other situation he would have drawn his blackjack or his gun and beaten the man to a pulp. Perhaps it was the sand under his feet that made him uncertain, or perhaps it was the utter fearlessness of Skannet.

Boz was smiling at him. "You'll have to shoot me," he said. "I'm stronger than you. Big as you are. And if you shoot me, you won't have probable cause."

Losey admired the man's perceptiveness. In a physical struggle the issue might be in doubt. And there was no cause to draw a weapon.

"Okay," he said. He folded up his chair and started to walk away. Then he turned and said admiringly, "You're really a tough guy. You win. But don't give me a good probable cause. You see I haven't measured your distance from the house, you may be just out of range of the judge's order. . . ."

Boz laughed. "I won't give you cause, don't worry."

He watched Jim Losey walk off the beach to his car and drive away. Boz put his blanket into the beach bag and returned to his own car. He put the beach bag in the trunk, took the car key off its ring, and hid it under the front seat. Then he went back to the beach for his swim around the fence.

CHAPTER 5

ATHENA AQUITANE had earned her way to stardom in the traditional way that the public seldom appreciates. She spent long years in training: acting classes, dance and movement classes, voice lessons, extensive reading in dramatic literature, all necessary to the art of acting.

And of course the scut work. She made the rounds of agents, casting directors, mildly lecherous producers and directors, the more dinosaur-like sexual advances of studio wheels and chiefs.

In her first year she earned her living by doing commercials, and some modeling, as a skimpily clad hostess for automotive expositions, but that was only her first year. Then her acting skills began to pay off. She had lovers who showered her with gifts of jewelry and money. Some of them offered marriage. The affairs were brief and ended on friendly terms.

None of this had been painful or humiliating to her, not even when the buyer of a Rolls-Royce assumed she came with the car. She had put him off with the joke that she had the same price as the car. She was fond of men, she enjoyed sex, but only as a treat and reward for more serious endeavor. Men were not a serious part of her world.

Acting was Life. Her secret knowledge of herself was serious. The dangers of the world were serious. But acting came first. Not the tiny movie roles that enabled her to pay expenses, but the great acting parts in great plays put on by local theater groups and then the plays at the Mark Taper Forum that finally propelled her toward major film roles.

Her real life was the parts she played, she felt more alive as she brought her characters to life, carried them around inside her while living out her ordinary existence. Her love affairs were like amusements, playing golf and tennis, dining with friends, dreamlike substances.

Real life was only in the cathedral-like theater: putting on makeup, adding one splash of color to her costume, her face contorting with emotions of the lines of the play running through her head, and then, looking into that deep blackness of the audience—God finally showing his face—she pleaded her fate. She wept, fell in love, screamed with anguish, begged forgiveness for her secret sins, and sometimes experienced the redemptive joy of happiness found.

She hungered for fame and success to obliterate her past, to drown her memories of Boz Skannet, of the child they had together, of the betrayal by her beauty; a sly fairy godmother's boon.

Like any artist, she wanted the world to love her. She knew she was beautiful—how could she not, her world constantly told her so—but she knew also she was intelligent. And so from the beginning she believed in herself. What she really could not believe, at the beginning, was that she had the indispensable ingredients of true genius: enormous energy and concentration. And curiosity.

Acting and music were Athena's true loves, and to be able to concentrate on these things she used her energy to make herself expert in everything else. She learned to fix a car, became a superb cook, excelled at sports. She studied lovemaking in the literature and in life, knowing how important it was in her chosen profession.

She had a flaw. She could not bear to inflict pain on a fellow human being, and since in this life this was impossible to avoid, she was an unhappy woman. Yet she made hard-nosed decisions that furthered her place in the world. She used her power as a Bankable Star; she sometimes had a coldness that was as intense as her beauty. Powerful men beseeched her to appear in their movies, men begged to climb into her bed. She influenced, even demanded, the choosing of directors and costars. She could commit minor crimes without punishment, outrage custom, defy nearly all moralities, and who was to say who was the real Athena? She had the inscrutability of all

MARIO PUZO • 130

Bankable Stars, she was a twin, you could not separate her real life from the lives she lived on screen.

All this and the world loved her, but that was not enough. She knew her inner ugliness. There was one person who did not love her and that caused her to suffer. It is part of the definition of an actress that she will despair if she gets one hundred positive reviews and a single hateful one.

At the end of her first five years in Los Angeles, Athena got her first starring role in film and made her greatest conquest.

Like all top male stars, Steven Stallings had a veto over the female leading role of each of his pictures. He saw Athena in a Mark Taper Forum play and recognized her talent. But even more he was struck by her beauty, and so he chose Athena to costar with him in his next film.

Athena was completely surprised and flattered. She knew this was her big break, and initially she did not know why she had been chosen. Her agent, Melo Stuart, enlightened her.

They were in Melo's office, a wonderfully decorated room with Oriental bric-a-brac, gold-threaded carpets, and heavy comfortable furniture all bathed in artificial lights since the curtains were closed to cut out daylight. Melo liked an English tea in his office rather than going out for lunch and picked up the little sandwiches and popped them into his mouth as he talked. He only went out to lunch with his really famous clients.

"You deserve this break," he told Athena. "You're a great actress. But you've only been in this town a few years and despite your intelligence you're a little green. So don't take offense about what I'm going to say—here's what happened." He paused for a moment. "Usually I would never explain this, usually it's not necessary."

"But I'm so green," Athena said smiling.

"Not green exactly," Melo said. "But you're so focused on your art, you sometimes seem unaware of the social complexities of the industry."

Athena was amused. "So tell me how I got the part."

Melo said, "Stalling's agent called me. He said Stallings saw you in the Taper play and was knocked out by your performance. He def-

initely wants you in the picture. Then the producer called me to negotiate and we made the deal. Straight salary, two hundred grand, no
points, that comes later in your career, and no strings for any other
picture. That's a really great deal for you."

"Thank you," Athena said.

"I really shouldn't have to be saying this," Melo said. "Steven has
a habit of falling madly in love with his costars. Sincerely, but he's a
very ardent wooer."

Athena interrupted him. "Melo, don't spell it out."

"I feel I must," Melo said.

He gazed at her fondly. He himself, usually so impervious, had
fallen in love with Athena at the beginning, but since she had never
acted seductively, he had taken the hint and not revealed his feelings.
She was, after all, a valuable piece of property that would in the future earn him millions.

"Are you trying to tell me that I'm supposed to jump on his bones
the first time we're alone?" Athena said dryly. "Isn't my great talent
enough?"

"Absolutely not," Melo said. "And absolutely. A great actress is a
great actress, no matter what. But you know how someone becomes
a great star in film? At some time they have to get the great part at
exactly the right moment. And this is that great part for you. You
cannot afford to miss it. And what's so hard about falling in love
with Steven Stallings? A hundred million women all over the world
love him, why not you? You should be flattered."

"I'm flattered," Athena said coolly. "But if I really hate him, then
what?"

Melo popped another tea sandwich into his mouth. "What's to
hate? He's really a sweet man, I swear to you. But at least dally with
him until they've shot you enough in the picture so they can't cut
you out."

"What if I'm so good they won't want to cut me?" Athena said.

Melo sighed. "To tell the truth, Steven won't wait that long. If
you're not in love with him after three days, you'll be out of the picture."

"That's sexual harassment," Athena said, laughing.

"There can be no sexual harassment in the movie business," Melo said. "In one form or another you're offering your ass for sale by just going in."

"I meant the part where I have to fall in love with him," Athena said. "Straight screwing is not enough for Steven?"

"He can get all the screwing he wants," Melo said. "He's in love with you so he wants love in return. Until the shoot is over." He sighed. "Then you'll both fall out of love because you'll be too busy working." He paused for a moment. "It won't be insulting to your dignity," he said. "A star like Steven indicates his interest. The recipient, yourself, responds or shows a lack of interest in that interest. Steven will send you flowers the first day. The second day after rehearsal he invites you to dinner to study the script. There's nothing forced about it. Except, of course, that you will be cut from the picture if you don't go. With a full payoff, I can do that for you."

"Melo, don't you think I'm good enough to make it without selling my body?" Athena said with mock reproach.

"Of course you are," Melo said. "You're young, only twenty-five. You can wait two or three, even four or five years. I have absolute faith in your talent. But give it a chance. Everybody loves Steven."

It went exactly as Melo Stuart predicted. Athena received flowers the first day. They second day they rehearsed with the whole company. It was a dramatic comedy where laughter led to tears, one of the hardest things to do. Athena was impressed with Steven Stallings's skill. He read his part in a monotone with no effort to impress but still the lines came alive, and on the variations he invariably picked the one most true. They played one scene a dozen different ways and responded to each other, followed each other like dancers. At the end, he muttered, "Good, good," and smiled at her with respectful acknowledgment that was purely professional.

At the end of the day Steven finally turned on his charm.

"I think this may be a great movie because of you," he said. "How about getting together tonight and really doing a number on this script?" He paused for a moment and then said with a boyish smile that was endearing, "We were really good together."

"Thank you," Athena said. "When and where?"

Immediately Steven's face expressed a polite, playful horror. "Oh, no," he said. "Your choice."

At that moment Athena decided to accept her role and to play it as a true professional. He was the superstar. She was the newcomer. But all the choices were his and it was her duty to choose what he wanted. Ringing in her ears was Melo saying, "you wait two, three, four, five years." She couldn't wait.

"Would you mind coming to my place?" Athena asked. "I'll make dinner simple so we can work while we eat." She paused for a moment, then said, "At seven?"

Because she was a perfectionist, Athena prepared for the mutual seduction physically and mentally. Dinner would be light so it would not affect their work or their sexual performance. Though she rarely touched alcohol, she bought a bottle of white wine. The meal would show off her talent as a cook, but she could prepare while they worked.

Clothes. She understood that the seduction was supposed to be accidental, with no prior intent. But they should not be used as a signal to ward him off either. As an actor, Steven would be looking to interpret every sign.

So she wore faded blue jeans that showed her buttocks to advantage, the mottled blue and faded white invitingly cheerful. No belt. Above, a frilly white silk blouse that though it showed no cleavage, indicated the milkier color of her breasts beneath. Her ears she decorated with small round clip-ons, green to match her eyes. Still it was just a little too severe, a little standoffish. It left room for doubt. Then she had a stroke of genius. She painted her toenails a scarlet red and greeted him barefoot.

Steven Stallings arrived carrying a bottle of good red wine, not super but very good. He was also dressed for business. Baggy brown corduroy trousers, blue denim shirt, white sneakers, his dark black hair carelessly combed. Under his arm was the script with yellow note slips peeking out demurely. The only thing that gave him away was the faint scent of cologne.

They ate casually at the kitchen table. He complimented her on the food, as well he should. And as they ate they leafed through their scripts, comparing notes, changing dialogue for smoother delivery.

After dinner they moved to the living room and played out specific scenes they had targeted as trouble areas in the script. Through all this they were very conscious of each other, and it affected their work.

Athena noticed that Steven Stallings was playing his part perfectly. He was professional, respectful. Just his eyes betrayed his genuine admiration of her beauty, his appreciation of her talent as an actress, of her mastery of the material. Finally he asked her if she was too tired to play the crucial love scene in the movie script.

By that time the dinner had been comfortably digested. By that time they had become close friends, like the characters in the script. They played the love scene, Steven kissing her slightly on the lips but leaving out the body gropings. After the first chaste kiss, he looked deeply and sincerely into her eyes, and with perfect husky emotion in his voice, he said, "I wanted to do that the first time I saw you."

Athena held his eyes with her own. Then she lowered them, pulled his head down gently and gave him a chaste kiss. The necessary signal. They were both surprised by the genuine passion with which he responded. Which proved she was the better actor, Athena thought. But he was skillful. As he undressed her, his hands smoothed her skin and his fingers probed, his tongue tickled the inside of her thigh and her body responded. This wasn't so terrible, she thought as they moved into the bedroom. And Steven was so startlingly handsome, his classic face, suffused with passion, had an intensity that could not be duplicated on film, indeed on film this would be degraded into lecherousness. When he made love on screen it was far more spiritual.

Athena had now worked herself into the part of a woman overcome with mad physical passion. They were perfectly in sync and in one blinding moment rose to a simultaneous climax. Lying back in exhaustion, both wondered how the scene would have appeared on film and decided it would not have been good enough for a take. It had not revealed character as it should, or advanced the story as it should. It had lacked the inner tender emotion of true love or even true lust. There would have to be another take.

Steven Stallings fell in love, but he often did that. Athena, despite the fact that it was in some sense professional rape, felt pleased that things had turned out so well. There was no real downside except the question of free will. And it could be said of any life that the suppression of free will, judiciously exercised, was often necessary for human survival.

Steven was happy that now in the shooting of his new film he had all his ducks in a row. He had a good working partner. They would have a pleasant relationship, he wouldn't have to look around for sex. Also, he had rarely had a woman so blessed with talent and beauty as Athena, and also so good in bed. And obviously madly in love with him, which of course could be a problem later on.

What happened next cemented their love. They both jumped out of bed and said, "Let's go back to work." They picked up their scripts and, naked, perfected their readings.

However, one disconcerting note for Athena was when Steven put on his shorts. They were scalloped pink, especially designed to show off his shapely buttocks, those buns that were the source of ecstasy to his female fans. Another odd note was when he proudly told her that he had used a condom made especially for him, manufactured by a company he had invested in. You could never detect he was wearing one. They were also absolutely impregnable. And he asked her what would be the best marketing name for them: Excalibur or King Arthur. He liked King Arthur. Athena thought it over for a moment.

Then she said with mock seriousness, "Maybe a more politically correct name?"

"You're right," Steven said. "They're so expensive to make we have to sell them to both sexes. Our tag marketing line will be 'Condom of the Stars.' How about that for a name? Star Condoms."

. . .

The movie and their affair were both huge successes. Athena had successfully climbed the first rung of the ladder to stardom, and each picture she made over the next five years solidified that success.

The affair, as most star affairs go, was also a success but naturally short-lived. Steven and Athena loved each other with help from the script, but their love had the humor and detachment made necessary by his fame and her ambition. Neither could afford to be more in love than the other and this equality in love was death to their passion. Also there was the question of geography. The affair ended when the picture ended. Athena went on location to India, Steven on location to Italy. There were phone calls and Christmas cards and gifts, they even flew to Hawaii for a weekend of ecstasy. Working together on a movie was like being Knights at the Round Table. Searching for fame and fortune was looking for the Holy Grail, you had to do it on your own.

There had been speculation that they might marry. Of this there was no possibility. Athena enjoyed the affair but always saw its comic side. Though she made it her business as a professional actor to appear more in love than Steven, it was almost impossible for her not to giggle. Steven was so sincere, so perfect as an ardent and sensitive lover, that she could just as well have gone to one of his films.

His physical beauty could be enjoyed but not constantly admired. His constant use of drugs and liquor was so controlled it was impossible to pass judgment. He treated cocaine as a prescription drug, alcohol made him more charming. Even his success had not made him willful or moody.

So it was a great surprise when Steven proposed marriage. Athena refused with good humor. She knew that Steven screwed everything that moved, on location, in Hollywood, and even at the rehabilitation clinic when his drug problem got out of control. He was not a man she wanted to have as a semipermanent part of her life.

Steven took her refusal well. It had been a momentary weakness springing from an excess of cocaine. He was almost relieved.

Over the next five years, as Athena shot up to the top rank of stardom, Steven began to fade. He was still an idol to his fans, especially women, but he was unlucky or unintelligent in picking his roles. Drugs and alcohol made him more careless in his work habits. Through Melo Stuart, Steven had asked Athena for the male lead in *Messalina*. The shoe was now on the other foot. Athena had approval of her costar and she gave him the role. She said yes out of a perverse sense of gratitude and because he was perfect for the part, however with the proviso that he did not have to sleep with her.

During the last five years Athena had had short affairs. One had been with a young producer, Kevin Marrion, the only son of Eli Marrion.

Kevin Marrion was her age but a veteran of the movie business. He had produced his first major film at the age of twenty-one and it had been a hit. Which convinced him he had a genius for movies. Since that time he had produced three flops, and now only his father gave him credibility in the industry.

Kevin Marrion was extremely good-looking; after all, Eli Marrion's first wife had been one of the greatest beauties in the business. Unfortunately his looks iced out in the camera and he failed all his screen tests. As a serious artist his future was as a producer.

Athena and Kevin met when he asked her to star in his new film. Athena listened to him in rapt wonder and horror. He talked with the particular innocence of the very serious-minded.

"This is the best movie script I have ever read," Kevin said. "I must tell you in all honesty that I helped rewrite it. Athena you are absolutely the only actress that deserves this role. I could have any actress in the industry but I want you." He looked sternly at her to convince her of his sincerity.

Athena was fascinated by his pitching of the script. It was the story of a homeless woman living on the streets who is redeemed by the finding of an abandoned infant in a garbage pail and who then goes on to become the leader of the homeless in America. Half of the film consisted of her pushing the shopping cart that held all her possessions. And after surviving alcohol, drugs, near starvation, rape, and a government attempt to take away her foundling, she goes on to run for president of the United States on an independent ticket. Not winning, however—that was the class of the script.

Athena's fascination had really been horror. This was a script that would require her to be a homeless, despairing woman in a desolate background in old clothes. Visually, a disaster. The sentimentality was rank, the intelligence level of dramatic construction, idiotic. It was a bewildering, hopeless mess.

Kevin said, "If you play this part, I will die happy."

And Athena thought, Am I crazy or is this guy a moron? But he was a powerful producer. Obviously sincere, and obviously a man who could get things done. She looked despairingly at Melo Stuart, and he smiled back at her encouragingly. But she could not speak.

"Wonderful. Wonderful idea," Melo said. "Classic. Rise and fall. Fall and rise. The very essence of drama. But Kevin, you know how important it is for Athena after her breakthrough to select the proper follow-up. Let us read the script and we'll get back to you."

"Of course," Kevin said and handed both of them copies of the script. "I know you'll love it."

Melo took Athena to a small Thai restaurant on Melrose. They ordered their meal and flipped through the script.

"I'll kill myself first," Athena said. "Is Kevin retarded?"

"You still don't understand the movie business," Melo said. "Kevin has intelligence. He's just doing something he is not equipped to do. I've seen worse."

"Where? When?" Athena said.

"I can't recall offhand," Melo said. "You're a big enough star to say no but you're not big enough to make unnecessary enemies."

"Eli Marrion is too smart to back his son up on this one," Athena said. "He must know how terrible this script is."

"Sure," Melo said. "He even jokes that he has a son who makes flop commercial movies and a daughter who makes serious movies that lose money. But Eli has to make his children happy. We don't. We say no to this movie. But there's a catch. LoddStone owns the rights to a big novel that has a great role for you. If you turn Kevin down, you may not get that other part."

Athena shrugged. "This time I'll wait."

"Why not take both parts? Make it a condition you do the novel first. Then we'll find an out on making Kevin's picture."

"And that won't make enemies?" Athena asked him smiling.

"The first picture will be a big hit so it won't matter. Then you can afford to make enemies."

"Are you sure I can get out of Kevin's picture afterwards?" Athena said.

"If I don't get you out, you can fire me," Melo said. He had already made the deal with Eli Marrion, who could not give the direct no to his son and had chosen this way out of the disaster. Eli wanted to make Melo and Athena the villains. And Melo didn't mind. Part of any movie agent's job was to be the villain in the script.

Everything worked out. The first part, the film of the novel, made Athena an absolutely first-rank star. But unfortunately the consequences made her decide on a period of celibacy.

During the sham of the preproduction of Kevin's movie that would never be made, it was predictable that he would fall in love with Athena. Kevin Marrion was a relatively innocent young man for a producer, and he pursued Athena with unabashed sincerity and ardor. His enthusiasm and his social conscience were his greatest charm. One evening, in a moment of weakness compounded by the guilt she felt about betraying the picture, Athena took him to bed. It was enjoyable enough and Kevin insisted on marriage.

Meanwhile Athena and Melo had persuaded Claudia De Lena to rewrite the script. She rewrote it as farce and Kevin fired her. He was so angry that he became a bore.

For Athena the affair was convenient. It fitted in nicely with her working schedule. And Kevin's enthusiasm was pleasurable in bed. And his insistence on marriage even without a prenuptial agreement was flattering, since he would inherit LoddStone Studios one day.

But one night after listening to him talk incessantly about the movies they were going to make together, a sudden insight flashed through Athena's mind: "If I have to listen to this guy one more minute, I will kill myself." Like many kind people exasperated into being unkind, she went all the way. Knowing she would feel guilty, she made it a package. In that moment, she told Kevin that not only would she not marry him, but she would not sleep with him anymore and that also she would not appear in his movie.

Kevin was stunned. "We have a contract," he said. "And we'll enforce it. You are betraying me in every way."

"I know," Athena said. "Just talk to Melo." She was disgusted with herself. Of course, Kevin was right, but she found it interesting that he was more worried about his movies than his love for her.

It was after this affair, her film career assured, that Athena lost interest in men. She remained celibate. She had more important things to do, things in which the love of men had no part.

Athena Aquitane and Claudia De Lena became close friends solely because Claudia was persistent in her pursuit of friendship with women she liked. She first met Athena while rewriting the script of one of her early movies, when Athena was not quite yet a great star.

Athena insisted on helping her with the script, and although this was usually a scary process for the writer, she proved to be intelligent and a great help. Her instincts on character and story were always good and nearly always unselfish. She was intelligent enough to know that the stronger the characters around her, the more she would have to play with in her own role.

They often worked in Athena's home in Malibu, and it was there they discovered they had many things in common. They were athletes: strong swimmers, top amateur golfers, and very good on the tennis court. The two of them played doubles together and beat most of the male doubles on the Malibu Beach tennis courts. So when the picture finished shooting, they continued their friendship.

Claudia told Athena everything about herself. Athena told Claudia little. It was that kind of friendship. Claudia recognized this but it didn't matter. Claudia told of her affair with Steve Stallings. Athena laughed delightedly and they compared notes. They agreed, yes, Steve had been great fun, great in bed. And so talented, he was a marvelously gifted actor and a really sweet man.

"He was almost as beautiful as you," Claudia said. She generously admired beauty in others.

Athena seemed not to have heard. It was a habit she had when somebody mentioned her beauty.

"Is he a better actor though?" Athena said teasingly.

"Oh no, you're a really great actor," Claudia said. And then to provoke Athena into revealing more of herself, she added, "But he's a lot happier person than you."

"Really?" Athena said. "That may be. But someday he will be a hell of a lot unhappier than I ever will be."

"Yeah," Claudia said. "The cocaine and booze will get him. He's not going to age well. But he's intelligent, maybe he'll adapt."

"I don't ever want to become what he's going to be," Athena said. "And I won't."

"You're my hero," Claudia said. "But you're not going to beat the aging process. I know you don't drink and booze or even fool around much but your secrets will get you."

Athena laughed. "My secrets will be my salvation," she said. "My secrets are so banal they're not even worth telling. We movie stars need our mystery."

Every Saturday morning when they were not working, they went shopping together on Rodeo Drive. Claudia was always amazed at how Athena could disguise herself so that she would not be recognized by fans or the clerks in the stores. She wore a black wig and loose clothes to disguise her figure. She changed her makeup so her jaw seemed to be thicker, her lips fuller, but most interesting of all, it seemed as if she could rearrange the features on her face. She also wore contact lenses that changed her brilliant green eyes to a demure hazel. Her voice became a soft Southern drawl.

When Athena bought something, she put it on one of Claudia's charge cards and then reimbursed her with a check when they had their late lunch. It was wonderful to relax in a restaurant as complete nobodies; as Claudia joked, no one ever recognized a screenwriter.

Twice a month Claudia spent the entire weekend at Athena's Malibu beach house for swimming and tennis. Claudia had let Athena read the second draft of *Messalina,* and Athena had asked for the lead role. As if she were not a top star and Claudia should not be begging her.

. . .

So when Claudia arrived in Malibu to persuade Athena to go back to work on the picture, she felt some hope for success. After all, Athena would not only ruin her own career but damage Claudia's.

The first thing that shook Claudia's confidence was the tight security around Athena's house, in addition to the usual guards at the Malibu Colony gates.

Two men with Pacific Ocean Security Company uniforms were at the gate of the house itself. Two additional guards patrolled the huge garden inside. When the little South American housekeeper led her to the Ocean Room, she could see two more guards on the beach outside. All the guards had batons and holstered guns.

Athena greeted Claudia with a tight hug. "I'll miss you," she said. "In a week I'll be gone."

"Why are you being so crazy?" Claudia said. "You're going to let some jerk of a macho man ruin your whole life. And mine. I can't believe you're so chicken. Listen, I'll stay with you tonight and tomorrow we'll get gun permits and start training. In a couple of days we'll be sharpshooters."

Athena laughed and gave her another hug. "Your Mafia blood is coming out," she said. Claudia had told her about the Clericuzio and her father.

They made drinks and sat in the stuffed chairs that gave them a view of the ocean that was like looking at some deep blue-green portrait of water.

"You can't change my mind and I'm not chickenshit," Athena said. "Now, I'll tell you the secret you wanted to know and you can tell the Studio and then maybe you'll both understand."

Then she told Claudia the whole story of her marriage. Of Boz Skannet's sadism and cruelty and deliberate humiliation and of her running away. . . .

With her astute, storyteller mind, Claudia felt there was something missing in Athena's story, that she was deliberately leaving out some important elements.

"What happened to the baby?" Claudia asked.

Athena's features arranged themselves into a movie-star mask. "I can't tell you anything more about that right now, in fact what I did tell you about me having a baby is just between you and me. That's the one part you mustn't tell the Studio. I trust you with that."

Claudia knew she couldn't press Athena on this. "But why are you quitting the picture?" Claudia asked. "You'll be protected. Then you can disappear."

"No," Athena said. "The Studio will only protect me while the picture's shooting. And that won't matter. I know Boz. Nothing will stop him. If I stay, I'll never finish the picture anyway."

At that moment they both noticed a man in bathing trunks walking up from the water to the house. The two security guards intercepted him. One of the guards blew a whistle and the two guards in the garden came running around. With the odds at four to one, the man in the bathing trunks seemed to retreat slightly.

Athena was standing up, obviously shaken. "It's Boz," she said to Claudia quietly. "He's doing this just to scare me. It's not his real move." She went out onto the deck and looked down at the five men. Claudia followed her.

Boz Skannet looked up at them, his eyes squinting, his bronzed face painted by the sun. His body, in the bathing trunks, looked lethal.

He smiled and said, "Hey, Athena, how about inviting me in for a drink?"

Athena gave him a brilliant smile. "I would if I had poison. You've broken the court order—I could have you locked up."

"Nah, you wouldn't," Boz said. "We're too close, we have too many secrets together." Though he smiled, he looked savage.

Claudia was reminded of the men who came to the Clericuzio feasts in Quogue.

One of the guards said, "He swam around the fence from the public beach. He must have a car there. Or we can have him locked up."

"No," Athena said. "Take him to his car. And tell the Agency I want four more guards around my house."

Boz still had his face tilted up, his body seemed to be a great statue rooted in the sand. "See you, Athena," he said. And then the guards led him away.

"He is frightening," Claudia said. "Maybe you're right. We would have to shoot cannons to stop him."

"I'll call you before I *flee,*" Athena said, making it actressy. "We can have one last dinner together."

Claudia was almost in tears. Boz had really frightened her, had reminded her of her father. "I'm going to fly to Vegas and see my brother Cross. He's smart and knows a lot of people. I'm sure he can help. So don't leave until I come back."

"Why should he help?" Athena said. "And how? Is he in the Mafia?"

"Of course not," Claudia said indignantly. "He'll help because he loves me." She said this with pride in her voice. "And I'm the only person he really loves except for my father."

Athena looked at her with a frown. "Your brother sounds just a little shady. You're very innocent for a woman working in the movies. And, by the way, how come you sleep with so many men? You're not an actress and I don't think you're a tramp."

"That's no secret," Claudia said. "Why do men screw so many women?" Then she hugged Athena. "I'm off to Vegas," she said. "Don't move till I get back."

That night Athena sat on the deck and watched the ocean, black beneath the moonless sky. She went over her plans and thought fondly of Claudia. It was really funny that she could not see through her brother, but that's what love did.

When Claudia met with Skippy Deere later that afternoon and told him Athena's story, they both sat in silence for a while. Then Deere said, "She left some things out. I went to see Boz Skannet to buy him off. He refused. And he warned me that if we tried any funny stuff, he'd give the papers a story that would ruin us. How Athena dumped their kid."

Claudia flew into a rage. "That's not true," she said. "Anyone who knows Athena knows she couldn't do such a thing."

"Sure," Deere said. "But we didn't know Athena when she was twenty."

"Fuck you too," Claudia said. "I'm going to fly to Vegas and see my brother Cross. He has more brains and more balls than any of you guys. He'll straighten this out."

"I don't think he can scare Boz Skannet," Deere said. "We already gave it a good try." But now he saw another opportunity.

He knew certain things about Cross. Cross was looking to get into the movie business. He had invested in six of Deere's pictures and lost money overall, so Cross wasn't that smart. It was rumored Cross was "connected," that he had some influence in the Mafia. But everybody was connected with the Mafia, Deere thought. That didn't make them dangerous. He doubted that Cross could help them with Boz Skannet. But a producer always listened, a producer specialized in long shots. And besides he could always pitch Cross to invest in another picture. It was always a great help to have minor partners who had no control over the making of the picture and the finances.

Skippy Deere paused, then said to Claudia, "I'll go with you."

Claudia De Lena loved Skippy Deere despite the fact that Deere had once screwed her out of a half-million dollars. She loved Deere for his faults and the diversity of his corruption and because Skippy was always good company, all admirable qualities in a producer.

Years ago they had worked on a picture together and had been buddies. Even then, Deere had been one of the most successful and colorful producers in Hollywood. One time on a set, the star of the movie had boasted of fucking Deere's wife and Deere, listening off a ledge on the set three stories above him, had jumped and landed on the star's head and broken his shoulder in addition to then smashing his nose with a good right-hand punch.

Claudia had another memory. The two of them had been walking down Rodeo Drive and Claudia had seen a blouse in the window. It was the most beautiful blouse Claudia had ever seen. It was white with almost invisible stripes of green, so lovely it could have been painted by Monet. The store was one of those that required an appointment before you could even go in and shop, as if the owner were some great physician. No problem. Skippy Deere was a personal friend of the owner as he was a great friend of studio chiefs, the great corporate heads, the rulers of countries throughout the Western world.

When they were in the store, the clerk told them the blouse was five hundred dollars. Claudia staggered back, held her hands on her chest. "Five hundred dollars for one blouse?" she asked. "Don't make me laugh."

The clerk was staggered in his turn by Claudia's impudence. "It's of the finest fabric," he said, "handmade. . . . And the green stripe is a green like no other fabric in the entire world. The price is very reasonable."

Deere was smiling. "Don't buy it, Claudia," he said. "Do you know how much it costs to get it laundered? At least thirty bucks. Every time you wear it, thirty bucks. And you have to take care of it like a baby. No food stains, and definitely you can't smoke. If you burn a hole, bang, there goes your five hundred."

Claudia smiled at the clerk. "Tell me," she said, "do I get a free gift if I buy the blouse?"

The clerk, a beautifully dressed man, had tears in his eyes and said, "Please leave."

They walked out of the store.

"Since when can a store clerk throw a customer out?" Claudia asked, laughing.

"This is Rodeo Drive," Skippy said. "You're lucky you even got in."

The next day when Claudia arrived for work at the studio, there was a gift box on her desk. In it were a dozen of the blouses and a note from Skippy Deere: "Not to be worn except at the Oscars."

Claudia knew that the clerk at the store and Skippy Deere were both full of shit. She had later seen that same beautiful green stripe on a woman's dress and on a special hundred-dollar tennis bandanna.

And the picture she was working on with Deere was a schlock love-action film that would never come closer to an Academy Award than Deere's appointment to the Supreme Court. But she was touched.

And then there was the day that the picture they had worked on reached the magical one-hundred-million-dollar gross and Claudia had thought she would be rich. Skippy Deere invited her to dinner to celebrate. Skippy was bubbling over with good humor. "This is my lucky day," he said. "The picture goes over a hundred, I got a great blow job from Bobby Bantz's secretary, and my ex-wife got killed in a car accident last night."

There were two other producers at dinner with them and they both winced. Claudia thought Deere was making a joke. But then Deere said to the two producers, "I see your eyes green with envy. I save five hundred grand a year in alimony and my two kids inherit her estate, the settlement she got from me, so I don't have to support them anymore."

Claudia was suddenly depressed and Deere said to her, "I'm being honest, it's what every man would think but never say out loud."

Skippy Deere had paid his dues in the movie business. The son of a carpenter, he had helped his father work on the houses of movie stars in Hollywood. In one of those situations that are probable only in Hollywood, he became the lover of a middle-aged female star, who got him a job as an apprentice in her agent's company, a prelude to getting rid of him.

He worked hard, learning to control his fiery nature. Most of all, how to coddle Talent. How to beg hot new directors, fast-talk fresh young stars, become best friend and mentor to horseshit writers. He made fun of his own behavior, citing a great Renaissance cardinal pleading the Borgia Pope's cause with the King of France. When the King exposed his derriere, then defecated to show his contempt for the Pope, the Cardinal exclaimed, "Oh, the ass of an angel," and rushed to kiss it.

But Deere mastered the indispensable hardware. He learned the art of negotiation, which he simplified to "Ask for everything." He became literate, developing an eye for those novels that would make good movies. He could spot acting talent. He scrutinized the details of production, the different ways to steal money from the budget of a film. He became a successful producer, one who could put 50 percent of the script and 70 percent of the budget on the screen.

It was helpful that he enjoyed reading and also that he could screen-write. Not on a totally blank piece of paper, but he was adept at crossing out scenes and revising dialogue, and could actually create pieces of action, little set pieces, which sometimes played brilliantly but were seldom necessary to the story being told. What he prided himself on, what helped his pictures achieve financial success, was that he was especially good at endings, which were almost always triumphant, the exaltation of good over evil—and if that didn't fit, the sweetness of defeat. His masterpiece had been the ending of a film that dealt with the atom-bomb destruction of New York, in which all the characters came out as better human beings dedicated to the love of their fellow man, even the one who had exploded the bomb. He had to hire five extra writers to get that done.

All this would have been worth very little to him as a producer if he had not been especially astute about finance. He pulled investment money out of thin air. Rich men doted on his company, as did the beautiful women who hung on his arm. Stars and directors enjoyed his honest and bawdy appreciation of the good things in life. He charmed development money out of studios, and he learned that it was possible to get a green light out of some studio heads with an enormous bribe. His Christmas card and Christmas gift lists were endless, to stars, to critics on newspapers and magazines, even to high-ranking law enforcement people. He called them all dear friends and when they no longer became useful he cut them from the gift list but never from the card list.

One of the keys to being a producer was to own a property. It could be an obscure novel, unsuccessful in print, but it was something concrete you could talk about to the studio. Deere secured rights to these with five-year options at five hundred dollars a year. Or he would option a screenplay and work with the writer to shape it into something a studio would buy. That was real ditch-digging work, writers were so fragile. "Fragile" was his favorite word for people he thought jerks. It was especially useful with female stars.

One of his most successful relationships had been with Claudia De Lena, and one of the most enjoyable. He had really liked the kid, wanted to teach her the ropes. They had spent three months together working on the script. They went out to dinner together, they played golf together (Deere had been surprised when Claudia beat him). They went to the Santa Anita race track. They swam in Skippy Deere's pool with secretaries in bathing suits to take dictation. Claudia had even taken Deere to Vegas for a weekend at the Xanadu to meet her brother, Cross. They sometimes slept together, it was convenient.

The picture was a great financial success, and Claudia assumed she would earn a great deal of money on the back end. She had a percentage of Skippy Deere's percentage, and she knew that he was always positioned "upstream," as Deere liked to call gross percentage. But what Claudia did not know was that Deere had two different percentages, one on gross, the other on net. And Claudia's back end deal called for a piece of Skippy Deere's net position. Which, though the picture made over $100 million, came to nothing. The Studio's accounting procedure, Deere's percentage of the gross, and the cost of the picture easily wiped out net profits.

Claudia sued, and Skippy Deere settled for a small sum to preserve their friendship. When Claudia reproached him, Deere said, "This had nothing to do with our personal relationship, this is between our lawyers."

Skippy Deere often said, "I was human once, then I got married." More than that, he had fallen truly in love. His excuse was that he was young, and that he had married her because even then his keen eye knew she was a talented actress. In this he was correct, but his wife, Christi, did not have that magic quality on film that translated into a star. The best she could achieve was the third female lead.

But Deere really loved her. When he became a power in the movie industry, he did his best to make Christi a star. He called in favors from other producers, from directors, from studio chiefs, to get her big parts. In a few pictures he got her up to second female lead. But as she got older, she worked less. They had two children, but Christi became more and more unhappy and this took up a fair amount of Deere's work time.

Skippy Deere, like all successful producers, was insanely busy. He had to travel all over the world supervising his pictures, getting financing, developing projects. Coming in contact with so many beautiful, charming women, and needing companionship, he often had romantic liaisons, which he enjoyed with gusto, but still he loved his wife.

One day a Development girl brought him a script that she said was perfect for Christi, a foolproof star role that would exactly suit her talent. It was a dark movie, a woman who murdered her husband for love of a young poet and then had to escape the grief of her children and the suspicions of her in-laws. Then of course found redemption. It was very outrageous baloney, but it could work.

Skippy Deere had two problems: convincing a studio to make the movie and then convincing it to cast Christi in the part.

He called in all his favors. He took all his money on the back end. He persuaded a top male star to take a part that was really a featured role and got Dita Tommey to direct. Everything went like a dream. Christi played the part perfectly, Deere produced the film perfectly, that is to say, 90 percent of the budget actually got up on the screen.

During that time Deere was never unfaithful to his wife except for one night he spent in London arranging distribution, and then he fell only because the English girl was so thin he was intrigued by the logistics.

It worked. The picture was a commercial success, he made more on the sacrificial back end than he would have on a straight deal, and Christi won the Academy Award as best actress.

And, as Skippy Deere later said to Claudia, that was where the movie should have ended: Happily Ever After. But now his wife had found real self-esteem, now she sensed her true worth. The proof was that she became a vehicle star, she now received scripts delivered by messenger, with roles for beautiful, celluloid-magic personalities. Deere advised her to look for something more suited to her, the next picture would be crucial. He had never worried about her being faithful, indeed had conceded her the right to have fun when she was on location. But now in the few months after her Award— the toast of the town, invited to all the top parties, appearing in all the showbiz columns, courted by young actors struggling to get roles—she blossomed into a fresh young womanhood. She went out, openly, on dates with actors fifteen years her junior. The gossip journalists took note, the feminists among them cheering her on.

Skippy Deere seemingly took this very well. He understood the whole thing. After all, why did he himself keep screwing young girls? So why begrudge his wife equal pleasure? But then again why should he continue his extraordinary efforts to further Christi's career? Especially after she actually asked him for a role for one of her young lovers. He stopped looking for scripts for her, he stopped campaigning for her with other producers and directors and studio heads. And they, being older men, took umbrage for him in masculine brotherhood and no longer gave Christi any special consideration.

Christi made two more pictures in a starring role; both were flops because she was miscast. And so she spent the professional credit the Award had earned for her. In three years, she was back to playing third female leads.

By this time she had fallen in love with a young man who aspired to be a producer, indeed was very much like her husband, but he needed capital. So Christi sued for divorce, winning a huge settlement and $500,000 a year in alimony. Her lawyers never found out about Skippy's assets in Europe, so they parted friends. And now, seven years later, she had died in an automobile accident. By that time, although she had remained on Deere's Christmas card list, she was on his famous "Life Is Too Short" list, signifying he would not return her phone calls.

So Claudia De Lena had a twisted affection for Deere. For his exposing his true self to others, for his living his life so blatantly in his own self-interest, for his ability to look you in the eye and call you his friend while not caring that you knew he would never perform a true act of friendship. That he was such a cheerful, ardent hypocrite. And besides, Deere was a great persuader. And he was the only man she knew who could match wits with Cross. They took the next plane to Vegas.

BOOK IV

Cross De Lena
The Clericuzio

CHAPTER 6

BY THE TIME Cross reached the age of twenty-one, Pippi De Lena was impatient for Cross to follow his destiny. The most important fact in a man's life, conceded by all, was that he must make a living. He must earn his bread, put a roof over his head and clothes on his back, and feed the mouths of his children. To do that without unnecessary misery, a man had to have a certain degree of power in the world. It followed then, as night the day, that Cross must take his place in the Clericuzio Family. To do that, it was absolutely necessary he "make his bones."

Cross had a good reputation in the Family. His answer to Dante when Dante told him that Pippi was a Hammer was quoted happily by Don Domenico himself, who savored the words almost with ecstasy. "I don't know that. You don't know that. Nobody knows that. Where did you get that fuckin' hat?" What an answer, the Don exclaimed with delight. So young a man to be so discreet, and so witty, what a credit to his father. We must give this boy his chance. All this had been related to Pippi, and so he knew the time was ripe.

He started to groom Cross. He sent him out on collection assignments that were difficult and required force. He discussed the old history of the Family and how operations were executed. Nothing fancy, he stressed. But when you had to get fancy, it must be planned in extreme detail. Simple was extreme simplicity. You sealed off a small geographic area and then you caught the target in that area. Surveillance first, then car and hit man, then blocking cars for any pursuers, then going to ground for a time afterward so that you could not be immediately questioned. That was simple. For fancy, you got fancy. You could dream up anything but you had to back it up with solid planning. You only got fancy when it was absolutely necessary.

He even told Cross certain code words. A "Communion" was when the victim's body disappeared. That was fancy. A "Confirmation" was when the body was found. That was simple.

Pippi gave Cross a briefing on the Clericuzio Family. Their great war with the Santadio Family, which established their dominance. Pippi said nothing of his part in that war and was indeed scarce on details. Rather he praised Giorgio and Vincent and Petie. But most of all he praised Don Domenico for his farsightedness.

The Clericuzio had spun many webs, but its most extensive was gaming. It dominated all forms of casino and illegal gambling in the United States. It had a very subtle influence on the Native American casinos, it had a serious influence on sports betting, legal in Nevada and illegal in the rest of the country. The Family owned slot machine factories, had an interest in the manufacture of dice and cards, the supply of chinaware and silverware, the laundries for the gambling hotels. Gambling was the great jewel of their empire, and they ran a public relations campaign to make gambling legal in every state of the union.

Legal gambling all over the United States by federal law was now the Holy Grail of the Clericuzio Family. Not only casinos and lotteries but also wagering on sports: baseball, football, basketball, and all others. Sports were holy in America, and once gambling was legalized that holiness would descend on gambling itself. The profits would be enormous.

Giorgio, whose company managed some of the state lotteries, had given the Family a breakdown on the expected numbers. A minimum of two billion dollars was bet on the Super Bowl all over the United States, most of it illegally. The sports books in Vegas, legal betting alone ran up over fifty million. The World Series, depending on how many games were played, totaled about another billion. Basketball was much smaller, but the many playoff games carried another billion, and this was not counting the everyday betting during the season.

Once made legal, all this could be easily doubled or tripled with special lotteries and combination betting, except for the Super Bowl, whose increase would be tenfold and might even provide a net revenue for one day of $1 billion. The overall total could reach $100 billion, and the beauty was that there was no productivity involved, the only expenses were marketing and administration. What a great deal of money for the Clericuzio Family to rack up, a profit of at least $5 billion a year.

And the Clericuzio Family had the expertise and the political connections and pure force to control a great deal of this market. Giorgio had charts to show the complicated prizes that could be constructed based on big sports events. Gambling would be a great magnet to draw the money from the huge gold mine that was the American people.

So gambling was low-risk and had great growth potential. To achieve legal gambling, cost was no object and even greater risks were considered.

The Family was also made rich with income from drugs, but only at a very high level, it was too risky. They controlled European processing, provided political protection and judicial intervention, and they laundered the money. Their position in drugs was legally impregnable and extremely profitable. They dropped the black money in a chain of banks in Europe and a few banks in the United States. The structure of the law was outflanked.

But then, Pippi cautiously pointed out, despite all this there came times when risks had to be taken, when an iron fist must be shown. This the Family did with the utmost discretion and with terminal ferocity. And that was when you must earn the good life you led, when you truly earned your daily bread.

Shortly after his twenty-first birthday, Cross was finally put to the test.

One of the most prized political assets of the Clericuzio Family was Walter Wavven, the governor of Nevada. He was a man in his early fifties, tall and lanky, who wore a cowboy hat but dressed in perfectly tailored suits. He was a handsome man and though married had a lusty appetite for the female sex. He also enjoyed good food and good drink, loved to bet sports, and was an enthusiastic casino

gambler. He was too tender of public feelings to expose these traits,
or to risk romantic seductions. So he relied on Alfred Gronevelt and
the Xanadu Hotel to satisfy these appetites while preserving his political and personal image of the God-fearing, steadfast believer in
old-fashioned family values.

Gronevelt had recognized Wavven's special gifts early on and provided the financial base that enabled Wavven to climb the political
ladder. When Wavven became governor of Nevada and wanted a relaxing weekend, Gronevelt gave him one of the prized Villas.

The Villas had been Gronevelt's greatest inspiration. . . .

Gronevelt had come to Vegas early, when it was still basically a
western cowboy gambling town, and he had studied gambling and
gamblers as a brilliant scientist might study an insect important to
evolution. The one great mystery that would never be solved was
why very rich men still wasted time gambling to win money they did
not need. Gronevelt decided they did so to hide other vices, or they
desired to conquer fate itself, but more than anything it was to show
some sort of superiority to their fellow creatures. Therefore he reasoned that when they gambled they should be treated as gods. They
would gamble as the gods gambled or the kings of France in Versailles.

So Gronevelt spent $100 million to build seven luxurious Villas
and a special jewel-box casino on the grounds of the Xanadu Hotel
(with his usual foresight he had bought much more land than the
Xanadu needed). These Villas were small palaces, each could sleep
six couples in six separate apartments, not merely suites. The fur-
nishings were lavish: hand-woven rugs, marble floors, gold bath-
rooms, rich fabrics on the walls; dining rooms and kitchens staffed
by the Hotel. The latest audiovisual equipment turned living rooms
into theaters. The bars of these Villas were stocked with the finest
wines and liquors and a box of illegal Havana cigars. Each Villa had
its own outdoor swimming pool and inside Jacuzzi. All free to the
gambler.

In the special security area that held the Villas was the small oval
casino called the Pearl, where the high rollers could play in privacy

and where the minimum bet in baccarat was a thousand dollars. The chips in this casino were also different, the black one-hundred-dollar chip was the lowest denominator; the five hundred, pale white threaded with gold; a gold-barred blue chip for the thousand; and the specially designed ten-thousand-dollar chip, with a real diamond embedded in the center of its gold surface. However, as a concession to the ladies, the roulette wheel would change hundred-dollar chips into five-dollar chips.

It was amazing that enormously wealthy men and women would take this bait. Gronevelt figured that all these extravagant RFB comps ran the Hotel fifty thousand dollars a week on the cost sheet. But these were written off on tax reports. Plus the prices of everything were inflated on paper. Figures (he kept a separate accounting) showed that each Villa made an average profit of a million dollars a week. The very fancy restaurants that served the Villas' and other important guests also made a profit as tax write-offs. On the cost sheets, a dinner for four totaled over a thousand dollars, which since the guests were comped, was written off as business expense for that amount in taxes. Since the meal cost the Hotel no more than a hundred dollars counting labor, there was a profit right there.

And so, to Gronevelt, the seven Villas were like seven crowns that he bestowed on the heads of only those gamblers who risked or made a Drop of over a million dollars on their two- or three-day stay. It didn't matter that they won or lost. Just that they gambled it. And they had to be prompt in paying their markers or they would be relegated to one of the suites in the Hotel itself, which, however plush, were not comparable to the Villas.

Of course there was a little more. These were Villas where important public men could bring their mistresses or boyfriends, where they could gamble in anonymity. And strange to say there were many titans of business, men worth hundreds of millions of dollars, even with wives and mistresses, who were lonely. Lonely for carefree feminine company, for women of exceptional sympathy. And for these men, the Villas would be furnished by Gronevelt with the proper beauty.

Governor Walter Wavven was one of these men. And he was the only exception to Gronevelt's rule of the million-dollar Drop. He

gambled modestly and then with a purse supplied privately by Gronevelt, and if his markers exceeded a certain amount they were put on
hold to be paid by his future winnings.

Wavven came to the Hotel to relax, to golf on the Xanadu course,
and to drink and court the beauties supplied by Gronevelt.

Gronevelt played it very long with the governor. In twenty years
he had never asked an outright favor, just the special access to
present his arguments for legislation that would help the casino business in Vegas. Most of the time his point of view prevailed; when it
did not, the governor gave him a detailed explanation of the political
realities that had denied him. But the governor provided a valuable
service in that he introduced Gronevelt to influential judges and
politicians who could be swayed with hard cash.

Gronevelt nurtured in his secret heart the hope that, against long
odds, Governor Walter Wavven might someday be the president of
the United States. Then the rewards could be enormous.

But Fate foils the most cunning of men, as Gronevelt always acknowledged. The most insignificant of mortals become the agents of
disaster to the most powerful. This particular agent was a twenty-
five-year-old young man who became the lover of the governor's eldest child, a young woman of eighteen.

The governor was married to an intelligent, good-looking woman
who was more fair, more liberal in her political views than her husband, though they worked well as a team. They had three children,
and this family was a great political asset for the governor. Marcy,
the eldest, was attending Berkeley, her choice and her mother's, not
the governor's.

Freed from the stiffness of a political household, Marcy was entranced by the freedom of the university, its orientation toward the
political left, its openness to new music, the insights offered by
drugs. A true daughter of her father, she had a frankness of sexual interest. With that innocence and the natural instinct for fair play in the
young, her sympathies were with the poor, the working class, the
suffering minorities. She also fell in love with the purity of art. It
was therefore very natural for her to hang out with students who
were poets and musicians. It was even more natural that after a few

casual encounters she fell in love with a fellow student who wrote plays and strummed the guitar and was poor.

His name was Theo Tatoski and he was perfect for a college romance. He had dark good looks, he came from a family of Catholics who worked in Detroit's auto factories and, with a poet's alliterative wit, always swore he would rather fuck than fit a fender. Despite this he worked part-time jobs to pay his tuition. He took himself very seriously, but this was mitigated by the fact that he had talent.

Marcy and Theo were inseparable for two years. She brought Theo to meet her family in the governor's mansion and was delighted that he was unimpressed by her father. Later in their bedroom in the state mansion, he informed her that her father was a typical phony.

Perhaps Theo had detected their condescension; the governor and his wife had both been extra friendly, extra courteous, determined to honor their daughter's choice, while privately deploring so unsuitable a match. The mother was not worried; she knew Theo's charm would fade with her daughter's growth. The father was uneasy but tried to make up for it with a more-than-common affability, even for a politician. After all, the governor was a champion of the working class, per his political platform, the mother was an educated liberal. A romance with Theo could only give Marcy a broader view of life. Meanwhile Marcy and Theo were living together, and planned to get married after they graduated. Theo would write and perform his plays, Marcy would be his muse and a professor of literature.

A stable arrangement. The young people did not seem to be heavily into drugs, their sexual relationship was no big deal. The governor even thought idly that if worse came to worst their marriage would help him politically, an indication to the public that despite his pure WASP background, his wealth, his culture, he democratically accepted a blue-collar son-in-law.

They all made their adjustments to a banal situation. The parents just wished that Theo was not such a bore.

But the young are perverse. Marcy, in her final year of college, fell in love with a fellow student who was rich and socially more acceptable to her parents than Theo. But she still wanted to keep Theo as a friend. She found it exciting to juggle two lovers without committing the technical sin of adultery. In her innocence, it made her feel unique.

The surprise was Theo. He reacted to the situation not as a tolerant Berkeley radical, but like some beknighted Polack. Despite his poetic, musical bohemianism, the teachings of feminist professors, the whole Berkeley atmosphere of sexual laissez-faire, he became violently jealous.

Theo had always been moodily eccentric, it was part of his youthful charm. In conversation, he often took the extremely revolutionary position that blowing up a hundred innocent people was a small price to pay for a free society in the future. Yet Marcy knew Theo could never do such a thing. Once when they came to their apartment after a two-week vacation, they had found a litter of newborn mice in their bed. Theo had simply put the tiny creatures out into the street unharmed. Marcy found that endearing.

But when Theo found out about Marcy's other lover, he struck her in the face. Then he burst into tears and begged her forgiveness. She forgave him. She still found their lovemaking exciting, more exciting because now she held more power with his knowledge of her betrayal. But he became progressively more violent, they quarreled often, life together was no longer such fun, and Marcy moved out of their apartment.

Her other lover faded. Marcy had a few other affairs. But she and Theo remained friends and slept together occasionally. Marcy planned to go East and do her master's in an Ivy League university, Theo moved down to Los Angeles to write plays and look for movie-script work. One of his short musical plays was being produced by a small theater group for three performances. He invited Marcy to come to see it.

Marcy flew to Los Angeles to see the play. It was so terrible half the audience walked out. So Marcy stayed over that night in Theo's apartment to console him. What exactly happened that night could never be established. What was proven was that sometime in the early morning, Theo stabbed Marcy to death, knife wounds in each eye. Then he stabbed himself in the stomach and called the police. In time to save his life, but not Marcy's.

The trial in California was, naturally, a huge media event. A daughter of the governor of Nevada murdered by a blue-collar poet who had been her lover for three years and was then dumped.

The defense lawyer, Molly Flanders, successfully specialized in "passion" murders, though this case proved to be her last criminal case before she entered entertainment law. Her tactics were classic. Witnesses were brought in to show that Marcy had at least six lovers, while Theo believed they were to be married. The rich, socially prominent, sluttish Marcy had dumped her sincere blue-collar playwright, whose mind then snapped. Flanders pleaded "temporary insanity" on her client's behalf. The most relished line (written for Molly by Claudia De Lena) was "He is forever not responsible for what he has done." A line that would have incited Don Clericuzio into a fury.

Theo looked properly stricken during his testimony. His parents, devout Catholics, had persuaded powerful members of the California clergy to take up the cause, and they testified that Theo had renounced his hedonistic ways and was now determined to study for the priesthood. It was pointed out that Theo had tried to kill himself and was therefore self-evidently remorseful, thus proving his insanity, as if the two went together. All this was varnished by the rhetoric of Molly Flanders, who painted a picture of the great contribution Theo could make to society if he was not punished for a foolish act triggered by a woman of loose morals who broke his blue-collar heart. A careless rich girl, now unfortunately dead.

Molly Flanders loved California juries. Intelligent, well-educated enough to understand the nuances of psychiatric trauma, exposed to the higher culture of theater, film, music, literature, they pulsed with empathy. When Flanders got through with them, the outcome was never in doubt. Theo was found not guilty by reason of temporary insanity. He was immediately signed to appear in his life story for a miniseries, not as the primary actor but as a minor one who sang songs of his own composition to link the story together. It was a completely satisfactory ending to a modern tragedy.

But the effect on Governor Walter Wavven, the girl's father, was disastrous. Alfred Gronevelt saw his twenty-year investment going down the drain, for Governor Wavven in the privacy of his Villa announced to Gronevelt that he would not stand for reelection. What was the point of acquiring power when any son-of-a-bitch low-life white trash could stab his daughter to death, almost cut off her head, and live his life a free man? Even worse, his beloved child had been dragged through the papers and TV as a silly cunt who deserved to be killed.

There are tragedies in life that cannot be cured, and for the governor this was one of them. He spent as much time as possible at the Xanadu Hotel but was not his old jolly self. He was not interested in showgirls, or the roll of the dice. He simply drank and played golf. Which posed a very delicate problem for Gronevelt.

He was deeply sympathetic to the governor's problem. You cannot cultivate a man for over twenty years, even out of self-interest, without having some affection for him. But the reality was that Governor Walter Wavven, resigning from politics, was no longer a key asset, had no future potential. He was simply a man destroying himself with booze. Also, when he gambled he did so distractedly, Gronevelt held two hundred grand of his markers. So now had come the time when he must refuse the governor the use of a Villa. Certainly he would give the governor a luxury suite in the Hotel, but it would be a demotion, and before doing that Gronevelt took a last stab at rehabilitation.

Gronevelt persuaded the governor to meet him for golf one morning. To complete the foursome he recruited Pippi De Lena and his son, Cross. Pippi had a crude wit the governor always appreciated, and Cross was such a good-looking and polite young man that his elders were always glad to have him around. After they played they went to the governor's Villa for a late lunch.

Wavven had lost a great deal of weight and seemed to take no pride in his appearance. He was in a stained sweatsuit and wore a baseball cap with the Xanadu logo. He was unshaven. He smiled often, not a politician smile, but a sort of shameful grimace. Gronevelt noticed that his teeth were very yellow. He was also extremely drunk.

Gronevelt decided to take the plunge. He said, "Governor, you are letting your family down, you are letting your friends down, and you are letting the people of Nevada down. You cannot go on like this."

"Sure I can," Walter Wavven said. "Fuck the people of Nevada. Who cares?"

Gronevelt said, "I do. I care about you. I'll put the money together and you must run for senator in the next election."

"Why the hell should I?" the governor said. "It doesn't mean anything in this fucking country. I'm governor of the great state of Nevada and that little prick murders my daughter and goes free. And I have to take it. People make jokes about my dead kid and pray for the murderer. You know what I pray for? That an atom bomb wipes out this fucking country and especially the state of California."

Pippi and Cross remained silent during all this. They were a little shaken by the governor's intensity. Also, both understood Gronevelt was working to a purpose.

"You have to put all of that behind you," Gronevelt said. "Don't let this tragedy destroy your life." His unctuousness would have irritated a saint.

The governor threw his baseball cap across the room and helped himself to another whiskey at the bar.

"I can't forget," he said. "I lie awake at night and dream about squeezing that little cocksucker's eyes out of his head. I want to set him on fire, I want to cut off his hands and legs. And then I want him to be alive so I can do it again and again." He smiled drunkenly at them, almost fell, they could see the yellow teeth and smell the decay in his mouth.

Wavven now seemed less drunk, his voice became quiet, he spoke almost conversationally. "Did you see how he stabbed her?" he asked. "He stabbed her through the eyes. The judge wouldn't let the jury see the photos. Prejudicial. But I, her father, could see the photos. And so little Theo goes free, with that smirk on his face. He stabbed my daughter through the eyes but he gets up every morning and he sees the sun shining. Oh, I wish I could kill them all—the judge, the jurors, the lawyers, all of them." He filled his glass and then walked around the room furiously, his speech a crazy ramble.

"I can't go out there and bullshit about what I no longer believe. Not while the little bastard is alive. He sat at my dinner table, my wife and I treated him like a human being even though we disliked him. We gave him the benefit of the doubt. Never give anybody the benefit of the doubt. We took him into our home, gave him a bed to sleep in with our daughter and he was laughing at us all the time. He was saying, 'Who gives a fuck if you're the governor? Who gives a fuck if you have money? Who gives a fuck that you are civilized, decent human beings? I will kill your daughter whenever I like and there is nothing you can do. I'll bring you all down. I'll fuck your daughter, then I'll kill her, and then I'll stick it up your ass and go free.' " Wavven staggered and Cross quickly went to hold him. The governor looked up beyond Cross, to the high mural-decorated ceiling above, all pink angels and white-clad saints. "I want him dead," the governor said and burst into tears. "I want him dead."

Gronevelt said quietly, "Walter, it will all go away, give it time. File for senator. You have the best years of your life ahead of you, you can still do so much."

Wavven shook himself away from Cross and said quite calmly to Gronevelt, "Don't you see, I don't believe in doing good anymore. I'm forbidden to tell anyone how I really feel, not even my wife. The hatred I feel. And I'll tell you something else. The voting public has contempt for me, they perceive me as a weak fool. A man who lets his daughter get murdered, then can't get him punished. Who would trust the welfare of the great state of Nevada to such a man?" He was sneering now. "That little fuck could get elected easier than me." He paused for a moment. "Alfred, forget it. I'm not running for anything."

Gronevelt was studying him carefully. He was catching something that Pippi and Cross did not. Passionate grief so often led to weakness, but Gronevelt decided to take the risk. He said, "Walter, will you run for senator if the man is punished? Will you be the man you were?"

The governor seemed not to understand. His eyes rolled slightly toward Pippi and Cross, then stared into Gronevelt's face. Gronevelt said to Pippi and Cross, "Wait for me in my office."

Pippi and Cross quickly left. Gronevelt and Governor Wavven were alone. Gronevelt said to him gravely, "Walter, you and I must be very direct for the first time in our lives. We've known each other twenty years, have you ever found me to be indiscreet? So answer. It will be safe. Will you run again if that boy is dead?"

The governor went to the bar and poured whiskey. But he did not drink. He smiled. "I'll file the day after I go to that boy's funeral to show my forgiveness," he said. "My voters will love that."

Gronevelt relaxed. It was done. Out of relief, he indulged his temper. "First, go see your dentist," he told the governor. "You have to get those fucking teeth cleaned."

Pippi and Cross were waiting for Gronevelt back in his penthouse office suite. He led them into his living quarters so that they could be more comfortable, then told them what had been said.

"The governor is okay?" Pippi asked.

"The governor was not as drunk as he pretended," Gronevelt said. "He gave me the message without really implicating himself."

"I'll fly East tonight," Pippi said. "This must get the Clericuzio OK."

"Tell them I think the governor is a man who can go all the way," Gronevelt said. "To the very top. He would be an invaluable friend."

"Giorgio and the Don will understand that," Pippi said. "I just have to lay everything out and get the OK."

Gronevelt looked at Cross and smiled, then he turned to Pippi. He said gently, "Pippi, I think it's time Cross joined the Family. I think he should fly East with you."

But Giorgio Clericuzio decided to come West to Vegas for the meeting. He wanted to be briefed by Gronevelt himself, and Gronevelt had not traveled for the last ten years.

Giorgio and his bodyguards were established in one of the Villas, though he was not a high roller. Gronevelt was a man who knew how to make exceptions. He had refused the Villas to powerful politicians, financial giants, to some of the most famous movie stars in Hollywood, to beautiful women who had slept with him, to close personal friends. Even Pippi De Lena. But he gave a Villa to Giorgio Clericuzio, though he knew Giorgio had spartan tastes and did not really appreciate extraordinary luxuries. Every mark of respect counted, mounted up, and one breach, no matter how tiny, could be remembered someday.

They met in Giorgio's Villa. Gronevelt, Pippi, and Giorgio . . .

Gronevelt explained the situation. "The governor can be an enormous asset to the Family," Gronevelt said. "If he pulls himself together, he may go all the way. First, senator, then the presidency. That happens and you have a good shot at getting sports gambling legalized all over the country. That will be worth billions to the Family and those billions will not be black money. It will be white money. I say it's something we have to do."

White money was far more valuable than black money. But Giorgio's great asset was that he was never stampeded into rash decisions. "Does the governor know you are with us?"

"Not for sure," Gronevelt said. "But he must have heard rumors. And he's not a dummy. I've done some things for him that he knows I couldn't do if I were alone. And he's clever. All he said was that he would run for office if the kid were dead. He didn't ask me to do anything. He's a great con, he wasn't that drunk when he broke down. I think he figured the whole thing out. He was sincere, but he was faking it too. He couldn't figure out his revenge but he had the idea I could do something. He is suffering, but he's also scheming." He paused for a moment. "If we come through, he'll run for senator and he will be our senator."

Giorgio prowled uneasily in the room, avoiding the statues on their pedestals, the curtained Jacuzzi whose marble seemed to shine through the fabric. He said to Gronevelt, "You promised him without our OK?"

"Yes," Gronevelt said. "It was a matter of persuasion. I had to be positive to give him a sense that he still has power. That he could, still, cause things to happen, and so make power appeal to him again."

Giorgio sighed. "I hate this part of the business," he said.

Pippi smiled. Giorgio was so full of shit. He had helped wipe out the Santadio Family with a savageness that made the old Don proud.

"I think we need Pippi's expertise on this," Gronevelt said. "And I think it's time for his son, Cross, to join the Family."

Giorgio looked at Pippi. "Do you think Cross is ready?" he asked.

Pippi said, "He's had all the gravy, it's time for him to earn his living."

"But will he do it?" Giorgio asked. "It's a big step."

"I'll talk to him," Pippi said. "He'll do it."

Giorgio turned toward Gronevelt. "We do it for the governor, then what if he forgets about us? We take the risk and it's all for nothing. Here's a man who is governor of Nevada, his daughter gets killed and he lies down. He has no balls."

"He did do something, he came to me," Gronevelt said. "You have to understand people like the governor. That took a lot of balls for him."

"So he'll come through?" Giorgio said.

"We'll save him for the few big things," Gronevelt said. "I've done business with him for twenty years. I guarantee he comes through if he's handled right. He knows the score, he's very smart."

Giorgio said, "Pippi, it has to look like an accident. This will get a lot of heat. We want the governor to escape any innuendos from his enemies or the papers and that fucking TV."

Gronevelt said, "Yes, it's important that nothing can be implied about the governor."

Giorgio said, "Maybe this is too tricky for Cross to make his bones on."

"No, this is perfect for him," Pippi said. And they could not object. Pippi was the commander in the field. He had proved himself in many operations of this kind, especially in the great war against the Santadio. He had often told the Clericuzio Family, "It's my ass on the line, if I get stuck, I want it to be my fault, not somebody else's."

Giorgio clapped his hands. "Okay, let's get it done. Alfred, how about a round of golf in the morning? Tomorrow night I go on business to L.A. and the day after I go back East. Pippi, let me know who you want from the Enclave to help, and tell me if Cross is in or out."

And with that Pippi knew that Cross would never be admitted to the inside of the Clericuzio Family if he refused this operation.

Golf had become a passion for Pippi's generation of the Clericuzio Family; the old Don made malicious jokes that it was a game for *Brugliones*. Pippi and Cross were on the Xanadu course that afternoon. They didn't use driving carts; Pippi wanted the exercise of walking and the solitude of the greens.

Just off the ninth hole there was an orchard of trees with a bench beneath. They sat there.

"I won't live forever," Pippi said. "And you have to make a living. The Collection Agency is a big moneymaker but tough to keep. You have to be in solid with the Clericuzio Family." Pippi had prepared Cross, had sent him on some tough collecting missions where he had to use force and abuse, had exposed him to Family gossip; he knew the score. Pippi had waited patiently for the right situation, for a target that would not arouse sympathy.

Cross said quietly, "I understand."

Pippi said, "That guy that killed the governor's daughter. A punk prick and he gets away with it. That's not right."

Cross was amused by his father's psychology. "And the governor is our friend," he said.

"That's right," Pippi said. "Cross, you can say no, remember that. But I want you to help me on a job I have to do."

Cross looked down the rolling greens, the flags above the holes dead still in the desert air, the silvery mountain ranges beyond, the sky reflecting the neon signs of the Strip he could not see. He knew his life was about to change and he felt a moment of dread. "If I don't like it I can always go to work for Gronevelt," he said. But he let his hand rest on his father's shoulder for a moment to let him know it was a joke.

Pippi grinned at him. "This job is for Gronevelt. You saw him with the governor. Well, we're going to give him his wish. Gronevelt had to get the OK from Giorgio. And I said you would help me out."

Far away on one of the greens, Cross could see a foursome of two women and two men shimmering cartoonlike in the desert sun. "I have to make my bones," he said to his father. He knew he had to agree or live a completely different life. And he loved the life he led, working for his father, hanging out at the Xanadu, the direction of Gronevelt, the beautiful showgirls, the easy money, the sense of power. And once he did so he should never be subject to the fates of ordinary men.

"I'll do all the planning," Pippi said. "I'll be with you all the way. There's no danger. But you have to be the shooter."

Cross rose from the bench. He could see the flags on the seven Villas flapping, though there was no breeze on the golf course. For the first time in his young life he felt the ache of a world that was to be lost. "I'm with you," he said.

In the three weeks that followed, Pippi gave Cross an indoctrination. He explained that they were waiting for a surveillance team report on Theo, his movements, his habits, recent photos. Also, an operations team of six men from the Enclave in New York were moving into place in Los Angeles where Theo was still living. The whole operation plan would be based on the report of the surveillance team. Then Pippi lectured Cross on the philosophy.

"This is a business," he said. "You take all the precautions to prevent the downside. Anybody can knock somebody off. The trick is never to get caught. That is the sin. And never think of the personalities involved. When the head of General Motors throws fifty thousand people out of work, that's business. He can't help wrecking their lives, he has to do it. Cigarettes kill thousands of people, but what can you do? People want to smoke and you can't ban a business that generates billions of dollars. Same with guns, everybody has a gun, everybody kills everybody, but it's a billion-dollar industry, you can't get rid of it. What can you do? People must earn a living, that comes first. All the time. You don't believe that, go live in the shit."

The Clericuzio Family was very strict, Pippi told Cross. "You have to get their OK. You can't go around killing people because they spit on your shoe. The Family has to be with you because they can make you jailproof."

Cross listened. He only asked one question. "Giorgio wants it to look like an accident? How do we do that?"

Pippi laughed. "Never let anybody tell you how to run your operation. They can go fuck themselves. They tell me their maximum expectations. I do what is best for me. And the best is to be simple.

Very, very simple. And when you have to get fancy, get very, very fancy."

When the surveillance reports came, Pippi made Cross study all the data. There were some photos of Theo, photos of his car showing its license plates. A map of the road he traveled from Brentwood up to Oxnard to visit a girlfriend. Cross said to his father, "He can still get a girlfriend?"

"You don't know women," Pippi said. "If they like you, you can piss in the sink. If they don't like you, you can make them the Queen of England and they'll shit on you."

Pippi flew into L.A. to set up his operations team. He came back two days later and told Cross, "Tomorrow night."

The next day, before dawn, to escape the heat of the desert, they drove from Las Vegas to Los Angeles. Driving across the desert, Pippi told Cross to relax. Cross was mesmerized by the glorious sunrise that seemed to melt the desert sand into a deep river of gold lapping at the foot of the distant Sierra Nevadas. He felt anxious. He wanted to get the job done.

They arrived in a Family house in the Pacific Palisades where the six-man crew from the Bronx Enclave was awaiting them. In the driveway was a stolen car that had been repainted and had false license plates. Also at the house were the untraceable guns that were to be used.

Cross was surprised at the luxuriousness of the house. It had a beautiful view of the ocean across the highway, a swimming pool, and a huge sundeck. It also had six bedrooms. The men seemed to know Pippi well. But they were not introduced to Cross nor he to them.

They had eleven hours to kill before the operation started at midnight. The other men, ignoring a huge TV set, started a card game on the sundeck; they were all in bathing suits. Pippi smiled at Cross and said, "Shit, I forgot about the swimming pool."

"That's OK," Cross said. "We can go swimming in our shorts." The house was secluded, shielded by enormous trees and an encircling hedge.

"We can go bare-assed," Pippi said. "Nobody can see except the helicopters and they'll be looking at all the broads sunbathing outside their Malibu houses."

Both of them swam and sunbathed for a few hours and then ate a meal prepared by one of the six-man crew. The meal was steak, cooked on the sundeck grill, and a salad of arugula and lettuce. The other men drank red wine with their food, but Cross had a club soda. He noticed that all the men ate and drank sparingly.

After the meal, Pippi took Cross on a reconnaissance in the stolen car. They drove to the western-style restaurant and coffee shop farther down the Pacific Coast Highway where they would find Theo. The surveillance reports showed that on Wednesday nights Theo, on his way to Oxnard, had made a habit of stopping at the Pacific Coast Highway Restaurant at around midnight for coffee and ham and eggs. That he would leave about one in the morning. That night a surveillance team of two men would be tailing him and would report by telephone when he was on the way.

Back at the house Pippi rebriefed the men on the operation. The six men would have three cars. One car would precede them, another would bring up the rear, the third car would park in the restaurant lot and be prepared for any emergency.

Cross and Pippi sat on the sundeck waiting for the phone call. There were five cars in the driveway, all black, shining in the moonlight like bugs. The six men from the Enclave continued their card game, playing with silver coins: nickels, dimes, and quarters. Finally at eleven-thirty the phone call came: Theo was on his way from Brentwood to the restaurant. The six men got in three cars and drove away to take up their appointed posts. Pippi and Cross got into the stolen car and waited another fifteen minutes before they left. Cross had in the pocket of his jacket a small .22 pistol, which, though it had no silencer, only gave off a sharp little pop; Pippi carried a Glock that would make a loud report. Ever since his only arrest for murder, Pippi always refused to carry a silencer.

Pippi drove. The operation had been planned in the most specific detail. No member of the operations team was to go into the restaurant. Detectives would question the help about all the customers. The surveillance team had reported what Theo was wearing, the car he was driving, the license plates. They were lucky that Theo's car was a flaming red and that it was a cheap Ford, easily identifiable in an area where Mercedeses and Porsches were commonplace.

When Pippi and Cross arrived in the parking lot of the restaurant, they could see Theo's car was already there. Pippi parked next to it. Then he turned off the car lights and ignition and sat in the darkness. Across the Pacific Coast Highway they saw the ocean shimmering, parted with streaks of gold that were the moonlight. They saw one of their team cars parked on the far side of the lot. They knew their other two teams were at their stations on the highway waiting to shepherd them back to the house, ready to cut off any pursuers and intercept any problems before them.

Cross looked at his watch. It was twelve-thirty. They had to wait another fifteen minutes. Suddenly Pippi hit his shoulder. "He's early," Pippi said. "Go!"

Cross saw the figure emerging from the restaurant, caught in the glow of the door lights. He was struck by the boyishness of the figure, slight and short, a shock of curly hair above the pale, thin face. Theo looked too frail to be a murderer.

Then they were surprised. Theo, instead of going to his car, walked across the Pacific Coast Highway, dodging traffic. On the other side, he strolled out onto the open beach to the very edge, daring the waves. He stood there gazing at the ocean, the yellow moon setting on the horizon so far away. Then he turned and came back across the highway and into the parking lot. He had let the waves reach him, and there was the squish of water in his fashionable boots.

Cross slowly got out of the car. Theo was almost on him. Cross waited for Theo to go past, then smiled politely to let Theo get into his car. When Theo was inside, Cross drew the gun. Theo, about to put his key into the ignition, his car window down, raised his eyes, aware of the shadow. At the moment Cross fired, they looked into each other's eyes. Theo was frozen as the bullet smashed into his face, which instantly became a mask of blood, the eyes staring out. Cross yanked open the door and fired two more bullets into the top of Theo's head. Blood sprayed into his face. Then he threw a pouch of drugs on the floor of Theo's car. He slammed the door shut. Pippi had started up the motor of his car just as Cross fired. Now he opened the car door, and Cross hopped in. According to plan he had not dropped the pistol. That would have made it look like a planned hit instead of a drug deal gone sour.

Pippi drove out of the lot, and their cover car pulled out behind them. The two lead cars swung into position, and five minutes later they were back at the Family house. Ten minutes after that, Pippi and Cross were in Pippi's car heading toward Vegas. The operations team would get rid of the stolen car and the gun.

When they drove past the restaurant there were no signs of police activity. Obviously Theo was still undiscovered. Pippi turned the car radio on and listened to the news broadcasts. There was nothing. "Perfect," Pippi said. "When you plan right, it always goes perfect."

They arrived in Las Vegas as the sun was coming up, the desert a sullen red sea. Cross never forgot that ride through the desert, through the darkness, through the moonlight that never seemed to end. And then the sun coming up and then, a little later, the neon lights of the Vegas strip shining like a beacon heralding safety, the awakening from a nightmare. Vegas was never dark.

At almost that exact moment, Theo was discovered, his face ghostly in a paler dawn. Publicity centered on the fact that Theo was in possession of half a million dollars worth of cocaine. It was obviously a drug deal gone sour. The governor was in the clear.

Cross observed many things from this event. That the drugs he had planted on Theo cost no more than ten thousand dollars, although the authorities had placed the value at half a million; that the governor was praised for the fact that he sent condolences to Theo's family; that in a week the media never referred to the matter again.

Pippi and Cross were summoned East for an audience with Giorgio. Giorgio commended them both for an intelligent and well-executed operation, making no mention of the fact that it was supposed to look like an accident. And Cross was aware on this visit that the Clericuzio Family treated him with the respect due the Family Hammer. The primary evidence of this was that Cross was given a percentage of the income of the gambling books, legal and illegal, in Las Vegas. It was understood that he was now an official member of the Clericuzio Family, to be called to duty on special occasions with bonuses calculated on the risk of the project.

. . .

Gronevelt, too, had his reward. After Walter Wavven was elected senator, he took a weekend retreat at the Xanadu. Gronevelt gave him a Villa and went to congratulate him on his victory.

Senator Wavven was back in his old form. He was gambling and winning, he had little dinners with the showgirls of the Xanadu. He seemed completely recovered. He made only one reference to his earlier crisis. He said to Gronevelt, "Alfred, you have a blank check with me."

Gronevelt said, smiling, "No man can afford to carry blank checks in his wallet, but thank you."

He didn't want checks that paid off all the senator's debt. He wanted a long, continuing friendship, one that would never end.

In the next five years, Cross became an expert on gambling and running a casino hotel. He served as an assistant to Gronevelt, though his primary job was still working with his father, Pippi, not only in running the Collection Agency, which he was now certified to inherit, but also as the number two Hammer for the Clericuzio Family.

By the age of twenty-five, Cross was known in the Clericuzio Family as the Little Hammer. He himself found it curious that he was so cold about his work. His targets were never people he knew. They were lumps of flesh enclosed in defenseless skin; the skeleton beneath gave them the outline of wild animals he had hunted with his father when he was a boy. He did fear the risk but only cerebrally; there was no physical anxiety. There were moments in his life's repose, sometimes when he awoke in the morning with a vague terror as if he had some terrible nightmare. Then there were times when he was depressed, when he called up the memory of his sister and his mother, little scenes from childhood and some visits after the breakup of the family.

He remembered his mother's cheek, her flesh so warm, her satin skin so porous that he imagined he could hear the blood flow underneath, contained, safe. But in his dreams the skin crumbled like ash, blood washing over the obscene breaks into scarlet waterfalls.

Which triggered other memories. When his mother kissed him with cold lips, her arms embracing him for tiny moments of politeness. She never held his hand as she did Claudia's. The times he visited and left her house short of breath, his chest burning as if bruised. He never felt her loss in the present, he only felt her lost in his past.

When he thought of his sister, Claudia, he did not feel this loss. Their past together existed and she was still part of his life, though not enough. He remembered how they used to fight in the winter. They kept their fists in their overcoat pockets and swung at each other. A harmless duel. All was as it should be, Cross thought, except that sometimes he missed his mother and his sister. Still, he was happy with his father and the Clericuzio Family.

So in his twenty-fifth year Cross became involved in his final operation as a Hammer of the Family. The target was someone he had known all his life. . . .

A vast FBI probe destroyed many of the titular Barons, some true *Brugliones*, across the country, and among them was Virginio Ballazzo, now the ruler of the largest Family on the Eastern Seaboard.

Virginio Ballazzo was a Baron of the Clericuzio Family for over twenty years and had been dutiful in wetting the Clericuzio beak. In return the Clericuzio made him rich; at the time of his fall, Ballazzo was worth over $50 million. He and his family lived in very good style indeed. And yet the unforeseen happened. Virginio Ballazzo, despite his debt, betrayed those who had raised him so high. He broke the law of *omertà*, the code that forbade giving any information to the authorities.

One of the charges against him was murder, but it was not so much fear of imprisonment that made him turn traitor; after all, New York had no death penalty. And no matter how long his penalty, if indeed he was convicted, the Clericuzio would get him out in ten years, would ensure that even those ten years would be easy time. He knew the repertoire. At his trial, witnesses would perjure themselves in his behalf, jurors could be approached with bribes. Even after he had served a few years, a new case would be prepared, presenting new evidence, showing that he was innocent. There was one famous case in which the Clericuzio had done such a thing after one of their clients had served five years. The man had gotten out and the state had presented him with over a million dollars as reparation for his "false" imprisonment.

No, Ballazzo had no fear of prison. What made him turn traitor was that the Federal Government threatened to seize all his worldly goods under the RICO laws passed by Congress to crush crime. Ballazzo could not bear that he and his children would lose their palatial home in New Jersey, the luxurious condo in Florida, the horse farm in Kentucky that had produced three also-rans in the Kentucky Derby. For the infamous RICO laws permitted the government to seize all worldly goods of those arrested for criminal conspiracy. The stocks and bonds, the antique cars might be taken. Don Clericuzio himself had been angered by the RICO laws, but his only comment was "the rich will rue this thing, the day will come when they will arrest the whole of Wall Street under this RICO law."

It was not luck but foresight that the Clericuzio had removed their old friend Ballazzo from its confidence in the last few years. He had become too flashy for their tastes. *The New York Times* had run a story on his collection of antique cars, Virginio Ballazzo at the wheel of a 1935 Rolls-Royce, a debonair visored cap on his head. Virginio Ballazzo, on the TV at the running of the Kentucky Derby, riding crop in hand, talked about the beauty of the sport of kings. There he was identified as a wealthy importer of rugs. All this was too much for the Clericuzio Family, they became wary of him.

When Virginio Ballazzo opened discussions with the United States District Attorney, it was Ballazzo's lawyer who informed the Clericuzio family. The Don, who was semiretired, immediately took charge from his son Giorgio. This was a situation that required a Sicilian hand.

A Family conference was held: Don Clericuzio; his three sons, Giorgio, Vincent, and Petie; and Pippi De Lena. It was true that Ballazzo could damage the Family structure, but only the lower levels would suffer greatly. The traitor could give valuable information but no legal proof. Giorgio suggested that if worse came to worst, they could always set up headquarters in a foreign country, but the Don dismissed this angrily. Where else could they live but in America? America had made them rich, America was the most powerful country in the world and protected its rich. The Don often quoted the saying, "Rather a hundred guilty men go free than one innocent man be punished," then added, "What a beautiful country." The trouble was that everyone got soft because of such good living. In Sicily Ballazzo would never have dared become a traitor, would never even have dreamed of breaking the law of *omertà*. His own sons would have killed him.

"I'm too old to live in a foreign country," the Don said. "I will not be driven from my home by a traitor."

A small problem in and of himself, Virginio Ballazzo was a symptom, an infection. There were many more like him, who did not abide by the old laws that had made them all strong. There was a Family *Bruglione* in Louisiana, another in Chicago, and another in Tampa, who flaunted their wealth, who showed off their power for all the world to see. And then these *cafoni* when they were caught sought to escape the punishment they had earned by their own carelessness. By breaking the law of *omertà*. By betraying their fellows. This rot must be eradicated. That was the Don's position. But now he would listen to the others; after all, he was old, perhaps there were other solutions.

Giorgio outlined what was happening. Ballazzo was bargaining with the government attorneys. He would willingly go to jail if the government promised not to invoke the RICO laws, if his wife and children could keep his fortune. And of course he was bargaining not to go to jail, for that he would have to testify in court against the people he betrayed. He and his wife would be placed in a Witness Protection Program and would live the rest of their lives under false identities. Some plastic surgery would be performed. And his children would live the rest of their lives in respectable comfort. That was the deal.

Ballazzo, whatever his faults, was a doting father, they all agreed. He had three well-brought-up children. One son was graduating from the Harvard School of Business, the daughter, Ceil, had a fancy cosmetics store on Fifth Avenue, another son did computer work in the space program. They were all deserving of their good fortunes. They were true Americans and lived the American dream.

"So," the old Don said, "we will send a message to Virginio that will make sense to him. He can inform on everyone else. He can send them all to jail or to the bottom of the ocean. But if he speaks one word about the Clericuzio, his children are forfeit."

Pippi De Lena said, "Threats don't seem to scare anybody anymore."

"The threat will be from me personally," Don Domenico said. "He will believe me. Promise him nothing for himself. He understands."

It was Vincent who spoke up then. "We'll never be able to get near him once he's in the Protection Program."

The Don spoke to Pippi De Lena. "And you, *Martèllo* of mine, what do you say to that?"

Pippi De Lena shrugged. "After he testifies, after they hide him away in the Protection Program, sure we can. But there will be a lot of heat, a lot of publicity. Is it worth it? Does it change anything?"

The Don said, "The publicity, the heat, is what makes it worth doing. We will send the world our message. In fact when it is done it should be done a *bella figura*."

Giorgio said, "We could just let events take their course. No matter what Ballazzo says, it can't bury us. Pop, your answer is a short-term answer."

The Don pondered that. "What you say is true. But is there a long-term answer to anything? Life is full of doubts, of short-term answers. And you doubt that punishment will stop those others who will be trapped? It may or may not. It will certainly stop some. God himself could not create a world without punishment. I will talk personally to Ballazzo's lawyer. He will understand me. He will give the message. And Ballazzo will believe it." He paused for a moment and then sighed. "After the trials, we will do the job."

"And his wife?" Giorgio asked.

"A good woman," the Don said. "But she has become too American. We cannot leave a bereaved widow to shout her grief and secrets."

Petie spoke for the first time. "And Virginio's children?" Petie was the true assassin.

"Not if it's not necessary. We are not monsters," Don Domenico said. "And Ballazzo never told the children his business. He wanted the world to believe that he was a horse rider. So let him ride his horses at the bottom of the ocean." They were all silent. Then the Don said sadly, "Let the little ones go. After all, we live in a country where children do not avenge their parents."

The following day the message was transmitted to Virginio Ballazzo by his lawyer. In all these messages, the language was flowery. When the Don spoke to the lawyer he expressed his hope that his old friend Virginio Ballazzo had only the fondest memories of the Clericuzio, who would always look out for their unfortunate friend's interests. The Don told the lawyer that Ballazzo should never fear for his children where danger lurked, even on Fifth Avenue, but that the Don himself would guarantee their safety. He, the Don, knew how highly Ballazzo prized his children; that jail, the electric chair, the devils in hell, could not frighten his brave friend, only the specter of harm to his children. "Tell him," the Don said to the lawyer, "that I, personally, I, Don Domenico Clericuzio, guarantee that no misfortune will befall them."

The lawyer delivered this message word for word to his client, who responded as follows. "Tell my friend, my dearest friend, who grew up with my father in Sicily, that I rely on his guarantees with utmost gratitude. Tell him I have only the fondest memories of all the Clericuzio, so profound that I cannot even speak of them. I kiss his hand."

Then Ballazzo sang, "Tra la la . . ." at his lawyer. "I think we better go over our testimony very carefully," he said. "We do not want to involve my good friend. . . ."

"Yes," the lawyer said, as he reported later to the Don.

Everything proceeded according to plan. Virginio Ballazzo broke *omertà* and testified, sending numerous underlings to jail and even implicating a deputy mayor of New York. But not a word of the Clericuzio. Then the Ballazzos, man and wife, disappeared into the Witness Protection Program.

The newspapers and TV were jubilant, the mighty Mafia had been broken. There were hundreds of photos, live TV action shots of these villains being hauled off to prison. Ballazzo took up the whole centerfold of the *Daily News*, TOP MAFIA DON FALLS. It showed him with his antique cars, his Kentucky Derby horses, his impressive London wardrobe. It was an orgy.

When the Don gave Pippi the assignment of tracking down the Ballazzo couple and punishing them, he said, "Do it in such a way that it will get the same publicity as they are getting now. We don't want them to forget our Virginio." But it was to take the Hammer more than a year to complete this assignment.

Cross remembered Ballazzo and had fond memories of him as a jovial, generous man. He and Pippi had had dinner at the Ballazzo house, for Mrs. Ballazzo had a reputation as a fine Italian cook, particularly for her macaroni and cauliflower with garlic and herbs, a dish Cross still remembered. He had played with the Ballazzo children as a child and had even fallen in love with Ballazzo's daughter, Ceil, when they were teenagers. She had written him from college after that magical Sunday, but he had never answered. Alone with Pippi now, he said, "I don't want to do this operation."

His father looked at him and then smiled sadly. He said, "Cross, it happens sometimes, you have to get used to it. You won't survive otherwise."

Cross shook his head. "I can't do it," he said.

Pippi sighed. "OK," he said. "I'll tell them I'm going to use you for planning. I'll make them give me Dante for the actual operation."

Pippi set up the probe. The Clericuzio Family, with huge bribes, penetrated the screen of the Witness Protection Program.

The Ballazzos felt secure in their new identities, false birth certificates, new social security numbers, marriage papers, and the plastic surgery that had altered their faces so that they looked ten years younger. However, their body builds, their gestures, their voices, made them more easily identifiable than they realized.

Old habits die hard. On a Saturday night Virginio Ballazzo and his wife drove to the small South Dakota town near their new home to gamble in the small-time joint operating under the local option. On their way home, Pippi De Lena and Dante Clericuzio, with a crew of six other men, intercepted them. Dante, violating the plan, could not resist making himself known to the couple before he pulled the trigger of his shotgun.

No attempt was made to conceal the bodies. No valuables were taken. It was perceived as an act of retaliation, and it sent a message to the world. There was a torrent of rage from the press and television, the authorities promised justice would be done. Indeed, there was enough of a furor to make the whole Clericuzio Empire seem to be in jeopardy.

Pippi was forced to hide in Sicily for two years. Dante became the number one Hammer of the Family. Cross was made the *Bruglione* of the Western Empire of the Clericuzio. His refusal to take part in the Ballazzo execution had been noted. He did not have the temperament to be a true Hammer.

Before Pippi disappeared into Sicily for two years, he had a final meeting and bon voyage dinner with Don Clericuzio and his son Giorgio.

"I must apologize for my son," Pippi said. "Cross is young and the young are sentimental. He was very fond of the Ballazzos."

"We were fond of Virginio," the Don said. "I never liked a man better."

"Then why did we kill him?" Giorgio asked. "It's caused more trouble than it's worth."

Don Clericuzio gave him a stern look. "You cannot live a life without order. If you have power, you must use it for strict justice. Ballazzo committed a great offense. Pippi understands that, no, Pippi?"

"Of course, Don Domenico," Pippi said. "But you and I are of the old school. Our sons don't understand." He paused for a moment. "I wanted to thank you also for making Cross your *Bruglione* in the West while I'm gone. He will not disappoint you."

"I know that," the Don said. "I have as much trust in him as I have in you. He is intelligent and his squeamishness is that of youth. Time will harden his heart."

They were having a dinner cooked and served by a woman whose husband worked in the Enclave. She had forgotten the Don's bowl of grated Parmesan cheese, and Pippi went into the kitchen for the grater and brought the bowl to the Don. He carefully grated the cheese into the bowl and watched the Don dip his huge silver spoon into the yellowish mound, put it in his mouth, and then sip from his glass of powerful homemade wine. This was a man with a belly, Pippi thought. Over eighty years old and he could still order the death of a sinner, and also eat this strong cheese and harsh wine. He said casually, "Is Rose Marie in the house? I'd like to say good-bye to her."

"She's having one of her fucking spells," Giorgio said. "She's locked herself in her room, thank God, or else we wouldn't be able to enjoy our dinner."

"Ah," Pippi said. "I always thought she'd get better with time."

"She thinks too much," the Don said. "She loves her son Dante too much. She refuses to understand. The world is what it is, and you are what you are."

Giorgio said smoothly, "Pippi, how do you rate Dante after this Ballazzo operation? Did he show any nerves?"

Pippi shrugged and remained silent. The Don gave a little grunt and looked at him sharply. "You can be frank," the Don said. "Giorgio is his uncle and I am his grandfather. We are all of one blood and are permitted to judge each other."

Pippi stopped eating and looked directly at the Don and Giorgio. He said almost regretfully, "Dante has a bloody mouth."

In their world this was an idiom for a man who went beyond savageness, an intimation of bestiality while doing a necessary piece of work. It was strictly forbidden in the Clericuzio Family.

Giorgio leaned back in his chair and said, "Jesus Christ." The Don gave Giorgio a disapproving look for his blasphemy and then waved a hand at Pippi to continue. He did not seem surprised.

"He was a good pupil," Pippi said. "He has the temperament and the physical strength. He's very quick and he is intelligent. But he takes too much pleasure in his work. He took too much time with the Ballazzos. He talked to them for ten minutes before he shot the woman. Then he waited another five minutes before shooting Balazzo. That's not to my taste but more important you never can tell when it might lead to danger, every minute might count. On other jobs he was unnecessarily cruel, a throwback to the old days when they thought it clever to hang a man on a meathook. I don't want to go into details."

Giorgio said angrily, "It's because that prick of a nephew is short. He's a fucking midget. And then he wears those fucking hats. Where the hell does he get them?"

The Don said good-humoredly, "The same place the blacks get their hats. In Sicily when I was growing up everybody wore a funny hat. Who knows why? Who cares? Now, stop talking nonsense. I wore funny hats, too. Maybe it runs in the family. It's his mother who put all kinds of nonsense in his head ever since he was little. She should have married again. Widows are like spiders. They spin too much."

Giorgio said with intensity, "But he's good at his job."

"Better than Cross could ever be," Pippi said diplomatically. "But sometimes I think he's crazy like his mother." He paused. "He even scares me sometimes."

The Don took a mouthful of cheese and wine. "Giorgio," he said, "instruct your nephew, repair his fault. It could be dangerous to all of us in the Family someday. But don't let him know it comes from me. He is too young and I am too old, I would not influence him."

Pippi and Giorgio knew this was a lie but also knew that if the old man wanted to hide his hand, he had a good reason. At that moment they heard steps overhead and then someone coming down the stairs. Rose Marie came into the dining room.

The three men saw with dismay that she was having one of her fits. Her hair was wild, her makeup was bizarre, and her clothing was twisted. Most serious, her mouth was open but no words were coming out. She used her body and hand flailing to take the place of speech. Her gestures were startlingly vivid, better than words. She hated them, she wanted them dead, she wanted their souls to burn in hell for eternity. They should choke on their food, go blind from the wine, their cocks should fall off when they slept with their wives.

Then she took Giorgio's plate and Pippi's plate and smashed them on the floor.

This was all permitted, but the first time, years ago, when she had her first fit, she treated the Don's plate in the same fashion and he had ordered her seized and locked in her room and then had her dispatched for three months to a special nursing home. Even now the Don quickly put the lid on his cheese bowl; she did a lot of spitting. Then suddenly it was over, she became very still. She spoke to Pippi. "I wanted to say good-bye. I hope you die in Sicily."

Pippi felt an overwhelming pity for her. He rose and took her in his arms. She did not resist. He kissed her on the cheek and said, "I wish to die in Sicily rather than come home and find you like this." She broke out of his arms and ran back up the stairs.

"Very touching," Giorgio said, almost sneering. "But you don't have to put up with her every month." He gave a slight leer with this, but they all knew that Rose Marie was far past menopause and she had the fits more than once a month.

The Don seemed the least upset by his daughter's fit. "She will get better or she will die," he said. "If not I will send her away."

Then he addressed Pippi. "I'll let you know when you can come back from Sicily. Enjoy the rest, we're all getting older. But keep your eyes open for new men to recruit for the Enclave. That is important. We must have men we can count on not to betray us, who have *omertà* in their bones, not like the rascals born in this country who want to lead a good life but not pay for it."

The next day, with Pippi on his way to Sicily, Dante was summoned to the Quogue mansion to spend the weekend. The first day Giorgio let Dante spend all his time with Rose Marie. It was touching to see their devotion to each other, Dante was a totally different person with his mother. He never wore one of his peculiar hats, he took her on walks around the estate, took her out for dinner. He waited on her like some eighteenth-century French gallant. When she broke into hysterical tears, he cradled her in his arms, and she never went into one of her fits. They spoke to each other constantly in low, confidential tones.

At supper time, Dante helped Rose Marie set the table, grate the Don's cheese, kept her company in the kitchen. She cooked his favorite meal of penne with broccoli and then roast lamb studded with bacon and garlic.

Giorgio was always struck by the rapport between the Don and Dante. Dante was solicitous, he spooned the penne and broccoli into the Don's plate and ostentatiously wiped and polished the great silver spoon he used to dip into the grated parmesan. Dante teased the old man. "Grandfather," he said, "if you got new teeth, we wouldn't have to grate this cheese. The dentists do great work now, they can plant steel in your jaw. A miracle."

The Don was playful in kind. "I want my teeth to die with me," he said. "And I'm too old for miracles. Why should God waste a miracle on an ancient like me?"

Rose Marie had prettied herself for her son, and traces of her young beauty could be seen. She seemed happy to see her father and her son on such familiar terms. It banished her constant air of anxiety.

Giorgio, too, was content. He was pleased that his sister seemed happy. She was not so nerve-racking and she was a better cook. She didn't stare at him with accusing eyes and she would not be subject to one of her fits.

When the Don and Rose Marie had both gone to bed, Giorgio took Dante into the den. It was the room that had neither phones nor TV and no communication lines to any part of the house. And it had a very thick door. Now it was furnished with two black leather couches and black studded leather chairs. It still contained a whiskey cabinet and a small wet bar equipped with a small refrigerator and a shelf of glasses. On the table rested a box of Havana cigars. Still, it was a room with no windows, like a small cave.

Dante's face, too sly and interesting for so young a man, always made Giorgio uneasy. His eyes were too cunningly bright and Giorgio didn't like it that he was short.

Giorgio made them both a drink and lit up one of the Havana cigars. "Thank God you don't wear those weird hats around your mother," he said. "Why do you wear them anyway?"

"I like them," Dante said. "And to make you and Uncle Petie and Uncle Vincent notice me." He paused for a moment and then said with a mischievous grin, "They make me look taller." It was true, Giorgio thought, that hats made him look handsomer. They framed his ferretlike face in a flattering way, his features were strangely uncoordinated when seen without his hat.

"You shouldn't wear them on a job," Giorgio said. "It makes an identification too easy."

"Dead men don't talk," Dante said. "I kill everybody who sees me on a job."

"Nephew, stop fucking me around," Giorgio said. "It's not smart. It's a risk. The Family doesn't take risks. Now one other thing. The word is getting around that you have a bloody mouth."

Dante for the first time reacted with anger. Suddenly he looked deadly. He put down his drink and said, "Does Grandfather know that? Does this come from him?"

"The Don knows nothing about it," Giorgio lied. He was a very expert liar. "And I won't tell him. You're his favorite, it would distress him. But I'm telling you, no more hats on the job and keep your mouth clean. You're the Family number one Hammer now and you take too much pleasure in the business. That's dangerous and against Family rules."

Dante seemed not to hear. He was thoughtful now and his smile reappeared. "Pippi must have told you," he said amiably.

"Yes," Giorgio said. He was curt. "And Pippi is the best. We put you with Pippi so you could learn the right way to do things. And do you know why he's the best? Because he has a good heart. It's never for pleasure."

Dante let himself go. He had a laughing fit. He rolled onto the sofa and then onto the floor. Giorgio watched him sourly, thinking he was as crazy as his mother. Finally Dante got to his feet, took a long swig from his drink, and said with great good humor, "Now you're saying I don't have a good heart."

"That's right," Giorgio said. "You're my nephew but I know what you are. You killed two men in some sort of personal quarrel without the Family OK. The Don wouldn't take action against you, he wouldn't even reprimand you. Then you killed some chorus girl you were banging for a year. Out of temper. You gave her a Communion so she wouldn't be found by the police. And she wasn't. You think you're a clever little prick, but the Family put the evidence together and found you guilty though you could never be convicted in a court of law."

Dante was quiet now. Not from fear but from calculation. "Does the Don know all this crap?"

"Yes," Giorgio said. "But you're still his favorite. He said to let it pass, that you're still young. That you will learn. I don't want to bring this bloody mouth business to him, he's too old. You're his grandson, your mother is his daughter. It would just break his heart."

Dante laughed again. "The Don has a heart. Pippi De Lena has a heart, Cross has a chickenshit heart, my mother has a broken heart. But I don't have a heart? How about you, Uncle Giorgio, do you have a heart?"

"Sure," Giorgio said. "I still put up with you."

"So, I'm the only one who doesn't have a fucking heart?" Dante said. "I love my mother and my grandfather and they both hate each other. My grandfather loves me less as I grow older. You and Vinnie and Petie don't even like me though we share family blood. You think I don't know these things? But I still love all of you though you put me down lower than that fucking Pippi De Lena. You think I don't have any fucking brains either?"

Giorgio was astonished by this outburst. He was also made wary by its truth. "You're wrong about the Don, he cares about you just as much. The same with Petie, Vincent, and me. Have we ever not treated you with the respect of family? Sure, the Don is a little remote but the man is very old. As for me, I'm just giving you a caution for your own safety. You're in a very dangerous business, you have to be careful. You cannot let personal emotions in. That's disaster."

"Do Vinnie and Pete know all this stuff?" Dante asked.

"No," Giorgio said. Which was another lie. Vincent had also spoken to Giorgio about Dante. Petie had not, but Petie was a born assassin. Yet he, too, had shown a distaste for Dante's company.

"Any other complaints about how I do my job?" Dante asked.

"No," Giorgio said, "and don't be so tough about this. I'm advising you as your uncle. But I'm telling you from my place in the Family. You do not anymore make anybody do their Communion or Confirmation without the Family OK. Got it?"

"OK," Dante said, "but I'm still the number one Hammer, right?"

"Until Pippi comes back from his little vacation," Giorgio said. "Depends on your work."

"I'll enjoy my work less if that's what you want," Dante said. "OK?" He tapped Giorgio on the shoulder affectionately.

"Good," Giorgio said. "Tomorrow night take your mother out to eat. Keep her company. Your grandfather will like that."

"Sure," Dante said.

"Vincent has one of his restaurants out by East Hampton," Giorgio said. "You could take your mother there."

Dante said suddenly, "Is she getting worse?"

Giorgio shrugged. "She can't forget the past. She holds on to old stories that she should forget. The Don always tells, 'The world is what it is and we are what we are,' his old line. But she cannot accept it." He gave Dante an affectionate hug. "Now let's just forget this little talk. I hate doing this stuff." As if he had not been specifically instructed by the Don.

After Dante left on Monday morning, Giorgio reported the whole conversation to the Don. The Don sighed. "What a lovely little boy he was. What could have happened?"

Giorgio had one great virtue. He spoke his mind when he really wanted to, even to his father, the great Don himself. "He talked too much to his mother. And he has bad blood." They were both silent for a time after this.

"And when Pippi comes back, what do we do with your grandson?" Giorgio asked.

"Despite everything, I think Pippi should retire," the Don said. "Dante must have his chance to be foremost, after all he is a Clericuzio. Pippi will be an advisor to his son's *Bruglione* in the West. If necessary he can always advise Dante. There is no one better versed in those matters. As he proved with the Santadio. But he should end his years in peace."

Giorgio muttered sarcastically, "The Hammer Emeritus." But the Don pretended not to understand the joke.

He frowned and said to Giorgio, "Soon you will have my responsibilities. Remember always that the task is that the Clericuzio must one day stand with society, that the Family must never die. No matter how hard the choice."

And so they left. But it was to be two years before Pippi returned from Sicily, the killing of Ballazzo receding into the bureaucratic mist. A mist manufactured by the Clericuzio.

BOOK V

Las Vegas
Hollywood
Quogue

CHAPTER 7

⚃

CROSS DE LENA received his sister, Claudia, and Skippy Deere in the executive penthouse suite of the Xanadu Hotel. Deere was always impressed by the difference between the two siblings. Claudia, not quite pretty and yet so likable, and Cross, so conventionally handsome with a slim but athletic body. Claudia, so naturally amiable, and Cross, so rigidly affable and distant. There was a difference between amiable and affable, Deere thought. One was in the genes, the other, learned.

Claudia and Skippy Deere sat on the couch, Cross sat opposite them. Claudia explained about Boz Skannet and then leaned forward and said, "Cross, please listen to me. This isn't only business. Athena is my dearest friend. And she is truly one of the best people I have ever known. She helped me when I needed help. And this is the most important favor I've ever asked you to do. Help Athena out of this fix and I'll never ask you for anything again." Then she turned to Skippy Deere. "You tell Cross the money part."

Deere always took the offensive before he asked a favor. He said to Cross, "I've been coming to your hotel over ten years, how come you never give me one of the Villas?"

Cross laughed, "They've always been full."

Deere said, "Throw somebody out."

"Sure," Cross said. "When I get a profit statement from one of your pictures and when I see you lay down a ten-grand bet at baccarat."

Claudia said, "I'm his sister and I never got one of the Villas. Stop fucking around, Skippy, and lay out the money problem."

When Deere finished, Cross, reading off a pad on which he had made notes, said, "Let me get this straight. You and the Studio lose fifty million in cash, plus the two hundred million in projected profit, if this Athena doesn't go back to work. She won't go back to work because she's so afraid of an ex-husband called Boz Skannet. You can buy him off but she still won't go back to work because she doesn't believe he can be stopped. Is that the whole thing?"

"Yeah," Deere said. "We promised her she'd be protected better than the president of the United States while she's making this picture. We have surveillance on this guy Skannet even now. We have her guarded twenty-four hours. She still won't come back to work."

"I don't really see the problem," Cross said.

"This guy comes from a powerful political family in Texas," Deere said. "And he's a really tough guy, I tried to get our security people to lean on him . . ."

"Who's your security agency?" Cross asked.

"Pacific Ocean Security," Deere said.

"Why are you talking to me?" Cross asked.

"Because your sister said you could help," Deere said. "It wasn't my idea."

Cross said to his sister, "Claudia, what made you think I could help?"

Claudia's face twisted up in discomfort. "I've seen you solve problems in the past, Cross. You're very persuasive, and you always seem to come up with a solution." She smiled her innocent grin. "Besides you're my older brother, I have faith in you."

Cross sighed and said, "Same old bullshit," but Deere noticed the easy affection between the two.

The three of them sat silently for a while, then Deere said, "Cross, we came here as a long shot. But if you're looking for another investment, I have a project coming up that's very, very good."

Cross looked at Claudia, then at Deere, and said thoughtfully, "Skippy, I want to meet this Athena and after that maybe I can solve all your problems."

"Great," Claudia said, relieved. "We can all fly out tomorrow." She hugged him.

197 • THE LAST DON

"OK," Deere said. He was already trying to figure out how he could get Cross to take some of his loss on the *Messalina* film.

The next day they flew into Los Angeles. Claudia had talked Athena into seeing them, then Deere had taken the phone. That conversation had convinced him that Athena would never return to the picture. He was infuriated by this, but he diverted himself on the plane by scheming how he would get Cross to give him one of his fucking Villas when he visited Vegas again.

The Malibu Colony, where Athena Aquitane lived, was a section of beach that was located about forty minutes north of Beverly Hills and Hollywood. The Colony held a little over a hundred dwellings, each one of which was worth from three to six million dollars but looked very ordinary and ramshackle from the outside. Each house was enclosed by fencing and sometimes ornate entry gates.

The Colony itself could only be entered through a private road guarded by security men in a large hut who controlled the swinging barriers. The security personnel screened all visitors by phone or checklist. Residents had special car stickers that were changed every week. Cross recognized this as a "nuisance" security barrier, not a serious one.

But the Pacific Ocean Security men around Athena's house were another matter. They were uniformed, armed, and looked to be in very tough physical condition.

They entered Athena's house from the sidewalk parallel to the beach. It had its own additional security controlled by Athena's secretary, who buzzed them in from a small guest house nearby.

There were two more men with Pacific Ocean uniforms, and another at the door of the house. Passing the guest house, they walked through a long garden filled with flowers and lemon trees, which scented the salty air. They finally arrived at the main house which looked out over the Pacific Ocean itself.

A tiny South American maid let them in and led them through a huge kitchen into a living room that seemed to be filled with the ocean filtered through the huge windows. A room with bamboo furniture, glass tables, and deep-sea-green sofas. The maid led them through this room to a glass door that opened onto a terrace overlooking the ocean, a wide, long terrace that had chairs and tables and an exercise bike that glittered like silver. Beyond all of this was the ocean itself, blue-green, slanting to the sky.

Cross De Lena, when he saw Athena on that terrace, felt a shock of fear. She was far more exquisite than on film, which was very rare. Film could not capture her coloring, the depth of her eyes or their shade of green. Her body moved as a great athlete's moved, with a physical grace that seemed effortless. Her hair, cut into a rough, golden crop that would have been ugly on any other woman, crowned her beauty. She was wearing a powder-blue sweat suit that should have concealed the shape of her body but did not. Her legs were long in proportion to her torso, her feet were bare, there was no polish on her toenails.

But it was the look of intelligence on her face, the focusing of attention, that impressed him most.

She greeted Skippy Deere with the customary kiss on the cheek, embraced Claudia with a warm hug, and shook hands with Cross. Her eyes reflected the ocean waters behind her. "Claudia always talks about you," she said to Cross. "Her handsome, mysterious brother who can make the earth stop when he wants to." She laughed, a completely natural laugh, not the laugh of a woman frightened.

Cross felt a wonderful delight, there was no other word. Her voice was throaty, pitched low, a bewitching musical instrument. The ocean framed her, the fine-planed cheekbones, the lips unadorned, generous and the color of red wine, the radiating intelligence. Flashing through Cross's mind was one of Gronevelt's short lectures. *Money can make you safe in this world, from everything except a beautiful woman.*

Cross had known many beautiful women in Vegas, as many as in Los Angeles and Hollywood. But in Vegas the beauty was beauty as of itself with only a slight degree of talent; many of those beauties had failed in Hollywood. In Hollywood, beauty was married to talent and, less often, artistic greatness. Both cities attracted beauty from all over the world. Then there were the actresses who became Bankable Stars.

These were the women who in addition to their charm and beauty had a certain childlike innocence and courage. A curiosity in their craft that could be raised to an art form, which gave them a certain dignity. Though beauty was commonplace in both cities, in Hollywood Goddesses arose and received the adoration of the world. Athena Aquitane was one of those rare Goddesses.

Cross said coolly to Athena, "Claudia told me you are the most beautiful woman in the world."

Athena said, "What did she say about my brain?"

She leaned over the balcony of the deck and stuck one leg in back of her in some sort of exercise. What would be an affectation in another woman seemed perfectly natural with her. And indeed throughout the meeting she continued doing exercises, bending her body forward and backward, stretching a leg over the railing, her arms pantomiming some of her words.

Claudia said, "Thena, you'd never think we were related, right?"

Skippy Deere said, "Never."

But Athena looked at them and said, "You both look very much alike," and Cross could see she was serious.

Claudia said, "Now you know why I love her."

Athena stopped her motions for a moment and said to Cross, "They tell me you can help. I don't see how."

Cross tried not to stare at her, tried not to look at the flaming-sun gold of her hair set against the green behind her. He said, "I'm good at persuading people. If it's true that the only thing keeping you from going back to work is your husband, maybe I can talk him into a deal."

"I don't believe in Boz keeping his deals," Athena said. "The Studio has already talked a deal."

Deere said in what was for him a subdued voice, "Athena you really have nothing to worry about. I promise you." But for some reason he was unconvincing even to himself. He watched them all carefully. He knew how Athena overwhelmed men, actresses were the most charming people in the world when they wanted to be. But Deere detected no change in Cross.

"Skippy just won't accept that I can leave movies," Athena said. "It's so important to him."

"And not to you?" Deere said angrily.

Athena gave a long, cool look. "It was once. But I know Boz. I have to disappear, I have to start a new life." She gave them a mischievous smile. "I can get along anywhere."

"I can make an agreement with your husband," Cross said. "And I can guarantee that he'll abide by it."

Deere said confidently, "Athena, in the movie business, there are hundreds of cases like this, harassment of stars by crazies. We have foolproof procedures. There really is no danger."

Athena continued her exercises. One leg flew improbably above her head. "You don't know Boz," she said. "I do."

"Is Boz the only reason you won't go back to work?" Cross asked.

"Yes," Athena said. "He'll track me forever. You can protect me until I finish the picture but then what?"

Cross said. "I've never failed to make a deal. I'll give him whatever he wants."

Athena stopped her exercises. For the first time, she looked Cross directly in the eye. "I'll never believe in any deal Boz makes," she said. She turned away in dismissal.

Cross said, "I'm sorry I wasted your time."

"I didn't waste my time," Athena said cheerfully. "I did my exercises." Then she looked directly into his eyes. "I do appreciate your trying. It's just that I'm trying to look fearless like in one of my movies. Really, I'm scared to death." Then she quickly regained her composure and said, "Claudia and Skippy are always talking about your famous Villas. If I come to Vegas, would you give me one to hide out in?"

Her face was grave, but her eyes were dancing. She was showing off her power to Claudia and Skippy. She obviously expected Cross to say yes, if merely out of gallantry.

Cross smiled at her. "The Villas are usually taken," he said. He paused for a moment then said, with an utmost seriousness that startled the others, "But if you come to Vegas, I can guarantee no one will harm you."

Athena spoke to him directly. "Nobody can stop Boz. He doesn't care if he gets caught. Whatever he does he'll do in public so everybody can see."

Claudia spoke out impatiently, "But why?"

Athena said laughingly, "Because he loved me once. And because my life turned out better than his." She looked at them all a moment. "Isn't it a shame," she said, "that two people in love can grow to hate each other?"

At this moment the meeting was interrupted by the South American maid, who was leading a man onto the terrace.

The man was tall, handsome, and formally dressed with a touch-all-bases style: an Armani suit, Turnbull & Asser shirt, Gucci tie, and Bally shoes. He immediately murmured his apologies. "She didn't tell me you were busy, Miss Aquitane," he said. "I guess she got scared by my shield." He showed her the badge. "I just came to get some information on that incident the other night. I can wait. Or come back."

His words were polite but his look was bold. He glanced at the other two men and said, "Hello, Skippy."

Skippy Deere looked angry. "You can't talk to her without a PR and legal person around," he said. "You know better than that, Jim."

The detective offered his hand to Claudia and Cross and said, "Jim Losey."

They knew who he was. The most famous detective in Los Angeles, whose exploits had even been the basis of a miniseries. He also had appeared in very minor roles in films, and he was on Deere's Christmas gift and card lists. So Deere was emboldened to say, "Jim, give me a call later and I'll arrange a meeting with Miss Aquitane properly."

Losey smiled at him amiably and said, "Sure, Skippy."

But Athena said, "I may not be here much longer. Why not ask me now? I don't mind."

Losey would have been suave except for that constant wariness in his eyes, an alertness of his body that many years of crime work had planted in him.

He said, "In front of them?"

Athena's body was no longer in motion, and she had erased all her charm when she said quietly, "I trust them far more than I do the police."

Losey took that in stride. It was familiar. "I just wanted to ask you why you dropped the charges against your husband. Did he threaten you in any way?"

"Oh, no," Athena said scornfully. "He just threw water in my face in front of a billion people and yelled 'acid.' The next day he was out on bail."

"OK, OK," Losey said, and held up his arms in a placating gesture. "I just thought I could help."

Deere said, "Jim, give me a call later."

This raised an alarm bell in Cross. He looked thoughtfully at Deere, avoided looking at Losey. And Losey avoided looking at him.

Losey said, "I will." He saw Athena's handbag on one of the chairs and picked it up. "I saw this on Rodeo Drive," he said. "Two thousand dollars." He looked directly at Athena and said with a contemptuous politeness, "Maybe you can explain it to me, why anyone would pay that kind of money for something like this?"

Athena's face was like stone, she moved out of the frame of the ocean. She said, "That's an insulting question. Get out of here."

Losey bowed to her and left. He was grinning. He had made the impression he wanted.

"So you're human after all," Claudia said. She put her arm around Athena's shoulders. "Why did you get so mad?"

"I wasn't mad," Athena said. "I was sending him a message."

After the three visitors left, they drove from Malibu to Nate and Al's in Beverly Hills. Deere insisted to Cross that it was the only place west of the Rockies where you could get edible pastrami, corned beef, and Coney Island–style hot dogs.

As they ate Deere said reflectively, "Athena won't get back to work."

"I always knew that," Claudia said. "What I don't get is why she got so mad at that detective."

Deere laughed and said to Cross, "Did you get it?"

"No," Cross said.

Deere said, "One of the great legends of Hollywood is how anybody can get to fuck the stars. Now, male stars it's true, that's why you see the girls hanging around locations and the Beverly Wilshire Hotel. Female stars, not so much . . . a guy works on their house, a carpenter, a gardener, can get lucky, maybe she gets horny, it happened to me. Stunt men score good and other guys on the crew can get lucky. But that's fucking below the line and hurts female stars in their careers. Unless, of course, they are Superstars. Us old guys who run the show don't like that. Hell, doesn't money and power mean anything?" He grinned at them. "Now, you take Jim Losey. He's a big, handsome guy. He really kills tough guys, he's glamorous to people who live in a make-believe world. He knows that. He uses it. So he doesn't beg a star, he intimidates her. That's why he made that crack. In fact that's why he came out. It was his excuse to meet Athena and he figured he could take a shot. That insulting question was a declaration he wanted to fuck her. And Athena froze him out."

"So she's the Virgin Mary?" Cross said.

"For a movie star," Deere said.

Cross said abruptly, "You think she's scamming the Studio, trying to get more money?"

"She would never do anything like that," Claudia said. "She's absolutely straight."

"She got any grudges she's paying off?" Cross asked.

"You don't understand the business," Deere said. "First thing, the Studio would let her scam them. Stars always do that. Second, if she has a grudge, it's right out in the open. She's just weird." He paused for a moment. "She hates Bobby Bantz and she's not crazy about me. We've both been after her ass for years but never a tumble."

"Too bad you couldn't help," Claudia said to Cross. But he didn't answer her.

All during the trip from Malibu, Cross had been thinking hard. That this was the opportunity he was looking for. It would be dangerous, but if it worked he could finally make a break from the Clericuzio.

"Skippy," Cross said, "I have a proposition I want to make to you and the Studio. I'll buy your picture right now. I'll give the fifty million you've invested, put up the money to complete it, and let the Studio distribute it."

"You've got a hundred million?" Skippy Deere and Claudia both asked in astonishment.

"I know people who have it," Cross said.

"You can't get Athena back. And without Athena, there's no picture," Deere said.

"I said I'm a great persuader," Cross said. "Can you get me a meeting with Eli Marrion?"

"Sure," Deere said, "but only if I stay on as producer of the picture."

The meeting was not so easy to arrange. LoddStone Studios, that is to say, Eli Marrion and Bobby Bantz, had to be convinced that Cross De Lena was not just another big-mouth hustler, that he had the money and the credentials. Certainly he owned part of the Xanadu Hotel in Vegas, but he had no personal recorded financial worth that indicated he could swing the deal he proposed. Deere would vouch for him, but the clincher was when Cross showed a fifty-million-dollar letter of credit.

On the advice of his sister, Cross De Lena hired Molly Flanders as his lawyer for the deal.

Molly Flanders received Cross in her cave of an office. Cross was very alert, he knew certain things about her. In the world he had lived all his life, he had never met a woman who wielded power in any way, and Claudia had told him that Molly Flanders was one of the most powerful people in Hollywood. Studio chiefs took her calls, monster agents like Melo Stuart sought her help on the biggest deals. Stars like Athena Aquitane used her in their quarrels with studios. Flanders had once stopped production of the top miniseries on TV when her star client's check had been delayed in the mail.

She was much better looking than Cross had expected. She was large but well-proportioned and dressed beautifully. But on that body was the face of an elfin blond witch, the aquiline nose, the generous mouth and fierce brown eyes that seemed to squint with intense, intelligent combativeness. Her hair was braided into snakes around her head. She was forbidding until she smiled.

Molly Flanders, for all her toughness, was susceptible to handsome men and liked Cross as soon as she saw him. She was surprised because she had expected Claudia's brother to be homely. More than the handsomeness, she saw a force that Claudia did not have. He had a look of awareness that the world held no surprises. All this, however, did not convince her that she wanted to take Cross on as a client. She had heard rumors about certain connections, she didn't like the world of Vegas, and she was dubious as to the extent of his determination to take such a horrendous gamble.

"Mr. De Lena," she said, "let me make one thing clear. I represent Athena Aquitane as a lawyer not an agent. I've explained the consequences she must bear if she persists in her course of action. I'm convinced she will persist in it. Now, if you make your deal with the Studio and Athena still doesn't go back to work, I will represent her if you pursue legal action against her."

Cross looked at her intently. He had no way he could read a woman like this. He had to put most of his cards on the table. "I'll sign a waiver that I won't sue Miss Aquitane if I do buy the picture," he said. "And I have a check for two hundred thousand dollars here if you take me on. That's just for openers. You can bill me for more."

"Let's see if I understand this," Molly said. "You pay the Studio the fifty million they invested. Right now. You put up the money to complete the picture, minimum another fifty million. So you're going to gamble a hundred million that Athena goes back to work. Plus you're gambling that the picture will be a hit. It could be a flop. That's an awful risk."

Cross could be charming when he wanted to be. But he sensed that charm would not help with this woman. "I understand that with the foreign money, video, and TV sales, the picture can't lose money even if it's a flop," he said. "The only real problem is getting Miss Aquitane back to work. And maybe you can help on that."

"No, I can't," Molly said. "I don't want to mislead you. I've tried and failed. Everybody tried and failed. And Eli Marrion doesn't ever bullshit. He'll close down the picture and take the loss, then he'll try to ruin Athena. But I won't let him."

Cross was intrigued. "How will you do that?"

"Marrion has to get along with me," she said. "He's a smart man. I'll fight him in the courts, I'll make his Studio miserable on every deal. Athena won't be able to work again but I won't let them take her to the cleaners."

"If you represent me, you can save your client's career," Cross said. From the inside of his jacket he took an envelope and handed it to her. She opened it, studied it, then picked up the phone and made some calls that established the check was good.

She smiled at Cross and said, "I'm not insulting you, I do this with the biggest movie producers in town."

"Like Skippy Deere?" Cross said, laughing. "I invested in six of his pictures, four of them were hits and still I haven't made money."

"Because you didn't have me representing you," Molly said. "Now before I agree, you have to tell me how you can get Athena back to work." She paused. "I've heard some rumors about you."

Cross said, "And I've heard about you. I remember years ago when you were a criminal defense lawyer, you got some kid off a murder rap. He killed his girlfriend and you got an insanity plea. He was walking the streets less than a year later." He paused for a moment, deliberately letting his irritation show. "You didn't worry about his reputation."

Molly looked at him coldly. "You have not answered my question."

Cross decided that a lie should carry a little charm. "Molly," he said. "May I call you Molly?" She nodded her head. Cross went on. "You know I run a hotel in Vegas. I've learned this. Money is magic, you can overcome any kind of fear with money, so I'm going to offer Athena fifty percent of any money I make from the movie. If you structure the deal right and we're lucky, that means thirty million for her." He paused for a minute and said earnestly, "Come on, Molly, would you take a chance for thirty million?"

Molly shook her head. "Athena doesn't really care about money."

"The only thing that puzzles me is why the Studio doesn't give her the same deal," Cross said.

For the first time in their meeting, Molly smiled at him. "You don't know movie studios," she said. "They worry that all the stars will pull the same stunt if they set such a precedent. But let's go on. The Studio will take your deal, I think, because they will make a great deal of money just distributing the film. They will insist on that. Also, they will want a percentage of the profits. But I'm telling you again, Athena will not take your offer." She paused, then said with a teasing smile, "I thought you Vegas owners never gambled."

Cross smiled back at her. "Everybody gambles. I do when the percentages are right. And besides I plan to sell the Hotel and make a living in the movie business." He paused for a minute, letting her look into him to see the desire to be part of that world. "I think it's more interesting."

"I see," Molly said. "So this is not just a passing fancy."

"A foot in the door," Cross said. "Once I do that, I'll need your help further on."

Molly was amused by this. "I'll represent you," she said. "But as for us doing business further on, let's see first if you lose that hundred million."

She picked up the phone. She spoke into it. Then she hung up and said to Cross, "We have our meeting with their Business Affairs people to set out the rules before then. And you have three days to reconsider."

Cross was impressed. "That was fast," he said.

"Them, not me," Molly said. "It's costing them a fortune to tread water on this picture."

"I don't have to say this, I know," Cross said. "But the offer I plan to make Miss Aquitane is confidential, between you and me."

"No, you didn't have to say it," Molly said.

They shook hands, and after Cross left, Molly remembered something. Why had Cross De Lena mentioned that long-ago case when she had gotten that kid off, that famous victory of hers. Why that particular case? She had gotten plenty of murderers off.

There days later Cross De Lena and Molly Flanders met in her office before going to LoddStone Studios so that she could check over the financial papers that Cross was bringing to the meeting. Then Molly drove both of them to the Studio in her Mercedes SL 300.

When they had been cleared through the gate, Molly said to Cross, "Check the lot. I'll give you a dollar for any American car you see."

They passed a sea of sleek cars of all colors, Mercedeses, Aston Martins, BMWs, Rolls-Royces. Cross saw one Cadillac and pointed it out. Molly said cheerily, "Some poor slob of a writer from New York."

LoddStone Studios was a huge area on which were scattered small buildings housing independent production companies. The main building was only ten floors and looked like a movie set piece. The Studio had kept the flavor of the 1920s when it had started up, with only the necessary repairs being done. Cross was reminded of the Enclave in the Bronx.

The offices in the Studio Administration Building were small and crowded except for the tenth floor, where Eli Marrion and Bobby Bantz had their executive suites. Between the two suites was a huge conference room with a bar and bartender far off to one side and a small kitchen adjoining the bar. The seats around the conference table were plush armchairs of dark red. Framed posters of Lodd-Stone movies hung on the wall.

Waiting for them were Eli Marrion, Bobby Bantz, Skippy Deere, the chief counsel of the Studio, and two other lawyers. Molly handed the chief counsel the financial papers, and the three opposing lawyers sat down to read them through. The bartender brought them drinks of their choice, then disappeared. Skippy Deere made the introductions.

Eli Marrion, as always, insisted that Cross call him by his first name. Then told them one of his favorite stories, which he often used to disarm opponents in a negotiation. His grandfather, Eli Marrion said, had started the company in the early 1920s. He had wanted to call the firm Lode Stone Studios, but he still had a severe German accent that confused the lawyers. It was only a ten-thousand-dollar company then and when the mistake was discovered, it didn't seem worth the trouble to change it. And here now it was a seven-billion-dollar company with a name that didn't make sense. But, as Marrion pointed out—he never told a joke that didn't make a serious point—

the printed word was not important. It was the visual image with the lodestone attracting light from every corner of the universe that made the company logo so powerful.

Then Molly presented the offer. Cross would pay the Studio the fifty million it had spent, would give the Studio distribution rights, keep Skippy Deere as producer. Cross would put up the money to finish the picture. LoddStone Studios would also get 5 percent of the profits.

They all listened intently. Bobby Bantz said, "The percentage is ridiculous, we would have to have more. And how do we know that you people and Athena are not in a conspiracy? That this isn't a stickup?"

Cross was astonished by Molly's reply. For some reason he had assumed that negotiations would be much more civil than he had been used to in his Vegas world.

But Molly was almost screaming, her witchlike face blazing with fury. "Fuck you, Bobby," she said to Bantz. "You have the fucking balls to accuse us of a conspiracy. Your insurance doesn't cover you on this, you take this meeting to get off the hook and then insult us. If you don't apologize, I'll take Mr. De Lena right out of here and you can eat shit."

Skippy Deere broke in, "Molly, Bobby, come on. We're trying to save a picture here. Let's talk this through at least. . . ."

Marrion had observed all this with a quiet smile but did not say anything. He would speak only to give a yes or no.

"I think it's a reasonable question," Bobby Bantz said. "What can this guy offer Athena to make her come back that we can't?"

Cross sat there smiling. Molly had told him to let her answer whenever possible.

She said, "Mr. De Lena obviously has something special to offer. Why should he tell you? If you offer him ten million to give you that information I'll confer with him. Ten million would be cheap."

Even Bobby Bantz laughed at this.

Skippy Deere said, "They think Cross wouldn't be risking all that money unless he had a sure thing. That makes them a little suspicious."

"Skippy," Molly said, "I've seen you lay out a million for a novel that you never made into a picture. How is this different?"

Bobby Bantz broke in. "Because Skippy gets our studio to put up the million."

They all laughed. Cross wondered about this meeting. He was losing patience. Also, he knew he must not look too eager, so it wouldn't hurt if he showed his irritation. He said in a low voice, "I'm going on a hunch. If it's too complicated, we can just forget the whole thing."

Bantz said angrily, "We are talking about a lot of money here. This picture could gross a half billion worldwide."

"If you could get Athena back," Molly shot in quickly. "I can tell you I talked with her this morning. She already cut off all her hair to show she's serious."

"We can wig her. Fucking actresses," Bantz said. Now he was glowering at Cross, trying to read him. He was pondering something. He said, "If Athena does not come back and you lose your fifty million and can't go on to finish the picture, who gets the footage already done?"

"I do," Cross said.

"Aha," Bantz said. "Then you just release it the way it is. Maybe as soft porn."

"That's a possibility," Cross said.

Molly shook her head at Cross, warning him to keep quiet. "If you agree to this deal," she said to Bantz, "everything can be negotiated on foreign, video, TV, and profit participation. There's only one deal-breaker. The agreement must be secret. Mr. De Lena only wants credit as a coproducer."

"That's OK with me," Skippy Deere said. "But my money deal with the Studio still stands."

For the first time Marrion spoke. "That's separate," he said, meaning no. "Cross, do you give your lawyer full discretion on negotiations?"

"Yes," Cross said.

"I want to go on record on this," Marrion said. "You must know we planned to scrap the picture and take the loss. We are convinced Athena will not come back. We do not represent to you that she may come back. If you make this deal and pay us fifty million, we are not liable. You would have to sue Athena and she doesn't have that kind of money."

"I would never sue her," Cross said. "I'd forgive and forget."

Bantz said, "You don't have to answer to your money people?"

Cross shrugged.

Marrion said, "That is a corruption. You can't let your personal attitude betray the money people who trust you. Just because they're rich."

Cross said, straight-faced, "I never think it's a good idea to get on the wrong side of rich people."

Bantz said in exasperation, "This is some kind of trick."

Masking his face with benign confidence, Cross said, "I've spent my whole life convincing people. In my Vegas hotel I have to convince very smart men to gamble their money against the odds. And I do that by making them happy. That means I give them what they really want. I'll do that with Miss Aquitane."

Bantz disliked the whole idea. He was sure his studio was being screwed. He said bluntly, "If we find out Athena has already agreed to work with you, we will sue. We will not honor this agreement."

"I want to be in the movie business for the long haul," Cross said. "I want to work with LoddStone Studios. There's money enough for everyone."

Eli Marrion had been studying Cross all during the meeting, trying to come to an assessment. The man was very low key, not a bluffer or a bullshit artist. Pacific Ocean Security could not establish any real link with Athena, there was no likely conspiracy. A decision had to be made, but it was not really as difficult a decision as the people in this room were pretending. Marrion was so weary now he could feel the weight of his clothing on his skeletal frame. He wanted this to be over.

Skippy Deere said, "Maybe Athena is just nuts, maybe she's gone over the edge. Then we can bail out with the insurance."

Molly Flanders said, "She's saner than anyone in this room. I can have all of you certified before you get her."

Bobby Bantz looked Cross directly in the face. "Will you sign papers that you have no agreement with Athena Aquitane at this point in time?"

"Yes," Cross said. He let his dislike for Bantz show.

Marrion, observing this, felt satisfaction. At least this part of the meeting was going according to plan. Bantz was now established as the bad guy. It was amazing how people almost instinctively disliked him, and it really wasn't his fault. It was the role chosen for him to play, though admittedly it suited his personality.

"We want twenty percent of the profits of the picture," Bantz said. "We distribute it domestic and foreign. And we will be partners in any sequel."

Skippy Deere said in exasperation, "Bobby, they are all dead at the end of the picture, there can be no sequel."

"OK," Bantz said, "rights in any prequel."

"Prequel, sequel, bullshit," Molly said. "You can have them. But you get no more than ten percent of the profits. You'll make a fortune on distribution. And you have no risk. Take it or leave it."

Eli Marrion could endure no more. He rose, standing very straight, and spoke in a measured, serene voice. "Twelve percent," he said, "We have a deal."

He paused and then looking directly at Cross, he said, "It's not so much the money. But this could be a great picture and I don't want to scrap it. Also, I'm very curious to see what will happen." He turned to Molly. "Now, yes or no?"

Molly Flanders, without even looking at Cross for a sign, said, "Yes."

Later, Eli Marrion and Bobby Bantz sat alone in the conference room. They were both silent. They had learned over the years that there were things that must not be said aloud. Finally Marrion said, "There's a moral question here."

Bantz said, "We've signed to keep the agreement secret, Eli, but if you feel we must, I could make a call."

Marrion sighed. "Then we lose the film. This man Cross is our only hope. Plus if he found out the leak came from you there might be some danger."

"Whatever he is, he doesn't dare touch LoddStone," Bantz said. "What I worry about is letting him get a foot in the door."

Marrion sipped his drink, puffed his cigar. The thin, woody-smelling smoke made his body tingle.

Eli Marrion was really tired now. He was getting too old to worry about long-term future disasters. The great universal disaster was closer.

"Don't make the call," he said. "We have to keep the agreement. And besides, maybe I'm getting into my second childhood, but I'd love to see what the magician pulls out of his hat."

Skippy Deere, after the meeting, went back to his house and made a call summoning Jim Losey to meet with him. At their meeting he swore Losey to secrecy and told him what had happened. "I think you should put a surveillance on Cross," he said. "You might find out something interesting."

But he said this only after he had agreed to sign Jim Losey to play a small part in a new movie he was making about serial murders in Santa Monica.

As for Cross De Lena, he returned to Las Vegas and in his penthouse suite pondered the new course of his life. Why had he taken the risk? Most important, the winnings could be huge: not only the money but a new way of life. But what he questioned was an underlying motive, the vision of Athena Aquitane framed by the sea-green water, her constantly moving body, the notion that one day she might come to know him and love him, not forever, but just for a moment of time. What had Gronevelt said? "Women are never more dangerous to men than when they have to be saved. Beware, beware," Gronevelt said, "of Beauty in Distress."

But he dismissed all this from his mind. Looking down on the Vegas Strip, the wall of colored light, the throngs moving through that light, ants carrying bales of money to bury in some great nest, he analyzed the whole problem for the first time in a coldly neutral way.

If Athena Aquitane was such an angel, why then was she demanding, in effect if not in words, that the price for her returning to the picture was that someone kill her husband? Surely that had to be clear to anyone. The Studio's offer to protect her while she completed the picture was worth less because she would be working toward her own death. After the picture was done and she was alone, Skannet would come after her.

Eli Marrion, Bobby Bantz, Skippy Deere, they knew the problem and knew the answer. But no one would dare speak it aloud. For people like them, the risk was too great. They had risen so high, lived so well, that they had too much to lose. For them the gain did not equal the risk. They could accommodate the loss of the picture, for them it was only a minor defeat. They could not afford the great tumble from the highest level of society to the lowest. That risk was mortal.

Also, to give them their due, they had made an intelligent decision. They were not expert in this field of endeavor; they could make mistakes. Better to treat the fifty million dollars like a loss of points in their stock on Wall Street.

So now there were two main problems. The execution of Boz Skannet in a manner that would not injure the picture or Athena in any way. Problem number two, and far more important, was winning the approval of his father, Pippi De Lena, and the Clericuzio Family. For Cross knew the whole arrangement would not remain secret to them very long.

CHAPTER 8

⚃

CROSS DE LENA pleaded for Big Tim's life for many different reasons. One, he contributed between five hundred grand and one million to the Xanadu cage every year. Second, he had a sneaking affection for the man, for his lust for life, his outrageous buffooneries.

Tim Snedden, known as the Rustler, was the owner of a string of shopping malls that stretched over the northern part of the state of California. He was also a Las Vegas high roller who usually stayed at the Xanadu. He was particularly fond of and extraordinarily lucky at sports betting. The Rustler made big bets, fifty grand on football and sometimes ten grand on basketball. Thinking he was being clever, he lost small bets but almost invariably won his big bets. Cross was on to that immediately.

The Rustler was very big, nearly six and a half feet and over three hundred fifty pounds. His appetite matched his physique, he ate everything in sight. He boasted he had had a partial stomach bypass so that food passed directly through his system and he never gained weight. He was gleeful about this as an ultimate scam on nature itself.

For the Rustler was a natural-born scam artist, which was how he earned his nickname. At the Xanadu he fed his friends free under his comp, he absolutely destroyed room service. He tried to pay his call girls and the purchases at the gift shop under his comp. And then when he lost and had a cage full of markers, he stalled payment until his next visit to the Xanadu, instead of paying them within a month as a gentleman gambler would do.

Though he was very lucky with his sports gambling, the Rustler was less fortunate with casino games. He was skillful, he knew the odds and bet correctly, but his natural exuberance carried him away, and his winnings on sports would be wiped out and more. So it wasn't because of the money but because of long-range strategic reasons that the Clericuzio took an interest.

Since the Family's ultimate goal was the legalization of sports gambling all over the United States, any gambling scandal involving sports would hurt that aim. So an inquiry into the life of Big Tim Snedden the Rustler was launched. The results were so alarming that Pippi and Cross were summoned East to the mansion in Quogue for a conference. It was Pippi's first operation after his return from Sicily.

Pippi and Cross took the flight back East together. Cross worried that the Clericuzio had already found out about his movie deal on *Messalina* and that his father would be angry he had not been consulted. For Pippi, at fifty-seven, though retired, still was consigliere to his son the *Bruglione*.

So on the plane Cross told his father about the movie and reassured him that he still valued his counsel but had not wanted to put him in a bad light with the Clericuzio. He also voiced his anxiety about being summoned back East because the Don had learned about his Hollywood plans.

Pippi listened without saying a word, then sighed with disgust. "You're still too young," he said. "It won't be about the movie deal. The Don would never show his hand this quick. He'd wait to see what happened. It looks like Giorgio runs things, that's what Vincent and Petie and Dante think. But they're wrong. The old man is smarter than all of us. And don't worry about him, he's always fair in these things. It's Giorgio and Dante you have to worry about." He paused for a moment as if reluctant to talk about the Family even with Cross.

"You notice that Giorgio and Vincent and Petie's kids know nothing about Family business? The Don and Giorgio have all planned that the children will be strictly legit. The Don planned that for Dante too, but Dante was too smart, figured everything out, and he wanted in. The Don couldn't stop him. Think of all of us—Giorgio, Vincent, and Petie, you and me and Dante—as the rear guard, fighting so that the Clericuzio clan can escape to safety. That's the Don's planning. It's his strength, what makes him great. So he may even be glad you're making your escape, it's what he hoped Dante would do. That's what it is, isn't it?"

"I think so," Cross said. Not even to his father would he confess his terrible weakness. That he was doing it for the love of a woman.

"Always play it long, like Gronevelt," Pippi said. "When the time comes, tell the Don directly and make sure the Family wets its beak on the deal. But watch out for Giorgio and Dante. Vincent and Petie won't give a shit."

"Why Giorgio and Dante?" Cross asked.

"Because Giorgio is a greedy prick," Pippi said. "And Dante, because he's always jealous of you and because you're my son. Besides, he's a fucking lunatic."

Cross was surprised. It was the first time he had heard his father criticize any of the Clericuzio. "And why won't Vincent and Petie care?" he asked.

"Because Vincent has his restaurants and Petie has his construction business and the Bronx Enclave. Vincent wants to enjoy his old age and Petie likes the action. And both of them like you and respect me. We did jobs together when we were young."

Cross said, "Pop, you're not mad I didn't clear it with you?"

Pippi gave him a sardonic look. "Don't bullshit me," he said. "You knew I would disapprove and the Don would disapprove. Now when are you going to kill this Skannet guy?"

"I don't know yet," Cross said. "It's very tricky, has to be a Confirmation so that Athena will know she doesn't have to worry about him anymore. Then she can come back to the picture."

"Let me plan it for you," Pippi said. "And what if this broad, Athena, doesn't come back to work? Then you lose fifty mil."

"She'll come back to work," Cross said. "She and Claudia are close friends and Claudia says she will."

"My darling daughter," Pippi said. "She still doesn't want to see me?"

"I don't think so," Cross said. "But you can always drop around when she's staying at the Hotel."

"No," Pippi said. "If this Athena doesn't come to work after you do the job, I'll plan her Communion for her, no matter how big a movie star she is."

"No, no," Cross said. "You should see Claudia. She's much prettier now."

"That's good," Pippi said. "She had such an ugly mug when she was a kid. Like me."

"Why don't you make up with her?" Cross asked.

"She wouldn't let me go to my ex-wife's funeral, and she doesn't like me. So what's the point? In fact, when I die I want you to bar her from my funeral. Fuck her." He paused for a moment. "She was a ballsy little kid."

"You should see her now," Cross said.

"Remember," Pippi said. "Don't volunteer anything to the Don. This meeting is about something else."

"How can you be sure?" Cross asked.

"Because he would have met with me first to see if I would give you away," Pippi said.

As it turned out, Pippi was right.

At the mansion, Giorgio, Don Domenico, Vincent, Petie, and Dante waited to greet them in the garden by the fig trees. As was the custom they all had lunch together before they got down to business.

Giorgio laid it out. An investigation had shown that Rustler Snedden was fixing certain college games in the Midwest. That he possibly shaved points in the pro football and pro basketball games. He did this by bribing the officials and certain players, a very tricky and dangerous business. If this came out, it would cause a tremendous scandal and uproar that would give a near fatal blow to the Clericuzio Family's effort to have sports gambling legalized in the United States. And it would eventually be found out.

"The cops throw more manpower into a sports fix than into a serial murder," Giorgio said. "Why, I don't know. What the hell difference does it make who wins or loses? It's a crime that hurts nobody except the bookmakers and the cops hate them anyway. If the Rustler fixed all the Notre Dame games so that they always won, the whole country would be happy."

Pippi said impatiently, "Why are we even talking about this? Just have somebody warn him off."

Vincent said, "We already tried that. This guy is a special piece of work. He doesn't know what fear is. He's been warned, he still keeps doing it."

Petie said, "They call him Big Tim, and they call him the Rustler, and he loves all that shit. He never pays his bills, he even stiffs the IRS, he fights with the California state authorities because he won't pay the sales tax of the stores he owns in his malls. Hell, he even stiffs his ex-wife and his kids on support payments. He's a thief in his heart. You cannot talk sense to him."

Giorgio said, "Cross, you know him personally from his gambling in Vegas. What do you say?"

Cross considered. "He's very late paying his markers. But he finally pays. He's smart gambling, not degenerate. He's one of those guys who is hard to like, but he's very rich so he has lots of friends that he brings to Vegas. Actually even fixing the games and winning some of our money, he is a big plus for us. Just let it go." As he said this he noticed Dante smiling, knowing something he didn't know.

"We can't let it go," Giorgio said. "Because this Big Tim, this Rustler, is fucking nuts. He's laying down some crazy scheme to fix the Super Bowl game."

Don Domenico spoke for the first time and directly to Cross, "Nephew, is that possible?"

The question was a compliment. It was the Don acknowledging that Cross was the expert in the field.

"No," Cross said to the Don. "You can't fix the Super Bowl officials because no one knows who they will be. You can't fix the players because the important ones make too much money. Also, you can never fix one game in any sport a one hundred percent sure thing. If you are a fixer you have to be able to fix fifty or a hundred games. That way if you lose three or four, you don't get hurt. And so unless you can do a lot of them it's not worth the risk."

"Bravo," the Don said. "Then why does this man, who is rich, want to do something so foolhardy?"

"He wants to be famous," Cross said. "To fix the Super Bowl he would have to do something so risky he is sure to be found out. Something so crazy I can't even think what it will be. The Rustler will think it clever. And he is a man who believes he can get out of every jam he gets in."

"I have never met a man like that," the Don said.

Giorgio said, "They grow them only in America."

"But then he is very dangerous to what we want to do," the Don said. "From what you tell me, he is a man who will not listen to reason. So there is no choice."

Cross said, "Wait. He means at least a half million dollars' profit every year to the casino."

Vincent said, "It's a matter of principle. The Books pay us money to protect them."

Cross said, "Let me talk to him. Maybe he'll listen to me. The whole thing is small potatoes. He can't fix the Super Bowl. It's not worth our taking action." But then he got a look from his father and he realized that in some way it was not proper for him to make such arguments.

The Don said with a terminal determination, "The man is dangerous. Don't talk to him, nephew. He doesn't know who you really are. Why give him the advantage? The man is dangerous because he is stupid, he is stupid as an animal is stupid, he wants to feed on everything. And then when he is caught he wants to wreak as much havoc as he can. He will implicate everyone whether true or not." He paused for a moment and then looked at Dante. "Grandson," he said, "I think you should do the job. But let Pippi do the planning on this one, he knows the territory."

Dante nodded.

Pippi knew he was on dangerous ground. If anything happened to Dante, he would be held responsible. And another thing was clear to him. The Don and Giorgio were determined some day Dante would head the Clericuzio Family. But at present they did not trust his judgment.

In Vegas Dante registered in a suite at the Xanadu. The Rustler, Snedden, was not due in Vegas for a week, and during that time Cross and Pippi indoctrinated Dante.

"Rustler is a high roller," Cross said. "But not high enough to rate a Villa. Not in the class of Arabs and Asians. His RFB is enormous, he wants everything free he can get. He puts friends on restaurant tabs, orders the best wines, he even tries to put the gift shop on his tab. We don't give that even to the Villa guys. He's a claim artist, so the dealers have to watch him. He'll claim he made a bet just before the number hit on the crap table. He'll try to make a bet in baccarat after the first card shows. At blackjack he'll claim he wanted to hit an eighteen when the next card is three. He's very late paying his markers. But he gives us a half million a year, even after we take off what he beats the sports book for. He's cute. He even draws chips for his friends and puts them on his marker so we'll think he gambles bigger than he actually does. All that chickenshit stuff like the garment center guys used to pull in the old days. But then he goes berserk when his luck goes bad. Last year he dropped two million and we made him a party and gave him a Cadillac. He bitched that it wasn't a Mercedes."

Dante was outraged. "He draws chips and money from the cage and doesn't gamble it?"

"Sure," Cross said. "A lot of guys do it. We don't mind. We like to look stupid. It gives them more confidence at the tables. They outsmart us again."

"Why do they call him the Rustler?" Dante asked.

"Because he takes things without paying for them," Cross said. "When he has girls he bites them as if he wants to take a chunk of their flesh. And he gets away with it. He's a great, great bullshit artist."

Dante said dreamily, "I can't wait to hear him."

"He could never talk Gronevelt into giving him a Villa," Cross said. "So I don't."

Dante looked at him sharply. "How come I didn't get a Villa?"

"Because it could cost the Hotel a hundred grand to a million bucks a night," Cross said.

Dante said, "But Giorgio gets a Villa."

"OK," Cross said, "I'll clear it with Giorgio." They both knew Giorgio would be outraged by Dante's request.

"Fat chance," Dante said.

"When you get married," Cross said, "you'll get a Villa for your honeymoon."

Pippi said, "My operational plan depends on Big Tim's character. Cross you have to cooperate just here in Vegas to set the guy up. You have to let Dante draw unlimited credit in the cage and then make his markers disappear. Timewise, the arrangements in L.A. are set. You have to make sure the guy gets here and doesn't cancel his reservation. So you give him a party to present him with a Rolls-Royce. Then when he's here you have to introduce him to Dante and me. After that you're through."

It took Pippi more than an hour to tell the plan in detail. Dante said admiringly, "Giorgio always said you were the best. I was pissed off when the Don put you over me on this. But I can see he was right."

Pippi took this flattery stone-faced. He said to Dante, "Remember this is a Communion not a Confirmation. It has to look as if he took it on the lam. With his record and all the lawsuits against him, that will be plausible. Dante, don't wear one of your fucking hats on this operation. People have funny memories. And remember that the Don said he would like the guy to give information about the fix, but it's not really necessary. He's the ringleader, when he's gone the whole fix will disappear. So don't do anything crazy."

Dante said coolly, "I feel unlucky without my hat."

Pippi shrugged. "Another thing, don't try to cheat on your unlimited credit. That comes from the Don himself, he doesn't want the Hotel to lose a fortune on this operation. They already have to put up the Rolls."

"Don't worry," Dante said. "My work is my pleasure." He paused for a moment and then said with a sly grin, "I hope you give me a good report on this one."

This surprised Cross. It was plain that there was some hostility between them. And he was also surprised that Dante would try to intimidate his father. That could be disastrous, grandson of the Don or not.

But Pippi seemed not to have noticed. "You're a Clericuzio," he said. "Who am I to report on you?" He clapped Dante on the shoulder. "We have a job to do together. Let's make it fun."

When Rustler Snedden arrived, Dante studied him. He was big and fat but the fat was hard, it stuck to his bones and didn't roll. His shirt was blue denim with large pockets on each breast, a white button in the middle. In one pocket he stuffed the black hundred-dollar chips, and in the other, the white-and-gold five hundreds. The red fives and green twenty-fives he stuffed into the pocket of his wide-trousered white canvas pants. On his feet were floppy brown sandals.

The Rustler played mostly craps, the best percentage game. Cross and Dante knew that he had already bet ten grand on two college basketball games and placed a five-thousand-dollar bet with the illegal books in town on a horse race in Santa Anita. The Rustler was not going to pay the taxes. And he seemed not to be worrying about his bets. He was having a grand time shooting craps.

He was the mayor of the crap table, telling other gamblers to ride with his dice, shouting good-humoredly at them not to be chicken. He was betting the blacks, stacks of them covering all the numbers, betting right all the way. When the dice came to him he hurled them vigorously so that they bounced off the opposite wall of the table and came back to his easy reach. He would then try to grab them, but the stickman was always alert to catch them in the claw of his stick and hold them so that other players could make their bets.

Dante took his place at the crap table and bet with Big Tim to win. Then he made all the ruinous side bets that would, unless he was very lucky, make him a sure loser. He bet the hard four and the hard ten. He bet the boxcars in one roll and the aces and eleven in one roll at odds of thirty and fifteen to one. He called for a twenty-thousand-dollar marker and, after signing for the black chips, spread them all over the table. He called for another marker. By this time, he had caught Big Tim's attention.

"Hey, you with the hat. Learn to play this game," Big Tim said.

Dante waved to him cheerily and continued his wild betting. When Big Tim sevened out, Dante took the dice and called for a fifty-thousand-dollar marker. He spread black chips all over the table hoping he wouldn't get lucky. He didn't. Now Big Tim was watching him with more than ordinary interest.

Big Tim the Rustler ate in the coffee shop, which was also the restaurant that served plain American fare. Big Tim rarely ate in the Xanadu's fancy French restaurant or its Northern Italian Restaurant or its authentic English Royal Pub restaurant. Five friends joined him for dinner, and Big Tim the Rustler made out Keno tickets for everybody so they could watch the numbers board while eating. Cross and Dante sat in a corner booth.

His short-cut blond hair made the Rustler resemble a Brueghel painting of a jolly German burgher. He ordered a great variety of dishes, the equivalent of three dinners, but to his credit he ate most of them while also dipping into his companions' plates.

"It's really too bad," Dante said. "I never saw a guy who enjoyed life so much."

"That's one way to make enemies," Cross said. "Especially when you enjoy it at other people's expense."

They watched Big Tim sign the check, which he did not have to pay, and order one of his companions to tip in cash. After they left, Cross and Dante relaxed over their coffee. Cross loved this huge room with glass walls showing the night lit outside by pink lamps, green from the grass and trees outside reflecting into the room, softening the chandeliers.

"I remember one night about three years ago," Cross said to Dante. "The Rustler had a great streak at the crap table. I think he won over a hundred grand. It was about three in the morning. And when the pit boss took his chips to the cage, the Rustler jumped up on the crap table and pissed all over it."

"What did you do?" Dante asked.

"I had the security guards take him to his room and charged him five grand for the piss on the table. Which he never paid."

"I would have ripped his fucking heart out," Dante said.

"If a man gives you a half million a year, wouldn't you let him piss on a table?" Cross said. "But to tell the truth, I always held it against him. In fact, if he had done that in the Villas' casino, who knows?"

The next day Cross had lunch with Big Tim to brief him on his party and the presentation of the Rolls-Royce. Pippi joined them and was introduced.

Big Tim always pushed for more. "I appreciate the Rolls but when do I get one of your Villas?"

"Yeah, you deserve it," Cross said. "The next time you come to Vegas, you get a Villa. That's a promise, even if I have to kick somebody out."

Big Tim the Rustler said to Pippi, "Your son is a much nicer man than that old prick, Gronevelt."

"He was a little funny in his last years," Pippi said. "I was maybe his best friend and he would never give me a Villa."

"Well, fuck him," Big Tim said. "Now that your son is running the Hotel, you can get a Villa whenever you want."

"Never," Cross said, "he's not a gambler." They all laughed.

But now Big Tim was on another tack. "There's a weird little guy who wears a funny hat and is the worst crapshooter I ever saw," he said. "This guy signed nearly two hundred grand in markers in less than an hour. What can you tell me about him? You know I'm always looking for investors."

"I can't tell you anything about my players," Cross said. "How would you like it if I gave out information about you? I can tell you he can get a Villa anytime, but he never asks. He likes to keep a low profile."

"Just give me an intro," Big Tim said. "If I make a deal, you'll get a piece."

"No," Cross said. "But my father knows him."

"I could use some dough," Pippi said.

Big Tim said, "Good. Give me a big buildup."

Pippi turned on his charm. "You two guys would make a great team. This guy has a lot of money but he doesn't have your flair for big business. I know you're a fair guy, Tim, so just give me what you think I deserve."

Big Tim beamed at this. Pippi would be another of his suckers. "Great," he said. "I'll be at the crap table tonight, so bring him around."

When the introductions were made at the crap table, Big Tim the Rustler startled both Dante and Pippi by snatching Dante's Renaissance cap off his head and replacing it with a Dodger baseball cap he was wearing. The result was hilarious. The Renaissance cap on Big Tim's head made him look like one of Snow White's dwarfs.

"To change our luck," Big Tim said. They all laughed but Pippi didn't like the malevolent gleam in Dante's eyes. Also, he was angry that Dante had ignored his instructions and was wearing the hat. He had introduced Dante as Steve Sharpe and had pumped Big Tim up with stories that Steve was the overlord of a drug empire on the Eastern Seaboard and had to "wash" many millions. Also that Steve was a degenerate gambler who had bet a million on the Super Bowl and had lost without batting an eye. And his markers in the casino cage were pure gold. Paid them right up.

So now Big Tim threw his massive arm over Dante's shoulders and said, "Stevie, we have to talk. Let's have a little bite in the coffee shop."

There, Big Tim took a secluded booth. Dante ordered coffee but Big Tim ordered a whole array of desserts: strawberry ice cream, napoleons, and banana cream pie plus a dish of assorted cookies.

Then he launched into an hour-long selling speech. He owned a small mall he wanted to get rid of, a long-term moneymaker, and he could arrange that the payment would be mostly under-the-table cash. There was a meat-packing plant and carloads of fresh produce that could be sold for undercover cash, then resold for a profit for white money. He had an "in" with the movie business so that he could help finance pictures that went direct to video or to porno theaters. "Great business," Big Tim said. "You get to meet the stars and fuck the starlets and turn your money white."

Dante enjoyed the performance. Everything Big Tim said was with such confidence and brio that the victim could only believe in future riches. He asked questions that betrayed his eagerness but made a show of coyness.

"Give me your card," he said. "I'll give you a call or have Pippi call you and then we can set up a dinner meeting and have a full discussion so I can make a commitment."

Big Tim gave him his card. "Let's do it real quick," he said. "I have one particular 'no lose' deal I'll cut you in on. But we would have to move fast." He paused for a moment. "It's a sports thing."

Now Dante showed an enthusiasm he had not shown before. "Jesus, that has always been my dream. I love sports. You mean maybe buy a major league baseball team?"

"Not that big," Big Tim said hastily. "But big enough."

"So when do we meet?" Dante asked.

Big Tim said proudly, "Tomorrow the Hotel is giving me a party and a Rolls. For being one of their best suckers. I go back to L.A. the day after. How about that night?"

Dante pretended to give the question some thought. "Okay," he said. "Pippi's coming to L.A. with me and I'll have him give you a call to set it up."

"Great," Big Tim said. He wondered a bit about the man's cautiousness but knew better than to queer a deal with unnecessary questions. "And tonight I'm going to show you how to shoot craps so that you have some chance of winning."

Dante made himself look sheepish. "I know the odds, I just like to fuck around. And then the word gets out and I can get a whack at the chorus girls."

"Then there's no hope for you," Big Tim said. "But you and me, we'll make some money together anyway."

The next day the party for Big Tim the Rustler was held in the great ballroom of the Xanadu Hotel, which was often used for special events: the New Year's Eve party, Christmas buffets, weddings for high rollers, presentations of special awards and gifts, Super Bowl parties, the World Series, and even political conventions.

It was a huge, high-ceilinged room, with balloons floating everywhere and two enormous buffet tables, splitting the room in half. The buffets were shaped like huge ice glaciers, and encrushed in the ice were exotic fruits of all colors. Crenshaw melons, split open to show their yellow-gold flesh, great purple grapes with their juice bursting against the skin, porcupine pineapples, kiwi and kumquat, nectarines and lichee nuts, and a huge log of watermelon. Buckets of twelve different kinds of ice cream were buried like submarines. Then there was a passageway of hot dishes: a baron of beef as big as a buffalo, a huge turkey, a white, fat-ringed ham. Then there was a tray of different pastas, sprinkled green with pesto and red with tomato sauce. And then a great red pot, as big as a garbage can, with silver handles and steaming with a "wild boar" stew that was really a pork, beef, and veal mixture. Then came bread of all kinds and rolls heavy with flour. Another bank of ice held desserts, cream puffs, whipped-cream-filled doughnuts, an assortment of tiered cakes decorated with replicas of the Hotel Xanadu. Coffee and hard liquor would be served to the guests by the best-looking waitresses at the Hotel.

Big Tim the Rustler was already wreaking havoc on these tables before the first guest arrived.

In the full center of the room, mounted on a ramp separated by ropes from the crowd, was the Rolls-Royce. Creamy, white, luxurious, with true elegance and a certain genius in design, it stood in sharp contrast to the pretensions of this Vegas world. A wall of the room had been replaced by heavy golden draperies to allow its entrance and departure. Then off in a corner of the room was a purple Cadillac that was to be awarded as a door prize to those with numbered invitations: high rollers invited to the party and casino managers of the biggest hotels. This had been one of Gronevelt's best ideas. These parties increased the Drop at the Hotel significantly.

The party was a huge success because Big Tim was so flamboyant. Attended by his two waitresses, he almost single-handedly destroyed the buffet table. He loaded up three plates and gave an exhibition of eating that nearly made Dante's mission unnecessary.

Cross made the presentation speech for the Hotel. Then Big Tim made his acceptance speech.

"I want to thank the Xanadu Hotel for this wonderful gift," he said. "That two-hundred-thousand-dollar car is now mine for nothing. It's my reward for coming to the Xanadu the last ten years, during which they treated me like a prince and emptied my wallet. I figure if they give me fifty Rolls we would be about even but what the hell, I can only drive one car at at time."

Here he was interrupted by applause and cheers. Cross grimaced. He was always embarrassed by these rituals that exposed the falseness of the Hotel's goodwill.

Big Tim threw his arms around the two waitresses flanking him. He squeezed their breasts in a friendly way. He waited like an experienced comic for the applause to die down.

"No kidding, I'm truly grateful," he said. "This is one of the happiest days of my life. Right up there with my divorce. One little thing. Who's going to give me gas money to drive this car back to L.A.? The Xanadu cleaned me out again."

Big Tim knew when to stop. As the applause and cheers broke out again, he climbed the ramp and got into the car. The golden draperies that had replaced the wall now parted, and Big Tim drove out.

The party speedily broke up after the Cadillac was won by a high roller. The festivities had lasted for four hours and everybody wanted to get back to the gambling tables.

That night Gronevelt's ghost would have been overjoyed with the results of the party. The Drop was nearly double the average. Sexual coupling could not be confirmed but the smell of semen seemed to seep out into the hallways. The great-looking call girls that had been invited to Big Tim's party had quickly snuggled into relationships with less dedicated high rollers, who gave them black chips to gamble.

Gronevelt had often remarked to Cross that male and female gamblers had different sex patterns. And that it was important for casino owners to know them.

First Gronevelt proclaimed the primacy of pussy, as he called it. Pussy could overcome anything. It could even make a degenerate gambler go straight. There had been many important men of the world who had been guests at the Hotel. Nobel Prize–winning scientists, billionaires, great religious revivalists, eminent literary icons. A Nobel Prize–winner in physics, the best brain maybe in the world, had frolicked with a whole line of chorus girls during his six-day stay. He didn't gamble much but it was an honor for the Hotel. Gronevelt himself had to give gifts to each of the girls, it had never occurred to the Nobel Prize–winner to do so. The girls had reported he was the best screw in the world, eager, ardent, and skillful, no tricks, with one of the most beautiful cocks they had ever seen. And best of all, amusing, never boring them with serious talk. As gossipy and bitchy as any of the girls. For some reason this cheered Gronevelt up. That such a brain could please the opposite sex. Not like Ernest Vail, such a great writer but a middle-aged kid with a perpetual hard-on and no small talk to go with it. Then there was Senator Wavven, a possible future president of the United States, who treated sex like a game of golf. To say nothing of the dean of Yale, the cardinal of Chicago, the leader of the Civil Rights National Committee, and the crusty Republican bigwigs. All of them reduced to children by pussy. The only possible exceptions were the gays or druggies, but after all they were not typically gamblers.

Gronevelt noted that male gamblers called for hookers *before* they set out to gamble. Women, however, preferred sex *after* they gambled. Since the Hotel had to cater to the sexual needs of everyone and there were no male hookers, just gigolos, the Hotel used barmen croupiers and junior pit boys for the women, and that was their report. So Gronevelt made a jump. Males need sex to prepare them to go into battle with confidence. Women need sex to assuage the sorrow of losing or as part of the reward for their victory.

It was true that Big Tim called for a hooker an hour before his party and then went to bed with his two waitresses in the early morning after losing a big sum of money. They were reluctant, they were straight girls. Big Tim solved the problem in his own particular way. He put up ten thousand dollars worth of black chips and told them it was theirs if they spent the night with him. Accompanied with his usual vague promise of more if they had a really good night. He loved the way they studied the chips thoughtfully before agreeing. The joke was they got him so drunk that he fell asleep, gorged with food and drink, before he got past the fondling stage. He fell asleep between the two of them, his huge frame pushing them to the edges, both girls clinging to him until finally they fell on the floor to sleep.

Late that night Cross received a call from Claudia. "Athena disappeared," she said. "The Studio is frantic and I'm worried. Except ever since I've known her Athena has disappeared at least one weekend a month. But this time I thought you should know. You better do something before she runs away forever."

"It's OK," Cross said. He didn't tell her he had his own men covering Skannet.

But that call focused his mind on Athena. That magical face, which seemed to show her every emotion; the long, beautiful stretch of her legs. And the intelligence of her eyes, the vibration from some invisible instrument of inner being.

He picked up the phone and called a chorus girl he sometimes dated called Tiffany.

Tiffany was the captain of the chorus line of the Xanadu's big cabaret show. This entitled her to extra pay and perks for keeping discipline and preventing the usual quarrels and outright fights the girls fell into. She was a statuesque beauty who had failed screen tests because she simply was too big for celluloid. Where on the stage her beauty was commanding, on film she looked huge.

When she arrived, she was surprised at the quickness of Cross's lovemaking. He simply grabbed her and stripped her of her clothes and then seemed to devour her body with kisses. He entered her quickly and came to a climax quickly. This was so different from his usual style that she said, almost ruefully, "This time it must be true love."

"It sure is," Cross said, and began to make love to her again.

"Not me, you dope," Tiffany said. "Who's the lucky girl?"

Cross was annoyed that he was so easy to read. And yet he could not stop his devotion to the flesh beside him. He could not have enough of her succulent breasts, her silky tongue, the velvet mound between her thighs, all radiating an irresistible heat. When finally, hours later, the lustful fever was gone, he could not stop thinking about Athena.

Tiffany picked up the phone and ordered room service for them both. "I pity that poor girl when you finally get her," Tiffany said.

After she left, Cross felt free. It was a weakness to be so much in love, but satisfied lust gave him confidence. At three in the morning he made his last tour of the casino.

In the coffee shop he saw Dante with three good-looking, vivacious women. Though one of them was Loretta Lang, the singer he had helped to break her contract, he did not recognize her. Dante waved him over, but he declined with a shake of his head. Up in his penthouse suite he took two sleeping pills before going to bed, but he still dreamed of Athena.

The three women at Dante's table were famous ladies of Hollywood, wives of Bankable Stars and minor stars in their own right. They had been guests at Big Tim's party, not by invitation but by having wangled their way in on their charms.

The oldest was Julia Deleree, who was married to one of the most famous Bankable Stars in the movies. She had two children, and the family often appeared in magazines as the exceptional couple that had no problems, were ecstatic with their marriage.

The second was Joan Ward. She was still very attractive, nearly fifty. She played second leads now, usually as the intelligent woman, the suffering mother of a doomed child, or in the role of a deserted woman whose tragedy leads to a second happy marriage. Or as a fiery fighter for the feminist viewpoint. She was married to the head of a studio who paid her charge cards without complaint, no matter how huge, and whose only demand on her was to be the hostess for the many social-business parties he gave. She had no children.

The third star was Loretta, who by now was first choice as the comedy lead in kooky comedies. She, too, had married well, to a Bankable Star of empty-headed action films that took him on location in other countries for the best part of the year.

These three had become friends by being cast in the same movies and by shopping on Rodeo Drive and having lunches at the Beverly Hills Hotel's Polo Lounge, where they compared notes on their husbands and their charge cards. About the cards, they had no complaints. It was like having a shovel to dig in a gold mine, and their husbands never questioned their bills.

Julia complained that her husband didn't spend enough time with her kids. Joan, whose husband was acclaimed as a discoverer of new stars, complained she was childless. Loretta complained that her husband should branch out into more serious roles. But there came a day when Loretta, with her usual vivaciousness, said, "Let's stop bullshitting ourselves. We're all happily and very suitably married to very important guys. What we really hate is that our husbands send us out on Rodeo Drive so they feel less guilty about fucking other women." The three of them laughed. It was so true.

Julia said, "I love my husband but he's been in Tahiti for a month shooting a picture. And I know he's not sitting on the beach masturbating. But I don't want to spend a month in Tahiti, so he's either screwing his leading lady or the local talent."

"Which he would be doing even if you were there," Loretta said.

Joan said wistfully, "And even though my husband hasn't the sperm of a fucking ant, his cock is like a water wand. How come most of the stars he discovers are females? He screen-tests them by finding out how much of his cock they can swallow."

They were all half tipsy by now. They believed that wine had no calories.

Loretta said crisply, "We can't blame our husbands. The most beautiful women in the world show it to them. They really have no choice. But why should we suffer? Fuck the charge cards, let's have some fun."

And so had followed their sacred once-a-month girl's night out. When their husbands were gone, which was often, they would go on overnight adventures.

Since they were recognizable to most Americans, they had to disguise themselves. This proved to be extraordinarily easy to do. They used wigs to change the style and color of their hair. They used makeup, thickened their lips or thinned them. They dressed in the style of middle-class women. They downgraded their beauty, which didn't matter because, like most actresses, they could be enormously charming. And they delighted in the role playing. They loved to listen to different kinds of men bare their hearts to them in hope of getting into bed with them, often successfully. It was a breath of real life, the characters still mysterious, not doomed to a written script. And there were delightful surprises. Sincere offers of marriage and true love; men sharing their pain because they thought they would never see them again. The admiration they received not because of their hidden status, but because of their innate charms. And they loved creating new personas for themselves. Sometimes they would be computer operators on vacation, sometimes off-duty nurses or dental technicians or social workers. They would bone up for their parts by reading about their new professions. Sometimes they would pretend to be legal secretaries in the office of a big showbiz lawyer in L.A. and spread scandal about their own husbands and other of their actor friends. They had great times but always went out of town; Los Angeles was too dangerous, they might run into friends who would easily recognize them despite their disguise. They discovered that San Francisco was also risky. Some gay men seemed to know their true identity at a glance. Their favorite place was Las Vegas.

Dante had picked them up at the Xanadu Club Lounge, where tired gamblers took a break and listened to a band, a comic, and a girl singer. Loretta had once performed there at the beginning of her career. There was no dancing. The Hotel wanted their customers to get back to the tables as soon as they were rested.

Dante was attracted to them by their vivaciousness, their natural charm. They were attracted to him because they had watched him gamble and lose enormous amounts of money with his unlimited credit. After the drinks, he took them to the roulette wheel and staked them each to a thousand dollars' worth of chips. They were charmed by his hat and the extravagant courtesy showed to him by the croupiers and the pit boss. And his sly charm, which was touched by a vicious humor. Dante was witty in a vulgar and sometimes chilling way. And the extravagance of his gambling excited them. Of course they themselves were rich, they earned enormous amounts of money, but his was hard cash and that had its own magic. Certainly they had spent tens of thousands on Rodeo Drive in one day, but they had received luxurious goods in return. When Dante signed a hundred-thousand-dollar marker, they were awed, though their husbands had bought them cars that cost more. But Dante was throwing away money.

They didn't always sleep with men they picked up, but when they went to the ladies room they conferred on which one would get Dante. Julia begged and she said she had a real yen to pee in Dante's funny hat. The others gave in.

Joan had hoped to score five or ten grand. Not that she really needed it, but it was cash, real money. Loretta was not as charmed as the others by Dante. Her life in Las Vegas cabaret had partly inured her to such men. They were too full of surprises, most of them not pleasant.

The women had a three-bedroom suite in the Xanadu. They always stuck close together on these outings, for reasons of safety and so they could gossip together about their adventures. They made it a rule not to spend the entire night with the men they picked up.

So Julia wound up with Dante, who had no say in the matter, though he preferred Loretta. But he insisted Julia go to his suite, which was just below hers. "I'll walk you up to your suite," he said coolly. "We'll just be an hour. I have to get up early in the morning." It was then Julia realized he thought they were soft hookers.

"Come up to my suite," Julia said. "I'll walk you down."

Dante said, "You got your two horny buddies up there. How do I know you won't all jump me and sodomize me? I'm just a little guy."

That amused Julia enough to go to his suite. She had missed the slyness of his smile. On their way to his room, she said jokingly, "I want to pee in your hat."

Dante said to her, stone-faced, "If it's fun for you, it's fun for me."

Once in his suite there was very little chitchat. Julia threw her purse on the sofa and then pulled down the top of her dress so that her breasts showed, they were her best feature. But Dante seemed to be the exception, a male who was not interested in breasts.

He led her into the bedroom and then pulled off her dress and underclothes. When she was naked, he shed his own clothes. She could see his penis was short, stubby, and uncircumcised. "You have to use a condom," she said.

Dante threw her on the bed. Julia was a robust woman, but he picked her up and threw her without seeming to make an effort. Then he straddled her.

"I insist you use a condom," she said. "I mean it."

In the next moment there was an explosion of light in her head. She realized he had slapped her so hard that she had almost lost consciousness. She tried to wriggle away but for so small a man he was incredibly strong. She felt two more slaps that suffused her face with a hot glow and made her teeth ache. Then she felt him enter her. His driving thrusts lasted for only a few seconds and then he slumped over her.

They lay entwined and then he began to turn her over. She could see that he still had an erection and she knew he wanted to penetrate her anally. She whispered to him, "I love that but I have to get some Vaseline from my purse."

He let her slide out from under him and she went into the living room. Dante came to the door of the bedchamber. They were both still naked and he still had an erection.

Julia fumbled in her purse and then, with a dramatic flourish, took out a tiny silver handgun. It was a prop from a movie she had worked in and she had always fantasized about using it in a real-life situation. She pointed it at Dante, took the crouch stance she had been taught in the movie, and said, "I'm going to dress and leave. If you try to stop me, I'll shoot."

To her surprise, the naked Dante burst out in a good-humored laugh. But Julia noted with satisfaction that he immediately lost his erection.

She was enjoying the situation. She was imagining that she was back upstairs with Joan and Loretta and how they would laugh about this. She tried to get up the courage to ask for his hat so she could pee in it.

But now Dante surprised her. He started walking toward her slowly. He was smiling, he said gently, "That's such a small caliber, it won't even stop me unless you get a lucky shot to the head. Never use a small gun. You can put three bullets to my body and then I'll strangle you. Also, you're holding that gun wrong, you don't need that stance, there's no kick in it. Plus the chances are you won't even hit me, those little bitty things are inaccurate. So throw it away and we'll talk this over. Then you can leave."

He continued walking toward her so she threw the gun on the sofa. Dante picked it up and looked at it, shook his head. "A fake gun?" he said. "That's the sure way to get killed." He shook his head in an almost affectionate disapproval. "Well, if you were a real hooker, this would be a real gun. So who are you?"

He pushed Julia down on the sofa and imprisoned her there with his leg, his toes pushed against her pubic hair. Then he opened her purse and spilled the contents onto the coffee table. He fished into the purse pockets and took out her wallet of credit cards and her driver's license. He studied them carefully and then grinned in pure delight. He said to her, "Take off that wig." Then he reached over with a doily from the sofa and wiped her face clean of makeup.

"Jesus Christ, you are Julia Deleree," Dante said. "I'm fucking a movie star." He gave another delighted laugh. "You can pee in my hat anytime."

His toes were searching her crotch. Then he pulled her to her feet. "Don't be scared," he said. He kissed her and then turned her around and pushed her so that she was bent over the back of the sofa, breasts hanging down, her buttocks presented, tilted up to him.

Julia said to him tearfully, "You promised to let me leave."

Dante was kissing her buttocks, his fingers probing. Then he entered her savagely and she gave a yell of pain. When he finished, he patted her buttocks tenderly.

"You can get dressed now," he said. "I'm sorry I broke my word. I just couldn't miss the chance of telling my friends that I fucked Julia Deleree up her great ass."

The next morning Cross had a wakeup call push him out of bed early. It would be a busy day. He had to pull all of Dante's markers out of the casino cage and do the necessary paperwork to make them disappear. He had to get the pit bosses' marker books out of their hands and have them redone. Then he had to make arrangements so that the papers on the Rolls for Big Tim would be revoked. Giorgio had had the legal papers prepared so that the official change of ownership would not be valid until a month in the future. That was vintage Giorgio.

In the middle of all this he was interrupted with a call from Loretta Lang. She was in the Hotel and urgently wanted to see him. Because he thought it might be something about Claudia, he had Security bring her up to the penthouse.

Loretta kissed him on both cheeks and then told him the whole story about Julia and Dante. She said the man had introduced himself as Steve Sharpe and had lost a hundred grand at the crap table. They were impressed, and Julia decided to sleep with him. The three of them had only come to relax and have a night of gambling. Now they were terrified that Steve might cause a scandal.

Cross nodded sympathetically. He was thinking, What a stupid thing for Dante to do before a big operation, and the son of a bitch was giving away black chips for his pickups to gamble with. He said to Loretta calmly, "I know the man, of course. Who are the two women with you?"

Loretta knew better than to dally with Cross. She told him the two names. Cross smiled. "Do you three do this often?"

"We have to have a little fun," Loretta said. Cross gave her a sympathetic smile.

"OK," he said. "Your friend went to his room. She undressed. She wants to scream rape? What?"

Loretta said hastily, "No, no. We just want him to keep quiet. If he talks it could be absolute disasters for our careers."

"He won't talk," Cross said. "He's a funny kind of guy. Keeps a low profile. But take my advice, don't get mixed up with him again. You girls should be more careful."

Loretta was annoyed by this last remark. The three women had decided to continue their outings. They were not going to be frightened by one mishap. Nothing really terrible had happened. She said, "How do you know he won't talk?"

Cross looked at her gravely. "I'll ask him the favor," he said.

When Loretta left, Cross called for the secret camera file that showed all the guests at the registration desk. He studied them. Now that he had the information, it was easy to penetrate the disguises of the two women with Loretta Lang. It was dumb for Dante not to have gotten that info.

Pippi came by the penthouse office to have lunch before he left for Los Angeles to check off the logistics of the Big Tim operation. Cross told him the story Loretta had told.

Pippi shook his head. "The little bastard could have ruined the whole operation by throwing the timing off. And he keeps wearing that fucking hat after I told him not to."

Cross said, "Be careful on this operation. Keep your eye on Dante."

"I planned it, he can't fuck it up," Pippi said. "And when I see him in L.A. tonight, I'll give him another briefing."

Cross told him about how Giorgio had prepared the papers on the Rolls so that Big Tim would not acquire legal ownership for a month and so that after his death, the Hotel could regain the car.

"Typical Giorgio," Pippi said. "The Don would have let the estate keep his car for his kids."

Big Tim the Rustler Snedden left Vegas two days later, owing sixty grand in markers to the Xanadu Hotel. He took the late-afternoon plane to Los Angeles, went to his office and worked for a few hours, and then drove to Santa Monica to have dinner with his ex-wife and his two children. His pockets had wads of five-dollar bills, which he gave to his kids along with a cardboard container, a quart of silver dollars. To his wife he gave the support and alimony check due, without which he would not be allowed to visit. He conned his wife with sweet talk after the children went to bed but she wouldn't give him a screw, which he didn't really want after Vegas. But he had to try, it was something for nothing.

The next day Big Tim the Rustler had a very busy day indeed. Two Internal Revenue Agents tried to frighten him into paying some disputed taxes. He told them he would go to tax court and threw them out. Then he had to visit a warehouse of canned foods and another warehouse of over-the-counter drugs, all acquired at rock-bottom prices because their expiration dates were coming up. Those expiration dates would have to be changed. At lunch he met with a supermarket-chain vice president who would accept the shipment of these goods. During lunch he slipped the executive an envelope that held ten thousand dollars.

After lunch he received a surprise call from two FBI agents who wanted to ask him about his relationship with a congressman who was under indictment. Big Tim told them to go fuck themselves.

Big Tim the Rustler had never known fear. Perhaps because of his bulk, or maybe there was a piece of his brain missing. For he not only lacked physical fear, he lacked mental fear. He had not only taken the offensive against man but against nature itself. When the doctors told him he was eating himself to death and he should seriously diet, he had opted instead for the stomach bypass operation, which was more hazardous. And it had turned out perfectly. He ate as he wished without apparent harmful effect.

He had built his financial empire the same way. He made contracts that he refused to honor when they became unprofitable, he betrayed partners and friends. Everybody sued him, but they always had to settle for less than they would have received on the original terms. It was a life of success for one who took no precautions for the future. He always thought he would win in the end. He could always collapse corporate entities, shmooze over personal animosities. With women he was even more merciless. He promised them whole malls, apartments, boutiques. Then they settled for a small piece of jewelry at Christmas, a small check on their birthdays. Significant sums but not up to the original promises. Big Tim did not want a relationship. He just wanted to make sure he could have a friendly screw when he needed it.

Big Tim loved all this rustling, it made life interesting. There had been an independent bookmaker in L.A. that he had stiffed for a seventy-grand bet on football games. The bookmaker held a gun to his head and Big Tim said, "Go fuck yourself," then offered ten grand to settle the debt. The bookmaker took it.

His fortune, his ruddy health, his imposing bulk, his lack of guilt made Big Tim successful in everything he touched. His belief that all humanity was corruptible gave him a certain air of innocence that was useful not only in a woman's bed but also in the courts of law. And his gusto for life gave him a certain charm. He was a con man who let you peek at his cards.

So Big Tim did not wonder at the mystery of the arrangement Pippi De Lena had made with him for that night. The man was a hustler like himself and could be dealt with appropriately. Big promises and small rewards.

As for Steve Sharpe, Big Tim smelled a great opportunity, a multi-year scam. The little guy had dropped at least a half million in one day at the tables that he observed. Which meant he had an enormous credit line at the casino and must be in a position to earn a great deal of black money. He would be perfect in the Super Bowl fix. Not only could he supply the betting money, but he had the confidence of bookmakers. After all, those guys didn't take mammoth bets from just anybody.

Then Big Tim daydreamed about his next visit to Vegas. Finally he would get a Villa. He pondered on who to bring with him as guests. Business or pleasure? Future scam victims or maybe all women? Finally it was time to go to dinner with Pippi and Steve Sharpe. He called his ex-wife and his two kids for a chat and then was on his way.

The dinner was at a small fish restaurant down in the L.A. dock area. There was no valet service. so Big Tim put his car in a parking lot.

In the restaurant he was greeted by a tiny maître d' who took one look at him and ushered him to a table where Pippi De Lena was waiting.

Big Tim was an expert of the *abraccio* and he took Pippi into his arms. "Where's Steve? Is he jerking me around? I haven't the time for that kind of bullshit."

Pippi turned on all his charm. He clapped Big Tim on the shoulder. "What am I, chopped liver?" he said. "Sit down and have the best fish dinner you ever ate. We'll be seeing Steve after."

When the maître d' came to take their order, Pippi told him, "We want the best of everything and the most of everything. My friend here is a champion eater and if he gets up from this table hungry, I'll talk to Vincent."

The maître d' smiled confidently; he knew the quality of his kitchen. His restaurant was part of Vincent Clericuzio's empire. When the police backtracked Big Tim's trail, they would meet a blank wall here.

They ate a progression of clams, mussels, shrimps, and then lobsters: three for Big Tim and one for Pippi. Pippi was finished long before Big Tim. He said to him, "This guy is a friend of mine and I can tell you now he is tops in drugs. If that scares you off, tell me now."

"That scares me as much as this lobster," Big Tim said, waving its huge, nibbled claws in Pippi's face. "What else?"

"He always has to launder black money," Pippi said. "Your deal will have to include that."

Big Tim was enjoying the food; all the briny spices of the ocean filled his nostrils. "Great, I know all that," he said. "But where the fuck is he?"

"He's on his yacht," Pippi said. "He doesn't want anybody to see you with him. That's to your interest. He's a very cautious guy."

"I don't give a flying fuck who sees me with him," Big Tim said. "I want to see *me* with *him*."

Finally Big Tim was finished. His dessert was fruit, with a cup of espresso. Pippi skillfully skinned a pear for him. Tim ordered another espresso. "To keep me awake," he said. "That third lobster nearly put me away."

No check was presented. Pippi left a twenty-dollar bill on the table and the two left the restaurant, the maître d' silently applauding Tim's performance at the table.

Pippi guided Big Tim to a small rental car that Tim squeezed into with difficulty. "Christ, can't you afford a bigger car?" Big Tim said.

"It's only a short distance," Pippi said soothingly. And indeed it was a five-minute ride. By that time it was really dark except for the lights of a small yacht moored to the pier.

The gangplank was down, guarded by a man almost as big as Tim. There was another man on the far deck. Pippi and Big Tim went up the gangplank and onto the deck of the yacht. Then Dante appeared on the deck and came forward to shake their hands. He was wearing his Renaissance hat, which he guarded good-naturedly from Big Tim's swipe.

Dante led them below deck to a cabin decorated as a dining room. They sat around a table in comfortable chairs screwed into the floor.

On the table was an array of liquor bottles, a bucket of ice, and a tray with drinking glasses. Pippi poured them all a brandy.

At that moment the engines started and the yacht began to move. Big Tim said, "Where the hell are we going?"

Dante said smoothly, "Just a little spin for some fresh air. Once we're out on the open sea, we can go up on the deck and enjoy it."

Big Tim was not that unsuspicious, but he had faith in himself, that he could handle anything that happened in the future. He accepted the explanation.

Dante said, "Tim, my understanding is that you want to go into business with me."

"No, I want you to go into business with *me*," Big Tim said with boastful good humor. "I run the show. You get your money washed without paying a premium. And make a good bit extra. I have a mall I'm building outside Fresno and you can get a piece for five million or ten. I have a lot of other deals all the time."

"That sounds very good," Pippi De Lena said.

Big Tim gave him a cold stare. "Where do you shine in? I've been meaning to ask."

"He's my junior partner," Dante said. "My advisor. I have the money but he has the brains." He paused and then said sincerely, "He's told me a lot of good things about you, Tim, that's why we're talking."

The yacht was moving very swiftly now, the glasses trembled on the tray. Big Tim debated whether he should cut this guy in on the Super Bowl fix. Then he had one of his hunches, and they were never wrong. He leaned back in his chair, sipped his brandy, and gave both men a serious questioning look, which he often gave and had in fact rehearsed. The look of a man about to bestow his trust. In a best friend. "I'm going to let you guys in on a secret," he said. "But first, are we going to do business? You want a piece of the mall?"

"I'm in," Dante said. "Our lawyers will get together tomorrow and I'll put up some good faith money."

Big Tim emptied his brandy glass and then leaned forward. "I can fix the Super Bowl," he said. With a dramatic flourish he signaled to Pippi to fill his glass. He was gratified to see the look of astonishment on their faces. "You think I'm full of shit, right?" he said.

Dante took off his Renaissance hat and looked at it thoughtfully. "I think you're peeing in my hat," he said with a reminiscing smile. "A lot of people try. But Pippi is the expert on this stuff. Pippi?"

"Can't be done," Pippi said. "The Super Bowl is eight months away and you don't even know who'll be in it."

"Then fuck you," Big Tim said. "You don't want part of a sure thing, that's okay with me. But I'm telling you I can fix it. If you don't want it okay, let's do the mall. Turn this boat around and stop wasting my fucking time."

"Don't be so touchy," Pippi said. "Just tell us how the fix works."

Big Tim gulped his brandy and said in a regretful voice, "I can't tell you that. But I'll give you a guarantee. You bet ten million and we split the winnings. If anything goes wrong, I'll give you ten million back. Now is that fair?"

Dante and Pippi looked at each other with amused grins. Dante ducked his head, and his Renaissance hat made him look like a cunning squirrel. "You give me the money back in cash?" he asked.

"Not exactly," Big Tim said. "I'll make it up on another deal. Take ten million off the price."

"Do you fix the players?" Dante asked.

"He can't," Pippi said. "They make too much money. It must be the officials."

Big Tim was enthusiastic now. "I can't tell you but it's foolproof. And never mind the money. Think of the glory. It will be the biggest fix in sports history."

"Sure, they'll toast us in jail," Dante said.

"That's the beauty of me not telling you anything," Big Tim said. "I go to jail, you guys don't. And my lawyers are too good and I have too many connections."

For the first time, Dante varied Pippi's script. He said, "Are we far enough out?"

Pippi said, "Yeah, but I think if we talk a little more, Tim will tell us."

"Fuck Tim," Dante said pleasantly. "You hear that, Big Tim? Now I want to hear how the fix works and no bullshit." His tone was so contemptuous that Big Tim's face flushed red.

"You little prick," he said, "you think you can scare me? You think you're tougher than the FBI, and the IRS, and the toughest shylock on the West Coast? I'll *shit* in your hat."

Dante leaned back in his chair and banged on the wall of the cabin. A few seconds later two large, tough-looking men opened the door, then stood guard. In answer, Big Tim stood up and swept the table clean with one huge arm. Liquor bottles, the bucket of ice, and the tray of glasses crashed to the cabin floor.

"No Tim, listen to me," Pippi shouted. He wanted to spare the man unnecessary suffering. Also, he did not want to be the shooter, that was not part of the plan. But Big Tim was rushing toward the door, ready to do battle.

Then suddenly Dante was slipping inside Big Tim's arms, nestled against his huge body. They broke apart and Big Tim sagged to his knees. It was a frightening sight. Half his shirt had been sliced away and where once his hairy right breast had been there was just a huge red patch from which an enormous gush of blood poured, staining half the table.

In Dante's hand was the knife he had used, the blood crimson on its broad blade up to the hilt.

"Put him in a chair," Dante said to the guards, and then he took the cloth off the table to staunch Big Tim's bleeding. Big Tim was nearly unconscious with shock.

Pippi said, "You could have waited."

"No," Dante said. "He's a tough guy. Let's see how tough."

"I'll get things ready on the deck," Pippi said. He didn't want to watch. He had never done torture. There were really no secrets so important that justified that kind of work. When you killed a man, you merely separated him from this world so that he could do you no harm.

Up on the deck he saw that two of his men had already prepared. The steel cage was ready on its hook, the slatted bars closed. The deck was covered with a plastic sheet.

He felt the balmy air fragrant with salt, the night ocean purple and still. The yacht was slowing down and then it stopped.

Pippi gazed down at the ocean for a full fifteen minutes before the two men who had stood guard at the door appeared, carrying Big Tim's body. It was so terrible a sight that Pippi averted his eyes.

The four men put Big Tim's body into the cage and then lowered it over the water. One of the men adjusted the slats so that the cage was open for the denizens of the ocean deep to slide between the bars and feast on the body. Then the hook was released and the cage plunged to the bottom of the sea.

Before the sun rose, there would be only the skeleton of Big Tim's body swimming eternally in its cage on the ocean floor.

Dante came up on deck. He had obviously taken a shower and changed his clothes. Underneath the Renaissance hat his hair was slick and wet. There was no trace of blood.

"So he already made his Communion," Dante said. "You could have waited for me."

Pippi said, "Did he talk?"

"Oh yeah," Dante said. "The fix was really simple. Except maybe he was full of shit right up to the end."

The next day Pippi flew East to give the Don and Giorgio a full report. "Big Tim was crazy," he said. "He bribed the caterer who supplies the food and drink to the teams in the Super Bowl. They were going to use drugs to make the team they bet against weaker as the game went on. The coaches and players would notice even if the fans didn't, and the FBI, too. You were right, Uncle, the scandal would have set back our program maybe forever."

"Was he an idiot?" Giorgio asked.

"I think he wanted to be famous," Pippi said. "Rich wasn't enough."

"What about the others involved in the scheme?" the Don asked.

"When they don't hear from the Rustler, they'll be scared off," Pippi said.

Giorgio said, "I agree."

"Very good," the Don said. "And my grandson, did he perform well?"

It seemed an offhand remark, but Pippi knew the Don well enough to understand that this was a very serious question. He answered as carefully as he could but with a certain purpose.

"I told him not to wear his hat on this operation in Vegas and L.A. He did anyway. Then he didn't follow the script of the operation. We could have got the information with more talk but he wanted blood. He cut the guy to pieces. He cut off his cock and nuts and breasts. That wasn't necessary. He enjoys doing it and that is very dangerous for the Family. Somebody really has got to talk to him."

"It will have to be you," Giorgio said to the Don. "He doesn't listen to me."

Don Domenico pondered this a long time. "He's young, he'll grow out of it."

Pippi saw that the Don would not do anything. So he told them about Dante's indiscretion with the movie star the night before the operation. He saw the Don flinch and Giorgio grimace with distaste. There was a long silence. Pippi wondered if he had gone too far.

Finally, the Don shook his head and said, "Pippi, you have planned well, as always, but you can set your mind at rest. You will never have to work with Dante again. But you must understand, Dante is my daughter's only child. Giorgio and I must do our best with him. He will grow wiser."

C ross De Lena sat on the balcony of his executive penthouse suite in the Xanadu Hotel and examined the dangers of the course of action he was taking. From his vantage point he could see the full length of the Strip, the line of luxury casino hotels on either side, the crowds of people in the street. He could see the gamblers on the Xanadu golf course, superstitiously trying for a hole in one to ensure the victory at the gaming tables later.

First danger: In this Boz operation he was making a crucial move without consulting the Clericuzio Family. It was true that he was the administrative Baron of the Western District, which comprised

Nevada and the southern part of California. It was true that the Barons operated independently in many areas and were not strictly under the Clericuzio Family as long as they wet the Clericuzio beak with a percentage of earnings. But there were very strict rules. No Baron, or *Bruglione*, could embark on an operation of such magnitude without the approval of the Clericuzio. For one simple reason. If a Baron did so and got into trouble, he would receive no prosecutorial indulgence, no judicial intervention. In addition, he would receive no support against any rising chief in his own territories, and his money would not be laundered and tucked away for his old age. Cross knew he should see Giorgio and the Don for an OK.

This operation could be enormously sensitive. And he was putting up part of his 51 percent equity in the Xanadu, left to him by Gronevelt, to finance the movie deal. It was true it was his own money, but it was money allied to the hidden interest that the Clericuzio shared in the Hotel. And it was money that the Clericuzio had helped him earn. It was a peculiar and yet somehow very human quirk of the Clericuzio that they felt a proprietary interest in the fortunes of their subordinates. They would resent his investing this money without their advice. Their quirk, though it had no legal foundation, resembled a medieval courtesy: no baron could sell his castle without royal consent.

And the magnitude of the money involved was a factor. Cross had inherited Gronevelt's fifty-one points, the Xanadu was worth a billion dollars. But he was gambling fifty million, investing another fifty million for a total of a C million. The economic risk was enormous. And the Clericuzio were notoriously prudent and conservative, as indeed they had to be to survive the world they moved in.

Cross remembered another thing. Long ago, when the Santadio and Clericuzio Families were on good terms, they had gained a foothold in the movie business. But it had not turned out well. When the Santadio Empire was crushed, Don Clericuzio had ordered that all attempts to infiltrate the movie business be halted. "Those people are too clever," the Don said. "And they have no fear because the rewards are so high. We should have to kill them all and then we would not know how to run the business. It is more complicated than drugs."

No, Cross decided. If he asked permission it would be denied. And then it would be impossible to proceed. When it was done he could do penance, he could let the Clericuzio beak drown itself in his profits, success often excused the most impudent of sins. And if he failed, then most likely he would be finished anyway, approval or not. Which brought up a final doubt.

Why was he doing this? He thought of Gronevelt's "Beware of damsels in distress." Well, he had met damsels in distress before and had left them to their dragons. Vegas was full of damsels in distress.

But he knew. He yearned for the beauty of Athena Aquitane. It wasn't just for the loveliness of her face, her eyes, her hair, her legs, her breasts. He yearned to see the look of intelligence and warmth in her eyes, in the very bones of her face, in the delicate curve of her lips. He felt that if he could know her, be in her presence, the whole world would take on a different light, the sun a different heat. He saw the ocean behind her, rolling green and capped with white flume, like a halo around her head. And the thought strayed into his mind: Athena was the woman his mother had dreamed of becoming.

Astonished, he felt a well of longing to see her, to be with her, to listen to her voice, to watch her move. And then he thought, Oh shit, is this why I'm doing this?

He accepted it and was pleased that finally he knew the real reason for his actions. It made him resolute and it made him focus. At the present time the main problem was operational. Forget Athena. Forget the Clericuzio. There was the difficult problem of Boz Skannet, a problem that had to be solved quickly.

Cross knew he had put himself in too naked a position, another complication. To publicly profit if anything happened to Skannet was dangerous.

Cross resolved on the three people he needed for the planned operation. The first was Andrew Pollard, who owned Pacific Ocean Security and was already involved in the whole mess. The second was Lia Vazzi, the caretaker of the Clericuzio hunting lodge in the Nevada mountains. Lia headed a crew of men who also served as caretakers but were on call for special duties. The third man was Leonard Sossa, a retired counterfeiter on Family retainer to do odd jobs. All three came under Cross De Lena's control as the Western *Bruglione.*

It was two days later that Andrew Pollard got the phone call from Cross De Lena. "I hear you're working too hard," Cross said. "How about coming to Vegas for a little vacation? I'll comp you RFB — room, food, beverage. Bring the wife. And if you get bored pop up to my office for a chat."

"Thanks," Pollard said, "I'm pretty busy right now, but how about next week?"

"Sure," Cross said. "But then I'll be out of town, so I'll miss you."

"I'll come tomorrow then," Pollard said.

"Great," Cross said and hung up.

Pollard leaned back in his chair, pondering. The invitation had been a command. He would have to walk a very thin line.

Leonard Sossa enjoyed life as only a man reprieved from a terrible death sentence can enjoy life. He enjoyed the sunrise, he enjoyed the sunset. He enjoyed the grass growing and the cows who ate the grass. He enjoyed the sight of beautiful women and confident young men and clever children. He enjoyed a crust of bread, a glass of wine, a knob of cheese.

Twenty years before, the FBI had arrested him for making hundred-dollar bills for the now-extinct Santadio Family. His confederates had copped a plea, sold him out, and he had believed the flower of his manhood would wither in prison. Counterfeiting money was a far more dangerous crime than rape, murder, arson. When you counterfeited money, you attacked the machinery of government itself. When you committed the other crimes you were only some scavenger taking a bite out of the carcass of the huge beast that composed the expendable human chain. He expected no mercy and was given none. Leonard Sossa was sentenced to twenty years.

Sossa did only a year. A fellow inmate, overcome with admiration for Sossa's skills, his genius with ink and pencil and pen, recruited him for the Clericuzio Family.

Suddenly he had a new lawyer. Suddenly he had an outside doctor he had never met. Suddenly there was a hearing for clemency on the ground that his mental capacity had deteriorated to that of a child and he was no longer a menace to society. Suddenly Leonard Sossa was a free man and an employee of the Clericuzio Family.

The Family had a need for a first-rate forger. Not for currency, they knew that to the authorities counterfeiting was an unforgivable crime. They needed a forger for far more important tasks. In the mountains of paperwork Giorgio had to handle, juggling different national and international corporations, signing legal documents by nonexistent corporate officers, making deposits and withdrawals of vast sums of money, a variety of signatures and imitations of signatures were needed. Then, as time went on, other uses were found for Leonard.

The Xanadu Hotel used his skills very profitably. When a very rich high roller died and had markers in the cage, Sossa was brought in to sign another million dollars. Of course the dead man's estate would not pay the markers. But then the whole amount could be charged as loss on the Xanadu's taxes. This happened far more often than was natural. There seemed to be a high mortality rate in pleasure. The same was done to high rollers who reneged on their debts or settled dimes on the dollar.

For all this Leonard Sossa was paid a hundred thousand dollars a year and barred from doing any other kind of work, especially counterfeiting currency. This fit in with Family policy in general. The Clericuzio had an edict that prohibited all crime-family members from engaging in counterfeiting and kidnapping. These were the crimes that made all the Federal enforcement agencies come down with crushing force. The rewards were simply not worth the risk.

So for twenty years Sossa enjoyed life as an artist in his little house that nestled in Topanga Canyon, not far from Malibu. He had a small garden, a goat, a cat, and a dog. He painted during the day and drank at night. There was an endless supply of young girls who lived in the Canyon and were free spirits and fellow painters.

Sossa never left the Canyon except to shop in Santa Monica or when he was called to duty by the Clericuzio Family, which was usually twice a month for a period of no more than a few days. He did the work they wanted him to do and never asked questions. He was a valued soldier in the Clericuzio Family.

So when a car came to pick him up and the driver told him to bring his tools and clothes for a few days, Sossa turned his goat, dog, and cat loose into the Canyon and locked his house. The animals could take care of themselves; after all, they were not children. It was not that he was not fond of them, but animals had a short life span, especially in the Canyon, and he had gotten used to losing them. His year in prison had made Leonard Sossa a realist, and his unexpected release had made him an optimist.

Lia Vazzi, the caretaker of the Clericuzio Family's hunting lodge in the Sierra Nevada, had arrived in the United States when he was only thirty years old and the most wanted man in Italy. In the ten years since then he had learned to speak English with only a very slight accent and could read and write it to a fair degree. In Sicily he had been born to one of the most learned and powerful Families on the island.

Fifteen years before, Lia Vazzi had been the leader of the Mafia in Palermo, a Qualified Man of the first rank. But he had reached too far.

In Rome, the government had appointed an examining magistrate and given him extraordinary powers to wipe out the Mafia in Sicily. The examining magistrate had arrived in Palermo with his wife and children, protected by army troops and a horde of police. He gave a fiery speech, promising to show no mercy to those criminals who had ruled the beautiful island of Sicily for centuries. The time had come for the law to rule, for the elected representatives of the people of Italy to decide the fate of Sicily, not the ignorant thugs with their shameful secret societies. Vazzi took his speech as a personal insult.

The examining magistrate was heavily guarded day and night, as he heard the testimony of witnesses and issued arrest orders. His court was a fortress, his living quarters rimmed by a perimeter of army troops. He was seemingly impregnable. But after three months Vazzi learned the magistrate's itinerary, which had been kept secret to prevent surprise attacks.

The magistrate traveled to the big towns in Sicily to gather evidence and issue arrest warrants. He was scheduled to return to

Palermo to be given a medal for his heroic attempt to rid the island of its Mafia scourge. Lia Vazzi and his men mined a small bridge that the magistrate had to pass over. The magistrate and his guards were blown into such tiny bits that the bodies had to be brought out of the water with sieves. The government in Rome, infuriated, replied with a massive search for the culprits responsible, and Vazzi had to go underground. Though the government had no proof, he knew that if he fell into their hands he would be better off dead.

Now the Clericuzio sent Pippi De Lena to Sicily every year to recruit men to live in the Bronx Enclave and soldier for the Clericuzio Family. The bedrock of the Don's faith was that only Sicilians with their centuries-long tradition of *omertà* could be trusted not to turn traitor. The young men in America were too soft, too lightheaded with vanity, could be too easily turned into informants by the more ferocious of the district attorneys who were sending so many of the *Brugliones* to prison.

As a philosophy, *omertà* was quite simple. It was a mortal sin to talk to the police about anything that would harm the Mafia. If a rival Mafia clan murdered your father before your eyes, you were forbidden to inform the police. If you yourself were shot and lay dying, you were forbidden to inform the police. If they stole your mule, your goat, your jewelry, you were forbidden to go to the police. The authorities were the Great Satan a true Sicilian could never turn to. Family and the Mafia were the avengers.

Ten years before, Pippi De Lena had taken his son, Cross, on his trip to Sicily as part of his training. The task was not so much recruiting as screening, there were hundreds of willing men whose greatest dream was to be picked to go to America.

They went to a little town fifty miles from Palermo, into the countryside of villages built of stone, decorated with the bright flowers of Sicily. There they were welcomed into the home of the mayor himself.

The mayor was a short man with a rounded belly, the belly figurative as well as literal, for "a man with a belly" was the Sicilian idiom for a Mafia chief.

The house had a pleasant garden with fig and olive and lemon trees, and it was here that Pippi did his interviews. The garden strangely resembled the Clericuzio garden in Quogue, except for the brilliantly colored flowers and the lemon trees. The mayor was obviously a man who loved beauty, for in addition he had a comely wife and three lusciously pretty daughters who, though in their early teens, were fully developed women.

But Cross saw that his father, Pippi, was a different man in Sicily. There was none of his carefree gallantry here, he was soberly respectful to the women, his charm erased. Late that night, in the room they shared, he lectured Cross. "You have to be careful with Sicilians. They distrust men who are interested in women. You screw one of their daughters, we'll never get out of here alive."

Over the next few days men came to be interviewed and screened by Pippi. He had criteria. The men could not be older than thirty-five or younger than twenty. If they were married, they could not have more than one child. Finally, they had to be vouched for by the mayor. He explained this. If the men were too young, they might be too influenced by the American culture. If they were too old, they could not make the adjustment to America. If they had more than one child, they would be of too cautious a temperament to take the risks their duties would demand.

Some of the men who came were so seriously compromised in the eyes of the law that they had to leave Sicily. Some were simply seeking a better life in America no matter the cost. Some were too clever to rely on fate and desperately wanted to soldier for the Clericuzio, and these were the best.

At the end of the week Pippi had his quota of twenty men, and he gave his list to the mayor, who would approve them and then arrange for their emigration. The mayor crossed out one name on the list.

Pippi said, "I thought he would be perfect for us. Have I made a mistake?"

"No, no," the mayor said. "You have done cleverly as always."

Pippi was puzzled. All of the recruits would be treated very well. The single men would be given apartments, the married men with a child a small house. They would all have steady jobs. They would all live in the Bronx Enclave. And then some would be chosen as soldiers in the Clericuzio Family and make a handsome living with a bright future. The man whose name had been crossed out by the mayor had to be in very bad odor. But then why had he been cleared for an interview? Pippi sensed a Sicilian rat.

The mayor was observing him shrewdly, seeming to read his mind and pleased by what he read.

"You are too much of a Sicilian for me to deceive you," the mayor said. "The name I crossed out is a man my daughter intends to marry. I want to keep him here a year longer for my daughter's happiness, then you can have him. I could not refuse his interview. The other reason is that I have a man who I think you should take in his place. Will you do me the favor of seeing him?"

"Of course," Pippi said.

The mayor said, "I don't want to mislead you, but this is a special case and he must leave immediately."

"You know I have to be very careful," Pippi said. "The Clericuzio are particular."

"It will be to your interest," the mayor said. "But it is a little dangerous." He then explained about Lia Vazzi. The assassination of the magistrate had made world headlines, so Pippi and Cross were familiar with the case.

"If they have no proof, why is this situation so desperate for Vazzi?" Cross said.

The mayor said, "Young man, this is Sicily. The police are also Sicilians. The magistrate was a Sicilian. Everybody knows it was Lia. Never mind your legal proof. If he falls into their hands, he will be dead."

Pippi said, "Can you get him out of the country and into America?"

"Yes," said the mayor. "The difficulty is keeping him hidden in America."

Pippi said, "He sounds like he's more trouble than he's worth."

The mayor shrugged. "He's a friend of mine, I confess. But put that aside." He paused and smiled benignly to make sure that it was not put aside. "He is also an ultimate Qualified Man. He is expert in explosives and that is always a very tricky business. He knows the rope, an old and very useful skill. The knife and gun of course. Most important of all he is intelligent, a man of all parts. And steadfast.

Like a rock. He never talks. He listens and has the gift of loosening tongues. Now tell me, can you not use a man like that?"

"An answer to my prayers," Pippi said smoothly. "But still why does such a man run away?"

"Because in addition to all his other virtues," the mayor said, "he is prudent. He does not challenge fate. His days are numbered here."

"And a man who's qualified," Pippi said, "can he be happy as a mere soldier in America?"

The mayor bowed his head in a sorrowful commiseration. "He is a true Christian," he said. "He has the humility that Christ has always taught us."

"I must meet such a man," Pippi said, "if only for the pleasure of the experience. But I can guarantee nothing."

The mayor made a wide, expansive gesture. "Of course he must suit you," he said. "But there is another thing I must tell you. He forbade me to deceive you about this." For the first time the mayor was not so confident. "He has a wife and three children and they must go with him."

At that moment Pippi knew his answer would be no. "Ah," he said, "that makes it very difficult. When do we see him?"

"He will be in the garden after dark," the mayor said. "There is no danger, I have seen to that."

Lia Vazzi was a small man but with that wiry toughness that many Sicilians inherited from long-ago Arab ancestors. He had a handsome, hawklike face, a dark brown, dignified mask, and he spoke English to a degree.

They sat around the mayor's garden table with a bottle of homemade red wine, a dish of olives from the nearby trees, and bread, crusty and freshly baked that evening, round, still warm, and beside it a whole leg of prosciutto, studded with grains of whole pepper, like black diamonds. Lia Vazzi ate and drank and said nothing.

"I have received the highest recommendations," Pippi said respectfully. "But I worry. Can a man of your education and qualification be happy in America in the service of another man?"

Lia looked at Cross and then said to Pippi, "You have a son. What would you do to save him? I want to have my wife and children safe and for that I will do my duty."

"There will be some danger for us," Pippi said. "You understand that I have to think of the benefits that justify the risk."

Lia shrugged. "I can't be the judge of that." He seemed resigned to being refused.

Pippi said, "If you come by yourself, it will be easier."

"No," Vazzi said. "My family will live together or die together." He paused for a moment. "If I leave them here, Rome will make it very difficult for them. I would rather give myself up."

Pippi said, "The problem is how to hide you and your family."

Vazzi shrugged. "America is vast," he said. He offered the plate of olives to Cross and said almost mockingly, "Would your father ever desert you?"

"No," Cross said. "He is old-fashioned, like yourself." He said it gravely but with a tiny trace of a smile. Then he said, "I hear you're a farmer also."

"Olives," Vazzi said. "I have my own press."

Cross said to Pippi, "How about the Family hunting lodge in the Sierras? He could take care of it with his family and earn his keep. It's isolated. His family can help." He turned to Lia. "Would you live in the woods?" Woods as the idiom for anything not urban. Lia shrugged.

It was the personal force of Lia Vazzi that persuaded Pippi De Lena. Vazzi was not a big man, but his body put out an electric dignity. He had a chilling effect, a man who was not daunted by death, feared neither Hell nor Heaven.

Pippi said, "It's a good idea. Perfect camouflage. And we can call on you for special jobs and let you earn extra money. Those jobs will be your risk."

They could see the muscles on Lia's face loosen when he realized that he had been chosen. His voice trembled slightly when he spoke. "I want to thank you for saving my wife and children," he said, and looked directly at Cross De Lena.

Since then Lia Vazzi had more than earned the mercy that had been shown to him. He had risen from soldier to leader of all of Cross's operational crews. He supervised the six men who helped him care for the Hunting Lodge estate, on whose grounds he owned his own house. He had prospered, he had become a citizen, his children went away to the university. All this earned by his courage and good sense, and most of all, his loyalty. So when he received the message to meet Cross De Lena in Las Vegas, it was with a goodwill that he packed his suitcase in his new Buick and made the long drive to Vegas and the Xanadu Hotel.

Andrew Pollard was the first to arrive in Las Vegas. He flew from L.A. on the noon flight, relaxed by one of the Hotel Xanadu's huge pools, gambled small-time craps for a few hours, then was secretly whisked into Cross De Lena's penthouse office suite.

They shook hands and Cross said, "I won't keep you long. You can fly back tonight. What I need is all the information you have on the Skannet guy."

Pollard briefed him on everything that had happened and informed him that Skannet was now staying in the Beverly Hills Hotel. He told of his conversation with Bantz.

"So they don't really give a shit about her, they just want to get the picture done," he told Cross. "Also, the Studio doesn't take characters like that seriously. I have a twenty-man section in my company that just handles harassers. Movie stars really have to worry about people like him."

"What about the cops?" Cross asked. "Can't they do something?"

"No," Pollard said. "Not until after the damage."

"What about you?" Cross asked. "You have some good personnel working for you."

"I have to be careful," Pollard said. "I could lose my business if I get tough. You know how the courts are. Why should I stick my neck out?"

"This Boz Skannet, what kind of guy is he?" Cross said.

"He won't scare," Pollard said. "In fact he scares me. He's one of those genuinely tough guys who doesn't care about consequences.

His family has money and political power so he figures he can get away with anything. And he really enjoys trouble, you know, how some guys do. If you're going to get into this you have to be serious."

"I'm always serious," Cross said. "You have Skannet under surveillance now?"

"I sure have," Pollard said. "He is definitely capable of pulling bad shit."

Cross said, "Pull off your surveillance. I don't want anyone watching him. Understand?"

"OK, if you say so," Pollard said. He paused for a moment, then said, "Watch out for Jim Losey, he's keeping an eye out on Skannet. Do you know Losey?"

"I've met him," Cross said. "I want you to do one other thing. Lend me your Pacific Ocean Security ID for a couple of hours. You'll have it back in time to catch the midnight flight to L.A."

Pollard was worried. "You know I'll do anything for you Cross, but be careful; this is a very touchy case. I've built up a very good life out here and I don't want it to go down the drain. I know I owe it all to the Clericuzio Family, I'm always grateful, I'm always paid back. But this is a very complicated business."

Cross smiled at him reassuringly. "You're too valuable to us. One other thing, if Skannet calls up to check on men from your office talking to him, you just verify it."

At this, Pollard's heart sank. This was going to be real trouble.

Cross said, "Now tell me anything else you can about him." When Pollard hesitated, Cross added, "I'll do something for you. Later on."

Pollard thought for a moment. "Skannet claims he knows a big secret that Athena would do anything not to have anyone find out. That's why she dropped the charges against him. A terrific secret, Skannet loves that secret. Cross, I don't know how or why you're involved, but maybe knowing that secret can solve your problem."

For the first time Cross looked at him without affability and suddenly he knew why Cross had acquired his reputation. The look was cold, judging, a judging that could result in death.

Cross said, "You know why I'm interested. Bantz must have told you the story. He hired you to do a background on me. Now do you have any of this big secret or does the Studio?"

"No," Pollard said. "Nobody knows. Cross, I'm doing my best for you, you know that."

"I do know that," Cross said, suddenly gentle. "Let me make it easier for you. The Studio is hot to know how I'm going to get Athena Aquitane back to work. I'll tell you. I'm going to give her half the profits of the movie. And it's okay by me for you to tell them. You can make points, they may even give you a bonus." He reached into his desk and took out a round leather bag and put it in Pollard's hand. "Five grand of black chips," he said. "I always worry when I ask you up here on business that you'll lose money in the casino."

He need not have worried. Andrew Pollard always turned the chips into the casino cage for cash.

Leonard Sossa was just getting settled into a secured business suite at the Xanadu when Pollard's ID was brought to him. With his own equipment he carefully forged four sets of Pacific Ocean Security IDs, complete with special flap-open billfolds. They would not have passed an inspection by Pollard, but that was not necessary, Pollard would never see these IDs. When Sossa finished the job several hours later, two men drove him to the Sierra Nevada Hunting Lodge, where he was installed in a bungalow deep in the woods.

On the porch of the bungalow that afternoon, he watched a deer and bear that wandered by. At night he cleaned his tools and waited. He didn't know where he was or what he was going to do and he didn't want to know. He got his hundred grand a year and lived the life of a free man in the open air. He killed time by sketching the bear and the deer he had seen on a hundred sheets of paper and then riffling them together to give the impression of the deer chasing the bear.

Lia Vazzi was greeted in an altogether different fashion. Cross embraced him, gave him dinner in his suite. During Vazzi's years in America, Cross had been his operational chief many times. Vazzi, despite his own force of character, had never tried to usurp authority, and Cross in turn had treated him with the respect that a man gave his equal.

Over the years Cross had gone to the Hunting Lodge for weekend vacations and the two of them had gone hunting together. Vazzi told stories of the troubles in Sicily and the difference in living in America. Cross had reciprocated by inviting Vazzi and his family to Vegas, comped RFB at the Xanadu plus a credit rating of five thousand in the casino, which Lia was never asked to pay.

Over dinner they talked generally. Vazzi marveled still at his life in America. His oldest son was taking a degree at the University of California and had no knowledge of his father's secret life. Vazzi was uneasy with this. "Sometimes I think he has none of my blood," he said. "He believes everything his professors tell him. He believes women are equal to men, he believes peasants should be given free land. He belongs to the swimming team at college. In all my life in Sicily, and Sicily is an island, I have never seen a Sicilian swimming."

"Except a fisherman thrown off his boat," Cross said laughing.

"Not even then," Vazzi said. "They all drowned."

When they had finished eating, they talked business. Vazzi never really enjoyed the food in Vegas, but he loved the brandy and Havana cigars. Cross always sent him a case of good brandy and a box of thin Havana cigars once a year at Christmas.

"I have something very difficult for you to do," Cross said. "Something that must be done very intelligently."

"That is always difficult," Vazzi said.

"It must be at the Hunting Lodge," Cross said. "We will bring a certain person there. I want him to write some letters, I want him to give a piece of information." He paused to smile at Vazzi's dismissive gesture. Vazzi had often commented on American movies where the hero or villain refused to give information. "I could make them speak Chinese," Vazzi would say.

"The difficulty," Cross said, "is that there must be no mark on his body, no drugs inside his body. Also this certain person is very strong-willed."

"Only women can make a man talk with kisses," Vazzi said amiably, savoring his cigar. "It sounds to me that you are going to be personally involved in this story."

Cross said, "There is no other way. The men working will be your crew but first the Lodge must be cleared of the women and children."

Vazzi waved his cigar. "They will go to Disneyland, that blessing in happiness and trouble. We always send them there."

"Disneyland?" Cross asked, and laughed.

"I have never been," Vazzi said. "I hope to go there when I die. Will this be a Communion or a Confirmation?"

"Confirmation," Cross said.

Then they got down to business. Cross explained the operation to Vazzi and why and how it should be done. "How does it sound to you?" he asked.

"You are far more Sicilian than my son and you were born in America," Vazzi said. "But what happens if he remains stubborn and won't give you what you want."

"Then the fault will be mine," Cross said. "And his. And then we must pay. In that, America and Sicily are the same."

"True," Vazzi said. "As in China and Russia and Africa. As the Don often says, then we can all go swim in the bottom of the ocean."

CHAPTER 9

⊞

ELI MARRION, Bobby Bantz, Skippy Deere, and Melo Stuart assembled in emergency session in Marrion's home. Andrew Pollard had reported to Bantz Cross De Lena's secret scheme to get Athena back to work. This information had been corroborated by the detective Jim Losey, who refused to divulge his source.

"This is a stickup," Bantz said. "Melo, you're her agent, you're responsible for her and all your clients. Does this mean when we are in the middle of a big picture your star refuses to go to work until they get half the profits?"

"Only if you're crazy enough to pay it," Stuart said. "Let this De Lena guy do it. He won't stay in the business long."

Marrion said, "Melo, you're talking strategy, we're talking right this minute. If Athena goes back to work, then you and your client are sticking us up like bank robbers. Will you permit that?"

They were all astonished. It was rare that Marrion cut so quickly to the bone, at least since his younger days. Stuart was alarmed.

"Athena knows nothing about this," he said. "She would have told me."

Deere said, "Would she take the deal if she knew?"

Stuart said, "I would advise her to take it and then in a side letter split her half with the studio."

Bantz said crisply, "Then all her protestations of fear would be a mockery. Bullshit, in short. And Melo, you're full of shit. You think this studio would settle for half of what Athena gets from De Lena? All that money rightfully belongs to us. And she may get away rich with De Lena but it means the end of her career in the movies. No studio will ever hire her again."

"Foreign," Skippy said. "Foreign would take a chance."

Marrion picked up the phone and handed it to Stuart. "This is all to no purpose. Call Athena. Tell her what Cross De Lena is going to offer and ask if she is going to accept."

Deere said, "She disappeared over the weekend."

"She's back," Stuart said. "She often disappears on weekends." He pushed the buttons on the phone.

The conversation was very brief. Stuart hung up and smiled. "She said she has received no such offer. And no such offer would make her come back to work. She doesn't give a shit about her career." He paused for a moment and then said admiringly, "I'd like to meet this guy Skannet. Any man who can scare an actress out of her career has some good in him."

Marrion said, "It's settled then. We've recouped our loss out of a hopeless situation. But it's a pity. Athena was such a great star."

Andrew Pollard had his instructions. The first had been to inform Bantz of Cross De Lena's intention regarding Athena. The second was to pull the surveillance team off Skannet. The third was to visit Boz Skannet and offer a proposition.

Skannet was in his undershirt when he let Pollard into his Beverly Hills Hotel suite, and he smelled of cologne. "Just finished shaving," he said. "This hotel has more bathroom perfumes than a whorehouse."

"You are not supposed to be in this town," Pollard said reproachfully.

Skannet slapped him on the back. "I know, but I'll leave tomorrow. I just have a few loose ends to tie up." His malicious glee while saying this, his massive torso, would have frightened Pollard before, but now that Cross was involved it only evoked pity. But he would have to be careful.

"Athena is not surprised that you haven't left," he said. "She feels the Studio doesn't understand you but she does. So she would like to meet with you personally. She thinks that just the two of you alone can strike a deal."

When he saw the momentary rush of joy on Skannet's face, he knew that Cross had been right. This guy was still in love, he would buy the story.

Boz Skannet was suddenly wary. "That doesn't sound like Athena. She can't stand the sight of me, not that I blame her." He laughed. "She needs that pretty mug of hers."

Pollard said, "She wants to make a serious offer. A lifetime annuity. A percentage of her earnings for the rest of her life if you want. But she wants to talk to you personally and secretly. There's something else she wants."

"I know what she wants," Skannet said. Skannet had a curious look on his face. Pollard had seen that look on the faces of wistfully repentant rapists.

"Seven o'clock," Pollard said. "Two of my men will come to pick you up and bring you to the meeting place. They will stay with her to be her bodyguards. Two of my best men, armed. Just so you won't get any funny ideas."

Skannet smiled. "Don't worry about me," he said.

"Right," Pollard said and left.

When the door closed, Skannet shot his right hand up in the air. He would see Athena again with only two half-assed private detectives to protect her. And he would have proof that she initiated the meeting, he would not be violating the judge's restraining order.

For the rest of the day he dreamed of their reunion. It was really a surprise to him, and thinking about it he knew that Athena would use her body to persuade him into the bargain. He lay on his bed imagining how it would be to be with her again. The image of her body was clear. Her white skin, the gentle curve of her belly, her breasts with their pink nipples, her eyes so green they were another kind of light, her warm delicate mouth, her breath, her flaming hair like the sun turning into smoky brass under a night sky. For a moment his old love swept over him, his love of her intelligence and her brave character that he had broken down into fear. Then for the first time since he was sixteen, he was fondling himself. His mind formed clear figures of Athena urging him on, until he climaxed. For that one moment he was happy and he loved her.

And then everything turned around. He felt a sense of shame, of humiliation. He hated her again. Suddenly he was convinced it was some sort of trap. What did he really know about this guy Pollard, anyway. Skannet dressed hurriedly and studied the card Pollard had given him. The office was only a twenty-minute drive from the hotel. He rushed down to the hotel entrance and a valet brought his car.

When he entered the Pacific Ocean Security Building, he was surprised at the size and opulence of the operation. He made his way to the reception desk and stated his business. An armed security guard escorted him to Pollard's office. Skannet noticed that the walls were decorated with awards from the L.A. Police Department, the Association to Help the Homeless, and other organizations, including the Boy Scouts of America. There was even some sort of a movie award.

Andrew Pollard was regarding him with surprise, and a little concern. Skannet reassured him.

"I just wanted to tell you," he said, "I'll drive to the meeting in my car. Your men can ride with me and give me directions."

Pollard shrugged. This would be none of his business. He had done what he had been instructed to do. "Fine," he said. "But you could have called me."

Skannet grinned at him. "Sure, but I just wanted to check on your offices. Also, I want to call Athena to make sure this is on the up-and-up. I figured you can get her on the phone for me. She might not take my call."

"Sure," Pollard said agreeably. He picked up the phone. He didn't know what was going on and in his heart he hoped that Skannet would abort the meeting and he would no longer be involved in whatever Cross was planning to do. He also knew Athena would not speak to him directly.

He dialed the number and asked for Athena. He put the loudspeaker on so that Skannet could hear the call. Athena's secretary told him that Miss Aquitane was out and was not expected back until the next day. He put down the phone and raised an eyebrow to Skannet. Skannet looked happy.

And Skannet was. He had been right. Athena was planning to use her body to make the deal. She was planning to spend the night with him. The red skin of his face took on an almost bronze sheen with the rush of blood to his brain, remembering when she was young, when she had loved him, when he had loved her.

At seven that evening, when Lia Vazzi arrived at the hotel with one of his soldiers, Skannet was waiting for him and ready to go immediately. Skannet was dressed very neatly in a boyish way. He wore heavy blue jeans, a faded blue denim shirt, and a white sports jacket. He had shaved carefully, and his blond hair was combed straight back. His red skin seemed paler, his face softened by the paleness. Lia Vazzi and his soldier showed Skannet their forged Pacific Ocean Security IDs.

Skannet was not impressed by the men. Two runts, one with a slight accent he thought might be Mexican. They would give him no trouble. These private dick agencies were so full of shit, what kind of protection was this for Athena?

Vazzi said to Skannet, "I understand you want to drive your own car. I will go with you and my friend will follow in our car. Is that agreeable to you?"

"OK," Skannet said.

When they got out of the elevator and entered the lobby, they were stopped by Jim Losey. The detective had been waiting on a sofa by the fireplace and intercepted them on just a hunch. He had staked out there to keep an eye on Skannet just in case. Now he held his ID out to the three men.

Skannet looked at the ID and said, "What the fuck do you want?"

Jim Losey said, "Who are these two men with you?"

"None of your fucking business," Skannet said. Vazzi and his companion remained silent as Losey studied their faces.

"I'd like to have a few words with you in private," Losey said.

Skannet brushed him aside and Losey grabbed his arm. They were both big men. Skannet was frantic to be away. He said to Losey, his voice furious and loud, "The charges were dropped, I don't have to talk to you. And if you don't get your hands away, I'm going to kick the shit out of you."

Losey dropped his hand. He was in no way intimidated, but his mind was working. The two men with Skannet seemed strange to him, there was something going on. He stepped aside but followed them to the archway where cars were brought to hotel guests. He watched Skannet get into his car with Lia Vazzi. Somehow the other man had vanished. Losey noted this and waited to see if another car pulled out of the parking lot, but there was none.

There was no use trying to follow and there was equally no purpose to be served in putting out an alert for Skannet's car. He debated on whether to report this incident to Skippy Deere and decided against it. One thing was for certain, if Skannet got out of line again, he would regret his insults today.

It was a long drive, Skannet kept complaining and asking questions and even threatening to turn back. But Lia Vazzi was reassuring. Skannet had been told that the meeting place was a hunting lodge Athena owned in the Sierra Nevada, and the instructions were that they were to spend the night. Athena had insisted she wanted the meeting a secret from everyone, that she would settle the whole problem to everyone's satisfaction. Skannet didn't know what that meant. What could she do to dissolve the hatred that had grown over the last ten years? Was she stupid enough to think that a night of lovemaking and a bundle of cash would soften him? Did she think he was that simple? He had always admired her intelligence but maybe now she was just one of those arrogant Hollywood actresses who thought she could buy anything with her body and her money? And yet the thought of her beauty haunted him. Finally after all these years, she would smile at him, charm him, submit to him. No matter what happened he would have this coming night.

Lia Vazzi was not worried about Skannet's threats to turn back. He knew there were three cars on the road behind him as escort and he had his instructions. As a last resort he could simply have Skannet killed. But his instructions were also clear that Skannet should not suffer any injury short of death.

They drove through the open gate, and Skannet was surprised at the size of the Hunting Lodge. It looked like a small hotel. He got out and stretched his arms and legs. There were five or six cars parked alongside the lodge, which made him wonder for a moment.

Vazzi led him to the door and opened it. At that moment Skannet heard more cars pulling into the driveway. He turned thinking that Athena had arrived. What he saw were three cars parking and two men getting out of each one. Then Lia led him through the main entry of the lodge and into the living room with its huge fireplace. There, sitting on the sofa waiting for him, was a man he had never seen. The man was Cross De Lena.

What happened next was very quick. Skannet asked angrily, "Where's Athena?" then two men grabbed his arms, another two men put guns to his head, and the seemingly harmless Lia Vazzi pulled his legs out from under him so that he toppled to the floor.

Vazzi said, "You can die now if you don't do exactly as you are told. Don't struggle. Lie still."

Still another man shackled Skannet's legs together and then they pulled him to his feet so that he was facing Cross. Skannet was surprised how helpless he felt even when the men released his arms. His imprisoned feet seemed to neutralize all his physical powers. He reached out to at least punch the little bastard, but Vazzi stepped back, and though Skannet gave a little hop he could not get leverage with his arms.

Vazzi regarded him with quiet contempt. "We know you are a violent man," he said, "but now is the time to use your brain. Strength is of no use here. . . ."

Skannet seemed to take his advice. He was thinking hard. If they had wanted to kill him they would have done so. This was some process of intimidation to make him agree to something. Well and good, he would agree. And then he would take precautions in the future. One thing he was sure of. Athena was not involved in such an operation. He disregarded Vazzi and turned to the man sitting on the sofa.

"Who the hell are you?" he said.

Cross said, "I have a few things I want you to do and then you will be allowed to drive home."

"And if I don't, you'll torture me, right?" Skannet laughed. He was beginning to think this was some jerk-off Hollywood scene, some bad movie the Studio was using.

"No," Cross said simply. "No torture. No one will touch you. I want you to sit down at that table and write four letters for me. One to Lodd-Stone Studios promising never to go near their lot. One to Athena Aquitane apologizing for your previous conduct and swearing never to go near her again. Another to the police authorities admitting you purchased acid to be used in another attack on your wife, and another letter to me stating what secret you hold over your wife. Simple."

Skannet took a hobbling leap toward Cross and was pushed by one of the men so that he went sprawling onto the opposite sofa.

"Don't touch him," Cross said sharply.

Skannet used his arms to push himself to his feet.

Cross pointed to the desk where there was a stack of paper.

"Where's Athena?" Skannet said.

"She's not here," Cross said. "Everybody out of the room, except Lia," he said. The other men went out the door.

"Go sit at the desk," Cross said to Skannet. Skannet did so.

Cross said to him, "I want to talk to you very seriously. Stop trying to show how tough you are. I want you to listen. Don't do anything foolish. You have your hands free and that may give you illusions of grandeur. All I want you to do is write those letters and you'll be free."

Skannet said contemptuously, "You can go fuck yourself."

Cross turned to Vazzi and said, "No use wasting time. Kill him."

Cross had kept his voice even and yet there was something terrible in his casualness. In that moment Skannet felt a fear he had not known since he was a child. He realized for the first time the significance of all the men in the lodge, all the forces that were arrayed against him. Lia Vazzi had not yet made a move. Skannet said, "OK. I'll do it." He picked up a sheet of paper and began to write.

Cunningly, he wrote the letters with his left hand; like some good athletes, he could perform almost equally well with either hand. Cross came up behind him and watched. Skannet, ashamed of his sudden cowardice, braced his feet against the floor. Confident of his physical coordination, he switched the pen to his right hand and sprang up to stab Cross in the face, hoping to get the bastard in the eye. He exploded into action, his arm coming around, the whole torso of his body propelled, and was surprised that Cross had easily moved out of range. Still Skannet tried to move with his leg shackles.

Cross regarded him quietly and said, "Everybody is entitled to his once. You've had that. Now put down the pen and give me those sheets."

Skannet did so. Cross studied the sheets of paper and said, "You haven't told me the secret."

"I won't put it on paper. Get rid of that guy," he motioned to Vazzi, "and I'll tell you."

Cross handed the sheets of paper to Lia and said, "Take care of these."

Vazzi went out of the room.

"OK," Cross said to Skannet, "let's hear this big secret."

When Vazzi left the Hunting Lodge he ran the hundred yards to the bungalow that housed Leonard Sossa. Sossa was waiting. He looked at the two sheets of paper and said disgustedly, "This is left-handed. I can't do left-handed script. Cross knows that."

"Look at it again," Vazzi said. "He tried to stab Cross with his right hand."

Sossa studied the pages again. "Yeah," he said. "This guy is not a real lefty. He's just dicking you around."

Vazzi took the sheets and went back to the Hunting Lodge and entered the library. By Cross's face he knew something had gone wrong. Cross had a look of bewilderment, and Skannet was lying down on the sofa, his shackled legs extended over the arm, smiling happily up at the ceiling.

"These letters are no good," Vazzi said. "He wrote them left-handed and the analyst says he's a rightie."

Cross said to Skannet, "I think you're too tough for me to handle. I can't scare you, I can't make you do what I want. I give up."

Skannet rose from the sofa and said malevolently to Cross, "But what I told you is true. Everybody falls in love with Athena, but nobody knows her the way I do."

Cross said quietly, "You don't know her. And you don't know me." He went to the door and motioned. Four men came into the room. Then Cross turned to Lia. "You know what I want. If he doesn't give it to me, then just get rid of him." He walked out of the room.

Lia Vazzi gave a visible sigh of relief. He admired Cross, had been a willing subordinate all these years, but Cross was too patient. It was true that all the great Dons in Sicily excelled in patience, but they knew when to stop. Vazzi suspected that there was an American softness in Cross De Lena that would prevent his rise to greatness.

Vazzi turned to Skannet and said silkily, "You and I, we begin." He turned to the four men. "Secure his arms, but gently. Don't hurt him."

The four men pounced on Skannet. One of the men produced handcuffs, and in a moment Skannet was completely helpless. Vazzi pushed him to the floor on his knees, the other men forced Skannet to stay in place.

"The comedy is finished," Vazzi said to Skannet. His wiry body seemed relaxed, his voice was conversational. "You will scribble those letters with your right hand. Or you can refuse." One of the men produced a huge revolver and a box of bullets and handed them to Lia. He loaded the revolver, showing each of the bullets to Skannet. He went to the window and fired into the forest until the gun was empty. Then he went back to Skannet and put one bullet in. Spinning the cylinder, he put the gun under Skannet's nose.

"I don't know where the bullet is," Lia said. "You don't know where it is. If you still refuse to write the letters, I pull the trigger. Now is it yes or no?"

Skannet looked into Lia's eyes and did not answer. Lia pulled the trigger. There was just the click of an empty chamber. Lia nodded approvingly. "I was rooting for you," he said to Skannet.

He looked into the cylinder and put the bullet in the first chamber. He went to the window and fired. The explosion seemed to rock the room. Lia went back to the table, took another bullet from the box, loaded the gun with it, spinning the cylinder.

"We will try again," Lia said. He put the revolver beneath Skannet's chin. But this time Skannet flinched.

"Call back your boss," Skannet said. "I have a few more things I can tell him."

"No," Lia said, "that foolishness is over. Now answer yes or no."

Skannet looked into Lia's eyes and saw not a threat but a mournful regret. "OK," Skannet said. "I'll write."

He was immediately hauled to his feet and seated at the writing desk. Vazzi sat on the sofa while Skannet busied himself writing. He took the papers from Skannet and went to Sossa's bungalow. "Is that OK?" he asked.

"This will do fine," Sossa said.

Vazzi went back to the Hunting Lodge and reported to Cross. Then he went to the library and said to Skannet, "It's all over. I'll drive you back to L.A. as soon as I'm ready." Then Lia walked Cross out to his car.

Cross said, "You know everything you have to do. Wait until morning, I should be back in Vegas by then."

"Don't worry," Vazzi said. "I thought he would never write. What an animal." He could see that Cross was preoccupied. "What did he tell you when I was away?" Vazzi asked. "Something I should know?"

Cross said, with savage bitterness Vazzi had never seen before, "I should have killed him straight out. I should have taken my chances. I hate being so fucking clever."

"Ah well," Vazzi said, "it's done now."

He watched Cross drive through the gates. For one of the few times in ten years, he was homesick for Sicily. In Sicily men never became so distraught about a woman's secret. And in Sicily there would never have been all this fuss. Skannet would have been swimming at the bottom of the ocean a long time ago.

As dawn broke, a closed van pulled up to the Hunting Lodge.

Lia Vazzi collected the forged suicide notes from Leonard Sossa and put him into the car that would take him back to Topanga Canyon. Vazzi cleaned up the bungalow, burned the letters Skannet had written, removing all traces of occupancy. Leonard Sossa had never seen either Skannet or Cross during his stay.

Then Lia Vazzi prepared for the execution of Boz Skannet.

Six men were involved in this operation. They had blindfolded and gagged Skannet and put him in the van. Two of the men got into the van with him. Skannet was completely helpless, shackled hand and foot. Another man drove the van, and another man rode shotgun for the driver. The fifth man drove Skannet's car. Lia Vazzi and the sixth man drove another car that went in front.

Lia Vazzi watched the sun slowly rise from the shadows of the mountains. The caravan drove nearly sixty miles and then turned into a road deep in the woods.

Finally the caravan halted. Vazzi directed exactly how Skannet's car should be parked. Then he had Skannet taken out of the van. Skannet made no resistance, he seemed to have accepted his fate. Well, he's finally figured it all out, Vazzi thought.

Vazzi took the rope out of the car. He measured the length carefully and hung one end to the thick limb of a nearby tree. Two men were holding Skannet up straight so that he could slip the noose around the man's neck. Vazzi took out the two suicide notes that Leonard Sossa had forged and slipped them into Skannet's jacket pocket.

It took four of the men to lift Skannet to the roof of the van and then Lia Vazzi threw his fist out in the direction of the driver. The van shot ahead and Skannet flew off the roof and dangled in the air. The sound of his neck cracking resounded through the forest. Vazzi checked the corpse and removed the shackles from the body. The other men removed the blindfold and the gag. There were little scrapes around the mouth, but a couple of days hanging in the forest and they would not be significant. He checked the arms and legs for signs of restraint. Again, there were slight marks, but they would not be conclusive. He was satisfied. He did not know if it would work, but everything Cross ordered had been done.

Two days later, alerted by an anonymous tip, the county sheriff found Skannet's body. He had to scare off an inquisitive brown bear who was hitting the rope to make the body sway back and forth, and when the coroner and his assistants arrived, they found the body's rotting skin eaten by insects.

BOOK VI

A
Hollywood
Death

CHAPTER 10

TEN BARE female asses rose in harmony to greet the camera's blinking eye. Despite the picture still being in limbo, Dita Tommey was auditioning actresses on the *Messalina* soundstage for an ass to double for Athena Aquitane's.

Athena had refused to do nudes, that is, she would not show full tits and ass, an astonishing modesty in a star but not a fatal one. Dita would simply substitute tits and ass from some of the different actresses she was now auditioning.

Of course she had given the actresses full scenes with dialogue, she wouldn't demean them by posing them as if they were pornography. But the determining factor would be in the culminating sex scene, when rolling around in bed they would thrust their bare buttocks up to the camera eye. Her sex-scene choreographer was sketching out the rolls and twists with the male actor, Steve Stallings.

Watching the tests with Dita Tommey were Bobby Bantz and Skippy Deere. The only other people on the set were the necessary crew members. Tommey didn't mind Deere watching, but what the hell was Bobby Bantz doing here. She had considered briefly barring him from the set, but if *Messalina* was abandoned she would be in a very weak power position. She could use his goodwill.

Bantz asked fretfully, "What exactly are we looking for here?"

The sex-scene choreographer, a young man named Willis, who was also the head of the Los Angeles Ballet Company, said cheerfully, "The most beautiful ass in the world. But also with great muscles. We don't want sleaze, we don't want the crack open."

"Right," Bantz said, "Nothing sleazy."

"How about the tits?" Deere asked.

"They cannot be allowed to bounce," the choreographer said.

"We audition tits tomorrow," Tommey said. "No woman has perfect tits and a perfect ass, except maybe Athena, and she won't show them."

Bantz said slyly, "You should know, Dita."

Tommey forgot her weak power position. "Bobby, you're the perfect asshole, if that's what we're looking for. She won't fuck you so you assume she's a dyke."

"OK, OK," Bantz said. "I've got a hundred phone calls I have to return."

"Me too," Deere said.

"I don't believe you guys," Tommey said.

Deere said, "Dit, have a little sympathy. Bobby and I, what recreation do we get? We're too busy to play golf. Watching movies is work. We don't have the time to go to the theater or opera. We can squeeze maybe an hour a day for fun after we spend time with our families. What can you do with just one hour a day? Screw. It's the least labor-intensive recreation."

"Wow, Skippy, look at that," Bantz said. "That's the most beautiful ass I have ever seen."

Deere shook his head in wonder. "Bobby's right. Dita, that's the one. Sign her up."

Tommey shook her head in disbelief. "Jesus, you guys are morons," she said. "That's a black ass."

"Sign her up anyway," Deere said with exuberant joy.

"Yeah," Bantz said. "An Ethiopian slave girl for Messalina. But why the hell is she auditioning?"

Dita Tommey observed both men with curiosity. Here were two of the toughest men in the movie business, with over a hundred phone calls to return, and they were like two teenagers looking for their first orgasm. She said patiently, "When we send out casting calls we're not allowed to say we just want white asses."

Bantz said, "I want to meet that girl."

"Me too," Deere said.

But all this was interrupted by Melo Stuart coming on the set. He was smiling triumphantly. "We can all go back to work," he said.

"Athena is going back on the picture. Her husband, Boz Skannet, hung himself. Boz Skannet, off the picture." As he said this he clapped his hands as the crew always clapped when an actor finished work on a movie, his part finished. Skippy and Bobby clapped with him. Dita Tommey stared at the three of them with disgust.

"Eli wants the two of you right away," Melo said. "Not you, Dita," he smiled apologetically. "This will just be a business discussion, no creative decisions." The men left the soundstage.

When they were gone, Dita Tommey summoned the girl with the beautiful ass to her trailer. She was very pretty, truly black rather than tan, and she had an impudent vivacity that Dita identified as natural and not an actor's put-on.

"I'm giving you the part of an Ethiopian slave girl to the Empress Messalina," Dita said. "You'll have one line of dialogue but mainly we'll be showing your ass. Unfortunately we need a white ass to double for Miss Aquitane and yours is too black, otherwise you might steal the picture. She gave the girl a friendly smile. "Falene Fant, that's a movie name."

"Whatever," the girl said. "Thank you. For both the compliments and the job."

"One more thing," Dita said. "Our producer, Skippy Deere, thinks you have the most beautiful ass in the world. So does Mr. Bantz, the president and head of production for the Studio. You'll be hearing from them."

Falene Fant gave her a wicked grin. "And what do you think?" she said.

Dita Tommey shrugged. "I'm not into asses as much as men are. But I think you're charming and a very good actress. Good enough so that I think you can carry more than one line in this picture. And if you come to my house tonight, we can talk about your career. I'll give you dinner."

That night, after Dita Tommey and Falene Fant spent two hours in bed, Dita cooked dinner and they discussed Falene's career.

"It was fun," Dita said, "but I think from now on we should just be friends and keep this night a secret."

"Sure," Falene said. "But everyone knows you're dykey. Is it my black ass?" She was grinning.

Dita ignored the word *dykey*. That was a deliberate impudence to pay back for the seeming rejection. "It's a great ass, black, white, green, or yellow," Dita said. "But you have real talent. If I keep casting you in my pictures, you won't get credit for your talent. And I only make a picture every two years. You have to work more than that. Most directors are male and when they cast somebody like you they're always hoping for a little screw. If they think you're dykey, they may pass."

"Who needs directors if I have a producer and the head of a studio," Falene said cheerfully.

"You do," Dita said. "The other guys can get you a foot in the door, but the director can leave you on the cutting-room floor. Or he can shoot you so that you look and sound like shit."

Falene shook her head woefully. "I have to fuck Bobby Bantz, Skippy Deere, and I've already fucked you. Is this absolutely necessary?" She opened her eyes wide, innocently.

Dita really felt fond of her at the moment. Here was a girl who didn't try to be indignant. "I had a very good time tonight," she said. "You hit exactly the right note."

"Well, I never understood the fuss people make about sex," Falene said. "It's no hardship for me. I don't do drugs, I don't drink a lot. I have to have a little fun."

"Fine," Dita said. "Now, about Deere and Bantz. Deere is the better bet and I'll tell you why. Deere is in love with himself and he loves women. He will really do something for you. He'll find you a good part, he's smart enough to see your talent. Now Bantz doesn't like anybody except Eli Marrion. Also he has no taste, no eye for talent. Bantz will sign you to a studio contract and then let you rot. He does that with his wife to keep her quiet. She gets a lot of work for top dollar but never a decent part. Skippy Deere, if he likes you, will do something for your career."

"This sounds a little cold-blooded," Falene said.

Dita tapped her on the arm. "Don't bullshit me. I'm a dyke but I'm a woman too. And I know actors. They will do anything, male or female, to go up the ladder. We all play for big stakes. Do you want to go to a nine-to-five job in Oklahoma or do you want to become a movie star and live in Malibu? I see by your sheet that you're twenty-three years old. How many have you fucked already?"

"Counting you?" Falene said. "Maybe fifty. But all for fun," she said in mock apology.

"So a few more won't traumatize you," Dita said. "And who knows, it may be fun again."

"You know," Falene said, "I wouldn't do it if I wasn't so sure I'd be a star."

"Of course," Dita said. "None of us would."

Falene laughed. "What about you?" she asked.

"I didn't have the option," Dita said. "I made it on sheer overwhelming talent."

"Poor you," Falene said.

At LoddStone Studios, Bobby Bantz, Skippy Deere, and Melo Stuart were meeting with Eli Marrion in his office. Bantz was enraged. "That silly prick, he scares everybody to death and then commits suicide."

Marrion said to Stuart, "Melo, your client is coming back to work I assume."

"Of course," Melo said.

"She has no further requests, she doesn't need any extra inducements?" Marrion asked in a quiet, deadly voice. For the first time, Melo Stuart became aware that Marrion was in a rage.

"No," Melo said. "She can start work tomorrow."

"Great," Deere said. "We may still come in under budget."

"I want you all to shut up and listen to me," Marrion said. And this rudeness, so unprecedented in him, made them silent.

Marrion spoke in his usual low, pleasant voice, but there was now no mistaking his anger.

"Skippy, what do we give a fuck if the picture comes in on budget? We don't own the picture anymore. We panicked, we made a stupid mistake. All of us are at fault. We do not own this film, an outsider does."

Skippy Deere tried to interrupt him. "LoddStone will make a fortune on distribution. And you get a percentage on profits. It's still a very good deal."

"But De Lena makes more money than we do," Bantz said. "That's not right."

"The point is that De Lena did nothing to solve the problem," Marrion said. "Surely our studio has some sort of legal basis to regain the picture."

"That's right," Bantz said. "Fuck him. Let's go to court."

Marrion said, "We threaten him with court and then we cut a deal. We give him his money back and ten percent of the adjusted gross."

Deere laughed. "Eli, Molly Flanders won't let him take your deal."

"We'll negotiate directly with De Lena," Marrion said. "I think I can persuade him." He paused for a moment. "I called him as soon as I got the news. He will be joining us very shortly. And you know he has a certain background, this suicide is too fortunate for him, I don't think he will care for the publicity of a court case."

Cross De Lena, in his penthouse suite at the Xanadu Hotel, read the newspaper reports of Skannet's death. Everything had gone perfectly. It was a clear case of suicide, the two farewell notes on the body clinched it. There was no possibility the handwriting experts could detect the forgery, Boz Skannet had not left any great body of correspondence and Leonard Sossa was too good. The shackles on Skannet's legs and arms had been purposely loose and had left no marks. Lia Vazzi was an expert.

The first call Cross received was expected. Giorgio Clericuzio summoning him to the Family mansion in Quogue. Cross had never deceived himself that the Clericuzio would not find out what he was doing.

The second call Cross received was from Eli Marrion asking him to come to Los Angeles and without his lawyer. Cross said he would. But before he left Las Vegas he called Molly Flanders and told her about the phone call from Marrion. She was enraged. "Those slimy bastards," she said. "I'll pick you up at the airport and we'll go in together. Never even say good morning to a studio head unless you've got a lawyer with you."

When the two of them walked into LoddStone Studios and Marrion's office they knew there was trouble. The four men waiting there had the seriously truculent look of men about to commit strong-arm.

"I decided to bring my lawyer," Cross said to Marrion. "I hope you don't mind."

"As you wish," Marrion said. "I merely wanted to save you a possible embarrassment."

Molly Flanders, stern-faced and angry, said, "This is going to be really good. You want the picture back but our contract is iron."

"You're correct," Marrion said. "But we are going to appeal to Cross's sense of fair play. He did nothing to solve the problem, whereas LoddStone Studios has invested considerable time and money and creative talent without which this movie would not have been possible. Cross will get his money back. He gets ten percent of the adjusted gross and we will be generous in determining the adjustments. He will not be at risk."

"He has already survived the risk," Molly said. "Your offer is insulting."

"Then we will have to go to court," Marrion said. "Cross, I'm sure you will find that as distasteful as I do." He smiled at Cross. It was a kindly smile that made his gorilla-like face angelic.

Molly was furious. "Eli, you go to court twenty times a year and give depositions because you're always pulling crap like this." She turned to Cross and said, "We're leaving."

But Cross knew that a long court case was something he could not afford. His buying the film followed by Skannet's opportune death would be held up to scrutiny. They would dig up everything about his background, they would paint him in such a way that he would become too much of a public figure, and that was something the old Don had never tolerated. There was no mistaking that Marrion knew all this.

"Let's stick around," Cross said to Molly. Then he turned to Marrion, Bantz, Skippy Deere, and Melo Stuart. "If a gambler comes into my hotel and plays a long shot and wins, I pay him the full odds. I don't say I'll pay him even money. That's what you gentlemen are doing here. So why don't you reconsider this?"

Bantz said with contempt, "This is business not gambling."

Melo Stuart said soothingly to Cross, "You will make conservatively ten million dollars on your investment. Surely that's fair."

"And you didn't even do anything," Bantz said.

Only Skippy Deere seemed to be on his side. "Cross, you deserve more. But what they offer is better than a court fight, the risk of losing. Let this one go and you and I will do business again without the Studio. And I promise you'll get a fair shake."

Cross knew it was important to seem nonthreatening. He smiled in resignation. "Maybe you're all right," he said. "I want to stay in the movie business on good terms with everybody and ten million profit is not a bad start. Molly, take care of the papers. Now I have to catch a plane so please excuse me." He left the room and Molly followed him.

"We can win in court," Molly told him.

"I don't want to go to court," Cross said. "Make the deal."

Molly studied him carefully, then she said, "OK, but I'll get more than ten percent."

When Cross arrived at the mansion in Quogue the next day, Don Domenico Clericuzio, his sons Giorgio, Vincent, and Petie, and the grandson, Dante, were waiting for him. They had lunch in the garden, a lunch of cold Italian hams and cheeses and an enormous wooden bowl of salad, long loaves of crispy Italian bread. There was the bowl of grated cheese for the Don's spoon. As they ate, the Don said conversationally, "Croccifixio, we hear you have become involved in the moving picture business." He paused to sip his red wine. He then took a spoonful of the grated Italian Parmesan cheese.

"Yes," Cross answered.

Giorgio said, "Is it true that you pledged some of your shares in the Xanadu to finance a movie?"

"That is within my right," Cross said. "I am, after all, your *Bruglione* in the West." He laughed.

" 'Bruglione' is right," Dante said.

The Don shot a disapproving look at his grandson. He said to Cross, "You got involved in a very serious affair without Family consultation. You did not seek our wisdom. Most important of all, you carried out a violent action that might have severe official repercussions. On that, custom is clear, you must have our consent or go your own way and suffer consequences."

"And you used resources of the Family," Giorgio said harshly. "The Hunting Lodge in the Sierra. You used Lia Vazzi, Leonard Sossa, and Pollard with his Security Agency. Of course, they are your people in the West but they are also Family resources. Luckily everything went perfectly but what if it had not? We would all have been at risk."

Don Clericuzio said impatiently, "He knows all that. The question is why. Nephew, years ago you asked not to take part in that necessary work some men must do. I granted your request despite the fact that you were so valuable. Now you do it for your own profit. That is not like the beloved nephew I have always known."

Cross knew then that the Don was sympathetic to him. He knew he could not tell the truth, that he had been seduced by Athena's beauty; that would not be a reasonable explanation, indeed it would be insulting. And possibly fatal. What could be more inexcusable than that the attraction to a strange woman outweighed his loyalty to the Clericuzio Family. He spoke carefully. "I saw an opportunity to make a great deal of money," he said. "I saw a chance to get a foothold in a new business. For me and the Family. A business to be used to turn black money white. But I had to move quickly. Certainly I did not wish to keep it a secret and the proof is that I used Family resources which you must come to know. I wanted to come to you with the deed done."

The Don was smiling at him when he asked gently, "And is the deed done?"

Cross immediately sensed that the Don knew everything. "There is another problem," Cross said, and explained the new deal he had made with Marrion. He was surprised when the Don laughed aloud.

"You did exactly right," the Don said. "A court case might be a disaster. Let them have their victory. But what rascals they are. It's a good thing we always stayed out of that business." He paused for a moment. "At least you've made your ten million. That's a tidy sum."

"No," Cross said. "Five for me and five for the Family, that is understood. I don't think we should be discouraged so easily. I have some plans but I must have Family help."

"Then we must discuss better shares," Giorgio said. He was like Bantz, Cross thought, always pressing for more.

The Don interrupted impatiently. "First catch the rabbit then we will share it. You have the Family blessing. But one thing. Full discussion on everything drastic that is done. You understand me, nephew?"

"Yes," Cross said.

He left Quogue with a feeling of relief. The Don had shown his affection.

Don Domenico Clericuzio, in his eighties, still commanded his Empire. A world he had created with great endeavor and at great cost and so therefore felt he had earned.

At a venerable age, when most men are obsessed with sins inevitably committed, the regrets of lost dreams, and even doubts of their own righteousness, the Don was still as unshakable in his virtue as when he was fourteen.

Don Clericuzio was strict in his beliefs and strict in his judgments. God had created a perilous world, and mankind had made it even more dangerous. God's world was a prison in which man had to earn his daily bread, and his fellow man was a fellow beast, carnivorous and without mercy. Don Clericuzio was proud that he had guarded his loved ones safely in their journey through life.

He was content that, at his advanced age, he had the will to pass the sentence of death on his enemies. Certainly he forgave them, was he not a Christian who maintained a holy chapel in his own home? But he forgave his enemies as God forgives all men while condemning them to inevitable extinction.

In the world Don Clericuzio had created, he was revered. His family, the thousands who lived in the Bronx Enclave, the *Bru-*

gliones who ruled territories and entrusted their money to him and came for his intercession when they got into trouble with the formal society. They knew that the Don was just. That in time of need, sickness, or any trouble, they could go to him and he would address their misfortunes. And so they loved him.

The Don knew that love is not a reliable emotion no matter how deep. Love does not ensure gratitude, does not ensure obedience, does not provide harmony in so difficult a world. No one understood this better than Don Clericuzio. To inspire *true* love, one also had to be feared. Love alone was contemptible, it was nothing if it did not also include trust and obedience. What good was love to him if it did not acknowledge his rule?

For he was responsible for their lives, he was the root of their good fortune, and so he could not falter in his duty. He must be strict in his judgment. If a man betrayed him, if a man damaged the integrity of his world, that man must be punished and restrained even if it meant a sentence of death. There could be no excuse, no mitigating circumstance, no appeal to pity. What must be done must be done. His son Giorgio had once called him archaic. He accepted that this could not be otherwise.

Now he had many things to ponder. He had planned well over the last twenty-five years since the Santadio war. He had been farsighted, cunning, brutal when necessary, and merciful when it was safe to be so. And now the Clericuzio Family was at the height of its power, seemingly safe from any attack. Soon it would disappear into the legal fabric of society and become invulnerable.

But Don Domenico had not survived so long by being optimistically shortsighted. He could spot a malignant weed before it popped its head above the ground. The great danger now was internal, the rise of Dante, his growing into manhood in a manner not entirely satisfactory to the Don.

Then there was Cross, enriched by the Gronevelt legacy, actually making a major move without Family supervision. The young man had started so brilliantly, nearly becoming a Qualified Man, like his father, Pippi. Then the Virginio Ballazzo job had turned him finicky. And after being excused from operational duties by the Family because of his tender heart, he had gone back into the field for his own personal gain and executed that man Skannet. Without the permission of the Don himself. But Don Clericuzio excused himself for condoning these actions, for his rare sentimentalities. Cross was trying to escape his world and enter another. Though these actions were or could be the seeds of treason, Don Clericuzio understood. Still, Pippi and Cross combined would be a threat to the Family. Also, the Don was not unaware of Dante's hatred for the De Lenas. Pippi was too clever not to know this also, and Pippi was a dangerous man. An eye must be kept on him despite his proven loyalty.

The Don's forbearance sprang from a fondness for Cross and a love for Pippi, his old and faithful soldier, his sister's son. After all, they had Clericuzio blood. He was truly more worried about the danger to the Family presented by Dante.

Don Clericuzio had always been a fond and loving grandfather to Dante. The two had been very close until the boy was about ten years old and a certain disenchantment had settled in. The Don detected traits in the boy's character that troubled him.

Dante at the age of ten was an exuberant, slyly humorous child. He was a good athlete with great physical coordination. He loved to talk, especially with his grandfather, and he had long secret conversations with his mother, Rose Marie. But then, after the age of ten, he became malicious and crude. He fought with boys his own age with inappropriate intensity. He teased girls mercilessly and with an innocent lewdness that was shocking though funny. He tortured small animals—not necessarily significant with small boys, as the Don knew—but he tried once to drown a smaller boy in the school swimming pool.

Not that the Don was particularly judgmental of these things. After all, children were animals, civilization had to be drummed into their brains and backsides. There had been children like Dante who had grown up to be saints. What disturbed the Don was his loquacity, his long conversations with his mother, and most of all, his small disobediences to the Don himself.

Perhaps what disturbed the Don as well, who was in awe of the vagaries of nature, was that at the age of fifteen, Dante stopped growing. He remained at the height of five feet three inches. Doctors were consulted and agreed that at the most he would grow three more inches, and not to the usual Clericuzio family height of six feet. The Don considered Dante's short stature to be a danger signal, as he also considered twins. He claimed that while birth was a blessed miracle, twins were going too far. There had been a soldier in the Bronx Enclave who had fathered triplets, and the Don, horrified, bought them a grocery store in Portland, Oregon, a good living but a lonely one. The Don also had superstitions about left-handed people, and those who stuttered. Whatever anyone said, these could not be good signs. Dante was naturally left-handed.

But even all this would not have been enough to make the Don wary of his grandchild or lessen his affection; anyone of his blood was naturally exempt. But as Dante grew older he grew more contrary to the Don's dreams of his future.

Dante quit school in his sixteenth year and immediately pushed his nose into Family affairs. He worked for Vincent in his restaurant. He was a popular waiter and earned huge tips because of his quickness and his wit. Tiring of that, he worked for two months in Giorgio's Wall Street office but hated it and showed no aptitude, despite Giorgio's earnest attempts to teach him the intricacies of paper wealth. Finally he settled in with Petie's construction company and loved working with the Enclave soldiers. He was proud of his body, which grew more and more muscular. But in all this he acquired to some degree certain characteristics of his three uncles, which the Don noted with pride. He had Vincent's directness, Giorgio's coolness, and Petie's ferocity. Somewhere along the way, he established his own personality, what he truly was: sly, cunning, devious, but with a sense of fun that could be charming. And it was then he began wearing his Renaissance hats.

The hats—nobody knew where he got them—were made of colorful iridescent thread; some were round, some were rectangular, and they rode on his head as if they were on water. They seemed to make him taller, handsomer, and more likable. Partly because they were clownlike and disarming, partly because they balanced his two profiles. The hats suited him. They disguised his hair, jet black and ropey as with all the Clericuzio.

One day in the den, where Silvio's photo still occupied the place of honor, Dante asked his grandfather, "How did he die?"

The Don said shortly, "An accident."

"He was your favorite son, right?" Dante asked.

The Don was startled by all this. Dante was still only fifteen. "Why would this be true?" the Don asked.

"Because he's dead," Dante said with a sly grin, and it took the Don a few moments to realize that this raw youth had dared to make such a joke.

The Don also knew that Dante roamed and searched his office suite in the house when the Don was down at dinner. This did not disturb him, children were always curious about the old and the Don never had anything on paper that would divulge information of any kind. Don Clericuzio had a huge blackboard in a corner of his brain that was chalked with all necessary information, including the totals of all the sins and virtues of those dearest to him.

But as Don Clericuzio became more wary of Dante, he showed him even more affection, assuring the boy he was to be one of the heirs to his Family Empire. And rebukes and admonitions were given the boy by his uncles, primarily Giorgio.

Finally, the Don despaired of Dante joining the retreat into a legal society and gave his permission for Dante to train to be a Hammer.

The Don heard his daughter, Rose Marie, calling him to dinner in the kitchen where they ate when it was just the two of them. He went in, sat in the chair in front of the large, colorful bowl of angel hair pasta covered with tomatoes and fresh basil from his garden. She put the silver bowl of grated cheese before him, the cheese was very yellow, which proved its nutty sweetness. Rose Marie came to sit opposite him. She was gay and cheerful, and he was delighted by her good humor. Tonight there would be none of her terrible fits. She was as she had been before the Santadio War.

What a tragedy that had been, one of the few mistakes he had made, one that proved a victory was not always a victory. But who would have thought that Rose Marie would remain forever a widow?

Lovers always loved again, he'd always believed that. At that moment the Don felt an overpowering affection for his daughter. She would excuse Dante's small sins. Rose Marie leaned over and gave the Don's grizzled head an affectionate caress.

He took a huge spoonful of the grated cheese and felt its nutty heat against his gums. He sipped his wine and watched Rose Marie carve the leg of lamb. She served him three crusty brown potatoes, glossy with fat. His troubled mind cleared. Who was better than him?

He was in such a good mood that he let Rose Marie persuade him to watch television with her in the sitting room for the second time that week.

After watching four hours filled with horror, he said to Rose Marie, "Is it possible to live in such a world where everyone does what he pleases? No one is punished by God or man and no one has to earn a living? Are there such women who follow every whim? Men such foolish weaklings, who succumb to every little desire, every little dream of happiness? Where are the honest husbands who work to earn their bread, who think of the best ways to protect their children from fate and the cruel world? Where are the people who understand a piece of cheese, a glass of wine, a warm house at the end of the day is reward enough? Who are these people who yearn for some mysterious happiness? What an uproar they make of life, what tragedies they brew up out of nothing." The Don patted his daughter on the head and waved at the television screen with a dismissive hand. He said, "Let them all swim at the bottom of the ocean." Then he gave her a final piece of wisdom. "Everyone is responsible for everything he does."

That night, alone in his bedroom, the Don stepped out on his balcony. The houses in the compound were all brightly illuminated; he could hear the thwack of tennis balls on the tennis court and see the players underneath its bank of lights. There were no children playing outdoors so late. He could see the guards on the gate and around the house.

He pondered what steps he could take to prevent future tragedy. His love for his daughter and grandson washed over him, that was what made old age worthwhile. He would simply have to protect them as best he could. Then he was angry with himself. Why was he always foreseeing tragedy? He had solved all the problems in his life and he would solve this one.

Still, his mind whirled with plans. He thought of Senator Wavven. For years he had given the man millions of dollars to get legislation passed to ensure legalized gambling. But the senator was slippery. It was too bad that Gronevelt was not still alive; Cross and Giorgio did not have the necessary skill to prod him. Perhaps the gambling empire would never come to pass.

Then he thought of his old friend David Redfellow, now living so comfortably in Rome. Perhaps it was time to bring him back into the Family. It was all very well for Cross to be so forgiving of his Hollywood partners. After all, he was young. He could not know that one sign of weakness might be fatal. The Don decided he would summon David Redfellow from Rome to do something about the movie business.

CHAPTER 11

A WEEK AFTER the death of Boz Skannet, Cross received, through Claudia, a dinner invitation to Athena Aquitane's house in Malibu.

Cross flew from Vegas to L.A., rented a car, and arrived at the Malibu Colony guarded gatehouse as the sun began to fall into the ocean. There was no longer any special security, though there was still the secretary in the guest house who checked and buzzed him in. He walked through the longitudinal garden to the house on the beach. There was still the little South American maid, who led him to the sea-green living room that seemed just out of reach of the Pacific Ocean waves.

Athena was waiting for him, and she was even more beautiful than he remembered. She was dressed in a green blouse and slacks, and she seemed to melt and become part of the mist over the ocean behind her. He could not take his eyes off her. She shook his hand in greeting, not the usual Hollywood kiss on both cheeks. She had drinks ready and she handed him one. It was Evian water with lime. They sat in the large, mint green upholstered chairs that faced the ocean. The descending sun scattered gold coins of light in the room.

Cross was so aware of her beauty that he had to bow his head to avoid looking at her. The golden helmet of hair, the creamy skin, the way her long body sprawled in her chair. Some of the gold coins fell into her green eyes, fleeting shadows. He felt an urgent desire to touch her, to be closer to her, to own her.

Athena seemed unaware of the emotions she was causing. She sipped her drink and said quietly, "I wanted to thank you for keeping me in the movie business."

The sound of her voice further entranced Cross. It was not sultry or inviting. But it had such a velvet tone, it had such regal confidence and yet was so warm, that he just wanted her to keep talking. Jesus Christ, he thought, what the hell is this? He was ashamed of her power over him. His head still down, he murmured, "I thought I could get you back to work by appealing to your greed."

"That is not one of my many weaknesses," Athena said. Now she turned her head from the ocean so that she could look directly into his eyes. "Claudia told me the Studio reneged on their deal once my husband killed himself. You had to give them back the picture and take a percentage."

Cross kept his face impassive. He hoped to banish everything he was feeling about her. "I guess I'm not a very good businessman," he said. He wanted to give her the impression that he was ineffective.

"Molly Flanders wrote your contract," Athena said. "She's the best. You could have held on."

Cross shrugged. "A matter of politics. I want to get into the movie business permanently and didn't want enemies as powerful as Loddstone Studios."

"I could help you," Athena said. "I could refuse to return to the picture."

Cross felt a thrill that she would do that for him. He considered the offer. The Studio might still take him to court. Also, he could not bear to make Athena put him in her debt. And then it occurred to him that though Athena was beautiful that didn't mean she was not clever.

"Why would you do that?" he asked.

Athena got up from her chair and moved to stand close to the picture window. The beaches were gray shadows, the sun had disappeared, and the ocean seemed to reflect the mountain ranges behind her house and the Pacific Coast Highway. She gazed out toward the now blue-black water, the small waves rippling in slyly. She did not turn her head to him when she said, "Why would I do that? Simply because I knew Boz Skannet better than anybody. And I don't care if he left a hundred suicide notes, he would never kill himself."

Cross shrugged. "Dead is dead," he said.

"That's true," Athena said. She turned to face him, looked directly at him. "You buy the picture and suddenly Boz conveniently commits suicide. You're my candidate as the killer." Even stern, her face was so beautiful to Cross that his voice was not as steady as he would have wished.

"How about the Studio?" Cross said. "Marrion is one of the most powerful men in the country. What about Bantz and Skippy Deere?"

Athena shook her head. "They understood what I was asking them. Just as you did. They didn't do it, they sold the picture to you. They didn't care if I was killed after the picture was finished, but you did. And I knew you would help me even when you said you couldn't. When I heard about you buying the picture, I knew exactly what you would do, but I must say I didn't think you could be so clever."

Suddenly she came toward him and he rose from his chair. She took his hands in hers. He could smell her body, her breath.

Athena said, "That was the only evil thing I have ever done in my life. Making somebody commit murder. It was terrible. I would have been a much better person if I had done it myself. But I couldn't."

Cross said, "Why were you so sure I would do something?"

Athena said, "Claudia told me so much about you. I understood who you were but she's so naïve, she still hasn't caught on. She thinks you're just a tough guy with a lot of clout."

Cross became very alert. She was trying to get him to admit his guilt. Something he would never do even to a priest, not even to God himself.

Athena said, "And the way you looked at me. A lot of men have looked at me that way. I'm not being immodest, I know I'm beautiful, people have been telling me that since I was a child. I always knew I had power, but I could never really understand that power. I'm not really happy with it but I use it. What they call 'love.' "

Cross let go of her hands. "Why were you so afraid of your husband? Because he could ruin your career?"

For one moment there was a flash of anger in her eyes. "It wasn't my career," she said, "and it wasn't out of fear, though I knew he would kill me. I had a better reason." She paused, then said, "I can make them give you the picture back. I can refuse to keep working."

"No," Cross said.

Athena smiled and said with a brilliant, gay cheerfulness, "Then we can just go to bed together. I find you very attractive and I'm sure we'll have a good time."

His first reaction was one of anger, that she could think she could just buy him off. That she was acting a part, using her skill as a woman the same way a man would use physical force. But what really bothered him was that he could hear a faint bit of mockery in her voice. Mockery of his gallantry, and turning his true love into a simple screw. As if she was telling him that his love for her was as fake as her love for him.

He said to her coolly, "I had a long talk with Boz, trying to make a deal. He said he used to fuck you five times a day when you were married."

He was pleased that she seemed startled. She said, "I wasn't counting, but it was a lot. I was eighteen and I really loved him. Isn't it funny that now I wanted him dead?" She frowned a moment and said, casually, "What else did you talk about?"

Cross looked at her grimly. "Boz told me the terrible secret you had between you. He claims you confessed that when you ran away, you buried your baby in the desert."

Athena's face became a mask, her green eyes went dull. For the first time that night, Cross felt she could not possibly be acting. Her face had a pallor no actress could achieve. She whispered to him, "Do you really believe I murdered my baby?"

"Boz said that's what you told him," Cross said.

"I did tell him that," Athena said. "Now, I'm asking you again. Do you believe I murdered my baby?"

There is nothing so terrible as to condemn a beautiful woman. Cross knew that if he answered truthfully, he would lose her forever. Suddenly he put his arms around her very gently. "You're too beautiful. Nobody as beautiful as you could do that." The eternal worship of men for beauty against all evidence. "No," he said. "I don't believe you did."

She stepped away from him. "Even though I'm responsible for Boz?"

"You're not responsible," Cross said. "He killed himself."

Athena was gazing at him intently. He took her hands. "Do you believe I killed Boz?" he asked.

And then Athena smiled, an actress who finally realized how to play a scene. "No more than you believe I killed my baby."

They smiled, they had declared each other innocent. She took his hand and said, "Now, I'm cooking dinner for you and then we're going to bed." She led him into the kitchen.

How many times had she played this scene, Cross thought jealously. The beautiful Queen performing housewifely duties like an ordinary woman. He watched her cook. She wore no protective clothing and she was extraordinarily professional. She spoke to him as she chopped vegetables, prepared a skillet, and set the table. She gave him a bottle of wine to open, holding his hand and brushing against his body. She saw him looking with admiration when the table was laden after just a half hour.

She said, "I played a woman chef in one of my first roles, so I went to school to get everything right. And one critic wrote, 'When Athena Aquitane acts as well as she cooks, she will be a star.' "

They ate in the alcove of the kitchen so they could look at the rolling ocean. The food was delicious, little squares of beef covered with vegetables and then a salad of bitter greens. There was a platter of cheeses and warm short loaves of bread, plump as pigeons. Then there was espresso with a small, light lemon tart.

"You should have been a cook," Cross said, "My cousin Vincent would hire you for his restaurants any day."

"Oh, I could have been anything," Athena said with mock boastfulness.

All through dinner she had touched him casually in a way that was sexual, as if she were searching for some spirit in his flesh. Cross with every touch yearned to feel her body on his. By the end of the meal, he no longer could taste what he was eating. Finally they were done and Athena took him by the hand and led him out of the kitchen and up the two flights of stairs to her bedroom. She did it gracefully, almost shyly, almost blushing, as if she were an eager virginal bride. Cross marveled at her acting ability.

The large bedroom was at the very top of the house and had a small balcony that looked out over the ocean. The walls were covered with a weird, garish painting that seemed to light up the room.

They stood on the balcony and watched the room illuminate the beach sand with a spooky yellow glow, the other Malibu houses squatted along the water showing little boxes of light. Tiny birds, as if playing a game, ran in and out of the incoming waves to escape getting wet.

Athena put her hand on Cross's shoulder, around his body, the other hand reaching out to pull his mouth down to hers. They kissed for a long time as the warm ocean air washed over them. Then Athena led him inside the bedroom.

She undressed quickly, slipping out of her green blouse and slacks. Her white body flashed in the moon-ridden darkness. She was as beautiful as he had imagined. The rising breasts with their raspberry nipples seemed spun of sugar. Her long legs, the curve of her hips, the blond hair at her crotch, her absolute stillness, limned by misty ocean air.

Cross reached out for her body and her flesh was velvet, her lips filled with the scent of flowers. The sheer joy of touching her was so sweet he could not do anything else. Athena began to undress him. She did so gently, running her hands over his body as he had over hers. Then, kissing him, she gently pulled him onto the bed.

Cross made love with a passion he had never known or even dreamed existed. He was so urgent that Athena had to stroke his face to gentle him. He could not let loose of her body, even after they climaxed. They lay intertwined until they began again. She was even more ardent than before, as if it was some sort of contest, some sort of avowal. Finally they both drifted off into slumber.

Cross awoke just as the sun showed above the horizon. For the first time in his life, he had a headache. Naked, he moved onto the balcony and sat on one of the straw chairs. He watched the sun slyly rise slowly from the ocean and begin its ascent to the sky.

She was a dangerous woman. The murderer of her own child, whose bones were now filled with desert sand. And she was too skillful in bed. She could be the end of him. At that moment he decided he would never see her again.

Then he felt her arms around his neck and his face twisted around to kiss her. She was in a white fluffy bathrobe, and her hair was held in place by pins that glittered like jewels in a crown. "Take a shower and I'll make you breakfast before you go," she said.

She led him into the double bathroom, two sinks, two marble counters, two bathtubs, and two showers. It was stocked with men's toilet articles, razors, shaving cream, skin toners, brushes, and combs.

When he had finished and was out on the balcony again, Athena brought a tray with croissants, coffee, and orange juice to the table. "I can make you bacon and eggs," she said.

"This is fine," Cross said.

"When will I see you again?" Athena asked.

"I have lots of things to do in Las Vegas," Cross said. "I'll call you next week."

Athena gave him an appraising look. "That means good-bye, doesn't it?" she asked. "And I really enjoyed last night."

Cross shrugged. "You paid off your obligation," he said.

She gave him a good-humored grin and said, "And with amazing goodwill, don't you think? It wasn't begrudging."

Cross laughed. "No," he said.

She seemed to read his mind. Last night they had lied to each other, this morning the lies had no power. She seemed to know that her beauty was too much for him to trust. That he felt in danger with her, and with her confessed sins. She seemed deep in thought and ate silently. Then she said to him, "I know you're busy but I have something to show you. Can you spare this morning and catch an afternoon plane? It's important. I want to take you someplace."

Cross could not resist spending one last time with her and so he said yes.

Athena drove them in her car, a Mercedes SL 300, and took the highway south to San Diego. But just before they reached the city, she turned off into a thin road that led inland through the mountains.

In fifteen minutes they came to a compound enclosed by barbed wire. Inside the compound were six redbrick buildings separated by green lawns and connected by sky blue painted walkways. In one of the green squares, a group of about twenty children were playing with a soccer ball. On another green about ten children were flying kites. There was a group of three or four adults standing around watching them, but something seemed odd about the scene. When the soccer ball flew through the air, it seemed most of the children ran away from it, while on the other square the kites flew up, up, into the sky and never returned.

"What is this place?" Cross asked.

Athena looked pleadingly at him. "Just come with me please for now. Later, you can ask your questions."

Athena drove to the entry gate and showed a gold ID badge to the security guard. Passing through, she drove to the largest building and parked.

Once inside at the reception desk, Athena asked the attendant something in a low voice. Cross stood back, but still he heard the answer. "She was in a mood so we gave her a hug in her room."

"What the hell was that?" Cross asked.

But Athena didn't answer. She took his hand and led him through a long, shiny tile hallway to an adjoining building and into some sort of dormitory.

A nurse sitting at the entrance asked their names. When she nodded, Athena led Cross down another long hallway of doors. Finally, she opened one.

They were standing in a pretty bedroom, large and full of light. There were the same strange, dark paintings as on the wall in Athena's house, but here they were strewn on the floor. On the wall a small shelf held a row of pretty dolls dressed in starched Amish costumes. Also on the floor were several other scraps of drawings and paintings.

There was a small bed covered with a pink fuzzy blanket, the pillows white with red roses stitched all over them. But there was no child in the bed.

Athena walked toward a large box that was open at the top, its walls and base covered with a thick, soft pad colored light blue, and when Cross looked inside he saw the child lying there. She didn't notice them. She was fiddling with a knob at the head of the box, and Cross watched as she forced the pads together, almost crushing herself.

She was a small girl of ten, a tiny copy of Athena, but without emotion, devoid of all expression, and her green eyes were as unseeing as those of a porcelain doll. Yet each time she turned the controls to make the panels squeeze her tight, her face shone with complete serenity. She did not acknowledge them in any way.

Athena moved to the top of the wooden box. She switched the controls so that she could lift the child out of the box. The child seemed to weigh almost nothing.

Athena held her like an infant and bent her head to kiss the child's cheek, but the child flinched and pulled away.

"It's your mommy," Athena said. "Won't you give me a kiss?"

The tone of her voice broke Cross's heart. It was an abject pleading, but now the child was churning wildly within her arms. Finally Athena gently put her down on the floor. The child scrambled to her knees and immediately picked up a box of paints and a huge cardboard sheet. Completely absorbed, she began to paint.

Cross stood back and watched as Athena tried all her acting skill to establish a rapport with the child. First she kneeled down next to the little girl and was the loving playmate helping her daughter paint, but the child took no notice.

Athena then sat up, tried to be a confiding parent telling the child what was happening in the world. Then Athena became a fawning adult praising the child's paintings. To all this the child merely kept moving away. Athena picked up one of the brushes and tried to help, but when the child did see, she grabbed the brush away. She never said a word.

Finally Athena gave up.

"I'll come back tomorrow, darling," she said. "I'll take you for a ride and I'll bring a new paint box. See," she said, tears welling in her eyes, "you're running out of reds." She tried to give the child a farewell kiss but was held away by two small, beautiful hands.

Finally Athena rose and led Cross out of the room.

Athena gave him the keys to the car so he could drive back to Malibu, and during the ride, she held her head in her hands and wept. Cross was so stunned he could not say a word.

When they got out of the car, Athena seemed to have control of herself. She pulled Cross into the house and then turned and faced him. "That was the baby I told Boz I buried in the desert. Now do you believe me?" And for the first time Cross really believed she might love him.

Athena led him into the kitchen and made coffee. They sat in the alcove to watch the ocean. As they drank their coffee, Athena started speaking. She talked casually, no emotion in her voice or on her face.

"When I ran away from Boz, I left my baby with some distant cousins, a married couple in San Diego. She seemed a normal baby. I didn't know she was autistic then, maybe she wasn't. I left her there because I was determined to be a successful actress. I had to make money for both of us. I was sure I was talented and God knows everybody told me how beautiful I was. I always thought that when I was successful, I could take my baby back."

"So I worked in Los Angeles and visited her in San Diego whenever I could. Then I began to break through and I didn't see her that often, maybe once a month. Finally when I was ready to bring her home I went to her third birthday party with all kinds of presents, but Bethany seemed to have slipped into another world. She was a blank. I couldn't reach her at all. I was frantic. I thought maybe she had a brain tumor, I remembered when Boz had let her fall on the floor, that maybe her brain had been injured and it was now beginning to show. For months after that I brought her to doctors, she underwent a battery of tests of all kinds, I took her to specialists and they checked everything. Then someone, and I don't remember whether it was the doctor in Boston or the psychiatrist in Texas Children's Hospital, told me she was autistic. I didn't even know what that meant except that I thought it was some kind of retardation. 'No,' the doctor said. It meant she lived in her own world, was unaware of other people's existence, had no interest in them, could feel nothing for anything or anyone. It was when I brought her to the clinic here to be close to me that we found she could respond to that hugging machine you saw. That seemed to help, so I had to leave her there."

Cross sat without a word, while Athena continued. "Being autistic meant she could never love me. But the doctors told me some autistic people are talented, even geniuslike. And I think Bethany is a genius. Not only with her painting. Something else. The doctors tell me that after many years of hard training some autistic people can be taught to care for some things, then some people. A few can even live a near-to-normal life. Right now, Bethany can't stand listening to music or any noise. But at first she couldn't bear to have me touch her, and now she's learned to tolerate me, so she's better than she used to be.

"She still rejects me but not as violently. We've made some progress. I used to think it was punishment for my neglect of her because I wanted to be a success. But the specialists say that sometimes though it seems hereditary, it can be acquired, but they don't know what really makes it happen. The doctors told me it had nothing to do with Boz dropping her on her head or me deserting her, but I don't know if I believe that. They kept trying to reassure me that we were not responsible, that it was one of the mysteries of life, maybe it was preordained. They insisted nothing could have prevented it from happening and nothing can ever change it. But again something inside me refuses to believe any of that.

"Even when I first found out, I thought about it constantly. I had to make some hard decisions. I knew I would be helpless to rescue her until I made a lot of money. So I put her in the clinic and visited her at least one weekend a month and some weekdays. Finally, I got rich, I was famous and nothing that mattered before mattered any longer. All I wanted was to be with Bethany. Even if this hadn't happened, I was going to quit after *Messalina* anyway."

"Why?" Cross asked. "What were you going to do?"

"There's a special clinic in France with this great doctor," Athena explained. "And I was going to go there after the picture. Then Boz showed up and I knew he would kill me and Bethany would be all alone. That's why I sort of put a contract out on him. She has nobody but me. And well, I'll bear that sin." Athena paused now and smiled at Cross. "It's worse than the soaps, isn't it?" she said with a small smile.

Cross looked out over the ocean. It was a very bright oily blue in the sunlight. He remembered the little girl and her blank, masklike face that would never open up to this world.

"What was that box she was lying in?" he asked.

Athena laughed. "That's what gives me hope," she said. "Sad, isn't it? It's a hug box. A lot of autistic children use it when they get depressed. It's just like a hug from a person but they don't have to connect or relate to another human being." Athena took a deep breath and said, "Cross, someday I'm going to take the place of that box. That's the whole purpose of my life now. My life has no meaning except for that. Isn't that funny? The Studio tells me that I get thousands of letters from people who love me. In public people want to touch me. Men keep telling me they love me. Everybody but Bethany, and she's the only one I want."

Cross said, "I'll help you in any way I can."

"Then call me next week," Athena said. "Let's be together as much as we can until *Messalina* is finished."

"I'll call," Cross said. "I can't prove my innocence, but I love you more than anything in my life."

"And are you truly innocent?" Athena asked.

"Yes," Cross said. Now that she had been proven innocent, he could not bear for her to know.

Cross thought about Bethany, her blank face so artistically beautiful with its sharp planes, its mirror eyes; the rare human being totally free of sin.

As for Athena, she had been judging Cross. Of all the people she knew, he was the only one who had ever seen her daughter since the child had been diagnosed as autistic. It had been a test.

One of the greatest shocks of her life came when she found out that though she was so beautiful, though she was so talented (and, she thought with self-mockery, so kind, so gentle, so generous), her closest friends, men who loved her, relatives who adored her, sometimes seemed to relish her misfortunes.

It was when Boz had given her a black eye, and though everyone called Boz a "no-good bastard," she caught in all of them a fleeting look of satisfaction. At first she thought she had imagined it, was too sensitive. But when Boz had given her the second black eye, she caught those looks again. And she had been terribly hurt. For this time she had understood completely.

Of course they all loved her, she did not doubt that. But it seemed no one could resist a little touch of malice. Greatness in any form arouses envy.

One of the reasons she loved Claudia was because Claudia had never betrayed her with that look.

It was why she kept Bethany so secret from her day-to-day life. She hated the idea that people she loved would have that fleeting look of satisfaction, that she had been punished for her own beauty.

So though she knew the power of her beauty and used that power, she despised it. She longed for the day when lines would cut deep into her perfect face, each showing a path she had taken, a journey survived, when her body would fill out, soften and enlarge her to provide comfort for those she'd hold and care for, and her eyes would grow more liquid with mercy from all the suffering she'd witnessed and all the tears she'd never shed. She'd grow smile lines around her mouth from laughing at herself, and at life itself. How free she would be when she no longer feared the consequences of her physical beauty and instead delighted in its loss as it was replaced by a more enduring serenity.

And so she had kept careful watch on Cross De Lena when he met Bethany, saw his slight recoil at first but then afterward nothing. She knew he was helplessly in love with her and she saw he did not have that certain look of satisfaction when he knew of her misfortune with Bethany.

CHAPTER 12

CLAUDIA WAS DETERMINED to cash in on her sexual marker with Eli Marrion; she would shame him into giving Ernest Vail the points he wanted on his novel. It was a long shot, but she was willing to compromise her principles. Bobby Bantz was implacable on gross points, but Eli Marrion was unpredictable and had a soft spot for her. Besides, it was an honorable custom in the movie business that sexual congress, no matter how brief, demanded a certain material courtesy.

Vail's threat of suicide had been the trigger for this meeting. If carried out, the rights to his novel would revert to his former wife and her children, and Molly Flanders would drive a hard bargain. Nobody believed in the threat, not even Claudia, but Bobby Bantz and Eli Marrion, operating from their knowledge of what they would do for money, always had to worry.

When Claudia, Ernest, and Molly arrived at LoddStone, they found only Bobby Bantz in the executive suite. He looked uncomfortable, though he tried to disguise it with effusive greetings, especially to Vail. "Our National Treasure," he said and hugged Ernest with respectful affection.

Molly was immediately alert, wary. "Where's Eli?" she said. "He's the only one who can make the final decision on this."

Bantz's voice was reassuring. "Eli's in the hospital, Cedar Sinai, nothing serious, just a checkup. That's confidential. The LoddStone stock goes up and down on his health."

Claudia said dryly, "He's over eighty, everything is serious."

"No, no," Bantz said. "We do business every day in the hospital. He's even sharper. So present your case to me and I'll tell him your story when I visit."

"No," Molly said curtly.

But Ernest Vail said, "Let's talk to Bobby."

They presented their case. Bantz was amused but did not laugh outright. He said, "I've heard everything in this town but this is a beauty. I ran it by my lawyers and they say that Vail's demise does not affect our rights. It's a complicated legal point."

"Run it by your PR people," Claudia said. "If Ernest does it and the whole story comes out LoddStone will look like shit. Eli won't like that. He has more moral sense."

"Than me?" Bobby Bantz said politely. But he was furious. Why didn't people understand that Marrion approved everything he did. He turned to Ernest and said, "How would you knock yourself off? Gun, knife, out the window?"

Vail grinned at him. "Hara-kiri on your desk, Bobby." They all laughed.

"We're getting nowhere," Molly said. "Why can't we all go to the hospital and see Eli?"

Vail said, "I'm not going to a sick man's hospital bed and argue about money."

They all looked at him sympathetically. Of course in conventional terms it seemed insensitive. But men in sickbeds planned murders, revolution, frauds, studio betrayals. A hospital bed was not a true sanctuary. And they knew that Vail's protest was basically a romantic convention.

Molly said coldly, "Keep your mouth shut, Ernest, if you want to remain my client. Eli has screwed a hundred people from his hospital bed. Bobby, let's make a sensible deal. LoddStone has a gold mine in the sequels. You can afford to give Ernest a couple of gross points, for insurance."

Bantz was horrified, a hot stab went through his bowels. "*Gross points?*" he shouted incredulously. "Never."

"OK," Molly said. "How about a structured five percent of the net? No advertising charges, no interest deductions or gross points to the stars."

Bantz said contemptuously, "That's almost gross. And we all know that Ernest won't kill himself. That's too stupid and he is too intelligent." What he really wanted to say was that the guy didn't have the balls.

"Why gamble?" Molly said. "I've gone over the figures. You plan at least three sequels. That's at least a half billion in rentals including foreign but not the videos and TV. And God knows how much money you fucking thieves make in video. So why not give Ernest points, a measly twenty million. You would give that to any half-assed star."

Bantz thought it over. Then he turned on the charm. "Ernest," he said, "as a novelist you are a National Treasure. No one respects you more than me. And Eli has read every one of your books. He absolutely adores you. So we want to come to an accommodation."

Claudia was embarrassed at how Ernest obviously swallowed this bullshit, though to his credit, he shuddered a bit at the "National Treasure."

"Be specific," he said. Now Claudia was proud of him.

Bantz spoke to Molly. "How about a five-year contract at ten grand a week to write original scripts and do some rewrites and of course on the originals we only get first look. And for every rewrite he gets an additional fifty grand a week. In five years he could make as much as ten million."

"Double the money," Molly said. "Then we can talk."

At this point Vail seemed to lose his almost angelic patience. "None of you are taking me seriously," he said. "I can do simple arithmetic. Bobby, your deal is only worth two and a half. You'll never buy an original script from me and I'll never do one. You'll never give me rewrites. And what if you make six sequels? Then you make a billion." Vail began to laugh with genuine enjoyment. "Two and a half million dollars doesn't help me."

"What the fuck are you laughing about?" Bobby said.

Vail was almost hysterical. "I never dreamed in my life of even one million and now it doesn't help me."

Claudia knew Vail's sense of humor. She said, "Why doesn't it help you?"

"Because I'll still be alive," Vail said. "My family needs the points. They trusted me and I betrayed them."

They would have been touched, even Bantz, except that Vail sounded so false, so self-satisfied.

Molly Flanders said, "Let's go talk to Eli."

Vail lost his temper completely and stormed out of the door shouting, "I can't deal with you people. I won't beg a man on a hospital bed."

When he was gone, Bobby Bantz said, "And you two want to stick up for that guy?"

"Why not?" Molly said. "I represented a guy who stabbed his mother and his own three kids. Ernest is no worse than him."

"And what's your excuse?" Bantz asked Claudia.

"We writers have to stick together," she said wryly. They all laughed.

"I guess that's about it," Bobby said. "I did the best I could, right?"

Claudia said, "Bobby, why can't you give him a point or two, it's only fair."

"Because over the years he's screwed a thousand writers and stars and directors. It's a matter of principle," Molly said.

"That's right," Bantz said. "And when they have the muscle they screw us. That's business."

Molly said to Bantz with fake concern, "Eli is okay? Nothing serious?"

"He's fine," Bantz said. "Don't sell your stock."

Molly pounced. "Then he can see us."

Claudia said, "I want to see him anyway. I really care about Eli. He gave me my first break."

Bantz shrugged them off. Molly said, "You will really kick yourself if Ernest knocks himself off. Those sequels are worth more than I said. I softened him up for you."

Bantz said scornfully, "That schmuck won't kill himself. He doesn't have the balls."

"From 'National Treasure' to 'schmuck,' " Claudia said musingly.

Molly said, "The guy is definitely a little crazy. He'll croak out of sheer carelessness."

"Does he do drugs?" Bantz asked, a little worried.

"No," Claudia said, "but Ernest is full of surprises. He's a true eccentric who doesn't even know he's eccentric."

Bantz pondered this for a moment. There was some merit in their argument. And besides he never believed in making unnecessary enemies. He didn't want Molly Flanders to carry a grudge against him. The woman was a terror.

"Let me call Eli," he said. "If he gives the okay, I'll take you to the hospital." He was sure that Marrion would refuse.

But to his surprise, Marrion said, "By all means, they can all come to see me."

They drove to the hospital in Bantz's limo, which was a big stretch job but by no means luxurious. It was fitted with a fax, a computer, and a cellular phone. A bodyguard supplied by Pacific Ocean Security sat next to the driver. Another security car with two men followed behind.

The brown-tinted windows of the limo presented the city in a beige monochrome of old-time cowboy movies. As they progressed inward, the buildings became taller, as if they were penetrating a deep stone forest. Claudia was always amazed how in the short space of ten minutes she could go from a mildly bucolic small-town green to a metropolis of concrete and glass.

In Cedars Sinai, the hospital corridors seemed as vast as the halls of an airport, but the ceiling compressed like a bizarre camera shot in a German impressionist movie. They were met by a hospital coordinator, a handsome women dressed in a severe but high-couture suit who reminded Claudia of the "Hosts" in Vegas hotels.

She led them to a special elevator that took them nonstop to the top penthouse suites.

These suites had huge carved black oak doors that reached from floor to ceiling, with shiny brass knobs. The doors opened like gates, to a suite of a hospital bedroom, a larger, open-walled room with dining table and chairs, a sofa and lounge chairs, and a secretarial niche that held a computer and fax. There was also a small kitchen space and guest bathroom in addition to the bathroom for the patient. The ceiling was very high and the absence of walls between the kitchen niche, the living room area, and the business nook gave the whole room the look of a movie set.

Lying on a crisp, white hospital bed, propped up by huge pillows, was Eli Marrion. He was reading an orange-covered script. On the table beside him were business folders with budgets of movies in production. A pretty young secretary seated on the other side of the bed was taking notes. Marrion always liked pretty women around him.

Billy Bantz kissed Marrion on the cheek and said, "Eli, you look great, just great." Molly and Claudia also kissed him on the cheek. Claudia had insisted on bringing flowers, and put them on the bed. Such familiarities were excused because the great Eli Marrion was ill.

Claudia was noting all the details as if researching a script. Medical dramas were almost financially foolproof.

In fact, Eli Marrion was not looking "great just great." His lips were ridged with blue lines that seemed drawn with ink, he gasped for air when he spoke. Two green prongs grew from his nostrils, the prongs attached to a thin plastic tube that ran to a bubbling bottle of water that was plugged into the wall, all connected to some oxygen tank hidden there.

Marrion noted her gaze. "Oxygen," he said.

"Only temporary," Bobby Bantz said hurriedly. "Makes it easier for him to breathe."

Molly Flanders ignored them. "Eli," she said, "I've explained the situation to Bobby and he needs your OK."

Marrion seemed to be in good humor. "Molly," he said, "you were always the toughest lawyer in this town. Are you going to harass me on my deathbed?"

Claudia was distressed. "Eli, Bobby told us you were okay. And we really wanted to see you." She was so obviously ashamed that Marrion raised his hand with acceptance and benediction.

"I understand all the arguments," Marrion said. He made a motion of dismissal to the secretary and she left the room. The private duty nurse, a handsome, tough-looking woman, was reading a book at the dining room table. Marrion gestured to her to leave. She looked at him and shook her head. She resumed reading.

Marrion laughed, a low wheezing laugh. He said to the others, "That is Priscilla, the best nurse in California. She's an intensive care nurse, that's why she's so tough. My doctor recruited her especially for this case. She's the boss."

Priscilla acknowledged them with a nod of her head and resumed reading.

Molly said, "I'll be willing to limit his points to a maximum of twenty million. It will be insurance. Why take the risk? And why be so unfair?"

Bantz said angrily, "It's not unfair. He signed a contract."

"Fuck you, Bobby," Molly said.

Marrion ignored them. "Claudia, what do you think?"

Claudia was thinking many things. Obviously Marrion was sicker than anyone was admitting. And it was terribly cruel to put pressure on this old man who had to make such an effort to even speak. She was tempted to say that she was leaving, then she remembered that Eli would never have let them come except for some purpose of his own.

"Ernest is a man who does surprising things," Claudia said. "He is determined to provide for his family. But Eli, he's a writer and you always loved writers. Think of it as a contribution to art. Hell, you gave twenty million to the Metropolitan Museum. Why not do it for Ernest?"

"And have all the agents on our ass?" Bantz said.

Eli Marrion took a deep breath, the green prongs seemed to go deeper into his face. "Molly, Claudia, we will have to keep this our little secret. I'll give Vail two gross points to a max of twenty million. I'll give him a million up front. Will that satisfy you?"

Molly thought it over. Two gross points on all the pictures should yield a minimum of fifteen million but maybe more. It was the best she could do, and she was surprised that Marrion had gone so far. If she haggled he was quite capable of withdrawing the offer.

"That's wonderful, Eli, thank you." She leaned over to kiss him on the cheek. "I'll send your office a memo tomorrow. And Eli, I do hope you get well soon."

Claudia could not restrain her emotion. She clasped Eli's hand in hers. She noticed the brown specks that mottled the skin, the hand chilly with approaching death. "You saved Ernest's life."

At that moment Eli Marrion's daughter came into the room with her two small children. The nurse, Priscilla, rose from her chair like a cat scenting mice and moved toward the children, interposing herself between them and the bed. The daughter had been twice divorced and did not get on with her father, but she had a production company on the LoddStone lot because Eli was so fond of his grandchildren.

Claudia and Molly took their leave. They drove to Molly's office and called Ernest to tell him the good news. He insisted on taking them out to dinner to celebrate.

Marrion's daughter and two grandchildren stayed only a short time. But long enough for the daughter to get her father to promise to buy her a very expensive novel for her next movie.

Bobby Bantz and Eli Marrion were alone. "You're a soft touch today," Bantz said.

Marrion felt the weariness in his body, the air being sucked into it. He could relax with Bobby, he never had to act with him. They had been through so much together, used power together, won wars, traveled and schemed through the wide world. They could read each other's minds.

"That novel I'm buying for my daughter, will it make a movie?" Marrion asked.

"Low-budget," Bantz said. "Your daughter makes quote-unquote 'serious' movies."

Marrion made a weary gesture. "Why do we always have to pay for other people's good intentions? Give her a decent writer but no stars. She'll be happy and we won't lose too much money."

"Are you really going to give Vail gross?" Bantz asked. "Our lawyer says we can win in court if he dies."

Marrion said smilingly, "If I get well. If not, it will be up to you. You'll be running the show."

Bantz was astonished at this sentimentality. "Eli, you'll get well, of course you will." And he was absolutely sincere. He had no desire to succeed Eli Marrion, indeed he dreaded the day that inevitably had to come. He could do anything as long as Marrion approved it.

"It's going to be up to you, Bobby," Marrion said. "The truth is that I'm not going to make it. The doctors tell me I need a heart transplant and I've decided not to get one. I can live maybe six months, maybe a year, maybe much less with this lousy heart I have. And besides, I'm too old to qualify for a transplant."

Bantz was stunned. "They can't do a bypass?" he asked. When Marrion shook his head, Bantz went on. "Don't be ridiculous, of course you'll get a transplant. You built half the hospital, they have to give you a heart. You have another good ten years." He paused for a moment. "You're tired, Eli, we'll talk about this tomorrow." But Marrion had dozed off. Bantz left to check with the doctors and then to tell them to start all procedures to harvest a new heart for Eli Marrion.

Ernest Vail, Molly Flanders, and Claudia De Lena celebrated by having dinner at La Dolce Vita on Santa Monica. It was Claudia's favorite restaurant. She had memories of herself as a little girl being brought there by her father and being treated like royalty. She had memories of the bottles of red and white wine being stacked in all the window alcoves, on the back rails of banquettes, and in every vacant space. The customers could reach out and pluck a bottle as if they were grapes.

Ernest Vail was in good spirits, and Claudia wondered again how anybody could believe he would commit suicide. He was bubbling over with glee that his threat had worked. And the very good red wine put them all into a merry mood that was slightly boastful. They were very pleased with themselves. The food itself, robustly Italian, fueled their energy.

"Now what we have to think about," Vail said, "is two points good enough or should we push for three?"

"Don't get greedy," Molly said. "The deal is made."

Vail kissed her hand movie-star style and said, "Molly you're a genius. A ruthless genius, true. How could you two browbeat a guy sick on his hospital bed?"

Molly dipped bread into tomato sauce. "Ernest," she said, "you will never understand this town. There is no mercy. Not when you're drunk, or on coke, or in love, or broke. Why make an exception for sick?"

Claudia said, "Skippy Deere once told me that when you're buying, take people to a Chinese restaurant, but when you're selling, take them to an Italian restaurant. Does that make any sense?"

"He's a producer," Molly said. "He read it someplace. It doesn't mean anything without a context."

Vail was eating with the gusto of a reprieved criminal. He had ordered three different kinds of pasta just for himself but gave small portions to Claudia and Molly and demanded their opinions. "The best Italian food in the world outside Rome," he said. "About Skippy, it makes a certain kind of movie sense. Chinese food is cheap, it brings the price down. Italian food can put you to sleep and make you less sharp. I like both. Isn't it nice to know that Skippy is always scheming?"

Vail always ordered three desserts. Not that he ate all of them, but he wanted to taste many different things at one dinner. In him it did not seem eccentric. Not even the way he dressed, as if clothes were to shield skin from wind or sun, or the way he carelessly shaved, one sideburn cut lower than the other. Not even his threat to kill himself seemed illogical or strange. Nor his complete and childish frankness, which often hurt people's feelings. Claudia was not unused to eccentricity. Hollywood abounded with eccentrics.

"You know, Ernest, you belong to Hollywood. You're eccentric enough," she said.

"I am not an eccentric," Vail said. "I'm not that sophisticated."

"You don't call wanting to kill yourself over a dispute about money eccentric?" Claudia said.

"That was an extremely cool-headed response to our culture," Vail said. "I was tired of being a nobody."

Claudia said impatiently, "How can you think that? You've written ten books, you've won the Pulitzer. You're internationally famous."

Vail had polished off his three pastas and was looking at his entrée, three pearly slices of veal covered with lemon. He picked up a fork and knife. "All that means shit," he said. "I have no money. It took me fifty-five years to learn that if you have no money, you're shit."

Molly said, "You're not eccentric, you're crazy. And stop whining because you're not rich. You're not poor either. Or we wouldn't be here. You're not suffering too much for your art."

Vail put down his knife and fork. He patted Molly's arm. "You're right," he said. "Everything you say is true. I enjoy life from moment to moment. It's the arc of life that gets me down." He drank his glass of wine and then went on matter-of-factly. "I'm never going to write again," he said. "Writing novels is a dead end, like being a black-smith. It's all movies and TV now."

"That's nonsense," Claudia said. "People will always read."

"You're just lazy," Molly said. "Any excuse not to write. That's the real reason why you wanted to kill yourself." They all laughed. Ernest helped them to the veal on his dish and then to the extra desserts. The only time he was courtly was over dinner, he seemed to take pleasure in feeding people.

"That's all true," he said. "But a novelist can't make a good living unless he writes simple novels. And even that is a dead end. A novel can never be as simple as a movie."

Claudia said angrily, "Why do you put movies down? I've seen you cry at good movies. And they are art."

Vail was enjoying himself. After all, he had won his fight against the Studio, he had his points. "Claudia, I really agree," he said. "Movies are art. I complain out of envy. Movies are making novels irrelevant. What's the point of writing a lyrical passage about nature, painting the world in red heat, a beautiful sunset, a mountain range coated with snow, the awe-inspiring waves of great oceans." He was declaiming, waving his arms. "What can you write about passion and the beauty of women? What's the use of all that when you can see it on the movie screen in Technicolor? Oh, those mysterious women with full red lips, their magical eyes, when you can see them bare-assed, tits as delicious-looking as beef Wellington. All much better than real life even, never mind prose. And how can we write about the amazing deeds of heroes who slay their enemies by the hundred, who conquer great odds and great temptation, when you can get it all in gouts of blood before your eyes, tortured, agonized faces on the screen. Actors and cameras doing all the work without processing through the brain. Sly Stallone as Achilles in the Iliad. Now the one thing the screen can't do is get into the minds of their characters, it cannot duplicate the thinking process, the complexity of life." He paused for a moment, then said wistfully, "But you know what's worst of all? I'm an elitist. I wanted to be an artist to be something special. So what I hate is that movies are such a democratic art. Anybody can make a movie. You're right, Claudia, I've seen movies that moved me to tears and I know for a fact that the people who made them are moronic, insensitive, uneducated, and with not an iota of morality. The screenwriter is illiterate, the director an egomaniac, the producer a butcher of morality and the actors smash their fists into the wall or a mirror to show the audience they are upset. But then the movie works. How can that be? Because a movie uses sculpture, painting, music, human bodies, and technology to form itself, while a novelist only has a string of words, black print on white paper. And to tell the truth that's not so terrible. That's progress. And the new great art. A democratic art. And art without suffering. Just buy the right camera and meet with your friends."

Vail beamed at the two women. "Isn't it wonderful, an art that requires no real talent? What democracy, what therapy, to make your own movie. It will replace sex. I go to see your movie and you come to see mine. It's an art that will transform the world and for the better. Claudia, be happy that you are in an art form that is the future."

"You are a condescending prick," Molly said. "Claudia fought for you, defended you. And I've been more patient with you than any murderer I've defended. And you buy us dinner to insult us."

Vail seemed genuinely astonished. "I'm not insulting, I'm just defining. I am grateful and I love you both." He paused for a moment and then said humbly, "I'm not saying I'm better than you."

Claudia burst out laughing. "Ernest, you're so full of shit," she said.

"Just in real life," Vail said amiably. "Can we talk business a little bit? Molly, if I were dead and my family regained all the rights, would LoddStone pay five points?"

"At least five," Molly said. "Now you're going to kill yourself over extra points? You lose me entirely."

Claudia was looking at him, troubled. She distrusted his high spirits. "Ernest, are you still unhappy? We got you a wonderful deal. I was so thrilled."

Vail said fondly, "Claudia, you have no idea what the real world is all about. Which makes you perfect to do screenplays. What the hell difference does it make if I'm happy? The happiest man who ever lived is going to have terrible times in his life. Terrible tragedies. Look at me now. I've just won a great victory, I don't have to kill myself. I'm enjoying this meal, I'm enjoying the company of you two beautiful, intelligent, compassionate women. And I love it that my wife and children will have economic security."

"Then why the fuck are you whining?" Molly asked him. "Why are you spoiling a good time?"

"Because I can't write," Vail said. "Which is no great tragedy. It's not really important anymore but it's the only thing I know how to do." As he was saying this, he was finishing the three desserts with such evident enjoyment that the two women burst out laughing. Vail grinned back at them. "We sure bluffed out old Eli," he said.

"You take writer's block too seriously," Claudia said. "Just take some speed."

"Screenwriters don't have writer's block because they don't write," Vail said. "I cannot write because I have nothing to say. Now let's talk about something more interesting. Molly, I've never understood how I can have ten percent of the profit of a picture that grosses one hundred million dollars and costs only fifteen million to make, and then never see a penny. That's one mystery I'd like to solve before I die."

This put Molly in good spirits again; she loved to teach the law. She took a notebook out of her purse and scribbled down some figures.

"It's absolutely legal," she said. "They are abiding by the contract, one you should not have signed in the first place. Look, take the one-hundred-million gross. The theaters, the exhibitors, take half, so now the studio only gets fifty million, which is called rentals.

"OK. The studio takes out the fifteen million dollars the picture costs. Now there's thirty-five million left. But by the terms of your contract and most studio contracts, the studio takes thirty percent of the rentals for distribution costs on the film. That's another fifteen mil in their pockets. So you're down to twenty mil. Then they deduct the cost of making prints, the cost for advertising the picture, which could easily be another five. You're down to fifteen. Now here's the beauty. By contract, the studio gets twenty-five percent of the budget for studio overhead, telephone bills, electricity, use of sound-stages etc. Now you're down to eleven. Good, you say. You'll take your piece of eleven million. But the Bankable Star gets at least five percent of the rentals, the director and producer another five percent. So that comes to another five million. You're down to six million. At last you'll get something. But not so fast. They then charge you all the costs of distribution, they charge fifty grand for delivering the prints to the English market, another fifty to France or Germany.

And then finally they charge the interest on the fifteen million they borrowed to make the picture. And there they lose me. But that last six million disappears. That's what happens when you don't have me for a lawyer. I write a contract that really gets you a piece of the gold mine. Not gross for a writer but a very good definition of net. Do you understand it now?"

Vail was laughing. "Not really," he said. "How about TV and video money?"

"TV you'll see a little," Molly said. "Nobody knows how much money they make in video."

"And my deal with Marrion now is straight gross?" Vail asked. "They can't screw me again?"

"Not the way I'll write the contract," Molly said. "It will be straight gross all the way."

Vail said mournfully, "Then I won't have a grievance anymore. I won't have an excuse for not writing."

"You really are so eccentric," Claudia said.

"No, no," Vail said. "I'm just a fuckup. Eccentrics do odd things to distract people from what they do or are. They are ashamed. That's why movie people are so eccentric."

Who would have dreamed that dying could be so pleasant, that you could be so at peace, that you could be so without fear? That best of all you had solved the one great common myth?

Eli Marrion, in the long hours of the sick at night, sucked oxygen from the tube in the wall and reflected on his life. His private duty nurse, Priscilla, working a double shift, was reading a book by the dim lamp on the other side of the room. He could see her eyes dart quickly up and then down, as if checking him after every line she read

Marrion thought how different this scene was from how it would be in a movie. In a movie there would be a great deal of tension because he was hovering between life and death. The nurse would be crouched over his bed, doctors would be coming in and out. There should sure as hell be a lot of noise, a lot of tension. And here he was in a room absolutely quiet, the nurse reading, Marrion easily breathing through his plastic tube.

He knew this penthouse floor held only these huge suites for very important people. Powerful politicians, real estate billionaires, stars who were the fading myths of the entertainment world. All kings in their own right and now, here in the night in this hospital, vassals to death. They lay helpless and alone, comforted by mercenaries, their power scattered. Tubes in bodies, prongs in nostrils, waiting for surgeon's knives to scour the debris from their failing hearts or, like himself, for a completely edited heart to be inserted. He wondered if they were as resigned as he.

And why that resignation? Why had he told the doctors he would not have a transplant, that he preferred to live only the short time his failing heart would give him. He thought that, thank God, he could still make intelligent decisions devoid of sentiment.

Everything was clear to him, like making a deal on a film: figuring the cost, the percentage of return, the value of subsidiary rights, the possible traps with stars, directors, and cost overages.

Number one: He was eighty years old and not a robust eighty. A heart transplant would disable him for a year, at the very best. Certainly he would never run LoddStone Studios again. Certainly most of his power over his world would vanish.

Number two: Life without power was intolerable. After all, what could an old man like himself do even with a fresh new heart? He could not play sports, run after women, take pleasure from food or drink. No, power was an old man's only pleasure, and why was that so bad? Power could be used for the good. Had he not granted mercy to Ernest Vail, against all prudent principles, against all his lifelong prejudices? Had he not told his doctors that he did not want to deprive a child or some young man the chance to have a new life by taking a heart? Was that not a use of power for the higher good?

But he had had a long life of dealing with hypocrisy and recognized it now in himself. He had declined a new heart because it was not a good deal; a bottom-line decision. He had granted Ernest Vail his points because he desired the affection of Claudia and the respect of Molly Flanders, a sentimentality. Was it so terrible that he wanted to leave an image of goodness?

He was satisfied in the life he had lived. He had fought his way from poverty to riches, he had conquered his fellow man. He had enjoyed all the pleasure of human life, loved beautiful women, lived in luxurious homes, worn the finest silks. And he had helped in the creation of art. He had earned enormous power and a great fortune. And he had tried to do good for his fellow man. He had contributed tens of millions to this very hospital. But most of all he had enjoyed struggling against his fellow man. And what was so terrible about that? How else could you acquire the power to do good? Even now he regretted the last act of mercy to Ernest Vail. You could not simply give the spoils of your struggle to your fellow man, especially under threat. But Bobby would take care of that. Bobby would take care of everything.

Bobby would plant the necessary publicity stories featuring his refusal of a heart transplant so that someone younger could have it. Bobby would recover all the gross points that existed. Bobby would get rid of his daughter's production company, which was a losing proposition for LoddStone. Bobby would take the rap.

Far off he could hear a tiny bell, then the snakelike rattling of the fax machine transmitting the box office receipts compiled in New York. The stuttering making a refrain for his failing heart.

The truth now. He had enough of life at its best. It was not his body that had ultimately betrayed him but his mind.

The truth now. He was disappointed in human beings. He had seen too many betrayals, too many pitiful weaknesses, too much greed for money and fame. The falseness between lovers, husbands, and wives, fathers, sons, mothers, daughters. Thank God for the films he had made that gave people hope and thank God for his grandchildren and thank God he would not see them grow up into the human condition.

The fax machine stilled its stutter, and Marrion could feel the fluttering of his failing heart. Early morning light filled his room. He saw the nurse flick off her lamp and close her book. It was so lonely to die with only this stranger in this room when he was loved by so many powerful people. Then the nurse was prying open his eyelids, putting her stethoscope to his chest. The huge doors to his hospital suite opened like the great door of some ancient temple and he could hear the rattling of dishes on the breakfast trays. . . .

Then the room filled with bright lights. He could feel fists thumping his chest and wondered why they were doing this to him. A cloud was forming in his brain, filling it with mist. Through that mist voices were screaming. A line from a movie penetrated his oxygen-starved brain. "Is this how the Gods die?"

He felt the electric shocks, the pummeling, the incision made to massage his heart with bare hands.

All of Hollywood would mourn but none more than the night duty nurse, Priscilla. She had done a double shift because she supported two small children, and it displeased her that Marrion had died on her shift. She prided herself on her reputation as one of the finest nurses in California. She hated death. But the book she had been reading had excited her and she had been planning how to talk with Marrion about making it into a movie. She would not be a nurse forever, she was a screenwriter on the side. Now she did not give up hope. This top floor of the hospital with its huge suites received the greatest men of Hollywood and she would stand guard for them against death forever.

But all this had happened in Marrion's mind before he died, a mind saturated with thousands of movies he had watched.

In reality, the nurse had gone to his bed some fifteen minutes after he was dead, so quietly had he died. She debated for maybe thirty seconds about calling an alert to try to bring him back to life. She was an old hand with death and more merciful. Why try to revive him to all the torture of reclaiming life? She went to the window and watched the sun rise and the pigeons strutting lustfully on the stone ledges. Priscilla was the final power deciding Marrion's fate . . . and his most merciful judge.

CHAPTER 13

SENATOR WAVVEN had great news, and it would cost the Clericuzio five million dollars. So said Giorgio's courier. That demanded a mountain of paperwork. Cross would have to extract five million from the casino cage and leave a long record to account for its disappearance.

Cross also had a message from Claudia and Vail. They were in the Hotel occupying the same suite. They wanted to see him as soon as possible. It was urgent.

There was also a call from Lia Vazzi in the Hunting Lodge. He requested to see Cross personally as soon as possible. He did not have to say it was urgent, any request from him had to be urgent or he would not call, and he was already on his way.

Cross started on the paperwork for the transfer of the five million dollars to Senator Wavven. The cash itself would have too much bulk for a suitcase or large overnight bag. He called the Hotel gift shop; he remembered an antique Chinese trunk for sale that was big enough to hold the money. It was dark green decorated with red dragons and superimposed false green gems, and it had a strong locking mechanism.

Gronevelt had taught him how to make the paper trail that legitimized money skimmed from the Hotel casino. It was long and laborious work that involved transfers of money to different accounts, the payment of different suppliers for liquor and food, special training projects and publicity stunts, and a roster of players who did not exist as debtors to the cage.

Cross worked an hour on this. Senator Wavven was not due in until the next day, a Saturday, and the five million had to be put in his hands before he left early Monday morning. Finally his concentration began to wander and he had to take a break.

He called down to Claudia and Vail's suite. Claudia picked up the phone. She said, "I'm having a terrible time with Ernest. We have to talk to you."

"OK," Cross said. "Why don't the two of you go down and gamble and I'll pick you up in the dice pit an hour from now." He paused. "Then we can go for dinner and you can tell me your troubles."

"We can't gamble," Claudia said. "Ernest went over his credit limit and you won't give me credit anymore except for a lousy ten grand."

Cross sighed. That meant Ernest Vail owed the casino a hundred grand that was just so much toilet paper. "Give me an hour and then come up to my suite. We'll have dinner here."

Cross had to make another phone call, to Giorgio to confirm the payment to the senator, not that the courier was suspect but it was one of the built-in routines. This they did with verbal code already established. The name was in arbitrary prearranged numbers, the money designated in arbitrary prearranged alphabetical letters.

Cross tried to continue his paperwork. But again his mind wandered. For five million, Senator Wavven was going to have something important to say. For Lia to make the long drive to Vegas, he had to have serious trouble.

There was a ring at the doorbell, Security had brought Claudia and Ernest to the penthouse. Cross gave Claudia an extra warm hug because he didn't want her to think he was mad at her for losing in the casino.

In the living room of his suite, he handed them the room service menu and then ordered for them. Claudia sat stiffly on the sofa, Vail slouched back disinterestedly.

Claudia said, "Cross, Vail is in terrible shape. We have to do something for him."

Vail didn't look so bad to Cross. He seemed truly relaxed, his eyes half closed, a pleased smile on his lips. This irritated Cross.

"Sure, first thing I'll do is cut off all his credit in this town. That will save money, he's the most incompetent gambler I've ever seen."

"It's not about gambling," Claudia said. And she told him the whole story about Marrion promising to give Vail gross on all the sequels to his book, and then dying.

"So?" Cross asked.

"Now Bobby Bantz won't honor that promise," Claudia said. "Since Bobby became head of LoddStone Studios, he's gone crazy with power. He's trying his best to be like Marrion but he just hasn't got the intelligence or the charisma. So Ernest is out in the cold again."

"Just what the hell do you think I can do?" Cross asked.

"You're partners with LoddStone in *Messalina*," Claudia said. "You must have some clout with them. I want you to ask Bobby Bantz to keep Marrion's promise."

It was at times like this that Cross despaired of Claudia. Bantz would never give way, that was part of his job and his character.

"No," Cross said. "I've explained to you before. I can't take a position unless I know the answer will be yes. And here there's no chance."

Claudia frowned. "I never understood that," she said. She paused for a moment. "Ernest is serious, he will kill himself so that his family can get back the rights."

At this, Vail took an interest. He said, "Claudia, you dumbbell, don't you understand about your brother? If he asks somebody for something and they say no, then he has to kill them." He gave Cross a big grin.

Cross was enraged that Vail would dare to speak that way in front of Claudia. Luckily, at that moment room service arrived with their rolling tables and set dinner up in the living room. Cross controlled himself as they sat down to eat, but he couldn't help saying, with a cold smile, "Ernest, you can solve everything if you knock yourself off, as I understand it. Maybe I can help. I'll move your suite up to the tenth floor and you can just step out the window."

Now Claudia was angry. "This is not a joke," she said. "Ernest is one of my best friends. And you're my brother who always claims to love me and will do anything for me." She was in tears.

Cross got up and went over to hug her. "Claudia, there's nothing I can do. I'm not a magician."

Ernest Vail was enjoying his dinner. No man looked less likely to kill himself. "You're too modest, Cross," he said. "Look, I haven't got the nerve to jump out of a window. I have too much imagination, I'd die a thousand deaths on the way down thinking how I would look splattered all over the place. And I might even land on some innocent person. I'm too chicken to cut my wrists, I can't stand the sight of blood and I'm scared to death of guns and knives and traffic. I don't want to end up a vegetable with nothing accomplished. I don't want that fuckin' Bantz and Deere laughing at me and keeping all my money. There is one thing you can do: Hire somebody to kill me. Don't tell me when. Just get it done."

Cross began laughing. He gave Claudia a reassuring pat on the head and went back to his chair. "Do you think this is a fuckin' movie?" he said to Ernest. "You think killing somebody is sort of a joke?"

Cross left the table and went to his office desk. He unlocked the drawer and took out a purse of black chips. He threw the purse at Ernest and said, "Here's ten grand. Take your last shot at the tables, maybe you'll get lucky. Just stop insulting me in front of my sister."

Vail was cheerful now. "Come on Claudia," he said. "Your brother is not going to help." He put the purse of black chips into his pocket. He seemed anxious to get started gambling.

Claudia seemed abstracted. She was adding up everything in her head but refused to come to a sum total. She looked at the serene handsome face of her brother. He could not be what Vail was saying he was. She kissed Cross on the cheek, and said, "I'm sorry, but I'm worried about Ernest."

"He'll be all right," Cross said. "He likes to gamble too much to die. And he is a genius, isn't he?"

Claudia laughed. "So he always says, and I agree," she said. "And he's such a terrible coward." But she reached out to touch Vail affectionately.

"Why the hell do you stick with him?" Cross said. "Why are you sharing a suite with him?"

"Because I'm his best and last friend," Claudia said angrily. "And I love his books."

. . .

After the two left, Cross spent the rest of the night completing the plan to transfer the five million to Senator Wavven. When he finished, he called the casino manager, a high-ranking member of the Clericuzio Family, and told him to bring the money to his penthouse suite.

The money was brought up in two huge sacks by the manager and two security guards who were also of the Clericuzio. They helped Cross stack the money into the Chinese trunk. The casino manager gave Cross a little grin and said, "Nice trunk."

After the men left, Cross took the huge quilt from his bed and wrapped it around the trunk. Then he ordered room service to bring two breakfasts. Within a few minutes, Security called to tell him Lia Vazzi was waiting to see him. He gave the OK to bring him up.

Cross embraced Lia. He was always delighted to see him.

"Good news or bad news?" Cross asked him after room service delivered breakfast.

"Bad," Lia said. "That detective who stopped me in the lobby of the Beverly Hills Hotel when I was with Skannet. Jim Losey. He showed up at the Hunting Lodge and asked me questions about my relationship with Skannet. I brushed him off. The bad part is how he knew who I was and where I was. I'm not in any police file, I've never been in trouble. So that means there's an informer."

That startled Cross. A turncoat was rare in the Clericuzio Family and was always mercilessly rooted out.

"I'll report it to the Don himself," Cross said. "How about you? Do you want to take a vacation down in Brazil until we find out what it's all about?"

Lia had eaten very little. He helped himself to the brandy and Havana cigars Cross put out.

"I'm not nervous, not yet," Lia said. "I'd just like your permission to protect myself against this man."

Cross was alarmed. "Lia, you can't do that," he said. "It's very dangerous to kill a police officer in this country. This is not Sicily. So I have to tell you something you shouldn't know. Jim Losey is on the Clericuzio pad. Big money. I think he's just nosing around to claim a bonus for laying off you."

"Good," Vazzi said. "But it remains a fact. There must be an informer."

"I'll take care of it," Cross said. "Don't worry about Losey."

Lia puffed on his cigar. "He's a dangerous man. Be careful."

"I will," Cross said. "But no preemptive strikes on your part, OK?"

"Of course," Lia said. He seemed to relax. Then he said casually, "What's under that quilt?"

"A little gift to a very important man," Cross said. "Do you want to spend the night in the Hotel?"

"No," Lia said. "I'll go back to the Lodge and you can tell me what you learn at your leisure. But my advice would be to get rid of Losey right now."

"I'll talk to the Don," Cross said.

Senator Warren Wavven and his entourage of three male aides were checked into their Xanadu Villa at three in the afternoon. As usual, he had traveled in an unmarked limo and without any sort of escort. At five, he summoned Cross to his Villa.

Cross had two of the security guards put the quilt-wrapped trunk in the back of a motorized golf cart. One of the guards drove and Cross sat in the passenger seat keeping an eye on the trunk, which rested in the cargo space that usually held golf clubs and ice water. It was only a five-minute run through the grounds of the Xanadu to the separately secured compound that held the seven Villas.

Cross always loved the sight of them, the sense of power. Small palaces of Versailles, each with a diamond-shaped emerald swimming pool, and in the center a square holding the pearl-shaped private casino for the Villa occupants.

Cross carried the trunk into the Villa himself. One of the senator's aides led him into the dining room where the senator was enjoying a sumptuous array of cold food and iced jugs of lemonade. He no longer drank alcohol.

Senator Wavven was as handsome and affable as ever. He had risen high in the political councils of the nation, was the head of several important committees, and was a dark horse in the next presidential race. He sprang up to greet Cross.

Cross whipped the quilt off the trunk and put it on the floor.

"A little gift from the Hotel, Senator," he said. "Have a pleasant stay."

The senator clasped Cross's hand with both of his. His hands were smooth. "What a delightful present," he said. "Thank you, Cross. Now, could I have a few confidential words with you?"

"Of course," Cross said and gave him the key to the trunk. Wavven slipped it into his trouser pocket. Then he turned to his aides and said, "Please put the trunk in my bedroom and one of you stay with it. Now, let me have a few moments alone with my friend Cross."

They left and the senator began to pace the room. He frowned, "I have good news naturally, but I also have bad news."

Cross nodded and said amiably, "That's usually the case." He thought that for the five mil the good news had to be a hell of a lot better than the bad.

Wavven chuckled. "Isn't that the truth? The good news first. And very good news it is. I've devoted my attention in the last few years to passing legislation that would make gambling legal all over the United States. Even the provision to make sports gambling legal. I think I finally have the votes in the Senate and the House. The money in the trunk will swing some key votes. It is five, isn't it?"

"It's five," Cross said. "And money well spent. Now, what's the bad news?"

The senator shook his head sadly. "Your friends won't like this," he said. "Especially Giorgio, who is so impatient. But he's a fabulous fellow, truly fabulous."

"My favorite cousin," Cross said dryly. Of all the Clericuzio he liked Giorgio least, and it was obvious the senator felt the same way.

Then Wavven delivered the bombshell. "The president has told me he will veto the bill."

Cross had been feeling jubilant over the final success of Don Clericuzio's master plan. To build a legitimate empire based on legal gambling. Now, he was confused. What the hell was Wavven babbling about?

"And we don't have enough votes to overcome a veto," Wavven said.

Just to give himself time to recover his composure, Cross said, "So the five mil is for the president?"

The senator was horrified. "Oh, no, no," he said. "We're not even in the same party. And besides, the president will be a very rich man when he retires into private life. Every board of directors of every big company will want him. He has no need for petty cash." Wavven gave Cross a satisfied smile. "Things work differently when you are the president of the United States."

"So we're nowhere unless the president drops dead," Cross said.

"Exactly," Wavven said. "He is a very popular president, I must say, though we are in opposing parties. He will surely be reelected. We must be patient."

"So we have to wait five years and then hope to get a president who won't veto?"

"That's not exactly true," the senator said, and here he faltered a bit. "I must be honest with you. In five years the composition of the Congress may change, I may not have the votes I have now." He paused again. "There are many factors."

Cross was completely bewildered now. What the hell was Wavven really saying? Then the senator tipped his hand. "Of course if something happens to the president, the vice president will sign the bill. So, as malicious as it sounds, you have to hope that the president has a heart attack or his plane crashes, or he has an incapacitating stroke. It could happen. All of us are mortal." The senator was beaming at him and then suddenly it all became clear to Cross.

He felt a flash of anger. This bastard was giving him a message for the Clericuzio: The senator had done his part, now they had to kill the president of the United States to get the bill passed. And he was so slick and so sly, he had not implicated himself in any concrete way. Cross was sure the Don would not go for it, and if he did, Cross would refuse to be part of the Family ever after.

Wavven was going on with an affable smile. "It looks pretty hopeless but you never know. Fate may take a hand and the vice president is a very close friend of mine, even though we're from different parties. I know for a fact, he will approve my bill. We just have to wait and see."

Cross could scarcely believe what the senator was saying. Senator Wavven was the personification of the virtuous All-American politician, though admittedly with a weakness for women and innocent golf. His face was honorably handsome and his voice patrician. He presented himself as one of the most likable men on earth. Yet he was implying that the Clericuzio Family assassinate his own president. This is a piece of work, Cross thought.

The senator was now picking at the food on the table. "I'm only staying for one night," he said. "I hope you have some girls in your show who would like to have dinner with an old geezer like me."

Back in his penthouse suite Cross called Giorgio and told him he would be in Quogue the next day. Giorgio told him the Family driver would pick him up at the airport. He didn't ask any questions. The Clericuzio never talked business on the phone.

When Cross arrived at the Quogue mansion, he was surprised to find a full attendance. Assembled in the windowless den were not only the Don, but also Pippi, and the Don's three sons, Giorgio, Vincent, and Petie, and even Dante, wearing a sky-blue Renaissance hat.

There was no food in the den, dinner was to come later. As usual the Don made everyone look at the photos of Silvio and the christening of Cross and Dante on the mantelpiece. "What a happy day," the Don always said. They all settled in on chairs and sofas, Giorgio handed out drinks, and the Don lit up his twisted black Italian cheroot.

Cross gave a detailed report: how he had delivered the five million to Senator Wavven and then, word for word, his conversation with him.

There was a long silence. None of them needed Cross's interpretation. Vincent and Petie looked the most concerned. Now that Vincent had his chain of restaurants, he was less inclined to take risks. Petie, though he was head of the soldiers in the Bronx Enclave, had his enormous construction business as his primary concern. They did not relish such a terrible mission at this stage of their lives.

"That fucking senator is crazy," Vincent said.

The Don said to Cross, "Are you sure that was the message the senator was sending us? That we should actually assassinate the leader of our country, one of his colleagues in government?"

Giorgio said dryly, "They're not in the same political party, the senator says."

Cross answered the Don. "The senator would never incriminate himself. He just presented the facts. I think he assumes we will act on it."

Dante spoke up. He was excited by the idea, by the glory, by the profit. "We can get the whole gambling business, legal. That would be worth it. That's the biggest prize."

The Don turned to Pippi. "And what do you think, *Martèllo* of mine?" he asked affectionately.

Pippi was obviously angry. "It can't be done and it shouldn't be done."

Dante said in a taunting voice, "Cousin Pippi, if you can't do it, I can."

Pippi looked at him contemptuously. "You're a butcher, not a planner. You couldn't plan something like this in a million years. This is too big a risk. This is too much heat. And the execution is too difficult. You cannot get away free."

Dante said arrogantly, "Grandfather, give me the job. I'll get it done."

The Don was respectful to his grandson. "I'm sure you could," he said. "And the rewards would be very great. But Pippi is right. The aftermath would be too risky for our Family. One can always make mistakes, but never make a fatal mistake. Even if we were successful and achieved our aim, the deed would hang over us forever. It is too great a crime. Also, this is not a situation that endangers our existence, it is simply one that achieves a purpose. A purpose that can be achieved with patience. Meanwhile, we sit in a pretty position. Giorgio, you have your seat on Wall Street, Vincent, you have your restaurants, Petie, you have your construction business. Cross, you have

333 • THE LAST DON

your hotel and Pippi, you can retire and spend your last years in peace. And Dante, my grandson, you must have patience, some day you will have your gambling empire, that shall be your legacy. And when you do, it will be without the shadow of a terrible deed hanging over your head. So—let the senator swim to the bottom of the ocean."

Everyone in the room relaxed, the tension broken; except for Dante, all were happy with the decision. And all agreed with the Don's curse that the senator should drown. That he had dared to put them in this dangerous dilemma.

Only Dante seemed to disagree. He said to Pippi, "You've got a lot of balls, calling me a butcher. What are you, a fucking Florence Nightingale?"

Vincent and Petie laughed. The Don shook his head disapprovingly. "Another thing," Don Clericuzio said. "I think we for now should continue all our ties with the senator. I don't begrudge him the extra five million, but I take it as an insult that he thinks we would kill the president of our country to further a business venture. Also, what other fish does he have to fry? How does this act benefit him? He seeks to manipulate us. Cross, when he comes to your hotel, build up his markers. Make sure he has a good time. He is too dangerous a man to have as an enemy."

Everything was settled. Cross was hesitant about bringing up another sensitive problem. But he told the story of Lia Vazzi and Jim Losey. "There could be an informer inside the Family," Cross said.

Dante said coolly, "That was your operation, that's your problem."

The Don shook his head decisively. "An informer cannot be," he said. "The detective found something by accident and he wants a bonus to stop. Giorgio, take care of it."

Giorgio said sourly, "Another fifty grand. Cross, that's your deal. You'll have to pay it out of your hotel."

The Don relit his cigar. "Now that we are all here together, are there any other problems? Vincent, how is your restaurant business?"

Vincent's granite features softened. "I'm opening three more," he said. "One in Philly, one in Denver, and another in New York City. High class. Pop, would you believe I charge sixteen dollars for a plate of spaghetti? When I make it at home, I figure out the cost is half a buck a plate. No matter how hard I try, I can't make it more than that. I even put in the cost of the garlic. And meatballs, I'm the only high-class Italian restaurant that serves meatballs, I don't know why, but I get eight dollars for them. And not big ones. They cost me twenty cents."

He would have gone on but the Don cut him off. He turned to Giorgio and said, "Giorgio, how goes your Wall Street?"

Giorgio said cautiously, "It goes up and down. But the commissions we get for trading are as good as the shylocks get on the streets if we churn it enough. And with no risk of deadbeats or jail. We should forget about all our other business, except maybe gambling."

The Don was enjoying these recitals, success in the legitimate world was dear to him. He said, "And Petie, your construction business? I hear you had a little trouble the other day . . ."

Petie shrugged. "I got more business than I can handle. Everybody's building something and we have a lock on the highway contracts. All my soldiers are on the payroll and make a good living. But a week ago, this eggplant shows up on my biggest construction job. He's got a hundred black guys behind him with all kinds of civil rights banners. So I take him into my office and all of a sudden he's charming. I just have to put ten percent blacks on the job and pay him twenty grand under the table."

That tickled Dante. "We're getting strong-armed?" he said with a giggle. "The Clericuzio?"

Petie said, "I tried to think like Pop. Why shouldn't they make a living? So I gave the eggplant his twenty grand and told him I'd put five percent on the job."

"You did well," the Don told Petie. "You kept a small problem from becoming a big problem. And who are the Clericuzio not to pay their share in the advancement of the other people and civilization itself?"

"I would have killed the black son of a bitch," Dante said. "Now, he'll come back for more."

"And we will give him more," the Don said. "Just so long as they are reasonable." He turned to Pippi and said, "And what troubles do you have?"

"None," Pippi said. "Except that now the Family is nearly nonoperational and I'm out of a job."

"That is your good fortune," the Don said. "You've worked hard enough. You've escaped many perils, so now enjoy the flower of your manhood."

Dante didn't wait to be questioned. "I'm in the same boat," he said to the Don. "And I'm too young to retire."

"Play golf like the *Brugliones*," Don Clericuzio said dryly. "And don't worry, life always provides work and problems. Meanwhile, be patient. I fear your time will come. And mine."

CHAPTER 14

ON THE MORNING OF Eli Marrion's funeral, Bobby Bantz was screaming at Skippy Deere.

"This is fucking crazy, this is what's wrong with the movie business. How the fuck can you allow this to happen?" He was waving a stapled bundle of pages in Deere's face.

Deere looked at it. It was the transportation schedule for a picture shooting in Rome. "Yeah, so what?" Deere said.

Bantz was in rage. "Everyone in the picture is booked first class on the flight to Rome . . . the crew, the bit players, the fucking cameo roles, the gofers, the interns. There is only one exception. You know who that is? The LoddStone accounting officer we sent there to control the spending. He flew economy."

"Yeah, again, so what?" Deere said.

Bantz became deliberate in his anger. "And the picture has on budget a school to be set up for the children of everybody on the picture. The budget has the renting of a yacht for two weeks. I just read the script carefully. There are twelve actors and actresses who have maybe two, three minutes in the film. The yacht is listed for just two days' shooting. Now explain to me how you allowed this."

Skippy Deere was grinning at him. "Sure," he said. "Our director is Lorenzo Tallufo. He insists his people travel first class. The bit players and cameo roles were written into the script because they were screwing the vehicle stars. The yacht is booked for two weeks because Lorenzo wants to visit the Cannes Film Festival."

"You're the producer, talk to Lorenzo," Bantz said.

"Not *me,*" Deere told him. "Lorenzo has four one-hundred-million-dollar-grossing pictures, he has two Academy Awards. I'll kiss his ass when I help him onto the yacht. You talk to him."

There was no answer to this. Technically, in the hierarchy of the industry, the head of the Studio outranked everybody. The producer was the person who got all the elements together and oversaw the budget and script development. But the reality was that once the picture started shooting, the director was the supreme power. Especially if he had a record of successful movies.

Bantz shook his head. "I can't talk to Lorenzo, not when I don't have Eli to back me up. Lorenzo would tell me to go fuck myself and we'd lose the picture."

"And he'd be right," Deere said. "What the hell, Lorenzo always steals five million off a picture. They all do it. Now calm down so we can show ourselves at the funeral."

But Bantz was now looking at another cost sheet. "On your picture," he said to Deere, "there's a charge of five hundred thousand dollars for Chinese take-out food. Nobody, *nobody,* not even my wife can spend a half million dollars on Chinese food. French food maybe. But Chinese? Chinese take-out?"

Skippy Deere had to think fast, Bobby had him there. "It's a Japanese restaurant, the food is sushi. That's the most expensive food in the world."

Bantz was suddenly calm. People were always complaining about sushi. The head of a rival studio had told him about taking a Japanese investor to dinner at a restaurant that specialized in sushi. "A thousand bucks for two people for twenty fucking fish heads," he had said. Bantz was impressed.

"OK," Bantz said to Skippy Deere, "but you have to cut down. Try to get more college interns on your next picture." Interns worked for free.

The Hollywood funeral of Eli Marrion was more newsworthy than even that of a Bankable Star. He had been revered by studio heads, producers, and agents, he had even been respected and sometimes loved by Bankable Stars, directors, and even screenplay writers. What had inspired this was his civility and an overpowering intelligence that had solved many problems in the movie business. He also had had the reputation of being fair, within reason.

In his later years, he was an ascetic, did not wallow in power, did not command sexual favors from starlets. Also, LoddStone had made more great movies than any other studio, and there was nothing more precious to people who actually made movies.

The president of the United States sent his chief of staff to give a brief eulogy. France sent its minister of culture, though he was an enemy of Hollywood movies. The Vatican sent a papal envoy, a young cardinal, handsome enough to receive offers for cameo roles. A Japanese group of business executives magically appeared. The highest executives of movie corporations from the Netherlands, Germany, Italy, and Sweden did Eli Marrion honor.

The eulogies began. First a male Bankable Star, then a female Bankable Star, then an A director; even a writer, Benny Sly, gave Marrion tribute. Then the president's chief of staff. Then, just so the show would not be judged pretentious, two of the movie's greatest comics made jokes about Eli Marrion's power and business acumen. Finally, Eli's son, Kevin, and his daughter, Dora, and Bobby Bantz.

Kevin Marrion extolled Eli Marrion as a caring father, not only to his own children, but to everyone who worked at LoddStone. He was a man who carried the torch of Art on a film. A torch, Kevin assured the mourners, that he would pick up.

Eli Marrion's daughter, Dora, gave the most poetic speech, written by Benny Sly. It was eloquent, spiritual, and addressed Eli Marrion's virtues and accomplishments with a humorous respect. "I loved my father more than any man I have ever known," she said, "but I'm glad I never had to negotiate with him. I only had to deal with Bobby Bantz and I could outsmart him."

She got her laugh and it was Bobby Bantz's turn. Secretly he resented Dora's joke. "I spent thirty years building LoddStone Studios with Eli Marrion," he said. "He was the most intelligent, the kindest man I have ever known. Under him, my service of thirty years has been the happiest time of my life. And I will continue to serve his dream. He showed his faith in me by leaving me in control of the Studio for the next five years and I will not fail him. I cannot hope to equal Eli's achievements. He gave dreams to billions of people all over the world. He shared his wealth and love with his family and all the people of America. He was indeed a lodestone."

The assembled mourners knew that Bobby Bantz had written the speech himself, because he had given an important message to the whole movie industry. That he was to rule LoddStone Studios for the next five years and that he expected everyone to give him the same respect they had given Eli Marrion. Bobby Bantz was no longer a Number Two man, he was a Number One.

Two days after the funeral, Bantz summoned Skippy Deere to the studio and offered him the job of head of production of LoddStone, the job he had held himself. Now he was moving up to Marrion's job as chairman. The rewards he offered Deere were irresistible. Deere would get a share of profits of every movie made by the Studio. He would be able to green-light any picture budgeted for less than thirty million dollars. He would be able to fold his own production company into LoddStone as an independent, and name the head of that company.

Skippy Deere was astounded by the richness of the offer. He analyzed this as a mark of insecurity on Bantz's part. Bantz knew he was weak on the creative side and counted on Deere to cover him.

Deere accepted the offer and appointed Claudia De Lena to head his production company. Not only because she was creative, not only because she really knew movie making, but because he knew she was too honest to undercut him. With her, he would not have to watch his back. In addition, and this was no small thing in making movies, he always enjoyed her company, her good humor. And their sex thing had been gotten out of the way a long time ago.

It gave Skippy Deere a glow to think of how rich they would all become. For Deere had been around long enough to know that even Bankable Stars sometimes came to old age in semipoverty. Deere was already very wealthy, but he thought that there were ten levels

MARIO PUZO • 340

of being rich and he was only on the first level. Certainly he could live in luxury the rest of his life, but he could not have his own private jet, he could not have five homes and keep them up. He could not keep a harem. He could not afford to be a degenerate gambler. He could not afford another five divorces. He could not afford to keep a hundred servants. He could not even afford to finance his own pictures over any period of time. And he couldn't afford an expensive collection of art, a major Monet or Picasso, as Eli had done. But now someday he would move up from the first level to perhaps as high as the fifth level. He would have to work very hard and be very cunning, and most important, study Bantz very carefully.

Bantz outlined his plans, and Deere was surprised at how daring they were. Obviously Bantz was determined to take his place in the world of power.

For starters, he was going to make a deal with Melo Stuart so that Melo would give LoddStone preferential access to all the Talent in his agency.

"I can handle that," Deere said. "I'll make it clear to him that I'll give him the green light on his favorite projects."

"I'm particularly interested that we have Athena Aquitane do our next picture," Bobby Bantz said.

Aha, Deere thought. Now that Bantz controlled LoddStone, he hoped to get Athena into bed. Deere thought that as head of production he had a shot, too.

"I'll tell Claudia to work on a project for her right away," Deere said.

"Great," Bantz said. "Now remember I always knew what Eli really wanted to do but couldn't because he was too soft. We are going to get rid of Dora and Kevin's production companies. They always lose money and besides I don't want them on the lot."

"You have to be careful on that one," Deere said. "They own a lot of stock in the company."

Bantz grinned. "Yeah, but Eli left me in control for five years. So you're going to be the fall guy. You will refuse to green-light their projects. I figure that after a year or two, they'll leave in disgust and blame you. That was Eli's technique. I always took the rap for him."

"I think you'll have a hard time moving them off the lot," Deere said. "It's their second home, they grew up on it."

"I'll try," Bantz said. "Another thing. The night before he died, Eli agreed to give Ernest Vail gross with some money up front on all the pictures we made from his shitty novel. Eli made that promise because Molly Flanders and Claudia nagged him on his deathbed, which was really a lousy thing to do. I've notified Molly in writing that I'm not bound legally or morally to keep that promise."

Deere pondered the problem. "He'll never kill himself but he could die a natural death in the next five years. We should ensure ourselves against that."

"No," Bantz said. "Eli and I consulted our lawyers and they say Molly's argument would lose in the courts. I'll negotiate some money but not gross. That's sucking our blood."

"So, has Molly answered?" Deere asked.

"Yeah, the usual bullshit lawyer letter," Bantz said. "I told her to go fuck herself."

Bantz picked up the phone and called his psychoanalyst. His wife had insisted for years that he go into therapy to become more likable.

Bantz said into the phone, "I just wanted to confirm our appointment for four P.M. Yes, we'll talk about your script next week." He hung up the phone and gave Deere a sly smile.

Deere knew that Bantz had a rendezvous with Falene Fant at the Studio's Beverly Hotel Bungalow. So Bobby's therapist served as his beard because the Studio had taken an option on the therapist's original screenplay about a serial murder psychiatrist. The joke was that Deere had read the script and thought it would make a nice low-budget movie, although Bantz thought it was shit. Deere would make the movie and Bantz would believe Deere was just doing him a favor.

Then Bantz and Deere chatted about why spending time with Falene made them so happy. They both agreed that it was childish for important men like themselves. They also agreed that sex with Falene was so pleasurable because she was so much fun, and because she made no claims on them. Of course there were implied claims, but she was talented and when the right time came she would be given her chance.

Bantz said, "The thing that worries me is that if she becomes some sort of half-assed star our fun may be over."

"Yeah," Deere said. "That's the way Talent reacts. But what the hell, then she'll make us a lot of money."

The two of them went over the production and release schedules. *Messalina* would be finished in two months and would be the Locomotive for the Christmas season. A Vail sequel was in the can and would be released in the next two weeks. These two LoddStone pictures combined might gross a billion dollars worldwide, including video. Bantz would see a twenty-million-dollar bonus, Deere probably five million. Bobby would be hailed as a genius in his first year as successor to Marrion. He would be acknowledged as a true Number One exec.

Deere said thoughtfully, "It's a shame we have to pay Cross fifteen percent of the adjusted gross on *Messalina*. Why don't we just pay him back his money with interest and if he doesn't like it, he can sue. Obviously, he's leery about going to court."

"Isn't he supposed to be Mafia?" Bantz asked. And Deere thought, This guy is really chickenshit.

"I know Cross," Deere said. "He's not a tough guy. His sister Claudia would have told me if he was truly dangerous. The one I worry about is Molly Flanders. We're screwing two of her clients at the same time."

"OK," Bobby said. "Christ, we really did a good day's work. We save twenty mil on Vail and maybe ten on De Lena. That will pay our bonuses. We'll be heroes."

"Yeah," Deere said. He looked at his watch. "It's getting close to four o'clock. Shouldn't you be on your way to Falene?"

At that moment the door to Bobby Bantz's office burst open and there stood Molly Flanders. She was in fighting garb, trousers, jacket, and white silk blouse. And in flat heels. Her beautiful complexion was a blushing red with rage. There were tears in her eyes and yet she had never looked more beautiful. Her voice was filled with gleeful malice.

"OK, you two cocksuckers," she said. "Ernest Vail is dead. I've got an injunction pending to prevent you from releasing your new sequel to his book. Now are you two fuckheads ready to sit down and make a deal?"

Ernest Vail knew his greatest problem in committing suicide was how to avoid violence. He was far too cowardly to use the most popular methods. Guns frightened him, knives and poisons were too direct and not foolproof. Head in a gas oven, death in his car by carbon monoxide, again left too much uncertainty. Slitting his wrists involved blood. No, he wanted to die a pleasurable death, quick, certain, leaving his body intact and dignified.

Ernest prided himself that his was a rational decision that would benefit everyone except LoddStone Studios. It was purely a matter of personal financial gain and the restoration of his ego. He would be regaining control of his life; that made him laugh. Another proof of sanity: He still had his sense of humor.

Swimming out into the ocean was too "movies," throwing himself in front of a bus was also too painful and somehow demeaning, as if he were some homeless bum. One notion appealed to him for a moment. There was a sleeping pill, no longer popular, a suppository, which you just slipped into your rectum. But again, it was too undignified and was not completely certain.

Ernest rejected all these methods and searched for something that would give him a happy certain death. This process cheered him up so much that he almost abandoned the whole idea. So did writing rough drafts of suicide notes. He wanted to use all his art not to sound self-pitying, accusatory. Most of all he wanted his suicide to be accepted as a completely rational act and not one of cowardice.

He started with the note to his first wife, whom he thought of as his only true love. The first sentence he tried to make objective and practical.

"Get in touch with Molly Flanders, my lawyer, as soon as you get this note. She will have important news for you. I thank you and the children for the many happy years you've given me. I do not want you to think that what I've done is a reproach to you in any way. We were sick of each other before we parted. Please do not think my action is because of a diseased mind, or any unhappiness. It is completely rational, as my lawyer will explain. Tell my children that I love them."

Ernest pushed the note aside. It would need a lot of rewrite. He wrote notes to his second and third wives, which sounded cold even to him, informing them that they were being left small portions of his estate and thanking them for the happiness they had given him and reassuring them they also were in no way responsible for his action. It seemed he was not really in a loving mood. So he wrote a short note to Bobby Bantz, a simple "Fuck you."

Then he wrote a note to Molly Flanders that read, "Go get the bastards." This put him in a better mood.

To Cross De Lena, he wrote, "I finally did the right thing." He had sensed De Lena's contempt for his waffling.

Finally his heart opened up when he wrote to Claudia. "You gave me the happiest times of my life and we weren't even in love. How do you figure that? And how come everything you did in life was right and everything I did was wrong? Until now. Please disregard everything I've said about your writing, how I demeaned your work, that's just the envy of an old novelist as out of date as a blacksmith. And thank you for fighting for my percentage even though finally you failed. I love you for trying."

He stacked up the notes, which he had written on yellow second sheets. They were terrible but he would rewrite them, and rewriting was always the key.

But composing the notes had stirred his subconscious. Finally he thought of the perfect way to kill himself.

Kenneth Kaldone was the greatest dentist in Hollywood, as famous as any Bankable Star within that small milieu. He was extremely skillful in his profession, he was colorful and daring in his private life. He detested the portrayal in literature and movies of dentists as extremely bourgeois and did everything to disprove it.

He was charming in dress and manner, his dental office was luxurious and had a rack of a hundred of the best magazines published in

America and England. There was another, smaller rack for magazines in foreign languages, German, Italian, French, and even Russian.

First-rate modern art hung on the walls of the waiting room, and when you went into the labyrinth of treatment rooms, the corridors were decorated with autographed pictures of some of the greatest names in Hollywood. His patients.

He was always bubbly with cheerful good humor and vaguely effeminate in a way that was strangely misleading. He loved women but did not understand in any way a commitment to women. He regarded sex as no more important than a good dinner, a fine wine, wonderful music.

The only thing Kenneth believed in was the art of dentistry. There, he was an artist, he kept up with all technical and cosmetic developments. He refused to make removable bridges for his clients, he insisted on steel implants to which an artificial series of teeth could be attached permanently. He lectured at the dental conventions, he was such an authority that he had once been summoned to treat the teeth of one of the royal bloods of Monaco.

No patient of Kenneth Kaldone's would be forced to put his teeth in a water glass at night. No patient would ever feel pain in his elaborately outfitted dental chair. He was generous in his use of drugs and especially in the use of "sweet air," the combination of nitrous oxide and oxygen inhaled by patients though a rubber mask, which remarkably killed any pain to the nerves and transported his patient into a semiconsciousness as nearly pleasurable as opium.

Ernest and Kenneth had become friends on Ernest's first visit to Hollywood almost twenty years before. Ernest had suffered an excruciating toothache at the dinner of a producer who was courting him for the rights to one of his books. The producer had called Kenneth at midnight, and Kenneth had rushed to the party to drive Ernest to his office to treat the infected tooth. Then he had driven Ernest to his hotel, instructing him to come back to the office the next day.

Ernest later commented to the producer that he must have a lot of clout for a dentist to make a house call at midnight. The producer said no, Kenneth Kaldone was just that kind of a guy. A man with a toothache was to him like a man drowning, he had to be rescued. But also Kaldone had read all of Ernest's books and loved his work.

The next day when Ernest visited Kenneth in his office, he was effusively grateful. Kenneth stopped him with an upraised hand and said, "I'm still in your debt for the pleasure your books have given me. Now let me tell you about steel implants." He gave a long lecture that argued it was never too early to take care of your mouth. That Ernest would soon lose some other teeth, and steel implants would save him from putting his teeth in a water glass at night.

Ernest said, "I'll think about it."

"No," Kenneth said, "I can't treat a patient who disagrees with me about my work."

Ernest laughed. "It's a good thing you're not a novelist," he said. "But OK."

They became friends. Vail would call him for dinner whenever he came to Hollywood and sometimes he made a special trip to L.A. just to be treated with sweet air. Kenneth spoke intelligently about Ernest's books, he knew literature almost as well as he knew dentistry.

Ernest loved sweet air. He never felt pain and he had some of his best ideas while he was in the semiconscious state it induced. In the next few years he and Kenneth built a friendship so strong it resulted in Ernest having a new set of teeth with roots of steel, which would accompany him to the grave.

But Ernest's main interest in Kenneth was as a character for a novel. Ernest had always believed that in every human being there was one startling perversity. Kenneth had revealed his, and it was sexual but not in the usual pornographic style.

They always chatted a bit before a treatment, before Ernest was given sweet air. Kenneth mentioned that his primary girlfriend, his "significant other," was also having sex with her dog, a huge German shepherd.

Ernest, just beginning to succumb to the sweet air, took the rubber mask off his face and said without thinking, "You're screwing a woman who screws her dog? Don't you worry about that?" He meant the medical and psychological complications.

Kenneth did not grasp what was implied. "Why should I worry?" he said. "A dog is no competition."

At first Ernest thought he was joking. Then he realized Kenneth was serious. Ernest put his mask back on and submerged himself in the dreaminess of the nitrous oxide and oxygen, and his mind, stimulated as usual, made a complete analysis of his dentist.

Kenneth was a man who had no conception of love as a spiritual exercise. Pleasure was paramount, similar to his skills in killing pain. Flesh was to be controlled while indulged.

They had dinner together that night, and Kenneth more or less confirmed Ernest's analysis. "Sex is better than nitrous," Kenneth said. "But like nitrous, you must have at least thirty percent oxygen mixed in." He gave Ernest a sly look. "Ernest, you really like sweet air, I can tell. I give you the maximum—seventy percent—and you tolerate it well."

Ernest asked, "Is it dangerous?"

"Not really," Kenneth said. "Unless you keep the mask on for a couple of days and maybe not even then. Of course, pure nitrous oxide will kill you in fifteen to thirty minutes. In fact about once a month I have a little midnight party in my office, carefully selected 'beautiful people.' All my patients, so I have their blood work. All healthy. The nitrous turns them on. Haven't you felt sexual under the gas?"

Ernest laughed. "When one of your technicians goes by I want to grab her ass."

Kenneth said with wry humor, "I'm sure she'd forgive you. Why don't you come by the office tomorrow at midnight? It's really a lot of fun." He saw Ernest looking scandalized and said, "Nitrous is not cocaine. Cocaine makes women sort of helpless. Nitrous just loosens them up. Just come as you would go to a cocktail party. You're not committed to any action."

Ernest thought maliciously, Are dogs allowed? Then he said he would drop in. He excused himself by thinking it would only be research for a novel.

He did not have any fun at the party and did not really participate. The truth was, the nitrous oxide made him feel more spiritual than sexy, as if it were some sacred drug only to be used to worship a merciful God. The copulation of the guests was so animal-like that for the first time he understood Kenneth's casualness about his significant other and the German shepherd. It was so devoid of human content that it was boring. Kenneth himself did not participate, he was too busy operating the controls on the nitrous.

But now, years later, Ernest knew he had a way of killing himself. It would be like painless dentistry. He would not suffer, he would not be disfigured, he would not be afraid. He would float from this world to the other in a cloud of benign reflections. As the saying goes, he would die happy.

The problem now was how to get into Kenneth's office at night and how to figure out how the controls operated. . . .

He made an appointment with Kenneth for a checkup. While Kenneth was studying his X rays, Ernest told him that he was using a dentist as a character in his new novel and asked to be shown how the controls for the sweet air worked.

Kenneth was a natural-born pedagogue and showed him how to work the controls on the tanks of nitrous oxide and oxygen, stressing the safe ratios, lecturing all the while.

"But couldn't it be dangerous?" Ernest asked. "What if you got drunk and screwed up? You could kill me."

"No, it's automatically regulated so that you always get at least thirty percent oxygen," Kenneth explained.

Ernest hesitated a moment, trying to look embarrassed. "You know I enjoyed that party years ago. Now I have a beautiful girlfriend who is acting a little coy. I need some help. Could you let me have the key to your office so I could bring her here some night? The nitrous would just tip the balance."

Kenneth studied the X rays carefully. "Your mouth is in terrific shape," he said. "I'm really a great dentist."

"The key?" Ernest said.

"A really beautiful girl?" Kenneth asked. "Tell me which night and I'll come and work the controls."

"No, no," Ernest said. "This is a really straight girl. She wouldn't do even the nitrous if you were around." He paused for a moment. "She really is old-fashioned."

"No shit," Kenneth said and looked directly into Ernest's eyes. Then he said, "I'll just be a minute," and he left the treatment room.

When he returned, he had a key in his hand. "Take this to a hardware store and get it duplicated," Kenneth said. "Make sure you let them know who you are. Then come back and give me my key."

Ernest was surprised. "I don't mean right now."

Kenneth packed away the X rays and turned to Ernest. For one of the few times since Ernest had known him, the cheerfulness in his face was gone.

"When the cops find you," Kenneth said, "dead in my chair, I don't want to be implicated in any way. I don't want my professional status jeopardized, or my patients deserting me. The cops will find the duplicate and track it down to the store. They will assume trickery on your part. I assume you're leaving a note?"

Ernest was stunned and then ashamed. He had not thought of harming Kenneth. Kenneth was looking at him with a reproachful smile tinged with sadness. Ernest took the key from Kenneth, then in a rare show of emotion, he gave Kenneth a tentative hug. "So you understand," he said. "I'm being completely rational."

"Sure I do," Kenneth said. "I've often thought about it for myself in my old age or if things go bad." He smiled cheerfully and said, "Death is no competition." They both laughed.

"You really know why?" Ernest asked.

"Everybody in Hollywood knows," Kenneth said. "Skippy Deere was at a party and someone asked if he was really going to do the picture. He said, 'I will try until Hell freezes over or Ernest Vail commits suicide.' "

"And you don't think I'm crazy?" Ernest said. "Doing it for money I can't spend . . ."

"Why not?" Kenneth said. "It's smarter than killing yourself for love. But the mechanics are not that simple. You have to disconnect this hose in the wall that supplies the oxygen, that disables the regulator and you can make the mixture more than seventy percent. Do it on Friday night after the cleaning people leave so you won't be discovered until Monday. There's always a chance you can be revived. Of course if you use pure nitrous oxide you'll be gone in thirty minutes." Again he smiled a little sadly. "All my work on your teeth wasted. What a shame."

Two days later, on a Saturday morning, Ernest woke very early in his Beverly Hills Hotel room. The sun was just coming up. He showered and shaved and dressed in a T-shirt and comfortable jeans. Over that he wore a tan linen jacket. His room was strewn with clothes and newspapers, but it would be pointless to tidy up.

Kenneth's office was a half-hour walk from the hotel, and Ernest stepped out feeling a sense of freedom. Nobody walked in L.A. He was hungry but was afraid to eat anything because it might make him throw up when he was under the nitrous.

The office was on the fifteenth floor of a sixteen-story building. There was only a single civilian guard in the lobby and no one in the elevator. Ernest turned the key in the door of the dental suite and entered. He locked the door behind him and put the key in his jacket pocket. The suite of rooms was ghostly still, the receptionist's window glinted in the early morning sun and her computer was ominously dark and silent.

Ernest opened the door that led to the work area. As he walked down the corridor, he was greeted by the photos of Bankable Stars. There were six treatment rooms, three on each side of the corridor. At the end was Kenneth's office and conference room where they had chatted many times. Kenneth's own treatment room was attached, with his special hydraulic dental chair, where he cared for his high-ranking patients.

That chair was extra luxurious, the padding thicker and the leather softer. On the mobile table beside the chair was the sweet air mask. The console, with its hose linked to the hidden nitrous oxide and oxygen tanks, had its two control knobs turned to zero.

Ernest adjusted the dials so that he would get half nitrous oxide and half oxygen. Then he sat in the chair and put the mask over his face. He relaxed. After all, Kenneth would not be sticking knives into his gums now. All the aches and pains left his body, his brain roamed over the entire world. He felt wonderful, it was ridiculous to think of death.

Ideas for future novels floated through his head, insights into many people he knew, none of them malicious, which was what he loved about nitrous. Shit, he had forgotten to rewrite the suicide notes, and he realized how, despite his good intentions and language, they were in essence insulting.

Ernest was now in a huge, sailing colored balloon. He floated over the world he had known. He thought about Eli Marrion, who had followed his destiny, achieved great power, was regarded with awe for his ruthless intelligence in using that power. And yet, when Ernest's best book came out and was bought for the movies, the one that earned him the Pulitzer, Eli had come to the cocktail party his publishers gave him.

Eli had put out his hand and said, "You are a very fine writer." His coming to the party was sensational Hollywood gossip. And the great Eli Marrion had shown him the final and absolute mark of respect, he had given him gross. No matter that Bantz had taken it away after Marrion died.

And Bantz was not a villain. His relentless pursuit of profit was a result of his experience in a special world. If truth be told, Skippy Deere was worse, because Deere, with his intelligence, his charm and his elemental energy, and his instinctive moves to betrayal in a personal sense, was more lethal.

Another insight came to Ernest. Why was he always knocking Hollywood and films, sneering at them? It was jealousy. Film was now the most revered art form, and he himself loved movies, good ones anyway. But he envied more the relationships in making a movie. The cast, the crew, the director, the Bankable Stars and even the "Suits," those crass execs, seemed to come together in a close if not ever-loving family, at least until the picture was finished. They gave each other presents then and kissed and hugged and swore eternal devotion. What a wonderful feeling that must be to have. He remembered when he wrote his first script with Claudia, he thought he might be admitted to this family.

But how that could be with his personality, his malicious wit, his constant sneering? But under the sweet nitrous oxide, he could not even judge himself harshly. He had a right, he had written great books (Ernest was an oddity among novelists because he really loved his books), and he had deserved to be treated with more respect.

Benignly saturated with forgiving nitrous, Ernest decided he really didn't want to die. Money was not that important, Bantz would relent or Claudia and Molly would find a way out.

Then he remembered all his humiliation. None of his wives had ever truly loved him. He had always been the mendicant, never enjoyed requited love. His books had been respected but never aroused the adoration that made a writer rich. Some critics had reviled him and he had pretended to take it in good sport. After all, it was wrong to get angry with critics, they were only doing their job. But their remarks hurt. And all his male friends, though they sometimes enjoyed his company, his wit and honesty, never became close, not even Kenneth. While Claudia was truly fond of him, he knew Molly Flanders and Kenneth felt pity for him.

Ernest reached over and turned off the sweet air. It took just a few minutes for his head to clear and then he went to sit in Kenneth's office.

His depression came back. He tilted back in Kenneth's lounge chair and watched the sun rise over Beverly Hills. He was so angry at the studio screwing him out of his money that he couldn't enjoy anything. He hated the dawning of a new day; at night he took sleeping pills early and tried to sleep as long as he could. . . . That he could be humiliated by such people, people he held in contempt. And now he could no longer even read, a pleasure that had never before betrayed him. And of course, he could no longer write. That elegant prose, so often praised, was now false, inflated, pretentious. He no longer enjoyed writing it.

For a long time now, he had awakened every morning dreading the coming day, too tired to even shave and shower. And he was broke. He had earned millions and had pissed it away on gambling, women, and booze. Or given it away. Money had never been important until now.

The last two months he had not been able to send his kids their support payments or his wives their alimony. Unlike most men, sending those checks made Ernest happy. He had not published a book for five years, and his personality had become less pleasant even to himself. He was always whining about his fate. He was like a sore tooth in the face of society. And this image itself depressed him. What kind of soapy metaphor was this for a writer of his talent? A wave of melancholy swept over him; he was completely powerless.

He sprang up and walked into the treatment room. Kenneth had told him what he must do. He pulled out the cable that held the two plugs, one for oxygen and one for the nitrous oxide. Then he plugged back only one. Nitrous. He sat in the dental chair, reached over and turned the dial. At that moment he thought that there must be some way to get at least a ten percent oxygen flow so that death would not be so certain. He picked up the mask and put it over his face.

The pure nitrous hit his body and he experienced a moment of ecstasy, a washing away of all pain and a dreamy content. The nitrous hit and scrubbed out the brain in his skull. There was one last moment of pure pleasure before he ceased to exist, and in that moment, he believed there was a God and a Heaven.

Molly Flanders savaged Bobby Bantz and Skippy Deere; she would have been more careful if Eli Marrion was still alive.

"You have a new sequel to Ernest's book coming out. My injunction will stop that. The property now belongs to Ernest's heirs. Sure, maybe you can override the injunction and release the picture but then I sue. If I win, Ernest's estate will own that picture and most of what it earns. And for a certainty we can prevent you from making other sequels based on the characters in his books. Now, we can save all that and years of trouble in court. You pay five million up front and ten percent of the gross of each picture. And I want a true and certified account of the money on home video."

Deere was horrified and Bantz enraged. Ernest Vail, a writer, would have a greater percentage of the profit on the pictures than anyone except a Bankable Star ever got, and that was a fucking outrage.

Bantz immediately called Melo Stuart and the chief counsel for LoddStone Pictures. They were in the meeting room within a half

hour. Melo was necessary to the meeting because he was the pack-
ager of the sequels and earned a commission on the Bankable Star,
the director, and the rewriter, Benny Sly. This was a situation that
could require him to give up some points.

The chief counsel said, "We studied the situation when Mr. Vail
made his first threat against the Studio."

Molly Flanders broke in angrily. "You call killing himself a threat
to the Studio?"

"And blackmail," the chief counsel said smoothly. "Now we've
completely researched the law in this situation, which is very tricky,
but even then I advised the Studio we could fight your claim in court
and win. In this particular case, the rights to the property do not revert back to the heirs."

"What can you guarantee?" Molly asked the counsel. "To a
ninety-five percent certainty?"

"No," the counsel said. "Nothing is that certain in the law."

Molly was delighted. She would retire with the fee she earned
when she won this case. She got up to go and said, "Fuck you all, I'll
see you in court."

Bantz and Deere were so terrified they could not speak. Bantz
wished with all his heart that Eli Marrion were still alive.

It was Melo Stuart who rose and restrained Molly with an affectionate and imploring hug. "Hey," he said, "we're just negotiating.
Be civilized."

He led Molly back to her chair, noticing there were tears in her
eyes. "We can make a deal, I'll give up some points in the package."

Molly said quietly to Bantz, "Do you want to risk losing everything? Can your counsel guarantee that you will win? Of course he
can't. Are you a fucking businessman or some degenerate gambler?
To save a fucking lousy twenty to forty mil, you want to risk losing
a billion?"

They cut the deal. Ernest's estate got four million up front and 8
percent of the gross on the picture about to be released. He would
get two million and 10 percent of adjusted gross on any other sequels. Ernest's three ex-wives and his children would be rich.

Molly's parting shot was, "If you think I was tough, wait until
Cross De Lena hears how you screwed him."

Molly savored her victory. She remembered how one night she had taken Ernest home from a party. She was pretty drunk and extremely lonely and Ernest was witty and intelligent and she thought it might be fun to spend a night with him. Then when they arrived at her home, sobered up by the drive, and she took him to her bedroom, she had looked around despairingly. Ernest was such a shrimp and so obviously sexually shy and he was really a homely man. At that point he was tongue-tied.

But Molly was too fair a person to dismiss him at such a critical time. So she got drunk again and they went to bed. And really, in the dark, it hadn't been too bad. Ernest enjoyed it so much that she was flattered and brought him breakfast in bed.

He gave her a sly grin. "Thank you," he said. "And thank you again." And she perceived that he understood everything she had felt the previous night and was thanking her not only for bringing him breakfast but also as his sexual benefactress. She had always been regretful that she had not been a better actress, but what the hell, she was a lawyer. And now she had performed for Ernest Vail an act of requited love.

Dottore David Redfellow received Don Clericuzio's summons while attending an important meeting in Rome. He was advising the prime minister of Italy on a new banking regulation that would impose severe penal sentences on corrupt bank officials, and naturally he was advising against it. He immediately wound up his arguments and flew to America.

In the twenty-five years of his exile in Italy, David Redfellow had prospered and changed beyond his wildest dreams. At the beginning, Don Clericuzio helped him buy a small bank in Rome. With the fortune he had made in the drug trade and deposited in Swiss banks, he bought more banks and television stations. But it was Don Clericuzio's friends in Italy who helped guide him and build his empire, helped him to acquire the magazines, the newspapers, the TV stations, in addition to his string of banks.

But David Redfellow was pleased also by what he had done on his own. A complete transformation of character. He acquired Italian citizenship, an Italian wife, Italian children, and the standard Italian mistress as well as an honorary doctorate (cost, two million) from an Italian university. He wore Armani suits, spent an hour every week at his barber, acquired a circle of all-male cronies at his coffee bar (which he bought), and entered politics as advisor to the cabinet and the prime minister. Still, once a year he made his pilgrimage to Quogue to fulfill any wishes of his mentor, Don Clericuzio. So this special summons filled him with alarm.

Dinner was waiting for him at the Quogue mansion when he arrived, and Rose Marie had outdone herself because Redfellow was always rapturous about the restaurants of Rome. Assembled to honor him was the entire Clericuzio clan: the Don himself; his sons, Giorgio, Petie, and Vincent; his grandson, Dante; and Pippi and Cross De Lena.

It was a hero's welcome. David Redfellow, the college-dropout drug king, the louche dresser with an earring in his ear, the hyena riding the kills of sex, had transformed himself into a pillar of society. They were proud of him. Even more, Don Clericuzio felt he was in Redfellow's debt. For it was Redfellow who had taught him a great lesson in morality.

In his early days Don Clericuzio had suffered a strange sentimentality. He had believed that the forces of law could not be generally corrupted in the matter of drugs.

David Redfellow was a twenty-year-old college student in 1960 when he first started dealing drugs, not for profit but simply so he and his friends could have a steady cheap supply. An amateur endeavor, just cocaine and marijuana. In a year it had grown so big he and his classmate partners owned a small plane that brought goods over the Mexican and South American borders. Quite naturally they soon ran afoul of the law, and that was where David first showed his genius. The six-man partnership was earning vast amounts of money, and David Redfellow laid on such massive bribes that he soon had on his payroll a roster of sheriffs, district attorneys, judges, and hundreds of police along the Eastern seaboard.

He always claimed it was quite simple. You learned the official's yearly salary and offered him five times that amount.

But then the cartel of Colombians appeared on the scene, wilder than the wildest of the Old West movie Indians, not just taking scalps but whole heads. Four of Redfellow's partners were killed, and Redfellow made contact with the Clericuzio Family and asked for protection, offering 50 percent of his profits.

Petie Clericuzio and a crew of soldiers from the Bronx Enclave became his bodyguards, and this arrangement lasted until the Don exiled Redfellow to Italy in 1965. The drug business had become too dangerous.

Now, gathered together over dinner, they congratulated the Don on the wisdom of his decision many years before. Dante and Cross heard the story of Redfellow for the first time. Redfellow was a good storyteller and he praised Petie to the skies. "What a fighter," he said. "If it wasn't for him I would never have lived to go to Sicily." He turned to Dante and Cross and said to them, "It was the day you both were christened. I remember you both never flinched when they almost drowned you in Holy Water. I never dreamed that someday we would be doing business together, as grown men."

Don Clericuzio said drily, "You will not be doing business with them, you will do business only with me and Giorgio. If you need help you can call on Pippi De Lena. I have decided to go on with the business I spoke to you about. Giorgio will tell you why."

Giorgio told David the latest developments, that Eli Marrion was dead and Bobby Bantz had taken over the Studio, that he had taken away all the points Cross owned in *Messalina*, and returned his money with interest.

Redfellow enjoyed that story. "He is a very clever man. He knows you will not go to court so he takes away your money. That's good business."

Dante was drinking a cup of coffee, and he eyed Redfellow with distaste. Rose Marie, who was sitting beside him, put her hand on his arm.

"You think that's funny?" Dante said to Redfellow.

Redfellow studied Dante for a moment. He made his face very serious. "Only because I know that in this instance it is a mistake to be so clever."

The Don observed this exchange and it seemed to amuse him. In any case he was frivolous, a rare occurrence, which his sons always recognized and enjoyed.

"So Grandson," he said to Dante, "how would you solve this problem?"

"Send him swimming to the bottom of the ocean," Dante said, and the Don smiled at him.

"And you, Croccifixio? How would you solve this situation?" the Don asked.

"I'd just accept it," Cross said. "I'd learn from it. I just got out-foxed because I didn't believe they'd have the balls."

"Petie and Vincent?" the Don asked.

But they refused to answer. They knew the game he was playing.

"You can't just ignore it," the Don said to Cross. "You will be known for a fool and men all over the world will refuse you any respect."

Cross was taking the Don seriously. "Eli Marrion's house still holds his paintings and they're worth about twenty or thirty million. We could hijack them and hold them for ransom."

"No," the Don said. "That would expose you, reveal your power, and no matter how delicately handled, could lead to danger. It is too complicated. David, what would you do?"

David puffed on his cigar, thoughtfully. He said, "Buy the Studio. Do a civilized businesslike thing. With our banks and communications companies, buy LoddStone."

Cross was incredulous. "LoddStone is the oldest and richest film studio in the world. Even if you could put up the ten billion, they wouldn't sell it to you. That's simply not possible."

Petie said in his joker's voice, "David my old buddy, you can get your mitts on ten billion? The man whose life I saved? The man who said he could never repay me?"

Redfellow waved him away. "You don't understand how big money works. It's like whipped cream, you get a small amount and whip it up into a big froth with bonds, loans, stock shares. Money is not the problem."

Cross said, "The problem is how to get Bantz out of the way. He controls the Studio and whatever his faults, he is loyal to Marrion's wishes. He would never agree to selling the Studio."

"I'll go out there and give him a kiss," Petie said.

Now the Don made his decision. He said to Redfellow, "Carry out your plan. Get it done. But with all caution. Pippi and Croccifixio will be at your command."

"One more thing," Giorgio said to Redfellow. "Bobby Bantz, by the terms of Eli Marrion's will, has total command over the Studio for the next five years. But Marrion's son and daughter have more stock in the company than Bantz. Bantz can't get fired but if the Studio is sold, the new owners will have to pay him off. So that's the problem you have to solve."

David Redfellow smiled and puffed on his cigar. "Just like the old days. Don Clericuzio, the only help I need is yours. Some of those banks in Italy may be reluctant to gamble on such a venture. Remember, we will have to pay a big premium over the actual worth of the Studio."

"Don't worry," the Don said. "I have a lot of money in those banks."

Pippi DeLena had watched all this with a wary eye. What disturbed him was the openness of this meeting. By procedure only the Don, Giorgio, and David Redfellow should have been present. Pippi and Cross could have been given orders separately to help Redfellow. Why had they been let in on these secrets? Even more important, why were Dante, Petie, and Vincent brought into the circle? All this was not like the Don Clericuzio he knew, who always kept his plans as secret as possible.

Vincent and Rose Marie were helping the Don up the stairs to go to bed. He had stubbornly refused to have a lift chair installed on the railings.

As soon as they were out of sight, Dante turned to Giorgio and said furiously, "And who gets the Studio when we own it? Cross?"

David Redfellow interrupted coolly. "I will own the Studio. I will run it. Your grandfather will have a financial interest. This will be documented."

Giorgio agreed.

Cross said laughing, "Dante, neither one of us can run a movie studio. We're not ruthless enough."

Pippi studied all of them. He was good at scenting danger. That's why he had lived so long. But this he couldn't figure out. Maybe the Don was just getting old.

Petie drove Redfellow back to Kennedy Airport where his private jet waited. Cross and Pippi had used a chartered jet from Vegas. Don Clericuzio absolutely forbade the owning of a jet by the Xanadu or any of his enterprises.

Cross drove their rented car to the airport. During the drive, Pippi said to Cross, "I'm going to spend some time in New York City. I'll just keep the car when we get to the airport."

Cross saw that his father was worried. "I didn't do well in there," he said.

"You were OK," Pippi said. "But the Don was right. You can't let anybody screw you twice."

When they arrived at Kennedy, Cross got out and Pippi slid across the seat to get behind the wheel. Through the open window, they shook hands. In that moment Pippi looked up at his son's handsome face and felt an enormous wave of affection. He tried to smile as he slapped Cross gently on the cheek and said, "Be careful."

"Of what?" Cross asked, his dark eyes searching his father's.

"Everything," Pippi said. Then, startling Cross, he said, "Maybe I should have let you go with your mother but I was selfish. I needed you around."

Cross watched his father drive away and for the first time he realized how much his father worried about him, how much his father loved him.

CHAPTER 15

MUCH TO HIS OWN DISMAY, Pippi De Lena decided to get married, not for love but for companionship. True, he had Cross, he had the cronies at the Xanadu Hotel, he had the Clericuzio Family and a vast network or relatives. True, he had three mistresses and he ate with good and sincere appetite; he enjoyed his golf and was down to a ten handicap, and he still loved to dance. But as the Don would say, he could go dancing to his coffin.

So in his late fifties, robust in health, sanguine in temperament, rich, semiretired, he longed for a settled home life and perhaps a new batch of kids. Why not? The idea appealed to him more and more. Surprisingly, he yearned to be a father again. It would be fun to raise a daughter, he had loved Claudia as a child, though they no longer spoke. She had been so cunning and so forthright at the same time, and she had made her way in the world as a successful screenplay writer. And who knows, maybe someday they would make up. In some ways she was as stubborn as he was, so he understood her and he admired the way she stood up for what she believed in.

Cross had lost the gamble he had taken in the movie business, but one way or another his future was assured. He still had the Xanadu and the Don would help him recover from the risk he had taken with his new venture. He was a good kid, but he was young and the young must take risks. That's what life was all about.

After dropping off Cross at the airport, Pippi drove to New York City to spend a few days with his East Coast mistress. She was a good-looking brunette, a legal secretary with a sharp New York wit, and a great dancer. True, she had a tongue that lashed out, she loved to spend money, she would be an expensive wife. But she was too old, over forty-five. And she was too independent, a great quality for a mistress but not for the kind of marriage that Pippi would demand.

It was a pleasurable weekend with her, though she spent half the Sunday reading the *Times*. They ate in the finest restaurants, went dancing in the nightclubs, and had great sex in her apartment. But Pippi needed something more placid.

Pippi flew to Chicago. His mistress there was the sexual equivalent of that brawling city. She drank a little too much, she partied too exuberantly, she was happy-go-lucky and a lot of fun. But she was a little lazy, a little too messy, Pippi liked a clean home. Again, she was too old to start a family, at least forty, she said. But what the hell. Was he up to running around with a really young broad? After two days in Chicago, Pippi crossed her off the list.

With both, he would have a problem settling them in Vegas. They were big-city women, and Vegas, Pippi knew in his heart, was really a hick cow town where casinos took the place of cattle. And there was no way that Pippi would live in any place but Vegas, for in Vegas nighttime did not exist. Electric neon banished all ghosts, the city shone like a rosy diamond in the desert at night, and after dawn the hot sun burned away all the wraiths that had escaped the neon.

His best shot was his mistress in Los Angeles, and Pippi was pleased that he had geographically positioned them so neatly. There could be no accidental confrontations, no mental struggles in choosing between them. They served a certain purpose and they could not interfere with any temporary love affairs. Indeed, looking back, he was pleased at how he had conducted his life. Daring but prudent, brave but not foolhardy, loyal to the Family and rewarded by them. His only mistake had been in marrying a woman like Nalene, and even there, what woman could have given him more happiness for eleven years. And what man could boast of having made only one mistake in his lifetime? What was it the Don always said, It was OK to make mistakes in life as long as it was not a fatal mistake.

He decided to go directly to L.A. and not stop in Vegas. He called to notify Michelle that he was on his way and refused her offer to pick him up at the airport. "Just be ready for me when I get there," he told her. "I've been missing you. And I've got something important to tell you."

Michelle was young enough, thirty-two, and she was more tender, more giving, more easy on the nerves, maybe because she had been born and raised in California. She was also good in bed, not that the others were not, for this was a primary qualification for Pippi. But she had no sharp edges, she wouldn't be trouble. She was a little kooky, she believed in New Age crap called channeling and being able to talk to spirits, and talked about all the past lives she had lived, but she could also be fun. Like many California beauties, she had dreamed of being an actress, but that had been knocked out of her head. She was completely wrapped up in yoga and channeling now, in physical health, running and going to the gym. And besides, she always complimented Pippi on his karma. For of course none of these women knew his true vocation. He was simply an administrative officer of the hotel association in Vegas.

Yes, with Michelle, he could stay in Vegas, they could keep an apartment in L.A. and when they got bored they could make the forty-minute flight to L.A. for a couple of weeks. And maybe to keep her busy, he would buy her a gift shop in the Hotel Xanadu. It could really work out. But what if she said no?

Something struck his memory: Nalene reading *Goldilocks and the Three Bears* when the children were small. He was just like Goldilocks. The New York woman was too hard, the Chicago woman was too soft, and the L.A. woman was just right. The thought gave him pleasure. Of course, in real life nothing was "just right."

When he deplaned in L.A., he breathed in the balmy air of California, not even noticing the smog. He rented a car and drove first to Rodeo Drive, he loved to bring his women little gifts as a surprise and enjoyed walking down the street of fancy shops that held the luxuries of the world. He bought a gaudy wristwatch in the Gucci store; a purse in Fendi's, though he thought it ugly; a Hermès scarf; and some perfume in a bottle that looked like an expensive sculpture. When he bought a box of expensive lingerie, he was in such good spirits that he kidded the saleswoman, a young blonde, that it was for himself. The girl gave him one look and said, "Right . . ."

Back in the car, three thousand dollars poorer, he headed for Santa Monica, the goodies in the passenger seat, gifts crammed into a gaily colored Gucci shopping bag. In Brentwood, he stopped in the Brentwood Mart, a favorite place. He loved the food stores that boxed an open square studded with picnic tables where you could have a cold drink and eat. The food on the plane had been terrible, and he was hungry. Michelle never kept food in the refrigerator because she was always dieting.

In one store he bought two roast chickens, a dozen barbecued spareribs, and four hot dogs with all the trimmings. In another shop, he bought fresh baked white and rye bread. At an open stand he bought a huge glass of Coke and sat down at one of the picnic tables for a final moment of solitude. He ate two of the hot dogs, half of one of the roast chickens, and some French fries. He had never tasted anything so good. He sat in the golden light of the late afternoon sun in California, the sweet balmy air washed his face clean. He hated to leave but Michelle was waiting. She would be bathed and scented and a little tipsy and she would take him to bed immediately before he could even brush his teeth. He would propose to her before they started.

The shopping bag holding the food was decorated with type telling some fable about food, an intellectual shopping bag as befitted the intellectual clientele of the Mart. When he put it into the car, he read only the beginning line, "Fruit is the oldest product of human consumption. In the Garden of Eden . . ." Jesus, Pippi thought.

He drove to Santa Monica and stopped in front of Michelle's condo, which was in a two-story-high series of Spanish-looking bungalows. When he got out of the car he carried the two bags automatically in his left hand, leaving his right hand free. Out of habit, he surveyed the street up and down. It was lovely, no cars parked, the Spanish styles provided commodious driveways and a mildly religious benignity. The runners along the curbs were hidden by flowers and grass, the heavy-branched trees made a canopy against the descending sun.

Pippi now had to walk down a long alleyway whose wooden, green-painted fences were draped with roses. Michelle's apartment was in the back, a relic of the old Santa Monica, which was still bucolic. The buildings themselves were of seemingly old wood, and each separated swimming pool was adorned by white benches.

Outside the alleyway, far down the other end, Pippi heard the growling motor of a stationary vehicle. It alerted him, he was always alert. At the same moment he caught sight of a man rising from one of the benches. He was so surprised that he said, "What the fuck are you doing here?"

The man's hand did not come out to greet him and in that instant everything was clear to Pippi. He knew what was going to happen. His brain processed so much information that he could not react. He saw the gun appear, so small and inoffensive, saw the tension on the killer's face. Understood for the first time the look on the faces of men he had put to death, their supreme astonishment that life was at an end. And he understood that finally he would have to pay the price for living his life. He even thought briefly that the killer had planned badly, that this was not how he would have done it.

He tried his best, knowing there was no mercy. He dropped the shopping bags and lunged forward, at the same time reaching for his gun. The man came forward to meet him, and Pippi in exultation reached for him. Six bullets carried his body into the air and flung it into a pillow of flowers at the foot of the green fence. He smelled their fragrance. He looked up at the man standing over him and said, "You fucking Santadio." Then the final bullet crashed into his skull. Pippi De Lena was no more.

CHAPTER 16

EARLY ON THE DAY Pippi De Lena was to die, Cross picked up Athena at her Malibu home and they drove to San Diego to visit Athena's daughter, Bethany.

Bethany had been prepared by the nurses, she was dressed to go out. Cross could see she was a blurry reflection of her mother, and tall for her age. There was still the blankness in her face and eyes, and her body was too slack. Her features did not seem to have real definition, as if partially dissolved, like a bar of used soap. She still wore the red plastic apron that she used to protect her clothes when she was painting. She had been painting on the wall since early that morning. She didn't acknowledge seeing them, and she received her mother's hug and kisses with a shrinking away of her body and face.

Athena disregarded this and hugged her even harder.

The day was to be a picnic at a wooded lake nearby. Athena had packed a lunch basket.

On the short drive, Bethany sat between them, with Athena driving. Athena frequently brushed back Bethany's hair and caressed her cheek while Bethany stared straight ahead.

Cross thought of how when the day was done he and Athena would be back in Malibu making love. He was imagining her naked body on the bed and him standing over her.

Suddenly Bethany spoke, and it was to him. She had never acknowledged him before. She stared at him with her flat green eyes and said, "Who are you?"

Athena answered, and her voice was perfect, as if it was the most natural thing in the world for Bethany to ask. She said, "His name is

Cross and he's my very best friend." Bethany seemed not to hear and retired into her world again.

Athena parked the car a few yards from a dazzling lake nestled in the forest, a tiny blue gem in a vast cloth of green. Cross took the basket of food, and Athena unpacked it onto a red cloth she spread over the grass. She also put out crisp green napkins and forks and spoons. The cloth was embroidered with musical instruments that caught Bethany's attention. Then Athena spread out a pile of different sandwiches, glass bowls of potato salad, and sliced fruits. Then a plate of sweet cakes oozing cream. And a platter of fried chicken. She had prepared everything with the care of a catering professional because Bethany loved food.

Cross went back to the car and took a case of soda from the trunk. There were glasses in the basket and he poured soda for them. Athena offered her glass to Bethany, but Bethany struck her hand aside. She was watching Cross.

Cross stared into her eyes. Her face was so rigid it could have been a mask instead of flesh, but her eyes were now alert. It was as if she was trapped in some secret cave, that she was being smothered but could not call for help, that her flesh was blistered and she could not bear to be touched.

They ate, and Athena took on the role of the insensitive chatterbox, trying to make Bethany laugh. Cross marveled at how skillful she was, affectedly irritating and boring, as if the autistic behavior of her child was perfectly natural, treating Bethany as a fellow gossip though the girl never answered. It was an inspired monologue she created to ease her own pain.

Finally it was time for dessert. Athena unwrapped one of the creamy cakes and offered it to Bethany, who refused it. She offered one to Cross and he shook his head. He was getting very nervous because, though Bethany had consumed an enormous amount of food, it was obvious she was very angry with her mother. He knew that Athena sensed it, too.

Athena ate the pastry and exclaimed enthusiastically about how delicious it was. She unwrapped another two and set them before Bethany. The girl usually loved sweets. Bethany took them off the tablecloth and put them on the grass. In a few minutes they were covered with insects. Then Bethany picked up the two cakes and shoved one into her mouth. She handed the other to Cross. Without a moment's hesitation, Cross put the pastry into his mouth. There was a tickling sensation all across his palate and on the sides of his gums. He quickly gulped some soda to wash it down. Bethany looked at Athena.

Athena had the studied frown of an actress planning to do a difficult scene. Then she laughed, a wonderfully infectious laugh, and clapped her hands. "I told you it was delicious," she said. She unwrapped another pastry, but Bethany refused and so did Cross. Athena threw the pastry onto the grass and then took her napkin and wiped Bethany's mouth and then did the same to Cross. She was enjoying herself, it seemed.

On the drive back to the hospital, she spoke to Cross with some of the same inflections she used with Bethany. As if he, too, were autistic. Bethany watched her carefully and then turned to stare at Cross.

When they dropped the child off at the hospital, Bethany took Cross by the hand for a moment. "You're beautiful," she said, but when Cross tried to kiss her good-bye, she turned her head away. Then she ran.

Driving back to Malibu, Athena said excitedly, "She responded to you, that's a very good sign."

"Because I'm beautiful," Cross said dryly.

"No," Athena said, "because you can eat bugs. I'm at least as beautiful as you are and she hates me . . ." She was smiling joyfully, and as always her beauty made Cross dizzy and alarmed him.

"She thinks you're like her," Athena said. "She thinks you're autistic."

Cross laughed, he enjoyed the idea. "She may be right," he said. "Maybe you should put me in the hospital with her."

"No," Athena said, smiling. "Then I couldn't have your body whenever I wanted it. Besides, I'm going to take her out after I finish *Messalina*."

When they arrived at her Malibu house, Cross went in with her. They had planned for him to spend the night. By this time he had learned to read Athena: The more vivacious she acted, the more disturbed she was.

"If you're upset, I can go back to Vegas," he said.

Now she looked sad. Cross wondered how he loved her most, when she was naturally exuberant, when she was stern and serious, or when she was melancholy. Her face changed so magically in its beauty that he always found his feelings matching hers.

She said to him fondly, "You've had a terrible day and you shall have your reward." There was a mocking tone to her voice, but he understood it was a mockery of her own beauty, she knew her magic was false.

"I didn't have a terrible day," Cross said. And it was true. The joy he felt that day, with the three of them alone by the lake in the vast forest, reminded him of his childhood.

"You love ants on your pastry . . ." Athena said sadly.

"They weren't bad," Cross said. "Can Bethany get better?"

"I don't know but I'll keep searching until I find out," Athena said. "I have a long weekend coming up when they won't need to shoot *Messalina*. I'm going to fly to France with Bethany. There's a great doctor in Paris and I'm going to take her for another evaluation."

"What if he says there's no hope?" Cross said.

"Maybe I won't believe him. It doesn't matter," Athena said. "I love her. I'll take care of her."

"Forever and ever?" Cross asked.

"Yes," Athena said. Then she clapped her hands together, her green eyes shining. "Meanwhile, let's have some fun. Let's take care of ourselves. We'll go upstairs and shower and jump into bed. We'll make mad passionate love for hours. Then I'll cook us a midnight supper."

For Cross, he was a child again waking up with a day of pleasure before him, the breakfast his mother prepared, the playing of games with his friends, the hunting trips with his father, then supper with his family, Claudia, Nalene, and Pippi. The card games afterward. It was that innocent a feeling. Before him was making love to Athena in the twilight, watching the sun disappear over the Pacific from the balcony, the sky painted with marvelous reds and pinks, the touch of her warm flesh and silky skin. Her beautiful face and lips to kiss. He smiled and led her up the stairs.

The phone in the bedroom rang, and Athena ran up ahead of Cross to answer it. She covered the mouthpiece and in a startled voice said, "It's for you. A man named Giorgio." He had never received a phone call at her house before.

This could only be trouble, Cross thought, and so he did something he never thought he was capable of doing. He shook his head.

Athena said into the phone, "He's not here. . . . Yes, I'll tell him to call you when he comes." She hung up the phone and asked, "Who's Giorgio?"

"Just a relative," Cross said. He was stunned by what he had done, and why: because he could not give up a night with Athena. That was a grievous crime. And then he wondered how Giorgio knew he would be here and what Giorgio wanted. It must be something important, he thought, but still it could wait until morning. More than anything else he was desperate for the hours of making love to Athena.

It was the moment they'd been waiting for all day, all week; they were stripping off their clothes before showering together but he couldn't resist embracing her, their bodies still sweaty from the picnic. Then she took his hand and led him under the spraying water.

They dried each other with the large orange towels and, wrapped in them, stood on the balcony to watch the sun slide gradually behind the horizon. Then they went inside to lay on the bed.

When Cross made love to her, it seemed that all the cells of his brain and body flew out and he was left in some feverish dream; he was a ghost whose wisps were filled with ecstasy, a ghost who entered her flesh. He lost all his caution, all his reason, he didn't even study her face to see if she was acting, if she truly loved him. It seemed to go on forever, until they fell asleep in each other's arms. When they woke they were still entwined, lit by a moon whose light seemed brighter than the sun's. Athena kissed him and said, "Did you really like Bethany?"

"Yes," Cross said. "She's part of you."

"Do you think she can get better?" Athena asked. "Do you think I can help her get better?"

At that moment Cross felt as though he would give up his life to make the girl well. He felt the urge to sacrifice for the woman he loved, which many men feel but which until that time had been completely alien to him.

"We can both try to help," Cross said.

"No," Athena said, "I have to do it by myself."

They fell asleep again, and when the phone rang the air was misty with the newly born dawn. Athena picked up the phone, listened, and then said to Cross, "It's the guard at the gate. He says four men in a car want to come and see you."

Cross felt a shock of fear. He took the phone and said to the guard, "Put one of them on the phone."

The voice he heard was Vincent's. "Cross, Petie is with me. We got some really bad news."

"OK, put the guard on," Cross said, and then, to the guard, "They can come in."

He had completely forgotten about Giorgio's call. That's what love does, he thought contemptuously. I won't live a year if I keep this up.

He slipped on his clothes quickly and ran downstairs. The car was just pulling up to the front of the house, the sun, still half hidden, threw its light from over the horizon.

Vincent and Petie were getting out of the back of a long limousine. Cross could see the driver and another man in front. Petie and Vincent walked the long garden path to the door and Cross opened it for them.

Suddenly Athena was standing beside him, clad in slacks and a pullover, nothing beneath. Petie and Vincent were staring at her. She had never looked more beautiful.

Athena led them all into the kitchen and started making coffee, and Cross introduced them as his cousins.

"How did you guys get here?" Cross asked. "Last night you were in New York."

"Giorgio chartered us a plane," Petie said.

Athena was studying them as she made the coffee. Neither of them showed any emotion. They looked like brothers, both were big men, but Vincent was pale as granite, while Petie's leaner face was tanned red with weather or drink.

"So what's the bad news?" Cross said. He expected to hear that the Don had died, that Rose Marie had really gone crazy, or that Dante had done something so terrible that the Family was in crisis.

Vincent said with his usual curtness, "We have to talk to you alone."

Athena poured them coffee. "I tell you all my bad news," she said to Cross. "I should hear yours."

"I'll just leave with them," Cross said.

"Don't you be so fucking condescending," Athena said. "Don't you dare leave."

At this Vincent and Petie reacted. Vincent's granite face flushed with embarrassment, Petie gave Athena a speculative grin, as if she was someone to be watched. Cross, seeing this, laughed and said, "OK, let's hear it."

Petie tried to soften the blow. "Something happened to your father," he said.

Vincent broke in savagely, "Pippi got shot by some punk eggplant mugger. He's dead. So is the mugger, a cop named Losey shot him as he was running away. They need you in L.A. to identify the body and do the paperwork. The old man wants him buried in Quogue."

Cross lost his breath. He wavered for a moment, trembling in some dark wind, then he felt Athena holding his arm with both her hands.

"When?" Cross asked.

"About eight last night," Petie said. "Giorgio called for you."

Cross thought, While I was making love, my father was lying in the morgue. He felt an extraordinary contempt for his moment of weakness, an overwhelming shame. "I have to go," he said to Athena.

She looked at his stricken face. She had never seen him so.

"I'm sorry," she said. "Call me."

. . .

In the backseat of the limousine, Cross heard the other two men offering condolences. He recognized them as soldiers from the Bronx Enclave. As they moved through the Malibu Colony gate and then onto the Pacific Coast Highway, Cross detected a sluggishness of movement. The car they were riding in was armored.

Five days later the funeral of Pippi De Lena was held in Quogue. The Don's estate held its own private cemetery as the mansion held its own private chapel, and Pippi was buried in the grave next to Silvio, to show the Don's respect.

Only the Clericuzio clan and the most valued soldiers of the Bronx Enclave attended. Lia Vazzi came from the Hunting Lodge in the Sierras at the request of Cross. Rose Marie was not present. On hearing of Pippi's death, she had one of her fits and was taken to the psychiatric clinic.

But Claudia De Lena was there. She flew in to comfort Cross and to say good-bye to her father. What she had not been able to do when Pippi was alive, she felt she must do after his death. She wanted to claim a part of him for herself, to show the Clericuzio that he was as much her father as he was part of their Family.

The lawn in front of the Clericuzio mansion was decorated with a huge floral wreath the size of a billboard, and there were buffet tables and waiters and a bartender at a makeshift table to serve the guests. It was strictly a day of mourning, and no Family business was discussed.

Claudia cried bitter tears for all the years she'd been forced to live without her father, but Cross received condolences with a quiet dignity and showed no signs of grief.

The next night he was on the balcony of his suite in the Xanadu Hotel watching the riot of colors on the neoned Strip. Even this far up he could hear the sounds of music, the buzz of gamblers crowd-

MARIO PUZO • 374

ing the Strip looking for a lucky casino. But it was quiet enough for him to analyze what had happened in the last month. And to reflect on the death of his father.

Cross did not believe for a moment that Pippi De Lena had been shot down by a punk mugger. It was impossible for a Qualified Man to meet such a fate.

He reviewed all the facts he had been told. His father had been shot by a black mugger named Hugh Marlowe. The mugger was twenty-three years old, with a record as a drug dealer. Marlowe had been killed while fleeing the scene by Detective Jim Losey, who had been trailing Marlowe in a drug case. Marlowe had a gun in his hand and pointed it at Losey who had therefore shot him down, a clean shot through the bridge of his nose. When Losey investigated, he discovered Pippi De Lena, and immediately called Dante Clericuzio. Before he notified even the police. Why would he do so even if he was on the Family payroll? A great irony—Pippi De Lena, the ultimate Qualified Man, the Clericuzio Number One Hammer for over thirty years, murdered by a raggedy drug-dealing mugger.

But then why had the Don sent Vincent and Petie to transport him with an armored car and guarded him until the funeral? Why had the Don taken such elaborate precautions? During the funeral he had asked the Don. But the Don said only that it was wise to be prepared until all the facts were known. That he had made a full investigation and it seemed all the facts were true. A petty thief had made a mistake and a foolish tragedy had ensued, but then, the Don said, most tragedies were foolish.

There was no doubting the Don's grief. He had always treated Pippi as one of his sons, had indeed given him some preference, and had said to Cross, "You shall have your father's place in the Family."

But now Cross on his balcony overlooking Vegas pondered the central issue. The Don never believed in coincidence and yet here was a case bursting with coincidence. Detective Jim Losey was on the Family payroll and out of the thousands of detectives and policemen in Los Angeles, it was he who stumbled on the killing. What were the odds on that? But put that aside. Even more important, Don Domenico Clericuzio well knew it was impossible for a street mugger to get that close to Pippi De Lena. And what mugger fired six shots before fleeing? Never would the Don believe such a case.

So the question came. Had the Clericuzio decided that their greatest soldier was a danger to them? For what reason? Could they disregard his loyalty and devotion as well as their own affection for him? No, they were innocent. And the strongest evidence in their favor was that Cross himself was still alive. The Don would never allow that if they had killed Pippi. But Cross knew that he himself must be in danger.

Cross thought about his father. He had truly loved him, and Pippi was hurt that Claudia had refused to speak to him while he was alive. Yet she went to the funeral. Why? Could it be that she had finally remembered how good he was to both of them before their family fell apart?

He thought of that terrible day when he had chosen to go with his father because he realized what his father really was, knew that he could really kill Nalene if she took both children. But he had stepped up and taken his father's hand, not because of love but because of the fear in Claudia's eyes.

Cross had always thought his father was protection against the world they lived in, always thought his father invulnerable. A giver of death, not a receiver. Now he himself would have to guard against his enemies, even perhaps the Clericuzio. After all, he was rich, he owned half a billion worth of the Xanadu, his life was now worth taking.

And that made him think of the life he was now leading. To what purpose? To grow old like his father, taking all risks and then still to be killed? True, Pippi had enjoyed his life, the power, the money, but now to Cross it seemed to have been an empty life. His father had never known the happiness of loving a woman like Athena.

He was only twenty-six years old; he could make a new life. He thought of Athena and that he would see her tomorrow working for the first time, observe her make-believe life and see all the masks she could wear. How Pippi would have loved her, he loved all beautiful women. But then he thought of the wife of Virginio Ballazzo. Pippi had been fond of her, eaten at her table, hugged her, danced with her, played boccie with her husband, then planned the killing of them both.

He sighed and rose to go back into his suite. Dawn was breaking, and its light misted the neon that hung like a great theater curtain over the Strip. He could look down and see the flags of all the great casino hotels, the Sands, Caesars, the Flamingo, the Desert Inn, and the shooting volcano of the Mirage. The Xanadu was greater than them all. He watched the flags flying over the Xanadu Villas. What a dream he had lived in, and now it was dissolving, Gronevelt dead and his father murdered.

Back in his room he picked up the phone and called Lia Vazzi to come up and have breakfast with him. They had traveled from the funeral in Quogue to Vegas together. Then he called for breakfast for both of them. He remembered that Lia was fond of pancakes, an exotic dish to him still after all his years in America. The security guard arrived with Vazzi the same time as breakfast did. They ate in the kitchen of the suite.

"So what do you think?" Cross asked Lia.

"I think we should kill this detective Losey," Lia said. "I told you that a long time ago."

"So you don't believe his story?" Cross asked.

Lia was cutting his pancakes into strips. "It's a disgrace, that story," he said. "There is no way a Qualified Man like your father would let a rascal get that close to him."

"The Don thinks it's true," Cross said. "He investigated."

Lia reached for one of the Havana cigars and the glass of brandy Cross had set out for him. "I would never contradict Don Clericuzio," he said. "But let me kill Losey just to make sure."

"And what if the Clericuzio were behind him?" Cross asked.

"The Don is a man of honor," Lia said. "From the old days. If he killed Pippi, he would have killed you. He knows you. He understands you will avenge your father and he is a prudent man."

"But still," Cross said, "who would you choose to fight for? Me or the Clericuzio?"

"I don't have a choice," Lia said. "I was too close to your father and I'm too close to you. They won't let me live if you go down."

Cross for the first time had brandy with Lia for breakfast. "Maybe it's just one of those foolish things," he said.

"No," Lia said. "It's Losey."

"But he has no reason," Cross said. "Still, we'll have to find out. Now I want you to form a crew of six men, those most loyal to you, none from the Bronx Enclave. Have them ready and wait for my orders."

Lia was unusually sober. "Forgive me," he said. "I have never questioned your orders. But on this I beg you to consult with me on the overall plan."

"Good," Cross said. "Next weekend I plan to fly to France for two days. Meanwhile find out all you can about Losey."

Lia smiled at Cross. "You're going with your fiancée?"

Cross was amused by his politeness. "Yes, and with her daughter."

"The one with the quarter of her brain missing?" Lia asked. He did not mean to be offensive. It was an idiom in Italian that also included brilliant people who were forgetful.

"Yes," Cross said. "There is a doctor there who may help her."

"Bravo," Lia said. "I wish you all the best. This woman, does she know about Family matters?"

"God forbid," Cross said, and they both laughed. And Cross was wondering how Lia knew so much about his private life.

CHAPTER 17

FOR THE FIRST TIME Cross was going to watch Athena work on a movie set, to see her act out false emotions, to be someone other than herself.

He met Claudia in her office at the LoddStone lot, they would watch Athena together. There were two other women in the office, and Claudia introduced them. "This is my brother Cross and this is the director, Dita Tommey. And Falene Fante, who is working today in the picture."

Tommey gave him a searching look, thinking he was handsome enough to be in the business except that he showed no fire, no passion, he would be stone cold dead on the screen. She lost interest. "I'm just leaving," she said as she shook his hand. "I'm very sorry about your father. By the way, you're welcome on my set, Claudia and Athena vouch for you even though you're one of the producers."

Cross became aware of the other woman. She was sort of dark chocolate with an outrageously insolent face and a terrific body, which her clothes flaunted. Falene was far less formal than Tommey.

"I didn't know Claudia had such a handsome brother—and rich, too, from what I hear. If you ever need somebody to keep you company at dinner, give me a call," Falene said.

"I will," Cross said. He was not surprised by the invitation. Plenty of the showgirls and dancers at the Xanadu had been just as direct. This was a girl who was naturally flirtatious, aware of her beauty, and not about to let a man she liked the looks of escape because of social rules.

Claudia said, "We were just giving Falene a little more to do in the film. Dita thinks she's talented and so do I."

Falene gave Cross a big grin. "Yeah, now I shake my ass ten times instead of six. And I get to say to Messalina, 'All the women of Rome love you and hope for your victory.'" She paused for a minute and said, "I hear you're one of the producers. Maybe you can get them to let me shake my ass twenty times."

Cross sensed something in her, something she was trying to hide, despite her vivaciousness.

"I'm just one of the money men," Cross said. "Everybody has to shake their ass at some time or another." He smiled and said with charming simplicity, "Anyway, I wish you luck."

Falene leaned over and kissed him on the cheek. He could smell her perfume, which was heavy and erotic, and then he felt the grateful hug for his goodwill. Then she leaned back. "I have to tell you and Claudia something but in secret. I don't want to get into trouble, especially now."

Claudia, sitting at her computer, frowned and did not answer. Cross took a step away from Falene. He did not like surprises.

Falene noticed these responses. Her voice faltered a little. "I'm sorry about your father," she said. "But there's something you should hear about. Marlowe, the guy who supposedly mugged him, was a kid I grew up with and I knew him really well. Supposedly that detective Jim Losey shot Marlowe who supposedly shot your father. But I know Marlowe never had a gun. He was scared shitless of guns. Marlowe did small-time drugs and played the clarinet. And he was such a sweet coward. Jim Losey and his partner, Phil Sharkey, used to pick him up sometimes and ride him around so that he could spot dealers for them. Marlowe was so scared of jail, he was a police informant. All of a sudden he's a mugger and a murderer. I know Marlowe, he wouldn't harm a soul."

Claudia was silent. Falene waved to her and went out the door, then came back. "Remember," she said, "it's a secret between us."

"It's all gone and forgotten," Cross said with his most reassuring smile. "And your story won't change anything."

"I just had to get it off my chest," Falene said. "Marlowe was such a good kid." She left.

"What do you think?" Claudia said to Cross. "What the hell could that be about?"

MARIO PUZO • 380

Cross shrugged. "Druggies are always full of surprises. He needed dope money and he does a stickup and he gets unlucky."

"I guess," Claudia said. "And Falene is so good-hearted she'll believe anything. But it is an irony, our father dying like that."

Cross looked at her stone-faced. "Everybody gets unlucky once."

He spent the rest of the afternoon watching scenes being shot. One scene showed the hero, unarmed, defeating three armed men. This offended him, it was ridiculous. A hero should never be put in such a hopeless position. All it proved was that he was too dumb to be a hero. Then he watched Athena do a love scene and a quarrel scene. He was a little disappointed, she seemed to do little acting, the other actors seemed to outshine her. Cross was too inexperienced to know that what Athena was doing would register much more forcefully on film, that the camera would work its magic for her.

And he did not discover the real Athena. The acting she did was only for a few short snippets of time, and then there were long intervals in between. You could not see any of the electricity that would flash across the screen. Athena even seemed less beautiful when she was acting before the camera.

He said nothing of this when he spent the night with her that night in Malibu. After they had made love and she was cooking their midnight supper, she said, "I wasn't very good today, was I?" She gave him her catlike grin, which always sent a shock of pleasure through him. "I didn't want to show you my best moves," she said. "I knew you'd be standing there trying to figure me out."

He laughed. Always he was delighted by her perception of his character. "No, you weren't much," he said. "Would you like me to fly with you to Paris Friday?"

Athena was surprised. He knew she was surprised by her eyes. Her face never changed, she was in control. She thought it over. "That could be a big help," she said. "And we could see Paris together."

"And we'll be back Monday," Cross asked.

"Yes," Athena said. "I have to shoot Tuesday morning. We have only a few weeks to go on the picture."

"And then?" Cross asked.

"Then I'll retire and take care of my daughter," Athena said. "Besides, I don't want to keep her a secret much longer."

"The doctor in Paris is the final word?" Cross asked.

"Nobody's the final word," Athena said. "Not on this stuff. But he's close."

On Friday evening they flew to Paris on a specially chartered plane. Athena was disguised in a wig, and her makeup veiled her beauty in such a way as to make her even look homely. She wore loosely fitting clothing that hid her figure entirely and in some ways made her look matronly. Cross was amazed. She even walked differently.

On the plane Bethany was fascinated to find herself looking down on the earth. She roamed the plane looking out all the different windows. She seemed a little startled, her usually blank expression became almost normal.

They went from the plane to a small hotel off Georges-Mandel Avenue. They had a suite with two separate bedrooms, one for Cross and one for Athena and Bethany, the sitting room between them. It was ten in the morning; Athena removed her wig and makeup and changed her clothes. She could not bear to be homely in Paris.

At noon the three of them were in the doctor's office, a small chateau set on its own grounds and enclosed by an iron fence. There was a guard at the gate, and after checking their names he let them in.

They were met at the door by a maid who led them into a huge sitting room, which was densely furnished. There the doctor awaited them.

Dr. Ocell Gerard was a huge, heavy man, carefully dressed in a beautifully cut suit of brown pin stripes, a white shirt, and a dark brown silk tie to match. He had a round face, which should have had a beard to hide his heavy jowls. His thick lips were a dusky red. He introduced himself to Athena and Cross but ignored the child. Both Athena and Cross felt an immediate aversion to the man. He did not look like a doctor suitable to the sensitive profession he practiced.

There was a table set for tea and pastries. A maid attended to them. They were joined by two nurses, young women clad in strict professional attire, white caps and ivory-colored blouses and skirts. The two nurses watched Bethany intensely all during the meal.

Dr. Gerard addressed Athena. "Madame, I would like to thank you for your very generous contribution to our Medical Institute for Autistic Children. I have observed your request for complete confidentiality, which is why I'm conducting this examination here in my own private center. Now tell me exactly what you expect of me." His voice was a mellow bass, it was magnetic. It attracted Bethany's attention, and she stared at him, but he ignored her.

Athena was nervous, she really didn't like the man. "I want you to evaluate. I want her to have some sort of normal life if possible and I will give up everything to achieve that. I want you to accept her into your Institute, I am willing to live in France and help in her schooling."

She said this with enchanting sadness and hope, with such an air of self-abnegation, that the two nurses gazed at her almost adoringly. Cross was aware she was using all her acting skills to convince the doctor to take Bethany into the Institute. He saw her reach her arm out to clasp Bethany's hand with a caressing gesture.

Only Dr. Gerard seemed unimpressed. He did not look at Bethany. He addressed himself directly to Athena. "Do not deceive yourself," he said. "All your love will not help this child. I have examined her records and there is no doubt she is genuinely autistic. She cannot return your love. She does not live in our world. She does not even live in the world of animals. She lives on a different star, absolutely alone."

He continued, "You are not at fault. Nor, I believe, is the father. This is one of those mysterious complexities of the human condition. Here is what I can do. I will examine and test her more thoroughly. Then I will tell you what we at the Institute can and cannot do. If I cannot help, you must take her home. If we can, you will leave her with me in France for five years."

He spoke to one of the nurses in French, and the woman left and returned with a huge book containing photographs of famous paintings. She gave the book to Bethany, but it was too big to fit on her lap. For the first time Dr. Gerard spoke to her. He spoke to her in French. She immediately put the textbook on the table and began to turn the pages. Soon she was lost in studying the pictures.

The doctor seemed ill at ease. "I don't mean to be offensive," he said. "But this is in the best interest of your child. I know Mr. De Lena is not your husband, but is it possible he is the father of your child? If so, I would want to test him."

Athena said, "I did not know him when my daughter was born."

"*Bon*," the doctor said. He shrugged. "Such things are always possible."

Cross laughed. "Maybe the doctor sees some symptoms in me."

The doctor's thick red lips pursed as he nodded and smiled amiably. "You do have certain symptoms. So do we all. Who knows? A centimeter either way, all of us could be autistic. Now I must make a thorough examination of the child and run some tests. It will take at the very least four hours. Why don't the two of you take a stroll through our lovely Paris. Mr. De Lena, your first time?"

"Yes," Cross said.

Athena said, "I want to remain with my daughter."

"As you wish, madame," he said and then spoke to Cross. "Enjoy your stroll. I detest Paris myself. If a city could be autistic, it would be Paris."

A taxi was called, and Cross went back to the hotel room. He had no desire to see Paris without Athena and he needed rest. Besides, he had come to Paris to clear his head, to think things out.

He pondered what Falene had told him. He remembered that Losey had come to Malibu alone, detectives usually worked in pairs. Before leaving Paris he had asked Vazzi to look into it.

At four, Cross was back in the doctor's sitting room. They were waiting for him. Bethany was poring over the book of paintings, Athena was pale, the only physical sign that Cross knew could not be acting. Bethany was also gobbling a plate of pastries, and the doctor took it away from her, saying something in French. Bethany did not protest. A nurse came then to take her to the playroom.

"Forgive me," the doctor said to Cross. "But I must ask you some questions."

"Whatever you like," Cross said.

The doctor rose from his chair and strode about the room. "I will tell you what I have told madame," the doctor said. "There are no miracles in these cases, absolutely none. With long training there could be enormous improvement, in some cases, not many. And with Mademoiselle, there are certain limits. She must stay in my institution in Nice for five years at least. We have teachers there who can explore every possibility. In that time we will know whether it is possible for her to live a nearly normal life. Or whether she must be institutionalized forever."

Here Athena began to weep. She held a small blue silk handkerchief to her eyes and Cross could smell its perfume.

The doctor looked at her impassively. "Madame has agreed. She will join the Institute as a teacher. . . . So."

He sat directly across from Cross. "There are some very good signs. She has genuine talent as a painter. Certain senses alert, not withdrawn. She was interested when I spoke French, a language she cannot understand but intuits. That is a very good sign. Another good sign: The child showed some signs of missing you this afternoon, she has some feeling for another human being and that may be extended. It is highly unusual, but can be explained in not so mysterious a way. When I explored this with her she said you were beautiful. Now, you must not be offended, Mr. De Lena. I ask this question only for medical reasons to help the child, not accuse you. Have you sexually stimulated the girl in any way, perhaps unintentionally?"

Cross was so startled he burst out laughing. "I didn't know she responded to me. And I never gave her anything to respond to."

Athena's cheeks were red with anger. "This is ridiculous," she said. "He was never alone with her."

The doctor persisted. "Have you at any time given her physical caresses? I don't mean clasping her hand, patting her hair, or even kissing her cheek. The girl is nubile, she would respond simply out of physicality. You would not be the first man tempted by such innocence."

"Maybe she knows about my relationship with her mother," Cross said.

"She doesn't care about her mother," the doctor said. "Forgive me, madame, that is one of the things you must accept—nor her mother's beauty or her fame. They literally do not exist for her. It is you who she extends herself to. Think. Perhaps an innocent tenderness, something inadvertent."

Cross looked at him coolly. "If I did it I would tell you. If that would help her."

"Do you feel tenderness for this girl?" the doctor asked.

Cross considered for a moment. "Yes," he said.

Dr. Gerard leaned back and clasped his hands. "I believe you," he said. "And that gives me great hope. If she can respond to you, she may be helped to respond to others. She may tolerate her mother someday and that will be enough for you, am I right, madame?"

"Oh, Cross," Athena said. "I hope you're not angry."

"It's OK, really," Cross said.

Dr. Gerard looked at him carefully. "You are not offended?" he said. "Most men would be extremely upset. One patient's father actually struck me. But you are not angry. Tell me why."

He could not explain to this man, or even to Athena, how the sight of Bethany in her hugging machine affected him. How it reminded him of Tiffany and all the showgirls he had made love to who had left him feeling empty. How his relationships with all the Clericuzio and even with his father left him with feelings of isolation and despair. And finally how all the victims he had left behind seemed the victims of some ghostly world that became real only in his dreams.

Cross looked the doctor directly in the eye. "Maybe because I'm autistic too," he said. "Or maybe because I have worse crimes to hide."

The doctor leaned back and said in a satisfied voice, "Ah." He paused and smiled for the first time. "Would you like to come in for some tests?" They both laughed.

"Now, madame," Dr. Gerard said. "I understand you catch a plane back to America tomorrow morning. Why not leave your daughter with me now. My nurses are very good, and I can assure you the girl will not miss you."

"But I'll miss her," Athena said. "Could I keep her tonight and bring her back tomorrow morning? We have a chartered plane so I can leave when I like."

"Certainly," the doctor said. "Bring her here in the morning. I will have my nurses escort her down to Nice. You have the phone number of the Institute and you can call me as often as you like."

They got up to go. Athena impetuously kissed the doctor on the cheek. The doctor flushed, he was not insensible to her beauty and fame, despite his ogreish appearance.

Athena, Bethany, and Cross spent the rest of the day strolling the streets of Paris. Athena bought new clothes for Bethany, a full wardrobe. She bought painting supplies and a huge suitcase to hold all the new things. They sent everything to the hotel.

They had dinner in a restaurant on the Champs Elysées. Bethany ate greedily, especially the pastries. She had not spoken a word all day or responded to any of Athena's gestures of affection.

Cross had never seen such a show of love as that Athena showed Bethany. Except when as a child he saw his own mother, Nalene, brushing Claudia's hair.

During dinner Athena held Bethany's hand, brushed the crumbs off her face, and explained that she would return to France in a month to stay with her at the school for the next five years.

Bethany paid no attention.

Athena was enthusiastic when she told Bethany how they could learn French together, go to museums together and see all the great paintings, and how Bethany could spend as much time as she wanted on her own paintings. She described how they would travel all over Europe, to Spain, to Italy, to Germany.

Then Bethany spoke the first words of the day. "I want my machine."

As always Cross was stricken by a sense of holiness. The beautiful girl was like a copy of a great portrait painting but without the soul of the artist, as if her body had been left empty for God.

It was after dark when they walked back to their hotel. Bethany was between them, and they swung her hands so that she lifted up in the air, and for once she allowed it, in fact seemed to delight in it so much that they continued past the hotel.

It was at this moment that Cross had the precise feeling of happiness he had had at the picnic. And it consisted of nothing more than the three of them linked together, holding hands. He was filled with wonder and horror at his sentimentality.

Finally they returned to the hotel. After Athena had helped Bethany to bed, she came into the sitting room of the suite, where Cross was waiting for her. They sat side by side on the lavender sofa holding hands.

"Lovers in Paris," Athena said, smiling at him. "And we never got to sleep together in a French bed."

"Are you worried about leaving Bethany here?" Cross asked.

"No," Athena said. "She won't miss us."

"Five years," Cross said, "is a long time. And you're willing to give up five years and your profession?"

Athena got up from the sofa and walked up and down the room. She spoke passionately. "I glory in being able to do without acting. When I was a kid I dreamed of being a great heroine, Marie Antoinette going to the guillotine, Joan of Arc burning at the stake, Marie Curie saving mankind from some great disease. And of course, also giving up everything for the love of a great man, most ridiculous of all. I dreamed of living a heroic life and knew I'd surely go to Heaven. That I would be pure in mind and body. I detested the idea of doing anything that would compromise me, especially for money. I was determined that under no circumstance would I ever harm another human being. Everyone would love me, including myself. I knew I was smart, everyone told me I was beautiful, and I proved to be not only competent but talented.

"So what did I do? I fell in love with Boz Skannet. I slept with men not out of desire but to further my career. I gave life to a human being who may never love me or anyone. Then I very cleverly maneuver or request the murder of my husband. Not so subtly I ask who will murder this husband of mine who is such a threat to me now." She pressed his hand. "And for this I thank you."

Cross said to reassure her, "You didn't do any of those things. It was just your destiny, as we say in my family. As for Skannet, he was a stone in your shoe, another family saying, so why shouldn't you get rid of him?"

Athena kissed him briefly on the lips. "Now I have," she said. "My knight errant. The only trouble is you don't stop at killing dragons."

"After five years, if the doctor says she can't improve, then what?" Cross asked.

"I don't care what anyone says," Athena said. "There's always hope. I'll be with her the rest of my life."

"And you won't miss your work?" he asked.

"Of course I'll miss it, and I'll miss you," Athena said. "But finally I'll do what I believe is right, not just be a heroine in a movie." Her voice was amused. Then she said with a flat tone, "I want her to love me, that's all I want."

They kissed each other good night and went into their separate bedrooms.

The next morning they took Bethany to the doctor's office. Athena had a difficult time saying good-bye to her daughter. She hugged the girl and wept, but Bethany would have none of it. She pushed her mother away and got ready to repulse Cross, but he did not move to embrace her.

Cross was momentarily angry with Athena for being so helpless with her daughter. The doctor, observing this, said to Athena, "When you return, you will need a great deal of training to cope with this child."

"I'll be back as quickly as I can," Athena said.

"You needn't hurry," the doctor said. "She lives in a world where time does not exist."

On the plane back to L.A., Cross and Athena agreed that he would go on to Vegas and not accompany Athena to Malibu. There had only been one terrible moment on the whole trip. For a full half hour Athena had doubled over in her grief, wordlessly crying. Then she became calm.

When they parted Athena said to Cross, "I'm sorry we never got to make love in Paris." But he understood she was being kind. That at this particular time, she was repulsed by the thought of them making love. That like her daughter, she was now separated from the world.

Cross was met at the airport by a big limo driven by a soldier from the Hunting Lodge. Lia Vazzi was in the back. Lia closed the glass partition so that the driver couldn't hear their conversation.

"Detective Losey was up to see me again," he said. "The next time he comes will be his last."

"Be patient," Cross said.

"I know the signs, trust me on this," Lia said. "Something else. A crew from the Bronx Enclave has moved into place in Los Angeles, I don't know by whose orders. I would say you need bodyguards."

"Not yet," Cross said. "You have your six-man crew together?"

"Yes," Lia said. "But they are men who will not act directly against the Clericuzio."

When they got to the Xanadu, Cross found a memo from Andrew Pollard, a complete file on Jim Losey, that made for interesting reading. And a piece of information that could be acted on immediately.

Cross drew a hundred grand from the casino cage, all in C notes. He told Lia they were going to L.A. Lia would be his driver and he wanted no one else with them. He showed him Pollard's memo. They flew to L.A. the next day and rented a car to drive to Santa Monica.

Phil Sharkey was mowing the lawn in front of his house. Cross got out of the car with Lia and identified himself as a friend of Pollard's who was in need of information. Lia carefully studied Sharkey's face. Then he went back to the car.

Phil Sharkey was not as impressive-looking as Jim Losey, but he looked tough enough. He also looked as if his years of police work had burned out his confidence in his fellow human beings. He had that alert suspiciousness, that seriousness of manner, that the best cops have. But he was obviously not a happy man.

Sharkey ushered Cross into his house, which was really a bungalow, the insides dreary and worn; it had the forlorn look of a womanless and childless dwelling. The first thing Sharkey did was call Pollard and confirm the identity of his visitor. Then without offering any courtesy, a seat, or a drink, he said to Cross, "Go ahead, ask."

Cross opened his briefcase and took out a packet of hundreds. "There's ten grand," he said. "That's just for letting me talk. But it will take a little time. How about a beer and a place to sit?"

Sharkey's face broke into a grin. It was curiously affable, the good cop in the partnership, Cross thought.

Sharkey shoved the money casually into his trouser pocket. "I like you," Sharkey said. "You're smart. You know it's money that talks, not bullshit."

They sat at a little round table on the back porch of the bungalow, which overlooked Ocean Avenue to the sandy beach and water beyond, as they drank their beers out of the bottle. Sharkey patted his pocket to make sure the money was still there.

Cross said, "If I hear the right answers, there's another twenty grand for you right after. Then, if you keep your mouth shut about me being here, I'll come around to see you in two months with another fifty grand."

Sharkey gave his grin, but now there was a hint of mischief in it. "In two months you won't care who I tell, is that it?"

"Yes," Cross said.

Sharkey was serious now. "I'm not telling you anything that gets anybody indicted."

"Hey, then you don't know who I really am," Cross said. "Maybe you better call Pollard again."

Sharkey said curtly, "I know who you are. Jim Losey told me I should always treat you right. All the way." And then he put on his sympathetic listening style that was part of his profession.

Cross said, "You and Jim Losey were partners for the last ten years and you were both making good money on the side. And then you retired. I'd like to know why."

"So, it's Jim you're after," Sharkey said. "That's very dangerous. He was the bravest and the smartest cop I ever knew."

"How about honest?" Cross asked.

"We were cops, and in Los Angeles," Sharkey said. "Do you know what the fuck that means? If we do our real job and kick the shit out of the spics and blacks, we could get indicted and lose our jobs. The only ones we could arrest without getting into trouble were the white schmucks who had money. Look, I got no prejudice, but why should I throw white guys in jail when I can't throw the other kind in jail? That's not right."

"But I understand Jim got a chest full of medals," Cross said. "You got some too."

Sharkey gave him a dismissive shrug. "You can't help being a hero cop in this town if you have just a little bit of balls. A lot of those guys didn't know they could do business if they talked nice. And some of them were out-and-out killers. So we had to defend ourselves and we got some medals. Believe me, we never looked for a fight."

Cross was doubting everything Sharkey was saying. Jim Losey was a natural-born strong-arm guy despite his fancy clothes.

"Were you two partners in everything?" Cross asked. "Did you know everything that was going on."

Sharkey laughed. "Jim Losey? He was the boss always. Sometimes I didn't even know exactly what we were doing. I didn't even know how much we were getting paid. Jim handled all that and he gave me what he said was my fair share." He paused a moment. "He had his own rules."

"So how did you make money?" Cross asked.

"We were on the pad for some of the big gambling syndicates," Sharkey said. "Sometimes a payoff for the drug guys. There was a time when Jim Losey wouldn't take drug money but then every cop in the world started taking it, so we did."

"Did you and Losey ever use a black kid named Marlowe to finger big shot drug dealers?" Cross asked.

"Sure," Sharkey said. "Marlowe. A nice kid scared of his own shadow. We used him all the time."

Cross said, "So when you heard Losey shot him running away from a mug-murder, you were surprised?" Cross asked.

"Hell, no," Sharkey said. "Druggies graduate. But they are so fucked up, they always botch it. And Jim, in that situation, never gives the warning we're taught to give. He just shoots."

"But wasn't it a strange coincidence," Cross said, "their paths crossing like that?"

For the first time Sharkey's face seemed to lose its toughness, grow sad. "It's fishy," he said. "The whole thing is fishy. But now I guess I have to give you something. Jim Losey was brave, women loved him and men held him in high regard. I was his partner and I felt the same way. But the truth is he was always a fishy guy."

"So it could have been some sort of setup," Cross said.

"No, no," Sharkey said. "You have to understand. The job makes you take graft. But it doesn't make you a hit man. Jim Losey would never do that. I'll never believe that."

"So why did you take your retirement after that?" Cross asked.

"It was just that Jim was getting me nervous," Sharkey said.

"I met Losey out at Malibu not long ago," Cross said. "He was alone. Does he often operate without you?"

Now Sharkey gave his grin again. "Sometimes," he said. "That particular time he went to take a shot at the actress. You'd be surprised how often he made a score with big stars in that business. Sometimes he had lunches with people and he didn't want me around."

"One other thing," Cross said. "Was Jim Losey a racist? Did he hate blacks?"

Sharkey gave him a look of amused astonishment. "Of course he did. You're one of those bullshit liberals, right? You think that's terrible? Just go out and put a year in on the job. You'll vote to put them all in the zoo."

"I have another question," Cross said. "You ever see him with a short guy wearing a funny hat?"

"An Italian guy," Sharkey said. "We had lunch and then Jim told me to get lost. Spooky guy."

Cross reached into his briefcase and took out another two packets of money. "Here's twenty grand," he said. "And remember, you keep your mouth shut and you get another fifty grand. OK?"

"I know who you are," Sharkey said.

"Sure you do," Cross said. "I instructed Pollard to tell you who I am."

"I know who you really are," Sharkey said with his infectious grin. "That's why I don't take your whole briefcase right now. And why I'll keep quiet for two months. Between you and Losey, I don't know who'll kill me faster."

CROSS De Lena realized he had enormous problems. He knew Jim Losey was on the Clericuzio Family "pad." That he received fifty thousand a year as a salary, and bonuses for special jobs, but none of these had included murder. It was enough for Cross to make a final judgment. Dante and Losey had killed his father. It was an easy judgment for him to make, he was not bound by the legal laws of evidence. And his whole training with the Clericuzio helped him make the verdict of guilty. He knew his father's competence and character. No mugger could get close to him. He also knew Dante's character and competence and Dante's dislike for his father.

The big question was this: Had Dante acted on his own or had the Don commanded the killing? But the Clericuzio had no reason; his father had been loyal for over forty years and an important factor in the Family ascension. He had been the great general in the war against the Santadio. And Cross wondered, not for the first time, why no one had ever told him the details of that war, not his father, not Gronevelt, not Giorgio or Petie or Vincent.

The more he thought about it, the more Cross was sure of one thing: The Don had no hand in the killing of his father. Don Domenico was a very conservative man of business. He rewarded loyal service, he did not punish it. He was extremely fair-minded, to the point of cruelty. But the clinching argument was this: He would never have let Cross live if he had killed Pippi. That was the proof of the Don's innocence.

Don Domenico believed in God, he sometimes believed in Fate, but he did not believe in coincidence. The coincidence of Jim Losey being the cop who shot the mugger who shot Pippi would be absolutely rejected by the Don. He had surely made his own investigation and discovered Dante's connection with Losey. And he would not only know Dante's guilt but his motive.

And what about Rose Marie, Dante's mother? What did she know? When she had heard of Pippi's death, she had had her most serious fit, screaming unintelligibly, weeping incessantly, so that the Don had sent her to the East Hampton psychiatric clinic he had funded many years ago. She would be there for at least a month.

Visitors to Rose Marie in the clinic had always been forbidden by the Don, except for Dante, Giorgio, Vincent, and Petie. But Cross often sent flowers and baskets of fruit. So what the hell was Rose Marie so upset about? Did she know about Dante's guilt, understand his motive? At that moment Cross thought about the Don saying that Dante would be his heir. That was ominous. Cross decided he would visit Rose Marie at the clinic, despite the Don's interdiction. He would go with flowers, and fruit, and chocolates and cheeses, with true affection, but with the purpose of tricking her into betraying her son.

Two days later, Cross entered the lobby of the psychiatric clinic in East Hampton. There were two guards at the door, and one escorted him to the reception desk.

The woman at the reception desk was middle-aged and well dressed. When he stated his business, she gave him a charming smile and said he would have to wait a half hour because Rose Marie was undergoing a minor medical procedure. She would notify him when it was done.

Cross sat down in the waiting room of the reception area, just off the lobby, where there were tables and soft armchairs. He picked up a copy of a Hollywood magazine. Reading it, he came across an article on Jim Losey, the detective hero of Los Angeles. The article detailed his heroic achievements, capped by his killing the mugger-murderer Marlowe. Cross was amused by two things. That his father was referred to as the owner of a financial service agency and a typical helpless victim of a brutal criminal. And by the tag line of the article, which asserted that if there were more cops like Jim Losey, street crime would be under control.

A nurse tapped him on the shoulder. She was an impressively strong-looking woman, but she said with a pleasant smile, "I'll bring you up."

Cross picked up the box of chocolates and the flowers he had brought and followed her up a short flight of stairs and then down a long corridor spaced by doors. At the last door the nurse used a master key and opened it. She motioned Cross inside and closed the door after him.

Rose Marie, clad in a gray robe, her hair neatly braided, was watching a small TV. When she saw Cross she jumped up from the couch and flew into his arms. She was weeping. Cross kissed her cheek and gave her the chocolates and flowers.

"Oh, you came to see me," she said. "I thought you hated me for what I did to your father."

"You didn't do anything to my father," Cross said, and led her back to the couch. Then he turned off the TV. He kneeled beside the couch. "I was worried about you."

She reached out and stroked his hair. "You were always so beautiful," she said. "I hated that you were your father's son. I was glad to see him dead. But I always knew terrible things would happen. I filled the air and the earth with poison for him. Now you think my father will let this pass?"

"The Don is a just man," Cross said. "He will never blame you."

"He has fooled you as he has tricked everyone else," Rose Marie said. "Never trust him. He betrayed his own daughter, he betrayed his grandson and he betrayed his nephew Pippi. . . . And now he will betray you."

Her voice had risen to a loud pitch and Cross was afraid she would go into one of her fits.

"Quiet down, Aunt Roe," Cross said. "Just tell me what upset you so that you had to come back here." He stared into her eyes and thought how pretty she must have been as a young girl, the innocence still in her eyes.

Rose Marie whispered, "Make them tell you about the Santadio War, then you will understand everything." She looked past Cross and then covered her head with her hands. Cross turned. The door opened. Vincent and Petie were standing there silently. Rose Marie jumped off the couch and ran into the bedroom and slammed the door shut.

Vincent's granite face showed pity and despair. "Jesus Christ," he said. He went to the bedroom door and knocked, then said through it, "Roe, open the door. We're your brothers. We won't hurt you . . ."

Cross said, "What a coincidence to meet you here. I was visiting Rose Marie too."

Vincent never had any time for bullshit. "We're not here to visit. The Don wants to see you in Quogue."

Cross appraised the situation. Obviously the receptionist had called somebody in Quogue. Obviously, it was a planned procedure. And just as obviously, the Don did not want him talking to Rose Marie. That Petie and Vincent had been sent meant that it was not a hit, they would not be so carelessly exposed.

This was confirmed when Vincent said, "Cross, I'll go with you in your car. Petie can go in his." A hit in the Clericuzio Family would never be one on one.

Cross said, "We can't leave Rose Marie like this."

"Sure we can," Petie said. "The nurse will just shoot her up."

Cross tried to make conversation while he drove. "Vincent, you guys sure got here fast."

"Petie drove," Vincent said. "He's a fucking maniac." He paused for a moment and then said in a worried voice, "Cross, you know the rules, how come you visit Rose Marie?"

"Hey," Cross said, "Rose Marie was one of my favorite aunts while I was growing up."

"The Don doesn't like it," Vincent said. "He's very pissed off. He says it's not like Cross. He knows."

"I'll straighten it out," Cross said. "But I was really worried about your sister. How's she doing?"

Vincent sighed. "This time it may be for keeps. You know she was sweet on your old man when she was a kid. Who could figure Pippi being killed would throw her so much?"

Cross caught the false note in Vincent's voice. He knew something. But Cross only said, "My father was always fond of Rose Marie."

"In the past years she wasn't so fond of him," Vincent said. "Especially when she got into one of her fits. You should hear the things she said about him then."

Cross said casually, "You were in the Santadio War. How come you guys never talk about it to me?"

"Because we never talk about operations," Vincent said. "My father taught us it served no purpose. You just go on. There's plenty of trouble in the present to worry about."

"My father was a big hero though, right?" Cross said.

Vincent smiled for just a moment, his stone face almost softened. "Your father was a genius," Vincent said. "He could plan an operation like Napoleon. Nothing ever went wrong when he planned it. Maybe once or twice because of bad luck."

"So he planned the war against the Santadio," Cross said.

"Ask the Don these questions," Vincent said. "Now talk about something else."

"OK," Cross said. "Am I going to be knocked off like my father?"

The usually cold and stone-faced Vincent reacted violently. He grabbed the steering wheel and forced Cross to park on the side of the highway. His voice choked with emotion when he said, "Are you crazy? Do you think the Clericuzio Family would do such a thing? Your father had Clericuzio blood. He was our best soldier, he saved us. The Don loved him as much as any of his sons. Jesus Christ, why do you ask something like that?"

Cross said meekly, "I just got scared, you guys popping up."

"Get back on the road," Vincent said disgustedly. "Your father and me and Giorgio and Petie fought together during really rough times There is no way we could go against each other. Pippi just got unlucky, a crazy jigaboo mugger."

They rode the rest of the way in silence.

At the mansion in Quogue, there were the usual two guards at the gate and one man sitting on the porch. There did not seem to be any unusual activity.

Don Clericuzio, Giorgio, and Petie were awaiting them in the den of the mansion. On the bar was a box of Havana cigars and a mug filled with twisted black Italian cheroots.

Don Clericuzio sat in one of the huge brown leather armchairs. Cross went to greet him and was surprised when the Don pushed himself up to stand, with an agility that belied his age, and embraced him. After which he motioned Cross to the huge coffee table on which various dishes of cheeses and dried meats were spread.

Cross sensed that the Don was not yet ready to speak. He made himself a sandwich of mozzarella cheese and prosciutto. The prosciutto was thin slabs of dark red meat fringed with very tender white fat. The mozzarella was a white ball so fresh it was still sweating milk. It was tied off on top with a thick salty knob like the knot in a rope. The closest that the Don had ever come to boasting was that he never ate a mozzarella that was more than thirty minutes old.

Vincent and Petie were also helping themselves to food, while Giorgio served as bartender, bringing wine to the Don and soft drinks to the others. The Don only ate the dripping mozzarella, letting it melt inside his mouth. Petie gave him one of the twisted cheroots and lit it for him. What a wonderful stomach the old man had, thought Cross.

Don Clericuzio said abruptly, "Croccifixio, whatever you seek now from Rose Marie, I will tell you. And you suspect something amiss about your father's death. You are wrong. I have had inquiries made, the story is true as it stands. Pippi was unlucky. He was the most prudent of men in his profession but such ludicrous accidents happen. Let me set your mind at rest. Your father was my nephew and a Clericuzio, and one of my dearest friends."

"Tell me about the war with the Santadio," Cross said.

BOOK VII

The
Santadio
War

BOOK VII

The Sarcastic War

CHAPTER 18

⌘

"I T IS DANGEROUS to be reasonable with stupid people," Don Clericuzio said, as he sipped from his wine glass. He put his cheroot aside. "Pay strict attention. It's a long story and everything was not what it seemed to be. It was almost thirty years ago . . ." He motioned to his three sons and said, "If I forget something important, help me." His three sons smiled at the idea that he would forget something important.

The light in the den was a soft golden haze tinged with cigar smoke, and even the smell of the food was so sharply aromatic that it seemed to affect the light.

"I became convinced of that after the Santadio . . ." He paused a moment to sip his wine. "There was a time when the Santadio were our equal in power. But the Santadio made too many enemies, they drew too much attention from the authorities and they had no sense of justice. They created a world without any values and a world without any sense of justice cannot continue to exist.

"I proposed many arrangements with the Santadio, I made concessions, I wanted to live in a world of peace. But because they were strong, they had a sense of power that violent people have. They believe that power is all. And so it came to war between us."

Giorgio interrupted. "Why does Cross have to know this story? How can it benefit him or benefit us?"

Vincent looked away from Cross, Petie stared at him, his head tilted back, appraising. None of the three sons wanted the Don to tell the story.

"Because we owe it to Pippi and Croccifixio," said the Don. And then he spoke directly to Cross. "Make of this story what you will but I and my sons are innocent of the crime you suspect. Pippi was a son to me, you are to me as a grandchild. All of Clericuzio blood."

Giorgio said again, "This can do all of us no good."

Don Clericuzio waved his arm impatiently, then said to his sons, "It's true, what I've said so far?"

They nodded and Petie said, "We should have wiped them out from the beginning."

The Don shrugged and said to Cross, "My sons were young, your father was young, none of them yet thirty. I didn't want to waste their lives in a great war. Don Santadio, God have mercy on his soul, had six sons but he thought of them more as soldiers than as sons. Jimmy Santadio was the oldest and he worked with our old friend Gronevelt, God have mercy on him as well. The Santadio then had half the Hotel. Jimmy was the best of the lot, the only one who saw that peace was the best solution for all of us. But the old man and his other sons were hot for blood.

"Now it was not to my interest for the war to be bloody. I wanted time to use reason, to convince them of the good sense of my proposals. I would give them all of the drugs, and they would give me all of the gambling. I wanted their half of the Xanadu and in return they would control all drugs in America, a dirty business that required a violent and firm hand. A very sensible proposal. There was far more money in drugs and it was a business that did not involve long-term strategy. A dirty business with a lot of operational work. All this added to the Santadio strength. I wanted the Clericuzio to control all of gambling, not as risky as drugs, not as profitable, but, managed cleverly, more valuable in the long term. And this added to the Clericuzio strength. I always aimed to finally be a member of society, and gambling could become a legal gold mine with none of the everyday risk and dirty work. In this, time has proved me justified.

"Unfortunately, the Santadio wanted everything. Everything. Think of it then, nephew, it was a very dangerous time for us all. By then the FBI knew we Families existed and cooperated with each other. The government, with its resources and technology, brought many Families down. The wall of *omertà* was cracking.

"Young men, born in America, were cooperating with the authorities to save their own skins. Luckily, I established the Bronx Enclave, and brought new people from Sicily to be my soldiers.

"The only thing I have never been able to understand is how women can cause so much trouble. My daughter, Rose Marie, was eighteen years old at this time. How did she become besotted over Jimmy Santadio? She said they were like Romeo and Juliet. Who were Romeo and Juliet? Who in Christ's name were those people? Certainly not Italians. When I was told of this, I reconciled myself. I reopened negotiations with the Santadio Family, I lowered my demands so that the two Families could exist together. In their stupidity, they read this as a sign of weakness. And so began the whole tragedy that has lasted all these years."

Here the Don broke off. Giorgio helped himself to a glass of wine, a slice of bread, and a chunk of the milky cheese. Then he stood behind the Don.

"Why today?" Giorgio asked.

"Because my great nephew here is worried about how his father died and we must dispel any suspicions he may have of us," the Don said.

"I have no suspicions of you, Don Domenico," Cross said.

"Everyone has suspicions of everything," the Don said. "That's human nature. But let me continue. Rose Marie was young, she had no knowledge of worldly affairs. She was heartbroken when at first both Families opposed the match. But she had no real idea why. And so she decided to bring everyone together, she believed love would conquer all, she later informed me. She was very loving then. And she was the light of my life. My wife died young, and I never remarried because I could not bear to share Rose Marie with a stranger. I denied her nothing and I had high hopes for her future. But a marriage with the Santadio, I could not bear. I forbade it. I was young then too. I thought my orders would be obeyed by my children. I wanted her to go to college, marry someone from a different world. Giorgio, Vincent, and Petie had to support me in this life, I needed their help. And I had hopes that their children could also escape to a better world. And my youngest son,

Silvio." The Don pointed to the photograph on the mantelpiece of the den.

Cross had never really taken a close look at the photo, he had not known its history. The photo was of a young man of twenty who looked very much like Rose Marie, only more gentle, his eyes grayer and more intelligent. It was a face that showed such a good soul that Cross wondered if it had been retouched.

The air in the windowless room was becoming more pungent with cigar smoke. Giorgio had lit a huge Havana.

Don Clericuzio said, "I doted on Silvio even more than on Rose Marie. He had a better heart than most people. He had been accepted to the university with a scholarship. There was every hope for him. But he was too innocent."

Vincent said, "He had no street smarts. None of us would have gone. Not like he did, without protection."

Giorgio took up the story. "Rose Marie and Jimmy Santadio were shacked up in this Commack Motel. And Rose Marie came up with the idea that if Jimmy and Silvio talked, they could bring the two Families together. She called Silvio and he went to the motel without telling anybody. The three of them discussed strategies. Silvio always called Rose Marie 'Roe.' His last words to her were, 'Everything is going to be okay, Roe. Dad will listen to me.' "

But Silvio was never to speak to his father. Unfortunately, two of the Santadio brothers, Fonsa and Italo, were doing a guardian-like surveillance on their brother Jimmy.

The Santadio with their violent paranoia suspected that Rose Marie was leading their brother Jimmy into a trap. Or at least luring him into a marriage that would lessen their own power in their Family. And Rose Marie was offensive to them with her ferocious courage and determination to marry their brother. She had even defied her own father, the great Don Clericuzio. She would stop at nothing.

Recognizing Silvio, when he left the motel they trapped him on the Robert Moses Causeway and shot him dead. They stripped him of his wallet and watch to make it look like a robbery. It was typical of the Santadio mentality, their act was one of savagery.

Don Clericuzio was not deceived for a moment. But then Jimmy Santadio came to the wake, unguarded and unarmed. He requested a private audience with the Don.

"Don Clericuzio," he said, "my sorrow is nearly equal to yours. I place my life in your hands if you think the Santadio are responsible. I talked to my father and he gave no such order. And he authorizes me to say to you that he will reconsider all your proposals. He gave me permission to marry your daughter."

Rose Marie had come to hold Jimmy's arm. And there was such a pitiful look on her face that for the moment the Don's heart melted. Sorrow and fear gave her a tragic beauty. Her eyes were startling, so dark and bright with tears. And there was a stunned, uncomprehending look on her face.

She turned from the Don and looked at Jimmy Santadio with such love that Don Clericuzio for one of the few times in his life thought of mercy. How could he bring sorrow to such a beautiful daughter?

Rose Marie said to her father, "Jimmy was so horrified that you might think his family had anything to do with it. I know they didn't. Jimmy promised me that his family would come to an agreement."

Don Clericuzio had already convicted the Santadio Family of the murder. He did not require any proof. But mercy was another matter.

"I believe and accept you," the Don said, and indeed he believed in Jimmy's innocence, though that would make no difference. "Rose Marie, you have my permission to marry but not in this house, nor will any of my family be present. And Jimmy, tell your father that we will sit down together and discuss business after the marriage."

"Thank you," Jimmy Santadio said. "I understand. The wedding will be in our Palm Springs house. In one month all my family will be there and all your family will be invited. If they choose not to come then it's their decision."

The Don was offended. "So quickly after this?" He gestured toward the coffin.

And then Rose Marie collapsed into the Don's arms. He could sense her terror. She whispered to him, "I'm pregnant."

"Ah," the Don said. He smiled at Jimmy Santadio.

Rose Marie whispered again. "I'll name him after Silvio. He'll be just like Silvio."

The Don patted her dark hair and kissed her cheek. "Good," he said. "Good. But I still will not attend the wedding."

Now Rose Marie had recovered her courage. She lifted her face to his and kissed him on the cheek. Then she said, "Dad, somebody has to come. Somebody has to give me away."

The Don turned to Pippi who was standing beside him. "Pippi will represent the Family at the wedding. He's a nephew and he loves to dance. Pippi, you will give your cousin away and then you can all dance to the bottom of the ocean."

Pippi bent to kiss Rose Marie's cheek. "I'll be there," he said with false gallantry, "and if Jimmy doesn't show up, we'll run away together."

Rose Marie gratefully raised her eyes and came into his arms.

A month later Pippi De Lena was on the plane from Vegas to Palm Springs to attend the wedding. That month had been spent with Don Clericuzio in the Quogue mansion, and in meetings with Giorgio, Vincent, and Petie.

The Don clearly instructed that Pippi was to be in charge of the operation. That his orders were to be treated as orders from the Don himself, no matter what the orders might be.

Only Vincent dared to question the Don. "What if the Santadio didn't kill Silvio?"

The Don said, "It doesn't matter, but it reeks of their stupidity, which will endanger us in the future. We will only have to fight them at another time. Of course, they are guilty. Ill will itself is murder. If the Santadio are not guilty then we must agree that Fate itself is against us. Which would you rather believe?"

For the first time in his life, Pippi noted that the Don was distraught. He spent long hours in the chapel in the basement of his house. He ate very little, and drank more wine, which was unusual for him.

And he put Silvio's framed photo in his bedroom for a few days. One Sunday he asked the priest saying Mass to hear his confession.

On the last day, the Don had a meeting with Pippi alone.

"Pippi," the Don said, "this is a very tricky operation. There may be a situation when the question comes up if Jimmy Santadio is to be spared. Do not. But no one is to know this is my order. That deed must be on your head. Not on mine, not Giorgio or Vincent or Petie. Are you willing to take the blame?"

"Yes," Pippi said. "You don't want your daughter to hate you or reproach you. Or her brothers."

"A situation may arise where Rose Marie is at risk," the Don said.

"Yes," Pippi said.

The Don sighed. "Do everything to safeguard my children," he said. "You must make the final decisions. But I never gave you the order to kill Jimmy Santadio."

"And if Rose Marie discovers it was . . ." Pippi asked.

The Don looked directly at Pippi De Lena. "She is my child and the sister of Silvio. She will never betray us."

The Santadio mansion in Palm Springs had forty rooms on just three floors, built in the Spanish style to harmonize with the surrounding desert. It was separated from that enormous field of sand by an encircling wall of redstone. The compound within held not only the house but a huge swimming pool, a tennis court, and a boccie alley.

On this wedding day there was a massive barbecue pit, a platform for the orchestra, and a wooden dance floor, laid over the lawn. This floor was surrounded by long banquet tables. Parked by the huge bronzed gates of the compound were three large catering trucks.

Pippi De Lena arrived early Saturday morning with a suitcase filled with wedding clothes. He was given a room on the second floor, the bright golden light of the desert sun pouring in the windows. He started to unpack.

The church ceremony would be held in Palm Springs only a half hour away. The religious rites would begin about noon. Then the guests would return to the house for the celebration.

There was a knock on the door and Jimmy Santadio came in. His face was shiny with happiness and he gave Pippi a vigorous hug. He was not yet dressed in his wedding clothes and looked very handsome in loose white slacks and a gray-and-silver silk shirt. He held Pippi's hands in his to show his affection.

"It's great you came," Jimmy said, "and Roe is thrilled you're giving her away. Now before everything starts, the old man wants to meet you."

Still holding his hand, he led Pippi down to the first floor and down a long corridor to Don Santadio's room. Don Santadio lay in bed clad in blue cotton nightclothes. He was far more decrepit than Don Clericuzio but he had the same sharp eyes, the alert listening manner; his head was round as a ball and bald. He beckoned Pippi close to him and held out his arms so that Pippi could embrace him.

"How just it is that you came," the old man said, his voice was hoarse. "I count on you to help our two Families embrace each other as we two have done. You are the dove of peace we must have. Bless you. Bless you." He sank back on the bed and closed his eyes. "How happy I am this day."

There was a nurse in the room, a stout middle-aged woman. Jimmy introduced her as a cousin. The nurse whispered that they should leave, the old Don was conserving his strength to join the celebration later in the day. For a moment Pippi reconsidered. It was obvious that Don Santadio did not have long to live. Then Jimmy would become the head of his Family. Perhaps things still could be worked out. But Don Clericuzio could never accept the murder of his son, Silvio; there never could be real peace between the two Families. In any case, the Don had given him strict instructions.

Meanwhile two of the Santadio brothers, Fonsa and Italo, were searching Pippi's room for weapons and communications equipment. Pippi's rental car had also been thoroughly checked.

The Santadio had prepared lavishly for the wedding of their prince. Huge woven baskets filled with exotic flowers were scattered all over the compound. There were colorful pavilions stocked with bartenders pouring champagne. There was a jester in a medieval costume doing magic tricks for the children, and music blasted out of speakers strung along the compound. Each guest was given a lotto ticket for a prize of twenty thousand dollars that was to be drawn later. What could be more splendid?

Huge gaily colored tents had been pitched all over the manicured lawn to protect the guests from the desert heat. Green tents over the dance floor, red over the orchestra. Blue tents over the tennis court, which held the wedding gifts. These included a silver Mercedes for the bride and a small private plane for the groom, from Don Santadio himself.

The church ceremony was simple and short, and the guests returned to the Santadio compound to find the orchestra playing. Food counters and three separate bars were put in their own tents, one decorated with scenes of hunters pursuing wild boars, another filled with highball glasses containing fruity tropical drinks.

The wedding couple danced the first dance in lonely splendor. They danced in the shade of the tent, the red desert sun peeked into the corners and bronzed their happiness as they ducked their heads into the patches of sunlight. They were so obviously in love that the crowd cheered and clapped. Rose Marie had never looked so beautiful, nor Jimmy Santadio so young.

When the band stopped playing, Jimmy plucked Pippi out of the crowd and presented him to the more than two hundred guests.

He said, "This is Pippi De Lena who gave the bride away, and he represents the Clericuzio Family. He is my dearest friend. His friends are my friends. His enemies are my enemies." He raised his glass and said, "We all drink to him. And he gets the first dance with the bride."

As Pippi and Rose Marie danced, she whispered to him, "You'll bring the Families together, won't you Pippi?"

"It's a cinch," Pippi said, and whirled her around.

Pippi was the marvel of the celebration, never had there been a more convivial wedding guest. He danced every dance, and was lighter on his feet than any of the younger men. He danced with Jimmy and then with the other brothers, Fonsa, Italo, Benedict,

Gino, and Louis. He danced with the children and the matrons. He waltzed with the orchestra leader, and sang with the band, rowdy songs in Sicilian dialect. He ate and drank with such abandon that his tux was spotted with tomato sauce and the fruity juice of the cocktails and the wine. He hurled the boccie balls with such élan that the court became the center of the wedding for an hour.

After boccie, Jimmy Santadio drew Pippi aside. "I'm counting on you to make everything work," he said. "Our two Families together, nothing can stop us. Me and you." It was Jimmy Santadio at his charming best.

Pippi mustered every ounce of sincerity for his answer. "We will. We will." And he wondered if Jimmy Santadio was as honest as he seemed. By now he must know that somebody in his Family had committed the murder.

Jimmy seemed to sense this. "I swear to you, Pippi, I had nothing to do with it." He took Pippi's hand in his. "We had nothing to do with Silvio's death. Nothing. I swear on the head of my father."

"I believe you," Pippi said and pressed Jimmy's hands. He had a moment of doubt, but it didn't matter. It was too late.

The red desert sun faded to twilight, and lights came on all over the compound. This was the signal for a formal dinner to be served. And all the brothers, Fonsa, Italo, Gino, Benedict, and Louis, proposed a toast to the bride and groom. To the happiness of the marriage, to the special virtues of Jimmy, to Pippi De Lena, their great new friend.

Old Don Santadio was too ill to leave his bed but sent his heartiest good wishes in which he mentioned the plane he had given his son, at which everybody cheered. Then the bride herself cut a huge slice of the wedding cake and brought it to the old man's bedroom. But he was asleep, so they gave it to his nurse, who promised to feed it to him when he woke up.

Finally, toward midnight, the party broke. Jimmy and Rose Marie retired to their bridal chamber, saying they would leave on their honeymoon to Europe the next morning and they needed their rest. At which the guests hooted derisively and made vulgar remarks. All in high spirits and good humor.

The hundreds of cars left the compound and sped off into the desert. The catering trucks were packed, the personnel pulled down the tents and assembled the tables and chairs, then pulled up the platform and even hastily policed the grounds to be certain there was no garbage. Finally they were through; they would finish it up the next day.

At Pippi's request, a ceremonial meeting had been arranged with the five Santadio brothers, to be held after the guests had left. They would exchange gifts to celebrate the new friendship of the two Families.

At midnight they gathered together in the huge dining room of the Santadio mansion. Pippi had a suitcase full of Rolex watches (genuine, not knockoffs). There was also a large Japanese kimono studded with hand-painted sexual scenes of Oriental lovemaking.

Fonsa shouted out, "Let's bring it up to Jimmy right now."

"Too late," Italo said cheerily. "Jimmy and Rose Marie are on their third round."

And they all laughed.

Outside, the desert moon isolated the compound in an icy white light. Chinese lanterns hanging on compound walls made red circles in the white moonbeams.

A large truck, the word CATERING limned in gold paint on its side, rumbled up to the gates of the Santadio compound.

One of the two guards approached the truck, and the driver told him they had come back to pick up a forgotten generator.

"This late?" the guard said.

As he spoke the driver's helper got out of the truck and moved toward the other guard. Both guards were sluggish with the food and drink from the wedding.

In one synchronized movement two things happened: The driver reached down between his legs and showed a gun with a silencer, then fired three times directly into the first guard's face. The driver's helper grabbed the other guard in a stranglehold and with a large, sharp knife in one swift motion cut his throat.

They were dead on the ground. The soft hum of a motor sounded as the large metal platform on the rear of the truck quickly descended and twenty soldiers of the Clericuzio sprang out. Stocking masked, dressed in black, armed with silenced guns, led by Giorgio, Petie, and Vincent, they spilled all over the compound. A special crew cut through the telephone lines. Another crew spread out to command the compound. Ten of the masked men with Giorgio, Petie, and Vincent crashed into the dining room.

The Santadio brothers held their wine glasses to toast Pippi, he stepped away from them. No words were spoken. The invaders opened fire and the five Santadio brothers were torn apart by a hail of bullets. One of the masked men, Petie, stood over them and gave all five the coup de grace, a bullet under the chin. The floor glittered with broken glass.

Another masked man, Giorgio, handed Pippi a mask and black trousers and sweater. Pippi quickly changed and threw his discarded clothes into a bag held by another masked invader.

Pippi, still unarmed, led Giorgio, Petie, and Vincent down the long corridor to the bedroom of Don Santadio. He pushed open the door.

Don Santadio had finally woken and was eating the bridal cake. He took one look at the four men, made the sign of the cross, and put a pillow over his face. The dish holding the cake slipped to the floor.

The nurse was reading in the corner of the room. Petie was on her like a great cat, gagging her and then tying her to the chair with thin nylon rope.

It was Giorgio who advanced to the bed. He reached out gently and pulled the pillow from Don Santadio's head. He hesitated a moment and then fired two shots, the first in the eye, the second, lifting up the round bald head, upward from under the chin.

They regrouped. Vincent finally armed Pippi, he handed over a long silver rope.

Pippi led them from the room down the long corridor and then up to the third floor, which held the bridal chamber. The corridor was littered with flowers and baskets of fruit.

Pippi pushed against the bridal chamber door. It was locked. Petie took off one of his gloves and produced a pick. With this he easily opened the door and pushed it back.

Rose Marie and Jimmy were sprawled on the bed. They had just finished making love, and their bodies were almost liquid with released sensuality. Rose Marie's see-through negligee was bunched above her waist, and the straps had slipped down, exposing her breasts. Her right hand was on Jimmy's hair, the left on his stomach. Jimmy was completely naked, but he sprang up as soon as he saw the men and pulled a bedsheet to use as a robe. He understood everything. "Not here, outside," he said, and advanced toward them.

Rose Marie, for a fraction of a second, was still uncomprehending. As Jimmy moved toward the door, she clutched at him but he evaded her. He went through the door surrounded by the masked Giorgio, Petie, and Vincent. And then Rose Marie said, "Pippi, Pippi, please don't." It was only when the three men turned to look at her that she realized that they were her brothers. "Giorgio, Petie, Vincent. Don't. Don't."

This was the most difficult moment for Pippi. If Rose Marie talked, the Clericuzio Family was doomed. His duty was to kill her. The Don had not specifically instructed him on this; how could he condone the killing of his daughter? Would her brothers obey him? And how did she know it was them? He made the decision. He closed the door behind him and was out in the corridor with Jimmy and Rose Marie's three brothers.

Here the Don had been explicit. Jimmy Santadio was to be strangled. It was perhaps the mark of mercy that there should be no penetrations of his body for his loved ones to weep over. It was perhaps from some tradition of not shedding a loved one's blood while consecrating him to death.

Suddenly Jimmy Santadio let the bedsheet drop, and his hands reached out and ripped Pippi's mask from his face. Giorgio grabbed one of his arms, Pippi the other. Vincent dropped to the floor and grabbed Jimmy's legs. Now Pippi had his rope around Jimmy's neck and bent him to the floor. Jimmy had a twisted smile on his lips, curiously pitying as he stared into Pippi's face: that this act would be avenged by Fate or some mysterious God.

Pippi pulled the cord tight, Petie reached to help with the pressure, and they all sank to the floor of the corridor, where the white bedsheet received Jimmy Santadio's body like a shroud. Inside the bridal chamber, Rose Marie began to scream . . .

The Don had finished speaking. He lit up another cheroot and sipped his wine.

Giorgio said, "Pippi planned the whole thing. We got away clean and the Santadio were wiped out. It was brilliant."

Vincent said, "It solved everything. We haven't had any trouble since."

Don Clericuzio sighed. "It was my decision and it was wrong. But how were we to know Rose Marie would go mad? We were in crisis and this was our only opportunity to strike a decisive blow. You must remember that at that time, I was not yet sixty, I thought too much of my power and intelligence. I thought then certainly it would be a tragedy for my daughter but widows do not grieve forever. And they had killed my son Silvio. How could I forgive that, daughter or no daughter? But I learned. You cannot come to a reasonable solution with stupid people. I should have wiped them out at the very beginning. Before the lovers met. I would have saved my son and daughter." He paused for a moment.

"So, you see, Dante is Jimmy Santadio's son. And you, Cross, shared a baby carriage with him when you were infants, your first summer in this house. All those years I have tried to make up to Dante for the loss of his father. I tried to help my daughter recover from her grief. Dante was brought up as a Clericuzio and he will, with my sons, be my heir."

Cross tried to understand what was happening. His whole body quivered with revulsion toward the Clericuzio and the world they lived in. He thought of his father, Pippi, playing the role of Satan, seducing the Santadio to their death. How could such a man be his father? He thought then of his beloved aunt, Rose Marie, living all those years with her heart and her mind broken, knowing that her husband had been murdered by her father and her brothers. That her own family had betrayed her. He even thought of Dante with some pity, now Dante's guilt was established. And then he wondered about the Don. Surely he did not believe the story of Pippi's mugging. Why did he seem to accept it, a man who had never believed in coincidence. What was the message here?

Cross could never read Giorgio. Did he believe in the mugging killing? It was obvious that Vincent and Petie believed it. But now he understood the special bond between his father and the Don and his three sons. They had been soldiers together in the massacre of the Santadio. And his father had spared Rose Marie.

Cross said, "And Rose Marie never talked?"

"No," the Don said, sardonically. "She did even better. She became crazy." There was just a hint of pride in his voice. "I sent her to Sicily and brought her back in time for Dante to be born on American soil. Who knows, someday he might be president of the United States. I had dreams for the little boy but the combination of Clericuzio and Santadio blood was too much for him.

"And you know the most terrible thing?" the Don said. "Your father, Pippi, made a mistake. He should never have spared Rose Marie, though I loved him for it." He sighed. He took a sip of wine and, looking Cross full in the face, he said, "Be aware. The world is what it is. And you are what you are."

On the flight back to Vegas, Cross pondered the riddle. Why had the Don finally told him the story of the Santadio War? To prevent him from visiting Rose Marie and hearing a different version? Or was he warning him off, telling him not to avenge his father's murder because Dante was involved. The Don was a mystery. But of one thing Cross was sure. If it was Dante who killed his father, then Dante must kill him. And surely Don Domenico Clericuzio knew that, too.

CHAPTER 19

D ANTE CLERICUZIO did not have to hear this story. His mother, Rose Marie, had whispered it into his tiny ear from the time he was two years old: whenever she had one of her fits, whenever she felt her grief for the lost love of her husband and her brother Silvio, whenever her terror of Pippi and her brothers overcame her.

It was only when Rose Marie had her worst fits that she accused her father, Don Clericuzio, of the death of her husband. The Don always denied giving the order, as he denied that his sons and Pippi had carried out the massacre. But after she accused him two times, he packed her off to the clinic for a month. After that, she only ranted and raved, and never accused him directly again.

But Dante remembered her whisperings always. As a child he loved his grandfather and believed in his innocence. But he schemed against his three uncles though they always treated him tenderly. Especially, he dreamed of vengeance on Pippi, and though these were fantasies, he thought them for his mother's sake.

When Rose Marie was normal she took care of the widower Don Clericuzio with the utmost affection. To her three brothers she showed sisterly concern. With Pippi, she was distant. And because in those times she had such a sweet visage, it was difficult for her to express malice convincingly. The structure of the bones in her face, the curve of her mouth, and the gentle eyes of liquid brown denied her hate. To her child Dante she showed her overwhelming need to love, which she could no longer feel for any man. She showered him with gifts out of that affection, as did his grandfather and his uncles out of something less pure, a love muddied with guilt. When Rose Marie was normal, she never told Dante the story.

But in her fits she was foul-mouthed, full of curses, even her face could turn into an ugly mask of fury. Dante was always bewildered. When he was seven years old, a doubt entered his mind. "How did you know it was Pippi and my uncles?" he asked her.

Rose Marie cackled with glee. She seemed to Dante a witch out of his fairy-tale books. She told him, "They think they are so clever, that they plan for everything with their masks and special clothes and hats. Do you want to know what they forgot? Pippi was still wearing his dancing shoes. Patent leather and black string bows. And your uncles always grouped themselves together in a particular way. Giorgio always to the front, Vincent a little behind, and Petie always to the right. And the way they looked at Pippi to see if he would give the order to kill me. Because I had recognized them. The way they wavered, almost shrank back. But they would have killed me, they would have. My own brothers." She would then burst into such great weeping that Dante would be terrified.

Even as a small child of seven, he would try to comfort her. "Uncle Petie would never hurt you," he said. "And Grandpa would have killed them all if they did." He wasn't certain of his Uncle Giorgio or even Uncle Vinnie. But in his child's heart, it was Pippi he could never forgive.

By the time Dante was ten years old, he had learned to watch for his mother's fits, and so when she beckoned him to her to tell the Santadio story again, he would quickly take her away into the safety of her bedroom so his grandfather and his uncles would not hear.

By the time Dante grew into manhood, he was too clever to be fooled by all the disguises of the Clericuzio Family. He was of so humorously malicious a nature that he showed his grandfather and his uncles that he knew the truth. And he could perceive that his uncles were not that fond of him. Dante had been designated to join the legal social world, to perhaps take Giorgio's place and learn the financial complexities, but he showed no interest. He had even taunted his uncles that he had no interest in the sissy side of the Family. Giorgio listened to this with a coolness that for a moment frightened the sixteen-year-old Dante.

Uncle Giorgio said, "OK, you won't." There was sadness in his voice and some anger, too.

When Dante quit high school in his senior year, he was sent to work in Petie's construction company in the Bronx Enclave. Dante was a hard worker and developed huge muscles from the hard, grueling work on the building sites. Petie put him on crews of soldiers from the Bronx Enclave. When Dante was old enough, the Don decreed the boy would be a soldier under Petie.

The Don had come to his decision only after reports from Giorgio on Dante's character, and some acts committed by Dante. The young boy was accused of rape by a pretty high school classmate and of assault with a small knife by another fellow student, a boy his own age. Dante had begged his uncles not to let his grandfather know and they had promised him, but of course they had reported to the Don immediately. These charges were settled by large sums of money before Dante could be prosecuted.

And it was during his teenage years that his jealousy of Cross De Lena increased. Cross had grown into a tall, extraordinarily handsome youth with a mature courtesy. All the women in the Clericuzio clan adored him, fussed over him. His female cousins flirted with him, something they never did with the Don's grandson. Dante, wearing his Renaissance hats, with his sly humor and his short and hugely muscular body, was frightening to these young girls. Dante was too clever not to observe all this.

When Dante was taken to the Hunting Lodge in the Sierras, he enjoyed trapping more than shooting. When he fell in love with one of the female cousins, as was perfectly natural in the close-knit Clericuzio clan, he was too direct in his advances. And he was too familiar with the daughters of the Clericuzio soldiers who lived in the Bronx Enclave. Finally Giorgio, who had the role of an instructive, punitive parent, enrolled him with the owner of a New York City high-class bordello to quiet him down.

But Dante's enormous curiosity, his cunning cleverness, made him the only one of his generation of the Clericuzio who really knew what the Family did. So it was finally decided he would be given operational training.

As time went on, Dante felt a growing separation from his Family. The Don was as fond of him as ever and made clear to him that he was an heir to the Empire, but he no longer shared his thoughts with his grandson, no longer gave him his insights, his secret little pearls of wisdom. And the Don did not support Dante's suggestions and ideas on strategy.

His uncles, Giorgio, Vincent, and Petie, were not as warm in their affection as when he was a child. Petie, it was true, seemed more of a friend, but then he had been trained by Petie.

Dante was clever enough to think that maybe the fault was his, because he had betrayed his knowledge of the massacre of the Santadio and his father. He even asked questions of Petie about Jimmy Santadio, and his uncle told him how much they had respected his father and how sad they had been about his death. It was never said openly, never admitted, but Don Clericuzio and his sons understood that Dante knew the true story, that Rose Marie, in her fits, had disclosed the secret. They wanted to make amends, they treated him as a child prince.

But what most formed Dante's character was his pity and love for his mother. In her fits she inflamed in him a hatred for Pippi DeLena; she exonerated her father and brothers.

All these things helped Don Clericuzio make his final decision, for the Don could read his grandson's mind as easily as he could read his prayer book. The Don judged that Dante could never take part in the final retreat to the cloak of society. His Santadio and (the Don was a fair man) Clericuzio blood was too ferocious a mixture. Therefore Dante would join the society of Vincent and Petie, of Giorgio and Pippi De Lena. They would all fight the final battle together.

And Dante proved to be a good soldier, though an irrepressible one. He had an independence that made him flout the Family rules, and indeed he sometimes did not comply with specific orders. His ferocity was useful when a confused *Bruglione* or an undisciplined soldier stepped over the Family line and had to be dispatched to a less complex world. Dante was not subject to control except by the Don himself, and mysteriously the Don refused to chastise him personally.

Dante feared for his mother's future. That future depended on the Don, and as her fits occurred more often, Dante could see the Don becoming more impatient. Especially when Rose Marie would make a grand exit by drawing a circle with her foot and then spitting in the middle while screaming she would never enter the house again. That was when the Don would ship her off to the clinic again for a few days.

So Dante would coax her out of her fits, restore her to her natural sweetness and affection. But there was always the dread that finally he could not protect her. Unless he became as powerful as the Don himself.

The only person in the world Dante feared was the old Don. It was a feeling that came from his experiences with his grandfather as a child. And it sprang, too, from his sense that the sons feared Don Clericuzio as much as they loved him. Which was amazing to Dante. The Don was in his eighties, he no longer had physical strength, he rarely left his mansion, and his height was diminished. Why fear him?

True, he ate well, he made an imposing appearance, the only physical disarray time had done was to soften his teeth so that his diet was reduced to pasta, grated cheese, stewed vegetables, and soups. Meats were simmered to shreds in tomato sauces.

But the old Don had to die soon, so there would be shifts of power. What if Pippi became Giorgio's right-hand man? What if Pippi seized power by sheer force? And if that happened, Cross would ascend, especially since he had acquired so much wealth with his share of the Xanadu.

So there were practical reasons, Dante assured himself, not his hatred of Pippi, who dared to criticize him to his own Family.

Dante had made his original contact with Jim Losey when Giorgio decided that Dante should have some points of power and designated him to deliver Losey's salary from the Family.

Of course precautions had been taken to protect Dante if Losey should ever turn traitor. Contracts were signed that showed Losey to be working for a Family-controlled security corporation as a consultant. The contract specified confidentiality and that Losey be paid in cash. But in the security corporation's tax filings, the money was reported as expenses, with Losey using a corporation dummy as recipient.

Dante had made special payments to Losey over several years before he initiated a more intimate relationship. He was not intimidated by Losey's reputation, he sized him up as a man who was at a juncture where he was thinking of accumulating a very large nest egg for his old age. Losey had a hand in everything. He was protecting drug dealers, taking Clericuzio money to protect gambling, was even dabbling in strong-arming certain high-powered retail merchants into paying extra protection fees.

Dante exerted all his charm to make a good impression on Losey; both his sly and vicious sense of humor and his disregard for accepted moral principles appealed to Losey. Dante reacted particularly well to Losey's bitter tales of his war against the blacks who were destroying Western civilization. Dante himself had no racial prejudices. Blacks had no influence on his life, and if they did they would be mercilessly removed.

Dante and Losey had a powerful common urge. They were both dandies interested in their looks, and they both had a similar sexual drive for the domination of women. Not so much erotic but as an expression of power. They took to spending time together when Dante was in the West. They went to dinner together and cruised the nightclubs. Dante never dared to bring him to Vegas and the Xanadu, and it was not to his purpose.

Dante loved to tell Losey of how he was first the abject extravagant courter of women, and the women were imperious in the power of their beauty. And then how he enjoyed the imperiousness by maneuvering them into a position where they could not escape the unwilling giving of sex. Losey, a little contemptuous of Dante's trick, would tell how he would break women down from the very beginning with his extraordinary macho presence, and then humiliate them.

Both of them declared that they would never force a woman to have sex who did not respond to their courtship. They both agreed that Athena Aquitane would be a grand prize if she ever gave them an opening. When they roved around the L.A. clubs together and picked up women, they would compare notes and laugh at those vain women who thought they could go to the utmost limit and then refuse the final act. Sometimes the protests would be too vehement, and then Losey would show his shield and tell the women he would bust them for prostitution. Since many of them were soft hookers, the threat worked.

They spent evenings of camaraderie, orchestrated by Dante. Losey, when not telling the "nigger" stories, tried to define the varieties of hookers.

There were first the out-and-out prostitutes who held one hand out for money and grabbed your cock with the other. Then there was the soft hooker who was attracted to you and gave you a friendly screw and then, before you left in the morning, asked you for a check to help pay the rent.

Then there was the soft hooker who loved you but loved others too and established a long-term relationship studded with gifts of jewelry for every holiday, including Labor Day. Then there were the freelance nine-to-five secretaries, airline stewardesses, shop clerks in fancy boutiques, who invited you up to their apartment for coffee after an expensive dinner and then tried to throw you out on your ass to freeze in the street without even a hand job. These were their favorites. Sex with them was exciting, fraught with drama, tears, and subdued cries for forbearance and patience, which produced a sex that was better than love.

One night after they had dinner at Le Chinois, a restaurant in Venice, Dante suggested they take a stroll along the boardwalk. They sat on a bench and watched the human traffic go by, beautiful young girls on Rollerblades, pimps of all colors pursuing them and shouting endearments, the soft hookers selling T-shirts decorated with sayings incomprehensible to the two men. Hare Krishnas with begging bowls, bearded groups of singers with guitars, family groups with cameras, and reflecting them, the black ocean of the Pacific, on whose sandy beaches isolated twosomes crouched under blankets they believed disguised their fornication.

"I could lock up everybody here for probable cause," Losey said, laughing. "What a fucking zoo."

"Even those pretty young kids on skates?" Dante asked.

"I'd just bust them for carrying pussies as a dangerous weapon," Losey said.

"Not many eggplants here," Dante said.

Losey stretched out on the beach, and when he spoke it was with a fair imitation of a Southern accent.

"I think I've been too hard on my black brethren," he said. "It's like the liberals always say, it all springs from their having been slaves."

Dante waited for the punch line.

Losey linked his hands behind his head and pulled back his jacket to let his gun holster show to scare off any reckless punks. Nobody paid attention, they had spotted him for a cop by his first step on the boardwalk.

"Slavery," Jim Losey said. "Demoralizing. It was too easy a life for them so it made them too dependent. Freedom was too hard. On the plantations they were taken care of, three meals a day, free rent, they were clothed and they were given good medical attention because they were valuable property. They weren't even responsible for their children. Imagine. The plantation owners fucked their daughters and gave those children jobs for the rest of their lives. Sure they worked but they were always singing, so how hard could they be working? I'll bet five white guys could do the work of a hundred niggers."

Dante was tickled. Was Losey serious? It didn't matter, he was expressing an emotional view not a rational one.

They were enjoying themselves, it was a balmy night, the world they observed gave them a comfortable feeling of security. These people were never a danger to them.

Then Dante said, "I've got a really important proposition to put to you. Do you want the rewards first or the risks first?"

Losey smiled at him. "Rewards first, always."

Dante said, "Two hundred grand cash up front. A year later, a job as head of security at the Xanadu Hotel. With a salary five times what you get now. Expense account. Big car, room, board, and all the pussy you can eat. You get to do all the background checks on the hotel showgirls. Plus bonuses like you make now. And you don't have the risk of being the primary shooter."

"Sounds too good," Losey said. "But somebody has to get shot. That's the risk, right?"

"For me," Dante said. "I'm the shooter."

"Why not me?" Losey asked. "I have the badge to make it legal."

"Because you wouldn't live six months after it," Dante said.

"And what do I do?" Losey asked. "Tickle your ass with a feather?"

Dante explained the whole operation. Losey whistled to express his admiration for the daring of the idea.

"Why Pippi De Lena?" Losey asked.

"Because he's about to turn traitor," Dante said.

Losey was still looking doubtful. It would be the first time he committed the crime of cold-blooded murder. Dante decided to give it something extra.

"You remember that Boz Skannet suicide?" he said. "Cross made that hit, not personally, but with a guy named Lia Vazzi."

"What does he look like?" Losey asked. When Dante had described Vazzi he realized it was the man accompanying Skannet when he had stopped him in the hotel lobby. "Where can I find this Vazzi guy?"

For a long moment Dante considered. He was doing something that broke the only really holy law of the Family. Of the Don. But it might get Cross out of the way, and Cross would be someone to fear after Pippi's death.

"I'll never tell anybody where it came from," Losey said.

Dante for a moment reconsidered, then he said, "Vazzi lives in a hunting lodge my family owns up in the Sierras. But don't do anything until we finish with Pippi."

"Sure," Losey said. He would do what he liked. "And I get my two hundred grand right up front, right?"

"Right," Dante said.

"Sounds good," Losey said. "One thing. If the Clericuzio come after me, I'll sell you down the river."

"Don't worry," Dante said amiably. "If I hear that, I'll kill you first. Now we just have to work out the details."

It all went as they planned.

When Dante fired the six shots into Pippi De Lena's body and when Pippi whispered, calling him a "fucking Santadio," Dante felt an exultation he had never felt before.

CHAPTER 20

⊞

LIA VAZZI, for the first time, deliberately disobeyed the order of his boss, Cross De Lena.

It was unavoidable. Detective Jim Losey had made another visit to the Hunting Lodge and had again asked questions about Skannet's death. Lia denied all knowledge of Skannet and claimed he had just happened to be in the hotel lobby at that particular time. Losey patted him on the shoulder, then lightly slapped him across the face. "OK, you little guinea prick," he said, "I'll get you soon."

In his mind Lia signed a death warrant for Losey. No matter what else happened, and he knew his future was in peril, he would make sure of Losey's fate. But he had to be very careful. The Clericuzio Family had strict rules. You never harmed a police officer.

Lia remembered driving Cross to the meeting with Phil Sharkey, Losey's retired partner. He had never believed that Sharkey would remain quiet on the promise of a future fifty grand. Now he was sure that Sharkey had informed Losey of that meeting and probably had seen Vazzi waiting in the car. If this was true, there would be a great danger to Cross and himself. In essence he distrusted the judgment of Cross, police officers stuck together like Mafioso. They had their own kind of *omertà*.

Lia recruited two of his soldiers to drive him down from the Hunting Lodge to Santa Monica, the home of Phil Sharkey. He was confident that just by talking to Sharkey he would know if the man had informed Losey of the visit by Cross.

The outside of Sharkey's house was deserted, the lawn empty except for an abandoned mower. But the garage door was open, a car in it, and Lia walked up the cement path to the door and rang the bell. There was no answer. He kept ringing. He tested the knob, the door was not locked, now there was a choice to be made. Did he go in or leave immediately? He wiped his prints off the knob and bell with the tail of his tie. Then he went through the door into the small hallway and called Sharkey's name in a shout. There was no answer.

Lia moved through the house; the two bedrooms were bare, he looked into the closets and under the beds. He went through the living room, looking under the sofa and through the cushions. Then he went into the kitchen and to the patio table where there was a container of milk and a paper plate that held a partially eaten cheese sandwich, white bread with dehydrated yellow mayo on the edges.

There was a slatted brown door in the kitchen, and Lia opened it to reveal a shallow basement only two wooden steps down, sort of a dropped room with no windows.

Lia Vazzi descended the two steps and looked behind a mound of used bicycles. He opened a closet with huge doors. In it was a policeman's uniform hanging all by itself, on the floor was a pair of thick black shoes, and resting on the shoes was a braided street policeman's cap. That was all.

Lia went to the one trunk on the floor and pulled up the lid. It was surprisingly light. The interior was filled to the top with neatly folded gray blankets.

Lia went back up the stairs and stood on the patio staring at the ocean. Burying a body in the sand was foolhardy, so he dismissed the idea. Maybe somebody had come by and picked Sharkey up. But for an assassin there would be a risk of being seen. Also, Sharkey would be a dangerous man to kill. So, Lia reasoned, if the man was dead he had to be in this house. Immediately he went back down to the basement and threw all the wool blankets out of the trunk. And sure enough, there at the bottom was first the large head, and then the lean body. There was a hole in Sharkey's right eye and over it a thin cake of blood like a red coin. The facial skin, waxy with long death, was pockmarked with black dots. Lia, as a Qualified Man, knew exactly what that meant. Someone trusted had been allowed to come very close to shoot point blank into the eye; those dots were powder marks.

Carefully, Lia folded the blankets, put them back over the body, and then exited the house. He had not left any fingerprints but was aware that fragments of the blankets must have adhered to his clothing. He would have to destroy the clothes thoroughly. His shoes, too. He had his soldiers drive him to the airport, and while he was waiting for a plane to take him to Vegas, he bought a change of clothing including new shoes in one of the stores in the airport mall. Then he bought a carry-on bag and put his old clothes into it.

In Vegas he checked into the Xanadu and left a message for Cross. Then he showered thoroughly and dressed again in his new clothes. He waited for Cross to call.

When the call came, he told Cross he would be up to see him. He brought the bag of his old clothing, and the first thing he said to Cross was "You just saved yourself fifty grand."

Cross looked at him and smiled. Lia, usually a natty dresser, had bought a flowery shirt, blue canvas pants, and a light jacket, also blue. He looked like a low-caste casino hustler.

Lia told him about Sharkey. He attempted to make excuses for his actions, but Cross dismissed them. "You're in this with me, you have to protect yourself. But what the hell does this mean?"

"Simple," Lia said. "Sharkey was the only one who could tie Losey with Dante. Otherwise it's just your say-so. Dante made Losey kill his partner."

Cross said, "How the hell could Sharkey be that dumb?"

Lia shrugged. "He figured he could get money from Losey and then get the fifty from you anyway. He knew that Losey must be playing for big stakes because of the money you gave him. After all, he was a detective for twenty years, he could figure these things out. And he never dreamed Losey would kill him, his old partner. He didn't figure on Dante."

"They were extreme," Cross said.

"In this situation you cannot allow an extra player," Lia said. "I must say I'm surprised that Dante could see that particular danger. He must have convinced Losey, who really would not want to kill an old partner. We all have our sentimentalities."

"So now Dante is controlling Losey," Cross said. "I thought Losey was tougher than that."

"You're talking about two different classes of animal," Lia said. "Losey is formidable, Dante is crazy."

"So Dante knows I know about him," Cross said.

"Which means I have to act very quickly," Lia said.

Cross nodded. "It will have to be a Communion," he said. "They will have to disappear."

Lia laughed. "Do you think that will deceive Don Clericuzio?" he said.

"If we plan it right, nobody can blame us," Cross said.

Lia spent the next three days with Cross going over plans. During that time he burned his old clothes in the hotel incinerator with his own hands. Cross exercised by shooting a lone eighteen holes of golf, with Lia accompanying him to drive the golf cart. Lia could not understand the popularity of golf in all the Families. To him it was a quaint aberration.

On the night of the third day they sat on the balcony of the penthouse. Cross had laid out the brandy and Havana cigars. They watched the crowds on the Strip below.

"No matter how clever they are, my death so soon after my father's would compromise Dante with the Don," Cross said. "I think we can wait."

Lia puffed on his cigar. "Not too long. Now they know you spoke with Sharkey."

"We have to get them both at the same time," Cross said. "Remember, it will have to be a Communion. Their bodies must not be found."

Lia said, "You're putting last things first. And first we have to be sure we can kill them."

Cross sighed. "It's going to be very difficult. Losey is a dangerous man and careful. Dante can fight. We have to isolate them in one place. Can it be done in Los Angeles?"

"No," Lia said. "That is Losey's territory. He is too formidable there. We will have to do it in Vegas."

"And break rules," Cross said.

"If it's a Communion then nobody will know where they were killed," Lia said. "And we are already breaking the rule by killing a police officer."

"I think I know how to get them to Vegas at the same time," Cross said. He explained the scheme to Lia.

"We will have to use more bait," Lia told Cross. "We have to make sure Losey and Dante come when we want them here."

Cross drank another brandy. "OK, here's some more bait." He told Lia, and Lia nodded in agreement. "Their disappearance will be our salvation," Cross said. "And it will deceive everyone."

"Except Don Clericuzio," Lia said. "He is the only one to fear."

BOOK VIII

Communion

CHAPTER 21

VERY LUCKILY Steve Stallings did not die until his final close-up scene in *Messalina* was shot. It could have cost millions of dollars in reshooting.

The last scene to be shot was a battle scene that actually took place in the middle of the film. A desert town had been erected fifty miles from Vegas to denote the base of the Persian army that was to be destroyed by the Emperor Claudius (Steve Stallings) accompanied by his wife, Messalina (Athena).

At the end of the day, Steve Stallings retired to his hotel suite in the small town. He had his cocaine and his booze and two female companions for the night, and he was going to kick everybody's ass, he was pissed off. For one thing, his part in the picture had been cut to a character part, not a star. He realized he was shifting into a secondary career, an inevitable fate for aging stars. Another thing, Athena had been distant from him all during the shoot, he had hoped for more. Also—and this was, he himself felt, a little childish—at the wrap party and showing of the rough cut, he was not getting star treatment; he had not been given one of the Xanadu Hotel's famous Villas.

After his long years in the movie business, Steve Stallings knew how the power structure worked. When he was a Bankable Star, he could override everyone. Theoretically, the studio chief was boss, he gave the green light for a picture. A powerful producer who brought a "property" to the studio was also the boss, he got the elements together—i.e., stars, director, screenplay—supervised the development of the script, and raised independent money from people who were given a credit as associate producers but had no power. For that period he was the boss.

But once the picture started shooting, it was the director who was the boss. Providing he was an A director or the even more powerful Bankable Director (that is, one who would assure an audience in the film's opening weeks and attract Bankable Stars to appear in the movie).

The director had complete charge over the picture. Everything had to go through him. The costumes, music, sets, how the actors played their parts. Also, the Directors Guild was the most powerful union in the movie business. No name director would accept the job of replacing another director.

But all these people, powerful as they were, had to bow to the Bankable Star. A director who had two Bankable Stars in the same movie was like a man riding two wild horses. His balls could be scattered to the four winds.

Steve Stallings had been such a star and knew he no longer was.

The day's shoot had been physically taxing and Steve Stallings needed relaxation. He showered, ate a big steak, and when the two girls came up, local talent and not bad looking at all, he fed them cocaine and champagne. For once he relaxed his prudence, after all his career was entering its twilight years, and he didn't really have to be careful anymore. He went heavy on the coke.

The two girls were wearing T-shirts emblazoned with STEVE STALLINGS ASS KISSERS, in tribute to his buttocks, admired by fans all over the world, male and female. They were properly awe-stricken, and it was only after the cocaine that they peeled off their T-shirts and bundled in with him. This cheered him up somewhat. He took another snort of cocaine. The girls were caressing him, stripping off his shorts and shirt. Stallings daydreamed as they fiddled, their fiddling putting him at ease.

Tomorrow at the wrap party, he would see all his conquests. He had screwed Athena Aquitane, he had screwed Claudia who had written the movie, he had even screwed Dita Tommey long ago, when she wasn't yet fully convinced of her true sexual orientation. He had screwed Bobby Bantz's wife and, though she no longer counted because she was dead, Skippy Deere's wife. It always gave him a feeling of virtuous fulfillment when at a dinner party he looked around and tallied up all the women who were now sitting so placidly with their husbands and lovers. He was an intimate of them all.

There was a distraction. One of the girls was sticking a finger up his ass and that always annoyed him. He had hemorrhoids. He rose from the bed to snort some more cocaine and take a full swig of champagne, but the wine upset his stomach. He felt nauseous and then disoriented. He didn't quite know where he was.

Suddenly, he was aware of a great fatigue: his legs sagged, the glass fell from his hand. He was bewildered. Very far away he heard one of the girls scream and he was furious with her for screaming, and then the very last thing he felt was a lightning bolt exploding in his head.

What happened next could only have happened with a combination of stupidity and malice. One girl had screamed because Steve Stallings had toppled over her onto the bed and had lain there, mouth open and eyes staring, so obviously dead that both girls panicked and just kept screaming. The screaming attracted the hotel personnel and a number of people who were gambling in the tiny hotel casino, which held only slots, a dice table, and a large, round poker setup. These people followed the screaming and came upstairs.

There were, outside Stalling's hotel room, with its now-open door, several people staring at his naked body sprawled out on the bed. In what seemed just a few minutes, an additional crowd gathered from the town, hundreds of them. They crowded into the room to touch his body.

At first there were just reverent touches for the man who had made women all over the world fall in love with him. Then some women kissed him, other women touched his testicles, his penis, one women took out a pair of scissors from her purse and cut off a great thatch of glossy black hair to expose the underlying fuzz of gray on his skull.

The malice came in because Skippy Deere had been one of the first to arrive and had failed to call the police immediately. He watched the first wave of women approach Steve Stallings's body. He had a clear view. Stallings's mouth was open as if he had been caught in the act of singing and there was a look of astonishment on his face.

The first woman who reached him—Deere saw her clearly—gently closed his eyes and pushed his mouth shut before she softly kissed him on the forehead. But she was pushed aside by the next wave who were not so restrained. And Deere felt the malice within him, the horns Stallings had given him years ago seemed to tingle, and he let the invasion continue. Stallings often boasted that no women could resist him and he was certainly on the mark. Even dead, women were caressing his body.

Only when a piece of Stallings's ear vanished and he had been turned sideways to show his famous buttocks, his whole body deathly pale, did Deere finally call the police and take command of the situation and solve all the problems. That was what producers did. That was their forte.

Skippy Deere made all the arrangements for the body to be autopsied immediately and then shipped to Los Angeles, where the funeral would be held three days later.

The autopsy showed that Stallings had died of a cerebral aneurysm which, when it exploded, sent all his blood rushing through his head.

Deere hunted down the two young girls who had been with him and promised them they would not be prosecuted for cocaine use and that they would be signed for small parts in a new movie he was producing. He would pay them a thousand a week for two years. However, there was a moral turpitude clause that would end the contract if they talked to anyone about Stallings's death.

Then he took the time to call Bobby Bantz in L.A. and explain what he had done. He also called Dita Tommey to give her the news and have her tell all the *Messalina* personnel, above the line and below the line, to be sure to attend the showing in Vegas and the wrap party. Then, shaken more than he would admit, he took two Halcions and went to sleep.

CHAPTER 22

THE DEATH OF Steve Stallings did not affect the showing and wrap party in Vegas. That was Skippy Deere's expertise. And the emotional structure of movie making. It was true that Stallings had been a star, but he had ceased to be a Bankable Star. It was true that he had made love to many women in their bodies, and millions more in their minds, but his love had never been more than reciprocal pleasure. Even the women in the picture, Athena, Claudia, Dita Tommey, and the three other featured female stars, were less grieved than would be imagined by romantics. Everyone agreed that Steve Stallings would want the show to go on, nothing would distress him more than to have the wrap party and screening canceled because of his death.

In the film industry you said good-bye to most of your lovers at the end of a picture as politely as you did in the old days to your dancing partner at a ball.

Skippy Deere claimed it was his idea to hold the wrap party at the Xanadu Hotel and to show a very rough cut of the picture that same night. He knew that Athena would be leaving the country in the next few days and wanted to make sure that Athena did not have to reshoot any scenes.

But, in reality, it was Cross who proposed the idea of a wrap party and showing of the film at the Xanadu Hotel. He asked it as a favor.

"It will be great publicity for the Xanadu," Cross told Deere. "And here's what I'll do for you. I'll comp everybody on the picture and anybody you invite for one night—room, food, beverage. I'll give you and Bantz a Villa. I'll give Athena a Villa. I'll provide security so nobody gets to see the rough cut—like the press—that you don't want to. You've been screaming for years you wanted a Villa."

Deere pondered this. "Just for publicity?"

Cross grinned at him. "Also you get hundreds of people loaded with big cash. The casino will get a good part of it."

"Bantz doesn't gamble," Deere said. "I do. You'll get my money."

"I'll give you fifty grand in credit," Cross said. "If you lose we won't press for payment."

That convinced Deere. "OK," he said. "But it has to be my idea or I can't sell it to the Studio."

"Certainly," Cross said. "But Skippy, you and I have done a lot of things together. And I've always come out on the short end. This time it's different. This time you have to come through." He smiled at Deere. "This time you can't disappoint me."

For one of the few times in his life Deere felt a thrill of apprehension and did not quite know why. Cross was not making a threat. He seemed genial, he seemed to be just stating a fact.

"Don't worry," Skippy Deere said, "We finish shooting in three weeks. Make your plans for then."

Then Cross had to make sure that Athena would agree to come to the wrap party and showing of the rough cut. "I really need it for the Hotel and a chance to see you again," he said to her.

She agreed. Now Cross had to make sure that Dante and Losey would come to the party.

He invited Dante to come to Vegas to talk about LoddStone's and Losey's plan to make a picture based on Losey's adventures in the police department. Everybody knew that Losey and Dante were now good buddies.

"I want you to put in a word for me with Jim Losey," Cross told Dante. "I want to be a coproducer on his film and I'm willing to invest half the budget."

Dante was amused by this. "You're really serious about this movie business," he said, "Why?"

"Big money," Cross said. "And broads."

Dante laughed. "You've got big money and broads already," he said.

"Class. Big money and class broads," Cross said.

"How come you don't invite me to this party?" Dante asked. "And how come I never get a Villa?"

"Put the word in for me with Losey," Cross said, "and you'll get both. Bring Losey along. Plus if you're looking for a date I can fix you up with Tiffany. You've seen her show."

To Dante, Tiffany was the ultimate personification of pure lust, her breasts so full, her smooth, elongated face with its thick lips and wide mouth, her height and long, shapely legs. For the first time Dante was enthusiastic. "No shit," he said. "She's twice as big as me. Imagine? You've got a deal."

It was a little too obvious, but Cross was counting on the fact that the interdiction on violence in Vegas by all the Families would make Dante confident.

Then Cross added casually, "Even Athena is coming. And she's the main reason I want to stay in the movie business."

Bobby Bantz, Melo Stuart, and Claudia flew to Vegas on the Studio jet. Athena and the rest of the cast arrived from the shoot in their personal trailers, as did Dita Tommey. Senator Wavven would represent the state of Nevada, as would Nevada's governor, who had been handpicked for the job by Wavven himself.

Dante and Losey would have two apartments in one of the Villas. Lia Vazzi and his men would occupy the other four apartments.

Senator Wavven and the governor and their entourages would occupy another Villa. Cross had arranged a private dinner for them with selected showgirls. He hoped that their presence would help take the heat off any investigation of what was to happen. That they would use their political influence to smother any publicity and legal pursuit.

Cross was breaking all the rules. Athena had a Villa, but Claudia, Dita Tommey, and Molly Flanders also had apartments in that Villa. The remaining two apartments held a four-man crew of Lia Vazzi's men, to guard Athena.

A fourth Villa was assigned to Bantz and Skippy Deere and their entourages. The remaining three Villas were occupied by twenty of Lia's men, who would replace the usual security guards. However, none of the Vazzi crews were to be involved in the real action, they did not know Cross's true purpose. Lia and Cross were to be the only executioners.

Cross shut down the Villas' Pearl Casino for the two days. Most of the Hollywood personnel, no matter how successful, could not afford to play the casino's stakes. Those superrich guests who had already booked were informed that the Villas were undergoing repairs and renovations and could not accommodate them.

In their plan Cross and Lia Vazzi had determined that Cross would kill Dante and that Lia would kill Losey. If the Don decided on their guilt and determined that Lia had actually done the job on Dante, he might wipe out Lia's whole family. If the Don found the truth, he would not extend his vengeance to Claudia. She, after all, had Clericuzio blood.

Also, Lia had a personal vendetta against Jim Losey, he hated all representatives of government, and why not mix a little personal pleasure in with such a dangerous business.

The real problem was how to isolate the two men and make the bodies disappear. It had always been the rule of all the Families all over America that no execution could be carried out in Vegas, in order to preserve the public acceptance of gambling. The Don was a strong enforcer of that rule.

Cross hoped Dante and Losey would not suspect a trap. They did not know that Lia had discovered Sharkey's body and therefore knew of their intentions. The other problem was how to prepare for Dante's strike against Cross. And then Lia established a spy in Dante's camp.

Molly Flanders flew in early on the day of the party, she and Cross had business. She brought with her a justice of the Supreme Court of California and a monsignor of the Catholic Diocese of Los Angeles. They would serve as witnesses when Cross signed the will she had also prepared and brought. Cross knew that his chances of remaining alive were small, and he had carefully considered where his half of the Xanadu Hotel should go. His interest was worth $500 million, and that was nothing to be sneezed at.

The will left Lia's wife and children a comfortable pension for life. The rest he divided between Claudia and Athena, with Athena's portion held in trust for her daughter, Bethany. It struck him that there was no one else in the world he cared enough about to leave his money to.

When Molly, the judge, and the monsignor arrived in the penthouse suite, the judge congratulated him on his good sense for making a will at so young an age. The monsignor calmly surveyed the luxury of the suite as if to weigh the wages of sin.

They were both good friends of Molly's, who had done pro bono work for them. She had called in her markers at the special request of Cross. He wanted witnesses who could not be corrupted or intimidated by the Clericuzio.

Cross gave them drinks, and the signing of the will was completed. The two men left; though they had been invited, they did not want their reputations sullied by attending a movie wrap party in the gambling hell of Las Vegas. They were, after all, not elected officials of the state.

Cross and Molly were alone in the suite. Molly gave him the original of the will. Cross said, "You have a copy for yourself, right?"

"Of course," Molly said. "I must say I was surprised when you gave me your instructions. I had no idea you and Athena were so close. And besides she's pretty rich in her own right."

"She may need more money than she has," Cross said.

"Her daughter?" Molly said. "I know about her. I'm Athena's personal attorney. You're right, Bethany may need that money. I had you figured differently."

"You did?" Cross said. "How so?"

Molly said quietly, "I had the idea that you took care of Boz Skannet. I had you figured as a Mafia guy with no mercy. I remember about that poor kid I got off from a murder rap. And that you mentioned him. And that he was killed supposedly in some drug deal."

"And now you see how wrong you were," Cross said, smiling at her.

Molly looked at him coldly. "And I was very surprised when you let Bobby Bantz screw you out of your profit share in *Messalina*."

"That was small potatoes," Cross said. He thought of the Don and David Redfellow.

"Athena is going to France the day after tomorrow," Molly said. "For quite a while. Are you going with her?"

"No," Cross said. "I have too many things here."

"OK," Molly said. "I'll see you at the movie screening and the wrap party. Maybe the rough cut of the film will give you an idea of the fortune Bantz gypped you out of."

"It doesn't matter," Cross said.

"You know, Dita put in a card at the beginning of the rough cut. Dedicated to Steve Stallings. Bantz will be really pissed off at that."

"Why?" Cross asked.

"Because Steve screwed all the women Bantz couldn't," Molly said. "What shits men are," she added. Then she left.

Cross went to sit on his balcony. The Vegas street below him was crowded, people sifting into the hotel casinos that lined the strip on either side. The neon marquees flashed their signs: Caesars, the Sands, the Mirage, the Aladdin, the Desert Inn, the Stardust—purples, reds, and greens, a mixed rainbow to which there was no end until you lifted your eyes to the desert and mountains that lay beyond. The blazing afternoon sun could not subdue them.

The *Messalina* people would not begin to arrive until three, and then he would see Athena for the last time if things went wrong. He picked up the balcony phone and called the Villa where he had housed Lia Vazzi and told him to come up to the penthouse suite so that they could go over their plans one more time.

Messalina wrapped at noon. Dita Tommey had wanted the last shot of the rising sun illuminating a terrible slaughter of the Roman battlefield. Athena and Steve Stallings looking down. She shot a double for Stallings and used a shadow over his face for disguise. It was nearly three in the afternoon before the camera truck, the huge mobile trailers that served as homes on the set, the mobile catering kitchens, the wardrobe trailers and vehicles carrying weapons of the time before Christ, rolled into Vegas. Many others came as well, because Cross had treated this occasion in the Old Vegas style.

He had comped everyone who worked on *Messalina,* above the line and below the line, with room, food, and beverage. LoddStone Studios had supplied the list of over three hundred names. Certainly it was generous, certainly it created goodwill. But these three hundred people would leave a substantial part of their wages in the casino drop. This he had learned from Gronevelt. "When people feel good, when they want to celebrate, they gamble."

The rough cut of the movie *Messalina* would be played at ten P.M., but without music and special effects. After the screening would come the wrap party. The huge Xanadu ballroom where the party for Big Tim had been held was cut into two parts. One to show the film, the other, larger part for the buffet and orchestra.

By four in the afternoon, everybody was in the Hotel and the Villas. It was not to be missed by anyone: everything free in the convergence of two glamorous worlds, Hollywood and Las Vegas.

The press was infuriated by the tight security. Access was barred to the Villas and the ballroom. It was not even possible to photograph the players in this glamorous event. Not the stars of the film, the director, the senator and the governor, the producer and the head of the Studio. They could not even get into the screening of the rough cut of the film. They prowled around the casino and offered huge bribes to the gamblers below the line for their IDs to get into the ballroom. Some were successful.

Four crew members, two cynical stuntmen, and two women from the catering team sold their IDs to reporters for a thousand dollars apiece.

Dante Clericuzio and Jim Losey were enjoying the luxury of their Villa. Losey shook his head in wonderment. "A burglar could live for a year on just the gold from the bathroom," he said aloud.

"No, he couldn't," Dante said. "He'd be dead in six months."

They were sitting in the living room of Dante's apartment. They hadn't called room service because the huge kitchen refrigerator was stuffed with trays of sandwiches and caviar canapés, bottles of imported beer and the finest wines.

"So we're all set," Losey said.

"Yep," Dante said, "and when we're done, I'll ask my grandfather for the Hotel. Then we'll be set for life."

"The important thing is that we get him here alone," Losey said.

"I'll do that, don't worry," Dante said. "Worse comes to worst, we'll drive him out to the desert."

"How do you get him here in this Villa?" Losey said. "That's the important thing."

"I'll tell him Giorgio flew in secretly and wants to see him," Dante said. "Then I do the job and you clean up after me. You know crime scenes, what they'll look for."

He said musingly, "The best way is to drop him into the desert. They may never find him." He paused for a moment. "You know Cross ducked Giorgio the night Pippi died. He won't dare do it again."

"But what if he does?" Losey asked. "I'll be waiting here all night jerking off."

"Athena's Villa is next door," Dante said. "You just tap on it and get lucky."

"Too much heat," Losey said.

Dante said with a grin. "We can take her out into the desert with Cross."

"You're crazy," Losey said. And he realized this was true.

"Why not?" Dante said. "Why not have some fun? The desert is big enough to dump two bodies."

Losey thought of Athena's body, her lovely face, her voice, her regal air. Oh, he and Dante would have fun. He was already a murderer, he might as well be a rapist. Marlowe, Pippi De Lena, and his old partner, Phil Sharkey. He was a three-time murderer and too shy to commit rape. He was turning into one of those morons he had arrested all his life. And for a woman who sold her body to the whole world. But this little prick before him with the funny hat was really a piece of work.

"I'll give it a shot," Losey said. "I'll invite her in for a drink and if she comes, she's asking for it."

Dante was amused by Losey's rationalization. "Everybody asks for it," he said. "We ask for it."

They went over the details, and then Dante went back to his apartment. He ran a bath; he wanted to use the expensive scents in the Villa. As he lay in the hot, perfumey water, his black, horselike Clericuzio hair soaped into a white, heavy topknot, he thought about what his fate would be. After he and Losey dumped the body of Cross into the desert, miles from Vegas, the toughest part of the operation would begin. He would have to convince his grandfather that he was innocent. If worse came to worst, he could confess to Pippi's death also, and his grandfather would forgive him. The Don had always showed him a special love.

Also, now, Dante was the Family Hammer. He would apply for appointment as *Bruglione* of the West and the overlordship of the Xanadu Hotel. Giorgio would oppose him, but Vincent and Petie would be neutral. They were content to live on their legal enterprises. And the old man could not live forever, Giorgio was a white-collar guy. There would come a time when the warmaker would become the emperor. He would not retreat into society. He would lead the Family back to its glory. He would never give up the power over life and death.

Dante left the bath and showered to get all the soap out of his ropy hair. He anointed his body with the colognes from their fancy bottles, sculpted his hair from delicate tubes of aromatic gels, reading the directions carefully. Then he went to the suitcase that held his Renaissance hats and chose one encrusted with precious jewels that had the shape of a custard. Its threads were gold and purple. Lying there it looked ridiculous, but when he put it on his head, Dante was enchanted. It made him look like a prince. Especially the row of studded green gems sewed along the front. This was how Athena would see him tonight, or failing that, Tiffany. But the two could wait if necessary.

As he finished dressing, Dante thought of what his life would come to be. He would live in a Villa, as luxurious as any palace. He would have an inexhaustible supply of beautiful women, a self-supporting harem dancing and singing in the Xanadu Hotel showroom. He could eat in six different restaurants with six different national cuisines. He could order the death of an enemy, reward a friend. He would be as close to being a Roman emperor as modern times allowed. Only Cross stood in the way.

Jim Losey, finally alone in his apartment, was contemplating the course his life had taken. He had been, for the first half of his career, a great cop, a true knight defending his society. He'd had an intense hatred for all criminals, especially blacks. And then gradually he had changed. He resented the charges in the media that cops were brutal. The very society he was defending from scum was attacking him. His superiors, with their gold-braided uniforms, sided with the politicians who talked shit to the people. All that bullshit about how you couldn't hate blacks. What was so bad about that? They committed most of the crimes. And wasn't he a free American who could hate whoever he wanted to hate? They were the cockroaches who would eat away all civilization. They didn't want to work, they didn't want to study, burning the midnight oil was a joke to them unless it meant shooting basketball under the light of the moon. They mugged unarmed citizens, they turned their women into whores, and they had an intolerable disrespect for the law and its enforcers. It was his job to protect the rich from the malice of the poor. And his own desire was to become rich. He wanted the clothing, the cars, the food, the drink, and above all, the women the rich could afford. And surely that was American.

It had started with bribes to protect the gambling, then some frame-ups of drug dealers to make them pay protection. He had been proud of his "hero cop" status, the recognition he received for the courage he had shown, but there was no monetary reward. He was still buying cheap clothes, he still had to be very careful with his money to make his paycheck stretch out. And he, who guarded the rich against the poor, received no reward, indeed was one of the poor. But the final straw was that in public esteem he was lower than the criminal. Some of his friends, law enforcers, had been prosecuted and sent to jail for doing their duty. Or fired from their jobs. Rapists, burglars, lethal muggers, armed robbers in broad daylight, had more rights than cops.

Over the years, Losey sold himself his story in his head. The press and TV reviled law enforcers. The fucking Miranda rights, the fucking ACLU; let those fucking lawyers do patrol for six months, they'd grow a lynching tree.

After all, he used the tricks, the beatings, and the threats to get some scumbag to confess his crime and to put him away from society. But Losey could not sell himself completely, he was too good a cop. He could not sell himself on having become a murderer.

Forget all that; he would be rich. He would fling his badge and his bravery citations into the face of the government and the public. He would be security chief for the Xanadu Hotel at ten times the salary, and from this Paradise in the desert, he would watch with pleasure as Los Angeles crumbled under the assault of criminals he would no longer fight. Tonight he would see the movie *Messalina* and go to the wrap party. And maybe get a shot at Athena. Here his mind cringed, even as he felt his body ache with the thought of exercising such sexual power. At the party, he'd pitch a feature film to Skippy based on his career, the greatest hero cop in the LAPD. Dante had told him that Cross wanted to invest, which was really funny. Why kill off a guy who would invest in his movie? That was simple. Because he knew Dante would kill him if he backed out. And Losey, tough as he was, knew he could not kill Dante. He knew the Clericuzio too well.

For a flash he thought of Marlowe, a good nigger, really sweet, always so cheerful and cooperative. He had always liked Marlowe, and his murder was the one thing he felt sorry about.

Jim Losey still had hours to wait before the screening and the party. He could go gamble in the main casino, but gambling was a mug's game. He decided against it. He had a big night ahead. First the movie and the party, then at three in the morning he would have to help Dante kill Cross De Lena and bury him in the desert.

Bobby Bantz invited the above-the-line principals of *Messalina* to his Villa for celebratory drinks at five that evening: Athena, Dita Tommey, Skippy Deere, and as a courtesy, Cross De Lena. Only

Cross declined, claiming pressure of duties at the Hotel on this special night.

Bantz had brought his latest "conquest," a seemingly fresh young girl named Johanna, discovered by a talent scout in a small town in Oregon. She was signed to a five-hundred-dollar-a-week contract for two years. Beautiful but completely untalented, she gave off such a virginal air that the innocence was a separate attraction. And yet with a shrewdness beyond her years, she had refused to sleep with Bobby Bantz until he promised to bring her to Vegas for the showing of *Messalina*.

Skippy Deere, with an adjoining apartment in Bantz's Villa, chose to be a squatter in Bantz's place, and so prevented Bantz from getting in a quick screw with Johanna, which made Bantz irritable. Skippy was pitching an idea for a feature film that he really was crazy about. Being crazy for a property was a legitimate part of a producer's job.

Deere was telling Bantz about Jim Losey, the greatest hero cop in the LAPD, a big, handsome son of a bitch, who might even be able to play the title role himself, since it would be a story about his life. One of those great "true" life stories where you could invent anything bizarre.

Deere and Bantz both knew that Losey playing himself was a fantasy, invented to con Losey so that he would sell his story cheap, and also for public hype.

Skippy Deere outlined the story with great enthusiasm. Nobody could sell a nonexistent property better. In a moment of pure exhilaration, he picked up the phone and, before Bantz could protest, invited the detective to the five P.M. cocktail party. Losey asked if he could bring a friend, and Deere assured him he could, assuming it was a girlfriend. Skippy Deere, as a producer of films, liked to mix different worlds together. You never knew what miracle might emerge.

Cross De Lena and Lia Vazzi were in the Xanadu penthouse suite reviewing the details of what they would do that night.

"I have all the men in place," Lia said. "I control the Villa compound. None of them know what you and I will do, they will have no part in that. But I have word that Dante has a crew from the Enclave digging your grave in the desert. We have to be careful tonight."

"After tonight is what I worry about," Cross said. "Then we have Don Clericuzio to deal with. Do you think he'll buy the story?"

"Not really," Lia said. "But that is our only hope."

Cross shrugged. "I have no choice. Dante killed my father and so now he has to kill me." He paused for a moment and then said, "I hope the Don was not on his side from the beginning. Then we have no chance."

Lia said cautiously, "We could abort everything and lay our troubles in front of the Don. Let him decide and act."

"No," Cross said. "He can't decide against his grandson."

"You're right, of course," Lia said. "But still, the Don has gone a little soft. He let those Hollywood people cheat you, and that in his youth he would never have allowed. Not the money, the disrespect."

Cross poured more brandy into Lia's glass and lit his cigar. He did not tell him about David Redfellow. "How do you like your room?" he said jokingly.

Lia puffed on his cigar. "What nonsense. So beautiful. To what purpose? Why does anyone have to live like that? It is too much. It takes away your strength. It arouses envy. It's not clever to insult the poor like that. Why then would they not want to kill you? My father was a rich man in Sicily but never did he live in luxury."

"You don't understand America, Lia," Cross said. "Every poor man who sees the inside of that Villa rejoices. Because he knows in his heart someday he will live in just such a place."

At that moment the private phone in the penthouse rang. Cross picked it up. His heart gave a little jump. It was Athena.

"Can we meet before the movie shows?" she asked.

"Only if you come to my suite," Cross said. "I really can't leave here."

"How gallant," Athena said coolly. "Then we can meet after the wrap party, I'll leave early and you can come to my Villa."

"I really can't," Cross said.

"I'm leaving in the morning for L.A.," Athena said. "Then the day after, I fly to France. We won't meet in private until you come there . . . if you come."

Cross looked at Lia, who shook his head and frowned. So Cross said to Athena, "Can you come to me here, now? Please?"

He waited for a long time before she said, "Yes, give me an hour."

"I'll send a car and security for you," Cross said. "They'll be waiting outside your Villa." He hung up the phone and said to Lia, "We have to watch out for her. Dante is crazy enough to do anything."

The cocktail party in Bantz's Villa was graced by beauty.

Melo Stuart brought a young actress with a great stage reputation that he and Skippy Deere planned to cast as the female lead in the Jim Losey Story. She had a strong Egyptian beauty, bold features, an imperious manner. Bantz had his new find, Johanna, last name not decided, the innocent virgin. Athena, who had never looked so radiant, was surrounded by her friends: Claudia, Dita Tommey, and Molly Flanders. Athena was unusually quiet, but still Johanna and the stage actress, Liza Wrongate, looked at her almost in awe and envy. Both came to Athena, the Queen they hoped to replace.

Claudia asked Bobby Bantz, "Didn't you invite my brother?"

"Sure," Bantz said. "He was too busy."

"Thanks for giving Ernest's family his points," Claudia said, grinning.

"Molly robbed me," Bantz said. He had always liked Claudia, maybe because Marrion had liked her, so he didn't mind her kidding. "She held a cannon to my head."

"But you could have made it tough," Claudia said. "Marrion would approve."

Bantz stared at her blankly. He felt suddenly tearful. Never would he be the man Marrion had been. And he missed him.

Meanwhile Skippy Deere had cornered Johanna and was telling her about his new film, which had a great cameo of an innocent young girl grossly raped and killed by a drug dealer. "You look perfect for the part. You don't have much experience but if I can get it past Bobby, you can come and test." He paused for a moment and then said in a warm, confidential manner, "I think you should change your name. Johanna is too square for your career." Implying the stardom that lay ahead.

He noted how her face flushed; really it was touching how young girls believed in their beauty, desired to be stars, as passionately as Renaissance girls wanted to be saints. When Ernest Vail's cynical smile appeared before him, Deere thought: Laugh as much as you like, still it was a spiritual desire. In both instances it would lead more often to martyrdom than glory, but that was part of the deal.

Johanna went off predictably to talk to Bantz. Deere joined Melo Stuart and his new girlfriend, Liza. Though she was talented on stage, Skippy had doubts about her future on the movie screen. The camera was too cruel for her kind of beauty. And her intelligence would make her unfit for many roles. But Melo had insisted she be the female lead in the Losey picture, and there were times when Melo could not be denied. And the female lead was just a bullshit, carry-the-water-bag part.

Deere kissed Liza on both cheeks. "I saw you in New York," he said. "Marvelous performance." He paused for a moment and said, "I'll hope you take the part in my new movie. Melo thinks it will be your breakthrough on film."

Liza gave him a cold smile. "I have to see the script," she said. Deere felt that flash of resentment he always felt. She was getting the break of her life and she wanted to see a fucking script. He could see Melo smiling with amusement.

"Of course," Deere said. "But believe me I would not send you a script that was not worthy of your talent."

Melo, never as ardent a lover as he was a businessman, said, "Liza, we can guarantee you the leading female role in an A feature. The script is not a sacred text as in the theater. It can be changed to please you."

Liza gave him a slightly warmer smile. She said, "You believe that crap too? Stage plays are rewritten. What do you think we do when we try them out of town?"

Before they could answer, Jim Losey and Dante Clericuzio entered the apartment. Deere rushed over to greet them and introduce them to the others at the party.

Losey and Dante were an almost comical pair. Losey, tall, handsome, impeccably tailored—full shirt and tie, despite the intense July heat of Vegas. And Dante beside him, his hugely muscled body bulging out of a T-shirt, his brightly jeweled Renaissance cap crowning his black ropy hair, and so short. All the others in the room, experts in make-believe worlds, knew these two were not make-believe, despite their weirdness. Their faces were too blank and cold. That could not be duplicated with shadows.

Losey immediately addressed Athena and told her how he looked forward to seeing her in *Messalina*. He abandoned his intimidating style and was almost fawning. Women had always found him charming, could Athena be an exception?

Dante helped himself to a drink and sat on the sofa. No one came near him except Claudia. They had not seen each other more than three times over the years, all they had in common were childhood memories. Claudia kissed him on the cheek. When they were children he had tormented her, but she always remembered him with a certain fondness.

Dante reached up to give her a hug. "*Cugina,* you look beautiful. If you looked like that when we were kids I would never have beaten you up so much."

Claudia plucked his Renaissance hat from his head. "Cross told me about your hats. They make you look cute." She put the hat on her head. "Even the Pope doesn't have a hat this cute."

"And he has a lot of hats," Dante said. "Now who would have thought you'd become such a big wheel in the movie business."

"What do you do these days?" Claudia asked.

"I run a meat company," Dante said. "We supply the hotels." He smiled, then asked, "Listen, could you introduce me to your beautiful star?"

Claudia brought him over to Athena, who was still cornered by Jim Losey putting on his charm. Athena smiled at Dante's Renaissance hat. Dante made himself look disarmingly comical.

Losey continued on with his flattery. "I know your movie will be great," he told her. "After the wrap party maybe you'll let me be your bodyguard back to the Villa, then we can have a drink together." He was playing the good cop role.

Athena was at her best refusing an advance. She smiled at him sweetly. "I'd love to," she said. "But I'm only going to stay a half hour at the party and I wouldn't want you to miss it. I have to catch an early plane tomorrow, then I fly to France. I simply have too many things to do."

Dante was admiring her. He could see she loathed Losey and that she was afraid of him. But she had made Losey think he could some-how have a shot at her.

"I can fly with you to L.A.," Losey said. "What time is your flight?"

"You are nice," Athena said. "But it's a small private charter and all the seats are full."

When she was safely back in her Villa, she called Cross and told him that she was on her way over.

The first thing Athena was aware of was the security. There were guards on the elevator to the penthouse suite of the Xanadu Hotel. There was a special key to unlock the elevator. The elevator itself had security cameras in the ceiling, and its doors opened up into an anteroom that held five men. One was at the elevator door to greet her. Another man was at the lone desk that held a bank of TV screens, and there were two other men playing cards in the corner of the room. Another was seated at the sofa reading *Sports Illustrated*.

They all looked at her with a special appraising, slightly aston-ished look she had encountered many times, acknowledging that her beauty was of a special variety. But it had long since failed to rouse her vanity; now it only made her aware of some danger.

The man at the desk pushed a button that opened the door to Cross's suite, and she went in, the door swinging shut behind her.

She was in the office part of the suite. Cross met her and led her into the living quarters. He kissed her briefly on the lips and then led her into the bedroom. Without saying a word, they both undressed and held each other naked. For Cross it was such a relief to hold her flesh, to look into her radiant face, that he sighed. "I'd rather just look at you than do anything else in the world."

In reply, she caressed him, made him kiss her, drew him down on the bed. She felt that this was a man who truly loved her, would do anything she commanded, and in return she would give him his every wish. For the first time in a very long time, she responded both physically and mentally. She truly loved him and loved making love to him. Yet she always knew he was dangerous, even to her, in some way.

After an hour they dressed and went out onto the balcony.

Las Vegas was showered in neon lights, the late sun baked the streets and gaudy hotels in a great band of gold. Beyond was the desert and the mountains. Here in time, they were isolated; the green flags of the villas hung limply in the air.

Athena held his hand tightly. "Will I see you at the movie and the wrap party?" she asked.

"I'm sorry, I can't," Cross said. "But I'll see you in France."

"I've noticed it's very hard to get to see you," Athena said. "The locked elevator and all those guards."

Cross said, "It's just for the next few days, too many strange people in town."

"I met your cousin, Dante," Athena said. "That detective seems to be a buddy of his. They make a charming pair. Losey was very interested in my welfare, and my schedule. Dante offered his help too. They were so worried about my getting to L.A. safely."

Cross pressed her hand. "You will," he said.

"Claudia said you and Dante are cousins," Athena said. "Why does he wear those funny hats?"

"Dante is a nice guy," Cross said.

"But Claudia told me the two of you were enemies since you were kids," Athena said.

"Sure," Cross said amiably, "but that doesn't make him a bad person."

They were silent, the streets below were clogged with vehicles and walking people migrating to different hotels for dinner and gambling. Dreaming of pleasure fraught with risk.

"So this is the last time we will see each other," Athena said and pressed his hand as if to nullify what she said.

"I said I'll meet you in France," Cross said.

"When?" Athena asked.

"I don't know," Cross said. "If I don't come, you'll know I'm dead."

"Things are that serious?" Athena said.

"Yes," Cross said.

"And you can't tell me anything about it?" Athena asked.

Cross didn't answer for a moment. "You'll be safe," he said. "And I think I'll be safe. I can't tell you any more than that."

"I'll wait," Athena said. She kissed him and then walked out of the bedroom and out of the suite. Cross watched and then went out to the balcony to see her emerge from the Hotel and onto the colonnade. He saw the car with his security guards drive her to her Villa. Then he picked up the phone and called Lia Vazzi. He told Vazzi to tighten security around Athena even more.

By ten P.M. the theater section of the ballroom of the Xanadu Hotel was full. The audience was gathered waiting for the first rough cut showing of *Messalina*. There was a premiere seating section that consisted of soft armchairs with a telephone console in the middle. There was one empty seat with a wreath of flowers bearing Steve Stalling's name. The other seats held Claudia, Dita Tommey, and Bobby Bantz and his companion, Johanna. Melo Stuart and Liza. Skippy Deere immediately took possession of the phone.

Athena was the last to arrive and was cheered by the crew and stunt men below the line. The above-the-line people, the supporting cast, and all the people seated in the armchairs applauded and kissed her on the cheek as she made her way to the center armchair. Then Skippy Deere picked up the phone and told the projectionist to begin.

Against the black background the line "Dedicated to Steve Stallings" appeared, and the audience applauded in a muted, respectful fashion. The insertion had been opposed by Bobby Bantz and Skippy Deere, but Dita Tommey vetoed them, God only knew why, Bantz said. But what the hell, it was only a rough cut, and besides, the sentimentality would create some press.

Then the picture came on the screen . . .

Athena was mesmerizing, she had even more sexuality on screen than she had in real life and a wit that was no surprise to anyone who knew her well. Indeed Claudia had written lines specifically to show off this quality in her. No cost had been stinted, and the crucial sex scenes were done in good taste.

There was no question that *Messalina,* after all its troubles, would be a major hit. And that, without final music and special effects. Dita Tommey was ecstatic, she was finally a Bankable Director. Melo Stuart was calculating how much he would ask for Athena's next picture; Bantz, looking not too happy, was worrying about the same thing. Skippy was counting the money he would make; finally he could own his own jet.

Claudia was more thrilled than any of them. Her creation was up on the screen. She had sole credit and it was an original screenplay. Thanks to Molly Flanders, she had *gross* points. Of course, there had been a little rewrite by Ben Sly but not enough for a credit.

Everybody was clustered around Athena and Dita Tommey, congratulating them. But Molly had her eye on one of the stunt men. Stunt men were crazy bastards, but they had hard bodies and were great in bed.

The wreath for Steve Stallings had been brushed to the floor, and people were trampling it. Molly could see that Athena had detached herself from the crowd to pick it up and place it back on the chair. Athena caught Molly's eye and they both shrugged, Athena giving a shy smile as if to say, That's movies.

The crowd moved to the other side of the ballroom. A small band was playing, but everyone rushed the buffet tables. Then the dancing began. Molly went up to the stunt man, who was glowering around; it was at these parties they were most vulnerable. They felt their work was not appreciated, and they resented like hell when the flabby male star was allowed to punch them out on screen when they could kill the faggot bastard in real life. Just like a stunt man, his cock is already hard, Molly thought, as he led her onto the dance floor.

Athena only spent an hour at the party. Receiving everyone's congratulations, she was gracious, and yet she observed herself being gracious and she hated it. She danced with the "best boy" and other members of the crew and then with a stunt man whose aggressiveness made her decide to leave.

The Xanadu Rolls was waiting for her with an armed driver and two security guards. When she got out of the Rolls at her Villa, she was surprised to see Jim Losey coming out of the adjoining Villa. He approached her. "You were great in that movie tonight," he said. "I've never seen a better body on a woman. Especially that ass."

Athena would have been wary except that the driver and both security guards were already out of the car, positioned. It was part of her theatrical training, the blocking out of the stage where actors position themselves. She noted that they placed themselves so that none of the lines of fire would jeopardize any of them. She also noticed that Losey viewed them with a mild contempt.

"That was not my ass," Athena said, "but thank you anyway." She smiled at him.

Suddenly Losey was holding her hand. "You're the greatest-looking woman I ever met," he said. "Why don't you try a real guy instead of those phony actor faggots."

Athena took her hand away. "I'm an actor too, and we're not phonies. Good night."

"Can I come in for a drink?" Losey asked.

"I'm sorry," Athena said, and rang the bell to the Villa. The door was opened by a butler Athena had never seen before.

Losey took a step to go in with her, and then to her surprise, the butler walked outside and quickly pushed her into the Villa. The three security guards formed a barricade between Losey and the door.

Losey looked at them with contempt. "What the fuck is this?" he said.

The butler remained outside the door. "Miss Aquitane's security," he said. "You will have to leave."

Losey took out his police ID. "You see who I am," he said. "I'll kick the shit out of all of you, and then I'll lock you up."

The butler looked at the ID. He said, "You're Los Angeles. No jurisdiction." He pulled out his own ID. "I'm Las Vegas County."

Athena Aquitane had remained just inside the doorway. She was surprised her new butler was a detective, but now she was beginning to understand. "Don't make a big deal out of it," she said, and closed the door against all of them.

Both men put their IDs back into their jackets.

Losey gave each in turn a hard stare. "I'll remember you guys," he said. None of the men reacted.

Losey turned away. He had more important fish to fry. In the next two hours Dante Clericuzio would be bringing Cross De Lena to their Villa.

Dante Clericuzio, Renaissance hat perched on his head, was having a great time at the wrap party. He used fun to prepare himself for serious action. A girl in the catering crew had caught his attention, but she gave him no encouragement because she had focused on one of the stunt men. The stunt man had given Dante threatening looks. Lucky for him, Dante thought, I have business to do tonight. He looked at his watch, maybe good old Jim had managed to snare Athena. Tiffany had never showed, though she had been promised. Dante decided to start a half hour early. He called Cross, using the private number with the operator.

Cross answered.

"I have to see you right away," Dante said. "I'm in the ballroom. Great party."

"So, come up," Cross said.

"No," Dante said. "These are orders. Not on the phone and not in your suite. Come on down."

There was a long pause. Then Cross said, "I'll be down."

Dante stationed himself so that he could observe Cross making his way through the ballroom. There seemed to be no security around him. Dante patted down his hat and thought back to their childhood together. Cross had been the only boy who had made him fearful, and he had fought him often because of that fear. But he loved the way Cross looked, had often been envious. And he envied his cousin's confidence. It was just too bad . . .

Once he killed Pippi, Dante had known he could not let Cross remain alive. Now, after this, he would have to confront the Don. But Dante had never doubted that his grandfather loved him, he had always shown his love. The Don might not like this, but he would never invoke his awful power to punish his beloved grandson.

Cross was standing before him. Now he had to get Cross to the Villa where Losey was waiting. It would be simple. He would shoot Cross, and then they would drive his body out into the desert and bury him. Nothing fancy, as Pippi De Lena had always preached. The car was already parked behind the Villa for transport.

Cross said to him abruptly, "So what is it?" He did not look suspicious or even wary. "Nice new hat," he said and smiled. Dante had always envied that smile, as though the guy knew everything Dante was thinking.

Dante played it very slow, very low-voiced. He took Cross by the arm and led him outside, in front of the huge colored marquee that had cost the Xanadu Hotel ten million dollars. The flashing blue, red, and purple bathed their figures in cold light blanched by the desert moon. Dante whispered to Cross, "Giorgio flew in, he's at my Villa. Top secret. And he wants to see you right away. That's why I couldn't say anything on the phone."

Dante was delighted that Cross looked concerned. "He told me not to tell you anything, but he's pissed off. I think he found out something about your old man."

At this Cross gave Dante a somber look, almost one of displeasure. Then he said, "OK, let's go." And he led Dante through the grounds of the Hotel to the Villa compound.

The four guards at the compound gates recognized Cross and waved them through.

Dante opened the door with a flourish and doffed his Renaissance hat. He said, "After you," and smiled slyly, which gave his face a puckish humor.

Cross walked in.

. . .

Jim Losey was filled with cold rage when he turned away from Athena's guards and walked back to his own Villa. Yet there was a part of his brain that assessed the situation, gave out a warning signal. What were all those guards doing around? But, shit, she was a movie star and that experience with Boz Skannet must have scared the hell out of her.

He used his key to get into the Villa, it seemed to be deserted, everyone was at the party. He had more than an hour to get ready to receive Cross. He went to his suitcase and unlocked it. There was his Glock, gleaming, wiped clean of oil. He opened his other suitcase, which had a secret pocket. In there was the bullet-filled magazine. He put them together, put on a shoulder holster and tucked the gun inside. He was all set. He noted that he was not nervous, he was never nervous in these situations. That was what made him a good cop.

Losey left the bedroom and walked into the kitchen. There were sure a lot of hallways in this Villa. From the refrigerator, he took a bottle of imported beer and a tray of canapés. He crumbled one with his teeth. Caviar. He gave a little sigh of pleasure, he had never tasted anything so delicious. This was the way to live. This was his for the rest of his life, the caviar, the showgirls, maybe some day Athena. He just had to do his job tonight.

Carrying the tray and bottle, he went into the huge living room.

The first thing that startled him was that the floor and the furniture were covered with plastic sheeting, giving the whole room a ghostly white glow. And then, seated in a plastic-covered armchair, was a man smoking a thin cigar and holding a glass of peach brandy. It was Lia Vazzi.

Losey thought, What the fuck is this? He put the tray and bottle on the coffee table and said to Lia, "I've been looking for you."

Lia puffed his cigar, took a sip of brandy. "And now you've found me," he said. He stood up. "Now you can slap me again."

Losey was too experienced a man not to be alert. He was putting things together. He had wondered why the other apartments in the Villa were vacant, it had struck him as strange. He casually unbuttoned his jacket and grinned at Lia. More than a slap this time, he thought. It would be an hour before Dante arrived with Cross, he could work while waiting. Now that he was armed, he had no fear of being one-on-one with Lia.

Suddenly there was a flood of men in the room. They seeped in from the kitchen, the connecting foyer, from the video/TV room. They were all bigger than Jim Losey. Only two of them had drawn guns.

Losey said to them, "You know I'm a cop?"

"We all know that," Lia said in a reassuring voice. He stepped closer to Losey. At the same time, the two men pressed their guns against Losey's back.

Lia flipped his hand inside Losey's jacket and came out holding the Glock. He handed it to one of the men and then gave Losey a quick pat-down.

"Now," Lia said, "you always had so many questions to ask. Here I am. Ask."

Losey still had no real fear. He was just worried that Dante would arrive with Cross. He could not believe that a man like himself, who had had the great good fortune to remain alive in so many dangerous situations, could finally be overcome.

"I know you set that guy Skannet up," Losey said. "And I'll get you for it sooner or later."

"It will have to be sooner," Lia said. "There's no later. Yes, you are right and now you can die happy."

Losey still could not believe that anyone would dare to murder a police officer in cold blood. Sure, drug dealers would exchange bullets, and sure, some crazy nigger would blow you away because you showed a badge, as would fleeing bank robbers, but no mob guy would have the balls to execute a police officer. It would be too much heat.

He reached out to shove Lia away, to achieve a dominance over the situation. But suddenly there was a shocking line of fire slashing through his stomach and his legs trembled. He started to crumble to his knees. Something thick slapped against his head and his ear was on fire and he could not hear. He sank to his knees and the rug felt like an enormous cushion. He looked up. Standing over him was Lia Vazzi, and in his hands was a thin silk rope.

Lia Vazzi had spent two whole days sewing together the two body bags he would have to use. They were of dark brown canvas with a drawstring at the head. Each bag could contain a large body. There was no possible leakage of blood from the bag, and once you drew the string, you could sling it over your shoulder like an army duffel bag. Losey had not noticed the two bags lying on the sofa. Now the men stuffed his body into one, and Lia drew the string tight. He left the bag leaning upright against the sofa. He gave orders to the men that they were to surround the Villa but were not to appear until he summoned them explicitly. They knew what they were to do after that.

Cross and Dante strolled from the compound gates toward Dante's Villa. The night air was oppressive with the cauldron of heat spewed from the day's desert sun. They were both perspiring. Dante noted that Cross was dressed in slacks, open shirt, and buttoned jacket, that he could be armed . . .

The seven Villas, their green flags waving slightly, made a magnificent sight under the desert moon. They looked like edifices from another century with their balconies, their frilled green awnings over the windows, their huge white doors decorated with gold. Dante held Cross by the arm. "Look at that," he said. "Isn't it beautiful? I hear you're fucking that great-looking broad in the movie. Congratulations. When you get tired of her let me know."

"Sure," Cross said amiably. "She sort of likes you and your hat."

Dante took off his hat and said eagerly, "Everybody likes my hats. Did she really say she likes me?"

"She's enchanted by you," Cross said dryly.

"Enchanted," Dante said musingly. "That's really classy." He wondered for a moment if Losey had been able to get Athena into their Villa for a drink. That would be the icing on the cake. He was tickled that he had distracted Cross, he had noticed the slight irritation in his cousin's voice.

They were at the door of the Villa. There seemed to be no security guards around. Dante pressed the bell, waited, and then rang again. When there was no answer, he took out his key and opened the door. They entered Losey's suite.

Dante was thinking, Maybe Losey was in the sack with Athena. Which was a hell of a way to run an operation, but he would have done the same thing.

Dante led Cross into the living room and was astonished to see the walls and furniture covered with clear plastic sheets. Leaning against the sofa was a huge brown duffel bag standing upright. On the sofa was an empty duffel bag of the same kind. All under plastic. "Jesus Christ, what the hell is this?" Dante said.

He turned to face Cross. Cross was holding a very small gun in his hand. "To keep the blood off the furniture," Cross said. "I have to tell you, I never thought your hats were cute and I never believed that a mugger killed my father."

Dante was thinking, Where the hell is Losey? He called out to him, meanwhile thinking that such a small-caliber gun could never stop him.

Cross said, "All your life you were a Santadio."

Dante whirled sideways to give a smaller target and flung himself on Cross. His strategy worked; the bullet hit him in the shoulder. He had a fraction of a second of joy, that he would win, and then the bullet exploded, taking away half of his arm. And he realized there was no hope. Then he really surprised Cross. With his good arm, he began pulling up the plastic sheeting from the floor. Blood pouring from his body, his arms filled with plastic sheeting, he tried to stagger away from Cross, then held up the sheets of plastic as a silvery shield.

Cross stepped forward. Very deliberately he fired through the plastic, then fired again. The bullets exploded, and Dante's face was almost covered with tiny bits of plastic turned red. Dante's left thigh seemed to separate from his body as Cross fired again. Dante fell, the white rug now held concentric circles of scarlet. Cross knelt beside Dante and wrapped his head with plastic and fired again. The Renaissance cap still on his head exploded upward into the air but remained attached. Cross saw that the hat was secured to the head by some sort of clip but now it rested on an open skull. It seemed to float.

Cross stood up and put the gun in the holster in the small of his back. At that moment Lia came into the room. They looked at each other.

"It's done," Lia said. "Wash off in the bathroom and go back to the Hotel. And get rid of your clothes. I'll take the gun and clean up."

"And the rugs and the furniture?" Cross asked.

"I'll take care of everything," Lia said. "Wash up and go to that party."

When Cross left, Lia helped himself to a cigar that was on a marble-topped table and looked for bloodstains while he was at it. There were none. But the sofa and the floor were soaked. Well, that was it.

He wrapped Dante's body in the plastic sheeting and, with the help of two of his men, stuffed it into the empty canvas bag. Then he gathered all the plastic sheeting in the room and stuffed it into the same bag. When he had finished, he drew the strings tight. First, they carried the bag containing Losey into the Villa garage and threw it into the van. They made another trip with Dante's body bag.

The van had been modified by Lia Vazzi. It had double floors with a space between the two. Lia and his men squeezed the two bags into the hollow space and then rejoined the floor strips.

As a Qualified Man, Lia had prepared for everything. In the van were two cans of gasoline. He himself carried them back into the Villa and poured them over the floors and furniture. He set a fuse that would give him five minutes to get away. Then he got into the van and started the long drive to L.A.

Before him and after him were the members of his crew.

It was early morning before he pulled onto the pavement in front of the yacht that was waiting for him. He unloaded the two bags and brought them aboard. The yacht pulled away from shore.

It was nearly noon when, far out at sea, he watched the iron cage holding the two bodies slowly descend into the ocean. They had made their final Communion.

Molly Flanders disappeared with her stunt man, to his room in the Hotel rather than to the Villa, because Molly, despite her affection for the less worldly in power, had a tiny trace of the old Hollywood snobbism, she didn't want it known she was screwing below the line.

The wrap party began to filter out just as dawn appeared, the sun rising ominously clad in red, a thin trail of blue smoke rising to meet it.

Cross had changed his clothes and showered and then had gone to the party. He was seated with Claudia, Bobby Bantz, Skippy Deere, and Dita Tommey celebrating the sure success of *Messalina*. Suddenly there were shouts of alarm from outside. The Hollywood group ran out and Cross followed them.

A thin pillar of fire rose triumphantly over the neon lights of the Vegas Strip. It mushroomed into a great pillow of plum and rosy clouds against the sandy mountains.

"Oh my God," Claudia said, holding Cross tightly by the arm. "It's one of your Villas."

Cross was silent. He watched the green flag over the Villa being consumed by smoke and fire, heard the fire engines screaming down the Strip. Twelve million dollars going up in flames to hide the blood he'd shed. Lia Vazzi was a Qualified Man who spared no expense, courted no risks.

CHAPTER 23

BECAUSE HE WAS on official leave, Detective Jim Losey's dis-appearance wasn't noted until five days after the fire at the Xanadu. The vanishing of Dante Clericuzio was, of course, never re-ported to any authorities.

The investigation led to the police finding Phil Sharkey's body. Suspicion focused on Losey, and it was assumed he had fled to es-cape interrogation.

L.A. detectives came to interview Cross because Losey was last seen at the Xanadu Hotel. But there was nothing to show any con-nection between the two men. Cross explained he had only seen him briefly on the night of the party.

But Cross was not worried about the law. He was waiting to hear from Don Clericuzio.

Surely the Clericuzio knew that Dante was missing, surely they knew he had been at the Xanadu when last seen. Why then had they not contacted him for information. Could the whole matter be passed over so easily? Cross did not believe that for a moment.

He continued to run the Hotel day by day, busy with plans to re-build the burned-out Villa. Lia Vazzi had certainly taken care of the bloodstains.

Claudia came to visit him. She was brimming over with excitement. Cross arranged for dinner to be brought up to his suite so they could talk in private.

"You're not going to believe this," she said to Cross. "Your sister is going to be head of LoddStone Studios."

"Congratulations," Cross said, giving her a brotherly hug. "I always said you were the toughest of the Clericuzio."

"I went to our father's funeral for your sake. I made that clear to everyone," Claudia said with a frown.

Cross laughed. "You certainly did, and you pissed everybody off except the Don himself who said, 'Let her go make pictures and God bless her.' "

Claudia shrugged. "I don't care about them. But let me tell you what happened because it is so strange. When we all left Vegas in Bobby's jet, everything seemed perfect. But when we landed in L.A., all hell broke loose. Detectives arrested Bobby. For guess what?"

"Making lousy movies," Cross teased.

"No, listen, this is weird," Claudia said. "Remember that girl Johanna that Bantz had with him at the wrap party? Do you remember what she looked like? Well, it turns out she was only fifteen years old. They got Bobby on statutory rape and white slavery because he took her across the state border." Claudia's eyes were wide with excitement. "But it was all a setup. Johanna's mother and father were there screaming bloody murder that their poor daughter had been raped by a man forty years older."

"She sure didn't look fifteen," Cross said. "Though she did look like a good hustler."

"It would have made a terrible scandal," Claudia said. "But good old Skippy Deere took charge. He got Bantz off the hook for that moment. He kept him from being arrested and the whole thing getting into the media. So everything seems squared away."

Cross was smiling. Apparently good old David Redfellow had lost none of his skills.

"It's not funny," Claudia said reproachfully. "Poor Bobby was *framed*. The girl swore that Bobby forced her to have sex in Vegas. The father and mother swore they cared nothing for money but wanted to stop all future rapists of young and innocent girls. The whole Studio was in an uproar. Dora and Kevin Marrion were so upset that they talked about selling the Studio. Then Skippy took charge again. He signed the girl to star in a low-budget film, the script to be written by her father. For very good money. Then he got Benny Sly to rewrite the script in one day for a lot of money. Not bad, by the way, Benny is some kind of genius. We're all set. And then the district attorney of Los Angeles insists he's going to prosecute. The DA that LoddStone got elected, the DA who was treated like a king by Eli Marrion. Skippy even offered him a job at the Studio in Business Affairs at a million a year for five years and he turned it down. He insisted Bobby Bantz be fired as head of the Studio. Then he would make a deal. Nobody knows why he was being so hard-nosed."

"An unbribable public official," Cross said with a shrug. "It happens."

He thought of David Redfellow again. Redfellow would violently disagree that there was any such animal. And Cross envisioned how Redfellow had managed everything. Redfellow probably said to the DA, "I'm bribing you to *do* your duty?" And as for the money, Redfellow would have immediately gone to the limit. Twenty, Cross figured. On a ten-billion buy of the Studio, what the hell was twenty million? And with no risk for the DA. He would be acting strictly according to law. It was really elegant.

Claudia was still talking, fast. "Anyway, Bantz had to step down," she said. "And Dora and Kevin were happy to sell the Studio. Plus the deal for five green lights on their own movies, a billion dollars cash in their pockets. And this little Italian guy appears at the Studio, calls a meeting and announces he will be the new owner. And then right out of the blue, he makes me head of the Studio. Skippy was pissed. Now, I'm his boss. Is this crazy?"

Cross just watched her with amusement, then he smiled.

Suddenly, Claudia stood back and looked at her brother. And her eyes were darker, sharper, more intelligent than he had ever seen before. But she had a good-natured smile on her face when she said, "Just like the boys, right, Cross? Now, I'm doing it just like the boys. And I didn't even have to fuck anybody. . . ."

Cross was surprised. "What's the matter, Claudia?" he asked. "I thought you were happy."

Claudia smiled. "I am happy. I'm just not dumb. And because you're my brother, and I love you, I want you to know that I haven't been fooled."

She walked over and sat on the couch next to him. "I lied when I said I went to Daddy's funeral just for you. I went because I wanted to be part of something that he was part of, that you were part of. I went because I couldn't stay away any longer. But I do hate what they stand for, Cross. The Don as well as the others."

"Does that mean you don't want to run the Studio?" Cross asked.

Claudia laughed aloud. "No, I'm willing to admit I'm still a Clericuzio. And I want to make good movies and make a lot of money. Movies are great equalizers, Cross. I can make a good movie about great women. . . . Let's see what can happen when I use the Family talents for good instead of evil." They both laughed.

Then Cross took her in his arms. He kissed her on the cheek. "I think it's great, really great," he said.

And he meant it for himself as well as for her. For if Don Clericuzio had made her head of the Studio, he did not connect Cross with the disappearance of Dante. The whole scheme had worked.

They had finished dinner and had been talking for hours. When Claudia rose to leave, Cross took a purse of black chips from his desk. "Take a shot at the tables on the house," he said.

She gave him a soft slap on the cheek and said, "Only if you're not going to get into that big brother thing again and talk to me like a child. That last time I wanted to deck you."

He hugged her, it felt good to feel her so close. In a moment of weakness, he said, "You know, I left a third of my estate to you in case anything happens. And I'm very rich. So you can always tell the Studio to fuck off if you want to."

Claudia eyes were shining when she said, "Cross, I appreciate you worrying about me, but I can tell the Studio to fuck off anyway, without your estate . . ." Then suddenly she looked worried. "Is anything wrong? Are you sick?"

"No, no," Cross said. "I just wanted you to know."

"Thank God," Claudia said. "Now that I'm in, maybe you can get out. You can break away from the Family. You can be free."

Cross laughed. "I am free," he said. "I'm going away very soon, to live with Athena in France."

. . .

On the afternoon of the tenth day, Giorgio Clericuzio appeared at the Xanadu to see him, and Cross felt a sinking sensation in his stomach that he knew would lead to panic if he did not control it.

Giorgio left his bodyguards outside the suite with Hotel Security. But Cross was under no illusions, his own bodyguards would follow any order Giorgio gave. And he was not reassured by Giorgio's appearance. Giorgio seemed to have lost weight, and his face was very pale. It was the first time that Cross had seen him look as though he was not in complete control.

Cross greeted him effusively. "Giorgio," he said, "this is an unexpected pleasure. Let me call down and get a Villa ready for you."

Giorgio gave him a tired smile and said, "We can't locate Dante." He paused for a moment. "He's gone off the map and the last time he was seen was here at the Xanadu."

"Jesus," Cross said, "that's serious. But you know Dante, he was not always under control."

Now Giorgio didn't bother to smile. "He was with Jim Losey and Losey is gone too."

"They were a funny combo," Cross said. "I wondered about that."

"They were pals," Giorgio said. "The old man didn't like it but Dante was the guy's paymaster."

"I'll help any way I can," Cross said. "I'll check all the Hotel employees. But you know Dante and Losey weren't officially registered. We never do that for anyone in the Villas."

"You can do that when you get back," Giorgio said. "The Don wants to see you personally. He even chartered a plane to bring you back."

Cross paused for a long moment. "I'll pack a bag," he said. "Giorgio, is it serious?"

Giorgio looked him squarely in the face. "I don't know," he said.

On the chartered plane to New York, Giorgio studied a briefcase full of papers. Cross did not impose himself, though this was a bad sign. In any case Giorgio would never give him any information.

The plane was met by three closed cars and six Clericuzio soldiers. Giorgio got into one car and motioned Cross into another. Again a bad sign. Dawn was breaking when the cars rolled through the security gates of the Clericuzio compound in Quogue.

The door of the house was guarded by two men. Other men were scattered around the compound, but there were no women or children to be seen.

Cross said to Giorgio, "Where the hell is everybody, in Disneyland?" But Giorgio refused to acknowledge the joke.

The first thing Cross saw in the Quogue living room was a circle of eight men, and inside that circle two men were talking in a very amiable way. His heart gave a jump. They were Petie and Lia Vazzi. Vincent was watching them and he looked angry.

Petie and Lia seemed to be on the best of terms. But Lia was dressed only in slacks and a shirt, no jacket or tie. Lia usually dressed formally, so this meant he had been searched and disarmed. And indeed he looked like a cheerful mouse surrounded by merry, menacing cats. Lia gave Cross a sad nod of acknowledgment. Petie never glanced his way. But when Giorgio led Cross into the back den, Petie broke off and followed, as did Vincent.

There, Don Clericuzio was waiting for them. Seated in a huge armchair, he was smoking one of his crooked cigars. Vincent went to him and handed him a glass of wine from the bar. Cross was offered nothing. Petie remained at the door, standing. Giorgio sat down on the sofa next to the Don and motioned to Cross to sit with him.

The Don's face, drawn thin with age, had no trace of emotion. Cross kissed him on the cheek. The Don looked at him and his face softened as if with sadness.

"So Croccifixio," the Don said, "it was all cleverly done. But now you must explain your reasons. I am Dante's grandfather, my daughter is his mother. The men here are his uncles. You must answer to all of us."

Cross tried to keep his composure. "I don't understand," he said.

Giorgio said harshly, "Dante. Where is he?"

"Christ, how should I know?" Cross said as if surprised. "He never reported to me. He could be down in Mexico having a good time."

Giorgio said, "You don't understand. Don't fuck around. You are already judged guilty. Where did you dump him?"

At the bar, Vincent turned away as though he could not look into his face. Behind him Cross could hear Petie coming closer to the sofa.

"Where's the proof?" Cross said. "Who says I killed Dante?"

"I do." It was the Don who spoke. "Understand: I have pronounced you guilty. There is no appeal from that judgment. I brought you here to make your plea for mercy, but you must justify the killing of my grandson."

Hearing that voice, the measured tone, Cross knew that everything was over. For him and Lia Vazzi. But Vazzi already knew. It had been in his eyes.

Vincent turned to Cross, his granite face softened. "Tell my father the truth, Cross, it's your only chance."

The Don nodded. He said, "Croccifixio, your father was more than my nephew, of Clericuzio blood, as you are. Your father was my trusted friend. And so I will listen to your reasons."

Cross prepared himself. "Dante killed my father. I judged him guilty as you judged me guilty. And he killed my father out of revenge and ambition. He was a Santadio in his heart."

The Don did not respond. Cross went on. "How could I not avenge my father? How could I forget my father was responsible for my life? And I had too much respect for the Clericuzio, as my father had, to suspect your hand in the killing. Yet, I think you must have known Dante was guilty and did nothing. So how could I come to you to redress the wrong?"

"Your proof," Giorgio said.

"A man like Pippi De Lena could never be surprised," Cross said. "And Jim Losey at the other end is too much of a coincidence. There is not a man in this room who believes in coincidence. All of you know Dante was guilty. And Don, you yourself told me the story of the Santadio. Who knows what Dante planned after he killed me, as he surely knew he must. Next, his uncles." Cross did not dare to mention the Don. "He counted on your affection," he said to the Don.

The Don had laid his cigar aside. He face was inscrutable but held a touch of sadness.

It was Petie who spoke. Petie had been the closest to Dante. "Where did you dump the body?" Petie asked again. And Cross could not answer him, could not get the words out of his mouth.

There was a long silence and then finally the Don raised his head to all of them and spoke. "Funerals are wasted on the young," he said. "What have they done to celebrate them? How have they inspired great respect? The young have no compassion, no gratitude. And my daughter is already crazy, why should we compound her grief and erase hopes for her recovery. She will be told her son has fled and it will take years for her to know the truth."

And now it seemed that everyone in the room relaxed. Petie came forward and sat on the sofa beside Cross. Vincent, behind the bar, raised a glass of brandy to his lips in what could have been a salute.

"But justice or no, you have committed a crime against the Family," the Don said. "There must be a punishment. For you, money, for Lia Vazzi, his life."

Cross said, "Lia had nothing to do with Dante, for Losey, yes. Let me ransom him. I own half the Xanadu. I will transfer half that ownership to you as payment for me and Vazzi."

Don Clericuzio seemed to ponder this. "You are loyal," he said. He turned to Giorgio and then Vincent and Petie. "If you three agree, I will agree." They did not answer.

The Don sighed as if in regret. "You will sign over half your interest but you must move out of our world. Vazzi must return to Sicily with his family, or not, as he pleases. That is as far as I can go. You and Vazzi must never speak together again. And I order my sons, in your presence, never to avenge their nephew's death. You will have a week to arrange your affairs, to sign the necessary papers for Giorgio." Then the Don spoke in a less harsh voice. "Let me assure you that I had no knowledge of Dante's plans. Now, go in peace and remember I always loved your father like a son."

When Cross left the house, Don Clericuzio got out of his chair and said to Vincent, "To bed." Vincent helped him up the stairs, for the Don now had a certain weakness in his legs. His age was finally beginning to ravage his body.

EPILOGUE

Nice, France
Quogue

ON HIS LAST DAY in Vegas, Cross De Lena sat on his pent-house balcony and looked down on the sun-drenched Strip. The great hotels—Caesars Palace, the Flamingo, the Desert Inn, the Mirage, and the Sands—blazed their neon marquees to challenge the sun.

Don Clericuzio had been specific in his banishment: Cross was never to return to Las Vegas. How happy his father, Pippi, had been here, and Gronevelt had built the city into his own Valhalla, but Cross had never really enjoyed their ease. True, he had enjoyed the pleasures of Vegas, but those pleasures always held the cold flavor of steel.

The green flags of the seven Villas dropped in the desert stillness, but one hung from the burned building, a black skeleton, the ghost of Dante. But he would never see all of this again.

He had loved the Xanadu, he had loved his father, Gronevelt, and Claudia. And yet he had in some sense betrayed them. Gronevelt, by failing to be faithful to the Xanadu; his father, by not being true to the Clericuzio; and Claudia, because she believed in his innocence. Now he was free of them. He would begin a new life.

What could he make of his love for Athena? He had been warned of the dangers of romantic love by Gronevelt, by his father, and even by the old Don. That was the fatal flaw of great men who would control their worlds. Then why was he now ignoring their advice? Why was he placing his fate at the mercy of a woman?

Quite simply, the sight of her, the sound of her voice, the way she moved, her happiness and her sorrow, all made him happy. The world became dazzlingly pleasurable when he was with her. Food became delicious, the sun's heat warmed his bones, and he felt that sweet hunger for her flesh that made life holy. And when he slept with her he never feared those nightmares that preceded the dawn.

It was now three weeks since he had last seen Athena, but he had heard her voice just this morning. He had called her in France to tell her he was coming, and he had caught the happiness in her voice because now she knew he was still alive. It was possible she loved him. And now, in less than twenty hours he would see her.

Cross had faith that someday she would truly love him, that she would reward him for his love, that she would never judge him, and that like some angel she would save him from Hell.

Athena Aquitane was perhaps the only woman in France who put on her makeup and clothes to try to destroy her beauty. Not that she tried to look ugly, she was not a masochist, but she had come to regard her physical beauty as too dangerous for her inner world. She hated the power it gave her over other people. She hated the vanity that still spoiled her spirit. It interfered with what she knew would be her life's work.

On the first day of work at the Institute for Autistic Children in Nice, she wanted to look like the children, to walk like them. She was overcome with the sense of identification. That day, she relaxed her facial muscles to their soulless serenity and limped in the weird, lopsided way of some of the children who had motor damage.

Dr. Gerard observed this and said sardonically, "Oh, very good but you're going in the wrong direction." Then he took her hands in his and said gently, "You must not identify with their misfortune. You must fight against it."

Athena felt rebuked and ashamed. Again her actress vanity had misled her. But she felt herself at peace caring for these children. It did not matter to them that her French was imperfect, they did not grasp the meaning of her words anyway.

Even the distressing realities did not discourage her. The children were sometimes destructive, did not recognize the rules of society. They fought each other and their nurses, they smeared their feces on the walls, they urinated where they pleased. Sometimes they were truly frightening in their ferocity, their repulsion of the outside world.

The only time Athena felt helpless was at night in the small apartment she had rented in Nice, when she studied the literature of the Institute. They were reports on the progress of the children and they were frightening. Then she would crawl into bed and weep. Unlike the movies she had lived in, these reports had mostly unhappy endings.

When she received the call from Cross that he was coming to see her, she felt a surge of happiness and hope. He was still alive and he would help her. Then she had some trepidation. She consulted Dr. Gerard.

"What do you think would be best?" she asked.

"He could be of great assistance to Bethany," Dr. Gerard said. "I would very much like to see how she relates to him over a period of time. And it might be very good for you. Mothers must not be martyrs for their children." She thought about his words on her way to pick up Cross at the Nice airport.

At the airport, Cross had to walk from the plane to the low-slung terminal. The air was balmy and sweet, not the scorching sulfurous heat of Vegas. Along the borders of the concrete reception plaza grew masses of luxurious red and purple flowers.

He saw Athena waiting for him on that plaza, and he marveled at her genius in transforming her appearance. She could not completely hide her beauty, but she could disguise it. Gold-framed tinted glasses turned her eyes from brilliant green to gray. The clothes she was wearing made her look thicker and heavier. Her blond hair was tucked under a country-brimmed hat of blue denim that overlapped the side of her face. He felt a thrill of possession that he was the only one who knew how beautiful she really was.

As Cross approached, Athena took off her glasses and put them in the pocket of her blouse. He smiled at her irrepressible vanity.

Less than an hour later they were in the suite of the Negresco Hotel where Napoleon had bedded Josephine. Or so the hotel brochure on the door still claimed. A waiter knocked and brought in a tray with a bottle of wine and a delicate plate of tiny sandwiches. He left it on the balcony table that overlooked the Mediterranean.

At first they were awkward with each other. She held his hand trustingly yet as if she were in command, and the touch of her warm flesh gave him a rush of desire. But he could see she was not quite ready.

The suite was beautifully furnished, more opulent than any of the Xanadu Villas. The bed had a canopy of dark red silk, the matching drapes were studded with golden fleur-de-lis. The tables and chairs had an elegance that could never have existed in the Vegas world.

Athena led Cross out to the balcony, and as she did so Cross blindly kissed her on the cheek. And then she couldn't help herself, she picked up a wet cotton napkin that was wrapped around the wine bottle and scrubbed her face free of all the disfiguring cosmetics. Her face glistened with drops of water, the skin radiant and pink. She put one hand on his shoulder and kissed him gently on the lips.

From the balcony they could view the stone houses of Nice, tinted the faded greens and blues of paint from hundreds of years ago. Below, the citizens of Nice strolled on the Promenade des Anglais, on the stony beach young men and women, almost nude, splashed into the blue-green water while little children dug themselves into the pebbly sand. Farther out, hawkish white yachts, strung with lights, patrolled the horizon.

Cross and Athena had taken their first sip of wine when they heard the faint roar. From the stone seawall, from what looked like the mouth of a cannon but was really the great eastern pipe of the sewers, a great wave of deep brown water gushed into the pristine blue of the sea.

Athena turned her head away. She said to Cross, "How long will you be here?"

"Five years if you let me," he said.

"That's silly," Athena said frowning. "What will you do here?"

Cross said. "I'm rich, maybe I'll buy a small hotel."

"What happened to the Xanadu?" Athena asked.

"I had to sell my interest," he said. He paused for a moment. "We won't have to worry about money."

"I have money," Athena said. "You have to understand. I'm going to stay here for five years and then I'm going to bring her home. I don't care what they say, I will never put her back in an institution, I'll take care of her for the rest of her life. And if anything happens to her, my life will be with children like her. So you see we can never have a life together."

Cross understood her perfectly. He took a long time to consider his answer.

His voice was strong and determined when he said, "Athena, the only thing I'm sure about now is that I love you and Bethany. You have to believe that. It's not going to be easy, I know that, but we'll try our best. You want to help Bethany, not be a martyr. For that we have to take a final jump. I'll do everything I can to help you. Look, we'll be like gamblers in my casino. The odds are stacked against us, but there's always that chance to beat the odds."

Cross saw her weakening so he pressed on. "Let's get married," he said. "Let's have other children and live our lives like normal people. With our children let's try to make right what seems wrong with our world. All families have some misfortune. I know we can overcome it. Will you believe me?"

Finally Athena looked at him directly. "Only if you believe I truly love you," she said.

In the bedroom when they made love, they took each other on faith; Athena believed that Cross would truly help her save Bethany, and Cross, that Athena truly loved him. When finally she turned her body toward him, she murmured, "I love you. I really do."

Cross bowed his head to kiss her. She said it again, "I truly love you," and Cross thought, What man on earth could disbelieve her?

Alone in his bedroom, the Don pulled the cool sheets up to his neck. Death was approaching, and he was too wily not to detect its nearness. But everything had worked out according to his plans. Ah, how easy it is to outwit the young.

During the last five years he had seen Dante as the great danger to his master plan. Dante would resist the folding of the Clericuzio Family into society. And yet, what could he himself, the Don, do?

Order the killing of his daughter's son, his own grandson? Would Giorgio, Vincent, and Petie obey such an order? And if they did, would they think him some kind of monster? Would they then fear him more than they loved him? And Rose Marie, what would remain of her sanity then, for surely she would sense the truth.

But when Pippi De Lena was killed, the die was cast. The Don immediately knew the truth of the matter, investigated Dante's relationship with Losey and made his judgment.

He had sent Vincent and Petie to guard Cross, armored car and all. And then, to forewarn Cross, told him the story of the Santadio War. How painful it was to set the world straight. And when he was gone, who would there be to make these terrible decisions? He decided now, once and for all, the Clericuzio would make its final retreat.

Vinnie and Petie would deal strictly with their restaurants and construction businesses. Giorgio would buy companies on Wall Street. The withdrawal would be complete. Even the Bronx Enclave would not be replenished. The Clericuzio would finally be safe and fight against the new outlaws who were rising all over America. He would not blame himself for past mistakes, the loss of his daughter's happiness and the death of his grandson. And after all, he had set Cross free.

Before he fell asleep, the Don had a vision. He would live forever, the Clericuzio blood would be part of mankind forever. And it was he, himself, alone who had created this lineage, his own virtue.

But, oh, what a wicked world it was that drove a man to sin.

THE GODFATHER

Mario Puzo

'A novel about the Mafia written on the grand scale with an admirable ring of authenticity and a remarkable degree of sympathy with the gangsters' own standards of justice'
Sunday Telegraph

'A splendid and distinguished blood saga of the Cosa Nostra, the American Mafia, and of the whirl created by five families of mafiosi at war in New York'
Sunday Times

'Mario Puzo is an extremely talented storyteller, and his tale moves at breakneck speed without ever losing its balance. More important, Puzo proves to be a genuine social historian. The Godfather is fiction, but it is still a valid and fascinating portrait of America's most powerful and least understood subculture, the Mafia'
Newsweek

FOOLS DIE

Mario Puzo

Within the interconnecting worlds of bigtime gambling, publishing and the film industry, the power of corruption and the corruption of power are nowhere better explored. From New York to Las Vegas, Merlyn and his brother Artie obey their own code of honour in the ferment of contemporary America, where law and organised crime are one and the same . . .

'Fame and wealth, skulduggery and cheating and pimping, love affairs and carnal arrangements, one scene following another pell-mell, all written with unflagging vitality . . . bawdy, comic, highly coloured, hypnotic. It would be a very cool reader indeed to did not devour the whole mixture greedily'
New York Times

'Corruptly compulsive'
Daily Express

'Unforgettable . . . will rivet your attention'
Cosmopolitan

THE FORTUNATE PILGRIM

Mario Puzo

'From the barren farms of Italy to the cramped tenements of New York, the immigrant families struggle with an adopted life – none more so than the Angeluzzi-Corbos. At their head stands Lucia Santa, wife, widow and mother of two families. It is her formidable will that steers them through the Depression and the early years of war. But she cannot prevent the conflict between Italian and American values – nor the violence and bloodshed which must surely follow . . .

'I began reading The Fortunate Pilgrim yesterday afternoon and didn't stop reading until I had finished it. Puzo presents the convincing imagery of Thomas Wolfe with the economy of Nathaniel West. No one I know can create a city scene with more vivid accuracy'
Joseph Heller

'The novel's main tension comes from Lucia Santa's bewildered, proud and terrified response to her family's gradual Americanisation. Her passion holds together not just the family but the novel . . . Mr Puzo has refused to do any faking '
New Statesman

'Puzo has written a chronicle of Italian immigrant life which is a small classic'
New York Times

ALSO AVAILABLE IN PAPERBACK

❏ The Godfather	Mario Puzo	£5.99
❏ Fools Die	Mario Puzo	£5.99
❏ The Fortunate Pilgrim	Mario Puzo	£5.99
❏ The Dark Arena	Mario Puzo	£5.99
❏ The Silence of the Lambs	Thomas Harris	£5.99
❏ Red Dragon	Thomas Harris	£5.99
❏ Truth or Dare	Sara Sheridan	£5.99
❏ White Viper	Terence Strong	£5.99
❏ Nimitz Class	Patrick Robinson	£5.99
❏ Kilo Class	Patrick Robinson	£5.99
❏ HMS Unseen	Patrick Robinson	£5.99

ALL ARROW BOOKS ARE AVAILABLE THROUGH MAIL ORDER OR FROM YOUR LOCAL BOOKSHOP AND NEWS-AGENT.

PLEASE SEND CHEQUE/EUROCHEQUE/POSTAL ORDER (STERLING ONLY) ACCESS, VISA, MASTERCARD, DINERS CARD, SWITCH OR AMEX.

EXPIRY DATE .... SIGNATURE ....

PLEASE ALLOW 75 PENCE PER BOOK FOR POST AND PACKING U.K.

OVERSEAS CUSTOMERS PLEASE ALLOW £1.00 PER COPY FOR POST AND PACKING.

ALL ORDERS TO:

ARROW BOOKS, BOOKS BY POST, TBS LIMITED, THE BOOK SERVICE, COLCHESTER ROAD, FRATING GREEN, COLCHESTER, ESSEX CO7 7DW.

TELEPHONE: (01206) 256 000
FAX: (01206) 255 914

NAME: ....

ADDRESS ....

....

Please allow 28 days for delivery. Please tick box if you do not wish to receive any additional information ❏
Prices and availability subject to change without notice.